The Origin
of Sorrow

Cover created by Rhonda Ward <sprkward@yahoo.com>

Published by **Combustoica**, a prose project of About Comics.
www.COMBUSTOICA.com.
For rights inquiries, contact rights@aboutcomics.com

Combustoica edition published 2011.

Books by Robert Mayer

Fiction

Superfolks

The Execution

Midge and Decker

The Grace of Shortstops

Sweet Salt

The Search

I, JFK

The Ferret's Tale

Danse Macabre

Non-Fiction

The Dreams of Ada

Notes of a Baseball Dreamer
    (First published as *Baseball And Men's Lives*)

Praise for the Books of Robert Mayer

"Fascinating." — John Grisham

"Gripping." — Janet Malcolm, The New York Times

"He writes like an angel." — Newsday

"Exemplary." — Village Voice

"Pure, undiluted magic." — Washington Post

"Quiet brilliance." — Atlanta Journal-Constitution

"Strangely moving." — Cleveland Plain Dealer

"Genuinely compelling storytelling." — Chicago Tribune

"Wonderfully human." — Dallas News

"The poet's touch." — Detroit News

"A blend of the funny and the poignant." — St. Louis Post Dispatch

"Absorbing." — Sunday Oklahoman

"Heart-stopping" — Albuquerque Journal

"Ranks with the best." — Santa Fe Reporter

"Topnotch." — People Magazine

"Compelling." — Booklist

"Excellent." — Library Journal

"Wonderful, moving." — Publisher's Weekly

The Origin of Sorrow

Robert Mayer

Combustoica
packaged by About Comics - Camarillo, California

Ann Kelley

Kristin Reidy

Mary Bonney

Karen Chavez

And to the people of the Judengasse

Can you crawl out of asking
the origin of sorrow ... ?
—Dana Levin,
Hive

Contents

Book One: Guttle

The confinement, the dirt, the swarm of people, the accents of an unpleasant tongue, all made a disagreeable impression, even when one only looked in when passing outside the gate. It took a long time before I ventured in alone ... And yet, they were also human beings, energetic, agreeable, and even their obstinacy in sticking to their own customs, one could not deny it respect. Moreover, their girls were pretty.

— Goethe,
Poetry and Truth

1

In the beginning were the walls. Stone walls ten metres high. Erected on both sides of a dirt lane in Frankfurt-am-Main, in the Christian year 1458, after the Holy Father ordered the Emperor to confine all Jews in the city. Three hundred years later, the walls and their iron gates still were standing. The Jews had begat in number from 110 to 3,000. They now occupied every metre of the lane. They still were locked inside.

On the last Friday in March, in the Christian year 1769, Guttle Schnapper, a dark-haired girl with eyes black as olives — fifteen and a half years pretty she was — bare of foot that morning and wearing a blue cotton shift, came out from a neighbor's house at the northern end of the lane. She carried a small pitcher of milk. Her mind was in turmoil over an unwelcome marriage proposal she had received the night before from Viktor the Cantor, an overweight young man whose operatic voice had a teardrop in it, as the voices of all good cantors must. In the darkness of a cloud-ridden dawn she tripped upon the leg of a dead man. Milk flew from the pitcher, soaked the side of the man's face, his wisp of beard. Guttle stumbled, caught herself. Frightened, she nonetheless peered closer, to see if she knew the man. Her eyes took in his outstretched arm, his wooden hammer, which was clutched in his hand even in death.

"It's the Schul-Klopper!" she cried out.

As she stared, stunned, at the body, she was further upset by the sound of laughter. Three Gentile boys were peering through the bars of the north gate, making fun of the dead man. Guttle ran at them, shouting that they should show respect. The boys pranced away, still laughing. When she spun her head around, her braids tied with white ribbons whipping off her neck, she saw down the lane the men and boys walking towards the synagogue for the morning service, to which the Schul-Klopper's hammer only moments ago had summoned them. She knelt beside him. His face was pale as parchment. Pale not because he had just fallen dead, but because in all his fifty-nine years, may he rest in peace, the sun had rarely touched his forehead, his long nose, his cheeks that peeked soft as a baby's tush above the whiskers. The faces of everyone in the lane were pale; the sun, when it passed overhead precisely at noon each day, allowed its rays to warm the cobbles for four minutes, perhaps five. Then, as if in a rush to escape this stinking place, the rays climbed the walls of the gray houses and disappeared, leaving the Judengasse, as it was called — the Jews Lane — in the deeper gray of twilight, till the twilight itself disappeared into black of night.

The Schul-Klopper's brown eyes were open. He was staring as if in disbelief that he was dead. Guttle could hardly accept it, either. Only a few minutes before, she had heard his hammer pound on their door. She had heard him knocking on doors morning and evening every day of her consciousness. He was the most familiar figure in the lane, more familiar even than the Chief Rabbi. Now his face was twisted by pain he no longer felt. Guttle knew she needed to find help, even as she knew that Solomon Gruen was beyond all help but God's.

The pitcher still in her hand, she ran to fetch her mother, bare toes flinching like frightened kittens on the cold morning cobbles. Before she reached her house a neighbor boy, Isidor Kracauer, emerged from the adjoining door and grabbed her arm, spilling more of the milk. He was a year younger than she. His short blond hair stood up in front of his dark blue yarmulke like winter wheat.

"Why are you running?" he asked.

"It's the Schul-Klopper!"

"I know, I heard him knock, I'll hurry."

"Not schul! He's over there. He's dead."

She set the empty pitcher on the ground, took his hand, led him to the body. Isidor blushed at her touch, as only a fair-skinned boy of fourteen can blush. They'd been raised like cousins; Guttle had yet to notice the stress her curving body had begun to induce in him.

The Schul-Klopper, though wearing his usual long black coat, frayed at the wrists, was repellant in his twisted silence. Neither wanted to touch him. They'd seen dead bodies before, there was plenty of death in the lane, but usually in a bed, under covers. Isidor quickly invented an excuse to keep away; it was for good reason the boys at the yeshiva called him Izzy the Wise. "Don't touch him, he might have disease," the boy warned. "I'm going for the Doctor." He leaped across the sewage ditch, nearly a metre wide, which bisected the lane like a stinking brown snake, and stumbled off to the hospital.

"It's not the Doctor he needs," Guttle murmured, looking again at the Schul-Klopper. With his hand still clutching his curved hammer, he seemed to be knocking with patience on the door of Heaven.

Guttle hurried to the synagogue, half way down the lane. When she returned with the Chief Rabbi, the Doctor, Lev Berkov, was kneeling beside the body, holding Herr Gruen's wrist, touching fingers to Herr Gruen's throat. Izzy in his wisdom watched from several feet away, then ran off towards the schul. The Doctor glanced up at the Rabbi, and murmured, "He's dead."

Tears formed in Guttle's eyes. She did not know why — she already knew he was dead.

Rabbi Avram Eleazar folded her slim hand into his stubby one, and lifted her chin with a finger. "It's all right to cry, child," he said. "But also remember, death is the will of Elohim. Perhaps Solomon died so that another might live."

Hungry for comfort, Guttle asked, "He died so that who might live?"

The handsome young Doctor hid a smile with his fist. Lifting his eyebrows at the question, the Chief Rabbi shrugged, rotated the palms of his stubby hands skyward. Quickly he turned from her, so she would not see his own eyes watering at the passing of his dearest friend.

As she walked home carrying the empty pitcher, a darkness crossed Guttle's face, like the shadow of a large bird — but there were no birds in the Judengasse. The death of the Schul-Klopper, the shadow seemed to warn, would one day cast a dark mark on her own life. She shuddered. That was nonsense, just her unruly imagination, for which she was not yet known.

The Judengasse curved like a limp sausage for half a kilometre, sliding in a gentle slope toward the river Main. At each end of the lane were the gates of iron. Men were permitted to leave only for business, and were to be back inside each day by five on the clock. Women could only go to the nearby market. At night, and on Sundays, the gates were locked to everyone.

Why had the Jews put up with this for three hundred years? Because the Constables outside the gates had pistols. And muskets. And swords. And cold, hard eyes.

Along both sides of the lane, narrow houses of gray wood stood quietly, shoulder touching shoulder, like skinny men whispering Kaddish. Behind the front houses a second row had been wedged against the outer walls down through the centuries, to house the expanding number of families. The Schnapper home fronted the lane, in sight of the north gate.

"Where's the baby's milk?"

Her mother's question stung Guttle like a slap as she entered the kitchen and set down the empty pitcher. "I send you across the lane for milk, you let Bea Metzenbaum talk your ear off, you forget what you went for. You would forget your head if it wasn't attached."

"Mama, listen! The Schul-Klopper is dead."

She recited what had happened in the lane.

"You never watch where you're going!" her mother said. "You're always too busy thinking!" Then Emmie Schnapper dropped herself onto a chair like a load of wash. "The Schul-Klopper? That's terrible." She looked at Guttle, took her hand, rubbed it. "Are you all right, bubbelah?"

"I'm fine," Guttle said, though she had begun to tremble.

"Avra, watch little Benjy. I'm going to Ida's next door to borrow milk."

Emmie's heavy footsteps faded down the stairs. Avra, who was thirteen, two years younger than Guttle, thin as a spatula, said, "Was it disgusting? Were his insides hanging out? I'll bet you'll have nightmares tonight."

Guttle accommodated her, if that is the proper word. "His insides were bleeding onto the cobbles. His throat was slashed. His fingernails were long as claws. He said he'd come get me in my sleep tonight, and klop my head to pieces with his hammer. He forced me to tell him my name. I said I was Avra Schnapper."

"You didn't! I'm telling Mama you're scaring me!" She bolted down the stairs before Guttle could remind her she was supposed to be watching the baby. "I'm so awful, Benjy," Guttle said. "How could I say such things?"

"What things?" Benjy, still in his white nightshirt, was looking up at her with a sleepy face and slept-on hair. He was not yet three years old.

"Nothing, Benj. I'm just upset."

"At me?"

"Not you, sweetie." She sat on a chair by the kitchen table, pulled her only living brother onto her lap. "I'm mad at Herr Gruen for being dead."

"What's dead?"

She ignored his question. "And I'm angry at Viktor Marcus for wanting to marry me."

"What's marry?"

She tousled his silky hair. "Married is the same as dead, only you're not alone."

She set her brother down and dropped tea leaves into a glass and poured hot water over them from a kettle on the woodstove. Holding the glass with one hand and Benjy's fingers with the other, she led him upstairs to the small front bedroom she and Avra shared, and she set her tea on the windowsill. She needed to rid herself of the dead Schul-Klopper's image, needed to purge herself of her stupid joke. How do you apologize to the dead?

From her father's chair in the sitting room she fetched the newspaper he'd brought home the evening before, the Sachsen-Meiningen *Zeitung.* With editions of this newspaper, with her father's help, she had taught herself to read and write Hochdeutch, in addition to her Hebrew and the Judendeutch that was the language of the lane. Benjy climbed beside her onto the bed as she looked at the newspaper. Hardly a week went by when her father's name did not appear in it. Almost always it was the same sentence. "The profits of the Prince will be invested, to replenish the municipal treasury, by the Court Jew, Wolf Salomon Schnapper."

She tried to read, couldn't concentrate. But a small notice near the bottom caught her attention. It was headed, "Madame Antoine to Marry." It said: *"According to a dispatch from Vienna, Empress Maria Teresa has authorized negotiations to marry her youngest daughter, Archduchess Antoine, to the Dauphin of France. Such a match would create a rare alliance between the two leading powers of Europe. The lovely Madame Antoine is thirteen and one-half years of age, the French Dauphin is fifteen. He is heir to the throne of his grandfather, King Louis XV. The report caused much joy in Vienna, although no formal announcement has been made."*

Guttle sipped her tea while Benjy babbled, pretending to read. Madame Antoine might be going off to live in a grand palace, she mused, but they still had something in common, she and the Princess: neither one could choose whom they would marry. Although, she admitted to herself, marrying a Prince might not be altogether bad.

Her father had been looking at her in a new way of late, and Guttle knew why. He was measuring her for a husband. It would not be a boy, like the Dauphin, it would be a man of twenty-five years at least; that was the law shackled on Jewish men by the Frankfurt Council, who wanted to reduce the number of Jewish babies. Her marriage would not be for a political merger, like Madame Antoine's, but for a financial one; her father would decide whose family was wealthy enough, with enough useful acquaintances, to suit him.

In the street below, her mother and sister were arguing. The sister with the sharp nose and the sharper tongue. Avra was not so ugly, but the slight extra grinding of her nose, the thinness of her lips, a tightness to the skin of her face, a narrowness between the eyes — as if there had been a shortage of Schnapper flesh when she'd been born — gave her a sour appearance. No surprise that she was developing a personality to match.

Guttle carried Benjy down to the kitchen. "Ida already knew about Herr Gruen," her mother, Emmie, said as she climbed the last step ahead of Avra.

"Where's the milk?"

Her mother looked at her empty hands. "Oy, I got so caught up in talk. Guttle Schnapper, don't you say a word!"

"I'm not saying a thing, Mama." She tried to swallow a smile. Like a raw egg, it wouldn't go down.

"Avra, go borrow milk," Emmie said. "Try Frau Schlicter. She doesn't talk so much."

"And Avra," Guttle said.

"What? I'm not talking to you!"

"Don't spill it."

Avra stuck her tongue out at Guttle before stomping down the stairs.

"Do you feel all right from the Schul-Klopper?" Emmie asked.

Guttle wanted to curl up in bed and weep in her pillow. Tripping over a dead man should happen only in one of Viktor's operas, on a dimly lighted stage, while the audience gasped.

"You look upset. Maybe you shouldn't go to the bakery."

"I need to go," Guttle said. "At least there I can focus on the beetles."

A few minutes later she was at the north gate, waiting impatiently with her mother and two other bakery women; it was their turn to meet the flour wagon. Avra was home with the little ones; almost everywhere in the Judengasse there were little ones. Guttle heard the slow clopping of hoofs on the cobbles before the gray head of the old horse came into view around the ghetto wall. As the wooden wagon came closer, an escort of flies announced its approach, dipping and circling. The flour merchant pulled the horse to a stop. The small wagon could have been driven through the open gate and transported the flour sacks to the bakery, but the tradesman, tall, thin, emaciated, had made clear long ago that, like most Gentiles, he would never enter the Judengasse. As if the Jews carried germs. Instead, the women had to lift heavy sacks from the cart and place them in the two wheelbarrows they'd brought along.

To the left of the gate a young Constable stood erect as a pole in gray breeches and a dark blue coat with silver buttons. His musket was propped against the wall. He seemed uninterested in the flour transaction — though his gaze did flick to Guttle from time to time — as Frau Schnapper, the bakery treasurer, pulled a purse from the pocket of her apron. "The usual price?" she asked.

"The usual," the merchant said, brushing a fly from his drooping gray mustache.

Frau Schnapper reached up and handed him several coins. He examined them closely, as if counterfeiting might be a burgeoning art in the Judengasse, before shoving them into his trouser pocket. Guttle pulled her dark braids prettily around her chin. "And how much for the beetles?"

The merchant did not smile. Reaching for his tattered whip, he said, "For you, Mädchen, the beetles are free."

It was an old joke. What humor it may once have contained had long since faded. But the handsome young Constable, who was new at his post, turned his face to hide his grin. Perhaps it was for his benefit that Guttle had revived the joke.

The merchant flicked his whip and the swaybacked horse began to move slowly along the cobbles, accepting without protest the weight of the wagon and the nuisance of the flies, as if it had been pulling this same cart over these same stones for three hundred years. Perhaps it had. The other two women wrapped thick fingers around the wheelbarrow handles and pushed the flour through the gate. It would fill the bellies of the Judengasse for a week.

Guttle smiled at the clean-shaven guard. "Imagine," she said. "Free beetles. Perhaps a new day is dawning."

The Constable was not accustomed to speaking with Jews. He did not know how to respond. Guttle winked at him. Then she hurried back through the gate, raising her ankle length shift two inches so it would clear the churned-up mud. This new guard certainly seemed nicer than Leutnant Gruber, who wielded his sword as if were a fly swatter and the Jews an irritant buzzing around his head. Was it really possible, a kindhearted guard at the gate?

Above them, in the third-story front room of the first house inside the gate, Hiram Liebmann, the deaf mute, was noting on a sheet of paper what he had observed: that the flour wagon had arrived eleven minutes late, that the purchase of flour had taken three minutes. Lacking language, he made his notations with small drawings, like entries in an odd ledger: a cart for the horse and wagon, a sack of flour for the sale. When he was through, he would wind his pocket watch, as he did many times each day; it marked his passage though life, as a crutch serves a one-legged man.

Guttle's mother was waiting for her a few houses down, in front of the rag dealer's stall. Used coats, dresses and remnants of cloth hung from nails and were piled on a table. "What are you, meshuganah?" her mother said. "Talking to a guard holding a musket?"

"He wasn't holding it."

"Don't get smart with me. I heard what you said. 'Perhaps a new day is dawning.' What kind of talk is that? You want another Fettmilch riot? I would smack your face, if I didn't think finding the Schul-Klopper maybe affected your brain. And 'free beetles?' Enough with your jokes. Today is not a day for them."

Frau Schnapper led her towards the bakery. Guttle said nothing as they walked down the lane, in which merely breathing the humid, stagnant air was difficult. *Dishwater air,* the poet laureate of the Judengasse, Nahum Baum, had called it in a poem more than a century earlier. The air had not improved since.

"Just wait," Emmie said. "A new day, indeed! We'll see what your father has to say."

The aroma of browning challah and the putrid stink of the ditch battled for the air like warring armies. Half a dozen women in white aprons were baking with flour that remained from the previous week. Guttle went to her Friday work place, already cleared for her. The new sacks of flour were stacked beside a flat stone shelf.

The air in the bakery was warmer than the morning air outside, although that, too, was unusually mild. This was a time of renewal, the first week of spring, the Chief Rabbi had intoned in his Sabbath sermon, and the congregation had buzzed like a hive. Except for the men who went into the city on business, and passed the city parks, the Jews had few hints of the changing seasons. Not a tree, not a bush, not a flower, not a blade of grass grew in the Judengasse; there wasn't any room; there wasn't enough sun. Only in the cemetery did wildflowers bloom, in late summer mostly, and then wilted quickly, imitating the dead.

With knowing fingers Guttle wound her braids atop her head to keep them clear of the flour and the ovens. Slitting stitches on the top canvas sack, she dumped a pile of coarse brown flour onto the flat stone. The flour was speckled, as always, with red dots. Flour beetles. Sinking to her knees to see them better, she began to pick the beetles out, using a pair of tweezers donated long ago by a Doctor at the hospital. Each insect she removed she dropped into a pot of heated oil that smoked near the edge of the stone. The beetles, living creatures, sizzled as they touched the oil. Then they turned black. The work of cleaning the flour was tedious, was always assigned to one of the younger women, who still had strong knees and strong eyes, knees not yet burning from dozens of years of scrubbing floors, eyes not yet dimmed from reading the Books of Moses by oil lamp or candle light. Even young eyes, however, were not strong enough to spot all the beetle eggs in the flour. This was a secret made harmless by the heat of the ovens, a secret the world of women kept from the world of men. There was a saying every woman knew: in baking bread, you can't have too many eggs.

While Guttle searched for beetles and dropped them in the oil, other women added water and yeast to the already cleaned flour, molded it into braided loaves, and gossiped. The subject this day, of course, was the death of the Schul-Klopper.

"Who can replace him?" one of them asked. "It's hard to imagine anyone else knocking."

They agreed that at least Solomon Gruen had led a full life. A learned man, a Greek scholar, with all those shelves of books he loved. They wondered why he never had married — well, maybe his life had not been so full. But he'd been a good shammus — a good sexton — at the schul, they agreed, making sure everything was in good repair, that there was always enough oil for the lamps, helping the Rabbis teach the young boys the Talmud in the three *heders*. And he'd been a good influence, they agreed, on that wild Hersch Liebmann, a boy from the poorest family in the Judengasse, whom he'd given a job as janitor at the schul so he could take home a few kreuzer each week to his elderly parents. Life was unpredictable, the women agreed; who wanted to die in the street instead of in bed? But at least the Schul-Klopper had died doing what he most enjoyed: summoning the pious to services. And death had been quick, with little suffering. His heart, no doubt.

The chatter of the women stopped as the whining sound of a saw biting into board sliced through the air from the shop of the coffin maker across the lane. Yussel Kahn called himself a cabinet maker, which he was, but only the wealthiest in the Judengasse thought of him that way. To the rest he was the coffin maker. The women paused in their work, maintaining a respectful silence. They could guess what the coffin maker was doing. He was fashioning the plain spruce box in which Solomon Gruen would be buried before sundown. And when, a short time later, they heard him hammering nails they knew they were right. When he was making furniture, Yussel Kahn, who took pride in his craft, used only glue and dowels.

Except for the painful screaming of the saw, an unusual quiet had settled over the lane. News of the death of the Schul-Klopper had passed from house to house as if through the ether, even before it was passed by word of mouth. Saddened families kept noisy children indoors out of respect.

Rag pickers and moneylenders did not cry out to passersby; there were none. But now it was noon, the body of Solomon Gruen was resting in the hospital under a sheet, where it would remain until the funeral that evening, and Guttle could hear the Judengasse returning to life. The boys in the heders were out and about for their midday exercise. Young children innocent of death darted through the lane shouting as they played made up games, watched over by older sisters — the girls did not go to heder — or by no one at all. Groups of women, talking quietly, moved past the bakery toward the north gate, where they would pass the new Constable, then walk two by two in the direction of the market. The women could go to the stalls to buy fresh fruits and vegetables only after noon, after the Gentile women had taken their pick. Unlike the Gentiles, they were not allowed to touch the produce.

Guttle picked beetles out of the last pile of flour and dropped them into the oil. She packed the cleaned flour in ceramic canisters with tight-fitting lids. With a slatted spoon she lifted clumps of the dead beetles from the surface of the oil onto a rag. By the time the oil was clean — the same oil was used week after week — a knob of crisp beetles sat dripping on the cloth, waiting, like the body of Solomon Gruen, to be carried to its final resting place.

Perched on the edge of the stone, closing her tired eyes, Guttle found herself burrowing past the morning's sadness to the previous evening's absurdity. Viktor the Cantor proposing marriage to her, instead of first asking her father! Outrageous! He'd been shocked when she put him off, saying she was too young to marry. But he said he might ask her father tonight. Now she relived his proposal — in the cemetery! — as melodrama, as opera, which was Viktor's favorite subject; he'd studied it while away at school, talked about it incessantly. Beneath her breath, amid the baking bread, with the other women chattering outside, she softly sang an aria, which she invented as she sang. A creative person was Guttle Schnapper, and in the Judengasse this could be a curse, because what could you do with it? Guttle often painted dark moods into song .

> *He wants to marry me*
> *Though I am just fifteen;*
> *He wants to carry me*
> *Where I have never been;*
> *His voice, though very large,*
> *Does not exceed his paunch;*
> *I might be crushed to death*
> *Before we ever launch*
> *The dozen babes he seeks*

("Just six of each!")
Without a loving breeze
The eager Cantor can't
Prepare to sail my boat
However high his C's.
When Viktor seeks my hand,
Perhaps this very night,
Papa I beg of you:
My troth don't plight!
Now love's bare plot's afloat,
The naked scene is set;
How will fair Guttle fare?
I don't know yet!

She rubbed her eyes with her fists. She didn't know whether, in the half light of the lane, the libretto of her life would be comedy or tragedy.

Soon after the women returned to check the ovens, their talking broke off. There was an intaking of breath, several women at once began to say, "Shalom, shalom Doctor." Guttle turned to look. Doctor Lev Berkov, the tall, lean director of the hospital, had entered the bakery. To many of the women, Doctor Berkov was the catch of the Judengasse. Though he'd grown up in a poor family, he had managed to leave the Judengasse to go to medical school. Then he'd come back. He was thirty years old, and not yet married. And so nice, so dedicated. He had a full head of brown hair, and the way he wore his beard, trimmed very short in a dark triangle, the bakery women found (in their matronly euphemism) scintillating.

Doctor Berkov greeted the women with smiles and friendly nods even as he looked about. Spotting Guttle in the far corner, he approached her, asked if she would step outside for a moment. The whispers began as soon as she followed him into the lane: Was that his choice? Would Guttle Schnapper wed the handsome Doctor? But what would that do to poor Viktor Marcus, with whom she'd been seen keeping company? It was not the Doctor's place to choose, of course, nor the Cantor's. Guttle's father would arrange her marriage. But if the good Doctor hinted that he was interested, would any father say no? Guttle would be sixteen in the autumn, it was time she was spoken for.

Thus did the women speculate as the Doctor led her out of earshot. He asked her how she was feeling since finding the Schul-Klopper. She'd been shaky at first, she admitted, but felt fine now. She told him she was grateful he'd come to ask.

The Doctor replied that there was also something else he wanted to know. It was she who had spilled the milk on the deceased, was that correct?

"I didn't mean to … I stumbled over him."

"Where did you get the milk?"

"I borrowed it from Frau Metzenbaum. We had none left for my baby brother."

"And was Herr Gruen — the Schul-Klopper — already dead when this happened? As far as you could tell."

Guttle began to feel uneasy. She did not understand the point of the questions. "He was lying on muddy cobbles, that's why I stumbled. He wasn't making a sound. He wasn't moving. He wasn't breathing. I was afraid to touch him. That's why, when Isidor ran to get you at the hospital, I knew it was too late. I ran for the Rabbi instead."

"Was his mouth open at the time?"

"It was closed."

"When you left Herr Gruen lying there, was anyone else in the lane?"

"Nobody. The men were already off to schul." Her irritation grew. "Why are you asking these questions? Did we do something wrong?"

She began to feel nervous in her stomach. The Doctor saw her agitation, placed his hand on her shoulder. "That's all the questions. You and Izzy didn't do anything wrong. You did exactly the right thing, getting help. It's just that, when someone dies, we doctors are supposed to find out the cause."

Guttle looked at the Doctor's face. His searching eyes flicked away. There was, she knew, something he was not telling her.

A few minutes later, as the sun reached its apex, clean light sharp as a butcher's knife fell into the lane from overhead, brightening the cobbles. Guttle and the other women of the bakery — indeed, hundreds of women the length of the Judengasse — and some men, too — poured out into the lane, as they did at this time each sunny day, and turned their faces skyward, to feel the warm rays on their pale cheeks, their foreheads, the soft lids of their eyes. Motionless and silent, they stood that way, faces toward the blue sliver of sky, absorbing the sun's warmth like so many hungry flowers. Until, in four minutes, maybe five, the golden light climbed the east-side walls and disappeared, and the lane was in shadow again.

2

Guttle carried the oil-soaked beetles, wrapped in cloth, from the bakery to the sewage ditch. Every twenty metres a board lay across the trench so people could cross it without having to jump. She knelt on the nearest board, let go of two corners of the cloth, slid the black mess into the ditch. The viscous sewage was moving slowly downhill, and the clump of dead beetles moved with it. Children in the street had been waiting for her, as they did each Friday, and now they ran alongside the ball of beetles, shouting and making a game of it, throwing small stones in an attempt to shatter the clump, shouting, "Kill the Emperor," although for years there had been an Empress. The skull of beetles vanished around the curve. Guttle's shift was wet beneath her arms. She was frightened for the kinder. Constables sometimes walked the lane unexpectedly, and children in the Judengasse had been hanged for lesser offenses than shouting angry words. Children had been hanged for stealing a piece of cheese from the Gentile market.

She stood up on the board, but as she stepped onto the uneven cobbles, the words of the youngsters, circling like ravens, made her dizzy. She lost her balance, fell hard on her knees. She didn't want to move. Who had taught the children such a thing? People in the Judengasse did not curse the Gentiles. Life was life. You lived it as it came. You made the best of it. A dozen different sayings had taught her that. What was, was the will of Yahweh. Seeking to change the immutable was the wisdom of fools.

Still, she could not deny the anger within her. She wanted to see the locks on the gates disappear. She wanted to see the ghetto walls crumble. It was not the Gentiles she hated, it was the walls. She wanted to take an axe and hack at them until they cracked, work her fingers into the cracks and pull away chunks of rock. Stone by stone pull the wall apart until there was a hole that every person in the lane could climb through, to stream out into the city, to promenade in the parks, to smell the flowers and the trees, to play on the grass, to feel the warm sun on their faces. To do all the forbidden things.

It didn't matter that she was fifteen years old, and a girl. It didn't matter that no one had made the walls so much as tremble in three hundred years.

Pressing the back of her hands to her eyes, she thought: Yahweh has put up with the walls for all these centuries. Am I superior to Him? If I oppose His will — and me just a girl — am I mad! Not even a hundred men could tear down the walls.

Her eyes began to sting. The oily rag was clenched in her fist. She had the feeling that someone was watching her, perhaps judging her; she'd had this feeling before. Disregarding it, she knelt by the ditch and saw brown turds float by. Soon they would pass beneath the south gate and down the sluice, into the river laced with sailing vessels, where, in the mild current, Jewish waste would mingle with Gentile waste, and drift together towards the Rhine and the distant sea.

At first she had kept her reaction to the dead Schul-Klopper under control. Now, alone in her room, sprawled on the flowered print spread on the bed, she found the memory of his body making her skin itch, her head throb like the pounding of his hammer. When her mother peered into the room, Guttle blurted, "Why did we run out of milk? If we had milk, I wouldn't have stepped on him!"

"You're right, Guttle, it's my fault. Now come with me to the market."

"I don't want to go. Everyone keeps looking at me. As if it was me who made the Schul-Klopper die."

"No one is blaming you. No one is looking at you. What, are you planning to spend the rest of your life in this room?"

"You know something, Mama? There's not so much exciting happening outside."

"That again? You want a dead horse, maybe? Come, I need you to help me carry. I'll tell you what, bubbelah. Next time we run out of milk, I'll borrow some myself."

"There won't be a dead man to trip over!"

"I certainly hope not," Emmie Schnapper said.

On the third-floor of the first house inside the north gate, Yetta Liebmann, boney and haggard, heard footsteps on the stairs, then a knocking on the door. Emmie Schnapper and her daughter Guttle had returned from marketing, with the food Emmie had offered to bring.

"I got you a nice chicken," Frau Schnapper said, pulling a wrapped bird from one of two string bags. "And four small potatoes. And a little piece of sweet, for a treat."

Hiram Liebmann, the younger son, emerged from the front bedroom, holding his pocket watch and a piece of paper marked 1 + 10, which he showed to Frau Schnapper. It had taken her one hour and ten minutes for her to return, from the time he'd seen her leave through the gate.

Behind him appeared his older brother, Hersch, who scowled when he saw the food on the table. "What's all this?" he asked.

"Frau Schnapper brought it from the market," his mother said. "Wasn't that nice?"

"Give it back. We don't want charity."

"Oh, it's not charity," Frau Schnapper said. "You can pay for it when you have money."

"When do you think that will be? I don't get paid much for sweeping the schul."

"Don't you and your brother have a grave to dig?" his mother asked. "When you get paid for that, we'll have enough. Till then, your father could use a good meal. He's in there under the covers, he's always so cold."

Hersch said no more, but motioned to Hiram and led the way down the stairs. Watching them go, Guttle knew the brothers had seen her as a child, acting as if she were not there.

"I'm sorry," Yetta said to Emmie. "He's angry a lot these days. I don't know what dybbuk has gotten into him."

"This time of year, the spring air warming up, is worst on the young ones," Frau Schnapper said. "Guttle is the same. Sometimes I think their bodies have ancient memories, of trees and fields, of lakes in which to swim — and it makes them a little crazy. They haven't learned yet how to accept the walls."

"It's a hard thing to learn," Yetta said. "Sometimes I think my Hiram is the lucky one. He doesn't expect so much."

The women indulged themselves in a mutual sigh. Frau Schnapper left soon after, carrying her own purchases, to begin preparing the Sabbath meal. Guttle followed silently, feeling invisible.

Mentioning the grave her sons needed to dig had given Yetta an inspiration. She entered the small bedroom, where Leo peered from beneath covers pulled to his neck. "I have to go out," she said. "I'll be back soon."

She walked down the two flights of stairs slowly, holding tight to the rickety banister. In the lane she stayed close to the houses, ready to grab hold in case an uneven cobble twisted her ankle, or broke her shoe. Soon she reached her destination — the Judengasse hospital. It was a three-story building with examining rooms at street level and space for eight beds upstairs, twelve in an emergency. A Doctor's helper, seated at a table looking bored, asked what she needed. Yetta said she wanted to see the Doctor. When the assistant asked what the trouble was, Yetta told him it was a private matter.

In his office down the hall, Doctor Berkov stood from behind his writing table and helped her to a straight-backed chair. He, too, asked what the trouble was.

"There's no trouble," she replied. "I've come about the coat."

"What coat?"

"The Schul-Klopper's coat. When you bury him, you won't be needing his coat."

"You have a use for it?"

"My husband. You've seen him. He's cold all the time. For him I would like the coat."

The Doctor pondered. The deceased had not been diseased, he was fairly certain of that. "I don't see why not," he said, finally. "It's probably a good idea."

He went to another room, and returned with the worn black coat and handed it to her. At once she noticed a white stain near the collar.

"What's this?" she asked, pointing.

"Spilled milk."

"That I can wash out."

She thanked him, and with the coat folded under her arm she walked home, past the bakery with its warm smells of challah, past a pawn shop and a moneylender, past the rag picker's stall, till she climbed the steep stairs in her house. She found Leo sitting at the table in the kitchen, hoping she would fix a glass of tea.

"Better than tea, look what I got for you. A new coat!"

"A new coat? From where did you get a new coat?"

"It was the Schul-Klopper's. He won't be needing it."

Leo was a small man and seemed of late to be melting into nothing. He looked at the coat, stood, carefully put his arms through the sleeves, shrugged the collar onto his neck. The hem of the coat reached below his ankles. "Look, it fits," he said.

Yetta smiled, or at least one could say the corners of her mouth pulled back out of memory. She had done well. She moved to the kitchen, poured water from an earthen jar into the kettle for tea. She lit a few pieces of kindling in the stove.

"What are you doing?"

"I'm making you tea."

"I don't want tea. I'm going for a walk in my new coat."

With no further words Leo was out the door in his brown slippers, shuffling down the stairs, both feet touching each step, the way small children do. Yetta let the water boil for herself. She couldn't remember the last time he'd gone out.

He shuffled only as far as the rag dealer's shop, thinking: the coat of a dead man she wants me to wear! He shrugged off the coat, handed it to the skinny proprietor, Ephraim Hess. With a minimum of haggling they struck a deal. The rag dealer handed Leo a few kreuzer. He was still standing there, placing the coins in his pocket, one by one, when the rag dealer's waif of a wife, Eva, came out from inside the shop, carrying in a small blanket a newborn child. Handing the baby to her husband, she inspected the coat quickly. Just as quickly she pulled a faded dress from a nail at the front of the stall, and hung the coat there, the spot most visible to passersby.

"Eva, you can't put it out so fast," her young husband told her. "That's the Schul-Klopper's coat. He hasn't even been buried yet."

"All the better," his wife said. "Someone can dress nice for the funeral."

The infant started to squall. Eva took the baby, opened her blouse, gave the child a lovely breast on which to suck.

"That's a fine-looking child," Leo said. "What name do you call her?"

"It's a boy," the rag dealer said, the pride of a new father in his voice. "Our first child. Only eight hours old. We named him Solomon, after Israel's greatest king."

"After Israel's greatest poet," the wife said.

Leo offered a nod of understanding. "One Solomon dies, another Solomon is born. It's the way of the world."

He left them looking love into one another's eyes, and shuffled home with a new rhythm in his steps, humming to the music of the coins clinking in his pocket. He was not so old he could not remember young love. When he entered the apartment after a slow climb up the stairs, Yetta, appraising him as if she were a dealer in old men, said, "What did you do with your new coat? You didn't lose it already!"

"I didn't lose it. I sold it to the rag dealer." He jingled his pocket, and shook his elbows as if he were about to dance.

"You sold it? It was supposed to keep you warm."

"Now we have money to buy wood. To keep you warm, too, bubbelah. And to cook the chicken." He eased himself onto a chair. Both the chair and his knees creaked.

"We already have wood to cook the chicken," Yetta said.

"Then it's to buy wood for next week's chicken."

"Wood for next week's chicken? We don't have chicken for next week's chicken. Besides, the coffin maker gives us wood. He gives the boys his odds and ends, pieces too small to use. He doesn't charge for that."

"There you go. In case he starts to charge, we'll have money for wood."

Yetta shook her head, closing her eyes as she did, as she had been doing for thirty-five years. She approached her husband and pressed her lips to the top of his flaking head. He was bald except for a gray fringe that circled the back from ear to ear. "I don't know what to do, Leo. I tried to do something nice for you."

"What you can do nice for me?" He took her wrinkled hand and gently pulled her onto his boney knees, which had almost worn through his breeches. "What you can do nice for me, Yetta darling, is live with me until I die."

"All the way till then?" She tugged lightly at his chin. "That's a lot to ask, you know. That young Doctor has a *schön* tush."

He pushed her off of his lap. "In that case, make me a glass of tea before you run away with him."

Yetta kissed the whorls of his ear, from which small white hairs were growing, and made him a glass of tea. He chopped with a knife at a bowl of honey, and when a small piece broke off placed it between his lips. As he sipped the tea through the crystal honey, Yetta sat across from him and watched, saying nothing.

And if, as he drank his tea, he was thinking what lovely breasts the rag dealer's young wife has, what harm was being done?

Doctor Lev Berkov, wearing the brown breeches, loose-fitting white shirt and leather vest that was the fashion for younger men, caught up with the Chief Rabbi just as he was locking his study, and asked to speak with him. Rabbi Eleazar said he had no time just then, but when the Doctor said his problem was related to the forthcoming funeral, the Rabbi gave him a questioning, annoyed look, then reluctantly unlocked the door and motioned him inside. The Rabbi seated himself behind his desk, but did not put a match to the lamp; the only light in the room filtered in through the single curtained window that faced the lane. The Rabbi was dressed, as always, in black. The Doctor at first had difficulty seeing him.

The Origin of Sorrow 33

"It's about Solomon Gruen," Berkov said, seating himself on a wooden chair. He removed his three-cornered hat, making sure with his right hand that the yarmulke he wore underneath had remained in place.

"What about him, may he rest in peace?" the Chief Rabbi said. Avram Eleazar was sixty-two years old, not tall but broad-shouldered, looking more like a sea captain than a man of religion, except for the pallor above his full gray beard. He'd been the Chief Rabbi in the Judengasse for fifteen years, had carried its burdens on his shoulders more than people knew.

"I'm not certain that he died of heart seizure," the Doctor said.

The Rabbi frowned, his expression almost lost within his beard. "Heart seizure, brain seizure, what does it matter? Dead is dead — not to sound harsh. We still have to bury him before the sun sets."

In his four years at the hospital the Doctor had become used to giving bad news. He found what he needed to tell the Rabbi more difficult than he had expected. "The hospital is not set up to do an autopsy, as you know. We need all our space for the living. Most often there's no need, the cause of death usually has been lingering, and is plain to see. I do what little I can to look over the body without defiling it. I look in the nose, the mouth, the ears, as a matter of simple medical procedure. In Herr Gruen's case, there may be a problem."

"What sort of problem?" The powerful voice emanated disembodied from the dark.

"When his glands dried — his salivary glands — I found traces of a white residue on his tongue, and leading down into his throat. I don't know what it is."

The Rabbi pulled a gold pocket watch from his vest. It was a recent gift from a Rabbi from Weimar who had come to join the staff of the yeshiva, which, despite the walls, was known throughout the region for its Talmudic studies. He squinted at the watch, angling it toward the window so he could read the face. He did not return it to his pocket, but set it on his desk. "About this you're bothering me?" he asked, sounding more irritated than he'd intended. "White something that you don't know what it is? Salt is white. Milk is white. Cheese is white. Crystals of honey are white. You're the Doctor, why do you come to me?"

"It's none of those things. I'm afraid it's nothing he would normally ingest, or I wouldn't be here. It's the residue of a fine powder that reminds me of no food."

"Out with it, Doctor. What does it remind you of?"

Berkov hesitated. A carriage passing slowly on the cobbles rattled the window. There was no room for horses or coaches to be kept in the lane, but frail or wealthy residents sometimes paid a driver to deliver goods to their doors in narrow one-horse carriages. When the noise had faded, the Doctor said, "It reminds me of arsenic."

"Arsenic? Arsenic is a poison. Why would the Schul-Klopper swallow arsenic? Are you saying he killed himself? I don't believe that. Not for a moment!"

"I'm not saying that. I'm not even saying it's arsenic. I don't know what it is. If it is arsenic, I still wouldn't think he killed himself. If he were to do that, for whatever reason, he most likely would have done it in his room. Arsenic works quickly. I don't think he could have ingested it and then walked the length of the lane, pausing to knock on every door, and reached the end alive."

"I knew Solomon Gruen well," the Rabbi said, leaning his elbows on his desk. His words were spoken slowly, as if he were controlling great anger. "There was no indication he was troubled. If he were, he would have come to me. Besides, he was a pious man, and the Talmud forbids self slaughter. He did not kill himself." The Rabbi slapped the flat of his hand on the oak desk top. The pocket watch jumped. "Do you understand?"

Pulling a handkerchief from his pocket, wiping his face, the Doctor said, "I agree with you completely. I never meant to suggest that was the case."

"Then what is it you are suggesting?"

"I'm saying that if my guess is correct — and it is only a guess — somebody fed it to him."

"That's absurd," the Rabbi said, standing abruptly. "Who would do such a thing?"

"I have no idea."

"Why would anyone do such a thing?"

"I have no idea about that, either. I'm a physician, not a Constable. I'm only telling you of a possibility. People often gave the Schul-Klopper something to drink when he knocked on their doors, am I right? A glass of tea, a glass of milk. It was considered a mitzvah. The poison could have been mixed into something that he drank shortly before he died."

"Where would someone get arsenic without arousing suspicion? Without being reported to the police?"

"It's in every house in the lane. Ratsbane."

The Rabbi shook his head. "I won't listen to any more of this. A murderer in the Judengasse? I don't believe it. I won't believe it."

"I understand how you feel, Rabbi. But who would have thought that a son of Adam, the creation of Yahweh himself, would be a murderer?"

Deflated, the Rabbi lowered himself into his chair. His tone became softer. "You want to know something, Doctor? That's my least favorite story in the Torah. I never believed Cain had motive enough to kill his brother. And Abel certainly was not at fault in any way." He picked up a drinking mug on his desk and studied it, as if looking for an answer there. "I suppose Cain is meant as a symbol," he said. "A warning that we all have the capacity for evil."

"One of two brothers. Fifty percent evil. That's quite a warning."

"You forget Seth."

"Yes, there was also Seth. So two thirds of our human make-up is good."

"Most of the time." Wearily, the Rabbi moved his arm in a circle above his head, perhaps to indicate the stone walls that surrounded them. "But that's another matter. Are you asking me to delay the funeral?"

"Not at all. There's no need for that."

"You're not suggesting we call in the police? They disturb us enough on their own."

"No police, Rabbi. Certainly not till we have more information."

"So why have you told me this?"

"Medical ethics, in my view, requires that I pursue the matter. I plan to take the residue to a chemist in the town, to find out what it is. I just felt that, as the head of the community, you ought to be informed."

"What if you're right, and the chemist goes to the police?"

"He won't. We pay him hundreds of gulden a year for medicines. He'll do as I say. Besides, I won't tell him the circumstances."

From outside the window came the sound of another narrow carriage clattering along the cobbles. The Rabbi unfolded from his chair, looked at his watch, placed it in his vest pocket. "I suppose I should thank you for telling me," he said. "Now I'm sure to get heartburn from the Sabbath dinner my good wife has spent all day preparing. I hope I still have some soda powder upstairs."

"If you don't, we have plenty at the hospital. It's our most common request."

Moving to the door, the Rabbi stopped. "What about soda powder! That's white. Have you thought of that?"

"I'm afraid I have. But it fizzles when you drink it. I would expect to find residue on the roof of the mouth, perhaps inside the cheeks. Not just on the tongue and throat. That's just my surmise, of course. I could be wrong. Even so, why would Herr Gruen drink soda powder first thing in the morning?"

"It fits," the Rabbi said. "Solomon woke up with chest pains. He thought it must be indigestion. So he took some soda, to settle his stomach.

And he went out on his rounds. Only this time it was not indigestion. The pains were from his heart. When he reached the end of the lane, his heart failed."

"It's a tempting scenario."

"Of course that's what happened! You can dispose of your residue. I'm glad you came to me, Lev, to talk things out before you did anything rash."

"I'll pray that you are correct," the Doctor said. "But on Monday I'll take the residue to the chemist."

"Why stir up trouble that isn't necessary?"

"If Herr Gruen was poisoned, there is a sick murderer among us. He could kill again."

For the second time in the conversation the Rabbi felt deflated. "Go," he said. "I won't discuss this any further. My wife is waiting upstairs. No doubt she's angry already."

The Doctor opened the the door, and turned. "I'll keep you informed, Rabbi."

"I'm sure you will," the Rabbi said. Then, as if realizing he should not be so angry at the young Doctor, he said, "What you should do, Lev, if I may call you that, is take your mind off your work a little. It struck me this morning, when she found the body, how nicely the Schnapper girl has grown up. Maybe pay her some attention. She's got a brain in her, that one. She's become a jewel of the lane. "

"Rabbi, you sound like the women."

"They all want you to marry the Schnapper girl?"

"They all want me to marry their daughters."

Rabbi Eleazar smiled through his beard. He clamped the Doctor on the shoulder.

"I'll think about what you said," the Doctor told him

The Rabbi answered, "And I'll try not to think about what you've said."

3

The usual aromas of oak and wood oil in the shop of the cabinet maker were obscured by the smell of newly cut spruce from the coffin that stood upright against a wall. The janitor from the synagogue was supposed to come for it, but hadn't; perhaps he was at the cemetery, digging the grave. Through his open door Yussel Kahn saw the girl from the bakery kneeling motionless beside the trench. She looked as if she were praying, but Jews didn't kneel when they prayed, Catholics did. He wasn't sure about Lutherans.

Even Gentiles, he was certain, didn't pray to floating turds.

The coffin maker's story was well known to Guttle and to all the women in the bakery. From his earliest adult years, Yussel Kahn had been the finest carpenter in the Judengasse. He made tables and chairs and cabinets for all the wealthiest families (though wealthy in the Judengasse was not like wealthy outside.) Because his fine work was too expensive for some, he made coffins at no charge for every family that needed one. The boxes did not take long to make, the wood was the cheapest, he asked from the bereaved only a small donation to the temple, at which he prayed each morning, often walking the last few metres alongside the Schul-Klopper.

Yussel took his childhood love Lainie as a bride as soon as he turned twenty-five. Although the minimum age had been established to keep the Jewish population down, Yussel and his young bride learned quickly that Fate (they were reluctant to blame Yahweh) had other ways to achieve that end. In the first year of their marriage, Lainie gave birth to a boy, but he died after two days. Tears rolled down Yussel's cheeks and wet his beard as he banged together a tiny coffin in which to bury his first-born son. In the second year, Lainie gave birth to a sweet baby girl, the image of herself. The girl lived only a week. Yussel tearfully buried another child. But worse happened the third year. Another boy was conceived, and grew in his mother's womb, but this one was born dead, and in his posthumous birth he took his bleeding mother with him.

Yussel was near to crazy. For months he didn't work. Each morning and each evening in the synagogue he asked Yahweh what he had done to offend. He received no answer. He swore he would never marry again, would produce no more children. When finally he reopened his shop, he let it be known that he would no longer make coffins for infants. Adults were supposed to die, he said, but children were not.

This, of course, did not prevent the children of other families from dying — in infancy, or in their first year, or in their second. The Judengasse was so overcrowded, the sanitary conditions were so bad, the trench in the street like an open sore, that disease struck often, overwhelming the weakest, the little ones, first. But when the bereaved parents of a dead baby came to the coffin maker, he always turned them away.

"We have to bury her!" the crazed mother would wail.

"Take a drawer from a cabinet," Yussel would reply calmly, "and bury her in that." And he would give them a piece of board with which to cover the burial drawer, and he would send them on their way.

The people of the Judengasse were not happy with this, but the other two carpenters in the lane, both of whom had apprenticed with Yussel and loved him dearly, sided with the coffin maker. They would not break his rule. Someone, they said, needed to stand up to Gott.

Inevitably, what would happen is that month after month the bereaved parents would see the dark space for the missing drawer in their bedroom dresser or kitchen cabinet and be reminded again of their loss. They would come to Yussel again, and plead, and he would agree to make a drawer to match the one now buried in the cemetery. When it was done, and he gave it to them, and they paid him and thanked him, he would always tell them: "You think this will help you forget. Believe me, you will never forget."

They didn't argue with him; they knew his own sad story.

In time, a few cynics began to whisper that this was all a business ploy, that because the carpenter made coffins for free, but charged for replacing drawers, he emerged with a fatter purse. But none who knew the coffin maker believed that. Certainly not the women in the bakery. Certainly not Guttle Schnapper.

He wanted to go to her, seeing her kneeling by the trench, ask if something was wrong, but he held back. He would only torment himself. It was five years since his wife had died, since the third of their three babies had died, since he had vowed that he would never marry again. With the passing years his maleness had grown heavy; he needed release more loving than a twisted sheet. But he had made his vow. And the girl was young. She was the daughter of the Court Jew Wolf Schnapper, he knew, and would come with a fine dowry — but what did he, Yussel Kahn, have to offer? Only a small bedroom above the shop, with a small kitchen shared by three families. There was no reason her father would agree.

Turning from the doorway, he bumped his elbow on the coffin. With a fierce burst of strength he embraced the coffin, his chest hard against it, his arms tight around it, and carried it through the open doorway. Carefully he leaned it against the wall outside.

The girl didn't look at him. Her eyes might as well have been closed.

Had he, when his wife died, embraced a living death as firmly as he'd just embraced the coffin? Perhaps.

In the center of the workshop was a piece he'd been crafting all week, a new writing table commissioned by her father. Only the drawer for pens and paper was missing. He'd have finished it today had it not been for the interruptions. On his work bench lay a new hammer he had carved at the request of the Chief Rabbi, a gift from the synagogue for the next Schul-Klopper, whomever that might be. He'd donated a rare piece of mahogany he'd been saving for something special; it held a smoother, more graceful curve than oak as the hammer broadened from the narrow end that fit in the hand to the wide end that withstood the thumping on doors. Her father's writing table was lambent with light from the oil lamps. Perhaps he could invite her in to see it. But would she care? Would she think him strange? Would she be frightened?

He was thirty-three years old, and a fool. His rust-colored hair had begun to thin, his beak of a nose made him less than handsome. At his age he could not throw himself at a virgin. If he ever should marry again, a widow with hungry children to feed would make more sense. There were so many of those in the Judengasse.

Her hair had been in braids in the morning, wrapped atop her head. Now one braid had fallen, and hung behind her shoulder, with a white ribbon dangling. She seemed not to have noticed. One day the previous autumn, after she had washed her hair for the Sabbath, he'd seen her hanging her head out the window of her third-story room, apparently hoping the light breeze twisting above the street would dry it quickly. The long dark hair spilling loose, framing her innocent face, became imprinted on his pillow that night. Only on rare nights since had he not imagined her hair splayed there. It was an image, he assured himself, that was historical. He could imagine her in some ancient desert, wrapped head to foot in white, a shepherd's crook in her hands as she moved among a flock equally white. Behind her, in the distance, was a tent. It was an image from the Torah. Every Friday since, the cabinet maker had cut his eyes toward the bakery five, ten, twenty times, in hopes of catching a glimpse of her.

Back from the market, leaning against the Owl, Guttle watches Frau Liebmann walk by as if not seeing her. A few minutes later she returns, carrying a long black coat. It looks like the dead Schul-Klopper's coat. Moments after, Herr Liebmann shuffles past wearing the same coat — then returns without it. Guttle wonders what is happening, wonders if she is imagining things. Leaping about, her mind returns to the threat of marriage to the Cantor. His mother, Sophie Marcus, a contralto, begins to sing.

> Just look at her, beside the stinking ditch,
> A fit place for a bitch too good for Sonny.
> On her knees, the hussy is a tease,
> And yet the lad is hers, for love and money.
> Filled with gloom, he moons up in his room,
> There is no greater pain for any mortal;
> When word spreads that he won't be her groom
> He fears that all the lane will surely chortle.
> Now my Jake must to the Court Jew go
> And end my Viktor's woe with an arrangement —
> A future marriage match! And if he dare say no
> This cobbled lane will know a mean estrangement.
> See her sweat — she acts as if she's mute,
> As if she cannot see or hear me.
> Listen, sweet: if you don't change your tune
> I swear by God above, you'll fear me.
> Not high stone walls, not even iron gates,
> Can hurt like Sophie Marcus when she hates!

The shadowy image of Sophie Marcus slunk away. Feeling dazed, Guttle did not notice her friend Izzy approach.

"Your mind is far away," he said. "Do you want to tell me where it is?"

"Maybe some other time."

"Can I tell you about something, then?" Izzy asked. Focusing, she began to discern the excitement in his voice. "It's about the Torah. I've been thinking about about how it ends, with Moses leading the Jews to Eretz Yisroel. Moses dies, he never gets to enter the Promised Land. And his story just stops, more than two thousand years ago."

"What else should there be?"

"The Gentiles added their own New Testament. Which we don't believe happened, which we're not allowed to talk about. But what about the Jews? What happened to them? We're still here. Did our people forget how to write?"

Their homes were side by side, touching. On the Schnapper residence a blue owl, now faded, had been painted long ago. Guttle ran her fingers over it, trying to listen. Many of the tenements had pictures of animals on them, or colorful shields, to brighten the ghetto a bit, and to distinguish one adjoining house from the next. Only these small paintings kept the tenements from resembling two large rows of rotting teeth.

Izzy was still speaking. "When Herr Gruen died today" — that got her attention — "I thought: he knew everybody in the Judengasse, from being the Schul-Klopper for so long. He must know lots of stories. The histories of lots of families. Maybe some of them were important for us to know. Maybe angels spoke to some of those families. Maybe even Yahweh. But now the Schul-Klopper is dead, so he can't pass the stories on to anyone."

Guttle glanced impatiently at her door; she wanted to wash her hair. "Adonai, here in the Judengasse?"

"Why not? He talked to the Jews for thousands of years. All of a sudden He stopped. Why did He stop? Who says He stopped?"

"Maybe He can't find us behind these walls."

"I'm serious."

"I'm serious, too."

"Anyway," Izzy went on, "I had this idea. It's crazy, I know. But I worked my courage up, and I talked to Rabbi Simcha after class. About shouldn't somebody be writing another sacred book, about what's happened to the Jews since then? All the way to today. Even here in the Judengasse. Just the important stuff, of course."

"Like what? Moses parting the sewage?"

He ignored her jibe. "You know what Rabbi Simcha said? He thought it was an interesting idea. 'A powerful idea,' he said. He took me in to see the Chief Rabbi, without even an appointment, and he made me tell the whole thing again, with the Chief Rabbi sitting there in his big leather chair, with a red carpet on the floor. I never was in there before."

"And then?" She was getting excited for him now. She had an idea what was coming.

"I was scared. At first he didn't say anything. He just sat there, stroking his beard. When he finally spoke, he agreed it was an interesting idea. 'Especially coming from one so young.' He said it would involve a lot of research, it would take many years to finish. Which meant it was an undertaking only for a young man. He looked at me with those lentil eyes of his, with the centers hard, only now they seemed soft and kind somehow. I'm so stupid, I didn't understand what he meant. Then he said, 'I'm told the other boys call you Izzy the Wise.' I still didn't get it. So he said, 'What do you say, Izzy the Wise? Do you think you are up to the task?'"

Isidor began to cough, had to struggle to catch his breath. His freckled face reddened.

"And you said?"

"I began to cough and choke, just like now. I couldn't say anything. Then I blurted, 'Do you really think I'm worthy of doing this, Rabbi?' He sat there and looked at me, stroking his beard again. I think maybe he thinks with his beard. His eyes became like tiny woodstoves, bits of fire flaring in them. 'Whether you are worthy enough is between you and Yahweh,' he said. 'My question is, are you smart enough?'"

Guttle laughed, a short burst, and covered her mouth in apology. She placed a hand on his arm. "What could you say to that?"

"I didn't know what to say. But I got inspired. Maybe from the painting of Moses receiving the Ten Commandments, which is on the wall behind his desk. Or maybe from my own excitement. I had never meant for me to be the one to write such a book. That would be crazy. But all at once I wanted to. More than anything. The Chief Rabbi just sat there, waiting for me to answer. What I finally said was, 'If I am entrusted by you to attempt this, perhaps Yahweh will make me smart enough.'"

Guttle grinned, her eyes glistened. "We don't call you Izzy the Wise for nothing. I'll bet he ate it up."

"Like a freshly cooked chicken. That's my new task — my burden, is the word he used — for all my yeshiva years. Starting now. To gather old stories. To find out what happened to the Jews since the Temple was destroyed. To set it down. As if for a new holy book, for me to write later on, or for my descendants to write. He used that word. Descendants. I never thought about us having Descendants. Have you."

"That's wonderful!" Ignoring his question, she squeezed his hand. His breath stopped at the warmth of her touch. "I was going to kiss you on the cheek, for good luck," she said. "But now I don't think I'm allowed. Now that you're a holy man."

Isidor looked at the ground. Why did she always do that to him? Even in his time of triumph. Perhaps underneath, Guttle was cruel. He managed to mumble, "I don't think I'm holy yet. Writers aren't holy, anyway."

With his eye cast down at the cobbles, Isidor saw neither the smile that parted her lips nor the gleam in her eyes as she leaned close and kissed his cheek. By the time he looked up to see her face she had disappeared into the entrance of the Owl. He could hear her swift footsteps bounding up the stairs. He touched the cheek where for the merest of moments her lips had lightly pressed, where perhaps a wisp of her breath still lingered. It had happened so quickly, he wondered if he had only imagined it.

Guttle wished that Joan of Arc had been Jewish. Her name then would have been Jennie Aron, as in Aron Kodesh. She would have been revered in the lane, just as the women of the Pentateuch were. Guttle was happy for Izzy in part because history intrigued her. The Holy Roman Empire was so scattered that little of interest had happened there, as far as she knew, but neighboring France had been alive with heroes, with vast adventures. Sitting on her bed by the third-floor window, trying to put the dead Schul-Klopper out of her mind, she pulled from her shelf her favorite book, *The History of France from Hugh Cept to Louis IV*; her father, approving of her interest, had bought her a German translation for her fourteenth birthday. She had been enthralled by all of it, but nothing could equal the story of Jennie Aron. Jennie had been only seventeen when God told her to lead the armies of France into battle, to drive out the English, who had taken over her country. Covered head to toe in armor, sword in hand, Jennie had gone to war. Guttle herself still had a year and a half before she reached seventeen — plenty of time for Yahweh to speak to her, to tell her to tear down the gates. She would do it fiercely, if only He would show her how. She kicked off her shoes and stretched out on her bed, wiggling her toes, and opened the book to Jennie's story. When her chores were done she liked more than anything to read; her books allowed her to escape from the lane. But here was the terrible illustration — Jennie being burned at the stake. The French girl was looking toward the heavens while flames around her knees crept higher. Some of the spectators were laughing.

Guttle shivered, as not the voice of Yahweh but a chill wind blew through the open window. She thought again of what she had been trying to keep out of her mind. The questions the Doctor had asked her about the spilled milk. Later she had seen him going into the Rabbi's study. The Doctor was not very pious; she had never seen him go there before. She had a strong feeling that something was very wrong, and that it had to do with the death of the Schul-Klopper. She closed her eyes against the vision that assaulted her, and the terrible word: Disease. Had the Schul-Klopper died of the smallpox? Or the plague? Would pock marks blow through the lane like poisoned leaves, spreading pain and death?

She tried to calm herself. If that were the case, the Chief Rabbi or the Doctor would already have made an announcement about what should be done.

As Hiram and Hersch Liebmann strode the cobbles together, a stranger might have mistaken them for twins. Both were broad-shouldered, their arms and legs well-muscled. Both kept their hair long but their faces beardless. They wore faded clothes Yetta had bought at one of the rag picker shops. Their shirts were open at the neck, a tangle of chest hair poking through. Their sturdy faces were similar, though Hiram's features were leaner. Hersch at twenty-four was two years older. He wore a dark blue yarmulke pinned to his hair; his job at the synagogue required one. Hiram's head was bare; he would worship no God that had deprived him from birth of hearing, of speech.

An occasional rag picker or dealer in junk furniture waved at them as they passed. Most people in the street did not. The boys were not outcasts, there just seemed no reason for them to be included in other peoples' lives. When Solomon Gruen a few years back hired Hersch as janitor at the synagogue, most people accepted it, but nobody cheered.

Their first stop was at the coffin maker. They found the coffin leaning against the wall outside. Hersch pointed to the narrow lower end, grabbed the wider end himself, and together they carried the empty box down the lane and across the trench to the hospital. At the direction of Doctor Berkov, they placed it on a low table in a small room. Through the doorway of an adjoining room Hiram saw on another table a long shape covered by a sheet.

They left the hospital quickly and crossed to the synagogue. Hiram waited outside. He pulled his watch from his pocket. Barely more than a minute passed before Hersch emerged with Rabbi Simcha, the second in command, and together the three walked toward the south gate. Just before reaching it they turned right. The cemetery spread before them, the only piece of visible land remaining in the Judengasse. Gray tombstones, many listing at odd angles, seemed to grow in uneven rows all the way to the ghetto wall, which veered away in a slight arc to accommodate the graves. The burial ground was older than the Judengasse; it had been there when the Jews of Frankfurt were free to come and go. The oldest grave was from the Christian year 1234. More than five thousand graves had been dug since.

The boys grabbed weathered spades that lay inside the cemetery gate. They followed as Rabbi Simcha, walking among the stones, reading an epitaph here, another there, looking for a spot in which to fit Solomon Gruen. Near the center of the cemetery, he stopped. "Let's do it here," he said, looking at both, then realizing, speaking only to Hersch. "It's the Becker plot, but there are no more Beckers here. They moved to France years ago. The graves are tight, but Solomon Gruen had no family, we'll squeeze him in. He was a good man. I don't think the Beckers will mind."

"If they do, they won't complain," Hersch said.

The Rabbi put a hand to his lips to hide a small grin. He was not sure if Hersch was indulging in morbid humor or was just being crude.

Thirty-six years old, Rabbi Emil Simcha was a slim man, with a calm demeanor despite intense dark eyes that peered, ever curious, above his full brown beard. A pink scar ran from above his left eye to his left temple. His cheeks were pitted with souvenirs of smallpox. Pacing off where the grave should be, he took Hiram's spade and drew a narrow rectangle in the dirt. When he handed the spade back, Hiram waved his free hand in front of him, and made knocking motions with his fist. He pointed at the ground. When the Rabbi hesitated, uncertain, Hiram repeated the motions in reverse, pointing to the earth, knocking in the air, tapping his hand on his chest.

"Yes," the Rabbi said, nodding, mouthing his words slowly to Hiram, not knowing if he could read lips. "The grave is for the Schul-Klopper. You'll dig his grave here."

Hiram nodded vigorously. The Rabbi replied with two nods of his own. He was glad to have communicated, though he was not sure he understood all that had been said.

The Lord speaks in many tongues, the Rabbi thought as he left the brothers. We are deaf mutes in front of Him. We cannot hear, neither can we reply. Yet we pity the obviously deaf and dumb among us — but not ourselves.

Restless, Guttle asked her sister Amelia if she would help pump water for the Sabbath. Seven years old, with bright blue eyes that were unusual in the lane, and pale brown hair, Amelia did a skip and jump, indicating she was eager and ready. She loved working the hand pump, watching the water spurt as if by magic from beneath the ground. Guttle lifted a large bucket from beside the stove, handed a kettle to the child and took a larger kettle herself.

Together they went down the stairs and through a narrow passage three houses down the lane that led to the space in the rear where the pumps grew like a stunted iron tree between the front and rear rows of tenements. Guttle set the bucket in the mud under the spout. Amelia, using both hands, primed the pump vigorously, until water began to fall from the spout and splash into the bucket.

When it was almost full, Guttle, straining, lifted the heavy bucket away from the spout and set a kettle in its place, and Amelia began to pump again. They needed enough water till Sunday; pumping on the Sabbath would violate the day of rest.

"Will you dance with me tomorrow night?" Amelia asked as she pumped.

"I don't think there will be dancing this week."

"But there's always dancing on Saturday night."

"The Schul-Klopper died today. I don't think the men will bring out their fiddles. It wouldn't be appropriate."

The child stopped pumping as the kettle overflowed. Guttle replaced it with the smaller one.

"Didn't the Schul-Klopper go to heaven?" Amelia asked.

"I'm sure he did. He was a devout man."

"Isn't going to heaven good? Shouldn't people be happy for him?"

"That's a good thought. But grown-ups don't seem to look at it that way."

The child stopped pumping. The water had filled the second kettle.

"I've got an idea," Guttle said. "Why don't we dance now?"

"Here? People might see."

"They always see in the lane." She took the child's hands in hers, and led her a few metres from the pump, to where the ground was dry.

"There isn't any music."

"Listen to the music in your head."

Humming, Guttle began to turn her sister in a slow dance. Amelia heard her inner music, danced more rapidly, causing Guttle to spin. Guttle was hearing a waltz; the child seemed to hear a polka.

"Swing me, now!" Amelia said, and as she ran in a rapid circle around Guttle she lifted her legs off the ground and their arms stretched taut. Guttle, whirling in place, spun her about, the child's legs extended full out under her green dress, her hair flying behind her. Around and around she swung, her feet inches off the ground, till her arms tired and she let her legs sink and dragged the toes of her scuffed and muddy shoes, and stumbled to a stop. The grinning faces of both sisters were flushed. Wiping perspiration from her forehead, slightly dizzy, Guttle stepped backwards, and nearly bumped into Eva Hess, the rag picker's wife, who put a hand forward to prevent a collision, and placed an empty kettle on the ground.

"Looks as if you were going around in circles, Amelia," the slim young mother said.

"That's what Jews do."

"Why do you say that?"

"If we went in a straight line, we'd bump into a wall."

Guttle looked at Eva, but spoke to Amelia. "Who told you that, Ami?"

"Nobody told me. It's obvious."

Eva looked at the child. "The lane is a cruel teacher."

Climbing the stairs, Guttle felt confident she would not lay awake that night thinking of the Schul-Klopper's body. She had seen a body before, when her brother Joseph had taken ill and died; she'd been nine at the time, and Joseph four. But Amelia's picture of Jews walking in circles, exhausting circles with no end in sight, was an image new to her. A weary carousel, without color or destination — already it turned and turned before her eyes.

4

"He asked you for your hand? Surely he knows better."

"He thinks no father would turn him down."

"He may be right. A Cantor in the family would be sweet. So, if you feel that way, why do you lead him on?"

"I don't lead him on. I merely walk with him."

"At night!"

"In the evening. The lane is narrow, when you walk you are always walking with someone. Besides, we always go to the cemetery. That's hardly a place for courting."

"Then why do you go there?"

"It's deserted in the evening. He sings to me there."

"Guttle! You let him sing to you?"

"Not to me! He sings arias, from the operas he knows. He tells me stories, of Milan and Berlin, where he studied. He describes the operas. I view him as a teacher, and I his student."

"Your father took you to see opera once, at the Prince's court."

"You think I don't remember? Prevus and Euridyce, by Glock. The costumes were so beautiful — and the music. It soared! No doubt that's why I admire Viktor's songs."

"Perhaps tonight, after the funeral, his father will ask your Papa for your hand. I doubt your Papa would say no."

"No!"

"Viktor's father, Jacob Marcus, is a moneylender. He comes from a good family."

"You mean a wealthy one!"

"The boy himself may have come into wealth today, when his uncle passed away. Solomon Gruen had no children of his own."

"I didn't know the Schul-Klopper was Viktor's uncle. But his mother is a shrew."

"That may be true. But you will marry whom your Papa wishes. The Cantor, who is wealthy now, could be the perfect match."

"No."

"It's so."

"No!"

"It's so!"

"No, no, no, no, no!"

She selected Sabbath clothing and carried it to the washing-up closet. Pouring water from a kettle into the wash basin, she stripped off her clothes and began to scrub herself with a soapy cloth. She would have liked to go to the communal bath, but on Fridays it was reserved for men, so they could bathe before the Sabbath. She soaped under her arms, looked in the mirror above the wooden commode, lathered under her breasts. Nice enough, she thought, though she had never caught up in size with her friend Dvorah Schlicter; that contest she'd lost forever. She washed away the soap and dried herself with a towel and put on the clothes she'd chosen for the funeral: a black skirt to go with her black cloak, and a beige silk blouse, one of three silk blouses she owned. She could have made more but there wasn't any point; under Frankfurt law, Jewish women could wear silk only on the Sabbath.

She peered into the children's room. Avra had put the little ones down for a nap, and had fallen asleep herself. Until not long ago the children had been Guttle's responsibility; she'd read them stories from the Torah till their eye-lids grew heavy. It was a way to learn more of the Torah for herself. And it put them to sleep every time. What courageous chutzpah Izzy had, she thought. A companion book to the Torah! Well, if anyone could do it, Izzy could.

She told her mother she was going out. In the street, men who'd had business in the city were hurrying in through the gate to get ready for the funeral. As a little girl she used to wait for her father impatiently every afternoon and run to the gate when she saw him coming, and hug him around the knees, till he picked her up and she kissed his cheek and he carried her to the house. She hadn't met him there for a long time. He'd like that.

From the slaughterhouse beyond the gate came the sound of a cow lowing. She approached the gate and looked out. The new young guard from the morning still was there, his back to her. How long ago that seemed! The bell of the cathedral rang out over the city, the hourly mockery. It was not yet the Sabbath, perhaps she should go past the gate and taunt that new guard. See if he would arrest her for donning her silk blouse three hours early. But she was not feeling mischievous, just bored.

Jennie Aron, alias Jeanne d'Arc, alias Joan of Arc, stared at the entry. The high stone walls on either side curved together and formed an arch over the gates. The Maid of Orlean noticed something she'd never focused on before. Between the iron gates and the stone walls was pebble-filled cement to which the gates were attached. Cement was vulnerable. The carpenters would have tools that could chip away at it. In the dark of night the cement could be removed, and with her sword she could lead her people through the opening. A night guard with a musket was always stationed outside, he would hear the assault. She could overpower him — but what then? That was the larger question. Her fellow Jews could get outside the gates — but their homes, their shops, their schul would remain within. They would have no place to go. Only she, the leader, if caught, would have a destination — the Frankfurt prison across the river, with its narrow cells, its stench, its rats, its gallows. Jennie might be executed a second time.

Idling backwards, Guttle found herself on the precise spot where she'd discovered Herr Gruen's body. Quickly she jumped away, out of fear or respect. One shoe landed on the edge of a muddy cobble, her ankle turned, sprained; she shuddered, as if she had trod upon a soul.

Across the river from the Judengasse, not far from the Sachsenhauser Bridge and the Fahrtor Gate, which was the principal entrance to Frankfurt, a black carriage pulled by a snorting white horse rolled to a stop at a stable. The driver, who was the lone occupant, stepped down amid the smell of horses and manure. He handed the reigns to a stable boy and walked towards the office to settle his bill. He was a short, stout man with an ample belly packed into a tight-fitting blue coat and vest, gray knee-breeches and gray stockings. On his head was a black three-cornered hat, partially covering a stylish but unpowdered wig. His shoes had silver buckles, his white blouse was ruffled at the collar. The man was Wolf Schnapper — husband to Emmie, father to Guttle, Avra, Amelia, Rifka and Benjamin. He was a successful moneychanger, the trusted personal banker to the Prince of Sachsen-Meiningen. He handled the Prince's investments, changed money for him when he was going to travel, provided loans at low interest when the Prince needed a new stallion, a new carriage, a new mistress. The fact that the principality was a small one did not lessen Wolf Schnapper's pride in his position.

In the stable office, Wolf signed his name to a ledger. His credit was good here, he settled his account promptly at the end of the month. The stable manager put a mark beside the signature, indicating that horse and carriage had not been ill used.

As he stepped outside, Schnapper heard the pounding of a horse racing along the hard-packed dirt road. With a strong pull on the reins the rider tugged a stunning black stallion to a stop at the gate, and leaped off. He was a younger man, twenty-five, tall and lean, with a short brown beard, wearing a three-cornered hat much like Schnapper's, but no wig. He was dressed less formally than the Court Factor — brown knee-breeches, loose white blouse, leather vest, well-worn shoes. A small leather pouch hung from his waist.

"Meyer Amschel!" Schnapper called as he approached the younger man, a neighbor who lived a few houses away. "You were riding like a bandit. Look, you're out of breath."

"So's the horse," the young man said. He handed the reins to the stable boy and took several deep breaths. His smile suggested he was pleased with his ride, and also with his dismount. He wiped the sweat from his face, from the small trimmed beard on his chin.

"Is the public coach not dangerous enough for you?" Schnapper asked.

"Not fast enough. I wanted to be back for the funeral. I imagine that's why you're early as well."

"Exactly so. But there are cutthroats on the highway, it's not safe to ride alone."

"So they say."

Schnapper shook his head, disapproving of the young man's recklessness. He knew Meyer Amschel was an orphan, had been for many years, had no father to caution him. Then Schnapper realized that he himself had traveled alone today. But that was different, he felt protected by his closeness to the Prince.

"Will you walk across the bridge with me?"

Meyer Amschel replied that of course he would. First he went in to see the manager. He did not have the credit the Court Factor did, he had paid in coins for the rental of the horse; now he received back in coins the deposit he had left for its safe return.

"Will you be wanting Blacker again tomorrow?" the manager asked.

"Not tomorrow." Tomorrow would be the Sabbath.

Schnapper was waiting when Meyer stepped outside. Together they walked toward the bridge. A light breeze was raising ripples in the river as it flowed east towards its confluence with the Rhine less than thirty kilometres downstream. The bridge had been built as a series of fourteen stone arches under which the water flowed. Small boats could slip under the arches with their sails intact. For larger ships coming up from the Rhine, the journey ended at Frankfurt. They couldn't fit under the bridge.

Meyer Amschel strode briskly, then slowed his pace to accommodate the older man's shorter legs. As they began to cross they could see commercial buildings with gabled roofs lining the waterfront that stretched away to the west. Almost directly ahead, just west of the bridge, were the towers of the church of St. Bartholomew, where each new Emperor was crowned. Just east of the bridge were the walls of the Judengasse.

"So," Schnapper asked as they walked, "how is the antique coin business?"

"I can't complain," the younger man said. "I know it's not as good as the factor business."

"There's nothing better, for us Jews," Schnapper said. "Since I was named Court Factor a year ago, my business has tripled. Just the title of Court Jew — the fact that I'm the court's official banker, that people know the Prince is borrowing from me — makes me more in demand."

"Before, merchants wouldn't take your money?"

"Now they're willing to pay higher interest. Borrowing where a Prince borrows makes them feel better. They stop complaining. They stop calling it usury. They start admitting that interest is a cost of doing business."

The men reached the midpoint of the bridge. Here, if one looked over the sides, there was a feeling almost of floating as the river stretched endlessly in both directions before it curved out of sight. Light clouds scudding by overhead, reflected on the surface of the water, could cause a fleeting rush of motion, as if the bridge were a magic carpet. Sometimes, when he was alone, Meyer would stand here for a long time, letting the current take his mind to distant places, carrying with it his distant dreams. But today the men were in a hurry, and did not pause. Schnapper did not care to look in any case, being prone to attacks of dizziness

"So, where did that fine-looking horse carry you today?"

"Mainz," Meyer replied.

"Did you find any treasures in Mainz, if I may ask?"

"One in particular." Meyer lifted the leather pouch from his belt, stopped walking and searched through it. He pulled out a small, dirty coin.

"This is a treasure?" Schnapper asked.

"It will be, after I clean it better. It's ancient. From Mesopotamia."

"The land of the Torah," Schnapper said, nodding. "If you don't mind my prying, how much will you sell this for?"

Meyer took the coin back from him and returned it to the pouch. "That depends," he said. "Whatever Crown Prince Wilhelm is willing to pay for it."

"You're doing business with the Crown Prince?"

They resumed walking along the bridge. The shorter man looked at the other's face with a doubting smile.

"I intend to begin," Meyer Amschel said. "With this coin."

"What if his royal honor doesn't want it?"

"He's a collector. Any collector would want it."

"And if he won't meet your price?"

"Then I'll meet his."

"What if he offers you less than you paid for it? You'll take a loss?"

"I won't look at it as a loss. I'll consider it an investment." He looked off into the distance, seeing things that only he could see. A gull crossed his line of sight carrying a fish in its mouth. "It will be an investment in future business with the Crown Prince. At which time, I'll have such treasures that he'll meet my price."

Schnapper peered at him, trying to conceal any expression. This was an unorthodox approach to finance. They walked in silence. A small boat with its sail unfurled passed beneath the bridge. They could feel the river's current in their feet as it lapped against the arches.

"You know something, Meyer Amschel," Schnapper said. "I'm becoming a rich man. Not rich by Gentile standards, of course, but rich in the lane. My children, Dank Gott, will never go hungry. I can even give a bit to charity. I venture to guess I'm one of the twenty richest men in the Judengasse. But approaching the Crown Prince? Suddenly I have a feeling you may surpass me one day, if you're not careful."

"Then I must try not to be careful," Meyer said.

"You must also continue to have good luck. As you did in finding that coin."

Meyer paused to tighten his purse, which was hanging too low and banging against his thigh. "With all respect, sir, I don't believe in luck."

"In what, then? Fate? Were you fated to find that coin from Mesopotamia? Perhaps Abraham himself blessed it and said, One day Meyer Amschel in the Judengasse of Frankfurt shall have this coin."

"That would be nice to believe. The more modest explanation is this: I received word yesterday that a certain coin dealer in Mainz had obtained such a coin. Taking passage on the public coach today would have gotten me home too late for the funeral, as we have discussed. Tomorrow is the Sabbath, so I could not travel to Mainz. Sunday the gates of the lane remain locked. Monday would be the earliest I could go to see it. Possibly some

Gentile dealer would have bought it by then. That's why I rented the fastest horse in the stable, and rode him to weariness. So I would have the best chance to buy the coin. Luck was not involved. Those who trust to luck get second best."

"Ah," the court factor said. "But you happened to learn about the coin right away. Was that not luck?"

"I have made friends in various towns. They keep me informed by post of what is available. Luck, in my view, is three-fourths information."

"And these friends of yours in various towns. They are loyal to you, they keep you informed, because … ?"

"Because in the past I have sold them coins."

"Let me guess," Schnapper interrupted. "In the past you have sold them coins at whatever price they were willing to pay."

The younger man did not respond. The conversation ended suddenly. It was always thus as Jews approached the Fahrtor, the main gate to the city, which stood at the end of the bridge. The Fahrtor was a stone tower six stories high. The first two stories were pierced by a pointed archway through which foot and carriage traffic moved in and out of the city. On the face of the Fahrtor, travelers entering the city saw a large painted stone engraving. It was famous — or notorious — far and wide as the Judensau — the Jews' Sow. The engraving was dominated by a large female pig. Beneath the pig several human figures were seated, sucking at its teats. At the rear of the pig, one man was holding up its tail while another, with his tongue protruding, was preparing to eat the pig's emerging excrement. To the rear, two men with hats and long beards, clearly representing Jewish elders, were watching. All the figures were wearing the pointed yellow hats that until recently had been mandatory for Frankfurt's Jews. Lettering under and through the image said: "Drink it, Jew, drink its milk/ Rabbi, eat its excrement."

The engraving was not the work of an odd or obscene individual. It had been put there, and was maintained in good repair, by the City of Frankfurt.

The two men tried not to look at the image as they passed beneath it. Each could not help flicking his eyes to it for an instant. Each could not help noticing the other do the same. By now, seeing the Judensau should have no effect on them, they believed. It was only a drawing; the confinement of the Judengasse was life. But the engraving always seemed to fill the air they were breathing with a heaviness that precluded speech, and sometimes induced nausea. Rage flared in their chests that had no place to go but deep within them. Such bitterness could not be expressed. Such bitterness could not be discussed. It could only be absorbed as pain beside the heart, as helplessness behind the eyes. It could only be battled by each man alone.

From the Fahrtor arch they could see and hear and smell the busy port at work. The wharves were piled high with logs, with barrels of wine and cheeses and spices, with bales of cloth imported for the women of Frankfurt to turn into clothing. Seamen, coach drivers, food hawkers, money changers shouted, one voice above another, in a salty cacophony. Horses, donkeys, mules, oxen harmonized with their smells. Invisible by daylight but present nonetheless were thousands of brown rats that lived in the docks, sleeping by day in walls and under floors and burrowed into piles of garbage, crawling out at night to feast on spilled cheeses, meats, grains, rinds, whatever they deigned to eat. For the Judengasse, the nearness of the docks was a blessing — it kept the lane mostly free of rodents. That, and canisters of ratbane, and the diligence of the women in keeping their homes clean.

Passing under the tower, the men reached into their purses to pay the toll required of everyone entering or leaving the city. The toll for Christians was four kreuzer. The toll for Jews was eight. In a city ledger the men were required to sign their names. The older man signed first: Wolf Salomon Schnapper. The younger man followed, with his barely legible signature: Meyer Amschel Rothschild.

The stone steps from the bridge led to a narrow riverside beach. A path alongside the sloping sewage sluice climbed to the ghetto wall. The two men followed the wall and entered the Judengasse at the north gate, which was closest to their homes. Wolf Schnapper was delighted to find his daughter Guttle, in Sabbath finery, waiting for him inside the gate. He hugged her and put his arm around her shoulder and together they walked to the Owl. Meyer Amschel hurried off toward the Hinterpfann, his own house across the lane.

5

Consternation hovered over the lane like a Talmudic argument. In little more than an hour the Sabbath would begin; just before dark it would be time to light the lamps and candles, time to welcome the happiest day of the week, a day of rest and study and joy. The lamps and candles would illuminate every kitchen, every window, turning the Judengasse into a weekly festival. But was it proper, people were wondering, to celebrate when a funeral was soon to begin? Wouldn't that dishonor the deceased?

In the Schnapper household, as in many others, this question was delaying dinner. Guttle's father sat at one end of the oak table covered with its white Sabbath cloth, his wife Emmie at the other. Guttle and Avra sat side by side, the three younger ones across from them. All were wearing their best Sabbath clothes, ready to walk to the synagogue after the meal. It was traditional to light the festive lamps and candles before eating. Frau Schnapper did not know what to do.

"Maybe I should go ask the Rabbi," Guttle said.

Her father thought that was a good idea. Guttle tucked her braids under her black velvet cap and hurried down the stairs. In the deserted lane she walked quickly to the home of the Chief Rabbi, adjacent to the schul, and knocked on the door. She had not seen a Sabbath lamp in a single window along the way. None was burning in the Rabbi's window. Perhaps it was still too early.

She had to knock a second time before she heard his sturdy footsteps moving to the door. When it swung open the Chief Rabbi was putting on his glasses to see who had knocked at dinner time. He peered at her closely, taking a moment to put a name to her face.

"The Schnapper girl," he said. He added, after a pause, "You haven't found another one, I hope."

Guttle's hand flew to her mouth to hide an unstoppable smile. She hadn't known that Rabbis made jokes. Especially Chief Rabbis. Especially that kind of joke.

His question had stolen her voice. The Rabbi said, "Well, what is it? My dinner is waiting."

"The lamps," Guttle managed to blurt. "The candles. We don't know whether to light the Sabbath lamps, because of the funeral. We don't want to insult the dead."

The Rabbi stepped beside her into the street, looked in both directions, saw no Sabbath lights. He fell into his Socratic teaching method.

"What do you think should be done? Guttle, is it?"

She did not hesitate. "I think we should light the lamps."

"Why do you think that?"

"Because the Schul-Klopper — Herr Gruen — would have wanted us to."

"Why would he have wanted us to?"

"People die all the time. But the Sabbath must live forever — or else the Jews will die."

The Rabbi leaned forward and pressed his lips to her forehead. His broad beard tickled her nose. The Rabbi thought: Lev Berkov would be a fool not to grab this one. What he said was, "That's precisely the right answer, young lady."

He leaned into the hallway of his house and called out, "Gilda, light the Sabbath lamps now. So everyone will know."

He stepped farther out into the lane, Guttle with him. In a second-floor window they saw the Rabbi's wife spread the curtains apart. They could see the star-shaped metal lamp that hung just below the ceiling. A lamp much like it hung in every apartment. The Rabbi's wife lowered the lamp. As she lighted the oil in each of the five points of the star, the window brightened like a sunrise. When all five points were burning, she said a brief prayer, and lit two Sabbath candles from a point of the star. She set the candles in the window, and passed her hands over her eyes.

Almost at once, candles flared in a window directly across from the Rabbi's house. Then in the house next door to the Rabbi's, as if the family had seen the lights go on across the lane.

"Go home now," the Rabbi said to Guttle. "Don't keep your family waiting."

Flustered, Guttle thanked him. She wanted to ask him if the Shul-Klopper had been murdered, but it was such an absurd thought that she didn't have the nerve. The deep gray of twilight was filling the narrow lane quickly from the bottom up, like water filling a tub. She began to run home along the cobbles. As she ran it seemed to her that lighted candles were appearing in the windows of every house just as she passed by. As if she were an angel lighting up the stars.

In the house abutting the Owl on the left, Otto Kracauer was scrubbing blood from his hands. Standing in the bedroom in his dark breeches and gray undershirt he poured water from a clay pitcher into a mismatched wash basin. Lathering his thick hands with soap, he scrubbed at the dried blood on his knuckles and wrists, at blood that had splattered on his hairy arms as far as his elbows. In the kitchen, his wife, Ida, waited for him to finish so she could light the Sabbath lamps. The three boys, Isidor, Aaron and Eli, hungrily eyed the food their mother had prepared.

The washing off of blood was a nightly chore for Otto, but on Fridays he always found himself more splattered than usual. He was the kosher slaughterer for the Judengasse, and while some families ate chicken several times a week, even most of the poorest, with the aid of charity funds, managed to buy a fresh-killed bird for the Sabbath.

The slaughterhouse, along with a stable and a herring shop the only Jewish-owned businesses outside the walls, was just to the west of the north gate, a noisy sprawling chicken coop of half an acre filled with squawking birds, floating feathers, smelly droppings, plus a cow or two. Once it had been inside the walls, but for many years now there had been no room in the lane. The neighbors had not been sorry to see it go when the banker Emil Hecksher, said to be the richest man in the Judengasse, bought the business and obtained permission from the city fathers to move it just outside the walls. How much this had cost him in bribes the people could only guess. Otto Kracauer had been the slaughterer for twenty years.

Finally his hands and arms were clean enough. He dried them and pulled on a clean shirt and joined his family at the table, watching Ida light the five-pointed lamp, and from it the Sabbath candles. When she ratcheted the lamp back up to the ceiling, the overlapping shadows cast by the five copper points seemed to form blurred Hebrew letters she could not identify.

Lifting a goblet of wine, Otto said the brief blessing — *Baruch atau Adonai Eloheinu Melech Ha-Olam, bo-ray peree haguffin.* He took a sip. The Sabbath meal could begin. The boys attacked their plates as if they had just spent forty years in the desert. Aaron was eighteen years old, Eli sixteen, Izzy fourteen. All seemed determined to grow three inches that very night.

"Good chicken," Otto said to his wife. She knew he was praising not her cooking but the quality of the bird he had brought home. "So tell me, Isidor, what is this news you have?"

Isidor swallowed whole the piece of potato that was in his mouth. "I went to see the Rabbi today… "

"A very good chicken," Otto said.

Izzy fell silent, looking at his plate, pushing the roasted potatoes around with his fork.

"So let him tell you," Ida said.

"I'm listening. So tell me already," the butcher replied.

Isidor took a breath and started again. He told of all that had transpired with Rabbi Simcha, and with the Chief Rabbi. When he finished, his pride was fighting a bout of nerves that was making his freckled hands tremble.

"So that's your news? You're going to spend your life talking to people about what happened to the Jews since what's-his-name came." He wiped his greasy hands with the embroidered handkerchief on his lap. "For that I send you to yeshiva?"

The butcher's dark eyes peered across the table at his youngest son. The boy fought hard to hold his gaze, then looked away, into the flames of the candles. Otto shoved another forkful of food into his mouth. "Good chicken," he murmured, with his mouth still full.

He pointed with his empty fork at his other sons. "Look at Aaron and Eli," he said. "No private conversations with Rabbis. But in a few weeks they'll be starting their own business. Selling the feathers they gather at the slaughterhouse. And feather pillows and quilts sewn by your mother. That will bring in a nice few gulden. More than talking to old people about the suffering of the Jews." He paused to drink some wine. "By the way, boys, I've been thinking about the name you picked. *Kracauer Brothers, Feather Merchants*. I have a better idea. We're going to call it *O. Kracauer and Sons*."

Aaron and Eli, seated side by side, looked at one another, but said nothing. Their father chewed another mouthful of food, sipped again from his goblet. If he noticed how downcast Isidor had become, he didn't show it as he spoke to the boy.

"A banker, an importer, these would be good professions for a yeshiva boy. You could make some real gelt that way. But a scholar? Let me tell you something, Izzy the Wise. You want to know the history of the Jews? I can tell you in a sentence. The Talmud says we should eat only fresh-killed meat. Which I know you know. And they have to be killed a certain way, which you also know. They have to be stretched out, lying down, exposing their windpipe. I have to cut their throats in one stroke, with a sharp knife, so that it's not torture. They die instantly. But the chickens are screaming as we stretch them on the block, and the others smell the blood of the ones I already killed. When one is screaming, they all start screaming. When the Gentiles hear the screaming, when they see the blood on our hands, they make up stories. They tell each other we kill Christian babies, to drain their blood. That we use Christian blood in secret ceremonies. So what do they do? What they do is obvious. They build stone walls around us. They lock us in every night. To protect their Christian babies." He set his empty goblet on the table, poured himself more wine from the decanter. "So there you have it, Izzy. The history of the Jews in a thimble. Now you can go learn something useful."

Isidor was staring at his plate. Half his food remained. His mother stood and began to collect the empty plates of the others. As she passed behind Izzy's chair she wanted very much to rumple his hair. But she didn't do so; her husband might get upset.

"What I don't understand, Papa," Eli said, "is why can't they tell the difference between a chicken and a baby?"

"Because they're Christians," Izzy said. "They can't even tell the difference between a man and God."

Almost choking on his wine, Otto Kracauer nodded vigorously, and slapped the table with glee. He'd never said the boy wasn't smart.

The Liebmann family also had finished dinner. Yetta and Leo had eaten sparsely; they rarely ate much, especially in the evening; a full stomach undermined sleep; an empty stomach didn't cost much. The boys had devoured most of the food that Frau Schnapper had brought from the market. Pushing himself away from the table, Hiram motioned that he was going to wash his face and change his shirt. Frau Liebmann pulled Hersch into a corner of the kitchen, where Leo with his failing ears wouldn't hear them.

"What's with your brother?" Yetta asked, speaking softly. "He's going to the funeral, and then to evening services? Why is today different? He hardly ever goes to schul."

"Why ask me? Why don't you ask him?"

"Because I'm asking you."

Hersch looked around the kitchen, as if for a place into which he could disappear. "I don't know," he said.

"You do know. I've never seen him so excited. Tell me why."

Hersch's parents seemed unusually old to him today. During dinner Yetta had told the story of the overcoat. Sadness pressed him like a vise as he watched his father shuffling off to his room.

"Hiram's going to be disappointed tonight. He might be hurt badly."

"Hurt?" Her hand moved to her sunken cheek, her lips. It hovered there, shaking slightly, like a baby bird. Also like a dying one. "What do you mean, hurt?"

"Not physically hurt, Mama. Hurt inside."

"How could he hurt more than he already does?"

"He's gotten a strange idea into his head, I think. After the funeral, the Chief Rabbi is going to name the new Schul-Klopper."

"So nu? What has this to do with Hiram?"

"I think Hiram wants it to be him. He wants to be the new Schul-Klopper. No, it's worse. I think he expects to be the new Schul-Klopper."

"He told you this meshuganah thing?"

"He didn't tell me."

"Then why do you think such nonsense?"

Hersch picked up a plate from a shelf beside him, studied it front and back, put it down. Through an open window across the room he could hear a shuffling sound, the muffled noise of people beginning to move down the lane to the schul.

"When we were starting to dig the grave today, Hiram motioned to Rabbi Simcha. He pointed to the grave for the Schul-Klopper, then he knocked in the air, as if he held a hammer. And he pointed to his own chest. What the Rabbi took it to mean was Hiram saying he was digging the grave for the Schul-Klopper. As if Hiram was a simpleton, saying the obvious. I think what Hiram was telling him was that he wanted to be the new Schul-Klopper. And because the Rabbi nodded, he thinks he'll be chosen."

"Didn't you say anything to Hiram? Tell him the truth?"

"I was going to. But I changed my mind. It's bad enough he won't be chosen. He doesn't need to be embarrassed, too, by us knowing this notion of his. Not unless he wants to tell us."

Frau Liebmann pulled a handkerchief from her pocket and wiped her eyes. "My poor baby," she said.

Hersch had been a normal, happy infant when he'd been born to Leo and Yetta, a first child, late in their lives. Though poor, they doted on their little bundle of smiles. Often they went without to make sure the robust boy had milk and bread. Two years later another child arrived. Hiram at first appeared to be as healthy as his brother, but in time they realized to their terrible distress that the boy could not hear, and could not speak. The doctors at the hospital said nothing could be done. The baby would grow up a deaf mute.

The Liebmanns felt like ancient sinners from the Torah. Yahweh had punished them for the sin of being greedy, for not being satisfied with their first born, for having another child when Yetta was past her forty-seventh year. For months they could hardly eat; they shriveled.

At first, Hersch welcomed the birth of his brother. He accepted with his usual smiles the attention the new baby required. Unlike most children his age, Hersch was patient. He was awaiting the day when he and his brother could romp together, could wrestle, could run, shouting, up and down the stairs and along the lane, could share secrets. What a good boy Hersch was, the neighbors said. Until one day, when he was four years old, or five, he changed. He began hitting his little brother, shoving him across the floor. His smiles were replaced by wails of anguish. When Yetta sat him down and sought an explanation, his words erupted through wrenching sobs. Hiram wouldn't play with him. Hiram wouldn't listen to him, wouldn't speak to him. Yetta thought they had explained the situation to him long ago, to prepare him for this. But clearly they had not done a good job. Now, as his mother tried to calm him, and stroked his hair, he understood for the first time that Hiram would never change: would never listen, would never speak. It was as if he had no brother at all. It was worse than having no brother at all.

Inconsolable, Hersch became uncontrollable. He became like an animal, people said. He would run from the house at night and hide. He would scream for no reason, embarrassing Leo and Yetta, irritating the neighbors. At heder, when he started there, he would suddenly shove his books to the floor and run from the room. Often the place they found him hiding was the cemetery. He was always in the oldest section, where the lettering on the tombstones had been worn flat across the centuries by wind and rain that sometimes whipped across the river below and swirled inside the gate. The cemetery, too, was the one place where the sun wasn't blocked by gabled houses. Perhaps here, hugging himself, he was finding warmth. The parents encouraged the brothers to be friends. But when little Hiram tried to hug his big brother, or kiss him on the cheek, Hersch pushed him away. The other children shunned the silent boy altogether.

The Rabbis saw this from afar and pitied the Liebmanns. Hersch, that precious little boy, once always smiling, became known as the wild one. The deaf mute — no one seemed to know his name — was assumed to be mentally slow.

In time, however, as the boys grew older, their relationship changed. Hersch began to understand and accept that Hiram's shortcomings were beyond his or anyone's control. He began to reach out. Alone together in the small bedroom they shared, they began to communicate. Hiram did not go to heder because of his deafness; he could neither read nor write. But little by little the boys worked out simple hand motions with which to converse. Hersch did not understand that his former rage at his brother's infirmities had been misplaced love. Hiram seemed to have known it all along.

The changes at first were hardly noticed in the lane. But now the two strong young men who looked so much alike were as close to one another as any brothers in the Judengasse. The aging of their parents, who were nearing seventy, was bringing them even closer.

Yetta squeezed her handkerchief into her hand. "How could he think such a stupid thing? To be the Schul-Klopper?"

"When you think about it, Mama, it's not so stupid. He's got strong legs. He's got strong arms. He could knock on doors as well as anyone. He wouldn't have to speak, he wouldn't have to hear. It's a job where those things don't matter."

"But he's so shy. He's frightened of people."

"That's the point. All those hours he looks out the window, thinking, timing things. Timing even the Schul-Klopper. But separate from everyone, except me and you and Papa. He must have realized he would be perfectly able to knock on doors with a hammer. And that if he were the Schul-Klopper, he would earn respect. He would be serving the lane. People would give him glasses of milk, of tea. Who knows, maybe some pretty girl would give him a glass of juice. I don't know for sure what he's thinking. But he wouldn't be useless anymore, the way he sees himself now. The way everyone sees him. And he would bring home a few kreuzer each week to help you and Papa. That would make him proud."

Yetta turned to the wall. Her shoulders began to shake like a cart on cobbles. When she turned back, her handkerchief was translucent. "It's a good idea," she said.

"It's a wonderful idea. But it's not going to happen."

"Why not? Anything is possible."

She pressed her wet handkerchief to her quivering lips. The image of a new life for her youngest danced in front of her eyes like sunlight.

"Mama, if we never thought of it, why would the Chief Rabbi think of it?"

"Because he's the Chief Rabbi! Who knows, maybe Yahweh will give him a nudge."

Hersch put his arms around his mother. She was so thin; she really must eat more.

"Mama, don't you go off that way, too. Hiram's going to be very upset. We'll have to comfort him. So don't you start expecting a miracle. If Yahweh cared a chicken liver about Hiram, He wouldn't have made him deaf and dumb."

The words were like a slap. But Yetta knew he was right. She leaned her cheek for a moment against Hersch's sturdy chest. If only the lane knew what a good son he had become.

"I'd better go to your father," she said, disengaging herself. "See if he feels well enough to go to the funeral."

Guttle stared into the candle flames. They were the eyes of God. That's why you lighted two each Sabbath Eve — to invite His eyes into your home. To let Him observe closely. To show Him you were not ashamed.

This was not what the Rabbis said. The Rabbis said the candles symbolized the joy and lightness of the day that was beginning. Guttle believed they were more than that.

In the flames there was yellow and orange, blue and white. There were curves and points, and an inner shape that echoed the outer — just like the human eye, made in His image. There was a reaching and a settling back, a stretching and a shriveling. The candle flames did not crackle and devour, like the flames in the woodstove. They did not heat water or cook meat or warm the room. They accomplished nothing useful you could specify.

Stare into them long enough and they stayed with you. When you looked away the flames remained in your eyes and on the candles, both. Only the eyes of Yahweh could do that.

Here was the difficulty. Try as you might, you could not see with them. Eyes open or eyes closed, you saw nothing but flame. To see with His eyes was forbidden.

Guttle turned away from the candles. She closed her eyes and saw flames still. Quietly she breathed, waiting for them to disappear. She murmured a small prayer in the darkening — that Jacob Marcus would not approach her Papa this night to arrange her marriage to his son.

*M*adame Guttle, the famed Viennese chanteuse, is on stage in Paris, at the Comedie Francais. She raises her bright orange skirt — and reveals that beneath it she is wearing men's breeches. The audience, which includes King Louis XV and his grandson the Dauphin, roars with laughter

Holding a candle, she begins to sing, in a coquettish coloratura voice:

> If I'd been born a man
> I'd be a scholar,
> I'd learn a dozen tongues
> In which to holler,
> In which to pledge my love
> To my sweet bride-to-be.
> If I'd been born a man —

(She lifts her skirt to reveal the breeches)

> Would I choose me?

(She lowers her skirt)

> I learned to cook and sew,
> But I would rather read.
> The thing I do not know
> Is how to plant a seed
> That in nine months will grow
> To look the same as he.
> If I'd been born a man—

(She shows her breeches — then the skirt again)

> Would I choose me?
> If I'd been born a man
> I'd teach the girls to love,
> But I am just a girl
> And so by God above
> I am not ready yet
> To bare my private parts
> Until I teach myself

(She plunges a hand deep under her skirt)

> The manly arts!

The audience roars with laughter; the people clap and cheer. Madame Guttle is about to blow out her candle when she hears a female voice from stage right...

"Guttle, what are you doing? We'll be late for schul!"

6

The cupola atop the synagogue, much higher than the ghetto walls, was flashing refractions of the descending sun. Guttle admired its beauty most at moments like that. She envisioned the cupola as a beacon, reminding Yahweh not to forget His children who were locked behind the walls.

The synagogue was the largest structure in the Judengasse. Situated on the east side of the lane, half way between the north and south gates, it exceeded the width of sixteen houses. Front to back it extended from the cobbled lane three quarters of the way to the ghetto wall. Attached to the rear were the chamber of the Judengasse Council and the rooms of the yeshiva. Large as it was, however, Guttle knew it could not contain the crowd of men, women and children, all dressed in their Sabbath best, who were moving toward it like an incoming tide for the Schul-Klopper's funeral.

Inside the temple, the Aron Kodesh, the holy ark, stood two stories high against the eastern wall. It held twelve Torah scrolls, each one clothed in an embroidered velvet cover of white or blue or maroon. Sparkling gold and silver threads wove Hebrew letters into bright designs. Engraved gold or silver plates hung from the polished wooden handles, like jewels around the necks of queens. Further attempts, when they flashed in the lamplight, Guttle thought, to catch the eye of Elohim. Two of the Torahs, on the top shelf, were so fragile they were kept behind glass; they were two of the three original Torahs belonging to the synagogue, dating back centuries. The third had disappeared long ago.

Females were permitted, if not encouraged, to attend services, but they had to keep to themselves. They had to stand in the rear. Guttle had mixed feelings about this arrangement. Sometimes she accepted with equanimity the assurance of the Rabbis that this was what the Talmud prescribed. At other times she chafed that she could not sit in front with the men.

As the hour for the funeral neared, Guttle watched them enter the schul. All wore black coats or cloaks, and black yarmulkes. The regulars, who attended services every day, or at least every Sabbath, filled the specific seats they had come to think of as reserved for them. Each became silent, grim, as he saw on the platform the plain spruce coffin, resting on velvet. It was not far from where they sat. They could see the grain of the wood.

As the men straightened their talises and took their seats, the women, wearing muted dresses of black or gray or brown, and simple hats, gathered in the rear. But as more and more men crowded in, and all of the seats became filled, late-arriving men had to stand in the back. Because the genders could not mingle, this forced the women out through the wide doors into the street. Rabbi Simcha, assaying the situation, whispered into the ear of the Chief Rabbi. At once Rabbi Eleazar ordered that the doors be kept open, so women and children might follow the proceedings as best they could from the lane.

The service began with late afternoon prayers. This was standard, and since most of the women could not hear anyway, some of them began to talk among themselves while waiting for the funeral. Children began to play quietly on the cobbles. As Guttle tried to listen to the prayers, a group of her friends pulled her away from the door, eager to tease her with the latest gossip. Among them were her sister Avra, Dvorah Schlicter, and Sara Greinz, who worked at the bakery.

"So," Dvorah asked Guttle, "when will you be stepping out with the handsome Doctor?"

"What are you talking about?"

"Don't be coy, Guttle." Dvorah tucked under her mob cap a lock of auburn curls that had crept out. "Sara told us all about it. How Lev Berkov came to the bakery to speak to you. And took you into the lane where no one could hear. And when you came back he had his arm around you, and a big smile on his face."

"You told them that?" Guttle asked Sara.

"It's the truth, isn't it?" Sara had a narrow face, pale brown hair, and what Guttle felt was a whiny disposition not unlike Avra's.

"You want to know what we talked about?" Guttle asked. "We talked about spilled milk."

"What is that supposed to mean?" Avra asked.

"I have no idea," Guttle said. "I won't be 'stepping out' with the Doctor any time soon. He never said anything like that."

"That's too bad, then," Sara said. "Maybe he's just trying to make someone else jealous. Which won't work, of course. But at least it will make the coffin maker happy."

"The coffin maker?" Dvorah asked. "What's he got to do with Guttle?"

"You don't know? You should see the way he looks at her whenever she's at the bakery. He can't take his eyes off her."

Guttle decided she must be talking with Izzy too much, because for an instant she wondered if girls had gossiped this way in ancient Egypt, while they worked as slaves, or in Babylon. Probably they had. In Sodom and Gomorra for sure.

"Where do you get these ideas, Sara?" she said.

Dvorah fussed with her cap again. She loved her bright auburn curls. She was going to hate losing them some day. She did not want to go through life wearing a wig, or with her hair always covered, as custom required of married women. It was supposed to keep other men from wanting her. But would some future husband still want her? Eighteen months older than Guttle, Dvorah nonetheless often followed her lead, had painfully taught herself to read German, for instance, after Guttle had learned the language with ease.

"The coffin maker has never even spoken to me," Guttle said.

"The truth is," Avra put in, "my sister is already betrothed. To Isidor Kracauer."

"Avra, Izzy is fourteen. By the time he's old enough to marry, I'll be an old maid."

"If not Izzy, then it's the Cantor. Everyone knows he's after you."

"Who told you such a thing?"

"What you should do," Dvorah said, "is marry a rich old banker. Then, when he dies, Izzy can take his place."

"Think what nonsense you're talking," Guttle said. "You know that my father will arrange my marriage. Just as yours will arrange yours." As soon as she spoke she wanted to snatch back the words. Dvorah's father had died two years before. He'd been stabbed to death when he resisted highwaymen on the road to Wiesbaden.

"Doesn't matter," Dvorah said. "You've got your father wrapped around your finger like a piece of string. He'll let you marry whomever you want."

She wondered where Dvorah got such ideas. Maybe it was from missing — from idealizing — the father she no longer had. "You don't know my Papa," she said.

She squeezed Dvorah's hand. Her friend squeezed back. The slip of the tongue seemed to have been forgiven. "Now, if you ladies will excuse me," Guttle said, "I came to attend a funeral. And that's where I'm going."

"After all, I did find the body," Avra mimicked, in a flamboyant voice. She tried to imitate her older sister's walk. The others did not smile. Avra wished she were with her own friends.

Pulling her cloak tighter around her shoulders, Guttle stepped closer to the temple. Politely but firmly she threaded her way through the crowd of women. The required space of three feet remained between the first row of women and the last row of men. She could hear the rich voice of the Cantor flowing out over the assemblage like liquid velvet. His robust tones from afar could make her tingle in a way that his presence could not.

Perhaps because of the Sabbath wine she had imbibed at dinner, Guttle edged closer to the men. Her mother grabbed her arm and pulled her back.

When Rabbi Simcha completed the mincha service, his pink scar throbbing, the Chief Rabbi approached the lectern. To those who could see him he presented an intimidating image, with his stern features, his full gray beard, his tall black hat, his thick hands. A thunderous speaker, he let the silence stretch on, looking about, nodding to some of the men he knew well, among them the banker Kaspar Reis and the Court Factor Wolf Schnapper, the butcher Otto Kracauer, the cabinet maker Yussel Kahn seated beside his good friend, that young fellow — the Rabbi couldn't recall his name — who had started a coin business.

"My dear friends," Rabbi Eleazar began. "We have come together, as we do each week, to celebrate the joyous Sabbath, a respite from work and from earthly cares. But today we have also come to lay to rest one of our dearest friends, one of this congregation's most loyal members. Solomon Gruen. Our beloved Schul-Klopper.

"Solomon had a long life" — here the Rabbi stared at Doctor Berkov, as if daring him to disagree — "but I always believed he would be the one who would bury me. He was never sick. He was never late on his rounds. For a Schul-Klopper, there can be no higher praise.

"Some may mourn that our friend left no family here to mourn for him. He chose never to marry, he had no children. 'The Judengasse is crowded enough,' he used to say. Whether that was his real reason for abstaining from raising a family of his own I do not know. But perhaps he saw a more accurate picture than the rest of us. Because Solomon Gruen did have a family. A large one. Every one of us living here in the lane was part of it. He could never pass a little boy without patting his head, or a little girl without pinching her cheek. Or a grown-up without a wave and a smile. So we say farewell to him today not merely as the shammus of the synagogue, not merely as the Schul-Klopper, but as a father, a grandfather, a son, a brother, to us all. Look around you — not only here inside the schul but out in the street. I dare say that almost every person in the Judengasse who is not an invalid or an infant has come to bid him shalom.

"Those of you inside can see resting on his coffin the beautiful hammer that he wielded so diligently for all those years, until this very morning. Why, you might ask, do we not put the hammer in his casket, and bury it clasped in his hand, where it fit so perfectly? I will tell you why. The Lord told Moses, when He gave him the Ten Commandments on Mount Sinai, that we shall not worship golden idols. That we shall worship no other god before Him. To place the hammer in Solomon's coffin would be to make of it a golden idol. Naked we came into this world, the Torah says, and naked shall we leave it. The carpenter must leave his tools behind, the butcher his knife, the teacher his books. But there is another reason we leave his hammer outside the coffin. Because his sacred task must not go unfilled, not for a single day. Because we must pass the hammer along at once to the next Schul-Klopper.

"This I shall not do now — not before Solomon is laid to rest — that would be an insult to his memory — but afterward, when we return here for the Sabbath service. It will not be the very same hammer, because the new Schul-Klopper must have an identity of his own. This afternoon I asked our fine cabinet maker, Yussel Kahn, to carve a new hammer. He did a beautiful job." The Rabbi held up the new hammer, which had been out of sight on the shelf of his lectern. "You will all get to admire it soon enough, when the new Schul-Klopper awakens you. You may even want to hit him with it."

Some men in the congregation laughed. Others fought to stifle smiles.

"It's all right to laugh," the Rabbi said. "No one in the Judengasse loved a good joke better than Solomon Gruen.

"But now the difficult time has come, before the sun sets over the cemetery, to lay him to rest. I have asked to serve as head pallbearer Hersch Liebmann, in whom Solomon put so much faith when he made him the shammus's assistant, and who responded so well. The others whom Rabbi Simcha has spoken with can approach the platform now. The rest of you please wait outside. In just a moment we shall carry the coffin out to lead the way.

"To Solomon Gruen, here in the schul he loved so well, I say one final shalom aleichem. Peace be upon him."

Slowly the men began to file into the street, first those standing at the rear, then those who had been seated. One among them, moving within the muted shuffle, was conscious of a disturbing feeling. He could not recall ever seeing Solomon Gruen pat the head of a little boy, or pinch the cheek of a little girl. Doctor Lev Berkov had the sensation that the Chief Rabbi, for reasons of his own, was making the deceased more beloved than he was.

In the street, with Sabbath lights from the windows gilding the cobblestones, Guttle watched most of the women and older girls drift toward their homes with young children in tow. It was time to put them to bed; they didn't need to see the burial. Some of the men did the same. There would not be enough room for everyone at the cemetery; they would take a short break before returning to the temple for the evening service. Others remained in their seats, choosing to study their prayer books until the cortege returned.

The procession was led by the six pallbearers carrying the coffin braced against their shoulders. Behind the coffin walked all eight Rabbis of the Judengasse. After them came the dozen men who belonged to the Hevra Kadisha, the Holy Brotherhood. Isidor, watching them pass, could not imagine why anyone would want to be a member. What they did was take care of men who were close to death (women had their own sisterhood) and then prepare the bodies for burial — washing the body, dressing it in a burial shroud; no doubt they had done so that very afternoon with the body in the coffin. Izzy shuddered as they passed. Membership was considered a high honor — so much so that often it was inherited, passed on from father to son among the wealthy. For the first time in his life, Izzy was glad his father was only a butcher.

Those men who wanted to walk to the cemetery came next. A few women, including Guttle, trailed behind. She felt an obligation, having discovered the body. As she walked, she was aware of a gurgling sound emanating from the sewer ditch, accompanying the funeral cortege. Those women who had gone home were hurrying to empty wash basins, dishwater tubs and chamber pots before the Sabbath began.

A loud wailing from the front of the knot of walking women pierced the night air. Guttle saw that the woman keening was Sophie Marcus, the Cantor's mother, the Schul-Klopper's sister. She was surprised; she'd heard that Frau Marcus had not gotten along with her brother, that they rarely spoke. As two women rushed to support the bereaved by her elbows, Guttle thought: perhaps she's the kind of woman who needs attention. And then she thought: her brother is dead, I'm being unkind.

When the procession turned right, through the cemetery gate, a last streak of yellow sky was visible above the wall. It left in deep shade the inscribed faces of the chipped and weathered stones, the oldest of which dated to the Christian year 1234. In the Jewish cemetery in Mainz, thirty kilometres away, Guttle had heard from her father, there were stones from the year 1000.

The procession wended its way along the narrow dirt paths amid clusters of stones, to the place among the deceased Beckers where Hersch and Hiram Liebmann had dug the grave not long before. The pallbearers lowered the coffin onto two leather straps. Holding the ends of these, they lowered the coffin further, into the grave.

The concluding prayers, led by the Chief Rabbi, did not take long. When he was through, he took a handful of earth from the pile beside the grave and tossed it onto the coffin. To those watching, the dull thud as the earth struck the wooden lid resounded with a forbidding finality.

As the mourners filed back to the lane in the quick-falling dark, the brothers Liebmann hefted their spades and began to fill in the grave. Hersch worked slowly. His arms felt heavy, as if his prayer shawl were made of lead. Perhaps his muscles had tightened from the effort of digging the grave. Or perhaps he was in no hurry to learn the identity of the new Schul-Klopper. Pausing, looking up at the darkening sky, he took a deep breath. The air was brisk and clean. He realized, for the first time, an oddity: the center of the cemetery was the one place in the Judengasse to escape from human stench.

In contrast, his brother worked quickly, dumping one heavy spade load after another into the grave. His prayer shawl didn't hamper him at all. Was he hurrying because darkness, and thus the Sabbath, was approaching rapidly? Or was he in a rush to get back to the temple, expecting to see if not hear himself offered the sacred hammer — as if some teasing messenger had whispered into his useless ear that it would be so? Hersch dared not ask.

When the grave was full they patted it level with the back of the spades, then left the tools inside the cemetery gate. As they walked up the lane, Hersch was conscious of a dread to which he was not accustomed, while his brother, who usually lumbered through the lane slowly, with no destination outside his own imagining, kept moving two or three steps ahead, turning and waiting for Hersch to catch up, then moving ahead again. When they reached the synagogue, Hersch would have kept on going, would have walked straight home. But Hiram quickly crossed the trench toward the temple doors. Hersch knew he had no choice but to follow.

The last to leave the cemetery was Meyer Amschel Rothschild. When the burial service was done he walked alone in the stone-pocked darkness to the plot where his father and then his mother had been buried when he was barely twelve years old. Every funeral he had attended since had drawn him there with a pull on his leaden soul. He had not cried for his father. He had not cried for his mother. He had not known why, then. He did not know why now.

They had sent him away to school in Furth that year, in Bavaria, instead of to the yeshiva. It was almost as if they had foreseen what was coming. He was in mathematics class, he remembered, hunched over his desk working on a problem, when the Rabbi who headed the school summoned him from class. Seated in his office, the Rabbi said, "Sit down, Meyer Amschel. I have received today a letter from your mother. It is bad news, I'm afraid." The Rabbi had hesitated, then continued. "Smallpox has appeared in the Frankfurt Judengasse. Your father was one of those stricken. It appears that he has passed away."

Meyer felt stunned for a moment, then stood up. "I have to go back."

"Sit, son, sit. It takes at least three days for the post to reach here from Frankfurt. Your father passed away on Thursday evening. The funeral would have been Friday. There's nothing you can do now."

"I have to be with my mother. And visit his grave. How can this be, Rabbi? My father went to schul every day. When I was little he would take my hand, and I would walk with him, alongside the Schul-Klopper, Herr Gruen. Yahweh wouldn't do this to him. I have to go see."

"The journey takes three days," the Rabbi said. "More important, let me read from your mother's letter. 'Please tell Meyer Amschel I shall be writing to him directly as soon as I am able. Under no circumstances should you allow him to come home. I know that will be his desire, but the lane is rife with smallpox, and it would not be safe for him. I am praying that this plague will pass before the school year ends.'" The Rabbi put the letter on his desk. "You see now why I cannot let you go back?"

Meyer had nodded dumbly, and left the Rabbi's office and went back to class, where the numbers no longer had meaning. That night he slipped out of the dormitory with all his spending money and one change of clothes in a sack, and walked two miles to the stable, and hid amid new-cut hay, till he could board the morning coach. He slept two nights on ragged beds arranged by the coach driver in cheap way stations. In Frankfurt the driver left him not at the town square but one street away from the north gate. His mother hugged him and kissed him and cried tears into his hair, and was frightened. It was not safe for him to be here, she said.

He visited his father's freshly turned grave with her. He did not cry. He wanted to be strong. Four days he stayed before making the long journey back to school.

When he next returned to the lane, six months later, it was because his mother, too, had succumbed to the pox. He was too late for her funeral as well. His small consolation was that he had come to see her when his father died. Again, he forced himself to be strong. He did not cry. Perhaps he had been too angry at Yahweh to cry.

As he stood by their graves now, Meyer unexpectedly felt tears welling. They seemed to be rushing up from his chest to his eyes like water from an underground spring. This had never happened in his many visits to their graves through the years. He did not know why it was happening now. Perhaps the death of Herr Gruen, his father's good friend, had stirred old memories. Or perhaps because he had just become old enough to marry, and realized his parents never would meet his bride. Under the dark sky pocked with stars he sobbed for them. He sobbed until there were no more tears within him. He felt as if the tears had cracked a wall of stones in his chest. He could feel the stones crumbling. He could hear them.

Reaching for his handkerchief, he discovered his pocket was empty; he had forgotten to bring one. He wiped the last of his tears on his prayer shawl, and found his way among the stones to the lane, and back to the schul, to his own seat, which long ago had been his father's.

The synagogue was almost full, as it always was on a Friday night, but not nearly as crowded as before. Moving past a knot of standing women, Hersch was surprised to see his mother among them, wearing her best hat and her one good coat. She was holding the arm of their young neighbor, Guttle Schnapper. The dread in his chest reached deeper, like a small tree extending its roots. He should never have told her about Hiram's stupid hope. He slumped onto the nearest bench. Hiram sat beside him, his shoulders thrust back, looking around eagerly.

The Sabbath service was led by Rabbi Simcha. It lasted, Hiram guessed in his silence, about half an hour, though he did not take out his watch to check; that, he'd decided, would not be proper in schul. Upon its conclusion, the Chief Rabbi once again approached the lectern. He held up his hands for quiet. In one of them Hiram saw the new carved hammer with its sleek, sensual curve. Just by looking he could imagine touching it.

Hersch peered at his brother. For a moment he himself wanted to be not only deaf but blind. He did not want to see or hear what happened next. He covered his eyes with his hand. He didn't dare to cover his ears. Where had Hiram gotten such an absurd idea as becoming a deaf and dumb replacement for Herr Gruen?

"Now, it is my happy task to name the new Schul-Klopper," the Chief Rabbi intoned. "I will not be presenting this fine hammer to him tonight, because as you know, the hammer is a tool, and no tool can be used on the Sabbath. Tomorrow morning and tomorrow afternoon he will knock on your doors with his fist. But tomorrow evening, in the community room, at the conclusion of the Sabbath, we will drink wine and toast the health of the new Schul-Klopper, and present him with his hammer."

The Rabbi sipped water from a cup on the lectern. His eyes seemed to take in every face in the temple as he turned about to include them all.

"We were all shocked to learn this morning of the death of Solomon Gruen, our dear friend, whom we have just laid to rest. But soon after, my thoughts turned of necessity to the selecting of his replacement. The Lord giveth and the Lord taketh away. I must tell you, it was not an easy task. By tradition, a new Schul-Klopper is a young man, who can walk the lane with ease. We have many fine young men in this community; it made me proud to contemplate upon them. But which one to select? I was making little progress in coming to a decision — until this afternoon, the Lord, blessed be His name, delivered the answer into my hands. Rabbi Simcha brought into my study a young man from the yeshiva, who had approached him with an interesting notion. I will not dwell on what we talked about, except to say I thought the idea was extraordinary for a boy his age."

In his seat next to his father, Isidor Kracauer was having trouble accepting what he was hearing. He heard the words but his mind denied their content. In the knot of women at the rear, Guttle let go of the hand of Yetta Liebmann. Her eyes widened with disbelief.

"Some of you know this boy, many of you don't," the Chief Rabbi continued. "In some ways he is quite shy. That is one of the very reasons I have chosen him. By knocking on your doors every day, he will meet, sooner or later, every one of you. His shyness, I am confident, will disappear. This will make a serious work of scholarship upon which he is embarking that much more rewarding for all of us. He is also clever enough, his teachers assure me, to understand the records he will need to keep as shammus of the schul, which is an important part of the Schul-Klopper's job."

Izzy finally understood. He was breathing rapidly. He could scarcely believe what was happening — this joy that was filling his being. His father Otto, seated beside him, had taken hold of the boy's arm, high up near the shoulder. He was squeezing so hard — an act of both pride and dismay —

that Izzy felt real pain. At the rear, Guttle was having trouble standing in her place. Her feet kept wanting to dance.

"So without further delay," the Rabbi said, "I announce to you my choice to be the new Schul-Klopper. He is the fine son of our longtime friend and butcher, Otto Kracauer. His name is Isidor. Stand up, Isidor, bitte, so everyone can get a look at you."

Izzy did not stir. His father put both his strong arms around his son's slim waist and hoisted him into a standing position. The temple was filled with oohs and ahs and cries of Mazel-tov. Izzy smiled blankly. His father stood and waved to the men on one side and then the other, like one of those rare Jewish prize fighters acknowledging cheers.

Hersch Liebmann looked at his brother's face. He saw no change of expression. If Hiram was disappointed, he was not showing it. He rarely showed what he was feeling. But Hersch became aware of an odd sensation within himself. The dread that had taken root in his chest the past few hours had vanished. Instead, he felt almost exultant. He did not care to examine why. Perhaps he'd wanted desperately to remain the superior one.

In the women's place at the rear, giddy from wine and exultation, Guttle could not stop herself. She found herself running down the aisle, the faces of the congregation a blur, throwing her arms around Izzy the Wise, hugging him close, kissing his cheek, more firmly than the brush of her lips that afternoon. The embrace, the kiss, flushed Izzy's face. Extra blood may have rushed to his brain, because suddenly he was aware of where he was and what was happening. He smelled the perfume of Guttle's soap, felt her breasts pressed against his chest, marveled at the residual power of her kiss — and realized that hundreds of men in yarmulkes and prayer shawls were staring at them, including all eight Rabbis and the Cantor.

Guttle felt Izzy's body grow tense in her arms. With disbelief, she became aware of what she had done. She let him go. She looked around into staring eyes and open mouths. Shame inflamed her cheeks. But she stayed where she was. For several long seconds she stayed and looked at them, proud and defiant, as if daring them to come and get her, to physically throw her out of the men's section for congratulating her friend. If they tried, she'd make them carry her.

Her resolve and her knees weakened together. Rather than collapse in front of them, she ran, meeting no other eyes, ran down a red-carpeted aisle that seemed to extend for kilometres, stumbled out of the synagogue whose sacred maleness she had violated, ran across a wobbling board that bridged the sewage ditch — feeling it would have served her properly if she had fallen in — turned and ran on her sore ankle along the slick cobbles beneath glowing windows, many of the windows flickering now as the oil in the lamps burned low, ran toward her home as fast as she could run in her long Sabbath dress.

Pausing to catch her breath, she found herself at the south gate, beside the cemetery. In her shame, in her rush to get away, she had run in the wrong direction.

7

Short of breath, ankle pulsing, Guttle felt mortified when she realized where she was. To walk home at once, the length of the lane, she would encounter all the men and women strolling home from the schul. What if they laughed at her? What if they scolded her? She couldn't face them.

She would wait just a few minutes. The air had turned colder, people would be going inside, not idling in the street. Once they were in their houses she could quietly slink home. But her back was aching, she had been standing for so long, at the funeral service, in the cemetery, at the Sabbath prayers. There was no place nearby to sit, but she could stretch out there, on that small plot of dirt in the deep shadow between the cemetery and the gate. It was just big enough. She smoothed her skirts beneath her and lay down to rest, arm cradling her head. Just for a few minutes, till the lane was clear.

When she awoke, the world was fragmented, a diaspora of the brain. She didn't know where she was. Then the gradual acknowledgment of raw dirt under her palms. Of chill from lack of a quilt. Of sleeping fully clothed. As remembrance returned, she became aware of a subtle sound, rhythmic, liquid, lapping. Sleep-inducing. She sat up to fight its lull. It could only be the river, lapping against the quays, against the stone arches of the bridge, against the wooden hulls of boats anchored against the current. The sound was lovely, like flowers made audible. A sound impossible to hear in daylight, beneath the bustle in the lane and the tumult of the docks. She struggled to her feet, shook away the wrinkles in her clothes. The lane was deserted. The candlelight in the windows was gone. Only a few oil lamps still flickered. She looked up over the cemetery in this near-total darkness, hoping to see a star. She had never been at this end of the lane after dark, there was no telling what she might see. But the sky had clouded over. No stars were visible. Just a pale hint of butter moon.

Backing onto the cobbles, still scanning the sky, she was startled by a gruff voice: "Who's there? What are you doing here?"

Pressed against the gate, peering in with invisible eyes, was the silhouette of a Constable. A pale sheen of moonlight reflected dully off his sword.

"Who's there? Come closer to the gate!"

Frightened, Guttle moved a few steps nearer. "I'm just looking at the sky." She felt her voice trembling. "And listening to the river."

His eyes were adjusting to her form, her face. "Ah, the schön madchen. Listening to the river. It's the free beetles girl — isn't it?"

In the dark, the guard seemed older, more intimidating. But it was not the new Constable. "You were at the north gate this morning, Herr Kapitän?"

"Double duty for the leader. We're short an officer. So tell me, what does the river say when you listen?"

"It's just… beautiful. The sounds it makes." She still felt confused, half asleep.

The Kapitän said nothing for a time. She was about to turn and walk away. She was not certain if she had his permission to go.

He spoke again. "There's a new walk by the river. Have you seen it?"

"I've heard of the promenade. I've never seen it. It's forbidden."

"Ach, yes. It's forbidden." His voice was softer. She was surprised by this conversation. He must be bored. "But if you walked on it alone, in the dark, who would know? Who would tell?" She saw the silhouette of his head move, as if he were looking about. He turned back to face her. "You could walk on it now, if you desired. See the river up close. Hear those sounds."

"You forget something, Herr Kapitän. A small matter of the gate."

"You people make me laugh. You, too, are forgetting something. A small matter of the key." He jiggled musically a ring of keys hooked to his dark coat.

She could scarcely believe what he was offering. Anticipation battled with fear in her voice. "You would do that? You would let me out to look at the river? I would come back, I promise. Of course I would come back, where else would I go? I wouldn't be gone long. Ten minutes. Maybe fifteen, if that's all right."

Another adventure offered on one of the strangest days of her life! She moved closer to the gate. The Kapitän jiggled his keys in the dark. She waited for him to turn the lock. Her thumping heart blotted the river sounds. Why was he being so nice? The new young guard, maybe, but not the Kapitän. Was this a new, gentler policy, ordered by the Empress herself?

"There is one thing we have not yet discussed," the Kapitän said.

"What is that?"

"The barter."

"The barter? What does that mean, the barter?"

"The barter. The trade. The exchange. If I unlock the gate, what will you do for me?"

For a moment she did not understand. What could she possibly do for him? Then his words hit her like a leather strap across her face. Her eyes smarted.

"Come, I don't hear an answer. Should I suggest some ideas, from which you could choose?"

She was not hearing him any more. She heard instead the lapping of the river. The river Main was laughing at her. Horrified, she took one, two, three steps backward. She turned and began to run, first slowly, then faster. Ran as hard as she could for the length of a dozen dark houses before she felt it was safe to slow down, short of breath, ankle throbbing with a heartbeat of its own. She did not want to attract attention. She did not want to have to explain why she was running. Someone was walking towards her. She slipped into the synagogue to hide.

The angel of sleep was late in arriving at the Judengasse that night. In the small front bedroom above his workshop, the cabinet maker Yussel Kahn could not fall asleep for the blood that was dancing in his veins. He had seen her twice that evening. He had seen her standing by the grave in the fading light, her face as smooth as polished cherry. He had seen her in the temple, that marvelous tense moment when she violated the sanctum of the men, rushed in to hug that boy and kiss him and the collective face of the Judengasse dropped in astonishment. She looking at the men in defiance for just a moment, as if daring them to throw her out. Then rushing out flustered. It was just the kind of thing his dear Lainie might have done. He lay awake, at first happy to think of the Schnapper girl, then increasingly disturbed. The Judengasse was such a small place. He must find a way to overcome this obsession. Perhaps he ought to confess it to someone. Perhaps speaking of it would ease the pain.

The coin dealer Meyer Amschel Rothschild also had difficulty falling asleep. He kept glancing in the dark at the bag of treasures on his dressing table. He wanted to study the Mesopotamian again. But handling money on the Sabbath was forbidden. Instead he lay awake composing in his head the letter he would write when the Sabbath ended, the letter to Crown Prince Wilhelm of Hesse-Hanau. Frankfurt was one of fifty-one self-governing towns in the so-called Holy Roman Empire, but there were also 94 Kings and

Princes, and Crown Prince Wilhelm was among the most influential. The letter would have to be worded carefully: just the right amount of assertiveness that would be expected from a knowledgeable coin dealer; just the right amount of obsequiousness that would be expected from a Jew. He also would have to find someone to whom to dictate it. His handwriting in Judendeutsch, the mixed language of the lane, written in Hebrew letters, was clear enough. But his German writing was not. He thought of the Court Factor Schnapper, whom he'd run into at the bridge. Schnapper must have a secretary; perhaps for a few kreuzer the secretary would ink his letter to the Prince.

For the rag dealer Ephraim Hess and his young wife, Eva, sleeplessness was to be expected. A hungry infant — Solomon the Poet, Solomon the King — just twelve hours old, was nestled between them on their narrow bed. Eva fed him whenever he cried, and burped him when necessary, and wondered if her slim body would produce enough milk for the next two years. The proud father looked at his unplanned but already loved son, and nuzzled the soft pate to inhale the newborn smell, and wondered if he could wrest enough freedom from the uncaring world to give his son a finer place in which to grow, a place unfettered by walls and gates.

Isidor Kracauer was tormented the most by his inability to fall asleep. The events of the day were sailing through his brain on wind-blown seas. The dead body, the praise for his history study. Then, of all things, being named Schul-Klopper, and shammus! Not to mention the hug and kiss from Guttle in front of all the men. How was he to fall sleep? He had to, he absolutely had to, because he needed to be up at dawn, out in the lane knocking on doors. Solomon Gruen had never been late, the Chief Rabbi had said. So Izzy dared not be late. He had to fall asleep, quickly, so he would wake up in time. He had to. This refrain kept clicking in his brain like a metronome, kept him twisting and turning until the middle of the night. And made it predictable that on his first morning as Schul-Klopper, Izzy the Wise would oversleep. This was not unusual; nobody had ever called him Izzy the Early Bird.

In contrast, Hiram Liebmann was awake as always to see the first hint of gray in the morning sky. While his brother slept beside him, he moved to the window with his pocket watch and his image book. It was the Sabbath, he was not supposed to write on Saturday. He did not understand why. If you couldn't hear and you couldn't speak, he'd decided long ago, Yahweh had used up all the restrictions to which He was entitled. Hiram looked at his watch. It was time for the new Schul-Klopper to be off on his rounds. He should be knocking on the door downstairs at any moment. But there was no sign of the boy. Hiram was not surprised. The boy was never out early. He pulled on his clothes, making sure to put his largest handkerchief in his pocket. Quietly he went down the stairs. He walked three doors over to the Kracauer house. Hesitating only briefly, he pounded on the door with his fist.

Otto Kracauer and his wife slept upstairs in a small front bedroom on the top floor. Pounding downstairs woke the butcher. It's the Schul-Klopper, he thought. He got out of bed, crossed the narrow hallway and knocked on the door of the boys' room. "Time to get up, the Schul-Klopper just knocked," he said, opening the bedroom door.

The oldest boy, Aaron, sat up in his bed, rubbing his eyes. The next boy, Eli, did the same. Both turned sleepily toward Izzy, who was still asleep. Eli shook Izzy's shoulder to wake him. "It's the Schul-Klopper," he said.

The father, who had turned into the hallway, stopped. He rushed back to the room. He and Aaron and Eli all blurted the same words at the same time. "The Schul-Klopper? Izzy's the Schul-Klopper!"

"Get him up!" the butcher ordered.

"Who knocked?" his wife asked over his shoulder as she pulled on her robe.

Awakening, Izzy took a moment to assess the situation. All at once he understood. He jumped out of bed, striking his head on the low slanted ceiling. He threw off his nightshirt and pulled on his clothes.

"What time is it? Where's my hammer?"

"You don't have a hammer yet," Aaron said. "Today you use your fist."

He pulled on his shoes. Eli threw him a yarmulke. Izzy caught it and bounded out of the room toward the stairs. "See you at the synagogue," he said.

Leaping down two steps at a time, he burst out the front door, not seeing Hiram Liebmann standing beside it. He scurried across the cobbles, jumped over the sewage ditch, knocked hard on the door of the first house on the east side. He knocked on the door of the next house. And the next. And the next.

He stopped. He looked across the lane. He was already at the fifth house. He had not knocked on any doors on the other side. He crossed the cobbles, jumped the ditch, knocked on the first house, which was the Liebmanns, the second, which was the Kravitzes, the third, which was the Schnappers, the fourth, which was his own. He stopped again. If he kept going on this side, he would omit houses across the lane. If he kept crossing and recrossing the lane, the Sabbath service would be half over before he reached the south gate. Maybe he should run all the way down this side, knocking on doors. But then he would have to run all the way back from the south gate to awaken the men who were just across the lane.

How had the real Schul-Klopper done it? He didn't know. He'd always been asleep when the Schul-Klopper knocked.

Izzy was near to panic when he noticed the deaf mute standing beside his door, watching. Hiram motioned for Izzy to come closer. Izzy needed to ask someone what to do, but he could not ask Hiram Liebmann, who couldn't hear, and wouldn't know.

Hiram tapped Izzy on the chest. He pointed across the lane. He made a sweeping motion, pointing with his forefinger toward all the houses on the east side. He tapped himself on the chest. He made the same sweeping motion toward all the houses on the west side.

"You'll help me?" Izzy said. "You'll do this side while I do that side?" He was repeating Hiram's motions as he spoke.

Hiram nodded. "You've got a deal," Izzy said. He clapped Hiram on the upper arm, and hurried across the lane. He knocked on the door of the fifth house, the sixth, the seventh, with his bare fist. Hiram withdrew his large handkerchief from his trouser pocket. Carefully he wrapped it around his right fist. With his left hand he pulled out his watch. There was no need to run, there would be plenty of time now. He slipped the watch back into his pocket. He began to walk along the cobbles, knocking firmly on every door, front house and rear.

Izzy, in his haste and panic, forgot about the houses in the rear. He was too worried the job might be taken away on his first day. Everyone would laugh at him, and call him sleepyhead.

So it was that men on the east side of the lane, especially early risers such as the cabinet maker, were happy to greet the new Schul-Klopper and wish him well. While men on the west side of the lane were surprised to find pounding on their doors not the new Schul-Klopper but the deaf mute. With good reason, they did not ask him questions. But any number of them mentioned it to Rabbi Simcha as he greeted them at the schul. The Rabbi told them he had no idea why this was so, but that he would surely find out.

When they had reached the south gate, their task complete, and they turned to walk back to the synagogue, Hiram Liebmann was filled with gratification by the service he had performed. No matter that he was not pious himself; he had done something useful for the people. Izzy Kracauer was less than satisfied. He was, in fact, in pain. The knuckles on both his hands were bleeding, scraped and splintered from knocking hard on all those doors. The sides of his hands was bruised and turning purple. He had knocked with them after the pain in his knuckles became too great. He showed his hands, hanging limp as cabbage leaves, to Hiram. Hiram held out his own; they were not bloodied, not bruised. He pulled out his handkerchief, wrapped it around his fist, showed it to Isidor. The boy placed the flat of an aching hand to his forehead. He winced at the pain in his knuckles. "Izzy the Dummkopf," he said.

At the conclusion of the morning service, Izzy and Hiram were summoned to meet in Rabbi Simcha's study with that gentleman and the Chief Rabbi. Nervously, Izzy explained what had happened. The Chief Rabbi frowned into his beard.

"How can we be certain this won't happen again?"

"What I was thinking," Izzy said, knowing he might oversleep on any day, "is that the shammus — that's me — has an assistant. Hersch Liebmann. So perhaps the Schul-Klopper — which is also me — should also have an assistant. Hiram Liebmann. This gentleman here. If it's not against the rules."

Rabbi Simcha looked at his superior. He knew the Chief Rabbi would not want to admit a mistake to the community, would not want to admit so soon that he had chosen wrong. "Since this is about assistants, Rabbi," he said, "perhaps I should handle it."

"A good idea."

The Chief Rabbi strode out of the study in bad humor. But within his beard he was also chuckling. Poor lad with his bleeding hands. The wise aren't always wise in the ways of the world. A subject for his class at the yeshiva, perhaps. Surely he could find someone who illustrates that, in Genesis, or Leviticus. Somewhere in the Torah, it was his experience, he could find an illustration for just about anything. Also, a justification for almost anything.

In Rabbi Simcha's office, Izzy was examining the floor. It was plain wood here, no red carpeting as in the Chief Rabbi's study. Hiram Liebmann was looking at the ceiling, smiling at his private thoughts. Rabbi Simcha was burdened with that pink scar on his face, and also pox scars. Surely he would help a deaf mute. Yahweh had made freaks of them both.

"Can the Schul-Klopper have an assistant?" the Rabbi asked. "An interesting question. Looking at your hands, Isidor, I would say that, for this evening, you must have an assistant. For medical reasons. So I would urge you to walk together, and let Hiram do the knocking — with his hand wrapped in a rag. Just as Solomon Gruen, peace be upon him, always wrapped his hand on the Sabbath. This afternoon I will read in the Talmud. To make sure dividing the job is not forbidden. When the Sabbath is over, you both will meet here. Is that understood?"

Isidor said it was. He led Hiram out the door. Somehow with his aching hands he would find a way to explain.

Later, after dark, Rabbi Simcha presented Isidor Kracauer with the new hammer made by the cabinet maker. "You are still the official Schul-Klopper," he said. Then he presented Hiram Liebmann with the worn hammer that had been used by Solomon Gruen. "And you can help him," he said, pointing from one to the other, and knocking on air. Hiram nodded, smiled. The meaning was clear.

"There will be no formal ceremony," the Rabbi said to Izzy. "He's just your helper. Understood?"

Izzy said he understood. He thanked the Rabbi. As they left the study, he reached up and put his arm around the shoulders of his new assistant.

The next afternoon, Hiram, with a handful of kreuzer in his pocket, walked to the shop of the rag dealer Ephraim Hess. He pointed to a long black coat that was hanging in front of the stall. Indicating that he wanted to buy it, he held out his palm with coins on it. The rag dealer took eight of the coins. He lifted down the heavy coat with the frayed sleeves.

When they were being summoned to services that evening, people on the west side of the lane greeted a Schul-Klopper carrying the hammer of Solomon Gruen, and wearing the familiar long coat of Solomon Gruen. Some, before they saw his face, wondered for a moment if a miracle of resurrection had occurred. Quickly, however, they shed the notion; they did not believe in resurrections. Later, Yetta was startled to find the familiar black coat with the frayed cuffs and the milk stain back in her apartment. She sat on a kitchen chair, wiped her brow with her apron. She looked up at the ceiling. "Adonai," she said, "I'm an old lady. I have an old man to take care of. Bitte, don't play games with me."

You heard about the Schnapper girl?

—I heard! People were angry. Everyone was whispering. The nerve of her!

—Right into the schul she ran. Right down among the men. Then she hugged him!

—She hugged him? That I didn't hear. Whom did she hug?

—The new Schul-Klopper. Rubbed her breasts up against him, they say.

—In front of the Rabbi? The Schul-Klopper rubbed her breasts? Who says?

—Those who saw. Then it got worse. She lay down in front of the gate guard. In the dark!

—No!

—Afterward she stood right by the gate. Close enough to kiss him.

—She kissed the gate guard? You saw?

—I didn't see. I'm telling you what I heard.

—For shame! For shame!

—People saw through their windows. She was walking alone in the lane. When any good girl would have been home sleeping.

—It just goes to show. It's a curse on her father, the Court Jew, Schnapper.

—A curse? For what?

—For chutzpah. To name a girl Guttle. The Good. He was asking for trouble. Maybe she's not so good.

—I never thought of that. It looks as if she's Guttle die Schlecht.

— Guttle the Bad! I'll have to tell my wife. She always said the Schnapper girl was too come-hither, with those down-turned lips of hers.

—Too come-hither for what?

—It was dark, I didn't see. You're the one who saw.

All day Saturday she stayed in her room. She came out only to eat, which she could barely do, and to empty the chamber pot. When her mother asked what the matter was, she said her stomach hurt. Which was true. She felt as if she'd been kicked by a horse, so loathsome had been the words of the Kapitäin.

His invisible leer had drained her spirit. She'd always acted as if bereft of care, eager to take risks, to explore the unknown — as much as was possible between the ghetto walls. Never afraid to speak her thoughts. She did not know from where this penchant came; her mother was far more timid. Now she had to ask herself if her mother's way was better. If the Kapitäin had really wanted to have his way with her, she realized, he could have kept silent about barters. He could have quietly unlocked the gate. In her naiveté she would have gone out, to gaze at the river rippling in the light of the moon, at the trembling reflections of boats held fast in the current. But at what terrible cost?

Thirsty, she forced herself to stir from her bed, went to the kitchen of the empty house, poured herself water from a pitcher, and drank. In the vegetable basket on the counter were a large cabbage and three potatoes. Her mind made a connection, her rage began to build anew. With both hands, as if performing a ceremony, she lifted the cabbage out of the basket and set it on the cutting board. From a nail on the wall she took down a heavy cleaver with a large rectangular blade, the one they used for quartering chickens; the blade was thick and sharp enough to crunch through bones. Staring at the cabbage, pale green and white, tightly wrapped, she tried to find in it the face of the Kapitäin. She squinted, trying to resolve it into features. It was no use, the night had been dark, and the morning seemed long ago. Regardless, she lifted the cleaver high above her head. She tensed, ready to split the cabbage in half with a strong downward stroke

Her raised arm began to shake. She couldn't do it. She put the cleaver down.

Returning the cabbage to the basket, she turned away, humiliated, took two steps towards her room. Then, with a demonic smile, she turned back. She fondled the three potatoes, clutched the longest, slimmest of the three, set it on the cutting board. It wobbled slightly; she steadied it with her fingers. When it was still, she lifted the cleaver, and quickly, with a swift, downward thrust, lopped it in two. But her aim missed the point intended.

Her hands were trembling as she put the cleaver down. How could she have done such a thing? She wondered if, like Melka of the South Gate, she was going mad.

Melka, it was said, was locked in a fourth floor attic across from the cemetery, escaping sometimes at night to walk the lane while the people slept. She had been a rich girl, the legend went, who had lived in a fine house overlooking the river at the time the ghetto was built. As the walls went up around her, as the gates were installed and locked, she slowly went insane. That had been three hundred years ago, and still she lived in her attic, people said, mostly women, absorbing century after century the free-floating insanity induced by confinement within walls and gates, by the absence of sun, by inescapable stench. This the benefactress Melka did so that only she, not all those in the lane, would be mad. Some said her constant ingesting of the roots of madness had swollen her brain so large that her head could no longer fit through the door. Others said this could not be so, insanity has no mass, the human capacity for madness is infinite.

Hearing footsteps on the stairs, Guttle pulled off her night shift and shuddered into her clothes. Her sister Avra appeared in the doorway.

"Why did you cut a potato in half?"

Guttle straightened her skirt, slipped into her shoes. "It wasn't me, it was Melka. I only meant to circumcise it."

Avra stuck out her tongue and disappeared. Guttle returned to the mirror. As she pulled her comb through tangled locks they stung her scalp like the pricks of pins. She wondered if Melka, too, had longed to walk by the river — if that was how her madness had begun.

8

The weekly meeting of the Judengasse Council was held as always at three o'clock Sunday afternoon. It was a convenient time for everyone, the gates to the outside world being locked. The seven current members were seated around a long oak table in the council chamber at the rear of the synagogue. Through the back wall they could hear the muffled voices of the yeshiva boys.

The Chairman achieved the full attention of the members when, after several preliminaries, he said: "The next piece of business carries over from last week. You will recall that we decided by a vote of six to none, with one absent, to petition the Frankfurt Town Council for a liberalization of the laws regarding Jews. Specifically, that we be permitted to leave the ghetto on Sundays, and that we no longer be forbidden to enter public parks."

Thaddeus Levi, an importer of silks, motioned to the Chairman. "I was unable to attend the last meeting because of a family problem. I would like to speak out against this action."

"We've already voted," Wolf Schnapper said.

"You can still hear my views."

"Very well, Thaddeus, go on," the Chairman said.

Levi, an elderly man with a stringy gray beard, rose in his seat. "I did not hear the arguments in favor of this petition. I imagine they are obvious. How wonderful it would be if the Frankfurt Council agreed to change the rules. How wonderful to take our children and grandchildren to the parks on a Sunday afternoon. Let them see flowers they have never seen, and lakes. Who could argue against that? But my question is, Why would the Frankfurt Council agree to such a thing? Why would they change the rules that have been in place for hundreds of years?"

"The worst that can happen is they refuse," Schnapper said.

"That would be no small thing, Wolf. If we send this request, and they refuse, imagine the disappointment. Our people will be dreaming of precious freedoms, and their hopes will be broken. And we wouldn't be able to ask again for maybe another fifty years. Worse than that, the Gentiles could get angry. They could impose conditions that are even worse."

"They could crack down on the import trade," Max Kalter, a teacher, said.

Levi glared at Kalter. "That's not a fair remark. This is not about me or my business. It's what's good for the Judengasse."

Loud voices erupted next door. One yeshiva boy was shouting the brilliance of a certain point made centuries before by Rashi. Another trumpeted the "more current" views of Moses Mendelssohn. Nothing in the world gladdened the yeshiva more than a philosophical argument.

Levi resumed his seat. Chairman Kalman Reis, a banker, had to wait for the shouting next door to die down. Then he said, "All right, Thaddeus, you've had your say. Does anyone want to change his vote."

No one stirred. "Then the vote shall be recorded as six for and one against."

Joshua Lamb, a younger man with ginger hair and a short beard, slim and powerful from regular exercises as captain of the Fire Brigade, by trade a dealer in used furniture, rarely spoke at these meetings, but he did so now. "Herr Levi has one good point, I think. About the disappointment if we are refused. I am still in favor of the petition. But perhaps we could agree to keep it a private matter, within the council. Make no mention of it until we receive an answer. Then, if it's a joyous one, the entire Judengasse can celebrate. If we are turned down, no one needs to know."

Rabbi Simcha responded. "Our people have endured worse disappointments for centuries. They could endure this as well, if it happens. They should know what we are doing."

"I agree," Kalter, the teacher, said.

They took a vote. By a margin of five to two, they decided to keep the petition secret until an answer was received from Frankfurt. That could take months, they knew. Rabbi Simcha was asked to read aloud the draft petition he had written. He pulled a paper from his leather envelope, and he read:

"To the most noble and illustrious City Council of Frankfurt-am-Main:

"As a human being every Jew has the same rights as all others, and a just claim to freedom. There is no other place in Germany where Jews are so restricted in the enjoyment of fresh air and a clean street as we are. Jews in Vienna enter public promenades without hindrance. In Mainz and Mannheim and in nearby Hanau the parks are open to Jews. Only we are denied this right. We therefore do petition the Frankfurt Council to accord those rights to us, and to unlock the gates of the Judengasse on Sundays, when we can most readily exercise those rights.

With all appropriate humility, etc."

The council members sat silently, taking in what he had read. They debated whether the first sentence, asserting equal rights for Jews, went too far; they were by no means asking for equal rights. Rabbi Simcha argued that the assertion of equality was the basis for all that followed. "It shows how little we really are asking for," he said.

In the end the vote on the petition was six in favor of sending it and one against. The Chairman said he and the Chief Rabbi would sign the request on behalf of the Judengasse, and would send it by post the next day.

Another eruption of noise. Partisans of Rashi and Mendelssohn were shouting again. When their voice levels lowered, the Chief Rabbi spoke.

"If I may, Kaspar, I have something unfortunate to tell the council. It concerns the funds in the synagogue. This afternoon our new shammus — he avoided saying Schul-Klopper, but sly smiles circled the table — "our new shammus — he does have a good mind, whatever you may be thinking just now — he came to me with disturbing information. He told me — and I ask that what I say now be held in confidence, not to leave this room — the reason why will become clear — he told me that as his first act as shammus he checked the financial records of the schul. He compared the information in the ledger, as to cash on hand, with the actual cash on hand. He expected no discrepancy — but found one. A large one. He discovered that a hundred gulden are missing from the treasury."

An intaking of breath around the table led Rabbi Eleazar to pause.

"The shammus, Isidor Kracauer, came to me at once. I personally went over the ledger. I personally counted the funds. The boy is correct.

"I've known this information only a few hours. I felt the council should be told. But nobody else need know. Not now. We don't want to smear the reputations of innocent parties. Especially of the deceased."

He waited for his inference to sink in. "The easy line of suspicion would lead to the keeper of the money, Solomon Gruen, peace be upon him. There is no evidence at this juncture to suggest that Solomon was involved. On the contrary, had he been involved, he could easily have tampered with the books, to make the numbers agree. He did not do that. Besides, I knew him well. He was a humble man, but one of great integrity. He loved the schul, he would never steal from it. Gossips in the street, however, need little evidence. So I ask the solemn pledge of all of you that this will not be mentioned outside this room, until we complete an investigation."

The Rabbi, who had been leaning forward over the table, his eyes fixing each of them in turn, leaned back in his chair.

"What about that assistant of his, that Liebmann boy?" Thaddeus Levi said. "That's two years' salary for him. Didn't they used to call him the Wild One?"

"That was a long time ago," the teacher said.

"That was my first thought," the Chief Rabbi conceded, "since after Solomon he had the easiest access. I spoke with him. Hersch Liebmann claims to have no knowledge of the money."

"He could be lying," Levi said.

"Of course he could be lying. But as of now we have no proof of anything."

"He's not the only one with access," Joshua Lamb noted. "There is also Viktor Marcus."

"The Cantor?" Levi retorted. "Shame on you for suggesting such a thing. He is a young man of God."

Lamb replied, "He is more a young man of song."

"His father is a moneylender." Levi's face was reddening with anger. "The son of Jacob Marcus would hardly need to steal."

"Jacob Marcus is not renowned for sharing wealth. Not even with his son."

"Perhaps. But Viktor inherited plenty from his uncle Solomon. He wouldn't need to pilfer from the schul!"

A terrible thought flashed through the mind of the Chief Rabbi. *A motive for murder?*

"The theft most likely occurred before the Schul-Klopper's unexpected passing."

"Enough," the Chief Rabbi said. "Right now we have no evidence against anyone. We'll continue to look into the matter. Meanwhile, we have moved the schul funds to a locked strongbox, in a safer place. I have asked Rabbi Simcha to take charge of it. Our procedures have perhaps been too lax until now. We never expected a thief in the lane." He stroked his beard. "This matter, of course, should dissuade no one from making further contributions."

The men around the table laughed, some a bit hollowly. Some of them tithed their income to the synagogue, as tradition required; other did not. The Chairman lifted his gavel. "I'm sure I speak for all of us in pledging to honor the request of the Chief Rabbi. We shall maintain silence until the thief can be found and punished. I remind you, we've also voted to remain silent about the petition to the Frankfurt Council. Though I would think a few prayers would be in order.

"I have one other announcement. You will recall that last week we selected two new members of the council to fill our vacant seats. I'm happy to say that Doctor Lev Berkov has agreed to take the seat of his deceased father. And Meyer Amschel Rothschild has agreed to fill the seat vacated for health reasons by Samuel Krieg. They will join us at the next session. Now I am going to adjourn this meeting — before anyone else has news."

They tried to laugh, even to smile, but failed. The Chairman tapped the table with his gavel. None of the councilors had spirit enough to stir. They sat slumped in their chairs, the oil lamps illuminating only their faces, the dark tableau suggesting a painting by a Dutch master.

9

*T*he Cantor, Viktor Marcus, is pacing on the bemah in a vast, dimly lit synagogue. His ivory-colored talis, with black trim, is draped on his broad shoulders. He takes hold of the lectern, a hand on each side, as if to deliver a sermon. All of the seats are empty. Guttle, unseen, is standing in the shadows. The Cantor sings an aria.

> Now I rise in dudgeon high, and fury,
> To air my rage before this absent jury,
> For how am I to honor and condone
> What Guttle fair, deserving of a throne
> Ere fracturing the sanctity this night
> Of Torah, of the Talmud, and of right,
> Hath done, perhaps with meditated rancor,
> To stab the heart of such a loving Cantor?
> It's wound enough to make a wooer swoon,
> For morrow, on the upright stroke of noon
> I'd planned with silent gait and hidden carriage
> To hear my father seek her hand in marriage.
> Instead, to trump my hand, she bolted in
> Where woman does not enter without sin,
> And ere a single hand could reach to stop her
> Did hug the boyish flesh of the Schul-Klopper,
> Compounding with her lips upon his skin
> Dark trespass into bright vermillion sin.
> Then, fleeing from the sanctity of schul,
> Where God forgives the rashness of a fool,
> As if to prove she's made of darker meat,
> Rashly to the south gate did retreat,
> And earned the leers of goyim without number

By spreading legs in unprotected slumber,
Till guard, with stiffened sword and words of hate,
Did send her reeling home, but much too late
To stop the gossip and its careless pain
From poisoning opinion in the lane
Enough so that a prudent Cantor waits,
And cancels nuptial dreams, and hesitates,
For who can wed a teaser — fairest Guttle —
Who needs a whipping, firm and hard and brutal?
Still do I long to thrust myself upon her,
But cannot do so now and keep my honor;
I wonder at the days that I must live
Before I dare to wed her, and forgive.
Condemn, but then relent — is that the way?
I must now to my bed, and let it lay.

Footsteps are heard from a corner of the schul. The girl pushes open the outer door and hurries home, limping on her turned ankle.

She was trying to read the play Hamlet, by William Shakespeare, a new German edition her father had bought for her. She could not concentrate. Still upset by the confrontation with the Kapitäin, her mind kept returning to the only time she had gone outside the gates by herself. It happened late one afternoon when she was five years old. Her mother had sent her next door to play with Izzy, which she often did. Instead, curious as always, Guttle that day went the other way, a short distance to the open gate. The guard had left his post for a moment. Guttle wandered through. She strolled to the slaughterhouse and went inside, and ran happily towards the rear, to look at the live chickens; when she came here with her mother, the chickens always made her laugh, the way they strutted and clucked; she understood less than they their approaching fate. Emerging, she saw the guard back at the gate, and became frightened. What if he told her mother? Her mother had forbidden her to go outside the gate by herself. She would get a beating for sure.

There must be another way in, she reasoned in her precocious manner, the lane was very long. She scooted behind the slaughterhouse, making herself invisible to the guard, and came to the outside of the stone wall. Slowly she walked along it, in search of an opening, a door, an unlocked gate. As she walked and walked without finding one, a fear beyond her father's hand came over her. The sky was growing dark, she was alone, who knew what the Gentiles might do if they found her? She might be snatched up and put in a cage by a witch, like Hansel and Graetel, a witch who baked children in her oven.

The darkness descended rapidly. There were no lamps in the deserted fields outside the wall. Strange shapes stalked the arriving night. She heard faint scurrying in the weeds, either witches or rats. Terror took hold, she began to cry, began to claw at the wall as if to create a gate of her own. "Let me in," she cried, and then, braving the thought of a beating, "Mama, Mama, I'm sorry, let me in." She ran back and forth along the wall, tugging at a stone with both hands when she found a loose one, clawing, clawing, but it would not come out. "Mama, Mama, come get me," she cried, but no one heard through the wall.

The air was cooling rapidly, and in her thin cotton dress with its short sleeves she felt cold. She was desperate now to get home, but she had run back and forth so many times that she was not sure which way she had come. Choosing a direction, she walked, uncertainly, tears staining her face while she wiped her sniffling nose with dirty hands and then dried her hands on her dress   it was pale blue, freshly washed, her mother would be angry about that as well. At last she heard the dim sound of chickens squawking, and knew she was getting closer. Coming to the end of the wall, she peered around it, and saw by the guard's lantern that the gate was open despite the dark, saw the night guard talking with her mother. "Mama, Mama," she yelled, and went running and stumbling across the cobbles. Her mother scooped her up and kissed her head and carried her into the lane, as the guard locked the gate behind them.

"You were supposed to be at Izzy's," her mother said. "Why did you go out of the lane? Why didn't you come right back?"

She sniffled and wiped her nose. "The walls kept me out. I don't like them."

"You're not supposed to like them. You won't like your tush, either, when your father is done paddling it."

Shakespeare still in her lap, Guttle smiled ruefully. What a little adventuress she had been! She was grateful that although the memory was vivid, the pain of the beating was not. It was the only time her father had used a stinging birch.

Because Izzy for his new project asked them, the elder Liebmanns recalled a time when the Judengasse was a happier place. When the houses were three times as large, and each belonged to only one family, and were spaced far apart. When there was room within the ghetto walls for chicken coops, for flower gardens, for large vegetable plots, for pens holding goats. When children had grassy yards in which to play. Though it is not quite accurate to say they recalled it; they remembered being told of it by their grandparents or great grandparents — who had been told of it by their grandparents.

Seated at their kitchen table, Izzy was learning things about the early days of the Judengasse that he had never heard before. Guttle had suggested he might begin his research by speaking with them; surely they would cooperate, he had taken on their son as assistant Schul-Klopper. Indeed, the Liebmanns had felt honored to talk with him. While Hersch and Hiram played chess in their room, Izzy made notes with a new graphite pencil he'd borrowed from the yeshiva.

Leo and Yetta regaled him with tales. In the old days, they told him, long before they were born, before there was even a ghetto, Jews had to wear special clothing. They had to wear black cloaks and broad white collars, which made it look as if their heads were sitting on a platter. They had to wear wide, round, bright yellow "Jew hats," with a distinctive point about three inches high rising from the top. The men had to wear on their cloaks a badge of two concentric yellow circles. The women had to wear veils with yellow stripes. Groups of Gentiles sometimes set upon them and beat them, for no other reason than they were Jews. In the thirteen hundreds, mobs had killed three quarters of the Jews in Frankfurt. Seventy-five people had been left dead in the streets. When the city fathers put up the stone walls, and forced the Jews to move in, they said, with some truth, that it was for the Jews' own protection. They charged the ghetto for that protection, twenty-two thousand gulden each year, a tax that was still in effect.

Izzy asked, "If it was so nice and spacious back then, with chickens and goats and gardens, what happened?"

Leo put his hands through his suspenders, which were stark black against his threadbare white shirt. Yetta was amazed at how talkative he was being; she hadn't heard him go on like this in years, not since he was a teacher at the heder. Before his mind started wandering.

"What happened was the begats," Leo said. He sipped from a glass of tea that Yetta had set before him. The tea had grown cold while he talked. "At first there were eleven families, I think it was. But those families begat more families. And they begat more. Not much of a surprise. So more and more houses had to be built."

He told of the changes happening outside the Judengasse as well. How the town was growing. Frankfurt was becoming a commercial center, for importing and exporting. Jews for hundreds of miles heard about this, and decided that Frankfurt was the place to come to do business. Because that was all that they could do. The laws against Jews being farmers, or members of craft guilds, or owning shops, were the same all over. So they came to Frankfurt to make money to feed their families — and they had to live in the Judengasse. Not only live there, they had to own property there. But no houses were for sale. No one was moving out. So they bought a chicken coop, or a vegetable garden, and built a house on the land.

Yetta placed her hand on her husband's arm. "Don't talk so fast," she said. "He has to write it down."

Izzy had been making notes as quickly as he could, writing only the important words. He was learning he could not write quickly enough to keep up with people talking. He would reconstruct the details when he went home.

"So write, write," Leo said. And he went on with his story.

After many years, he said, people were still begatting. What else should they do? Soon there were no gardens left. No chicken coops. No goat pens. All the space was taken up by houses. People moving to the Judengasse began to buy half a house. Or a quarter of a house. To meet the requirement of ownership. Two families would live in the same house. Sometimes three families. Or four.

"Let me tell this part," Yetta said. "After a long time passed — a hundred, two hundred years — even that was not enough. What the people decided to do — the houses were nice and large, twenty-four feet wide back then — they began to tear down each house, and put up three in its place. Each new house maybe three metres wide. But three or four floors high. Those are the houses we have today. The city fathers didn't mind. They got more taxes from three small houses than from one big one."

"And the special clothing?" Izzy asked.

"The yellow hats, the special collars, that ended before we were born. But not the yellow circles, not the striped veils. We had to wear them as children, right Leo? As grown-ups, too. They only stopped that maybe thirty years ago."

For more than an hour they had been reciting. Izzy's hand, still bruised from his door-knocking misadventure, was aching. He put the graphite down; he could barely hold it anymore. He asked if perhaps he could come back another time. They agreed that was a good idea.

"Just one more question," Izzy said. "Why did the Gentiles make us do all this?"

Leo looked at Yetta before answering. "Why? I'll tell you why. Because the sky is blue. That's why."

Izzy closed his writing book. He set the graphite on top of it. "I've heard people say that. Is the sky really blue?"

A wry smile rearranged the wrinkles on Yetta's face. But her smile disappeared at once. He was a child of the lane; she could not be certain he was joking.

As he pushed his chair back to leave, it scraped harshly along the floor. Hersch came out of the front room, followed by Hiram. "The boss is leaving," Hersch said, with a grin. He looked at his brother, then at Izzy. "Hiram says you shouldn't sleep late tomorrow."

Izzy, too, grinned, his blue eyes twinkled. "Tell him if I didn't sleep late, I wouldn't need an assistant."

Hersch made rapid motions. Hiram, looking at Izzy, placed his palms together beside his cheek, and tilted his head., nodding. He was granting permission. Izzy the Wise could sleep as late as he wished.

D octor Berkov once again was in the office of the Chief Rabbi. He was not made to feel welcome. He was not offered a seat. On the contrary, the Rabbi himself stood and went to his window and pulled apart the curtains and looked out, his back to the Doctor. The street was alive as it had not been since the death of the Schul-Klopper three days before. Men and women were strolling up and down the lane. Shopkeepers were calling out their wares — used clothing, bolts of cloth, used furniture, antiques, homemade candy, jellies and jams, money at a low interest rate. Children too young for heder were running about noisily, sometimes crashing into the legs of passersby.

"I've been to the chemist this morning," the Doctor said.

The Rabbi did not turn around. He kept his eyes on the street. "Not enough sick people to keep you busy?"

"Nothing my helpers couldn't handle."

He pulled a sheet of paper from his pocket and unfolded it. "Would you like to see his report?"

"Not particularly."

"I'm afraid it confirms my suspicion. The residue in the throat of Solomon Gruen was arsenic. Which means he almost certainly was poisoned."

The Rabbi stiffened. In the street a group of sightseers was walking past. The Judengasse was notorious, not only through Frankfurt but through all of Europe, for its overcrowding, its narrowness, its stench. It was the ultimate ghetto. Gentiles who had heard of its degradations walked through occasionally to see it for themselves — perhaps to describe it to their friends at home, perhaps to challenge their fears. Children were surrounding them, pulling at their breeches or coats, asking for coins. The Rabbi wished they wouldn't.

"What do you expect me to do with this information?" he said. "Go to the Polizei? Give them an invitation to come in and torture a few people? Maybe hang a few people?"

"You could conduct an investigation."

"Make the information public? Turn the lane into a stew pot of suspicion?" The Rabbi turned from the street, letting his eyes grow accustomed to the dim light inside. "I'm sure you've thought about this matter, Doctor. Is there anyone you suspect of having done this?"

"No."

"Have you thought of a motive anyone might have had for killing the Schul-Klopper."

"No."

"Then it seems to me our investigation has reached a dead end. Wouldn't you agree?"

The Doctor could not think of an appropriate answer. "You're willing to let someone get away with murder?"

"It wouldn't be the first time."

"Don't you stand for justice in the lane?"

"When justice seems possible. When it doesn't, I stand for order."

Frustrated, still holding the chemist's report, the Doctor asked, "Shall I leave this on your desk?"

"I'd rather you didn't. I don't want it contaminating my holy books."

"Then I'll take it to my office. It won't contaminate my patients."

He folded the report into the pocket of his coat. The Rabbi gave him a curt nod. Lev took this to mean he should leave the study without shaking hands. Crossing the lane, he was blind to the pedestrians, to the running children, deaf to their noise. He was furious. Yet he could not deny there was truth in the Rabbi's words.

The Chief Rabbi closed the window curtain. He glanced at the rows and rows of books on the shelves. Endless dissections of almost every line in the Torah, by the wisest Rabbis who'd ever lived. He sat down in his large chair, put his elbows on his desk. He bent his head into his hands. His fingers clenched tufts of graying hair.

"Solomon," he murmured in despair. "Solomon, what have I done?"

10

A cloudburst was pouring rain into the lane. Rushing water was cleaning the cobbles in some places, covering them with mud in others. The muck in the sewage trench was running rapidly, the liquid level rising. Merchants with open stalls had moved their goods inside and shut their doors. In the house of Meyer Amschel Rothschild, fifth house rear from the north gate, east side, the carpenter Yussel Kahn was finishing a long confession to his friend. An eavesdropper might have called it a heartburst.

"Do you want to tell me her name?" Meyer asked.

He was perched on a desk in the first-floor shop that he shared with his two brothers, who were in the city on a buying trip. The one-room shop was crowded with file cases, with bolts of silk and cotton, as well as displays of coins. Samples of fabric hung on the walls. The rain pouring down was threatening to roll in under the door. Too agitated to sit, Yussel was pacing about, as he had done since he arrived before the rain began.

"Her name doesn't matter," he said. "It's not her fault." He picked up a coin from the desk, looked at it, tossed it back onto a pile. "I'll tell you how bad it has gotten. Friday night, when I couldn't sleep for thinking of her, I got out of bed and went to my window. I stood there for a long time, staring out into the dark. Trying to figure out what to do. And I saw her. I know you won't believe it. In the middle of the night. Walking up the lane, all alone. I knew it wasn't possible. It was an apparition. This girl wouldn't be walking about at that time of night. But she looked so real. When I realized I wasn't dreaming, I decided I was going mad."

"I don't know what to tell you," Meyer said. "Have you spoken with her?"

A knock on the door cut through the sound of the downpour. "That must be my scribe. But stay till the rain stops. I'll make some tea. It's not a problem."

He moved to the door and pulled it open. A girl stepped inside, out of the rain. Her long brown hair was soaked. The shoulders of her white blouse were wet, as was the hem of her skirt.

"You must be Guttle," Meyer said. "Look at you! You're drenched."

He pushed the door closed behind her. Swelling from the moisture made it a tight fit.

"I couldn't find the house. Papa said the fifth house. He didn't tell me it was in the back. I knocked and knocked. I tried the fourth house, and the sixth. Till I found the alley leading here."

Her hair, her clothes, were dripping a small puddle onto the wood floor.

"You poor girl. Let me get you a towel." He turned to the carpenter, who had faded into the corner. "Do you know each other? Guttle Schnapper, this is Yussel Kahn."

Meyer ran up the staircase two steps at a time to the living quarters. When he came down he handed a towel to Guttle. She tossed her head to the side and began to dry her hair.

Meyer looked about. "Where's Yussel?"

"He said he had to go."

"In this rain?"

Guttle pulled lengths of hair through the towel. "He hurried out the door as if his tooth hurt. I had to push it closed."

"Mein Gott!" Meyer said.

"What's wrong?"

"Nothing. It's nothing." And he thought: Poor Yussel! This must be the girl!

"He's the coffin maker, isn't he?"

"I suppose he remembered an appointment. But look how wet you are. You should have waited until the rain stopped."

"Papa said it was important."

"It is important. But not so important it couldn't wait an hour."

She dried the nape of her neck. "We live just across the lane. In the Owl. I would hardly have gotten wet if Papa had told me the right place."

"Here, let me get you another towel." He hurried up the stairs, came down with a dry one. He handed it to her, draped the wet on the back of a chair. He thought: Laine has been gone a long time. Yussel ought to stop suffering and marry the girl.

"Is this your office?"

"Not much to look at, is it? I share it with my two brothers. The coins are mine, the cloth is theirs."

Rubbing her hair again, she looked at the coins set carefully in boxes divided into small compartments. "Is it a good business? The coins, I mean."

"It's getting better. I've loved coins since I was little. So it's almost like I'm still playing."

He wondered why he was prattling like an idiot.

"Do your brothers share the house as well?"

"They do. Also another family. The Bauers."

"What about your parents?"

He looked at his hands for a moment. She followed his gaze. She thought they were nice hands, long and thin.

"They're gone, may they rest in peace. They died when I was twelve. In a smallpox epidemic. I had been sent away to school at the time."

"I'm sorry."

"So. You're your father's secretary."

"Just a little. At home. Most of his work is at the court."

Finished with the second towel, she handed it to him. He tossed it on top of the first.

"Rothschild is an unusual name," she said. "I mean…" She grew flustered, but completed her thought. "I mean, it doesn't sound like Judendeutsch."

"It comes from a house."

"A house?"

"There used to be a house down the other end of the lane that had a red shield on it, for decoration. Like yours has the owl. Zum Roten Schild, the house was called. It was built about two hundred years ago, by my great great somebody — Isaak, son of Elchanan. In those days people didn't have surnames. They were called by their addresses as much as by their names. Isaak ben Elchanan began to be called Isaak Rothschild, after his house. When his grandson moved to this place later on, he brought the name Rothschild with him. It's a good thing."

"Why is it a good thing?"

"Because I'd hate to be named after this house. It's called the Hinterpfann. My name would be Meyer Amschel House-Behind-the-Saucepan."

Guttle laughed. Then she sneezed. "Hinterpfann." She reached in her pocket, pulled out a handkerchief, blew her nose. "You'd think my father would have known it was in the back." She sneezed again. "So the front house is the Saucepan. I always thought that carving was a loaf of bread." She folded her handkerchief, but kept it in her hand.

"It's not very clear, is it? Young lady, I hope you're not catching cold."

"I'm fine. What's this?" She picked up a small picture frame from the desk.

"An antique. I'm starting to branch out from old coins into all sorts of antiques. The collectors are the same people, so it makes sense. In that one is a poem by Nahum Baum. Written in his own hand, in 1626. You can read it."

She read it aloud: The poem was called *Gentiles.*

> *They see a race*
> *With every face*
> *The color*
> *Of its bones.*

"That's the whole poem? It doesn't say very much."

"If you think about it awhile, it can say a lot."

"Such as what?"

"Well, to me it says: The Gentiles create something they hate — and then they hate it."

Guttle put the framed poem back on the desk. "I like your way better."

"It's nice of you to say. But my way isn't worth twenty gulden. Even if I signed my name."

"Maybe you could sign it Hinterpfann."

Meyer grinned. Outside, the rain seemed to have stopped; he could hear individual drops falling heavily from the eaves. Time was passing quickly with this girl.

"Speaking of gulden, I guess we should get to work. Your family will think I kidnapped you. Sit here." He tossed the wet towels from the back of the chair onto the floor. "Here's paper, pens, ink." He took a sheet of paper from the drawer of the desk. "Oh, before I forget, I have a question. Do you know your neighbor Hersch Liebmann very well?"

"Not really."

"I'm thinking of hiring an assistant. To take things to and from the post. To deliver the antiques, if I start handling bigger objects. I know his family could use the money. And they were kind to my parents when they got sick. The fellow said he's interested, but I want to find out more about him first. Mostly if he is honest. He'd be handling some expensive coins."

"I really don't know," Guttle said. "Just that he seems to love his brother."

"Am I my brother's keeper? I suppose that's recommendation enough. He can work here when he's not too busy at the schul. Anyway. Here's the letter I want you to write. In a nice German hand. Can you read my writing, or shall I dictate it to you?"

She took the paper from him and looked at it. "I think you'd better dictate."

"You see the problem."

Meyer began to read the letter aloud, slowly. Guttle lifted a quill, dipped it in the ink, but did not write. Her mind had fled to what her father said just before she left the house. To the scary exchange they'd had.

"Let me know what you think of him."

"What does that mean, 'Let me know what you think of him?'"

"Nothing. Just what I said."

"Papa? Papa! What are you thinking?"

"Thinking? I'm not thinking anything."

"Yes you are! I know you. Papa, I'm not ready to get married. Not to Viktor Marcus, not to anyone."

"Married? Who said anything about married?"

"Ooooooh."

"Now hurry. Don't keep Meyer Amschel waiting."

Her anger returned as she recollected.

"You're not writing," Meyer said.

"I know. I like to hear the whole letter first. So I know how long it is. So I know how much space to leave."

"That makes sense." He read the letter aloud. "Are you ready now? Shall I begin again?"

"Please."

"To his Lofty Highness the Honorable Crown Prince Wilhelm. Your Gracious Sir… "

She began to write. She stopped and looked up at Meyer, who was standing beside and above her. "Are you writing this letter to impress me?"

Meyer lifted his white yarmulke, ran his hand through his hair, scratched his head, put the yarmulke back on. "To impress you? My dear young lady. I am writing this letter to impress Crown Prince Wilhelm, of Hesse-Hanau. He is the heir to the throne of Hesse-Kassel, one of the largest principalities in the region. I am hoping he will purchase some of my antique coins. Perhaps other things later on." He pulled a handkerchief from his pocket, wiped his hands. He picked a polished coin from a loose pile on the desk. "Do you have enough money to purchase antique coins?"

"No. Of course not."

"Well, when you do, I will write a letter to impress you."

She looked down at the desk, squeezed her eyes shut in embarrassment. She wanted to disappear into a wooden chest that sat against the wall. "I hope

I haven't offended you," she said softly, still looking down. "Perhaps you can begin the letter again. And I will write it."

"Yes, that's a good idea. That's why you're here… I suppose I should assure you that I am not offended. I am just… amused."

He began to read the letter, slowly. Guttle dipped the quill in the ink and began to write. She was careful not to make mistakes. When she was done she sprinkled sand onto it from a canister to blot the ink. She left it there for him to brush away when the ink was dry.

"A mused! He said he was amused!"

She was back in the Owl, shouting at her father, who was sunk in his soft chair near the window. A book of the Talmud lay open on his lap.

"Papa, did you hear me? Amused!" She was almost screaming. "Why didn't you tell me? Why didn't you tell me the house was in the back? I got soaking wet! My hair was hanging down in strings. Like a mop! I must have looked like a witch!"

She ran to her room, slammed the door behind her. The lamps in the house shook. The floor was jolted again as she threw herself onto her bed.

Emmie Schnapper emerged from the kitchen, wiping her pudgy hands on her apron. "What's the shouting about?"

Her husband looked casually into his book. "I think she likes him," he said.

11

In the ensuing days — weeks — months — unspoken measurings occurred between Guttle Schnapper and Meyer Amschel Rothschild.

Visiting the bakery on Friday (he went out to work later than usual that day, so he could catch a glimpse of her as she rid the flour of beetles) he noticed that when she was not smiling or speaking, when she was not aware that she was being observed, her lips turned down at the corners with a curve both pensive and sultry.

She was struck, stealing glances at him outside the synagogue that same night, with how unusually deep his dark brown eyes were set within his skull, grounded by crescent moons beneath that were darker than the rest of his lightly tanned face, shielded by long, dark lashes — eyes that suggested a sensitivity which, she suspected, even he himself could not articulate.

Taking a seat beside her one Sunday afternoon in the courtyard beside the synagogue, as she looked after her younger siblings while they played, he noticed how when she spoke she always seemed to be deferring to him — yet her words made clear that she was not. How she accomplished this he could not say.

She became aware that same afternoon of the way the skin at the corners of his eyes crinkled merrily when he smiled, or laughed, or made one of his subtle jests.

At home alone that evening he conceded that it was perhaps the contrast to her sorrowful lips that made her bright smile, when she flashed it at him, like an offering of heady wine.

Writing a letter for him, on a warm spring afternoon when his sleeves were rolled, she observed his muscular forearms, his large hands with prominent knuckles, and envisioned in them a place of safety for anything entrusted there.

When, as she wrote, a wisp of her hair fell out of place alongside her temple, he longed to ease it back where it belonged — except that, drifting free, it excited him. He dared not presume to touch it.

She tried to recall in her solitude the smell of his nearness, a distinctive scent all leather and honey, horse and sweat. Few men in the Judengasse roamed the surrounding towns for their business, fewer still rode on horseback. The aggregate of his aromas held the promise of sensuality. Perhaps also, in some obscure way, of freedom.

Each morning, because he might glimpse her that day, he awoke smiling, before he remembered the reason — as if he'd drunk deep of wine before he rubbed the cobbles from his eyes.

When she stood alone before the wash basin, it was his hands that soaped her breasts.

When one day he encountered her leaving the fruit market, just as he was returning from business in the city, he thanked Gott for paying attention. He noticed that when she was walking forward, her corseted breasts forthright, she often turned her head, then cocked it further, her eyes exploring the buzzing periphery, suggesting to him a fanciful canter though life, in contrast to his own blinkered gait.

She wondered if he had purposely arranged their meeting.

He recognized a layer of anger buried within her — buried, perhaps, not quite as deep as his own.

In the dark of midnight he kept seeing the sorrowful, sensual curve of her lips. That more than anything made him want to take care of her — also to make love to her.

Secretly, she cut a small circle from the edge of a dress pattern, and slipped it onto her finger, to see how it looked, to see how it would feel.

He became concerned about the ten-year difference in their ages.

She worried at the giddiness she felt beside his calm maturity.

When her hair was in braids atop her head his eyes kept darting compulsively to its tight, upswept origins at the nape of her neck.

She began to sleep with her pattern-paper ring in a small box under her pillow.

Agreeing to walk with him on a delightful May evening — if one ignored the stench from the ditch — she asked what the cities he visited on business were like — Mainz, for instance, or Hesse-Hanau — and he said he did not like to discuss what he saw outside, so as not to increase the frustration of those who were locked within.

In her presence he became less reluctant to speak of the world beyond the lane. He vowed to himself that one day he would take her to see these places, in a carriage of their own, drawn by a high-stepping filly.

One night she imagined him taking her to the cities of which he spoke, in a fiery chariot that crashed through the gates and set ablaze the roads as they passed.

He sensed in her a generosity of soul, which, if he could dwell within its circumference, would make him a better man.

She found herself seeking innocent pretexts under which to visit his office, to examine his coins.

He came to anticipate her tread in the alleyway, and his heart raced out to meet her, though he did not leave his chair; no sooner had she left than he began to hope she might find some excuse to return. And always he felt guilty about his shy friend Yussel. He was poaching on the cabinet maker's love.

She confessed to him that she would have liked to learn to sing, but she'd never asked her father for training in voice with Ansha Cohen, because she would be too nervous to perform.

He confessed to an ignorance of the arts — all the arts — but said that one day he would like to learn more.

"You don't have to say that on my account," she had replied, testing her temerity, waiting for a heavy shoe to fall.

"No, I suppose I don't," he'd said, and then, smiling, added, "though I find great beauty in antique coins — especially the Romans."

"If you could be somebody else, would you be a Roman?" she asked.

"Perhaps."

"I would be a Greek." And then, "I guess you would be Julius Caesar."

"I'd rather Marc Antony. You, I think, would be Helen of Troy."

"If I could not be Cassandra."

He smiled uncertainly; he did yet not know her at all; he did not know if she were joking or being serious. "You would like to make dire predictions?"

"Do any other kind come true?" She sensed she had upset him, and added, "I think of it more as truth-telling."

"Can you think of no happy prediction?"

Her face coloring pink, with points of red in her cheeks, she replied, "I can think of one. But I won't tell you."

"Does it have something to do with me?"

"Are you Marc Antony now, or Meyer Amschel ?"

"I think I'd best be Marc Antony."

"Then it doesn't have to do with you."

Nodding, he felt cold sweat on his forehead. "Deep inside, are you not a happy person?"

She expanded her chest with a deep breath, daring herself to take the risk, let her breath out slowly. "I'm happy when I'm with you," she said.

Her pillow at night, beneath her hands, across the lane from him, became his chest.

He began to make a special effort to acknowledge her mother in the lane.

She wondered if his dead parents would have approved of her.

A tiny brown mole on her right cheek, just below her ear, acquired for him a special significance. Without the mole, he decided, her face would have represented such perfection that Yahweh might have abandoned His clay and moved on. But Yahweh in His wisdom had left the mole there, to keep Himself interested in doing better.

On a dark Sunday in June, with the gates locked and the air heavy with anticipated rain, when he came calling she agreed to drink tea in his apartment and look at some new old coins. She was exhilarated — not just by the history of the coins themselves, but by the boyish pride with which he showed them to her.

He was relieved when he asked about her relationship with Viktor Marcus, and she replied that they had always been just friends, strained friends of late; that she enjoyed his tales of the operas he had seen in Milan and Berlin; that she was flattered when he sang to her in the cemetery; that was all.

He said, "I shall have to revise my opinion of the Cantor. I'd always heard he was something of a braggart." And she, her hand in front of her mouth to mute a delightful smile, replied, "Don't do anything hasty."

She thought he was going to kiss her. Instead, he said he could not sing to her in the cemetery like the Cantor, his voice would make the dead rise up and protest; what he could do there was show her the graves of his parents, if she cared. "What I mean to say," he explained, "is that it's the only place I can take you to meet them."

The rain held off, and in the cemetery, standing beside the soapstone markers, he told her the story of his two long journeys home from school at Furth during the pox — because his father had died, and then his mother. Seeing the glisten in his eyes, hesitating only an instant as a breeze brushed her face, she slipped her small hand into his.

Book Two: Jesters and Hangmen

Did I not tell you earlier that a Jew is such a noble, precious jewel that God and all the angels dance when he farts?

—Martin Luther,
The Jews and Their Lies

12

Heat was a plague that summer in the Rhine Valley, in Frankfurt, and in the Judengasse. The cloudbursts of spring had been followed by three months with little rain. The air was warmer than usual and had not cooled off with the arrival of September. For the first time anyone could remember, the absence of sunshine in the lane was a blessing. But not enough of one.

The elderly were suffering the most, sweating out their salts, their bodies unable to retain water no matter how much they drank. All twelve beds in the hospital were filled; pallets of straw had been set up in the corridors. Others among the elderly were bedridden in their homes under the care of spouses or children. The four Doctor's helpers, who normally were on duty two at a time, worked extra hours, applying cold cloths to the foreheads of the ill, giving them water and all manner of liquids. Doctor Berkov hardly slept as he went from house to house checking on the homebound sick. He developed a haggard look, with dark patches under his eyes and a thinning of his cheeks. His colleague, a Doctor Genschow, had left in June to do research at the university in Berlin. The replacement Lev sought had not yet arrived.

The lane's water pumps had become the focus of social life. Long lines proliferated as women and older children waited to fill kettles and basins and carry them back, water for cooking and washing dishes and for standing baths, but more and more for drinking, while thirst spread through the lane like a disease. The number of trips to the pump each family made doubled, then tripled. The pumps themselves became more difficult to use as the level of the wells dropped.

The bakery had become a fiery cave. The women could barely tolerate the heat as it reflected off the fire walls; a number of them fainted each week; the others were not far from doing so. Their foreheads dripped, their necks and the crevices beneath their arms cascaded rivulets of sweat under their clothing as they worked. The people were told to consume less bread; the number of loaves baked had to be reduced to protect the health of the bakers.

Food spoiled quickly in the heat, despite being moved into cellars. The women went to market through the steaming streets almost every day except the Sabbath to buy fresh milk and sorry-looking vegetables. At the slaughterhouse, Otto Kracauer hung blankets on ropes in the yard to catch any breeze that might fan his dolorous chickens as they lay in the dirt. As he reminded his helpers at least once a week, the chickens had to be alive before he killed them. Otherwise they weren't kosher.

In the lane, the stink from the ditch was worse than anyone could remember. It had attracted every house fly from Paris to Berlin, the people agreed, as they slapped at their necks and arms.

Most people — the Schnappers, the Schlicters, the Kracauers among them — found the heat in the lane, and the stronger stench, so oppressive that they stayed indoors as much as they could. Others, especially unmarried men such as Yussel Kahn and Hersch Liebmann, slept in the lane, after darkness had cooled the cobbles. Some men spent all day in the synagogue; its large, high-ceilinged space was cooler than the cramped houses. The Chief Rabbi announced that men and boys who wanted to sleep there could do so. A few wives sent their husbands off to the temple so they wouldn't be so crowded in their beds.

The communal baths were busy. Jewish custom called for the residents to bathe weekly — more than the average Frankfurt resident did. Doctor Berkov suggested they do so twice each week during the hot weather. For whatever reasons, by the start of September only one person in the Judengasse had died during the oppressive heat, an elderly man who had been ill since winter. Some were calling this a miracle. Others gave credit to the Doctor and his staff.

The only people who noticeably were not affected by the heat were the Schul-Klopper and his assistant. Every morning at dawn, Isidor Kracauer, awakened by Hiram's pounding, strode the west side of the lane with vigor, eager to begin a new day of research. Every morning, Hiram strode the east side wearing the long black coat with the frayed cuffs, no matter how warm the air had become. It was as if the coat had become his identity, and without it he would not have a title, a job — would not have the heady power of awakening the Judengasse each day.

And yet, despite all these tribulations, a feeling of excitement, of itchy anticipation, had gripped the lane. The Frankfurt Fall Fair was only a week away.

The town's annual fairs were the only times that Jewish merchants were allowed to sell their goods outside the Judengasse, alongside Gentile merchants. It was an old tradition. The September Fair had been held annually since the thirteenth century. Merchants and visitors came from throughout the German lands and from as far away as France and Switzerland. The more merchandise on display, the bigger the attraction, the Frankfurt Council knew. Visitors stayed in hotels and inns and ate in coffee houses and beer halls, pouring extra taxes into the town treasury. They increased the income of local merchants, including the Jews, who also paid taxes. For one week, nearly two hundred Judengasse residents carrying special passes would be permitted to spend five days in the city, at the Fair Grounds in the Town Square. There, they had heard from those who'd been there before, they would see jesters in outrageous costumes, acrobats doing daredevil stunts, bands playing, artists of every kind displaying their creations; they would smell sausages frying (they weren't kosher, but they smelled so good!), see tables laden with all manner of silks and linens and spices and jewelry and household creations, every kind of merchandise from near and far. It was all there to buy if you had the kreuzers or the gulden, to gape at in wonder and tell your friends about even if your pockets were empty. Good conversation, too, was a Jewish treasure.

But who in the Judengasse would get to attend? Those merchants who could afford the stall rental fee, for sure. But which were those? And some would need assistants for the week while their wives stayed home with the children. Whom would they choose? That question had set minds scheming, especially among the young. A pass to the Fair was a pass out of prison into the Gentile world. At least for five colorful days.

After mulling the problem, and discussing it with the invisible Melka, Guttle had thought of a way she might get to the Fair. The oppressive heat had given her the idea. She was on her way to the hospital to suggest it to Doctor Berkov when she was accosted by Meyer Amschel. He was not wearing a jacket or a collar, his shirt was unbuttoned at the top, she could see droplets of sweat clinging to the dark chest hairs below his neck.

"Guttle, do you have a moment? I need to ask you something. Two things, actually."

Glancing quickly down the lane, she saw no one nearby. She rubbed the drops of sweat into his chest. He ran his hand gently along her cheek. She took his hand and kissed his fingertips.

"I need you to write a letter to the crown Prince."

Guttle released his fingers reluctantly. "Are you trying to impress me?"

"Of course."

He wanted to touch her hair, her shoulders, her neck. He wanted to lead her to the privacy of the alleyway. But people were approaching.

"The other thing," he said. "Would you like to go to the Fair next week?"

"Me? The Fair?"

"Jesters, acrobats, Gentiles. I'm sure you've heard of it."

She wrinkled her nose at him. "I was just on my way … "

He interrupted her. "You'd be working with me. As my assistant. All week."

"You're serious?"

"Of course I'm serious. One doesn't make jokes about the Torah, the Talmud or the Frankfurt Fair."

"What about Hersch?"

"I don't need him running errands there. I need good handwriting." He touched her chin, wiping off a droplet of perspiration that may or may not have been there. "Good looks wouldn't hurt."

"Hersch will be upset."

"He's more than upset. He's angry. But this is business. I have to do what's necessary."

"You already told him I'd be going?"

"A few minutes ago."

"Wasn't that a bit presumptuous?"

"Absolutely. Of course, if you don't want to go, I could always ask your friend Dvorah. She of the bright red curls."

"You know, Meyer Amschel, if I weren't a lady, I would kick your knee."

"If you weren't a lady, Guttle Schnapper, I wouldn't be asking you."

She reached up and touched her braids, hiding her smile behind her shoulder. "Couldn't Hersch and I both go? Or him three days and me two?"

"We're only allowed two persons at each stall. The same two every day. We'll have passes with our names on them. The fines for cheating are large."

"That's so unfair." She looked over his shoulder at a common distraction, two merchants gesticulating, waving their arms about, like her father's shirts drying on a windy day. "I suppose you'll be wanting an answer."

"Before the Fair closes."

"Such impatience! But you do know how to impress a girl."

"Does that mean yes?"

His eyes were looking into hers. She did not look away. "I suppose it does," she said.

It had happened for him, he'd told her, the very first day, when she came to his office with her hair and her blouse dripping wet, looking like a fallen angel, and she had asked if he were trying to impress her. What innocence, what insouciance, what sweet promise he had seen. What desire he had felt. His first thought every morning since had been how to see her that day — that, and how some day she would be his bride.

She had perceived the same day through a looking glass — with a similar result. Entering his place looking like a drowning rat. Making a fool of herself while she wrote his letter. Running home and hurling herself onto her bed, hating herself because he would think her a mere child, a brash and forward one. Rushing to the window the next morning, shielding her face with the green curtain, hoping to get a glimpse of him walking to morning services, or walking home. Her heart palpitating with frustrated joy whether she saw him or not. Wanting to run down to him when he was there, but holding back — what could she say, how could she explain? Not knowing then how he would have welcomed it. A pure white spark had ignited within her that day, a new star in the night sky of her being. Months later, when she had placed her hand in his beside the graves of his parents, and he had touched her cheek with his fingertips, the spark had become a secret sun, vying to turn her inner night to inner day. Later still, a time in the alley when his lips discreetly, hesitantly, first brushed hers, the sun flamed violet, a fiery comet streaking to the female center of her. Love had been born like a new universe. As if Yahweh was bored with the old.

Meyer broke the eye connection before Guttle did. Several people in the lane had been watching them. The observers turned away and went about their business. One of them, Guttle saw, was Sophie Marcus.

Only Hiram Liebmann, from his third-floor window, continued to look. He'd rarely seen his brother as angry as when he'd stalked into the house a few minutes before, shouting and waving his arms, furious about not getting a pass to the Fair. For the first time, Hiram felt hostility toward the pretty Guttle girl, who was stealing Hersch's rightful place.

"About my letter to the crown Prince ... "

"Can it wait a little? I had an idea for the Fair. I want to give it to Dvorah." Guttle looked at him with a stern glare. "She of the bright red curls."

She hurried off before he could respond. Meyer didn't seem to mind the delay. Though it would be the most important letter he'd ever sent.

I sidor Kracauer was alone in the small library of the yeshiva. He sat slumped in the chair where he'd been working, his head resting in his hands. Sheets of paper were on the table, a quill, a jar of ink, a rolled parchment. When Rabbi Simcha passed the open door and saw him, he feared the boy might be ill, and he entered the room. Izzy didn't stir. The Rabbi approached, asked softly if he was feeling all right.

"Yes," the boy murmured, without looking up. "No. Yes." He raised his head from his hands. His yarmulke fell to the floor without his noticing. His eyes were rimmed with red.

"Which is it?" the Rabbi said. "Yes, or no?" He stooped and picked up the yarmulke and set it on the boy's blond head and smoothed it in place. Izzy wiped his eyes with the base of his palms and sat up straighter. "I've been working," he said.

"So I see."

"Reading the scrolls from the strongbox. The Chief Rabbi said I could, as long as I was careful. As long as they didn't leave this room. I could copy anything I wanted, he said. He even liked the idea of having copies made."

"And?"

"I was reading about Mainz. That parchment over there."

"Ah. Mainz."

"It was written in the year 1140. By a man in Mainz. I forget his name, I have it written down."

"Salamo bar Simeon."

"You know about it?"

The Rabbi saw that the boy was badly shaken, that he was more upset than he knew. An image came to the Rabbi's mind of a young bird leaving its nest before it was ready. "Tell me again," he said. "Refresh my memory."

"It was during what they called the Crusade. In the year 1096."

"The first one."

"There were more?"

"Several."

"Mein Gott!" the boy said.

"Some weren't as bad as the first. Go on, tell me what bar Simeon wrote."

Izzy pulled a handkerchief from his pocket, wiped his forehead. The small room had no windows — not that windows would have helped much with the intense heat.

"The leader of the Catholics, the Pope, called a conference in France. He asked the noblemen to make a crusade to the Holy Land, to free Jerusalem from the Muslims. They were in control of it back then. The people got excited. The nobles decided to go by sea, but the peasants and a few nobles started off by land. They marched beside the Rhine. Along the way they started accosting Jews — any Jews they came upon. They told the Jews they were Infidels, that they must become Christians. If they refused, they were tortured, and killed."

"Yes." Rabbi Simcha took a seat beside Izzy. "For a thousand years, since the destruction of the temple by the Romans, and the diaspora that followed, the Jews had been left in peace. Wherever they lived. For the most part. Except for a murder now and then. Until that crusade. But go on, Isidor. I interrupted your story."

"It's not a story, Rabbi. This man says it really happened. In Mainz. That's just thirty kilometres from here."

"Yes."

"As these crusaders marched down the Rhine, the Jews in Mainz came together. They agreed they would not become Christians. But they didn't want to be tortured, and they didn't want to be killed by the Christians. They would rather die by their own hands."

"Yes."

"They were prepared to fight. Some of them did. But there were eleven hundred Jews, and twelve thousand crusaders. There was no way they could win. So they gathered together and carried out their plan. The women cut the throats… "

He stopped.

"Yes."

"The women cut the throats of their own babies. Of babies at their breasts, he says. The men plunged swords and knives into the bellies, or the hearts, of their wives. And their mothers, even. They killed their own mothers!"

"Yes."

"Then the men killed themselves."

"Not only in Mainz," the Rabbi said. "In Worms, in Speyer, in other towns along the Rhine. But the most dead were in Mainz. Eleven hundred."

Izzy began to sniffle as he spoke.

"Do you know what those crusaders did? They stripped the clothes off all of the dead bodies. They dragged them through the town that way, and threw them into a ditch. The men and women and children all together. They did that just because they were Jews."

"When they got to Jerusalem, they mangled quite a few Muslims as well. But that's another story."

Izzy put his elbows on the table and lowered his head into his hands. Rabbi Simcha stood and moved behind the boy and placed his hands on the boy's shoulders and rubbed them. Izzy's muscles were knots. "You've taken on a difficult task, Isidor. It won't get easier. Perhaps you should stop. Wait till you get older."

"People need to know things," the boy said. His words were muffled by his hands. He turned in his chair and looked at the Rabbi, wiping his eyes. "Is it wrong to cry?"

"No." The old scar on the Rabbi's temple was throbbing. Because of Izzy, or the mass suicide at Mainz more than six hundred years before, he could not have said. "How can we hear of such things and not cry?"

Izzy took several slow, deep breaths. He pulled the papers on the table closer to him. He straightened the pile. He touched a small cloth to his tongue and wiped the ink from the point of his quill. "Then I want to keep on doing this," he said.

The Rabbi's reply was little more than a whisper.

"Yes."

Mournful moans drifted through the halls. The whitewashed walls were sweating. The hospital building itself seemed to be sick. Standing inside the front door, waiting for the Doctor, Dvorah Schlicter could see elderly patients lying on straw in the corridors. She recognized the nearest one, Herr Liebmann. The Doctor's helpers, all men, bent over them, sleeves rolled above hairy forearms, giving the patients sips of water, wiping their brows. The air she was breathing seemed not so much to smell of sweat as to be sweat. She wondered if Guttle's idea was a good one.

But a chance to go to the Fair! How could she pass it up?

Doctor Berkov loomed in front of her. "Come into my office. I'm busy with patients. I can spare two minutes." He perched on the edge of his desk. Wooden cabinets took up two side walls. Dvorah remained standing. She felt bad for intruding on the sick.

"Dvorah Schlicter, is that right? How can I help you?"

"It's about the Fair next week. I was wondering if the hospital will have a stall there."

"To sell what?"

He lifted a paper off his desk, a patient's record sheet, and glanced at it.

"Not to sell. To help the Jewish merchants. I've heard there will be more than a hundred merchants there from the Judengasse. With their helpers, that's more than two hundred people."

"So?" He continued to read as he listened.

"They'll be out in the bright sun, which they aren't used to. If this heat continues, they might need help. They could start fainting, like people here are doing. They might need water, cold compresses. If the hospital had a stall, it could provide those things."

"Also salt." Doctor Berkov placed the patient's record back on his desk. He looked at her with new interest. "I don't know that we've ever done that."

"Has it ever been this hot before? In September?"

The Doctor slid from the desk and began to pace in the small office. "It's a good idea. But I don't have the staff to do that. We're short of staff as it is."

"I could help. That's why I'm here. I could operate the stall."

The Doctor gazed at her. Sweat ran down her neck. Her head itched. She lifted off her cotton cap and placed it on a chair. Auburn curls tumbled around her face.

"How old are you?"

"Seventeen."

"Do you work?"

"I help my mother with sewing. She's a dressmaker."

"Can you roll bandages? Mix ointments to the proper measure?"

"There's a week till the Fair. I could learn."

The Doctor looked at his pocket watch. "It's an excellent idea. I should have thought of it myself. Come back in the morning, we'll try to fit in some training. I'll arrange for passes to the Fair."

He turned to leave his office, lifted her cap from the chair, held it out it to her. "It's a shame to hide that beautiful hair," he said. "Until you have to."

He was out the door too quickly to see her pale face flush.

Walking slowly home in the heat, cap in hand, Dvorah thought: I meant to tell him it wasn't my idea. He didn't give me the chance.

No one in the schul was praying more fervently than Yussel Kahn that the extraordinary heat not turn into an epidemic of deaths. The cabinet maker remembered the last epidemic, smallpox, thirteen years before. It had taken both of his parents and both of Meyer Amschel's, and more than a hundred others, in the space of a few months. He'd been twenty years old, had finished apprenticing and had just opened his shop. Two of the older carpenters had died of the pox. He had worked from sun-up till well past dark almost every day, making nothing but coffins, month after month. Only the Sabbath had saved him from exhaustion. He didn't want to face that again. Just one death, his own, would make more sense.

But the truth was, he was feeling somewhat better since Meyer Amschel had begun spending time with the Schnapper girl. He'd thought that when she found a beau he would fall into a pit of despair, perhaps never be able to climb out. Instead, the opposite had occurred. Now he could tell himself she was taken. This wasn't precisely true, but he believed it soon would be. He could stop berating himself over his own fear of approaching her; she was forbidden now in the real world as well as in his mind, and this decreased the internal pressure. The fact that it was his friend who had made her off limits made it easier, somehow. She might actually come into his life, if only as Meyer's wife. He could envision pleasant Sabbath dinners together over chicken that Guttle had cooked. They all could grow old together

But it hadn't taken long for his mind — or his manhood — to rise to the occasion, to find a replacement fantasy. If anything, this one was even prettier. In the popular plays of Shakespeare, which Yussel had been reading to pass the summer nights, Guttle could portray bright Cordelia, or Rosalind. In a Biblical drama, she would be Ruth, or Rebecca. But the sumptuous Dvorah Schlicter would be Delilah. Or the New Testament's Salomé, seven veils and all. Which he had begun removing in his mind several nights each week.

Even as he thought of her, there went the gorgeous Schlicter girl, walking up the lane, her cap in her hand, auburn curls framing her face like cherry. Pained by his pun — he needed to get his mind out of the ditch — he crossed the lane to speak with her. Dvorah's curves, he was surprised to discover, did not intimidate him the way Guttle's knowing eyes did.

He told her who he was — she knew — and that he was seeking an assistant to help at his stall at the Fair. Would she be interested? Selling coffins? she asked. No, not coffins. Selling cabinets, desks, tables. He had made miniature models of his work. He would display them, and take commissions.

Ten minutes ago she would have loved to, she said. But she had just agreed to run a hospital stall at the Fair. Because of the heat.

Ten minutes.

But I know of someone who would, she said. Who would that be? My mother.

Your mother? He tried to place her. Hannah Schlicter.

She's a seamstress, Dvorah said. She makes the most beautiful dresses. But with us five kids she can't afford to rent a stall at the Fair. Do you have room? Perhaps she could share your stall, and be your assistant as well.

He could say he didn't have room. But with just his miniatures…

Tell her I'll come by in an hour to look at her dresses. Across from the Owl, right?

That would be wonderful, the girl said.

As she walked off, recollection of her mother appeared in his mind. Her chubby arms. Short, squat, hair not quite as red as her daughter's. She probably outweighed him. And five children — though Dvorah was hardly a child.

Idiot! he thought as he crossed the cobbles to his shop. I'm not marrying the woman. I'm only doing a favor. For how could he tell her that her dresses were not good enough?

Yet, oddly, he was aware of a settling of his blood, of clear, cold water diluting the heat of his absurd ardors. As if, somewhere in Heaven, Lainie approved.

—D id you hear what happened to Meyer Rothschild?

—Something happened to Rothschild? I was going to ask if you heard about Hersch Liebmann.

—The shammus? What about him?

—He works for Rothschild. But Meyer won't take him to the Fair.

—I heard. It's terrible.

—The one chance of his life, and Rothschild said no. He's taking the Schnapper girl.

—She gets anything she wants, that one.

—Doesn't care whose feeling she hurts. Offended the Cantor, of all people, after leading him on. You should hear Sophie Marcus talk about her.

—A real Guttle die Schrect, like people say.

— So what happened to Rothschild? An accident?

—What you said.

—What I said? What did I say?

—Guttle the Bad. She's got her hooks into Rothschild. Very deep, they say.

—He let that happen? I thought he was smarter than that.

—He's twenty-five years old, I guess he's human.

—This would be the first sign of it.

— I say Mazel tov to both of them. It's his funeral.

—Not a bad way to go — if you get my meaning.

G uttle sat on her bed, fashioning a kerchief from a piece of fabric her mother had found at the rag dealer's. The cloth was yellow, with a pattern of red flowers, her favorite color. Sometimes it made her sad that there were more flowers on the kerchiefs of the women in the Judengasse than had ever bloomed within the walls. Only once that she remembered had real flowers graced their table — a bouquet of red roses. On the day he was named Court Jew, her father had brought them home to celebrate. Her mother had put them in water in a kettle on the kitchen table. Nine years old at the time, Guttle had never seen anything so beautiful. She asked if she could give one of the roses to Izzy. Her mother said that would be nice. Guttle recalled her disappointment when, only three days later, the roses had wilted, and died.

What Guttle did not know was that the rose she had given to Izzy six years earlier, though dead, still lived. In the attic room he shared with his two brothers, their straw mattresses side by side by side, with no room for space between, the rose still lay on a shelf, beside his hammer. It was a deep purple now, almost black, not the bright red it once had been, and it was covered with dust; Izzy did not want to touch it, to brush off the dust, fearing it might fall apart.

As she hemmed the kerchief, the image of the rose bouquet reminded Guttle of Baby R. The child had been born a year later — three years after Avra, three years before Amelia. Her parents had first liked Rifka for the new baby's name, then Rachel, but finally decided on Rose. She was a snuggly little thing, Baby R, perfectly formed. But one morning when Rose was only a week old, Guttle had looked into her crib and seen that something was wrong. The baby had twisted herself into an awkward position, and did not seem to be breathing. Guttle ran to the kitchen and pulled at her mother to come and see. Emmie had let out a desperate wail and scooped up the infant and run down the stairs and through the lane to the hospital, Guttle running behind her. In the examining room the Doctor unwrapped the baby's blanket and spanked her to get her breathing, and pushed on her tiny chest, and breathed into her mouth. Nothing worked. They did not notice Guttle watching from the doorway as the Doctor unwrapped the baby further, and inspected her body, and said that she was dead.

"You picked a bad name," Guttle remembered shouting at her distraught mother. "Roses die too soon."

Names. She'd been intrigued as a child how Adam, the first man, himself newly created, had come up with so many names — and how every one of them had been just right. A cow, with its fat flanks and drooping udders, could only be called a cow, nothing else. A chicken, with its skinny neck and yellow feet, obviously was a chicken; try a different name and it didn't work. With pin-sized heads and long, spidery legs, how could spiders be anything but? They surely weren't horses, or dogs, or trout.

If Adam had named human families, she would not be a Schnapper. A wolf could have been a schnapper. As could a wild boar. Or a viper. But not her. She was in constant conflict with her name.

She tried to keep a smile from surfacing. She felt a stirring in her breast. Yahweh's first man, she thought, would have given her a name with some red in it.

13

The Fahrgasse was the widest, busiest street in Frankfurt. Buildings with stone foundations and wooden upper stories rose on both sides. Late morning sun glared off the cobbles as Yussel and Meyer walked along, passing, beyond the slaughterhouse and Ziggy Zigmund's Z-Z horse stable, a market for salted meats and fish —which the Jews loved but was not to Lutheran taste — more stables, blacksmith stalls, farmers from the countryside selling fruit and vegetables from the backs of wagons, vendors tending small fires despite the heat, on which they were cooking sausages and veal chops. Gentile men and a few women were lining up at these stalls; the noon dinner hour was approaching. Further along, cafés and beer halls were filling with hungry diners. Wide, heavy carts drawn by six or eight horses rumbled by carrying stacks of lumber toward the town market. No doubt the lumber would be used to build the three hundred and fifty stalls for the Fair.

"So, who will be your assistant?" Meyer asked his friend. They were headed toward the Town Hall to obtain their passes.

"Hannah Schlicter."

"You mean Dvorah. Hannah is the mother."

"I mean Hannah."

Meyer looked at his friend as they walked, but said nothing.

"She's a seamstress. I went to see her work. The dresses are beautiful, she might get lots of orders. So I'm letting her share my stall."

"Good for you."

Before Yussel could reply, two boys, perhaps sixteen years old, stepped into their path. "Jud mach mores!" the boys shouted. Jews, pay your dues.

Yussel and Meyer took off their three-cornered hats. They bowed. They stepped aside to let the boys pass. All these things they were required by law when any Gentile uttered those words.

The gloom of repressed anger settled upon them, as it always did when this happened. They were silent as they turned off the Fahrgasse toward the Town Hall. Without thinking, they climbed the few steps to the front entrance of the Gothic building. A guard stepped in front of them. "Jews use the rear door," he reminded them.

They circled the building to the rear. "How do they always know?" Yussel asked.

"The badge of dishonor." Meyer patted Yussel's pallid cheek. "At home, we forget."

Meyer was the more accustomed to such insults. His coin and antiques business took him out into the city most every day. The cabinet maker left the Judengasse only when he needed to obtain more wood, or glue.

Inside the rear entrance to the Town Hall, an office had been set up to handle the business of the Fair. The two friends waited on a long line and paid the fees for their stalls, and were given two passes each. On one they wrote their own names. On the second pass, Meyer added Guttle's name, and Yussel added Hannah Schlicter's. The clerk recorded the names in his book.

The air in the dark corridor was cooler than it was outside. They were perspiring heavily, from walking in the unaccustomed sunlight, and from the debasement by the Gentile boys. They stood for a moment, carefully folding the passes into their pouches. As they turned to leave, they were stopped by a slim young man from the Judengasse. "Herr Rothschild is it? Herr Kahn? Don't go yet." He nodded down the corridor. "They're about to try a Jew. He's accused of robbery."

They recognized the man. It was the rag dealer with the new baby. Ephraim Hess.

"Why is that our business?"

"Ah, you've never been hauled into court, Herr Cabinet Maker. If you're a Jew, it's your business."

Yussel and Meyer glanced at one another. He had succeeded in making them curious. They followed him to a nearby courtroom. The door had been left open because of the heat, and the three of them slipped into seats in the last row. The benches nearer the front were filled.

The portly judge, cloaked in black, entered. The accused thief was called to the witness box, which was enclosed on three sides by wooden rails. He was a hearty looking fellow, about thirty years old, tanned, beardless except for the stubble of a day or two. The judge looked down from his raised bench, took in the rugged coloring of the defendant, and seemed uncertain. "Your name is Rafe Isaacs. You are a Jew?"

The accused said that he was.

The judge turned to a bailiff. "Bring in the skin."

Leaving through a rear door, the bailiff returned a moment later dragging the heavy, hairy skin of a large pig. The head and the tail were still attached. The men in the front seats murmured to one another and stretched their necks to see. The bailiff moved the suspect aside and placed the pig skin on the floor of the witness box. "Stand on that," he ordered.

The accused hesitated for a moment, looked around the courtroom as if in protest. Then he did as he'd been told.

"You are accused of being a highwayman," the judge intoned. "You are charged with robbing a Gentile merchant, who was driving alone in a carriage, of the sum of five gulden, by threatening to crack his head with an iron bar. How do you say, guilty or not guilty?"

"Not guilty."

"Very well. Before you are questioned you must take the Jews' oath. Place your right hand upon the Books of Moses in front of you, and repeat after me."

The judge moved a piece of paper on his lectern. As the accused repeated the judge's words, his tremulous voice seemed to clash with his powerful physique.

"Regarding such property of which the man accuses me, I know nothing of it, nor do I have it. I never had it in my possession, nor do I have it in any of my chests, I have not buried it in the earth, nor locked it with locks, so help me God who created heaven and earth, valley and hill, woods, trees, and grass. And so help me the Five Books of Moses, that if I dissemble I may nevermore enjoy a bite without soiling myself all over as did the King of Babylon.

"And may that sulphur and pitch flow down upon my neck that flowed over Sodom and Gomorra, and the same pitch that flowed over Babylon flow over me, but two hundred times more, and may the earth envelop and swallow me up.

"And may my dust never join other dust, and my earth never join other earth in the bosom of Master Abraham, if what I say is not true and right.

"If not, may a bleeding and a flowing come forth from me and never cease, as my people wished upon themselves when they condemned God, Jesus Christ, among themselves, and tortured Him and said, 'His blood be upon us and our children.'

"It is true, so help me God who appeared to Moses in a burning bush which yet remained unconsumed. It is true by the soul which I bring on the

Day of Judgment before the court of Abraham, Isaac and Jacob. It is true, so help me God."

All the time that the suspect was saying these words, he winced with pain, as the bailiff drew back and forth between his bare legs a rose branch covered with thorns.

"Very well, the accused Jew has sworn the oath," the judge said. "The city attorney may call his first witness."

In the back row, Meyer Rothschild leaned close to Yussel Kahn. "I've had enough of this," he whispered. Quietly he slipped from his seat and out into the corridor. Yussel followed. The rag dealer Ephraim Hess remained in his seat.

On the Fahrgasse, the cries of vendors, the smells of the stables and the beer halls, the rumbling of huge wagons carrying barrels of goods from the docks, the loading of other wagons in front of warehouses, all went unnoticed by the two men. Neither spoke until they were back in the Judengasse. The deprivations with which they had grown up they could accept; the unexpected cut deep.

They stopped outside the Pfann, where the alley led back to Meyer's apartment in the Hinterpfann. "I knew there was a special oath for Jews," Yussel said. "I never imagined anything like that."

They were ready to go their separate ways. But neither wanted to be alone. They perched on the warm cobbles, leaned their backs against the wall. They did not feel like working; Yussel did not trust the steadiness of his hands; Meyer, at the moment, had no interest in coins. The bustle of the lane swirled around them. Would things ever change? Thinking that way lay madness. Unless you had the power to make them change.

"The oath was bad enough," Meyer said. "And the pig. What was the need for ripping him with thorns?"

"I imagine that's their ironic joke. A crown of thorns upon his head. A branch of thorns between his legs."

"Highly comical."

Yussel wanted to alter the discussion, but hardly succeeded. "Are there many highwaymen on the roads?"

"So they say. I've never encountered one. I didn't know any were Jews."

Yussel closed his eyes, pressed his shoulder blades against the wall, recited a line of poetry — a line that resonated within his soul. "Desperation ignores no race, no faith, but gallops in on twin black steeds, swords flashing."

"Your beloved Shakespeare?" Meyer asked.

"Our beloved Nahum Baum. 1614."

"Before or after the Fettmilch attack?"

"During, if you believe the stories. Baum unable to go down and fight because of his withered leg. Watching from his window, writing poetry."

"The yeshiva teaches only Torah and Talmud. Where do you find your Shakespeare? Your Baum, for that matter?"

"A bookbinder and bookseller near the university, where I buy special glue for my wood. Shakespeare he displays in the window. The Baum he hides under the floor."

"And they sell?"

"I'm told 'The Merchant of Venice' does very well."

"A play about a merchant? That one you'll have to lend me, when I have the time. Maybe I'll learn something."

"That one you wouldn't like. Of course, the scribblings of Luther outsell them all."

"The devil in monk's clothing." Meyer spat on the cobbles.

Across the lane he saw Leo and Yetta Liebmann walking slowly toward their house near the gate. Leo was leaning on his wife's arm, apparently recovered from fainting spells that had sent him to the hospital. Meyer waved to them. Neither waved back. He could not tell if they had not seen him, preoccupied as they were with each uneven step on the cobbles, or if they, too, were angry because he wasn't taking their son Hersch to the Fair.

"That fellow in the court," Yussel said. "Do you think he's guilty?"

"His darkened, outdoor face could convict him."

"He could live in Mainz. In Mannheim. Anywhere there's sun in the Jewish quarter."

They envisioned the accused again. A sturdy, rugged man. He'd looked as if he could wrestle down a bull.

"One thing about highwaymen," Meyer said. "Whether they exist or not — I assume they do — I aim to make money off them."

"How can you do that?"

A woman emerged from the house next door to empty a chamber pot into the ditch. Both men turned away to diminish the smell. Etiquette said you shouldn't turn your nose, because everyone had chamber pots to empty. It was one rule of manners rarely obeyed.

"Merchants and Princes from all over will be coming to the Fair," Meyer said. "They'll want to buy jewelry, silks, antiques. But they don't like to carry gold or silver with them. Or a great deal of money. The metals are heavy to haul around. And there's a risk, because of these highwaymen. It could get stolen."

"How does that help you?"

"I've written to many of the richest merchants and Princes, offering them letters of credit."

"What's that?"

"I've told these wealthy men they can come here without any gold or silver, without much money. So they don't risk being robbed. For anything they want to buy at the Fair, I'll give them a letter of credit. They can use it just like gold. I will pay for their purchases. When they return home, they can send the money to me, safely. With interest, of course. Which is where I make a profit."

"Where will you get the money to lend them?"

"From the coins, the antiques. I've been saving cash exactly for this. There's money to be made in buying and selling all kinds of goods. There's more money to be made in banking. But there's a fortune to be made in combining both. Commerce can give you a stream of gold. With banking, you can turn the stream into a river."

Meyer loved to talk about business. Yussel was a willing listener.

"Look at the ships in the harbor," Meyer said. "Importing is growing fast — and it can't exist without loans, without credit. Importers have to pay for their goods first, and make their profits later. So they need to borrow money. Lending isn't new, most of the rich men in the lane are bankers. That doesn't make them brilliant..."

Yussel interrupted. "Don't tell that to them."

"I won't, believe me. But they did make the most of a sort of mercantile Judengasse. Some Pope or other decided way back that charging interest is unclean. The church forbid Catholics from doing it. That left the field to the Jews."

"Usury," Yussel said.

"Which is a stupid notion, unless the charge is excessive. The interest is because your money is locked up in the loan. You can't use it for anything else."

"It's hard to love the person you owe money to."

"Exactly. That's one reason the goyim hate us. But the idea of giving credit on a large scale isn't appealing to most bankers. A pawnbroker will give you a small amount, against your pawned item. Lending a lot of money, with nothing to back it up, no collateral — that's a gamble. Most Gentile bankers don't want to take the risk. Especially with fancy-living Princes they don't trust. Jews can't afford to be so choosy."

"Where'd those Gentile bankers come from?"

"Protestants don't listen to the Pope."

Yussel smiled, lifted his hat momentarily and ran his hand through his prematurely thinning ginger hair. "These letters of credit — when others see them, won't they offer the same thing?"

"Some of the braver ones will. But I'll charge lower interest."

"Then you'll make less money."

"Not if I get most of the business. Also, the merchants and Princes I give credit to now, because I trust them, will come to me in the future, when they need bigger loans."

"You were born to do business, Meyer Amschel. How do you think of such things?"

"I know one way. When I lie awake at night, I don't spend my time undressing Guttle Schnapper."

"You don't?"

"Not until recently."

At once, Meyer feared he'd misspoken, that he might have wounded his friend. But Yussel just grinned. He evinced no jealousy. This was one of the advantages of the Judengasse. With people living almost inside each other's shoes, the worst indulgences of the heart — envy, jealousy — had to be smothered quickly. Still, the mention of Guttle created a silence between them, until Yussel spoke. "I'm loathe to say this, but maybe you shouldn't be so ambitious about making a fortune."

"Why not?"

"There are thirty thousand people in Frankfurt. Ten times as many as there are Jews in the lane. Almost all of them are Lutherans. Including those in power."

"The rancid monk has been dead two hundred years."

"But not his diatribes. You want to know what's behind what we saw in the courtroom? I can lend you one of his books."

"That pleasure I'll skip. The way I look at it, they hate a Jew whether he's poor or rich. So I might as well be rich."

"Rich, you never know what they might do to you."

"Rich, you never know what I might do to them."

Yussel wiped the sweat from his forehead, rubbed his hand on his breeches. "It's impossible to talk to you."

"We're talking, aren't we? What's impossible, maybe, is convincing me."

Yussel smiled the smile of the eternally resigned. He made coffins, after all. Meyer shifted his position on the cobbles, extended a leg in front of him. The spring mud of the lane had long since dried into fine dust, and coated the cobbles with its paleness. A small cloud rose at his feet, like gnats. As the dust settled back, they saw at the northern gate the thin figure of the rag dealer, returning from town. Perhaps, unconsciously, that's who they had been waiting for.

"Ephraim Hess!" Yussel called out. "Back so soon? Come tell us what happened at the trial."

The rag dealer was happy to be summoned by these gentlemen, to be a bearer of information they did not have. "It was quick. There was only one witness. The Gentile who was robbed. He swore it was him. Said this Rafe Isaacs robbed him of five gulden.

"And the verdict?" Yussel asked.

"Guilty, of course."

"Why 'of course'?"

"A Gentile's word against a Jew's."

"He may well be guilty, Jew or not," Meyer said. "What did they fine him?"

"No fine."

"No fine? Then the oath was worse than the sentence."

"They're going to hang him."

Meyer and Yussel quit drawing breaths.

"Hang him?" Yussel asked. "For stealing five gulden?"

"He's a Jew," the rag dealer repeated.

"A Jewish thief," Meyer said. "Not a good marriage."

"The way the Gentiles see it, murder is only a crime against the person you kill. But robbery — that's a threat to all who own property."

From across the lane the rag dealer's young wife, Eva, came to greet her husband. She was holding the baby Solomon.

"This... deed... of supreme justice," Meyer said, selecting his words with care so as not to upset Eva. "Did they say when they will carry it out?"

"During the Fair. In the Town Square. They want to set an example."

The baby gagged. Eva patted his back until he burped.

Guttle had to press against the wall and slide sideways to get through the alley that led to the Hinterpfann, which had become the most colorful place in the lane, clogged with bolts of silk and cotton piled high on wooden pallets to keep them from touching the ground. Meyer's two brothers, Kalman and Moish, were adding more bolts to the piles. In anticipation of good sales at the Fair, they had imported from England more textiles than the house could hold. The alley was covered by an overhang, but still they hoped the weather didn't break into rain before they moved their stock. Dry goods didn't sell well wet.

Greeting the brothers, Guttle admired the fabrics, fingering the edges of a bright green silk, a beige silk, a burgundy. Any number she would have loved to shape into blouses, or have Dvorah's mother turn into a stunning dress — not that she had occasion to wear a stunning dress. Leaving the silks, she entered the house and found more fabric piled high on the office table. Two carrying cases on the floor, she figured, must hold the coins she and Meyer would sell at the Fair.

"Is that you, Guttle?" His voice came from up the stairs. "Come up to the kitchen. We'll write the letter here."

She had never been up the steep stairs. Climbing slowly, lifting her beige cotton skirt so she would not step on it, she gripped the coarse rope that passed for a balustrade. Rope splinters pricked her palms; she knew that Meyer's hands sometimes had sores from them. She found him seated at the kitchen table, on which he'd placed quills, ink, paper, like a meal for a scribe. He was reading a newspaper she did not recognize. Through an open door to the left she could see his narrow bedroom. The third and fourth floors, she knew, were occupied by Kalman, by Moish, his wife and three children, and by the Bauers. She'd heard from Meyer that the windows on the top floor were higher than the ghetto walls, and overlooked the city — but that they'd been boarded up, in accordance with Frankfurt law. Jews were not permitted to look out from their homes into the public gardens and the Christian streets. Constables made unannounced visits to make sure the laws were obeyed.

Hanging on the dingy yellow kitchen walls were blackened pots and pans. Dishes sat on a counter beside the woodstove. In a corner was a pile of newspapers higher than the table. Meyer folded the one he'd been reading and placed it on the pile.

"You look very nice today," he said, standing. She thanked him for the compliment. Knowing she was coming here, she had worn a white blouse with lace ruffles that circled her wrists and neck. It was her favorite blouse, one she usually reserved for the High Holy Days.

"You read a lot of newspapers," she said, looking at the pile. "Or maybe the problem is you don't read them."

"Oh, I read them. From Vienna, Berlin, Kassel, pretty much everywhere. The problem is that when they get here they're three weeks old. I need to get them sooner. For the latest exchange rates."

"I don't know what that means."

"All the money changers in the lane, do you know what they do?"

"Not really." She only knew that Viktor's father was one.

"You'll see it at the Fair. We'll be doing it as well. To buy anything in Frankfurt, you have to use Frankfurt money. Kreuzer, gulden. But every little town and principality mints it's own money. When people come to Frankfurt, they have to change their money in order to shop. Ducats, carolins, thalers, louis d'ors. Everything. The money changers do that. They charge a fee, of course, that's how they stay in business. But there's another way they can make a profit. Let's say they know what the exchange rate is for guldens in Hanau. If they give a traveler ten guldens for a certain amount of Hanau coins, and then go to Hanau and get eleven guldens back for the same coins, that's a nice profit."

"Let's write the letter," Guttle said.

"Yes, of course. I didn't mean to bore you with business." He pulled a chair out for her.

"You weren't boring me." As she sat she had her back to him. "Special couriers."

"What did you say?"

"Special couriers. If you don't want to wait for the newspapers, you could pay couriers in each town to ride here with the latest exchange rates. You'd have them ahead of anyone else."

Meyer tapped her temple lightly with his curled index finger. "You've got a head for business. I've been thinking about that very idea. Set up a relay system of our own couriers. Perhaps in time for next year's Fair. Depending on what it would cost."

She pulled up the sleeve on her right hand, to protect her lace cuffs. She lifted a quill and dipped it in the ink. "Shall we begin?"

Meyer became flustered. She seemed impatient to be done and leave his company. He did not know why. Clearly she had worn a special blouse to come see him. And her hair down over her shoulders, freshly washed and lustrous in the lamplight. Maybe she was going to see someone more important afterwards. Viktor Marcus, perhaps. He'd noticed the Cantor's eyes undressing her at every opportunity.

He did not like the thought. He could not help focusing on her shapely wrist with its small wrist bone. He picked up his scrawled notes and began to dictate the letter slowly, while Guttle wrote.

"It has been my particular and high fortune to make several deliveries to Your Lofty Princely Serenity… "

Guttle turned to look at him. "Your Lofty Princely Serenity?"

"Just write, bitte. I know what I'm doing."

She shrugged, returned to her writing as he continued.

"… to Your Highest gracious satisfaction. I now stand ready to exert all my energies and my entire fortune to serve Your Lofty Princely Serenity… "

She looked at him again. "More lofty serenity? Isn't that a bit obsequious?"

"You don't know these nobles, Guttle. They thrive on obsequious. Write, bitte."

"… whenever in the future it shall please You to Command me. A special and powerful incentive to this end would be given me if Your Lofty Princely Serenity… "

This time she set down her quill in protest, and turned. "How lofty do you plan to make him?"

"Lofty enough so he can look down from his high perch and see a Jewish supplicant. Which is how he sees the world. Which, unfortunately, is how the world is."

She frowned, but resumed writing, dipping her quill carefully into the ink.

"… deigned to grace me with an appointment as Court Factor."

She inhaled sharply, bit back a smile. And kept writing.

"I make bold to raise this request in the conviction that by so doing I am not giving any trouble."

He finished with the necessary salutations, leaned over her and signed the document. Carefully she wiped the quills on a bit of cloth. She stood to stretch her muscles.

"That's exciting, Meyer Amschel. Do you think he'll do it?"

"We'll have to wait and see."

"Is that like being a Court Jew, like my father?"

"Not exactly. But it's the first step. Wilhelm has bought a number of antique coins from me. He'll inherit a huge fortune from his father some day. He'll need someone who knows how to invest that money."

"He doesn't mind that you're a Jew?"

"Most of the Princes don't seem to. They know we're good at business."

Pulling down her sleeve, she looked at him, hesitated. She seemed to be struggling with something within herself. He saw this, and waited. Finally, she spoke. "Meyer Amschel, can I ask you something I shouldn't?"

Meyer tried to clear his throat. It remained dry. "If you shouldn't ask me, maybe you shouldn't ask me."

She looked at the floor — it could use a sweeping — then at him again. "But I want to."

"Then I imagine you're going to."

"I suppose I am. Are you planning to ask my father something any time soon?"

He frowned. So that's why she seemed irritable. He went to the counter and poured water into a glass from a pitcher. He drank. It wasn't very cold. Nothing remained cold in this heat.

"Guttle, that's not the way it works. You know that. With my father dead, your father has to come to me." He'd been about to say, "with an offer." He swallowed those words in time.

"But how will he get the idea?"

"Oh, he's already got the idea."

"But when? Maybe I should ask him."

"Don't do that, Guttle. Be patient. Your father needs to know he's in control. That he makes the choice. Besides... " He paused.

"Besides what?"

"Be patient till the Fair is over. If the Prince makes me a Court Agent... "

"Then my father will be impressed by your prospects!"

"Let's just say it wouldn't hurt."

"You're a sly one, Meyer Rothschild." She came to him and put her arms around his waist and rested her head on his chest.

"Is that bad? Being sly?"

"I like sly," she murmured.

He nuzzled his nose into her hair. The fragrance, the pliancy, offered sweet promise.

Footsteps resounded on the stairs. Guttle pulled away.

The doorway was dark. The footsteps grew louder. The boards creaked, the rope squealed. She thought of fairy Gentiles told their children. Of hungry giants coming up the stairs. Which she'd been forbidden by her mother to repeat. Which she used to tell Avra in their bed at night till Avra peed from fright. Which Avra no doubt was telling the little ones.

A sweating figure filled the doorway. It was only Kalman, seeking a drink of water.

Guttle had been holding her breath. She turned to Meyer. His face was a comfort. "How long will it take for the Prince to receive the letter?" She could tell he had been watching her.

"It's hard to say. You can never predict the post."

Mischief lit her eyes. With splayed fingers she lifted her dark locks high above her head, with all that did to stretch taut her torso, her blouse, and she said, with the most charming air of innocence she could muster, "Maybe you could send a courier."

14

Five September, the first morning of the Fair, Guttle rose early, as did most of the Judengasse. The merchants and their helpers who would be transporting goods on pushcarts or hired horse carts lined up inside the north gate while the sky still was dark, to move their merchandise before the heat became an extra burden. The line strung back along the cobbles as far as the bakery. Pressed against the gate and flanking the lines were hundreds of women and children and dozens of men who would not be going, who were there to watch the others leave and wave goodbye to them, as if they were setting off on a journey to another world. Which they were.

Peering through the gate, Guttle saw the night Constable salute his replacements by clapping his right hand crisply to his chest. Four Constables had arrived along with Kapitän Klaus. When dawn brightened the sky, the Kapitän pulled out his keys and unlocked the gate. The four Constables stood two on each side to check passes as the line began to creep slowly forward. No one without a pass to the Fair could move through the gate today.

In the borning half-light the line emerged like a procession of statues that had been there forever. Twenty metres back Guttle discerned the rag dealer Ephraim Hess beside a pushcart piled high with used clothing and fabrics. Near him his wife was holding their baby. As the line began to move Eva wrapped the infant in a thin blanket and placed him among the fabrics, and covered him with a dark dress. Clearly the woman was afraid the Constables would want to see a pass for the child. Guttle couldn't believe they would — but what if the baby began to cry as they passed the Constables? Then the couple surely would appear guilty — of something.

Not far behind them, Hannah Schlicter was piling her new dresses on the cart of the cabinet maker. Guttle walked down the line to greet them. The dresses dwarfed the small wooden models of desks and cabinets that Yussel Kahn would show at the Fair.

"Where's Meyer?" Yussel asked.

"In schul. He wouldn't skip morning services. But we have only his coins to carry, and a few small statues. We'll have plenty of time."

"I've seen his few small statues. A Greek head. A Roman. An Etruscan."

"He's been learning about ancient sculpture. You brought him the books."

The brightening sky washed the dusty cobbles with gray light. Guttle noticed a hand in a white sleeve waving at her. It was Dvorah. She hurried to greet her friend.

"My, don't you look nice," she said, taking in Dvorah's long white dress with lace at the collar, her auburn curls tumbling from beneath a white cap.

"I like your dress," Dvorah said.

When Guttle's mother Emmie heard Guttle would be going to the Fair she'd bought two yards of yellow cotton fabric. She'd fashioned a dress with white lace at the cuffs and a squared off neckline that would keep her throat cool, a style currently favored by the court ladies, her father had reported. Her mother had sewn scraps of yellow ribbon to an old white hat to complete the outfit.

"It's the latest fashion somewhere," Guttle said. She looked over Dvorah's hospital cart, which was laden with pitchers of water, jars of salt, ointments to protect against the sun. "I'm so glad this worked out for you."

"Isn't it exciting? I have to confess, Lev still thinks it was my idea."

"Lev? So it's Lev already, is it? You can let him think that, if you want. It makes no difference to me."

The line of carts was moving more easily. "Go find Izzy, he was looking for you," Dvorah said as she began to push her cart. "He seemed kind of sad."

"Because he's not going to the Fair?

"I think it was more than that."

They hugged briefly, and Guttle wandered off. The line alongside the ditch seemed to have gotten longer, not shorter. Izzy would be in schul, she thought, but she found him standing in the doorway of his house, idly watching the line move past. He did indeed look morose.

"What's wrong, Isidor?"

"Nothing."

"Don't say 'nothing.' You were looking for me."

The pushcarts creaked on the cobbles. Outside the gate, drivers with horse carts were yelling out their services. Special rates to the Fair, they shouted. The smell of horse manure drifted through the gate. Chickens in the slaughterhouse were clucking wildly at the bustle outside. Small children were beginning to cry, some to scream, as they saw both parents leaving through the gate with piles of goods, as if they would not be coming back. The little ones were left in the care of aunts, or neighbors.

"It's Hiram," Izzy said, over the noise.

"What's wrong with him? He's up there now, timing this little parade. I can see his hands in the window."

"He's worried about his brother."

"What's wrong with his brother? Can we get to the point? Meyer will be along any minute."

"Hersch has been acting wild. Breaking things. Yelling at his parents." Izzy hesitated. "Hiram thinks it's because of you."

"Me. What did... Oh."

"He expected to go to the Fair. He thinks Meyer chose you because... you know."

"I don't know! Besides, what's to be done? Meyer is the boss. He can choose whomever he likes."

"Yes."

"Well, Hersch will have to live with it. Meyer is paying him even though he doesn't have to work. That should make him happy. Look, the men are coming from schul. I have to go. I'll bring you something from the Fair. What would you like?"

"I don't need anything."

"I'll see what they have."

"Maybe... maybe just a flower, to go with the other one."

"What other one?"

She had never been to his room. She didn't know.

"Just a flower."

His voice dropped as she backed away, turned, moved off, looked back and waved to him as she hurried to meet Meyer. "Your dress is pretty," Izzy said, but she was far down the lane by then.

Upset with herself, Guttle thought: Izzy acts as if he's lost me. Viktor and his family despise me. Now Hersch does, too. I'm building quite a reputation.

When Meyer appeared, looking flustered, he apologized for being detained.

"Something is wrong," Guttle said.

"Not really."

"Meyer, don't lie. Your face shows everything."

"It's just the Cantor. His mother took me aside after services. She warned me to keep away from you. She said you and Viktor were as good as spoken for."

"She's a bit meshuganah."

"Of course."

"Did you tell her so?"

"What good would that have done? I just walked away."

"You said nothing?" Fury flushed Guttle's face.

"Look, everyone's gone," Meyer said. "Forget about Viktor. Let's go to the Fair."

She turned and stalked towards the gate ahead of him, more upset with Meyer than she had ever been, her mind spinning a cloth of it's own.

M*adame Guttle, the Viennese chanteuse, has returned to the stage of the Comedie Francais for another song. She is barefoot, wearing a white cotton dress. As the cheers and applause fade, she sings, in a mock-plaintive voice.*

> *He says we must wait until after the Fair,*
> *But what if by then I am no longer there?*
> *What if Viktor and I are already a pair?*
> *What's a poor girl to do?*
> *What's love got to do with being court agents*
> *Or visiting Fairs and similar pageants?*
> *Why can't he see that I'm losing my patience?*
> *What's a young lady to do?*
> *If I were a shiksa I'd go be a nun,*
> *But to tell you the truth I'd rather have fun;*
> *It's time my real life had already begun;*
> *What's a shy maiden to do?*
> *The Cantor my dowry just wants to be paid;*
> *With Meyer my future is always delayed;*
> *I'm a pretty young girl who just wants to get laid!*
> *Can't anyone help me? Can you?*

"W hat are you smiling about?" Meyer asked, catching up with her.

"Nothing," Guttle said. "Just... nothing."

A carousel of whirling colors stunned her as they rounded the corner into the Town Square. Strings of red and yellow pennants, hanging on every building, were flapping lazily in a mild breeze. Acrobats in green and orange costumes leapt upon one another's shoulders, building human castles against the bluing sky. Jugglers were keeping fountains of yellow balls aloft, and scary plumes of unsheathed knives that glinted silver, like warnings. Jesters in multicolored, striped outfits and pointy collars with bells on them ran to and fro, teasing the crowds that waited behind barricades. Musicians in blue uniforms, mostly red-faced men blowing brass horns, perched on chairs at the rear of a bandstand, playing marching tunes beneath flags of the Independent City of Frankfurt and the Holy Roman Empire. Cure mongers were hanging banners on their stalls heralding the latest elixirs for ague, plague, gout, boils, cramps, constipation, hangover, toothache, earache, headache and pox, only five kreuzer each; the bottles all looked the same. Everywhere Guttle turned were bright hues — red, blues, yellows, greens, purples, in the costumes of the jugglers and acrobats, in pennants that flew over many stalls. And everywhere she looked there were Gentiles — more Gentiles than she had seen in her life: hatless, clean-shaven men, some wearing powdered wigs. The women would arrive later, she assumed, to shop.

Threading among the stalls of fabrics, dolls, jewelry, ceramics, spices, coffees, teas, cut flowers and all manner of handiworks, she saw a fat organ grinder whose monkey was wearing a black coat, a black hat and a long gray beard. Judging by the train of laughter that followed him, the Jewish monkey already was a favorite. He was picking up lots of coins. She admired the skill of the jugglers, and found her eager body throbbing to the music; in the lane, when there was music at all, it was mostly fiddles. But it was the fantasia of bright colors that made her eyes sparkle. Of all the deprivations of the Judengasse, she realized, perhaps the least remarked upon was the absence of these brilliant hues, which seemed to speak to the spirit without need for words.

"Meyer, I never imagined anything like this," she told him, her anger forgotten. "Even my dreams are drab compared to this."

"Now you know why you're here," he answered. "It would mean nothing to Hersch."

The stalls were wood frames covered on the top and three sides with white linen to deflect the sun, and lined with wooden shelves for the display of merchandise. The three hundred and fifty stalls had been positioned by city workers in concentric squares out from the bandstand. Jewish merchants were restricted to the last three rows on the side nearest the Judengasse. They didn't mind. When the fairgoers were admitted from the five streets that fed into the square — where they already were waiting impatiently behind the barricades and the Constables — the stalls in the rear were the first they would encounter. The moneychangers, especially, knew this gave them an advantage. Out-of-towners would be anxious to exchange for the proper coins.

Meyer had chosen a stall between those of the cabinet maker and the rag dealer; he liked to be out of earshot of other dealers in coins and money. Each stall was allotted only one chair; Guttle sat on theirs amid her flounced yellow skirt while Meyer opened his display cases of coins and medallions. Cheaper coins he dumped onto a tray so visitors could rummage among them; the sense of touch, he knew, often brokered a sale. For money changing he had two metal boxes. One was filled with the kreuzers and gulden that Guttle would dispense after Meyer determined the rate of exchange. The other box, empty now, soon would clank with coins of the surrounding principalities. His letters of credit were tucked in his pocket. On the front shelf he set the three antique heads, placed to attract attention as well as to sell.

"How much time," Guttle asked, hands grasping the sides of the chair, legs swinging above the ground like an impatient child's. From a chain on his waistcoat Meyer lifted his pocket watch. "Any time now. They must be waiting for some nobleman to open the Fair."

"I'm nervous," Guttle said. "All this color, and music... it makes the lane seem... like a graveyard. Is that a terrible thing to say? And noblemen! What am I doing among noblemen who travel the world? Boiling beetles is what I do best."

"You'll be fine," Meyer said, squeezing her hand, threading an errant lock of hair back under her blue hat, lifting one of the ribbons from in front of her face.

"And look how many Gentiles!"

"They don't bite," Meyer said.

"You're making fun of me. I'm really scared."

"I know. The first time is always frightening. But I'm here with you."

The musicians broke off the march they were playing. The trumpeters stood and blasted a royal fanfare that resounded over the square and down all the intersecting streets. Cheers roared from the crowds behind the barricades. The cheers overwhelmed whatever the mayor of Frankfurt was saying on the platform. Nobody seemed to mind. When he was through he extended a welcoming hand to his right. Two Constables stepped onto the platform, and behind them a slightly pudgy man in the plumage of a male bird. His coat was bright red, his vest beige, his breeches yellow, his silk hose white to match his ruffled shirt, his shoes black with gold buckles. His wide hat was a bright yellow that matched his breeches; a red feather swept from it like a zephyr.

"Well, look who's there," Meyer said.

"Who is it?" Guttle stood on her toes to see.

"The great man himself. Crown Prince Wilhelm."

"My correspondent!" She strained her neck further. "Did you know he would be here?"

"Not to open the Fair. But he never misses a chance for bargains."

"Will he come see you?"

"Not me, especially. I'm nobody. But he's sure to tour Jews Row back here."

"I'm got up like a canary!"

"Don't worry, so is he."

The crown Prince was speaking. In the back row they could not hear his words. Most were drowned by cheers from merchants near the front. People were already beginning to perspire in the heat.

"You look beautiful," Meyer assured her. "Something the Prince has an eye for."

"How do you know that?."

"There are lots of stories. Also lots of children."

"He's married, then."

"He's married, yes, though the two facts don't connect."

"How can you say you're nobody? You may soon be a court agent. Do you think he'll have an answer to your letter?"

"He may not have received it yet. Even if he has, these things must be done in writing. The subject won't come up."

Guttle said nothing.

"Did you hear me, Guttle? The subject won't come up."

"You needn't worry, I know when to hold my tongue. If the crown Prince comes near here, I just might swallow it."

A loud cheer arose from the front, and the sound of a single long trumpet note that seemed to last beyond the breath of a man, the sound going on and on and drawing down upon the square the loudest roar yet from the people waiting behind the barricades. Hearing the long trumpet cry the Constables wrenched the barricades aside and the fairgoers poured into the square from five directions, swarmed among the stalls like grasshoppers in a field of barley. Guttle clutched tight to Meyer's arm. Soon the first customers arrived.

For half an hour they were too busy to talk, while the piles of kreuzer and gulden in one box dwindled and the other box filled up with every shape and denomination of foreign coin. Then business slowed as the visitors, armed with the proper currency, began to move among the displays. With Meyer's permission, Guttle went to visit Dvorah at the hospital stall.

"Has anyone fainted yet?" she asked.

"Not yet. I'm scared. What if it's a Gentile who faints? Lev and I didn't discuss that. Am I supposed to help Gentiles?"

"A true moral dilemma. Of course you are. Gentiles are people, too."

"I know. Still, I hope it's only Jews who get sick."

"The Chief Rabbi would be proud of you."

"Oh, you know what I mean. I'd be so nervous, touching them."

"Gentiles don't bite, silly."

Guttle looked up at the sky, more sky than you could see from anywhere else in Frankfurt, she imagined. Except perhaps the parks; that she didn't know. Clouds were approaching from the west. "Things may start cooling off," she said.

"I hope so. Of course, then I wouldn't be needed here."

Dvorah was rarely satisfied with anything in life. Guttle kissed her on the cheek and hurried back. When she found Meyer idle, she visited with Hannah Schlicter at the stall beside theirs. Dvorah's mother was bubbling over with news — she'd already sold a dress to a countess, who wanted to come for fittings and order more. "She took my name. She said she'll come to the Judengasse! A real countess! Can you imagine?"

As the bright sunlight and music and color and noise swirled like an operetta through her head, Guttle felt she could imagine anything.

The smell of wood smoke began to drift through the air like a refugee from a cooler place. Despite the heat the purveyors of sausages and sliced pork fried with onions had no course but to fire up the wood in their portable stoves. Smells of the not-kosher watered mouths in the back rows of stalls as well as those down front. Guttle wished she'd brought something tastier for them to eat than leftover chicken and challah. She'd thought of dried herring, but that would only make them more thirsty.

Her thoughts of food were banished by a jester dressed in lime and lemon stripes and a floppy hat, his face shiny with greasepaint, who was moving along the back row making mischief. Pausing at the stall beside theirs, he picked up one of Yussel Kahn's miniature carved chairs and tried to sit on it. He shook his head, it was much too small. The people who had gathered around laughed. He lifted a dress of Frau Schlicter's from the stall and held it at arm's length in front of him and began to dance with it. The small crowd applauded the lovely couple.

The jester put the dress back and approached Meyer's booth, and pulled three red balls from his pocket and began to juggle with them. He put one ball away, and with exaggerated theatrical motions lifted up one of the antique heads. It was the classic Greek, the most expensive of the three. Worth two hundred gulden, Meyer had said. The jester began to toss and catch the two balls in his other hand. He appeared to be preparing to juggle the balls and the Greek head. Guttle held her breath. She saw that Meyer was doing the same. The onlookers encouraged the jester. She saw Hannah and Yussel squirming, as if debating whether to step in. After feigning three times to throw the head in the air, the jester set it back on the shelf. It all had been a tease.

They breathed again as he moved on to the rag dealer's stall and began to play with the baby, tickling him with goose feathers, puzzling the infant by making strange faces. Ephraim Hess gave the jester a coin and he moved on to the next stall, and the next. Angry over his threat with the antique head, Guttle still was watching him when he left the line of stalls, crossed the cobbled street, spoke with a Constable. She tugged the sleeve of Meyer's coat as he concluded a deal with a young nobleman for a medal bearing the likeness of Julius Caesar; for many collectors, such medals were as valuable as coins.

"What is it?"

She leaned toward him so as not to be overheard. "Beware the jesters," she whispered.

She inclined her head toward the rag dealer's stall, which the Constable was approaching.

A moment later there was commotion on both sides. Ephraim Hess was exchanging loud words with the Constable, who apparently was insisting that the infant needed a pass to remain at the Fair. Meyer began to fear that the young man might get himself arrested. Once he was in jail, anything could happen. At the same time, in the other direction, fairgoers were crowding in and moving back like waves splashing on rocks as a small entourage swept grandly among the stalls. The wave broke again, and thrust in front of Meyer's stall was Crown Prince Wilhelm himself, in all his bemedalled plumage, along with four aides wearing black waistcoats and gray breeches: crows surrounding a peacock. While Meyer cast a concerned eye at the rag dealer and the Constable, the Prince lifted and inspected in order the Greek head, the Roman, the Etruscan.

"Do I know you, Herr Jew?" he asked.

Meyer bowed briefly from the waist. "I've sold you a number of coins, Your Serenity. Meyer Amschel Rothschild at your service."

"These are proper sculptings. I might be interested."

Meyer glanced away from the Prince and saw the Constable pulling Ephraim Hess by the sleeve of his coat while his wife Eva screamed and the baby Solomon cried. Meyer was torn, did not know what to do. He had to decide quickly.

"Your Royal Essence, if you will excuse me just a moment… a friend… I'll return in a moment. Guttle, entertain the Prince."

He pushed past her and left the stall.

Entertain the Prince? How could he do this to me?

She forced herself to smile, though beneath her dress her knees were shaking. She prayed that the Prince couldn't tell. Droplets of sweat ran down the hollow of her back.

"Leave the Prince unattended?" one of the crows exclaimed. "How dare the Jew! Make sure you get his name," he said to another crow. "He'll pay for this."

"Calm, calm, Hans, we are not unattended. And your name, lovely lady, is?"

"Guttle." She was barely able to speak, was blushing in front of royalty, astonished as much as the crows that Meyer had deserted him. Surprised also that the Prince appeared to be only about Meyer's age.

"Guttle… what was the fellow's name… Rothschild, may I ask?"

"Guttle Schnapper."

"Then the Jew is a fool."

"I mean, not yet. That is we're, well we, I was to say we're betrothed, but that is not true either. Yet, I mean."

"Easy, child. I see the picture. Perhaps he is not a fool."

"Of course he's a fool," Hans said to another crow. "Imagine, leaving the Prince like that. It's unheard of."

The Prince, looking at Guttle, smiled a small smile. "Now it's been heard of," he said. "Write down his name for me."

Guttle took up quill and paper. "He didn't mean anything, Your Lofty Serenity," she blurted. "He wants so much to be a court agent, he would never offend such as you. If he is granted the title, we can become betrothed." She wrote down Meyer's name. "But now he'll hate me, I wasn't supposed to speak of that."

The Prince looked beyond the stall, to where Meyer was speaking with the Constable. "I assure you, Fräulein, I heard not a word your lovely lips uttered. Hans! Paper and pen!"

Hans produced an embossed sheet of paper from the sack he carried, and a quill that he dipped in a jar of ink. At the rag dealer's stall the screaming had stopped; the dealer was hugging his wife, who held the baby at her side. Behind them Meyer was walking away a few steps, still speaking with the Constable.

"The effrontery," Hans said.

The Prince finished scrawling a note on the paper, which bore his coat of arms, and signed it with a flourish. He returned the writing tools to Hans, held the paper aloft so Hans could blow on it, waved it in the air so it would dry more quickly. He snapped his fingers and Hans produced an envelope, into which the Prince folded his note. Handing the envelope to Guttle, he said, "I hope we shall meet again, young lady."

Guttle thought: We shan't, unless you come to the Judengasse. She dared not say it. Uncertain what was expected of her, she curtsied, imitating etchings from her French history book. Wilhelm nodded, eyeing the shadowed valley of her bosom as she bowed, and without further word sauntered off, trailed by his pecking order.

Thirty metres away, his back to the stalls, the Constable pocketed a letter of credit for three gulden. "Buy something nice for your wife, your mistress," Meyer told him. "Should the question be asked, you can honestly swear you didn't accept cash."

Turning to hurry back, Meyer saw the Prince leaving. He wanted to run after him, to apologize, to explain. But that would be unseemly. Slowly he walked to the stall. The sea of people had closed, the crown Prince had vanished into the waves.

"What rotten timing!" Meyer muttered. "Yahweh is playing tricks."

"It wasn't Yahweh, it was you! How could you insult the Prince like that? More important, how could you leave me alone with him? I was terrified."

"I'm sorry, Guttle. Two reasons. I like that Hess fellow, he's got spunk. I didn't want to see him carted off. He's got a wife, a child."

She was not mollified. "And the second reason?"

"I didn't want you to think less of me."

"Me think less of you? I thought business always comes first."

"It does. Except when it comes second."

"So you tossed away your hopes."

"Was he that angry?" Meyer sat in the chair, disconsolate. He dropped his head toward his knees, but quickly raised it so as not to upset her. "There are other Princes out there. None as important as Wilhelm, none will ever be as rich. Still, latching onto a Prince here, a Prince there, I could do well enough."

They were interrupted by the approach of the rag dealer, carrying the baby. "I want to thank you, Herr Rothschild. For my wife, and my son. I don't know what you did — I can guess — but I wouldn't know how to do that. I am in your debt."

"Only people I do business with are in my debt. This was nothing. A gesture for a fellow Jew."

"My wife says I should offer you a coat. It would be secondhand, of course. But clean. I told her you are a gentleman, you have no need for a used coat."

"Thank your wife. Fortunes do change. I will accept your offer — in abeyance. Against the time I might need such a coat. So. Any debt you feel has been discharged."

"I do have a question. Might the Constable return tomorrow?"

"Not him or any others. Your baby is safe for the week — if he's a man of his word. I believe he is."

"A Constable?"

"Let's say I took a gamble. All life is a gamble. The trick is to get the odds in your favor."

"I hope you're right, sir."

He thanked Meyer again and went back to his wife at their stall, where customers were examining secondhand dresses and cloaks. The band on the center platform, which had been resting, erupted into another marching tune. Clouds covered the sun, creating an unearthly change of light, so rare in the Judengasse. A breeze came up, rippling the linen tops of the stalls.

"Perhaps I could write a letter to the crown Prince," Meyer said. "Explain the circumstances."

"I think he was aware of the circumstances," Guttle replied. "He left a note." She held it out to him.

"Have you read it?"

"No. It's for you."

"I don't have the stomach." The enormity of what he had done was closing in on him like the Judengasse walls. All his long-range plans — gone for a secondhand coat. "Read it to me, bitte."

She opened the envelope and held the paper in front of her. It fluttered in the breeze, she had to grasp it with both hands; they were trembling. "It says: 'We admire loyalty. Bring heads, best coins to Royal Hotel. Five by the clock. Wilhelm of Hesse-Hanau.'"

She handed him the note, knees shaky again. He read it through several times, his lips moving as he did, as if to give the words a third dimension. Around them the tumult of the Fair was as loud as rolling thunder. They heard none of it.

Meyer smiled ruefully. "It was you I wanted to please by making the moral choice. Instead, I impressed the Prince."

"A good lesson for life. Don't you think?"

"If I do what's right, I please the world?"

"No. If you please me, you please the world."

He glanced up at her, stood, put his hands on her shoulders. They looked into each other's eyes. She felt calmer now, as if a lightning storm had passed.

"We both know you didn't do it for me," she said, softly. "You did it because you couldn't not do it."

He reached his hands to his head, straightened his three-cornered hat. "You think you know me that well already?"

Guttle looked down, her fingers toyed with his sleeve. "It's my mission in life."

"A smart girl like you needs to aim higher." He tweaked her nose, gently.

"Perhaps Yahweh gave me the mission."

"Then He needs to aim higher."

She put her arms around him, snuggled her head against his chest. "I hear His aim is usually good," she said.

He held her quietly, contentedly, amid the swollen river of sound around them.

A man in the finery of a nobleman cleared his throat. Guttle left the stall to Meyer and basked in the warm sun, letting herself absorb again the colors, the aromatic air, the music, the chatter of human birdsong. She thought: how could the people who created all this also have created the Judengasse?

Dvorah kept glancing over her shoulder expectantly. It was mid-afternoon before Doctor Berkov arrived at the Fair. She saw him nodding to everyone he knew as he passed. When at last he arrived at the her stall she was busy handing out cups of water to a line of thirsty people, Jew and Gentile both. Perspiration had pasted her auburn curls to her temples. The Doctor lifted a kettle and began to help.

"You look tired," she said, as she put an empty kettle on the ground and reached for another.

"Tired, but happy."

Her chest swelled with contentment at the notion that he was happy being with her.

"My new physician finally arrived. That should make things easier."

"What's his name? Do you like him?"

"Not 'him.' Her. Doctor Rebecca Kirsch."

Dvorah's hand began shaking on the kettle.

"She seems quite nice," the Doctor said.

"A female Doctor? I've never heard of such a thing."

"They're becoming more common. Especially Jewish ones."

"And her husband, is he nice, too?"

"Doctor Kirsch isn't married. She's fresh out of medical school. Which is what I wanted. She'll know the latest techniques."

Dvorah thought of Guttle. Guttle would know how to respond to that double-edged remark. She wanted to cry. How could she hope to compete with a lady Doctor? She wanted to ask if this Rebecca was pretty, but she didn't dare.

"The lane is so crowded, where will she live?"

"In my father's old room, for now."

Her despair was complete. She hated this person already.

"I can't wait to meet her." Her voice was weak. She hoped it sounded sincere.

"Good, because she wants to meet you, too."

"Me? How does she even know I exist?"

An elderly Christian man was taking a mug of water. He asked if he might have one for his wife as well. Dvorah handed him a second cup, asking him to be sure to return them.

"I told her about you. She was concerned that all the hospital assistants are men. She said she wants a female helper, to work with female patients."

I told her about you.

"That makes sense." Trying to strengthen her voice.

"I told her about your idea for the Fair. She said it was forward looking. She wants to talk to you about working with her, if you're interested."

Your idea for the Fair.

"How could this Rebecca go to medical school? Women can't go to university."

"Neither can Jewish men." He poured water into several mugs. "The Gentiles don't think much of doctors. We're like butchers, or astrologers, compared to the academics, the philosophers. So medical school is permitted."

"Do you think she'd really hire me?"

So I can see you every day…

"I don't see why not."

On the bandstand the musicians swung from a military march into a zesty polka. People began to clap in time to the music. Gentiles began to dance in the aisles between the stalls, fat ladies with wobbling flesh, red-faced men perspiring, smiling girls with pigtails holding hands with grim-faced boys. Watching them, Dvorah found her hips swaying to the music. She noticed that Lev didn't seem to hear it at all.

The lane this day resembled a long, narrow home for orphans, alive with a myriad of young children running about scattershot, and no adults visible. All the shops were closed, their owners either doing business at the Fair or accepting that few customers would come to the Judengasse while the Fair was on. The shops were closed every Sabbath, but that was different; on the Sabbath, men, women and children would be walking in the lane after schul in their best clothes, or standing about exchanging jokes and gossip, looking forward to the evening when a few of the men might bring out their fiddles and start a dance. But today the men were not to be seen, most of the women were indoors cleaning or cooking, only small children were palpable, running races alongside the ditch, happy to have room to play without tripping over the legs of grown-ups. The bakery, the hospital, the synagogue and the schools were open as usual, but that was all.

When Izzy Kracauer, who had been doing research in the yeshiva, left to walk home for lunch, a line of young girls — the boys were in heder — formed behind him in single file, and began to mimic his Schul-Klopper stride, each of them knocking in the air with an imaginary hammer as they walked. Izzy stopped and turned to them; they had never done that before.

"What game is this?" he asked.

"Pied Piper of Hamelin," several girls shouted in unison.

The little ones never had been drawn to Solomon Gruen. The deaf mute many found frightening. But young Izzy, with his pale freckles and unkempt blond hair, they had bashfully adored ever since he became Schul-Klopper and started knocking importantly on their doors, like a passing Prince who could make their fathers jump.

"Who thought of it?" Izzy asked.

Several of the girls, each about seven years old, responded, "We did." Amelia Schnapper, Guttle's young sister, explained, "My Papa told me the story last night."

"Well, if you say I'm the Pied Piper, I guess I am," Izzy said, and as he turned and continued walking home he raised his hands to his mouth and played an imaginary flute, making musical piping sounds. The delighted girls fell in behind him and followed him to his door.

When Izzy came out again after eating his lunch, Amelia and the other girls were waiting. They lined up like baby geese following their mother, and marched and klopped and piped him to the yeshiva.

Inside, he told Rabbi Simcha what had happened. "How did this make you feel?" the Rabbi asked.

"It seems silly, but it made me happy. It made me want to laugh."

The Rabbi squeezed Izzy's shoulder. "After faith in Yahweh," he said, "fresh-scrubbed little faces are the answer to the past."

In the first house by the north gate, Hiram was bored. He had smiled broadly at Izzy's little parade, but when it had gone there was nothing worth watching. His parents were asleep in the heat. Hours remained before he would have to knock on doors for the evening service; first the men had to return from the Fair. He stretched out on his bed to nap.

His brother, however, was restless. Hersch left the apartment to find distraction. There were only the children running about; he did not care much for them. He walked to the south gate, where he could smell the river. He could imagine the moorings crowded with the small sailboats of wealthy merchants or nobles who had sailed up the Rhine or down the Main to the Fair, and with large sloops unloading still more goods. This made him only more agitated. Seeking peace, he walked to the Hinterpfann, and entered the familiar office where he had been working for Meyer Amschel for nearly six months.

The door was unlocked, it always was; Rothschild was a trusting man. The desk was clear. Most of the coins were at the Fair. Most of the cloth was at the Fair. He sat, pounded his hand on the desk. It was he who should be at the Fair.

He looked at the wooden chest against the wall. He knew what was in it, had seen its contents many times when Rothschild put pouches of money in or took them out. He knew the chest, too, never was locked.

There was no harm in lifting the lid. Just to look.

He was surprised. The level of the money was half what it had been a few days before; some of it must have been taken to the Fair, to use for money changing. He gazed at the pouches of cloth and leather. If one pouch were to disappear, would anyone notice? Rothschild rarely wrote anything down. There were no records of what was in the chest, except in Rothschild's head. How could anyone be sure if one pouch disappeared?

The bastard owed him something for stealing this week of his life.

He'd checked this morning in the mattress of his father's bed; he checked every few weeks. The pouch with a hundred gulden still was there. His plan was to have three hundred before he fled this place, set out on his own, or with Hiram if Hiram wanted to come, took a coach to some city far away that had no Jew laws. Find women. Live like a real person. If he took another hundred now he'd be more than half way. Maybe he didn't even need three hundred, maybe two hundred fifty would be enough. Especially if Hiram didn't come. He could start some kind of business. After fucking himself silly he could find a wife beyond the meager choice of Judengasse girls, who were either too fat or too arrogant. No more sweeping out the synagogue, no more digging graves, no more carting packages for Rothschild.

He stared at the chest. In a few days, after some of the profits from the Fair were dumped in, it would be nearly full; a single bag removed from near the bottom would never be missed. He needed to wait, just a little; there was no sense in being stupid. He closed the lid of the chest and went outside. At the end of the alley he encountered the busybody Sophie Marcus, who seemed to prowl everywhere in the lane, as if there were six of her. He was glad he had not stolen the money just now, with her as a witness.

"So, how was the goyishe Fair?" Sophie asked.

Was she innocent of his situation, and being pleasant, or was she being spiteful? With Frau Marcus he never knew. He walked by without responding.

"Look at him, he wants to be deaf as his brother."

Her words trailed after him like a curse.

At night, after the Fair had closed for the day, explosions of fireworks splattered the dark sky. From the Judengasse they could be heard, like rolling thunder, but not seen. More muted fireworks were touched off in the Schnapper household, when Guttle told her father, "Sophie Marcus is telling lies about you."

"Lies?"

"She told Meyer you are negotiating with her husband to arrange my marriage."

"I wouldn't use the word negotiating."

"You what? Papa!"

"Jacob Marcus came to me the other day, to discuss the subject."

"You sent him away, of course!"

"I did not send him away, of course."

"Are you trying to make me cry? What are you saying?"

"Jacob is an influential man. He lends money to influential men, both in and outside of the lane. You do not just send him away."

"So what did you tell him?"

"That I will think about it."

She approached her father, put her hand on his vest. "But you won't. Right, Papa?"

He lifted her hand and kissed it. "But I will."

"To drive me meshuganah?"

"To be true to my word. There are some good points to the idea."

"But I don't love him! I love Meyer."

"We're not talking about love. We're talking about marriage."

"Papa! What good points?"

"He's a religious young man. He would be good to you. He already has an inheritance."

"I don't care about his inheritance! What else?"

"You want more? I'll tell you. Having Jacob Marcus in the family wouldn't be bad."

Guttle stared at her father, her eyes growing wild.

"There are no good points!"

Shaking her head wildly, she ran from the room, down the stairs, across the lane, in search of Meyer.

15

On the second day of the Fair the gallows appeared. The chairs of the band had been moved to the front of the platform. Behind them, workmen had toiled during the night to erect a tall gibbet. The noose at the end of the rope could be seen dangling inside an iron cage that was taller and wider than a man. Here, posters around the square proclaimed, at three by the clock this very afternoon, a heinous Jew highwayman would be hanged by the neck until dead, as a warning to all others who would disrupt lawful travel to and from the city.

The noose seemed to hang over the heads of all the Jewish merchants. They didn't condone thievery, being easy targets themselves, but a public hanging seemed a relic of ancient times. Of stonings. Of burnings.

The performers leaped into the spirit of the day. As the acrobats climbed three high, the fellow on top would suddenly drop his head to the side, as if his neck had been snapped by a rope. Adults cheered, children laughed. A troupe of performing players created a human carriage pulled by two horses, with a handsome nobleman riding; a thief skulked up to rob the nobleman; the thief wore a yarmulke and had a long gray beard. Jesters ran about holding ropes, pretended to hang one another, and fell to the cobbles as if dead. People raised steins of beer and shouted their approval.

"It's madness," Meyer muttered. "They'll soon hang a man for stealing five gulden — and we've got a murderer walking free."

Guttle, tilting her head, squinted at him, certain she had not heard correctly. "What did you say?"

"Nothing, nothing." He clenched his teeth. "It's just the heat, I misspoke." He wiped his perspiring face with his handkerchief. He wanted to wipe away the words, but they hung in the humid air like a spider's web. He began to organize the unsold coins.

"You didn't misspeak. Tell me."

He saw a hint of hurt in her face. "I can't, I gave my pledge."

"You don't trust me?"

"Guttle, Guttle. I'll tell you what I know. It's not much. You must not repeat it."

"I promise." She touched his sleeve as if it were a sacred thing. "On the Torah."

"Listen, and then forget. When Lev Berkov and I joined the Judengasse Council — maybe a month after — he took me aside. He said he had a dilemma, he needed to confide in someone. A murder had been committed in the lane, he told me, and the Chief Rabbi was keeping it secret."

"That's not possible! Nobody in the lane could murder. We don't even have police. Besides, nobody's missing."

"He wouldn't say who it was. Someone whose death appeared natural. Neither Berkov or the Rabbi had any idea who the murderer was, or what the reason might be. They didn't want to bring in the Frankfurt police and have them beating people. So the Rabbi determined they should keep quiet, so as not to cause alarm. Berkov kept wondering whether to bring it before the council. He wanted my advice, it was keeping him awake at night."

"That's awful! And you told him?"

"It was his decision. I had no idea what he should do."

"He kept it to himself?"

"He never told the council, that's all I know."

"Who passed away around that time? Only Doctor Berkov's own father. And the Schul-Klopper. They think somebody killed Herr Gruen? That can't be, I don't believe it."

"I'm not sure I believe it myself."

A customer was approaching.

"But now you've forgotten the whole thing."

"On the Torah," Guttle said.

She stepped away from the stall. Sour thoughts blew through her mind like a curdling wind: Viktor Marcus got rich from his uncle's death!

Viktor wouldn't do such a thing.

But what if he did? He still wants to marry me!

She is wearing only a cotton chemise. Sticks and branches are piled around her, up to her knees. A priest is about to light the faggots into flames. She sings an aria.

> *Could he have killed for me?*
> *I know it cannot be;*
> *You do not take a life*

To help you gain a wife.
It hurts my anxious head,
It makes my stomach ill,
That I might share a bed
With someone who could kill.
Would Viktor be so rash
To slay his kin for cash
So Papa would say yes
On seeing his largesse?
(She looks at the flaming pyre, beginning to feel the heat.)
If my virginity
Did make him yearn for it
Am I then murder's cause?
And must I burn for it?
My legs my arms my hair
The torchlight of the Fair?
Or will they stretch my neck?
The thought of gallows galls;
A piece of heaven dies
Each time a virgin falls.
If I did lead him on
As though it were a game
I'll hang my head myself
—but just in shame.
So do not weep for me,
All life's a trial or three.
Except, a man was slain!
— That's still a mystery.

"You look pale," Meyer said. "I think you should go home before the hanging."

Yussel suggested the same to Hannah Schlicter. Hannah suggested it to Dvorah. None of the women left.

Guttle's father had not rented a booth. He was roaming the Fair, renewing acquaintances with bankers and other Court Jews. He had just come to visit with Guttle at Meyer's stall when from behind them a roar went up. They heard the rumble of a carriage on the cobbles; thinking some royalty had arrived, they turned — and saw two white horses pulling a cart in which four Constables sat with ready muskets, surrounding a prisoner who was standing tall, though his arms and legs were in chains.

"They'll go around three times, I think,' Wolf Schnapper said. "For their Son, their Father and their Holy Ghost."

He moved nearer to the roadway where the cart would pass if it came around again. Guttle and Meyer followed. The cabinet maker on one side, the rag dealer on the other, did the same. Everyone was curious to see the condemned man, horrible though the sentence might be.

They followed the progress of the cart by the cheers as it circled the Fair. Some people were hurling epithets at the prisoner, others were hurling rotten fruit they had brought for the occasion. The four Constables tried to tuck in their heads like turtles to avoid being hit, but were struck in the back of their gray uniforms nonetheless, more often than the lone prisoner. Perhaps this was a chance for the commoners of Frankfurt to vent their anger at the Polizei as well. One tomato did strike the prisoner's temple, and hung on the collar of his shirt, like a mark of blood.

The carriage came around a second time. As the Jewish merchants stood silently, Guttle's father focused his eyes on the manacled man: the thick arms, the tanned face, a yarmulke pinned to his dark, curly hair. The judge had permitted the yarmulke, he assumed, perhaps even ordered it, to emphasize that the condemned was a Jew.

"It's him!" Schnapper said as the cart rattled by, slower this time than last. He ran out into its wake, shouting. "That man is no highwayman! That man is the blacksmith from Mainz!"

Red-faced, he turned to Meyer and Guttle, who had joined him in the street. He spoke rapidly. "Two weeks ago, a horse on the Speyer coach threw a shoe — we were near Mainz, so the driver stopped to get it replaced. The smithy was a Jew, I talked with him as he worked. That's him, I'm sure of it! He's got a wife and children. He's no highwayman!"

The cart was turning the corner to more cheers. Schnapper ran to the first Constable he saw. It was the same officer from whom Meyer had rescued the rag dealer. "You have to stop the hanging!" Schnapper shouted. "I know that man, he's innocent."

"What did you say?"

"The man is innocent!"

As he leaned closer to make himself heard over the cheers a second Constable lifted his club and swung it hard into the back of Schnapper's neck. The Court Jew fell to his knees, then toppled sideways onto the cobbles. "Keep your Jew notions to yourself," the Constable warned, and turned away in disgust.

Guttle and Meyer ran to her father. He was struggling to his feet.

"Papa, Papa, are you all right?" Tears were watering her eyes.

"Don't worry for me. We've got to stop the hanging."

Ephraim Hess had come up to them and was listening. "It's a blacksmith from Mainz," Guttle told him. "He's no highwayman, Papa says."

"Rafe Isaacs?"

"That was the smithy's name. Rafe."

Ephraim ran to his wife and spoke with her. He began to move among the Jewish merchants, speaking rapidly. Eva, holding her baby, moved quickly in the other direction, doing the same. By the time the cart came around for the third time, moving even slower so the people could get a long look at the condemned, every Jewish merchant knew what Wolf Schnapper had said. "Stop the hanging!" they began to shout at the cart. And, "Free the innocent!" And, "Let the blacksmith go!" After the cart passed they stampeded down the aisles to the lip of the bandstand and shouted over and over: "Innocent! Innocent."

Some of the Gentile merchants began to drown them out with shouts of their own: "Hang the thief! Hang the thieving Jew! Guilty! Guilty!"

The horses came to a stop behind the platform. A drum roll rumbled through the square. It shuddered from the cobbles into the chests of every onlooker. The guards wrestled Rafe Isaacs onto a platform beneath the gallows, into the iron cage. Jewish merchants tried to climb onto the bandstand, young and old, in black suits and full beards, but a phalanx of Constables had formed in front of it and were driving the Jews back with swinging clubs, or pulling them down by legs or arms. Some tried to climb again. Others hit the cobbles and lay still.

Guttle and Meyer had helped her injured father to the chair at their stall. As he caught his breath, Guttle looked at Meyer, who had made no attempt to move toward the platform. She turned away, disappointed. Why wasn't he down there with the others?

Meyer put his arm around her, forgetting her father was there, or not caring. He seemed to know her thoughts. "It won't do any good," he said. "You fight the battles you can win. With weapons of your choice, not the enemy's."

She saw that Yussel Kahn also was holding back, was standing quietly next to Hannah, watching from afar.

The knot of the scratchy rope pressed into the back of his neck at the base of his skull. The front had caught on his Adam's apple. He tried to adjust his head slightly, to let the rope slip upward under his chin, but it didn't move. He thought: what is an Adam's apple? Of what is it made? What function does it serve in the process of life? Why do men have them and women not? What connection does this pebble in the throat have to the Garden of Eden?

What would he feel when his Adam's apple was crushed by the rope?

He stretched his neck. Still the rope did not move. He would not squirm more than that; it would not look proper.

Shouts from the crowd swept over him like a freezing wind, and he felt a chill. He could see old Jews being beaten by young Constables, and Christians cheering. But not all the Christians were cheering — he didn't think it was all of them. Perhaps there was comfort in that. Conflicting shouts fell around his head like sparks from his anvil. The executioner, his face covered with a black hood, except for slits for his blue eyes, spoke to him, said it was time for his last words.

He would say no last words. They had made certain of that. As surely as if they had cut out his tongue.

The executioner asked his forgiveness. He nodded. As if he had the power to forgive. As if he, Rafe Isaacs, with a rope around his neck, were God.

Brendel would be alone with the boys. He wondered if there was a heaven, if one day he would meet them there.

He did not think so.

He did not think Brendel would be alone for long.

He heard one of the Jews ask another, "Why doesn't he say who he is — the blacksmith from Mainz?"

He heard another, a thin fellow, reply, "Because they threatened to kill his wife. His children."

He wondered how the fellow knew such things.

It was a talent, such knowledge. Like shaping hot metal into shoes for horses. Or swords for Princes.

The door of the cage into which he had been put clanged shut behind him. The executioner had only to pull a lever, and the floor upon which he was standing would fall away. He would gag, choke, his Adam's apple would be crushed, he would kick his legs as he struggled in vain to breathe. He would soil himself, front and back. That is what happens, he knew.

Through the corner of his right eye he saw the executioner's arm move forward, saw his fingers wrap around the wooden lever. He saw the arm jolt backward.

Most of the Jews turned away before the platform in the cage dropped. Some could not keep from watching the deed done, to see what the Gentiles were seeing, before turning away. They straggled up the aisles to their stalls, bruised from the clubs of the Constables. Two supported their right arms with their left, bones broken. None had the stomach to do more business. In a long thin line they began to wend their way back to the Judengasse, like a defeated army.

They could leave their goods behind, the stalls were protected at night. This was necessary for merchants who came from other cities, and for the reputation of the Fair itself. It was held under the personal auspices of the Empress. Woe be to those who embarrassed her.

None of the merchants was in a hurry to face his wife, his children, to explain why he had returned early, to describe what he had seen. The two with broken arms went to the hospital, where Doctor Berkov set a splint on one and the new Doctor Kirsch took care of the other. Most drifted from habit to the center of the lane, to the synagogue, where they stood outside and talked among themselves. Guttle urged her father to go to the hospital, to have Doctor Berkov look at his neck, where he'd been struck. That could wait, he said; he was the one who'd identified the blacksmith; he wanted to hear what people were saying. Seeing the crowd outside the schul, others who had not been at the Fair left their homes to see what was happening.

Ephraim Hess vaulted onto the synagogue steps and waved his arms for quiet. People wondered who this rag dealer thought he was, to be taking charge like that. When the gossip had cooled to a murmur, Ephraim began to orate. They all knew what had happened today, he said. An innocent Jew had been hanged at the Fair. They as Jews could not ignore this. Business could not go on as usual. They must stick together. He urged them all to withdraw from the Fair; to get their merchandise back in the morning, and not return. The government and the Polizei must be shown that they could not do such things to Jews.

Shouts of agreement came from some in the gathering. "No more Fair!" they began to yell. "No more Fair!"

"Then do we all agree?" Ephraim asked the crowd.

Amid a mixed response, Wolf Schnapper slowly mounted the steps, rubbing his neck. He stood beside the rag dealer and asked for silence.

"I think most of you know who I am," he said. "Wolf Schnapper, currently Chairman of the Judengasse Council. Before we do anything precipitous, I think we should hear from other speakers." He looked about. "I see there in the rear another member of the council, Meyer Rothschild. Come up here, Meyer Amschel, and give us your thoughts."

On the edge of the throng, Meyer turned to Guttle. "Your father has a wicked streak."

He could hardly refuse to respond. They were waiting for him. He circled the crowd and climbed the steps and looked from face to face while focusing his thoughts.

"Except for reading from the Torah in schul," he began, "I have never spoken to a gathering such as this. I am a private person."

There was total stillness as they listened.

"I applaud the anger of my friend Ephraim Hess —" he turned to the rag dealer — "if I may call you my friend." Hess smiled, nodded. "I, too, am furious at what we witnessed today. I think we all share a natural urge to respond to this unnatural killing — perhaps even to hurt someone. I know I do."

"Revenge!" someone in the crowd yelled.

"But whom do we want to hurt?" Meyer continued. "Surely not ourselves. It has been my experience at the Fair that the most business is done the last few days. People have walked about with money in their pockets, looking at all the things they can buy. Now, in the next three days, they will do the spending. And on Friday they will want to change what money they have left back to their own currency. The money changers — I am one of them — will make profits."

"No, no, no!" someone cried out. "A man is dead!"

"This is not about business!" another yelled.

"There is a principle here," a third shouted.

Meyer held up his hand for silence. "Hear me out," he pleaded. "I haven't yet gotten to my point."

"Well, get to it, or close your mouth," a stout heckler yelled.

"The question," he intoned as they quieted, "is not whether to respond, but how to respond. My point about business was not that we would lose money — but that the Gentiles will know this. They will see our stalls empty, and they will laugh. Do you know why they will laugh? Because they will think we are afraid! They will think that the sight of a man dangling from a rope has frightened us away. They will think that a few blows from the clubs of their Constables have sent us packing up our goods and going home. Is that what we want them to think?"

There were murmurs in the crowd. He went on.

"For more than three hundred years we have been locked in this Judengasse. Have we survived because we are afraid? Of course not! We have survived because we are strong. In the year 1614, when the Fettmilch gang rampaged through the lane, looting shops and beating our people, did our forebears turn and run? They did not. They picked up cudgels and brooms and lit into the intruders and beat them back. Many a Gentile thug went home that day with a bleeding head or a broken bone. No thugs have attacked the lane since."

"That's right," someone yelled.

"That's because they hanged the ringleaders," someone else shouted.

"The man knows his history," Meyer said. "The emperor hanged Fettmilch and the other mob leaders. But would he have done that if our brave ancestors had cringed in fear, instead of fighting those thugs, and demanding justice afterward? I think not.

"Now we are on trial again, and once again we need to demonstrate our strength. We need to return to the Fair tomorrow as if nothing has happened. We must carry on business as usual, sick as we feel inside. That is the way to show them they cannot intimidate us."

"Rothschild makes sense," Jacob Marcus said.

Murmurs of agreement seemed to spread.

Meyer continued. "I hope, as you do, that these walls that surround us will come down in our lifetime. Not in our children's lifetime, or our children's children's, but in ours!" Cheers erupted among some of the spectators. He held up his hand. "But to see that happen, we cannot appear to be defeated. We cannot slink away like a beaten cur. We cannot abandon the field of battle. And if the field of battle happens to involve profits, as it does at the Fair, all the more reason not to run away. What kind of triumph is that?"

"He's right," came a cry from the crowd.

"Hot as it is," someone said, "winter will come. We'll need to feed our children when business slows."

Murmurs of agreement were everywhere now.

"We have survived worse," Meyer shouted, his voice growing hoarse. "There is no shame in surviving. There is no shame in being patient. But fleeing — that we must never do."

A roar of approval greeted these final words. Meyer felt euphoric as he turned away from them. Wolf Schnapper put a hand on his shoulder and said into his ear above the noise, "You will be very rich one day."

Meyer stepped back as if he'd been slapped. He glared for a moment, then turned away without responding and hurried down the steps. Behind him the rag dealer was asking for quiet.

"Rothschild is right!" someone else yelled.

Ephraim Hess help up his hands. "I agree with you. Herr Rothschild is right! I tend to be hot-headed sometimes. I want direct action. But going back to the Fair and facing them — that's direct action as well. Perhaps more courageous than what I suggested. I withdraw what I said before. Let's go back and take their money. Let's show we are not afraid."

The assent was unanimous. The men in the crowd felt better, their anger and frustration vented. They were ready to go home. They moved off in knots, to the south and to the north, eager to return to the Fair in the morning. Guttle hurried to Meyer. "You were wonderful," she said. "What did my father whisper to you?"

"Your father is a fool sometimes."

He saw the questioning hurt on her face. He took her hand. Together they walked toward the Owl and the Hinterpfann. Guttle did not understand.

They'd gone only a few steps when the Chief Rabbi called to Meyer from the doorway to his study. They crossed the sewage ditch to see what he wanted. Their hands were perspiring. They let them drop.

"I enjoyed how you threw cold water on that young hothead," the Rabbi said.

"Is that what I did, Rabbi? Ephraim Hess is a good man."

"Perhaps. But that's not why I called you over. I know this is not an appropriate time, the hanging must have been terrible to see; we'll say yizkor for the man in schul. Nonetheless, life must go on. Before this happened, my Gilda bought half a cow from the butcher. She's preparing a welcoming supper this evening for the new Doctor. Berkov will be there, and Rabbi Simcha. I thought perhaps you'd like to join us. Hear the latest folderol from the universities."

"I'd be honored, Rabbi."

Without thinking, Meyer looked at Guttle. Guttle blushed and peered at the ground. The Rabbi glanced from one to the other. "You may come, too, young lady. Right after evening service."

Rabbi Eleazar returned to his study. They resumed strolling in the dying heat of the lane.

"I feel awkward," Guttle said. "Does he really want me to come?"

"He likes you. He's the Chief Rabbi, he doesn't have to do things just to be polite."

They heard a thumping on the cobbles and saw Isidor Kracauer come running, cheeks puffing, blond hair akimbo. Guttle recalled her promise; she had not yet brought him a flower.

"Did you hear what they did to the blacksmith?" Izzy asked, breathless.

"We saw what they did to him," Meyer said.

"No. No. After the hanging."

"Hanging him wasn't enough?"

"The bastards cut off his head. It's stuck on a pike at the Fahrtor gate."

16

Ephraim Hess was tearing chunks off the bread, dipping them into his soup, forcing himself to eat, though he had no appetite. He did not know when he would get to eat again. He might never eat again; if they got caught, the penalty most likely would be death. Eva sat across from him, unable to swallow a morsel. The baby was asleep on the bed, which took up most of the kitchen of their two-room apartment; the front room was the rag shop.

The blacksmith's head would be facing the river, Ephraim assumed, facing the bridge across which travelers came. Beyond that he did not know what to expect. Would it still be dripping blood? Probably not. Would it be smiling at having escaped this difficult life? Would it be grimacing in the final pain of the hanging? Would it look still alive and ready to rejoin its body? Would the eyes be rolled back in the ghastly sightlessness of death? He did not know. All he knew was that the head of this innocent Jew murdered by the Gentiles could not be allowed to remain where it was, the eyes and lips pecked at by gulls till a disfigured face was thrown to the fish. It had to be rescued, be given a proper burial — with the rest of the body if that could be found, without it if necessary.

The way to retrieve it had come to him in a jolting image, as if he'd been physically struck, the entire plan visible at once. Quickly he had acquired the cooperation he needed. The cabinet maker would nail together a coffin this evening and leave it outside his shop. The slaughterer, with some misgivings, would leave the back door to the slaughterhouse unlocked. The Liebmann brothers, more muscular than he was, always ready for action, had agreed eagerly when he explained their roles. Everything was ready.

Eva had told him she feared he would not come back, that little Solomon would grow up fatherless. Ephraim replied that he could never be a proper father if he didn't listen to his heart.

"What about listening to your head?"

"Think about the blacksmith's head."

He'd taken her in his arms and their two thin bodies had pressed together and he'd reminded her that when they first became lovers they'd agreed to fight whatever battles needed to be fought to make the world better.

"We were so young then," she'd said.

"It was only two years ago."

"I know. We were so young then."

They weren't married in the records of the Judengasse. They couldn't be; Ephraim was still three years shy of twenty-five. Eva was nineteen. He called her his wife, and the lane accepted the fiction, especially after she became pregnant. The Rabbis weren't happy, but they were not about to make trouble for young lovers because of Frankfurt's laws. Frankfurt could enforce its laws itself if it found out.

Ephraim stepped into the lane and looked up at the sliver of sky visible above the tenements. It was weary with evening. By now the Liebmann brothers would be hidden in the slaughterhouse, having told the young guard Fritz they were going to buy a chicken. Before they returned the guard at the gate would have changed; the night guard wouldn't miss them. In the slaughterhouse they'd remove one of the two layers of clothing he'd told them to wear. He was confident they'd time it right, the deaf mute was precise with his pocket watch. When Otto Kracauer locked up his chickens and cows for the night, which he should be doing now — leaving the rear door unlocked — the brothers would remain inside.

In the rag shop, Ephraim took two dresses off their hooks. He folded them, stepped away and looked at them. He decided to add a third. He returned to the kitchen and sat beside Eva on the bed and held her hand. He asked if she were sure she wanted to come with him. She repeated that she was, that he would be safer with her and the baby along; a family man would attract less attention. But he could feel her bones trembling.

"Adonai will protect us," he said.

"Like He protected the blacksmith from Mainz?"

They sat in silence, hearing only their own thumping hearts. Ephraim lit a small lamp in the quick-falling dark. Solomon woke and began to cry. Eva gave him a breast.

The baby was almost sated when they heard a boom that sounded like thunder over the city. "The first fireworks," Ephraim said. "That's our signal."

Eva wrapped the child in a blanket. Ephraim took the bundle of dresses from the shop. He closed the door and together they walked toward the north gate. Ephraim showed their two Fair passes to the night guard, and held up the folded dresses. "Business was so good today, we have to replace our stock."

The sky was breaking up with exploding lights. Crackling leaped over the walls. The guard handed their passes back and waved them through. They walked from the lane, passing the darkened slaughterhouse on the left, and turned right at the first crossing. Eva touched his arm. "What if he'd asked why we couldn't wait till morning?"

"We have passes with the official seal. He's not supposed to stop us."

They moved along in the dark street, turned right a second time. Ahead of them was the forbidding outer face of the long ghetto wall. Beside it ran a cobbled walk. Across the street was a city park, appearing deserted in the darkness.

"Find a place that's comfortable," Ephraim said. "But don't fall asleep. You have to be watching for me when I come back." He handed her two of the three dresses in his bundle, keeping a dark blue one. He stripped off the outer of his two layers of clothing and gave her those.

"Do you really think I could fall asleep?"

"I hope not." He kissed her on the mouth, a long kiss, as if it might be their last. He pulled himself away and scurried into the deeper dark at the base of the wall.

He wondered why he needed to be a hero, to risk everything for a dead man. But what was his life for? To sell secondhand clothes?

If the timing was right, the mute would at this moment be moving in the dark outside the other wall. Hersch, keeping in the shadows, would be circling three blocks and joining him here.

Ephraim thought: it would be easy to escape from the Judengasse. But escape to where? You would have to leave your friends, go to another city. Perhaps to another Jewish ghetto. That's why, year after year, there was so little ferment in the lane. Rumor had it that the Judengasse Council had petitioned the city months ago to unlock the gates on Sundays, and allow Jews to enter the city parks. Rumor had it that the city had not even bothered to answer.

He heard the sound of faint footsteps on the cobbles. Before he realized it, Hersch was beside him; for a sturdy fellow he could be light of foot. They nodded to one another curtly; they were not great friends. Ephraim had selected the brothers because they fit his needs. Hersch was both strong and angry; Hiram would not be able to answer the Fahrtor guard's questions.

"Your brother is on his way?"

Hersch's nod was barely discernible.

"Follow me," Ephraim whispered.

They slipped quietly along the base of the wall. A pale quarter moon was visible intermittently between armadas of scudding clouds. Above and behind them, exploding fireworks battled for their attention, but they kept moving.

Ephraim paused, stuck out his arm to stop Hersch. "There's people in the park," he whispered. "Watching the sky."

"What should we do?"

"Keep going — and hope the fireworks last."

They shrunk into themselves and crept if possible more quietly than before, till they passed the end of the park and the end of the wall and could smell the river, heavy with the humid scent of fog and fish. They walked downhill beside the sloping sluice that carried the wastes from the lane. As they neared the river they could just make out the Fahrtor gate in front of shreds of fog that drifted above the water. They peered into the low darkness. Clouds slid like ice from in front of the sliver of moon. They could see the lone night guard on the stone platform this side of the gate, the outline of sailing vessels anchored behind him. The head would be just the other side of the stone arch, below the Judensau. The only way to get to it would be by wading through the water.

They crept near the river's edge. The lapping of the current became a booming in their ears. Sitting on wet dirt behind a cluster of leafy bush, they removed their shoes. Ephraim placed the rolled blue dress on the sand. By the hint of moon they could see rats drinking.

The guard on the Fahrtor platform was perhaps forty metres from them. The rag dealer thought: now everything rests on a deaf mute. Impatient, he whispered, "What's he waiting for?"

"He's timing it. He wants to make sure he doesn't start before we're here."

The croaking of a strange bird sounded along the narrow beach.

"What was that?"

"That's him."

"He's supposed to bang on a boat. What's he doing?"

"Improvising. Don't worry."

A moment later they heard the banging start, a stick hitting the wooden hull of a small boat. Interspersed was the croaking sound, if not a large bird than a strangling dog.

"It's the only sound he can make," Hersch said.

They stared at the guard silhouetted against the fog. He glanced in the direction of the sounds, then up at the fireworks he'd been watching. The knocking began again, louder, and the screeching. The guard looked along the shore. When the noise didn't stop, he climbed down from his platform onto the beach, and walked along the water's edge, to see what the problem was.

They knew what he would find: Hiram up to his neck in the water, banging with a stick for help, as if he were drowning. Trying to shout.

"Now," Ephraim urged.

Stooping low, they crept into the water. It was icy on their feet, their shins, shriveled their balls as it clawed at their waists, perhaps not as cold as it would have been were it not for the long hot spell, but cold enough to cut their breath short. They waded to the far side of the second arch, the water burdening their clothes, lapping at their chests. Ephraim reached his hands up to the side of the bridge. Hersch filled his lungs with air and bent beneath him. Ephraim found Hersch's knees with his feet and climbed. His wet clothing was heavy, was dripping into the water as he twisted to perch on Hersch's bent back. Holding his breath, he waited till he felt certain the guard was not coming back, then pulled himself onto the bridge. When he looked up, he had to grab onto the arch to keep his balance. The metal pike was directly in front of him. The face of the blacksmith, his dark hair in unruly curls, was staring down. The head seemed to be smiling grimly, the lower lip pulled down, the lower teeth showing, like gargoyles on Gentile buildings he'd seen on the way to the Fair.

Girding himself, Ephraim gripped the pike with both hands and strained to lift it from its iron holder. It came loose in his hands, but with the large head on top that end began to pull down towards the river. He tried to keep it upright but wasn't strong enough, the head was wrenching the pike from his hands. Beneath the clatter of the fireworks and the rumble of the river he thought he heard the severed head speaking, thought he saw the drooping lips moving.

Shma Yisroel, Adonai Eloheinu, Adonai Echud.

Hear O Israel, the Lord is our God, the Lord Is One.

"It's falling!" he whispered.

The iron pike clanged against the bridge. Standing below in the water, Hersch caught the loose head in his arms as it plummeted. He hoped a horde of rats wouldn't come swimming at the smell of blood. He didn't know if rats could swim.

"Who's there!" a voice shouted.

Ephraim leaped off the bridge into the water. They were hidden in shadow. Should they stay or run? The guard surely had a musket. But he might miss in the pale moonlight if they fled. If they ran in two directions, one of them, at least, would live.

They didn't move.

They heard a dull thunk, then footsteps on the stones. A white face appeared at the river's edge. It emitted a soft croak.

They hauled their heavy legs out of the water, Hersch still clutching the head to his chest. Hiram was there to meet them. Hersch gave the head to the rag dealer, and signaled with his fingers to his brother, "Where's the guard?" On one of his fingers a piece of cartilage clung like a leech. He shook his hand; it did not fly off, he had to use his other hand to pull it free. He was about to toss it into the river when Ephraim grabbed the sliver and pressed it up into the blacksmith's neck. "We have little enough of him," he said.

The guard? Hiram signaled to Hersch. He put his hands together and raised them above his head and made a clouting motion. He had hit the guard with a board.

"We're kaputt," Ephraim said. "Let's hope he isn't dead."

"We were kaputt if he caught us."

"Let's get out of here."

They hurried along the beach. Ephraim patted the sand in the dark till his fingers found the dress he had left there. As he lifted it, a rat with shiny wet fur spilled out and scurried away. Carefully he wrapped the head in the dress. He recited the Shma aloud, just as the drooping lips had done.

The fireworks had stopped. He could only hope the Gentiles had left the park without spotting Eva.

Hersch and Hiram took a step away.

"Wait," Ephraim said. "We have to change the plan. You shouldn't sleep in the slaughterhouse."

"Why not?"

"If that guard is dead, they'll be searching everywhere. You should sleep in your own beds."

"How can we get through the gate?"

"Change to your dry clothes at the butcher's. Hide the wet ones. Circle around and make it look like you're coming back from the Fair. Lean against each other like you're drunk. Slobber to the guard about how the fireworks were wonderful, too bad he had to work."

Ephraim set the wrapped head on the ground. He reached into his pocket, pulled out his and Eva's passes to the Fair. They were wet. He handed them to Hersch. "Wave these at the guard as you go in. He won't bother to check the names, not when you're coming back."

"You think they'll raid the lane, search every house?"

"Not for the head. Not with the Fair going on, too many foreigners here. But if the guard is dead… "

"Let's go," Hiram signaled to his brother.

They had scurried about ten steps in the dark of different directions when the voice of the guard shot over them from the river's edge. "Halt, who goes running there?" They bent their heads against musket fire that didn't come. Ephraim tightened his hold on his bundle and ran up beside the sluice to the ghetto wall, hoping he wasn't jarring the blacksmith too much; they had to get home before word reached the north gate that the head had been stolen.

He found Eva waiting as planned. "Danks Gott they didn't find you in the park."

"I hid in bushes. They didn't come near. Is that it?"

He nodded as he set it down, stripped off his wet clothing and put on the dry ones he'd left with her. The wet he wrapped around the severed head. They circled a deserted block and approached the north gate as if returning from the Fair. Eva cradled the baby. Ephraim held up his bundle to the guard. "They wouldn't let us go to our stall. Said we should restock our wares in the morning. What would it have hurt them if we … "

The guard was not interested in their problem. He waved them through the gate.

The coffin was waiting on the cobbles outside Yussel Kahn's shop. Together, with one hand each, they lifted the lid. Ephraim placed the head carefully inside. He lowered the lid, and with tools Yussel had left he hammered in one nail on each side — just enough so that a curious child couldn't lift the lid in the morning.

That was the plan, but now he changed his mind; if the Constables did come into the lane, the lonely coffin was the first place they'd look. He pried up the lid, took the wrapped head out and carried it with him. In the rag shop he placed it on the floor in a corner and covered it with coats. The Constables would have to be searching every house in the lane to find it.

Back in their room, they thought they would be sick. Eva wrapped the baby in his basket, and set him snugly in the shop, as far away as she could from the severed head. She poured two glasses of sweet wine. Instead of being sick they soon were overwhelmed by exhilaration for what they had done. They stripped away their clothes and burned their remnant fears in a fierce and driving love, stifling their moans with practiced hands so as not to wake the child, or those in the apartments on either side, or those above.

17

Portraits of Rashi and Rabbi Akiba and Maimonides looked down from the walls in the dining room, rich in woods and leathers. Guttle had never been in such a fine room before. Her eyes kept roaming, absorbing the furnishings, the velvet draperies, the cabinet filled with fine china, the glistening gold menorah. None of it belonged to Rabbi Eleazar, she knew — it went with the Chief Rabbi's house.

"Tell me," he was saying to the new Doctor, "if your family is from Berlin, where there is a fine university, I'm told, why did you choose to study in Göttingen?"

Guttle watched as Doctor Rebecca Kirsch chewed the last of her forshpice — her appetizer — before answering. It was too good to leave even a bite: a mix of small balls of ground meat with cabbage, in a sweet sauce such as Guttle had never tasted. She would have to ask her mother to make it; better still, request the recipe from the Rabbi's wife after dinner, if she were feeling brave, and try to make it herself.

Doctor Kirsch pressed her lips with her napkin, daintily yet firmly, Guttle noticed, as befitting a woman and a Doctor. "Göttingen is far more modern. Far more advanced."

She had black hair that was piled atop her head with pins, a curved ivory comb at the back. Her face was striking, with hollows in her cheeks that set off dark brown eyes. Her face retained the color of the outside world. Her fitted dress was satin, a rich, solid green.

"Advanced in what sense?" Rabbi Simcha asked.

"Well, they admit Jews. And women. Throughout the university, not just to the medical school."

"How did they manage that?" Meyer Amschel asked.

Gilda, the Chief Rabbi's wife, a black and white dotted babushka tied over her brown wig, was clearing the appetizer plates. Guttle, wearing her best white silk Sabbath blouse — breaking, for this occasion, Frankfurt's rules — thought to help, but she wanted to hear the answer.

"As you may know," Doctor Kirsch said, toying with her fork, "most universities have four divisions: theology, philosophy, science and medicine. Theology ranks at the top, and has the power of censorship over the others. It can keep out Jews, Calvinists, any religion it doesn't like. At Göttingen they declared all four divisions to be equal. This removed theology's right of censorship. Now anyone can attend."

"Why do you suppose they did that?" Lev Berkov asked.

"Because it's in line with the new thinking that's — how shall I say it? — beginning to ride in on the wind, from France, from England."

Gilda set a plate of boiled beef flanken with onions and potatoes in front of her husband. "Did you hear that, Gilda? After four thousand years, new thinking. I'm not sure I want to hear about it, Doctor. But if it's good news for the Jews, go ahead."

"It's a simple idea, but it's considered radical by some. It's what the French philosophers —Voltaire, Diderot, others — have been talking about for years. The idea that all people are equal. Rich and poor, nobleman and peasant, Christian and Jew."

Meyer leaned back in his seat while the Rabbi's wife set down his plate. "How is that possible? For instance, how can rich and poor be equal? That is a contradiction."

"And Christian and Jew," the Chief Rabbi said, chewing on his beef. "How can we be equal, when our culture is far superior? When the Gentiles around us are only a few centuries removed from barbarians."

"Some of them not that much," Rabbi Simcha said.

Rebecca Kirsch smiled. Nervous, Guttle dared to speak, the first comment she had offered. "In this advanced thinking, are men and women equal? I shouldn't think so."

Doctor Kirsch nodded and said "no" at the same time. "I'm afraid it's not that advanced."

"Of course not," the Chief Rabbi said. "Men and women can never be equal. Yahweh created them to be different."

His wife, who also had been silent till then, spoke as she took her seat. "This equalness is what they are teaching at the universities? Better our children should stay home. Not get meshuganah ideas."

The others began to cut into their boiled beef. The knives made squeaking sounds on the plates. Guttle could see that Doctor Kirsch was frustrated, that she did not want the conversation to end there.

"Perhaps I did not make clear what I meant by equal," the Doctor said. "Take rich and poor, as Herr Rothschild pointed out. A poor man will never be equal to a rich man in the things he can own. But they can be equal before the state. In an ideal society there would be no nobles, and no peasants. No one would be considered superior to anyone else as a matter of birth. Instead there would be what is being called a meritocracy. People would rise to prominence, to government service, on their own merits, not on their grandfather's blood lines. No matter how far they rose in terms of wealth, they still would have no more say than the poorest man in choosing the parliament, or in facing the courts. In matters of justice, for instance."

As they all listened intently, Rabbi Simcha closed his eyes, and seemed to be smiling at some inner vision.

"Look how things are now," Doctor Kirsch continued. "The nobles have power to influence the Empress. The peasants don't. The peasants are quite literally owned by the Princes. In Kassel, which is just twelve kilometres from Göttingen, Landgrave Friedrich conscripts the peasants into his army. He hires out his army to whatever country is fighting a war. The Prince gets paid, so much for each soldier supplied, so much for each one killed, so much for each one wounded. There is talk — in the wind, as I said — that the British colonists in America are tired of paying taxes to their king. There is talk they might rebel, and fight to have their own independent country. Should that happen, Friedrich most likely would lease his army to the British king, to fight his own colonists. No matter who wins that war, the Landgrave will become very rich from the blood of his peasants. And he's rather rich already."

Meyer, sitting to Guttle's right, discreetly squeezed her hand.

"A lot of farmers will die," Lev Berkov said.

"In a war in which they have no stake," Rabbi Simcha added.

"It's the way of the world," the Chief Rabbi said, mashing a piece of potato in his mouth. "A new idea doesn't change the way things are."

"Sometimes it does," Guttle blurted. "Look what Jesus did."

Silence struck the table like a storm. Guttle bit her lip, trying to bite back the words. The others, all except Doctor Kirsch, looked at their plates. Meyer Amschel rescued her. "That may be an unpleasant thought, but we all know it's the truth. Some ideas have power. If you go back further, the Jewish concept of one God swept across the world like a conflagration. It burned the pagan Gods to ash. It relegated them to myth."

"The problem is, even false ideas can flourish — like the premature Messiah," Rabbi Simcha said.

"Are you saying this concept of human equality is false?" Doctor Kirsch asked.

"Not at all. It's a wonderful notion. Just a bit… fanciful, perhaps."

Guttle, still upset with herself over her comment, was finding the beef hard to chew; some of the others were also. The Rabbi's wife noticed. "We have baked apples for dessert," she said, "so leave room. If I gave too much meat, you don't have to finish."

A sense of relaxation moved inaudibly around the table. Exhilarated though she was by these new arguments, Guttle realized she had just learned from the rebbetzin a lesson in grace. Her mother felt insulted if people didn't finish everything.

"If I may change the subject slightly," Meyer said, addressing the new Doctor, "Göttingen is a small town. How did it manage to build a university?"

"It didn't. There is only one building. The instructors teach in their homes. Very effectively."

"If I may change the subject even more," the Chief Rabbi said, "there is one other question I am curious about. I understand from Doctor Berkov that your credentials are impeccable. That being the case, there are many cities in which you could have gone to practice. Why did you come to us? To the Judengasse? Where you will be locked in at night, on Sundays, and so forth?"

"My father's answer is that I'm meshuganah. He may be right." She smiled, and put down her fork. "Seriously, I think there is a unique opportunity here to study what affects people's health. In addition to treating the sick along with Doctor Berkov, of course. The walls and the gates are terrible things, but medically, they provide a laboratory that could be useful."

"In what way?" Meyer asked.

"For instance, Rabbi Simcha was kind enough this morning to let me look through the Memory Book. Two things struck me at once. The first is that you have a terrible rate of infant deaths here. More than half the babies born alive die during the first year. Most in the first few weeks. The rate is high everywhere, but not as high as in the Judengasse. What is the cause of that? It becomes especially intriguing when you note, as I saw in the book, that a great number of the people here live to a very old age. Not only into their seventies, but into their eighties and even their nineties. This is very unusual."

"So you see a contradiction," Doctor Berkov said.

"Not so much a contradiction as a puzzle. There is something going on here that kills babies. But those infants who survive seem more fit to live a long life. Are these connected? Does it have to do with the sanitary conditions? With the diet? With the mere fact of being Jewish?"

"And you hope to find out?" the Chief Rabbi asked.

"Not really. I'm a Doctor, not a natural scientist. But exciting work is being done in science and medicine at the universities. Not only across Ashkenaz, but in England, in Denmark. I hope to keep up with the latest findings, and see if any of them apply here."

When nobody jumped in with a comment, Guttle summoned her courage. "Doctor Kirsch, something has been troubling me ever since I read it in Deuteronomy a few months ago."

"There's a lot that's troublesome in Deuteronomy," Rabbi Simcha said.

The Chief Rabbi gave him a harsh look. Guttle continued.

"It said that if mothers don't follow all of Yahweh's laws, their children will die. Do you think that could be what's happening in the lane, why so many babies die?"

"That's a good question, Guttle," the Chief Rabbi said. "I would like to hear your answer to that, Doctor."

"As I said before, I have no idea what's causing these deaths. Let's say I'm willing to accept that explanation — until we find a better one."

"Please hurry," Guttle said. But she had a morsel of tough beef in her mouth and was not understood.

"What was that? Speak up, young lady," the Chief Rabbi said. "We're interested in your opinion as well."

"I said, I hope they find a different explanation soon. Before I get married." They all laughed amiably; she wasn't sure she had been joking. "There are a lot of Yahweh's laws to follow in Deuteronomy. Also in Leviticus."

"You know your Torah," Rabbi Simcha said.

"But I don't trust that I can keep all the rules."

"Sounds to me as if you'll do just fine."

She hesitated, then spoke again. "Can I ask one last question?"

"Of course. You see, Doctor Kirsch, what inquiring minds we have here in the lane."

"So I'd heard. That was another attraction."

"What was your question?" Doctor Berkov said to Guttle.

She wiped her hands on her napkin. Gilda Eleazar was setting a huge baked apple in front of each of the diners, and a glass of tea

"At the Fair today," Guttle said, "an innocent man was hanged. He was a Jew. Because he wore a yarmulke, right to his death, I imagine he put his faith in Yahweh, as we all are taught to do. But if that's true, then Yahweh failed him. How are we to keep our faith in a Gott who allows such things — who lets us be confined to the Judengasse?"

The host toyed with his baked apple, then set down his spoon. "That is a question that has been with us since Job. Or before. It comes to most of us at some difficult time in our lives." He lifted the spoon, set it down again, took a sip of tea. "There is no doubt that terrible things happen. It is also true that all things, good and bad, emanate from Adonai. We can't deny that. We can't pick and choose what we ascribe to the Almighty. The only answer I have is a simple one. If we do not trust in Him who created the heavens and the earth, and gave us life, then in whom should we trust?"

"What about ourselves?" The comment came from the lady Doctor.

The Chief Rabbi's face darkened to a deep red. He pointed his spoon in her direction. "You may be fresh from the university, Rachel Kirsch, but that comment is close to blasphemy."

"It's Rebecca," the Doctor said.

Rabbi Simcha stood at his place. "Perhaps that is an answer — this lack of faith in Yahweh — that's also coming in the wind, as the Doctor has intimated. And perhaps in a way it answers part of Guttle's question. Perhaps Yahweh has placed us Jews within high walls so we'll be protected from these winds."

"Exactly so," the Chief Rabbi said. "Very good, Simcha. A postulation I had never considered in just that way. A new view of the walls, in fact. Perhaps a subject for my yeshiva class, where this Mendelssohn fellow seems to have a following. But now we have such sweet-smelling baked apples in front of us, I suggest we drop serious subjects. We'll tell some clever stories, to smooth the digestion."

Strolling home slowly, Guttle and Meyer discussed the evening. Somewhere above them was a half moon they could not see, providing just enough glare to outline the tops of the tenements. The lane was deserted, most people had gone to bed with the dark, as usual, so as not to burn much oil.

"The new Doctor seems very smart," Guttle said.

"Very intelligent. Making an enemy of the Chief Rabbi was not very smart."

"All she did was speak her mind. You like it when I speak my mind."

"You say different things."

"Dvorah wants to marry Lev Berkov. Do you think the new Doctor will be in her way?"

"Doctor Kirsch seems very serious. She came here to work. I doubt that marriage and children are on her mind. Besides, she's too intelligent for Lev."

"You think he's not intelligent?"

"He's very intelligent. But he thinks he's smart enough for two people. He wants Dvorah only for her body."

"What a terrible thing to say."

"I'm just speaking my mind."

"Is that why you want me? For my body?"

"I want you for your tantalizing soul."

"Oh."

"Of course, if your body came along in the bargain, I wouldn't object."

"You are such a romantic, Meyer Amschel Rothschild."

"I know. I can't help it."

"Be serious. Why do you like me?"

"Where did you get that idea?"

"Meyer!"

"Why do I like you? Because you make me laugh."

"That's all?"

"That's not all. But don't minimize it. Laughing is how we survive."

"The Jews?"

"The human race."

"Why does it have to be that way? The suffering?"

"Apparently that's the way Yahweh likes it."

They strolled in silence for a time. From one of the tenements they heard a baby cry.

"Why did Rabbi Eleazar get so angry at Doctor Kirsch?" Guttle asked. "I've never seen him like that. Is it blasphemy to believe in yourself?"

"I think he misunderstood. He thought she wanted to substitute ourselves for Yahweh. But she surely has faith. Otherwise she wouldn't have come to the Judengasse."

"Which do you believe in?"

"Me? I think we need to have faith in both. In Yahweh, and in ourselves. I think our lives are like the paintings on the Rabbi's walls. Yahweh provides the canvas, and the paint, and the brushes. But we have to paint the picture."

"What if we have no talent?"

"Then we do it with hard work."

She thought about that. "The picture doesn't always turn out very good."

"No, it doesn't. But it always gets finished, one way or another. Yahweh sees to that. So we have to keep trying while we can."

She leaned her head against his shoulder as they walked. "I want to help you paint your picture," she said.

He linked his arm through hers. "I want you to. But it will be our picture."

"If that's really true, can I tell you what I want in that picture? My secret dream? I've never told anyone. I'm afraid they would laugh at me."

"Tell me. You know I believe in secret dreams."

"I want to tear down the walls, so our people can be free. I want us to do it together."

They stopped walking. He ran a finger lightly across her lips, looked into her eyes. "I have a desire, too, which I've never told anyone."

"You do?"

"It's the same desire. But I don't think of it as a dream. I think of it as a goal."

She stood on her toes and kissed his lips. His breath smelled of wine and apples. Her own mouth still tasted of boiled beef. "When can we do it? How?"

"We can't do it by ourselves. Adonai will have to help. Perhaps Rebecca Kirsch's so-called wind will help."

They resumed strolling, hands entwined, feeling closer to one another than they ever had. "That's something your father doesn't understand about me. That I, too, have dreams — and not just of wealth. But as you said, we can't tell people. They'll think we're too puffed up."

They reached the front of the Owl. She turned to face him. "I have to ask you something. When my father called on you to speak today, you said he had a wicked streak. What did you mean?"

"He was putting me on the spot. It was a test, to see what I would say."

"That's good, isn't it?"

"I suppose you could look at it that way."

"After your speech, what did he whisper that got you so angry?"

"He said I would get very rich."

"That made you mad?"

"That wasn't what my speech was about. Sometimes, having principles and making money coincide. Not always — but today I was speaking for principle. Either he misjudged me, or he was being cynical. He meant I was manipulating that crowd for my own benefit. I was not."

"Maybe you have to sell yourself to him."

"Tell him I have ethics? He sees me in schul every day. When he's there. Tell him I tithe my income, as the Torah instructs? That's none of his business."

She squeezed his hand, hard. "When you two fight, I get afraid."

"Afraid of what?"

"Papa could make me marry someone else. Lev Berkov — though I don't have Dvorah's body. Or Viktor Marcus".

"They're both good men."

She dropped his hand and turned away, mumbling . Even if he were teasing, he had gone too far.

"What was that? I didn't hear."

She turned back. She repeated what she had said, enunciating every word. "I... don't... know... how... to... make... them... laugh."

He put his hands on her shoulders. "We have to be patient, Guttle. I know that's difficult at your age, but... "

"At my age?" She wanted to shriek, but controlled her voice. "What's wrong with my age?"

"Nothing. I love your age. I love everything about you. But we have to wait. Whatever Yahweh wants to happen will happen."

"You do?" Her voice was shy now.

"I do what?"

"Love me?"

"Of course. You know that."

"It's the first time you've said it."

He kissed her forehead, held his lips there. "I should have said it before."

She broke away in delayed reaction. "I hate that!"

"You hate what? What do you mean, you hate it?"

"I hate what you said about Yahweh. 'Whatever He wants to happen will happen.' It's what I hear in the lane every day. It's the opposite of what you said you believe."

Meyer took a deep breath, let it out slowly. "You're right. Sometimes I don't know what I believe. The point is this. Your father, though he is more open than most, is still of the old school. To him, marriage is not about love. It's about business. I have to prove to him that he, and you, will be getting a good deal."

"Do you believe marriage is about business?"

He rubbed his hand across his forehead. He knew he was about to wade into trouble. "You want me to be honest? A little."

"So if I were the rag picker's daughter, you wouldn't want to marry me." It was a statement, not a question.

"I still would love you."

"That's good to know."

"Guttle, that was a joke. Why are you being so difficult tonight?"

She pulled away from him. "I'm tired. I have to go to bed. Maybe it's that boiled beef speaking. Maybe I have trouble watching men hanged. Maybe I'm too young for you and the prevailing winds. Don't worry, I'll leave everything in your hands. And Yahweh's."

"Can you think of a better pair of hands?"

"That's four hands, not a pair."

Angrily, she turned towards the door.

"Goodnight, Guttle. When you're going to sleep, count Yahweh's hands. Maybe He has more than two. Maybe He has a thousand hands."

She opened the door to the Owl and disappeared into the dark, the humid dark of the house, the angry dark of herself. The dark she wanted no one — no one but Melka — to see. She wondered, not for the first time, if she even belonged with Meyer and his crowd. She wondered if their love was a game.

With her head on her pillow, she tried to count Yahweh's hands. Tears blurred her eyes, she couldn't see them.

O nly women lived in the Judengasse. Men did not live there at all.

The notion came to Guttle as she calmed.

The women emptied the chamber pots into the ditch, went to the market after the Christian ladies had picked the best vegetables, cooked the meals, washed the linens and the clothes and hung them to dry out back without benefit of sun, carried babies in mild or severe discomfort for nine months and bore them with terrible pain — Yahweh's everlasting punishment to Eve — only to see disappointment on the faces of their husbands if the child was a girl; only to watch in horror as half their babies died.

The men, the pious ones especially, did not live here. They lived in the years of the Torah — of Abraham and Joseph and Moses — which they read every day, morning and evening, in the schul. Or they lived in the abstract world of the Talmud, devouring and examining old arguments and theories, splitting niceties like slicing onions, till a woman could cry. At night, at home, they read aloud from the Talmud or chanted ancient prayers, the same prayers once chanted in the courts of Saul and David. When they were not dovaning in the desert of the Torah, they lived in the black forest of their work. This rubbed some of them with the coarse salt of life — the coffin maker, the rag picker. But the others, like her father, like Meyer Amschel, hid their heads in the mathematics of money. Her father, when his mind was not in his prayers, was at the court of Sachsen-Meiningen, making shrewd investments that added to the piles of coins in the Prince's vaults. Meyer Amschel, when he was not walking in the desert with Isaac or Jacob, lived in the antiquity of his coins and statues, in the marble times of the Greeks and the Romans — and in the countinghouse of Crown Prince Wilhelm, and in the vaults of his imagined future wealth. Both lived far from the grit and stink of the lane — the two men in whose hands her future rested.

That was all right, she told herself. She could be the gritty and sardonic and ever-faithful Sancho Panza if Meyer would be Don Quixote, riding into righteous battle with a shaving bowl for a yarmulke. He had the appearance for it — tall and lean, with a woeful countenance. She was well aware that, in fanciful books, prostitutes might become virgins — but even in fantasies women did not become knights.

What a strange book that was. Meyer had bought it for her, a gift, in the spring; it was long and difficult, she'd only just finished reading it. Every time her father had seen her with it he'd looked uncomfortable. She'd hoped he wouldn't think less of Meyer for giving her a Spanish fable; the Spaniards, everyone knew, had not been good to the Jews. When she finished the book she had urged Meyer to read it; he'd replied that he didn't have the time.

Sleepy at last, she turned onto her side, facing away from Avra, trying to put Meyer out of her mind. When she closed her eyes she saw him riding tall on his trusty steed Rozinante — or, if he preferred, Gulden. But their conversation during the stroll home still tormented her.

The young woman is walking barefoot through the dewy Spanish countryside, alongside the sea of sleep. Dawn is about to break. In her head she sings an aria:

> *The Cantor longs for me,*
> *Perhaps I ought to be*
> *Where he can sing to me*
> *Through all eternity.*
> *I know which one I love,*
> *And so does God above,*
> *But Meyer's always right —*
> *Which makes me want to fight!*
> *If I were Viktor's spouse*
> *We'd have the finest house,*
> *He'd buy the softest beds*
> *Where we would lay our heads;*
> *He'd not preserve my loins*
> *Like some historic coins;*

And when each child came
He'd sing its sacred name
In tones so proud and clear,
The lane itself would cheer.
Yet Meyer is my bliss,
Why do I think of this?
Why does a donkey hiss
That something is a miss.?
Because he waits and waits,
And does not link our fates!
He has not sought my hand;
I do not understand.
I left him in a huff,
Feeling not good enough.
He swears that I'm his prayer.
— I'm Dulcinea!

18

Awake at dawn as usual, Hiram Liebmann had just placed his chair at the third-floor window when by first light he saw the gates swing open and something — it resembled an animal — come flying through and land on the cobbles. A second thing followed, a third, a fourth, before the gates were pulled shut. After hitting the cobbles the things lay motionless.

In the faint light he could not see what they were. He pulled on his clothes and went downstairs and into the lane. When he saw what was there he fell to his knees beside the sewage trench, and vomited. He continued to throw up until he had nothing left to give. He wiped his mouth with his shirt and without looking at them again he made his way, sweating, to the house, up the two flights of stairs, and woke his brother. They had no hand signals for this. Hiram told him to get dressed quickly and come down, they needed to do something.

When Hersch saw the objects in the lane he bent over the ditch as well, but managed not to vomit. Hiram told him to follow, and he crossed the ditch and ran down the narrow alley leading to the Hinterpfann, and pounded on the door. He knew there was cloth in here. They had to cover those bloody things before women or children saw. He pounded with the side of his fist until Meyer Rothschild opened the door, wearing his gray sleep shirt, which came to his knees.

"What is it?" He knew Hersch still was angry with him.

"They've drawn and quartered the blacksmith. They threw his parts inside the gate. We need cloth to wrap him."

Meyer disappeared into a small back room, and returned with a bolt of canvas his brothers hadn't taken to the Fair. He grabbed a pair of shears from the table and handed them to Hiram. "I'll come as soon as I put clothes on," Meyer said.

"We can do this," Hersch said. "You round up a minyan. We have to bury him before the people see."

"What about a coffin?"

"There should be one in front of the coffin maker's, with his head in it."

"His head?"

"We stole it last night from the Fahrtor gate."

Hiram pulled at his brother's arm. Carrying the canvas and the shears, they hurried through the alley.

"This is their answer," Meyer muttered.

The four elongated segments of the body were strewn on the cobbles amid splashes of blood. Hiram unrolled part of the canvas and Hersch cut off a length. Together they lifted one of the arm-and-chest parts, trying not to look at the torn flesh. After they wrapped it Hersch knelt beside the trench and threw up. A moment later they were joined by Otto Kracauer, the butcher. His son Izzy, getting ready to knock on doors, had heard the commotion and looked out the window and awakened his father, who came bustling down with his stained apron tied over his sleeping gown.

"Cut the canvas and don't look," he told Hersch. "I can do the rest."

The brothers cut three more sections of cloth, and the butcher, who was used to this sort of thing with cows, wrapped the parts quickly. Meyer came stumbling along the lane carrying one end of the coffin. His brother Moish held the other end. They set it down near the bundles.

"It's empty," Meyer said.

"Not possible," Hersch sneered, and pulled off the lid. "The rag dealer!" he said, and ran off in that direction, and knocked on the door till Ephraim Hess, pulling on his clothes, opened it.

"The head's not in the coffin."

"I know."

"Where is it? We've got the rest."

"How... You've got the rest?"

"Never mind now, we need the head."

"It's here."

"We'll bring the coffin."

He ran back in the brightening lane and the butcher, Moish and the two brothers carried the coffin, heavy with the blacksmith's torn body, to the rag dealer's shop. Ephraim removed the wrapped head from the pile of coats and placed it in the coffin. They assured him the space they had left was the proper end.

A light drizzle began to fall. They noticed that the air was cooler than it had been only the day before. Hiram watched as Meyer went from door to door, pounded with his fist, explaining that they needed five more men to make a minyan for the blacksmith's funeral.

Hersch wondered if he and Hiram needed to invent a hand sign for drawn-and-quartered.

The men lifted the coffin onto their shoulders and began to carry it down the lane. Those that Meyer had awakened fell in behind them. More men, dressing for morning services, heard the footsteps on the cobbles and opened their doors and looked out and saw what was happening and, learning what was going on, followed. As they passed the synagogue the raindrops grew larger, the rain became steadier. The men continued walking, wearing hats or yarmulkes that darkened instantly. Rabbi Simcha heard the passing feet and looked out and saw the coffin, raindrops bouncing noisily upon it, and joined the line beside Meyer. By the time they neared the cemetery the coffin had a tail like a dark comet, of more than two hundred men.

"Rain at last," Meyer said to the Rabbi. "Yahweh is weeping for the blacksmith. He should have saved him instead."

He looked up and let the rain fall steadily onto his face, his chest. Yussel Kahn approached and asked what he was doing. "What does it look like I'm doing?" He swallowed rain as he spoke.

"It seems out of character. Something Guttle might do."

"There's no such thing as character unless you can step out of it. Otherwise, it's obsession."

"You know what, my friend? Guttle is good for you."

"This is news?"

The pallbearers paused at the cemetery gate. They didn't know where to take the coffin; no plot had been prepared. Rabbi Simcha spoke to Hersch. "Put him by the Beckers. I think they have room for one more."

Inside the north gate, where the rain had eased to a drizzle, Izzy and Guttle were on their knees. Between them was a pail of soapy water. With wet rags staining pink they were scrubbing away the blacksmith's blood.

"Why do you think the Christians hate us so?" Guttle asked, her eyes riveted to the dark stains. It was a question she had asked her father many times. His answers often varied, and never sufficed.

"Because of the church," Isidor said.

"What do you mean?"

Settling back on his haunches, Isidor said, "When the church was formed, it needed an enemy. People band together when they are against something, not when they are for something. So the church gave us horns and a tail, and made us children of Satan. By hating us, the Christians grew strong. Like an animal drinking blood."

That reasoning she had never heard. "How do you know such things?"

"I think a lot."

"You also talk a lot with Rabbi Simcha."

Izzy grinned, ran his hand through his hair, made sure his yarmulke had not fallen off.

"So what enemy has kept us Jews together for thousands of years?" Guttle asked.

"That's easy," the boy replied. "Everyone else."

They leaned forward then and worked quickly, dipping the rags into the water, scrubbing, wringing them out, scrubbing, till Izzy paused, wiped his brow with his sleeve. The drizzle had darkened his blond hair and pasted it to his head. "But a person could say this was Martin Luther's fault," he said.

Guttle braced for a welcome history lesson. "Why him?"

Izzy pulled a paper from his pocket. "Listen to what Luther wrote about the Jews:

"'The Catholics have dealt with the Jews as if they were dogs and not human beings. They have done nothing for them but curse them and seize their wealth. I would advise and beg everybody to deal kindly with the Jews.'"

"My goodness," Guttle said. "Let's invite him to dinner."

"Guttle, he's been dead for two hundred years."

"A Gentile says something nice about the Jews, we shouldn't be too picky."

"This is serious. He wrote that in 1523. Twenty years later, after the Jews had refused to convert to his new church, he had some different opinions."

She wrung out her rag, dipped it into the pail, continued scrubbing the cobbles while he read from his notes. The drizzle stopped entirely, as if Yahweh, too, wanted to hear.

"'The blind Jews are truly stupid fools,' Luther wrote. 'Be on your guard against the Jews, knowing that wherever they have their synagogues, nothing is found but a den of devils in which sheer self-glory, conceit, lies, blasphemy, and defaming of God and men are practiced most maliciously'."

"That's how he deals kindly?"

"It gets worse. 'They are nothing but thieves and robbers who daily eat no morsel and wear no thread of clothing which they have not stolen and pilfered from us by means of their accursed usury.'"

"Where did you find these things?" Guttle asked.

"The cabinet maker brought a book from his bookseller. I won't read everything I copied, there's too much. But listen to what he says should be done to the Jews:

"'Set fire to their synagogues or schuls and cover with dirt whatever will not burn, so that no man will ever again see a stone or cinder of them. This is to be done in honor of our Lord and Christendom, so that God might see that we are Christians, and do not condone or knowingly tolerate such public lying, cursing and blaspheming of his Son and of his Christians … If this does not help, we must drive them out like mad dogs. Eject them forever from this country.'"

Izzy folded the paper.

"He doesn't mention hanging us," Guttle said. "Or quartering us. I guess that's because he was a man of God." She stood and peered at the cobbles, to see if any trace of blood remained. Under the leaden sky it was hard to tell. Wringing her rag into the bucket, she dumped the pink water into the trench and watched it swirl away. "How can you stand to read that traif?"

"It's part of my studies."

"Maybe your father is right. Maybe you'd be better off cleaning up chicken shit."

"History has to acknowledge these things."

"Perhaps. Though sometimes I think we'd be better off burying the past with the dead."

"The present is the child of the past. It always will be."

Guttle knelt to clean the blood from a stone they had missed. "I suppose. But you made my head hurt. Sometimes I think Melka's head must always hurt — absorbing that kind of trash so we don't."

"Guttle, Melka of the South Gate isn't real. I can't find any proof that she ever lived."

"Did you find proof that she didn't? What's in that attic down there?"

"It's boarded up. The whole house is boarded up, no one wants to live there, because of the Melka stories. But that doesn't prove anything. Her name is not in the Memory Book."

"She belongs in your history regardless. There has to be some explanation for why we're not all insane."

"I can't write about her, she's not real."

"What the people believe — isn't that real? Aren't those the only facts in the Bible — what people used to believe?"

"Most people believe in Yahweh. Not in Melka."

"I think most people here believe in both. The women, anyway."

"Believing in Melka is blasphemous."

"No, it's not. Only worshipping her would be blasphemous. Maybe Yahweh created her. to do His work."

"A madwoman?" Izzy ran his hand across his chin, where the slight stubble of a blond beard had lately begun to grow. He seemed offended. "Maybe you should have my task."

"Don't be upset with me, Iz. You're doing wonderfully. That's what Rabbi Simcha says. Besides, a girl wouldn't be allowed to do it."

They began to walk toward their homes, side by side, Guttle carrying the bucket of stained rags. "Some day maybe we will," she said. "Some day maybe a girl will write what's happening to the Jews, and everyone will read it."

Izzy glanced at her, but didn't argue.

The merchants and their assistants, Guttle among them, had changed to dry clothes and were passing through the north gate to walk to the Fair when they saw two police wagons parked there, the horses standing quietly. Manacled in the rear of one wagon was the night guard from the south gate. When Kapitän Klaus arrived to oversee the north gate, he was quickly surrounded by other officers, manacled, and, blustering at the outrage, was hustled into the second wagon. Seated stiff as a pike on a white stallion, watching, several silver medals on the chest of his black uniform, was the mustached Kommandant of the Frankfurt Polizei.

Loitering nearby, pretending to repair the heel of his shoe, Yussel Kahn listened to the talk of the Constables. When he caught up with Meyer and Guttle, he told them what he had heard. "It seems the Kapitän was furious that the blacksmith's head had been stolen. He wanted to 'turn the Judengasse upside down' — those were his words, they said — to question everyone with the tip of his sword resting on their neck, find those who did it, kill those who would not speak. A stolen head massacre. But he couldn't do that, because the Fair is on. It would embarrass the Empress, with so many foreign nobles in the city. Instead, the Polizei Kommandant is replacing all of the guards — at the lane and at the Fahrtor Gate — for not preventing it. In case one was bribed to look the other way. Including the Kapitän. That's the gossip, anyway."

The news spread quickly through the line of merchants; there was no gossip better than police gossip. Guttle hoped the change was permanent; ever since the night six months before when he had spoken to her of barter, she had been uneasy passing near Kapitän Klaus, and always looked away, and felt his eyes burning into her back like a flame. Most were happiest to see him go. "Gott willing, we'll never see that bastard again," Meyer said.

After they'd walked two blocks, he moved Guttle out of the line. They were across from the Z-Z stable, the smell of horse manure especially pungent after the rain. "Do you think you could operate the stall by yourself today?" he asked. "Just the money changing. If anyone wants to haggle about coins, you can tell them to come back tomorrow."

"Where will you be?"

"I have to ride to Mainz."

"You have business in Mainz while the Fair is on?"

"Someone has to tell the blacksmith's widow that we buried her husband. To put her mind at ease."

"And the other reason?"

"There is no other reason."

"To make sure that she has money to feed her children?"

"Well, yes. That also."

Guttle squeezed his hand. "I'll be fine."

She watched him stride across the glistening cobbles and disappear into the stable. When he emerged he was sitting tall in a brown saddle, his back arched, atop a sturdy palomino whose blond mane ran down the sides of its neck like waterfalls. He waved goodbye to her and rode slowly down the crowded street. She watched until she could no longer see him, listened until the increasingly rapid hoof beats faded into the earth.

Book Three: A Flame of God

Toward your husband will be your lust, yet he will rule over you.

—Genesis, 3:16

19

On the day that Guttle turned sixteen years of age, the men in the Judengasse all wore their burial shrouds. The date of her birthday, 19 September, happened to fall that year on Rosh Hashanah, the Jewish New Year — the start of the year 5530 on the Jewish calendar. It was the custom in the German lands for the men to attend Rosh Hashanah services in shrouds, a reminder of their mortality, a reminder to remain free of sin during the coming year, because they could die at any time. The shrouds were gray, with round white collars, and hung loose almost to their ankles.

Because Rosh Hashanah nonetheless was a happy day, a day of celebration, a Yom tov, the women dressed in their most colorful finery and largest hats. The contrast as they mingled in the lane touched off metaphors in Guttle's brain: dead soldiers and ladies of the night; angels and devils; believers and atheists; shorn sheep and overgrown flowers. There was her father in his burial shroud. And Meyer. And Izzy. These were truths she could not accept, any more than she could accept the notion of her own death. All was carnival, the men mere players, like those she had seen at the Fair. A blasphemous thought danced in her head: perhaps all religion is carnival.

As she arrived outside the synagogue amid this odd commingling, wearing pale blue silk, Dvorah, in rustling burgundy, approached her, all aflutter, and asked, "Will tonight be the night?"

Guttle tried to appear calmer than she was. "Meyer Amschel is coming for dinner, to celebrate my birthday. It's the first time they've invited him. Anything more, I don't know."

"But something is going on. You said so."

"Papa has been giving me funny glances. Puffing his cheeks out, as if he's swallowed a bird. But I don't think he and Meyer have talked yet. And

I'm sure they won't discuss my dowry in front of me. I'm not even sure he's turned down the Marcuses yet."

"Don't you want to scream? It's been months with you and Meyer. With Lev and me it's been just a few weeks, and I can't stand it. I think he's going to ask me soon. Without a father… with no dowry… but that won't matter to Lev, do you think?" Guttle recalled Meyer's words. "With all you have to offer him, Dvorah, I doubt he'll miss a dowry."

Three bearded men emerged from the temple, walking together and talking, like some ancient tribunal debating the meaning of Yahweh's ambiguous words. Among them was Jacob Marcus, the Cantor's father. Guttle saw him glance at her as they passed. She could not define his expression.

"You know what I was thinking?" Dvorah said. "If we both get spoken for soon, we could get married together. A double wedding. Wouldn't that be fun?"

"We'd have to see what the men have to say."

"Don't be silly. Once we're betrothed, the men have no say."

"You're not jealous of Doctor Kirsch anymore?"

"Oh, no. Rebecca always has her nose in somebody's mouth, or ear, or chest. She doesn't even notice Lev, except as another Doctor."

The doors of the synagogue opened. The walking shrouds filed into the lane. Recess at the cemetery, Guttle thought. And shuddered. The coquettish noon sun glared off their white collars. Guttle hugged her father, Meyer, Izzy as she found them in the emerging throng. "Yom tov," each said to the other as they shook hands. Happy day.

The sun took its highlights and fled, the gray of afternoon settled in. Dvorah didn't see Lev, had no family men to greet. "Is this your first year?" she asked Izzy, fingering his rough shroud.

"I was already Bar Mitzvah'd, so I wore it last year. It fits better now."

"What a terrible thing to say."

"Don't worry about Izzy," Guttle said. "He's doing Yahweh's work. He'll probably live for nine hundred years."

The birthday dinner went smoothly. The gefilte fish, the cold beef with vinegar beets and asparagus, all prepared the day before, were superb, everyone agreed. Guttle felt the food clumping in her stomach, but the conversation flowed easily, mostly between her father and Meyer. When her mother brought out a raspberry cake, her father put up his hand. "The food is wonderful, Emmie, suitable to the occasion. But my breeches are splitting already. I want to walk in the lane with Meyer Amschel, to let our food go down. We'll have the cake and the birthday wishes when we return."

Wolf and Meyer folded their napkins and placed them on the table. Meyer followed her father to the door. He did not look back. Guttle was aware of her heart thumping noisily. She was afraid her food might come up, not go down. She listened to their footsteps descending the stairs, her father's heavy, Meyer's crisp. She looked across the table at her mother, who was still holding the raspberry cake. "Do you know anything? Will they be talking about me?" Emmie set the cake on the table, and shrugged her shoulders. "He never tells me anything."

"Can't we have birthday cake now?" one of the little ones asked.

Avra looked at Guttle with a sour smile. "After Papa's food goes down."

In the lane, pools of light rested on the cobbles like puddles of water, deeper in the centers than at the edges. In almost every kitchen people were eating their first supper of the New Year, the overflow light of their oil lamps spilling into the lane, brushing the shoulders of the two men as they strolled. Some of those who had finished their meals stood outside their doorways in Rosh Hashanah finery — the shrouds were gone — chatting with their neighbors. As Meyer and Wolf walked they were greeted by nods, or calls of Yom tov.

"Frau Schnapper is a good cook," Meyer said. "That was a wonderful meal."

"You're telling me? Why do you think I have this belly?" Wolf patted his ample waist. "I'll tell you a secret. Guttle cooks just as good. Maybe better." He leaned towards Meyer. "Don't tell Emmie I said that."

"Guttle is a fine young woman," Meyer said.

"They don't come any better. You like her a little, maybe?"

"I don't think that's a secret."

"You like her maybe a lot?"

Meyer laughed, kicked a stray chip of cobble into the ditch. "Have we started bargaining?"

Wolf clapped him on the shoulder. "I like you, Meyer Amschel. You come right to the point. She is a fine figure of a girl, don't you think?"

"Absolutely."

"Takes after her mother, not me, thank goodness. And smart."

"Like a whip." Meyer was enjoying the game. "I'll put my cards on the table, Herr Schnapper. I don't have one thing bad to say about your daughter."

"You don't? I could help you out. In the interests of a fair deal. Guttle does have her faults."

"She does? Tell me one."

"The truth is, she can be a little headstrong at times."

"I've noticed that. Tell me another."

"Well, let's see. At other times, she can be a lot headstrong."

"Now that's serious. Perhaps I'd be making a mistake."

"Now wait, wait. I may be exaggerating."

Meyer touched Wolf's arm. "Don't be alarmed, that was a joke. Guttle likes to think for herself. It's one reason I like her so much."

"It is?"

"Of course."

"That's good to hear you say. I remember when she was little, maybe four or five, I took her in a coach a few times on business trips, so she could see the world outside. We had a nice guard then, who sometimes would look the other way for a child. Everything she saw delighted her — the trees, the birds, the flowers, Butchers Lane, Jewelers Lane — even St. Bartholomew's church. Her questions were so intelligent that I encouraged her to read, to learn. Now I worry that it was a mistake."

"How could that be a mistake?"

"For a girl, a woman, too much thinking makes the lane even harder to bear."

They had reached the south gate, could hear the lapping of the river. Gulls circled in the distance, ghost birds in the moonlight, squawking their complaints. Meyer turned to begin strolling back.

"Wait a moment. Wait here."

Wolf pulled a handkerchief from his pocket, wiped perspiration from his brow. He put the handkerchief back, slipped his purse from his vest, tucked several coins into his hand. He approached the gate and tapped on it. Meyer watched the dark form of the night guard approach. Wolf spoke quietly with him — Meyer could not make out the words — and slipped his hand through the bars. A moment later the gate swung open.

"Come," Wolf said, and they both stepped through the gate before it closed behind them.

"Ten minutes," the guard said as they passed.

Meyer said over his shoulder, "Fifteen."

They walked downhill beside the sluice toward the docks. The river smell grew stronger. "Why did you tell him fifteen?"

Meyer could not tell if Schnapper was irritated or admiring. "I'm guessing you overpaid for ten."

The docks were dark, effusive with the smells of ox manure and spilt wine, silent except for two snarling cats fighting over a fish. Clouds that had been dimming the half moon drifted away, letting moonlight spill over them. To the left they could see the multiple arches of the bridge coiled like a sleeping serpent. Walking to the right, they came upon a stone stairway that led to the new and forbidden promenade. The walkway stretched invitingly along the river bank, flanked by a grassy slope on the river side and a line of linden trees on the other. As they strolled, Meyer noted how the broad ribbon of river thinned in the far distance, then vanished into the dark — like life.

He felt slightly guilty about enjoying this bought pleasure, smelling the grass, watching the river dance on broken glass. He knew he was already privileged in his freedom, like Wolf's, to leave the lane on most days, to travel on business, walking the streets of Frankfurt, or riding a coach or a stallion on roads that split meadows and farms with their fields of beets, potatoes, asparagus, cabbages, barley, sweet smelling hay in neat stacks, thousands of birds chirping overhead, or suddenly blanketing the fields like a crocheted quilt.

Wolf broke the silence. "We have a subject to discuss, Meyer Amschel. I think the New Year is an appropriate time. Especially as it is also Guttle's sixteenth birthday. This being Rosh Hashanah, I feel uncomfortable speaking of money. So I have a question to ask, if you will humor me. How many fish do you think are in this river? I think maybe fifteen hundred. Do you agree?"

"Oh, I think much more than that. I think three thousand at least."

"That many? That's a lot of fish."

"Perhaps. But it's a wide river."

Wolf pondered as they walked. "I'll tell you what. To keep things simple and friendly, we'll split the difference. We'll agree that there are twenty-two hundred and fifty fish."

Meyer stopped and looked at the river, as if he were actually peering into its depths. "It's been my experience that you never arrive at the correct solution to a problem by splitting the difference."

"Ah. So it's some kind of advantage you want? Very well. Twenty-three hundred."

"Twenty-four."

"Twenty-four?" The fish were gone with the moon as a passing cloud hid its face. "You would quibble over my daughter for a hundred gulden?"

"Over your Guttle I would not quibble a single kreuzer, Herr Schnapper. Over your hundred gulden, I will quibble."

They walked again, dragging the tension of their own footsteps, till Wolf stopped. "You drive a hard bargain, Meyer Amschel. I suppose that's a good quality in a son-in-law."

Meyer took a deep breath, let it out, smiled, offered his hand. Wolf took it and pumped it vigorously. "Done," he said.

A gull swept low over the water, broke the surface, came up shaking itself, with a fish in its beak. "Done," Meyer echoed.

The gull dropped the fish for an instant, caught it in midair, flew off across the river.

"We should go back," Wolf said. "Our time is almost up."

Both men breathed audibly as they walked on the promenade against the current of the river, hearing it whisper to the shore; it whispered of the future, a language they did not know. At the gate the guard displayed his pocket watch. "You are five minutes overdue."

"I suppose you'll have to shoot us," Meyer said.

The guard flushed, his eyes narrow with fury. His mouth seemed alive with words he didn't speak. Stonily, he unlocked the gate. When they had passed through he slammed it closed with a clang that rang through the lane.

"Why did you taunt him? It served no purpose. It was something Guttle would do."

"Yussel Kahn told me the same thing recently. Perhaps she's already a part of me."

The lane was deserted. In some windows the lamps had been turned off as people went to bed. The men walked in thought, undisturbed, exploring the emotions of their new roles: the pride of the father of the bride, the expectancy of the groom, also the bliss of a dealer with a dowry to invest.

"There's something else I've been wanting to ask you," Wolf said. "Have you heard from the crown Prince about becoming a court agent?"

"As a matter of fact, I received a letter just yesterday."

"And he said?"

"Meyer Amschel Rothschild is now a court agent to the Crown Prince of Hesse-Hanau. The cabinet maker will be carving a sign for me."

"That's a fine thing, Meyer Amschel. I wonder why Guttle didn't mention it?"

"I haven't told her. I wanted to surprise her on her birthday."

"It will be a help to your business."

"Gott willing. May I be blunt with you, Herr Schnapper?"

"Wolf. From now on you must call me Wolf. Of course you may be blunt. We aren't strangers anymore."

"To be truthful, I was surprised by our conversation tonight. I thought you would wait until you knew about the court appointment."

Wolf smiled with gratification. "To be blunt, you were right. I did know."

"How could you know?"

"You are not the only one with informants, young man."

Meyer took a moment to absorb the news. "And if the Crown Prince had refused my request? You would not have offered me Guttle's hand?"

Wolf stopped walking, and Meyer with him. "Of course I would have offered you her hand. She's meshuganah in love with you. What kind of father do you think I am?"

"But?"

"But you wouldn't have gotten a kreuzer more than fifteen hundred."

Tightening his lips against a smile, letting it burst forth in a broad grin that showed his teeth, Meyer stuck out his hand. He realized they had shaken hands already, and instead threw his arms around Wolf's shoulders. The two men hugged, their chests pressed firmly together, both of them squeezing tight.

"I'll take good care of her," Meyer said.

"Cake!" Benjy said, as at the sound of footsteps the three little ones came running from their room.

"Cake!" little Rifka echoed.

"Let's have cake!" Amelia, the seven-year-old, implored.

"In a moment, in a moment," their father said, holding up his hand. "Sit again around the table. Meyer Amschel and I have some announcements first."

The dinner plates had been cleared and washed. At each place was a flowered china cup and dessert plate — the best the Schnappers owned — and a napkin and a fork. In the center of the table was the coveted raspberry cake; in the icing on one side was a small furrow made by the finger of one of the little ones. With a scraping of chairs, the children, and Avra, Guttle and Emmie, settled into their seats. Guttle, feeling the flutter of a newborn bird in her chest, looked at Meyer standing beside her father. He seemed to be trying to control the hint of a smile. She could barely breathe from breathing too fast.

"The first announcement, you little ones won't understand. Take Papa's word, it's a good thing. Our Meyer Amschel has been granted the title of court agent by Crown Prince Wilhelm."

Our Meyer! Guttle's heart jumped.

"Hurrah for Meyer!" Benjy shouted. "Cake!"

"Meyer! You didn't tell me! That's wonderful," Guttle said, jumping up from her chair. She meant to hug him, but her father motioned her back to her seat.

"Now the second announcement."

Her heart was if possible beating faster than before.

"Hersch Liebmann has quit Meyer's employ. So Guttle, if she is willing, will take his place, after the holidays."

Her eyes were wide as she stared at them, first at her father, then at Meyer. That's all? her brain was shrieking. Nothing more?

"Now cake?" Benjy asked.

"Oh, yes. There is one other thing. Meyer and I have had a good discussion while walking by the river."

Guttle felt confused by the announcements. "By the river? How could you walk by the river?"

Rage at what had not been announced was pounding in her head. Even though she should not have expected it, not tonight. Impatience, she thought, would be her death one day.

Meyer rubbed his thumb and forefinger together, to indicate the bribe.

"Forget the river, the river is not important," her father said. "What's important is what we discussed. I have a feeling you might be interested." He winked at her, something he used to do when giving her a special treat when she was little. Guttle settled herself in her seat, clasped her hands on the table, looked down at them, trembling.

"What we discussed is one of the most important decisions of our lives. Because it involves taking a new member into our family. Tonight, I offered the hand of our lovely Guttle in marriage. To Meyer Amschel Rothschild."

His wife inhaled sharply. Avra gripped the table with both hands. Amelia clapped twice, then stopped. Guttle clasped her hands tighter and continued to look at them. Her head didn't swerve. She held her breath, felt her face flushing.

"Cake!" Rifka said.

"In a moment," Wolf replied. "When I asked Meyer Amschel if he would take Guttle as his bride, it was possible that he would say no. I am happy to report that he said yes. So, as of this moment, Guttle and Meyer are betrothed."

Guttle jumped up from her seat, and then Avra. Frau Schnapper rose slowly. Guttle rushed to Meyer and hugged him, pressed her face into his chest. Meyer kissed the top of her head. She let go of him and hugged her father and kissed his cheek. She hugged her mother, then came back to her father. "Thank you, Papa, thank you!"

"Not that it matters," he asked, "but is that all right with you?"

She hugged him again. "Not that it matters, Papa, but yes, it's all right with me."

Avra explained to the little ones what was happening. They all clapped this time. Wolf went to a cabinet and returned with a special bottle of schnapps he had purchased for the occasion. Emmie produced four small crystal glasses. Wolf poured the schnapps and offered a toast. "To Guttle and Meyer. May they be blessed by Elohim, and find happiness with one another. And may they have have many sons."

The four adults touched their glasses and drank. Guttle hugged her father again, and her mother, and Meyer. Everyone was smiling.

"When will the wedding be?" Avra asked.

"The Talmud prefers a marriage under the sky, if possible. The one month it never rains is August. So they shall be married then."

"August?" Guttle echoed. "That's almost a year away."

"You'll still be sixteen, Guttela. But an older sixteen."

"Some girls are married at twelve!"

"So I keep hearing from Avra. In our family, that won't be the case."

Guttle turned to Meyer. "What do you think?"

He drank the rest of his schnapps. "It's not for me to decide."

"Don't worry, Guttle," her mother said. "The betrothal months are the best part."

"That can't be," Guttle said, looking at Meyer.

Wolf's face darkened. For an instant he glared at his wife. But he must be mistaking her meaning, it was just a comment to comfort Guttle. This was a happy night, and schnapps was warming his belly. "Under the eyes of Elohim," he said, "you will be married in August."

Guttle took several deep breaths. She knew how stubborn her father could be. "Of course, Papa. Whatever you say." She took Meyer's hand, snuggled up to him.

"And you, Meyer Amschel?" Wolf asked. "Do you have anything to add?"

Meyer looked around the room, from one expectant face to the next, the scrubbed visages of his new family. He could think of only one thing to say. "Cake!"

ROBERT MAYER

The children applauded, bounced in their seats. Guttle's Meyer had won their hearts with a word. "A good idea," Emmie said. "Guttle, slice your birthday cake. I'll bring the tea."

Wolf disappeared into his bedroom. As the tea and cake were served, they began to hear the soft notes of a violin. Slowly Wolf emerged, bereft of his coat and vest, his shirt sleeves rolled to the elbows, his violin tucked into a handkerchief under his chin. The ancient melody filled the room as he drew the bow across the strings.

Meyer offered his hand to Guttle. She took it and he led her to the small space between the table and the bedrooms, and he put his arms around her, and she put her arms around him. There was no room to attempt an actual dance, so they stood that way, her head against his chest, and swayed ever so slightly to the vibrating strings. The children clapped, and stuffed cake into their mouths, getting their fingers sticky with raspberry frosting —"Children, use your forks,'" Emmie said — and they clapped again, spraying bits of cake across the table.

Wolf bowed faster, coaxed the violin into a livelier tune. Emmie and Avra clapped in rhythm. Guttle and Meyer did not change their own slow pace. After a time, hearing laughter from outside, Avra went to a window. A couple — she could not tell who they were — was dancing to the music, while two men clapped in time with the lively violin. She opened the window to see better. As the music flew louder over the lane, another couple, then another, emerged from the nearby tenements and joined in a dance, a peasant dance that was popular in the lane when the fiddlers brought out their instruments on Sabbath nights.

"What's the music for?" one of the men yelled up.

Avra yelled down, "Guttle and Meyer are betrothed!"

"A fine way to announce," Emmie said, pulling her away from the window. But when she looked down and saw half a dozen couples dancing and others watching she motioned to her husband. Without skipping a note Wolf came to the window and stood in front of it and bowed the fiddle louder. Slowly the dance party grew. Fat Otto Kracauer from next door seemed to shake the very cobbles as he pranced with his Ida. In the shadows at the edge of the lamplight even Yetta and Leo Liebmann could be seen, though they did not prance, as they had in their youth, instead holding one another quietly, much as the newly betrothed were doing.

Noticing that the whole family had vanished to the front rooms, Meyer touched his lips to Guttle's. They kissed again, long and slow, pressed their lips together till they heard giggling, opened their eyes, saw all three of the little ones watching. Guttle spoke to them without leaving Meyer's arms. "It's all right, you little sillies. We're betrothed."

Coming up behind them, Emmie said, "They'll be getting married, children. That's the important thing."

20

Gently, Guttle caressed her breasts, her ribs, her belly. She wished Avra were not in the bed beside her. How could her father be so cruel as to make them wait almost a year?

But she was also terrified that she would not like Meyer's weight upon her, would hate him thrusting inside her — where had Yahweh come up with that strange idea? Perhaps her mother was right, the long betrothal might be the best of times. They would be able to express affection openly. They could be together whenever they wanted, without starting talk. A happy time before the pain of bearing children, and the burden of rearing them, which might be more restricting than the walls. She would bear him children, of course — boys for him, girls for her — that's what women were for, but she was only sixteen years and a few hours old. What was the rush? How could her father be so smart as to make them wait almost a year? He was good at business, but she'd never before given him credit for being insightful about life.

The mattress shook. Avra was giggling. Guttle reached across and tickled her. Avra spun around, the two hugged, arms entangled. They fell asleep that way, in a sisterly embrace.

At the family breakfast table, Guttle asked her father a question that had kept her awake for part of the night. "What did Herr Marcus say when you told him I wasn't marrying Viktor? And Frau Marcus?" Forking a piece of cold kippered herring onto a crust of challah, her father replied, "I haven't told him yet. I'll tell him this morning, in schul."

"Papa! Why did you wait so long?"

"I wanted to make sure Meyer would accept. A spinster we don't need around here."

She saw him wink at Avra.

"That's not very nice. You gave them false hope."

"I gave them false hope? Listen to her. It wasn't me Viktor sang to in the dark."

"That again! Meshuganah Frau Marcus is going to kill me."

"Sophie Marcus kill? I don't think so. Maim, maybe."

"Wolf, stop it," Emmie Schnapper said.

"Papa thinks this is a joke. She watches me all the time already."

"Sophie Marcus is a bit strange, I'll grant," her father said. "But she wouldn't hurt a flea."

"Except when she eats them," Guttle said.

Avra, who had been drinking a glass of milk, convulsed with laughter, the milk spurting onto the table through her nose. The three little ones laughed, and clapped their hands.

"Children, behave yourselves, it's Rosh Hashanah!" Emmie ordered, standing and wiping the table with a rag.

"It's all right, today is a happy day," Wolf said. "Laughter is appropriate. Guttle is betrothed to Meyer Amschel Rothschild. That lad is going places."

"So," Guttle said, "you're not sorry that rich Jacob Marcus won't be joining the family?"

"About that, I'm sorry. But I realized that along with Jacob would come Sophie. That's why Meyer won out."

"Papa!"

Her father turned toward her mother. "What happened to your daughter's sense of humor?"

The room is white, windowless. The girl is wearing a gray shift. Languidly she pulls a comb through her long, dark hair as she sings an aria:

> *Over my shoulder I see her there;*
> *I know the why — not the when of her,*
> *At times it seems there are ten of her,*
> *Watching me eat, seeing me dress,*
> *Trying to multiply tristesse,*
> *Shadowing me throughout the lane*
> *Hoping to drive me quite insane.*
> *Watching me make the beetles burn*
> *She sees my ashes in an urn*
> *Which she could steal — nocturnal witch —*
> *And dump into the sewage ditch;*
> *Or set my dress to flaming fire*
> *To stop me from adoring Meyer;*
> *Or scar my face with blazing oils —*

So long as Viktor gets the spoils.
Attempt to talk with Sophie Marcus?
Sooner reason with a carcass.
Is it fair to be so loathed
Just because I am betrothed?

"He asked me, he asked me!" Dvorah said, rushing over to Guttle. She seemed to be jumping up and down in her white lace dress, though she was only rocking on her toes.

"He asked you what?"

They were outside the synagogue. Guttle wasn't sure why the New Year should be celebrated for two days, but it was. Once more the schul was filled with shrouded men, and the lane outside with women in silk and satin, and the poor in worn but neatly pressed cotton.

"He asked me to marry him!" Dvorah said. "He left schul early yesterday and talked with my mother, and she gave her permission, and last night after dinner he came and asked me. He said the New Year seemed like a good time to plan the future."

"What did you tell him?"

"What did I tell him? Are you crazy? I told him yes, of course."

"That's wonderful." Guttle hugged her friend. "You look like a a bride already, all dressed in white. So you're going to marry Izzy!"

"Not Izzy, silly! You can be terrible sometimes, Guttle Schnapper."

"I know. I'm sorry." She hugged Dvorah again, longer this time, and kissed her cheek. "I'm so happy for you."

She didn't want to compete with her friend's enthusiasm, but her own news was no secret; the Schlicters must have slept through the music. "Me, too," she said.

"Meyer? Last night?" They hugged yet again, both jumping up and down now while holding each other around the waist. "Dvorah Berkov and Guttle Rothschild! Let's do it! Let's have a double wedding."

"That would be fun. We're getting married in August."

"August? August is already passed."

"Next August."

"That's almost a year. Why wait so long?"

"My father said."

Dvorah frowned. She took off her brimmed hat, toyed with two white ribbons that hung from it. "Lev and I talked about November."

"That's all right," Guttle said. "Why have one celebration when we can have two?"

"You sure you won't mind?"

"There's an old saying. Never get in the path of a runaway horse."

"You mix me up sometimes. So it's all right with you if we get married first?"

"Of course it is." She reached out and touched Dvorah's hanging curls. "The only thing I'll soon miss is your hair. Maybe you'll pass it on to your daughters."

Dvorah pulled her hat on tight. "I'm not," she said.

"You're not going to shave your head?"

"I don't have to. I asked Rabbi Simcha last week. He said if I want to I can shave it and wear a wig, like our mothers do. But I can also just keep it covered in public, tucked under a big hat. As long as nothing shows."

"What does Lev say?"

"He loves my hair. The Talmud says you should shave your head so other men won't look at you. Lev said he trusts me. If other men look at me, I won't look back."

"Of course you won't."

From inside the synagogue they heard the wail of the shofar, the ram's horn. Again, again. Guttle loved this trumpeting that heralded the New Year. The doors of the temple swung open so the women and children could hear. The shofar blasted louder, in repeated bursts, short and long, seven short and one long, again, again. Till with one sustained wail that must have brought the trumpeter to his knees the service was over. The men filed out in their shrouds, their women came to meet them, "Yom tov." Milling about in the lane, families greeted one another, "Yom tov, Yom tov," till they drifted toward their homes, where their afternoon meals waited. Collaring Meyer, Emmie Schnapper said, "After you take off your shroud, bubbelah, why don't you come and eat with us?"

Guttle turned to say goodbye to Dvorah, but her friend had hurried off to greet the good Doctor. A few metres away, Guttle saw Sophie Marcus, dressed in black, glaring at her.

Meyer the following day showed his new assistant the brief letter he had received from Crown Prince Wilhelm: "We, Wilhelm, by the Grace of God Landgrave and Crown Prince of Hesse, Grand Duke of Fulda, Duke at Hersfeld, Count of Katzenelbogen, Dietz, Ziegelheim, Schaumburg & reigning Count of Hanau, etc etc etc Most Graciously bestow the title of Court Factor upon the Jew Meyer Amschel Rothschild of Frankfurt."

Guttle gave him back the letter. "He has a lot of titles for one person."

"I think I hear a joke coming."

"No joke. I can't think of one."

Meyer placed the letter in the single drawer of his desk. "My years in Hanover finally are paying off."

"What do you mean? You never told me much about them."

"When I was sent away from here, when I was thirteen, I was apprenticed to the Oppenheimer banking firm, in Hanover. The Oppenheimers had started out in the Judengasse. During the next hundred years, they branched out across the Ashkenaz, including Hanover. I stayed there five years. That's where I learned about finance. They had an antique coin department, where I learned about the coins."

"Did you like it there?"

"It was good. We weren't locked in a ghetto. No school boys taunted us in the street. It was near Göttingen. Much freer in their views than here."

"Why did you come back?"

"My visitor permit was about to expire. To stay, I would have had to become a permanent resident. And my brothers were here. But it was more than that. Frankfurt was becoming the big commercial center. I knew this would be the place to make money. Despite the walls and the gates."

"And now you'll be rich."

"Not yet. Wilhelm's letter just confirms that I do business with him. It's mostly an honorary title. To make money, I'll have to keep after him to get more of his business."

"But you're going to let people know?"

"Yussel is making a sign with the new title. I'll hang it on the door."

"Will people be jealous?"

"I don't think so. I'm the only coin dealer in the lane."

They were standing beside his desk. She moved closer to him, snuggled into his chest, as she loved to do. "I'm glad," she said.

"About the title?"

"Glad that you came back." She lifted his hand and kissed his knuckles. "But what you said about your brothers and the money, those aren't the only reasons you came back."

"They're not?"

"You knew that I was here, growing up for you."

He wrapped his arms around her, lifted her till she was sitting on the edge of the desk. "You may be right. If I wasn't aware of it, Adonai was."

Despite his lean body his lips were full. As he pressed them to hers she reveled in the exquisite tenderness, till, leaning back as he leaned forward, she nestled amid the papers on the desk. He kissed and nibbled at her lips and she at his until their backs ached as much as their loins and he stood and slowly pulled her upright, and stepped away lest they lose control utterly.

"August," he groaned, gripping a shelf of antique Geek and Roman figurines.

Though she could hardly speak with her breath pummeling her breasts, she echoed, "August."

The idea came to her after he said he'd be putting a sign on the door. Few would see it, because of the Hinterpfann's location in the rear row, down the alley from the lane. But if she made a banner for him they could hang it from a pole above the alley, and anyone looking for him would know where to go. When she had composed herself and straightened her clothing and fixed her braids she left him there and walked two houses away to Hannah Schlicter's, to buy the cloth. Red and yellow would be nice, she thought: a yellow flag, with his name and his new title in red.

She found Dvorah sweeping the cobbles in front of the tenement. They were expecting an important visitor, she said, the Countess Freya von Brunwald. She was the Gentile lady who'd bought three of her mother's dresses at the Fair. She was coming to order more.

As they chatted while Dvorah swept, a door clattered in the first house by the gate and Hersch Liebmann burst out and ran down the lane. They watched as just before the lane curved out of sight he disappeared into the hospital. Doctor Kirsch came out and walked swiftly in their direction. Behind her came Hersch and two male helpers holding a carrying board — a rectangle of wood padded with blankets. The Doctor scarcely noticed them as she hurried into the Liebmann house. Dvorah handed her broom to Guttle. "I'd better see if they need help."

Guttle stared at the Liebmanns' door, waiting to see who would come out, till she noticed a woman, a tanned, blonde stranger, standing inside the north gate, looking lost. Still glancing at the Liebmann house she leaned the broom against the tenement and approached the visitor.

"Are you the countess?" she asked.

The woman wore a simple gray dress and cap and would have been pretty if her face were not smudged with travel dust. Blonde ringlets peeped out of her cap. Her striking green eyes seemed to sparkle and burn at once. She wiped her sleeve across her forehead. "Do I look like a countess?"

Guttle was embarrassed, did not know how to respond. Either answer would be wrong.

"No matter, girl, perhaps you can help me just the same. My name is Brendel Isaacs. My late husband was a blacksmith. I've come from Mainz to see his grave. I've been told it's here."

"Yes, in the cemetery. Down at the south end."

"Thank you." She took a step in that direction.

"I'd better go with you. The Beckers are hard to find."

"The Beckers?"

"That's who he's buried with."

"Don't want to interrupt your sweeping. Your mistress will be angry. I know what that's like."

"I have no mistress," Guttle said, and led her down the lane. They crossed the sewage trench near the rag dealer's. Guttle thought she should introduce the widow to Ephraim Hess, who was outside his shop; Ephraim, everyone knew, had led the retrieval of… No, that would not be a good idea. Instead she merely waved to him as they passed.

Heavy footsteps sounded behind them. They moved out of the way as Doctor Kirsch led the two helpers by, with Dvorah following. Secured on the carrying board was Leo Liebmann, his eyes closed, his face white and glistening with sweat.

"What happened?" Guttle asked Dvorah.

"Some kind of seizure. She's not sure yet."

She was interrupted by Doctor Kirsch. "Come on, Dvorah, I'll need your help."

"Where's Doctor Berkov?" Guttle asked.

"In town, buying supplies."

"This is a busy place," Brendel Isaacs said as they resumed their walk toward the cemetery.

Guttle did not know what to talk about with the young widow. "Do you have children?"

"Two little ones."

They were silent till they entered the cemetery.

"I see what you mean," the widow said. "It's very big."

Guttle led her along the narrow gravel paths till they found the grave. Among the carved stones, a wooden marker said: "Rafe Isaacs. Blacksmith, Mainz. 1769. Yahweh Shall Make Him Whole."

The widow stood looking at the grave. Her knees buckled, and she collapsed to the pebbled earth. Guttle helped her up, helped her to a seat on one of the soapstone Beckers.

"I'm sorry for your loss," Guttle said.

"Don't be sorry for me. It was his own fault, the stupid fool."

"Excuse me?" Guttle knelt beside her to hear better.

"I know, I shouldn't be harsh with him. He was doing it for the children, they soon would've had nothing to eat. I told him I'd rather sell my body than let him risk his life." She twisted her torso as if to show it off. "I could have done it, my body is still good, despite the babes. I thought he was going to slap me. He almost did. He told me not to talk like that. Business would get better, he said; meanwhile, he was the man of the family, he would provide the food. 'One little robbery,' he said. He was certain he wouldn't be caught."

"You mean he was guilty?"

"Of course he was guilty. Who'd he pick to rob? A man whose horse he shod once. Stupid fool. They arrested him the next day. Fat lot that did to feed the babes. What did feed them was a purse from a man who lives here. Never did catch his name."

"What was he like, this man?"

"Now him I would give my body to. To say thanks. Maybe I'll find him, maybe he'll take on me and the babes. Tall and slim. He looked a gentle sort."

The tombstones began to whirl around Guttle. She grabbed the nearest Becker, closed her eyes. "You're saying the blacksmith from Mainz was guilty?"

"You have a problem with your hearing, dearie? Some man been boxing your ears? I've already said that, haven't I? Just this once, he said. And there he is, under the dirt. Hanged in the public square like a common thief. Maybe worse, I've heard, though I don't want to know."

Guttle saw again all those men storming the gallows, yelling "Innocent! Innocent!" Because her father had recognized him. "For stealing five gulden they didn't have to kill him," she said, "even if he was guilty." She put a hand to her forehead, opened her eyes, as the earth slowed to a stop.

"But there he lies," the widow said, nodding toward the grave. "Or so they tell me." She pulled a handkerchief from her sleeve and wiped the soot off her face. She took Guttle's hand. "Forgive me, young lady. I've come all the way from Mainz to say a prayer for him. To thank whoever it was that gave him a good Jewish burial. And listen to me, angry as a shrew. Perhaps you could thank the proper persons for me, who bought a coffin and buried my Rafe in his time of need. He was a good man, mostly. He only did it for the babes."

"Where are they now?"

"I've got an aunt watching 'em. I'll be taking the afternoon coach back. Unless I decide to go to the town square and earn some money. Don't look shocked, girl. I wouldn't be the first."

"But you're Jewish."

"Haven't heard that goyim are averse to Jewish twat."

Guttle pressed her hand over the widow's mouth. "Please don't talk like that."

"Who am I upsetting? These dead 'uns? These Beckers? Don't tell me you're a virgin — a girl with a shape like yours, and a pretty face to boot?"

"Of course not. I mean, yes. I'm betrothed."

"Make sure he can feed your babes without losing his head."

"You're very bitter."

"You've noticed that? In my place you might be bitter too, don't you think? But now, I might as well say a prayer for his soul. I've come this far."

Rising from the stone, she stood at the foot of her husband's grave. She pulled a small prayer book from the pocket of her skirt and opened it, and read the prayer for the dead:

Yisgadel v'yisgadosh sh'may rabo…

Guttle stood with head bowed, feeling feverish. There was something about this brash young widow, just a few years older than herself, that was making her heart melt.

When the prayer was done, Guttle led the woman out of the cemetery and up the lane. Ahead she could see the cabinet maker in front of his shop. Guttle greeted Yussel, and introduced him to Brendel Isaacs.

"You ladies look a bit peaked," Yussel said. "I've just made tea, would you like some?"

"I can't," Guttle replied, "Meyer will think I disappeared."

"Tea would be very nice," Brendel Isaacs said.

Guttle hurried on to Meyer's office. She found him bent over his desk with quill and paper, making lists of coins, with their descriptions. "Meyer, I'm sorry, I should be doing that. But you know what I just found out? You know the blacksmith from Mainz?"

"Of course."

"He was guilty! He was guilty after all."

"I know."

She was disappointed at his languid reaction. She saw again the men charging the gallows, shouting the man's innocence. Recalled her concern that Meyer was not joining in.

"The widow told you?"

Meyer continued writing as he spoke. "I knew before that. I knew at his trial."

"How did you know?"

"When we were leaving the courtroom, I saw the victim approaching the witness box. I recognized him, he's a man I've done business with. An honest man, who would not lie under oath. If the blacksmith were innocent, they would have needed to pay a perjurer."

"You never said anything."

"What was there to say, in the midst of all that emotion? To condemn him? The court already had done that."

"Even if he was guilty, for stealing five gulden they didn't have to hang him," Guttle said. "He had a wife, and children."

"You're right, they didn't. They were making him an example." Meyer set down his quill, turned his chair to face her. "It was cruel. But legally, they had the right. Robbery is a serious crime."

"I suppose." She drew in her breath, let it out slowly, knew she should not say what she was about to say; that only bad could come of it. "Did you get into bed with her?"

"With who?"

"The pretty widow. We weren't betrothed then, so it would have been all right. I just want to know."

Instantly she regretted asking, as she knew she would. For months she had worried that her father might choose someone other than Meyer. Now, betrothed not two days, she was questioning his faithfulness. Hidden in her heart, she feared, was a cruel beast.

"Where did you get an idea like that?"

"She's here. She's very... open. She said she had those thoughts about you."

"You're blaming me for someone else's thoughts? Don't be so strict, Guttle. Even Yahweh isn't that strict."

She stared at him in confusion. Ashamed and angry, she pulled the door open and fled down the alley. She cursed herself for being so jealous. She cursed Meyer for not really answering.

A t the north gate, a courier on horseback, come from the Frankfurt Council with a message six months in the crafting — or six months forgotten — asked the guard where he might find the Chairman of the Judengasse Council. The position rotated on a yearly basis, and was currently held by Wolf Schnapper, but having no knowledge of such things, and no reason to, the guard suggested that the courier inquire at the synagogue half way down the lane.

The courier never had been in the Judengasse. The stench from the ditch was assaulting his nose, a light drizzle was wetting his shirt. This was a place to get into and out of as quickly as possible. He dug his spurs into the flanks of the large black stallion he was riding, just as Guttle was bursting out of the Hinterpfann alley. The stallion was at half gallop as she ran out into the lane, her mind aflame with jealousy, her eyes clouded by the unexpected drizzle, by blurred flashes of color. She heard a horse's hooves clattering much too fast, turned, saw a mammoth horse and rider rushing at her, almost upon her. She threw herself to the ground just as the rider saw her and tried to stop his horse. Responding to the yank on the reins the galloping beast swerved to the right and lost its grip on the slick cobbles. Its front hoof caught the sloping edge of the ditch. A rear hoof, flailing out as the horse spun earthward, lashed the falling girl in the temple.

The stallion plummeted heavily onto its side into the trench of mud and slime. The courier, thrown across the ditch, landed hard beside his leather pouch. Guttle lay unconscious on the cobbles, eyes closed, a thin trickle of blood leaking from her temple into her hair.

21

The rag dealer saw it happen. Ephraim and Eva were moving their merchandise inside to keep it dry when he heard the clatter of hooves clopping too fast and looked in that direction just as the girl ran out from the alley and went down under the horse, the horse plummeting into the ditch, the rider flying across it and landing hard on the cobbles. He told Eva to run for a Doctor while he hurried to see who it was. When he recognized the Schnapper girl he knelt beside her. Her eyes were closed, her body limp.

From his third floor window Hiram Liebmann watched. He thought of running down to help but did not know what he could do. He and his brother had not been friendly with Meyer Rothschild since Hersch had quit his job, but it was hard not to like the girl. From many shops, merchants were running out to see. In his notebook he drew the horse, the rider, the girl, the children in the lane.

"Guttle!" Dvorah said, running up from the hospital with Doctor Kirsch, kneeling beside her friend.

"Don't move her," the Doctor said, and began gently to squeeze Guttle's fingers, her wrists, her ankles, to push back her hair and examine the wound that the horse's hoof had cut. Across the lane Doctor Berkov came rushing up and was kneeling beside the courier, who had raised himself to a sitting position on the cobbles. In the ditch the horse was writhing, trying to stand but unable to, whinnying and slapping his head from side to side in pain. From the north gate a guard came walking down, musket in hand. From the bakery a muffled shriek erupted, followed by Emmie Schnapper scurrying as fast as her stout body and short varicose legs would move. As she approached and her eyes confirmed what mouths had said she screamed, "Guttle!" In his shop in the Hinterpfann, in the back row with the door closed, Meyer Amschel writing on his papers the value of each coin was oblivious to the frenzy till Emmie Schnapper's scream pierced his consciousness like an arrow in his chest. Guttle! He dropped his quill, splattering ink on his lists, and ran down the alley, pushed his way through a cluster of spectators and knelt beside Doctor Kirsch, over the limp body of his betrothed.

"I don't think anything's broken," the Doctor said. "But she appears concussed." And to Dvorah, "Get her to a bed and remove her clothes. Gently as you can."

Dvorah and a Doctor's helper who'd brought a carrying board lifted Guttle carefully. Doctor Berkov, approaching, asked how she was. "I want to get her inside to look closer," Doctor Kirsch said. "It was an angled blow, the cut is superficial. I don't see any damage to the skull. But she might have injured her spine when she hit the cobbles. There could be paralysis."

Meyer listened, watched, barely able to move. Not since the year his parents died had he felt so helpless.

Yussel Kahn approached the group, the widow from Mainz at his side. They had just finished their tea when they heard the commotion. Doctor Kirsch stood and walked beside Guttle's supine figure as Dvorah and the male helper carried the board. Meyer, feeling faint, walked on the other side with Frau Schnapper, who was trying to stifle her sobs but not succeeding.

Half in and half out of the ditch, its right foreleg broken, the stallion flailed on its side. The guard pointed his musket in the air and fired, startling the onlookers; it was a call for help. Teachers and students in the yeshiva and the heders paused at the sound of the shot; the teachers followed their pupils into the lane to see what was happening. Isidor Kracauer, carrying one of his notebooks, hurried up alongside the chief Rabbi, who was wearing his high black hat. Seeing someone clearly of authority, the mud-stained courier, his hip and arm bruised but otherwise unharmed, handed the Rabbi his pouch. "From the Frankfurt Council," he said. "To the Judengasse Council." Rabbi Eleazar took the pouch, but said nothing.

The Constable was watching the flailing horse. "I have to shoot it to stop its pain," he said. From inches away he pointed his musket between the horse's pleading eyes.

"Wait!" the Chief Rabbi called out, an instant before the musket fired.

The horse's head erupted with blood and fell to the side of the ditch. The legs shuddered and became still. With the back resting at an angle on the slope, the belly and two legs disappeared under the muck.

"Did you want something, Rabbi?" the Constable asked.

"What I didn't want was a dead horse in my ditch."

"I had no choice."

"You could have tried to lead him out of the ditch, then shoot him."

"He'd be dead, either way. They'll come and pull him out with a wagon."

Flies already were landing on the horse, with no swishing tail to slap them away. The flow of the ditch was backing up behind it. The Chief Rabbi looked around. "Schul-Klopper," he called.

Izzy hurried to him.

"Knock on every door between here and the gate. Tell them not to dump any slops till after the horse is removed. Or else, to carry it below."

She was placed in a bed on the second floor, the women's ward. Dvorah pulled a curtain around her, began to unbutton her dress. Meyer paced anxiously outside the curtain. With Guttle naked and still unconscious, Doctor Kirsch examined her closely before covering her with a sheet and blanket. To the dried blood on her temple he applied a wet compress, another to her forehead.

She dreamed of devils, Rabbis, golden hyenas, mermaids who could dance. Barely awake, she tried to think what the strange dream meant. Her head hurt. Trying to understand the dream was making it hurt worse. She was no Joseph, and should not try to be. Dreams were random nonsense, mostly. Or Yahweh being childish, playing with imaginary toys. Or, if there were strange creatures in them, reviewing unworkable ideas He'd had before He was satisfied. When she slept again the nightmare came. A large black bird landed on the cobbles, beside the body of the Schul-Klopper. The dead man woke, raised his hammer, turned to her. The face was not that of Herr Gruen but of Hersch Liebmann. Sneering, with evil eyes, he came toward her, the hammer raised as if he would smash her face. She backed against the wall of the Owl. There was no place to run. She screamed, but could make no sound. Then, at the last instant a man's hand came down and stayed Hersch's arm. He was riding a white horse. She could not see who it was.

Fighting up from her nightmare as if from underwater, Guttle realized that the Schul-Klopper had been dead for six months. Only rarely did the name of Solomon Gruen arise in the lane any more. But not a day passed when Guttle did not, closing her eyes, see his black-clad body sprawled on the cobbles, his heavy hammer clasped in his hand. And wonder why, if someone had been attacking him — forcing him to drink rat poison, if that was truly the case — why had he not struck at them with his hammer? He was 59 years old, but he was strong.

She had never raised this question with anyone, not even Meyer. She was just a girl. The Chief Rabbi had not brought in the Frankfurt police to investigate — his friend was dead, nothing would bring him back, why make trouble for everyone in the lane? And in the lane itself, except for the Doctor's finding of poison, no one admitted knowing anything.

Breathing hard from the nightmare scare, Guttle murmured something unintelligible, and opened her eyes. Doctor Kirsch smiled. Dvorah clapped her hands, once, before remembering where she was. "Was that her?" Meyer asked, and pushed in through the opening in the curtain. When he saw that Guttle's eyes were open, her pupils moving about, he said, "Thank you, Adonai," and he knelt and caressed her arm. Guttle looked at him, trying to comprehend. Frau Schnapper, stepping through the curtains, pressed the back of her hand to her mouth.

"The white horse is gone," Guttle whispered.

Meyer looked anxiously at the Doctor. "The horse is black."

"I know." She peered closely into Guttle's eyes, holding up the lids, first one, then the other. "I think we should let her rest," she said.

The horse in the ditch mesmerized the lane. Children and adults alike stood around it as if waiting for it to levitate, though the weight of a thousand flies might have prevented that. "A shame, such a good-looking animal," Sophie Marcus said to Bea Metzenbaum. The courier and the Constable stood off to the side as they waited for help. Yussel Kahn took the arm of the widow from Mainz and led her out through the unattended gate, and walked with her to Jewelers Street, from which the afternoon coach to Mainz would be leaving. As she prepared to climb onto the coach, she thanked him for his hospitality. "If you're ever in Mainz, come visit. I brew a nice pot of tea."

"I'll consider that," Yussel said.

He could not help noticing the shapely curve of her stockinged calf as she climbed onto the coach. As the stage drew away, pulled by two brown horses, Brendel Isaacs looked out the side and waved.

Walking back alone, Yussel thought of Guttle — felled by the horse, but, he was confident, not badly hurt; Yahweh would not be that cruel, three days after her betrothal. Yussel had conquered his infatuation with her months before, and was pleased she would marry Meyer. He thought of Dvorah. That fantasy had not lasted long; he was mildly amused that Lev Berkov had taken her on; they seemed such opposites, scientific mind meeting voluptuous body; he wondered how long before there would be trouble. And he thought of Rebecca Kirsch. Since the new Doctor arrived, Yussel had been more content than at any time since before Lainie's death. Quickly they had discovered common interests. He exulted in news of the outside world — in science, in medicine, in philosophy. Rebecca had brought such news from the university; she loaned him journals from her collection; new ones kept arriving by post. Several evenings each week, both being alone, they shared a simple supper and discussed these unforeseen new turns that human knowledge was taking. She clearly had no interest in a physical relationship; seeing this, Yussel discarded, before they could rise, any such inclinations he might have had; what she gave him was equally stimulating. The world was on the brink of startling changes, and Rebecca seemed the only one in the lane who knew it. This was a slight exaggeration, he conceded; Lev Berkov kept up with medical advances, Meyer Amschel with trade and finance; a few others no doubt did the same; but Rebecca, much like himself, wanted to know everything.

Passing through the gate, Yussel found his old uneasiness returning. Brendel Isaacs was pretty, brash and enticing. She had made her interest clear. He could picture himself riding to Mainz once or twice each week for a sportive romp in the straw, while still spending other evenings discoursing with Doctor Kirsch. Some men would have found such twin blessings a kind of perfection. But depression was settling over the cabinet maker. Already, he had cast himself in a moral predicament. Such a tempting arrangement, he felt, would be a betrayal — but he was not sure of whom, or of what. Of Rebecca? Of the widow? Of his long-dead wife? Of the poor dead blacksmith lying in pieces among the Beckers? Or would it be something else — a betrayal of the centuries-old Jewish suspicion of excessive happiness? He ought to go to one of the Rabbis to discuss his dilemma, he told himself. He knew he would not. Instead, he would do what he always did. He would ruminate.

While Guttle slept, Meyer walked down the hospital stairs, stumbling as the ground floor came up to meet his legs unexpectedly, the phrase "she might be paralyzed" blocking all sense of time and space. Doctor Berkov and Frau Liebmann were emerging from a room at the far end. Out of remembered courtesy, he asked how Leo was doing.

"Not good," Yetta said. "My Leo can't move his arm, his leg. He talks meshuganah. 'Rabbits… money… rabbits… money.' That's all the words that come out, over and over. Then he's exhausted again."

"I'm sorry."

She might be paralyzed.

"Frau Liebmann has an interesting theory," the Doctor said.

"When Leo was a boy, he had a bed of straw in back of his house, where he raised rabbits. He'd sell them outside the gate, and give the money to his Mama and Papa. That's all I can think."

"Let's hope Leo recovers quickly," Meyer said. "Then he can tell you."

"From your lips to Gott's ear," Yetta said.

Unable to go home, needing to be near her, Meyer went back up the stairs to Guttle's bedside. She still was asleep. He sat in the wooden chair, gazing at her tender face, her down-curved lips at rest, the patch on her temple in his desperate view serving to highlight the perfection of the whole. Lowering his head into his hands, elbows on his knees, he closed his eyes. She will not be paralyzed! His tormented mind drifted from thought to prayer to promise to benediction; even when lucid he could not have said what it was:

Dear Yahweh, You permitted me to cry after the burial of the Schul-Klopper, to cry for the first time at the graves of my mother and my father. I do not know why my tears fell then, but those tears and sobs like eons of saltwater waves seemed to wash away a wall around my heart. No sooner was there a breach unto that wall, a wall made, I suspect, of the heavy stones of a child's anger, a child's abandonment, then You did let her, or cause her, or invite her, to rush into the temple, rush into the enclave of men, to hug her friend, and I saw in the tender face of this girl, this not yet molded woman, in that sweet innocent face, both terror and defiance. In that one instant she breached the broken wall and entered my heart. There, I soon learned, she belongs, as a Torah belongs in its embroidered covering, as the last piece of a puzzle completes the whole. Thank You Adonai for this gift, but please now let her be well. I shall always look after her, well or ill. I shall always obey Your commandments, be she well or ill. But let her be well and they shall be as a sacred covenant to me, as sacred as Your covenants with Abraham, with Moses. Have mercy, Elohim, Almighty God of Israel…

As the words drifted in his mind like a rudderless boat, he crossed the border into choppy sleep. He was startled awake when she said his name. He lifted his head too quickly, for a moment the floor dropped. He did not know how long he had slept in the chair. She was sitting up in the bed, holding the sheet under her neck, reaching out to him with her other arm. He rose from the chair and sat on the bed and slipped within her offered arm and enfolded her with his. Their cheeks pressed together. "I love you," he whispered, unable to find his voice. "With all my soul."

Her other arm went around him. The sheet she had been holding slid to her waist. Their close embrace found heat.

Clarity returned to him then, the rudderless boat finding shore. "You're sitting up!"

As he pulled away to look at her she lifted the fallen sheet. "Is that bad?"

"Move your legs. Raise your legs."

"Meyer, this is a hospital."

"Bitte, do as I say."

She wriggled her legs, raised her knees under the sheet.

"Danks Gott!"

"Meyer, what is it?"

"The Doctor thought you might be paralyzed."

They embraced fiercely. "That would have been terrible for you," Guttle said.

They remained that way, holding each other like lovers long parted, until Meyer said, "I ought to tell the Doctor." He kissed her nose. "I'll send Rebecca up. Then I should run home, straighten up a mess I left in the office. Maybe eat something. I'll be back in awhile."

"Don't run too fast," Guttle said. "Like some people."

As he left the hospital, his eyes watery with relief, he almost bumped into Sophie Marcus, who was standing idly outside, as she seemed to do much of the time of late, in one awkward place or another. "Yahweh took revenge for the Cantor," Frau Marcus said. "Is she dead?"

The horse was still in the ditch. Boys were throwing pebbles at it, or small clumps of mud, to watch the covering of flies rise into the air like devil's lace before descending again onto the horse. The Constable was growing impatient, help had not arrived. He walked outside the gate, so as not to frighten anyone. The sky had cleared, the sun was shining here. He discharged his musket into the air again. A flare of noise seeking aid.

As the shot was fired, a black carriage with a gold coat of arms on the doors was rounding into the square outside the gate, pulled by a prancing bay mare. Spooked by the musket shot, the mare reared; the driver had to struggle to steady her. When no shots followed, he tapped lightly with the reins and walked the bay across the square and through the gate, into the narrow lane, where the carriage just barely fit between the tenements and the trench. He pulled the mare to a stop outside the third house on the left; she reared again, whinnying. The driver leaped from his seat to the cobbles, patted her neck and fed her a carrot from his pocket to settle her. Four elegantly dressed people lowered themselves carefully from the coach on the tenement side — two women of middle age, two young men of about twenty years.

"Josef, what's upsetting Brunhilde?" Countess Freya von Brunwald asked. She had a long face with a sharp nose and a sharp chin, and was dressed in dark blue. The driver pointed ten metres ahead, to the stallion in the ditch. "Over there, missus."

"Oh, my, what is that?" the countess asked.

"Looks like a dead horse, half covered with turds," her son, Paul, replied.

The other woman, who had a round, fleshy face beneath a large straw hat, frowned. "It must be one of those Jewish rituals," she said. She pulled a beige handkerchief from the sleeve of her beige dress and held it to her nose.

The door to the tenement opened. Hannah Schlicter, the dressmaker, having heard the carriage pull up, anxiously stepped out to welcome them .

"This is my friend, Catharina Goethe," the countess told her. "This is her son, Wolf. And my son, Paul. The boys will explore the Judengasse while Frau Goethe and I examine your fabrics."

As Hannah led the women up the stairs to her shop, the young men looked about. Paul was dressed in brown, Wolf in a blue jacket over yellow breeches, and a yellow vest.

"Josef, my good fellow, you've got yourself into a fix," Paul said to the driver. "You'll never turn the carriage around in this space. Not with that ditch in the middle."

"Happily, lad, I inquired first. There's an exit gate at the other end."

The young men, both wearing the powdered wigs forbidden to Jews, mused about the dead stallion, wondered how it had gotten there. They became aware of the foul stench, the impossibly narrow houses, the incessant movement in the lane as men and women fingered used clothing at a rag dealer's table or bargained with pawn brokers or carried warm-smelling bread to their homes. The clean-shaven faces of the visitors, their fine city clothing, the powder on their wigs, their superior yet uneasy manner, identified them clearly as strangers — perhaps customers — and each shopkeeper nodded to his goods as the visitors passed.

Outside the stone synagogue, the young men stopped and admired its architecture, its soaring lines. "This place is awful, with the stench and the crowding," the fellow called Wolf said. "But I suppose it's admirable that they endure all this for the sake of their beliefs. And they do look human."

Paul said, "And this temple of theirs — it's not as tall, but it rises in an arc as fine as St. Bartholomew's."

A man dressed in black, wearing a black hat, emerged from the synagogue. He would have been good looking except for small pock marks that marred his face and a pink scar crossing his temple. The man nodded pleasantly to them, said "Shalom," and continued on his way.

"Prick them and they do bleed," Goethe murmured.

Gazing about, taking in every detail with his poet's eye, he saw a small hospital across the street, a bath house, a shoemaker's shop, several pawn brokers. Their carriage had rolled across the city in brilliant sunlight but here all was cloaked in a suffocating gray, as if a huge shroud had been strung from roof to roof.

"This," Goethe said, "is the physical embodiment of the Twenty-third Psalm."

"The valley of the shadow of death?"

"You can feel the rot in your bones."

"And yet, they live," Paul said. "But you're right. Look at their beards, their hats, their shining eyes. They seem to dwell mostly in the house of their Lord."

Reaching the south end, they looked down at the busy docks, at the boats in the river, sails flashing in the sun of a different world. A young Constable did not challenge them as they stepped beyond the gate. "Tell me, my good man," Paul said to the guard, "do you know why the Jews are kept under lock and key?"

"It's not my doing, sir."

"I understand that. But why, do you suppose?"

"I'm told they don't think like the rest of us."

"Who is it that tells you to guard this gate?"

"My Kapitän, sir."

"And who tells him?"

"The Polizei Kommandant."

"And he is told by?"

"I believe that would be the Frankfurt Council, sir."

"And the council listens to … ?"

"The Empress Maria Teresa. The city belongs, of course, to the Holy Roman Empire."

"Can anyone tell the Empress what to do?"

"There's only the Pope can do that."

"So. Do you think the same the way the Pope does?"

"Jesus, no! I'm a churchgoing Lutheran, myself."

"Yet here you are, outside the gate."

"Yet here I am."

"And doing a fine job of it."

"Thank you, sir."

"We can't allow those wrongful Jewish thoughts to get out and pollute the river, can we?"

"Actually, sir, if you follow your nose, the river already is… Oh, I see, you're having a bit of sport with me."

"Just a bit."

The visitors withdrew inside the gate, crossed the cobbles to the cemetery, and began to walk back. "You sounded sympathetic to the Jews," Goethe said.

Paul replied, "Just a bit."

As they passed the communal bath, and neared the hospital, they saw three young women walking a few paces up and a few paces back. They were struck by the image — one had red hair, one brown, one black. "I'll give them this," Wolf said. "Their girls are very pretty."

"Shall we speak with them?" Paul asked.

"Why not? You're in fine form today."

Coming closer, they saw that the girls — or women — on either side were partially supporting the one in the middle, who was wearing a robe over a hospital gown. The women moved aside as the men approached.

"Good afternoon," Paul said, pleasantly. "Shalom."

"I can't help noticing your plaster," Wolf said to the one in the middle. "I hope you weren't riding that poor horse back there."

She smiled wanly, but did not reply.

"She wasn't riding it, she stopped it with her head," the red-haired girl said.

The men raised their eyebrows. "I'd like to have seen that," Paul offered. "Is that a special talent of Jewish girls?"

"Guttle will be teaching the rest of us."

Guttle smiled weakly again.

"Excuse me, we did not introduce ourselves. I am Paul von Brunwald. This is my friend, Wolf Goethe. Our dear mothers have business with a dressmaker here, so we rode along."

"Your mother is the Countess?"

"That is she."

"My mother, that is she. The dressmaker, I mean. I am Dvorah Schlicter. This is Guttle Schnapper, and this is Doctor Kirsch."

"I hope you're not badly hurt," Wolf said.

"She just needs rest, and some fresh air."

The men inhaled the stench. Paul thought: perhaps we could take them out walking in a park…

"A female Doctor," Wolf said. "And Jewish. You cannot attend to Christians, I assume."

"That is the law."

"Yet one Jewish Doctor at all times is permitted to live outside the Judengasse. Do you know why? It's because the nobles and the Princes prefer a Jewish Doctor."

"Your words, not mine," Rebecca said.

Guttle raised her hand to her head.

"It still hurts?"

Guttle nodded, closing her eyes with weariness. She wondered how these Christian dandies with their powdered wigs had gotten into her white horse dream.

"We'd better get you back to bed. You still need rest."

"It was good to meet you gentlemen," Dvorah said. "I hope your mothers are pleased with their new dresses."

Paul reached into the pocket of his vest. "My card," he said, handing it to Dvorah. "If I can ever be of service."

The women displayed small smiles and turned to go. When they were inside, the young men walked on. "Who would have thought it?" Paul said. "The Three Graces live in the Judengasse."

For a moment Wolf felt dizzy, as if the tenements that seemed to lean together at their height were about to fall in on him. How could people exist like this? He found the half-light at mid-afternoon maddening. "Angels dwelling in hell," he murmured.

"You have to admit," Paul said, "that this place is filled with your kind of girl."

"What kind of girl is that?"

"Unavailable."

"You know how it is with me, my friend. I laugh at my own heart   and do what it wishes. But it wasn't me who just left a calling card."

They reached the fly-ridden horse. A Polizei Kapitäin was beside the Constable; he appeared to be giving instructions to another officer. The men paused to watch, to see if the officers would try to pull it out.

"Have you noticed something?" Goethe asked. "There is not one bit of nature in this place. Nothing natural at all. Not a tree. Not a flower. Not a blade of grass. You can barely see the sky. Look at that horse. A handsome stallion, the apex of nature. He should be galloping across green meadows in the dewy dawn, as he was born to do, and mounting lusty mares. Instead they rode him in here, and he's dead in a ditch of shit. A symbol, perhaps, of the absence of nature in the Jews."

Paul knew enough to keep his mouth shut when his friend took off on a flight of philosophy.

"Imagine, a state of total divorce from the natural world," Wolf went on. "How does one survive that? Unless… "

Paul waited. "Unless what?"

"Unless faith in the Creator is the internal equivalent of nature. Belief as a fertile field."

"Meaning this is a Garden of Eden?" Paul looked about him, sniffing at the air.

"Hardly. But what if the mind is a garden? What if the brain is not a machine in the service of reason, as the French philosophers would have it. Perhaps, in the believing mind, the Garden of Eden still resides. And blossoms with art, with literature."

"Why just in the believing mind?"

Goethe nodded appreciatively. "Good question. One I will have to think about."

"To my mind, that redhead Dvorah is built for more than inner faith. I could show her some lovely country gardens."

"There you go, bringing the discourse down to earthy essentials."

"I don't have poetry to warm my bed."

The dead horse apparently was going nowhere. The officers remained idle, waiting.

"I've heard of a race of horses," Wolf said, "who, when they're injured, bite into a vein, so they can breathe more freely — and thus gain eternal freedom. Much more noble than a musket ball between the eyes."

"Not every horse can be noble," Paul replied. "It's a lot to expect."

Wolf saw his mother waiting near the carriage up ahead, and hurried to her. Her handkerchief once more covered her nose. "Are we late? Where's the countess, Mother?"

"Up the stairs, paying a deposit."

"And you? Didn't you order a dress?"

"The seamstress is good," Frau Goethe said. "Her clothes are quite beautiful. But put a dress on my body that a Jewess has touched so intimately?" She closed her eyes, and shuddered. "I couldn't do that."

"Then why did you come?"

"To keep the Countess company, of course. In case of trouble."

"Trouble?"

His mother roamed her eyes over the entire Judengasse, and said, "You know."

The Chief Rabbi came to see Guttle after obtaining permission from Doctor Kirsch. When he stepped through the curtain she was startled at first by a bulky shape in black coming at her out of the white. Standing beside her bed, he expressed his concern. He inquired how the collision with the horse had occurred.

"Yahweh was punishing me. I was having bad thoughts."

"That's not correct Talmud, Guttle. Yahweh may punish us for our deeds, but not for our thoughts. He knows we cannot control our thoughts.

He made us that way. In fact, what happened to you could be looked at very differently. It could be that He was protecting you, not punishing you."

"By sending a horse to kick me in the head?"

"Galloping horses we don't see in the lane very often." The Rabbi eased himself onto the wooden chair beside the bed. "You were running in a reckless state, I gather. You might have tripped on a cobble and fell face first into the filth of the ditch. You might have broken your leg, much as the horse did. Perhaps Yahweh sent an angel in the form of a horse to protect you."

"An angel in the form of a horse?"

"In the form of an angel it would have caused a lot of talk." The Rabbi stroked his beard by way of grinning.

His words were comforting. She promised the Rabbi she would think about that.

She was propped up in bed, leaning on pillows, when Doctor Kirsch returned. She said her head felt better, and asked if the Doctor could stay. The Doctor sat on the edge of the bed, and waited.

"Why do people feel jealous?" Guttle asked.

Surprised, the Doctor took time to think. "I suppose it's a fear, emerging from deep inside us, that someone else will get what we want. Or take away what we have."

"If you're wondering why I'm asking, I got hurt because I was jealous."

"Perhaps you were punishing yourself. We have a bad conscience, and an accident happens. Perhaps we make it happen."

"It was stupid of me to be jealous of Meyer Amschel. Don't you think?"

"That's for you to decide, Guttle. Why were you jealous?"

"The widow from Mainz told me she likes him. She's very... appealing."

"Do you really think she could take Meyer from you? Meyer likes the way you look, the way you think, the way you make your jokes. Otherwise you wouldn't be betrothed."

Guttle looked down at the blanket covering her legs. "But what if..." She flushed, and could not complete the sentence.

"Oh, that's what you're concerned about — what if the widow is... appealing... at things you have never done."

"Meyer is twenty-six, he must have done those things. That alone makes me nervous."

"You should hope he has. A teacher has to learn his subject before he can teach it. I'm sure Meyer will be a good teacher."

"But the widow... ?"

"If you trust Meyer in other things, you need to trust him in this as well. Meyer travels a lot on business, does he not? There are lots of widows out there. Either you'll trust Meyer, or you'll make your life miserable."

Guttle leaned forward, pressed her forehead against the Doctor's shoulder, felt soothed by its warmth, its solidity.

"Perhaps because of the absence of sunlight," the Doctor said, "many people in the lane seem to burn with an inner fire. You do, Meyer does, Yussel Kahn, Ephraim Hess — lots of others. Don't waste your inner fire on things unworthy."

The Doctor caressed her cheek. Guttle closed her eyes. Sleepily, she lay her head on the pillow.

Her father had been away at the court of Sachsen-Meiningen. When he returned and learned what had happened he rushed to the hospital, and hugged Guttle tightly, almost desperately. He looked at the patch on her temple. "Mein Gott, you could have been killed!"

"I know, Papa. That's why I have to ask you something. I don't want to die without being married."

"Of course not. So?"

"So you should let Meyer and me get married right away."

"In case another horse comes galloping before August?"

"You never know what can happen."

"On the contrary, I do know what can happen. You can marry on the twenty-ninth of August, as planned. Not a day before."

"Oh, Papa!"

"I know you're not feeling well, but don't 'Oh, Papa' me. For one thing, I have to go see the Chief Rabbi, something about the message that courier brought. Then I'll come back. But first I have to ask you something. Some heder boys saw me passing just now. They didn't whisper, 'That's the Court Jew,' as they sometimes do. Do you know what they said?"

She waited.

"They said, 'That's the Papa of the girl who stopped the horse.'"

Guttle covered her face with her hands.

"Wait, there's more. Some of them applauded, and shouted, 'Hurrah, his daughter saved the children.'"

Uncomprehending, Guttle looked at him. "What are they talking about?"

"You're asking me? I'm the one who's asking you."

22

Rabbi Eleazar was seated at his desk, wearing a yarmulke instead of his tall round fur hat, when Wolf Schnapper knocked on the door and was told to enter. Rabbi Simcha sat in an upholstered armchair. Both appeared grim, as if another friend had died. Simcha asked how Guttle was recuperating, then the Chief Rabbi handed Schnapper a letter on yellow parchment. "From the Frankfurt Council," the Rabbi said. "By the courier your blessed daughter knocked off his horse. One would think she knew what he was carrying."

Wolf's insides churned beneath his waistcoat. The Frankfurt Council rarely if ever sent good news. He pulled his spectacles from an inner pocket, put them on and read the letter. His right hand fell to his side, limp. Lifting the parchment, he scanned it again, reading parts aloud, as if the others had not parsed it several times.

"Your request that we permit Jews to walk in the parks and promenades without hindrance is denied ... The request for equality is one more proof of the boundless arrogance of this nation which makes every effort at every opportunity to advance itself... If we granted the request, Christian women walking on the promenade might be harassed by hordes of Jews."

Simcha muttered, "Such boundless arrogance. The nerve of us."

Wolf handed back the letter. "Six months it took them to come up with that?"

"Apparently it was a difficult decision," Simcha said dryly.

"Now we have a difficult decision," the Chief Rabbi said. "Since you are Chairman of the council at present, you should be part of it. The question is, how to tell this to the congregation. Or whether to tell them at all."

"The request last spring was secret," Wolf said. "But there have been rumors."

"Everyone knows the courier was from the Frankfurt Council," Rabbi Simcha said. "People will want to know what it was about."

The Chief Rabbi stroked his beard, his stubby fingers idly combing errant hairs. "We'll have to let it be known. The question is, how? Should we summon a public meeting?"

"That would raise expectancy — and create serious disappointment," Wolf said. "Perhaps a lot of anger."

"Or I could announce it at morning services."

"It's not really a spiritual matter," Rabbi Simcha said.

The Chief Rabbi raised his eyebrows at this fine distinction, though he knew that was Simcha's way.

"You could fasten the letter to the door of the schul," Wolf said. "Everyone will read it soon enough. The disappointment will not be great, since no one expected more."

"Like Luther nailing his protests," Simcha said.

Rabbi Eleazar raised his eyebrows again. "That might be the simplest. I'll have the shammus do the nailing tomorrow, instead of me." He glanced wryly at Simcha. "So it won't look too spiritual."

Guttle spent the night in the hospital at the insistence of Doctor Kirsch, who wanted to be certain no delayed problems surfaced. When, the next morning, Guttle said she felt fine, the Doctor asked Dvorah to accompany her home.

As they walked slowly up the lane, they saw a knot of people gathered. The dead stallion still lay in the ditch, still covered with flies. Two city workers, stepping into the muck wearing high boots, were fastening belts and chains around the corpse. A strange predicament for an angel, Guttle thought. A heavy wagon pulled by four dray horses had been driven to the gate, but was too wide to fit into the lane on either side of the ditch.

As the friends reached the group of onlookers, people recognized them and opened a path. "It's the girl who stopped the horse!" someone said, and the others began to clap.

Guttle's face flushed. Her temple began to throb under her patch. She leaned toward Dvorah. "Why are they doing that?"

"I don't know."

Other people came to see what the applause was about. Word skirted among them like a weasel. "It's the girl who stopped the horse!"

Guttle saw Avra and her friends beside the ditch a bit further along. She pulled her sister aside. "What's the clapping about?"

"It's for you, silly."

"Why?"

"Because you saved those children."

"What children?"

"The little ones playing in the lane. You ran out and stopped that galloping horse with your head. If you hadn't, the children might have been killed."

"You saw me do that?"

"I didn't, but other people did. Izzy told me. The whole lane knows."

"I didn't do anything."

"Don't get modest now, Guttle, not when I'm finally proud to be your sister."

"I don't believe this!"

"Neither did I. But you've got a patch on your head to prove it."

Guttle walked back to Dvorah. "There's been a mistake. They think I saved some children by stopping the horse."

"Maybe you did."

"I didn't see any children."

"That doesn't mean they weren't there. Did you look down the lane?"

"Of course not. I heard the hoof beats, I turned toward the horse."

"There you are."

"But I wasn't trying to stop the horse. I was trying to avoid being trampled."

Meyer Amschel had come up beside them and was listening, smiling, grateful to see her on her feet. "Perhaps it's as you told me at the Fair," he said. "What's good for Guttle is good for the world."

She didn't smile. "I have to explain to them."

Meyer put a finger on her lips. "The Judengasse has few enough heroes. Why take a new one away? Besides, you may have saved some children, whether you intended to or not. Their mothers, I'm sure, don't care what was in your mind."

"Hold me," Guttle said.

He wrapped his arms around her. "By the way," he said, his lips almost touching her ear. "The answer to your question, which you ran from me too quickly to hear, is no. I didn't get into bed with her."

Who first read the document on the door after Izzy nailed it up is lost to history. Some say it was Sophie Marcus, but that is only legend. One man, then another, then as word spread small groups of other men, pressed close to read the Frankfurt Council's words excoriating them for seeking equality. They muttered and cursed, and in a rare lapse of equanimity about this continuing insult — this imprisonment — of three centuries, strode up the lane in the direction of the two police officers who had come to assess the horse problem, the two city workers, and the lifeless beast. Some of the men were shouting epithets against the Frankfurt Council. People stepped out of shops and looked out windows to see what was happening. Some added their presence to what was becoming a small protest. As they neared his rag shop, Ephraim Hess heard what they were shouting, heard what was posted at the synagogue. His face grew warm, his blood grew hot. He joined the line of men directly at the front, as was his way, holding a large green apple into which he had just bitten. As the men neared the Constables, the Kapitän, his muscles tensing, let his hand rest on the handle of the pistol in his belt. The junior officer fingered his musket. A man beside Ephraim bent and picked up a handful of mud and rolled it into a ball. Others did the same. Seeing what was happening in front of their shop, Eva ran to Ephraim and demanded that he come back inside. When he refused she tried to take the apple. Gently but firmly he pushed her away.

Shouts against the Frankfurt Council grew louder. The front line of men was ten metres from the officers and the horse. Ephraim sensed that a climax was approaching. Something had to happen now or all this pent-up fury would drain away, and the men would feel impotent. Not knowing if he was being a hero or a fool, and not caring, he stepped further in front of the others, reared his arm back in a clear indication that he was about to throw the apple. The Kapitän pulled his long-barreled pistol from his waistband, held it level in front of him with an outstretched arm, the barrel pointed directly at the rag dealer. Children who had been watching the horse, as if for signs of life, held their breath. The entire north end of the Judengasse seemed to hold its breath.

"No, no, no!" Eva cried out, but as she ran towards him Ephraim did what he had intended all along. He fired the green apple at the horse.

The apple smacked into the horse's flank, making a soft thud. It did not bounce off but remained imbedded in the muck with which the horse was covered. The captain lowered his pistol, held it at his side. The men beside Ephraim read the policeman's message: it was okay to assault the horse. Those who had made balls of mud hurled them at the dead animal. Some hit and stuck, others splattered on impact, a few missed altogether. From a third floor window an onion came hurtling down and made a direct hit on the stallion's back. Little boys picked up bits of mud and threw them as best they could at the beast. More food hurtled down from kitchen windows on both sides of the lane — a potato, a small green cabbage, another onion. Some hit the horse and stuck, others landed in the muck beside it. Children ran into their houses and came out with grapes to throw. The captain replaced his pistol under his coat. The two officers tried to hide smiles as the dead beast blossomed, under a rain of epithets, into a ripe vegetable garden.

The men whom a minute earlier had been an incipient mob began to point and laugh at their handiwork, and cheered the women at the windows. Draping arms over one another's shoulders, they sauntered back down the lane to their places of business, the decision of the Frankfurt Council defused, if not forgotten. "After all," they told one another, "what's new? From those swine, who could have expected more?"

Watching from in front of the Pfann, Meyer Amschel mused on Yahweh's curious ways. Where would the anger have been directed, and with what result, if the Council's horse had not been in the ditch?

Rebecca Kirsch had been busy in the hospital all morning. She was distressed to hear that the dead horse remained in the lane. "Who knows what's breeding in its sores?" she said to Dvorah. She hurried to where the two city workers were standing with hands on their hips. The policemen had left after the protesters dispersed.

"Why aren't you pulling out the horse?" the Doctor asked.

"The wagon won't fit in here. We need more men. We'll come back tomorrow."

The Doctor looked around for a face she recognized, and approached Avra. "Please go to the yeshiva. Tell them we need six strong boys to move the horse."

Avra ran off. Noting the stallion's new vegetable appointments, the Doctor rolled her eyes. She kneeled beside the blasted head, could see several kinds of vermin crawling in the dried blood, the broken eyes. With one of Leeuwenhoek's microscopes, she thought, she would see a lot more. All these animalcules, as the Dutchman had called them, swimming inside the horse, inside ourselves. Each a thousand times smaller than the eye of a louse, he'd written. God alone knew what they were for. And He wasn't telling.

As Rebecca shooed away three small children who had edged up close to look, Avra came running back, breathless, alone.

"Where are the boys?"

"Rabbi Jonah said no."

"He said no? How could he say no?"

"He said learning the Talmud is more important than dead horses."

The Doctor turned away, furious, trying not to spew out the phrases that came to mind. She could not go confront the director of the yeshiva; she was too new here. She glanced at the spectators; they were mostly children now. Pointing to one stout woman, she said, "You, come help me. Please. We can't wait till tomorrow."

"The bakery has lots of women," Avra reminded her. The girl had taken over Guttle's weekly job, the winnowing and boiling of the beetles.

"Go see if they can spare four strong women without ruining the bread."

Glad to be useful, Avra hurried off. She returned followed by her mother and Frau Metzenbaum and two other sturdy women. When they saw the beast, Frau Metzenbaum said, "Too bad a horse isn't kosher. There's everything we need for a stew."

"In your kitchen, not mine," Emmie Schnapper replied.

Pointing at the chains already affixed to the horse, Doctor Kirsch turned to the city workers. "You two grab the first links, in the ditch. You've got boots. We'll help you."

She lined up the women behind the two men, grabbing part of one chain herself. Avra saw that the lines were unbalanced, and took hold of the other chain.

"All right, prepare yourselves," the Doctor said. "Now, everyone, pull!"

At first they could not budge the horse. When it did inch forward, it slipped back deeper into the sewage as the women relaxed their muscles.

"We can do better!" Rebecca called out. "It's to prevent your children from becoming ill. Take a deep breath. Now, pull!"

The two men and the six women, straining, pulled together. The horse began to inch up out of the ditch. "Keep pulling!" Rebecca yelled, as the chain pressed into the bones of her slim fingers, as she felt her shoulders wanting to tear. "Brace yourselves with your legs!" she shouted, and they did. The horse, its skin oiled by greasy kitchen wastes, began gliding out more easily. "We've got it, keep pulling," she yelled, and little by little they inched the horse up out of the ditch and onto the cobbles.

Breathing hard, the women dropped the chains and blew into their hands. They wanted to lick the bruised spots but saw rust from the chains on their palms and fingers and wiped them on their skirts instead. "And thank you, too," Rebecca said to the city workers, not quite sarcastically.

"We're not done yet, missus," one of them said. "We have to get it to the wagon."

Rebecca looked to the north gate, and beyond, to where the wagon stood, the four dray horses growing uneasy as they smelled their dead stable mate. The distance was at least forty metres. It wasn't fair to ask these women to do that, Rebecca thought; her own hands wouldn't do her patients much good for a day or two, even now. But the screeching sounds of the chains scraping the cobbles, then the sight of the women hauling the turd-dripping horse, had summoned some of the nearby men. The rag dealer came, the cabinet maker, Meyer Rothschild, several others. Weary, with no breath left with which to speak, Rebecca pointed to the wagon. Eight men grabbed hold of the chains and bent their backs under them, and pulled the resisting horse along the cobbles, where it left a long smear of yellow-brown muck, out of the lane to the rear of the large wagon, onto a flat metal slab. The city workers took over from there.

Most of the men rarely did physical labor, and as they strolled back on the far side of the ditch, joking, they were proud of their accomplishment. They also felt good for having come to the aid of the women — whose burden now would be to clean the slimy cobbles.

After she had slept and bathed and changed her clothing, Guttle went to Hannah Schlicter's sewing room, and chose the red and yellow fabrics for Meyer's flag; she did not buy the cloth from his brothers because she wanted the banner to be a surprise. Frau Schlicter refused to charge her; she said the cloth was a betrothal gift. Guttle had been ordered by Doctor Kirsch to rest. While she did, she cut and sewed the banner.

The following morning, Yussel Kahn brought over the sign he had made proclaiming Meyer a court agent. With pride, Meyer nailed it to his door while Yussel and Guttle watched. When he was through inspecting it, Guttle unveiled her surprise: the same words in red on the yellow banner, on both sides:

Meyer Amschel Rothschild
Court Agent

In red in the center was the crown Prince's coat of arms.

Meyer held the banner like a treasure. "It's beautiful."

"It's to hang in the lane, above the alley. So people will know where to find you."

Yussel went to his shop and brought back his thickest wooden dowel. He and Meyer affixed the dowel to the wall above the alley, perpendicular to the tenement. When they hung the yellow banner from it, the flag was visible from the north gate to the point near the hospital where the lane curved. As they worked, first children, then some adults gathered to see what they were doing. When the adults could read the letters on the flag they began to cheer and applaud. Others heard, and came out from their shops, and looked, and joined in.

"I didn't know I was so popular," Meyer said.

Someone called out, "It's the girl who stopped the horse!" The cheering grew louder.

The hanging of the banner turned out to be a major event in the lane — not so much that day but in the days and weeks that followed. For years there had been only a few faded banners, so familiar as to be hardly noticed. Now Hannah Schlicter, seeing how cheerful Meyer's flag looked, and filled with confidence, because the Countess von Brunwald had ordered three expensive dresses, made a banner for herself, a simple one: *H. Schlicter, Dressmaker*. She chose white letters on dark green, so as not to compete with Meyer's flag, and she hung it from her second-floor window. Yussel thought such a banner might help his business, and paid Hannah to sew one for him, in blue and gold: *Yussel Kahn, Fine Wood Work*. Not to be outdone, Otto Kracauer told Ida to make one for the boys, in red on beige: O. *Kracauer & Sons, Feather Merchants*. Day after day, new banners appeared up and down the lane, hanging from the second story or the third or the fourth, over money-lenders, second hand clothing shops, junk shops, jewelers, wig makers, cake shops, tailors, dressmakers. Like a garden in spring, the Judengasse bloomed from a somber gray-brown into a multicolored festival.

When she was fully recovered from the horse's kick, and with Meyer taking the coach to Worms to look at coins and antiques, Guttle decided it was time to view her new job as his assistant more seriously. She'd asked for instruction from her father about books and ledgers; now she looked for Meyer's ledgers to make sure they were in order. She couldn't find them anywhere in the office. He might keep them up in his bedroom, she thought, but she didn't feel she should look up there. Instead, she opened the wooden money chest, on the floor against the wall, to do an accounting. The chest was three-quarters filled with small pouches. Some were made of leather, others of canvas or plain cotton. Each was heavy with coins and bills. On the outside of each were small ink notations of the amount of money in the pouch, followed by letters and numbers she did not understand. She guessed they were Meyer's symbols for who had paid the money, and what for. Also in the chest were a scattering of loose coins. They either had spilled from pouches that had opened, she figured, or were small payments Meyer had not bothered to wrap.

Adding up the money listed on the pouches, and noting the amounts on a sheet of paper, took much of the morning. When she realized the pouches might not contain what the notations said, she started again, opening each pouch to count the contents herself. All the notations turned out to be correct.

She was slumping over the desk wearily when Meyer returned in late afternoon, carrying a small Greek figurine — a fine Aphrodite, he said — and a sack of coins and medals. He kissed her hair. "What have you been doing?"

"Counting the money." She raised her head and shoulders from the desk. "I couldn't find your ledger."

"Probably because I don't have one."

"How can you do business without a ledger?"

"I keep it in my head. Looking at columns of numbers makes my brain hurt."

Guttle's eyes came into sharper focus. "Look at you! You bought a wig."

He took off his hat so she could see it better. The hair in the gray wig swept back over his ears and was knotted elegantly in the back. "I thought a court agent should look more proper. Do you like it?"

"It's wonderful. It's so distinguished."

"Exactly the image I was looking for. To insure confidence. I won't wear it in the lane, of course."

She stood to examine his new hair. Eyes sparkling, she said, "Now I have two men to kiss. I hope neither will be angry." She pressed her lips to his. Slowly lifting off his wig, and setting it carefully on the desk, she kissed him again.

"I like this game," Meyer said. "Which man is the better kisser? I think perhaps you need more samples."

Guttle laughed merrily, but turned away. "I think perhaps we should get back to business. You need to have a ledger. I know how to set it up."

"Then it will be both of my pleasures to allow you."

"Do you know how much money you have in the chest?"

"I can tell you exactly. Three thousand four hundred gulden and fifty-six kreuzer."

"That's close. Three thousand *three* hundred gulden and fifty-six kreuzer." She showed him the list she had compiled.

"I'm afraid you've made a slight mistake." From his waistcoat pocket he extricated a sheet of paper that had been folded and refolded so many times it was near to falling apart. He unfolded it carefully and handed it to her. On the sheet were several columns of numbers, each number with a line through it. Only the bottom number of the last column was not crossed out. "You see," Meyer said. "I'm right."

Guttle became upset. "I didn't ask you what number you had written on a piece of paper. I asked you how much money is in the chest. There's a hundred fewer gulden in the chest."

"Not possible. I'll tell you what. We'll count it again. Together."

"Meyer Amschel, I've spent all day counting it. Not once, but twice. You're welcome to count the money as many times as you like. It's almost time for supper, I hope you won't mind if I go and rest my eyes."

"I'm sorry, I didn't mean to doubt your work. If you counted it twice, you must be correct." He lifted her from the chair and hugged her, and kissed her cheek. She felt limp, and too weary to kiss him back. "You go rest, have a good supper," he said. "Give my regards to your family. I'll see you here in the morning."

Guttle walked slowly down the alley. Meyer watched her go. When she had disappeared from view, he knelt beside the wooden chest, and with a slight sense of guilt and a stronger sense of foreboding, he began to count the money.

A s Guttle approached the Owl, Izzy emerged from the adjacent house, curved hammer in hand. It was time for the Schul-Klopper to summon worshippers to evening service. She gave him a quick hug, as she always did these days upon encountering him; she knew he needed repeated assurances that, despite her betrothal, they still were best friends.

"I need to ask you something," she said. "When I got kicked by the horse, did you really see children in the lane?"

"I didn't, but Hiram did. From his window. He showed me the drawing in his book. The black horse charging, you throwing yourself in front of it, three little ones a few metres down the lane. Hiram's book is the truth, he draws only what he sees." A breeze curled up the lane from the river, raising dust, setting the new flags to flapping. "This horse episode is like a story from the Torah, which needs interpretation."

"A dead horse in the ditch — is that a heavenly sign? Do we all need to fast or something?"

"The real question is, if you didn't know children were in danger, why throw yourself in front of the horse? If the story were in Genesis, what would the Rabbis make of it?"

"Izzy … "

"I know! Perhaps an angel saved the children. Angels are incorporeal, they have no bodies. Perhaps a passing angel saw the children in danger, and invaded your body to stop the horse."

"That's very funny."

"Why?"

"The Chief Rabbi thinks the horse was an angel."

"See! We need a conclave of Rabbis. To get a Talmudic interpretation."

She reached up and smoothed an errant lock of his always errant hair. "Iz, this Torah project is warping your brain. You need to be a boy again."

He ignored her words. "What if both deductions are correct? An angel in a horse, and an angel in a girl, crashing together! What would the ancient Rabbis make of that?"

She saw movement over his shoulder, a figure in a black coat. "Here comes Hiram with his hammer. You'd better go do your Schul-Klopping. Some other time I'll tell you why I got kicked by the horse. When we're very old."

Hiram approached and stood beside Izzy. When the boy continued talking, his deaf assistant clenched a fistful of his shirt at the shoulder and pulled him away, toward the first house on their rounds.

Upstairs, resting on her bed, closing her eyes, Guttle tried to envision the moments before she and the horse collided. She remembers running through the alley, in a fury at Meyer. With her mind's eye now she sees small flashes of color far to the left. She hears again the onrushing hooves. Could those flashes of color have been children? Could she in fact have divined a terrible accident coming, and rushed out to stop the horse before it ran down and possibly killed the little ones? Could the image of the children have been jarred from her head by the horse's kick? Is that why she does not remember them? Perhaps in fact she had been trying to save them. Perhaps in fact she is deserving of applause. Could she tell this to people?

The notion caused her to squirm, induced sweat beneath her arms, between her thighs. To do so would appear as if she were belatedly seeking praise. They had already applauded her.

The rolling thoughts were making her head hurt. She doubted she had the courage to do such a thing. What if this new vision is a false memory, playing tricks? She did not know the truth of her actions. Perhaps there are often times when we don't.

Meyer tossed the last pouch of money into the chest and slumped in his chair. Guttle had been correct; he knew that would be the case, since she'd counted twice. But his figure was also correct, and the implications were grave. A hundred gulden was missing — and therefore stolen.

One possible thief came readily to mind. Hersch Liebmann. He'd had plenty of access, especially when they were at the Fair; he'd been angry at Meyer; he had quit his job right after.

Meyer realized he was still wearing his coat, his vest. He took them off and hung them properly, and felt his stomach rumble; he had not eaten since breakfast, he hadn't taken time to seek a kosher lunch in Worms. Now it was night and he felt not hunger but nausea. The notion of Hersch as a thief was eating his insides. To make such an accusation would be a serious affair. But a hundred missing gulden could not be ignored.

He went up the stairs and stretched out on his bed in his clothing — and sat up abruptly. If Hersch had taken this money, he might well have stolen from the synagogue when he worked there! What was it the stricken Leo Liebmann had been murmuring? Something about money. Money and rabbits. Meyer felt cold sweat form on his forehead.

There was little room upstairs to pace. Knowing he would not sleep, Meyer lit a candle in a lantern and carried it down to the lane. The night was dark, the lamps in most apartments had been extinguished for the night. The temperature had dropped sharply during the past few hours, the first hint of winter was in the air, but he did not go back for a coat. Lighting his way with the lantern, he walked slowly south, as far as the synagogue, crossed the ditch to the hospital, where lamps glowed faintly inside. Was Lev Berkov there? Perhaps he should go in and speak with him.

He decided not to. He began to walk back. Unwelcome new connections were splicing in his brain. If… then…

The ultimate thought was hardly tolerable.

Up ahead his love was asleep in her third-floor bed. He recalled his first time, in Hanover, when he was sixteen. A widowed dressmaker across from the bank had taken a liking to him, shy though he was, and had shown him once and then repeatedly the pleasures of the night. When he left Hanover two years later he had learned to enjoy more things than coins. But here in the lane such pleasures, unless you were married, were frowned upon; one learned to abstain. Until the desire in the loins became too severe, began to interfere with study, with work, with sleep, and then you either sought relief by yourself, and felt guilty afterward, or went to the whore-strewn streets near the town square and found unsatisfactory pleasure in the daylight of a ragged hotel. By setting the marriage age for men at twenty-five, the Frankfurt

Council seemed to think that Jews did not have urges. More likely, they didn't care.

"Meyer! Is that you? What are you doing out so late?"

The words were Guttle's, half whispered, half spoken, from her window above. "I can't sleep either. Wait, I'm coming down."

She emerged from the Owl a few moments later, tying a burgundy robe over her ivory sleeping gown. Her feet were bare, she realized when they touched the cold cobbles.

"You'll get a chill," Meyer said.

"I'm fine. There's money missing, that's why you're pacing so late."

They began to walk, slowly, Meyer holding the lantern that swung its pale light over the cobbles like a pendulum. "There's one likely thief," he said.

"I know. That's why I couldn't sleep. It would be a terrible thing to accuse him, Meyer Amschel. My mother is close with Yetta, helps with her marketing. Izzy dotes on Hiram. And with poor Leo in the hospital... "

"If he took the money, how can I not accuse him?"

"You don't know for sure."

"If the money is where I think it is, we'll know very soon."

"Hersch Liebmann a thief? It makes me want to cry."

"It's worse than that, Guttle."

"How can it be worse?"

Meyer pondered whether to tell her. He needed to confide in someone. Who better than his betrothed?

"He may also be a murderer."

"Meyer, what are you saying!"

"When the Schul-Klopper was killed, money was found missing from the schul. The Council kept that secret. If Solomon Gruen had caught Hersch stealing... then Hersch stood to lose everything."

"I don't believe that! Do you have proof? The punishment for murder is death. The Torah says so."

"I know."

Frightened, she threw her arms around him for comfort. He held her close. Their chests pressed together, he sensed a softness to her that he had not known before. Under her robe, her gown, were no stays, no corset. The blood began to stir his every organ. He withdrew his hand from her back, placed his palm against her breast. He thought he might swoon at the pliancy, at her nipple straining to meet him in the cold. She gasped. She did not remove his hand. Till feeling him growing against her thigh she pulled away. Both were breathing rapidly.

"I can't absorb this. You're wrong. I have to go back."

She dispelled a moment of tension between them by placing her bare feet on the tops of his shoes, her arms around his neck. Saying, "Walk me to the door."

They were not far from the Owl. He walked her there that playful way. Hersch Liebmann forgotten for the moment, she kissed him lightly on the lips, and went inside.

Meyer remained in the lane till his breath and his heartbeat slowed. August the twenty-ninth was still ten months away — her father's sadistic revenge for his extracting so large a dowry.

23

For two days Meyer debated within himself. Except for Guttle, he did not want to influence anyone's fate but his own. Since he was twelve years old, since his parents died, he'd been determined to create his own destiny, no matter how much work it took, no matter how much patience. Hersch Liebmann's future was not his concern. But if Hersch were indeed a thief — or worse — must this not be brought to the attention of the people?

He himself would not be robbed again. For the first time, though he did not like doing so, he had begun to lock the door to his office. Soon he would buy a strongbox for his coins, with a padlock of its own. If a thief were allowed to roam free, everyone in the lane would have to begin locking their doors, hiding their treasures. An oasis of morality, as he used to view the lane, would become a prison of suspicion. He could confront Hersch privately and demand the return of his money. But if he brought no charges, he would leave his unknowing friends and neighbors as Hersch's future victims.

He tested an idea on Guttle as she sat working at his desk. "The moral delinquency of stealing from your employer, of stealing from your synagogue, is betrayal. The basis of all civilization is trust. Precisely because the Gentile world cannot be trusted, we must retain our trust in one another within the walls."

She said nothing. He did not expect a response, just ears to listen.

"And that just refers to the stealing. What about the murder of Solomon Gruen? I don't want to be responsible for the taking of another man's life. That should be left to Elohim. But if Hersch murdered the Schul-Klopper, as logic suggests, how can I remain silent?"

"I don't know what you should do," Guttle said. "How could we face the Liebmanns if you brought such charges? The tension in the lane would be terrible."

"That's true. But our faith is based on the law. And the law is based on justice."

Over and over these thoughts twisted in his brain. Guttle worked quietly, preparing a set of ledgers for his business, not interrupting him as he pretended to study coins, climbed the stairs to his bedroom, prowled down again, up again. Until he came rushing down the stairs, waving a book, and said, "Look at this!"

"What is it?"

"In the Talmud. Look. The punishment for murder is death, we know that. But there's an exception. The exception is if there were no eyewitnesses to the murder. Then the punishment is not death, it's incarceration for life."

"No one saw the Schul-Klopper killed!"

"Exactly. Lev Berkov asked all the neighbors back then. No one saw. Not even Hiram from his window, if he's telling the truth. So Hersch would not be on trial for his life."

"But, incarceration? We have no jail. Where would he be kept?"

"I don't know. I suppose the council would have to decide. To build a small jail, maybe near the cemetery. Or perhaps to pay for a cell and his bread and water in the Frankfurt jail. That's what the Talmud specifies. A diet of bread and water."

"That's awful."

"Not so awful as killing another man. Not so awful as being hanged."

The discovery resolved Meyer's doubts. He would take at least the first step. "Is your father at home?"

"I think he is. Why my father?"

"As presiding Chairman of the council, he's the one who can authorize a search by the fire captain. To look for the missing gulden where I think they're hidden — in the mattress of Leo Liebmann's bed."

"Why do you think it's there?"

"First the synagogue's gulden, now mine — money breeding like rabbits. In the straw."

"You'll have to explain that," Guttle said.

In the early years of the century, parts of the Judengasse had been destroyed three different times by fire. Since then, in the absence of a constabulary, the captain of the fire brigade had become the supreme civil authority, reporting directly to the council. But never before in his ten years as captain, Joshua Lamb mused as he climbed the stairs, had he been called upon to search an apartment for other than fire violations, such as a woodstove installed too close to a wall. He hoped he would find nothing today — but his job would be validated if he found what he'd been told to seek.

"What's this?" Yetta Liebmann asked as the fire captain handed her a sheet of paper.

"Authorization from the council Chairman to search your husband's bed."

"To search my husband's bed? You won't find my husband in it."

"I'm not looking for Leo, Missus. I just need to look in his mattress. If you'll excuse me, is that the bedroom through there?"

"Bed bugs you're looking for? Lice? I didn't know they started fires. Keeping things clean, I do the best I can."

A door opened and Hersch and Hiram emerged from their room. "What's going on, " Hersch asked.

"This is the fire captain. He wants to search your father's bed for bugs."

"Not for bugs. Now, if you'll just let me look."

He stepped toward the open door of the bedroom. Hersch moved in front of him, blocking his way. "I think you should leave," Hersch said.

His mother handed him the paper the fire captain had brought. "Let him look," she said. "Only straw he'll find in the mattress. We're a poor family, Herr Fire Captain, we can't afford feathers."

Hersch continued blocking the way. "Are you planning to fight me?" the captain asked. "You have muscles, but I have training. I'd hurt you for sure. In front of your mother. She doesn't need that."

Hersch looked at the captain's determined face, his trim form, and at his mother. He was not afraid, he had suspected that some day they might come. It was as if a part of him wanted them to come — a desire he did not understand. Through his mind flashed the times when as a little boy he'd run away from heder and hidden in the cemetery; it had been cold among the stones, he had wanted to be found — that much he understood. "You're just doing it for attention," his mother used to tell him — but he did not recall, afterwards, getting more attention.

He stepped aside and let the captain pass. It would be stupid to want to get caught now, he thought. He had plans. But now only Yahweh could save him.

Frau Liebmann followed Joshua Lamb, a black yarmulke atop his ginger hair, into the bedroom. He approached the bed, where the sheet and blanket were folded neatly on top. Circling the bed, he examined the gray cotton mattress cover. On the first two sides he checked he saw nothing amiss. On the side nearest the wall, he found a hole in the cloth. It was the size of a fist. He knelt beside it, inserted his hand through the hole, felt around in the straw.

"Moths we sometimes have," Frau Liebmann said.

He pulled out a small leather pouch, then another. Standing, he showed them to Frau Liebmann, and clinked the coins within. "Wealthy moths," he said. He crossed to the kitchen, where Hersch and Hiram were waiting, and he showed the pouches to them. "When your father saw them, the knowledge his son was a thief caused a seizure. He's the one who gave you up."

The captain turned to leave with the pouches. Hersch reached for an iron pan, lifted it high, as if to slam it into the back of the captain's head. "Don't!" Frau Liebmann shrieked, just as Hiram grabbed his brother's arm and pulled it down. Hersch had hesitated just an instant. They all knew he would not have struck the blow. The captain's footsteps echoed on the stairs.

"What have you done?" Yetta asked, looking at her sons.

The clang of the heavy pan made their ears ring as Hersch slammed it onto the iron stove.

When the charges were announced, the word marched up and down the lane like the boots of barbarians. The foulest word in the language. Murder! Of Jew against Jew? Not possible! Yet it stuck to the skin like soot.

—Nobody was killed, how can there be murder?

—The Schul-Klopper.

—What, young Izzy? I saw him yesterday.

—No, the real Schul-Klopper. Solomon Gruen.

—A heart attack, they said. Not murder.

—Who said?

—We assumed.

— 'Murder without a witness.'

— How can you charge murder without a witness?

— Meyer Rothschild, the coin dealer at the north end.

—The one whose betrothed stopped the horse?

— Hersch Liebmann worked for him.

—The deaf mute?

—His brother.

—Oy vey, a wild one he used to be. But why murder? For what purpose? A murderer in the lane, it makes my hands shake.

—Probably he's innocent, don't get indigestion. So, did you see where Doctor Berkov got married yesterday?

— I didn't see, I heard. It rained, they had to go inside. Nobody saw.

—The bride looked beautiful, they say.

—Who says?

—Somebody who saw.

—I thought nobody saw.

—So they say. Too bad they spilled red wine on her dress. Right after he broke the glass.

—Who spilled?

—A dancer who fell. It's too bad. A bride should not wear red, it brings trouble.

—I beg to differ. If she had worn red, the wine wouldn't show.

—How could she know?

—Know not to wear red? She knew not to wear red. She wore white.

—It was ivory.

—It was white. I know somebody who knows the mother.

—What has the mother to do with it?

—She made the dress.

—I suppose she saw the murder, too.

— Nobody saw the murder. That's what I'm trying to tell you.

—For what reason would there be a murder?

—To cover up the stealing, they say.

—Somebody saw stealing?

—Nobody saw.

—So what's to cover up?

—Would Rothschild lie?

—But if he didn't see...

The lane was ulcerous with it. The accused walked about freely, they had no place to lock him up, and if he ran before the trial, good riddance. Where could he run to? To Berlin, to Hanover? A long run. He walked like a ghost of flesh, passersby avoiding his eyes. But they were extra pleasant to his brother, to show they held no bad feelings toward the Liebmanns. Guttle wary each day as she crossed from Meyer's office to the Owl. Hersch standing in front of his door, three metres away, glaring at her. Nothing to fear, she'd known him all her life. Frau Liebmann not speaking to her on the way to the hospital. Where Leo Liebmann heard the gossip, if he could hear. No talk of money, rabbits. No speech at all. Comatose, staring at the ceiling.

"The people seem very tense," Doctor Kirsch said to Doctor Berkov.

"They do," Doctor Berkov said to Doctor Kirsch.

Not me, the former Dvorah Schlicter, the new Frau Berkov, said to herself, sighing contentedly from the night before.

November became December. No one was thinking of Hanukah.

—That's him, over there!

—Don't look!

—He used to sweep the schul.

—He used to dig the graves.

—Still does. Look at his thick hands.

—Don't look!

—They could easily strangle someone.

—Poison. It was poison, they say.

The frightening word swirled like dead leaves in the winter wind.

—Poison that can kill?

—If it couldn't kill, how would it be murder?

The notion of one Jew taking another's life — this was too much to comprehend. If only spring would come, and all of this were gone, life would be good again in the Judengasse.

Guttle awoke from her dream just as she fed the ratbane to Frau Marcus. Her heartbeat was too fast, her forehead was cold with sweat. The perspiration spread to her thighs, to under her arms. She shivered as a cold wind rattled the window. Avra's even breathing beside her was the only peace in the room. Unable to sleep, she turned on her side, thinking about the dream, obsessing about it. How could she do such a thing, even in a dream? She became even more agitated when deep into the night she decided what it had meant, the message it had conveyed. She could not lie still. She needed to warn Meyer. At first light she slipped into her robe, and when she heard knocking in the lane she hurried downstairs, ran barefoot across the cobbles, almost ran into Hiram Liebmann, the Schul-Klopper's helper, as he emerged from the alley to the Hinterpfann. Hiram looked at her with eyes both pained and cold. Ignoring him, Guttle hurried past and pounded on the door until Meyer, saying, "I heard you already," opened it, barefoot in his sleep shirt, blinking sleepy eyes.

"I thought you were the Schul-Klopper."

"He was. I mean… Never mind. Let me in."

He stepped aside, closed the door behind her. "What's wrong?"

"I have to tell you a dream I had."

"Now?"

"Yes, now. Hersch Liebmann didn't kill the Schul-Klopper."

"He did."

She felt cold, pulled her robe tighter around her. Seeing this, he said, "I haven't lighted a fire yet. Do you want some tea?"

"No. First sit down and listen."

Meyer shrugged, tried to wipe the sleep from his eyes, pulled the chair from in front of his desk, sat. "So. What did you dream?"

"It was horrible. I dreamed I was feeding poison to Sophie Marcus. I woke up frightened. I couldn't get to sleep again."

"I can see that would be upsetting." He pulled her onto his lap. "But what has that to do with Hersch Liebmann? Was he in the dream?"

"No. Listen to me." She squirmed off his lap, paced about. "I would never poison anyone, of course, so the dream had to be about something else. Then it struck me. Our names have the same first letters. Guttle Schnapper. Solomon Gruen. They're just reversed. Maybe it wasn't me in the dream. Maybe I represented Solomon Gruen. He's the one who was poisoning Frau Marcus."

"But he's dead. She's alive."

"But our first letters were reversed, so the whole dream might be reversed. Like in a mirror. It could be Sophie Marcus who was giving the poison."

"Therefore?"

"That's what really happened. Frau Marcus is the murderer."

"Guttle, you're thinking too much. Twisting things around. You're nervous about the trial. We all are."

"I may be nervous, but I'm not crazy. Sophie Marcus is the crazy one."

"That's true. But Solomon Gruen was her brother. You're saying she poisoned her brother?"

"Remember, at the Fair, when you first told me Herr Gruen had been murdered? Immediately I thought, perhaps Viktor did it, for the money he would inherit. So my father would want me to marry him."

"Guttle, we talked about that. We agreed the Cantor wouldn't do such a thing. Even though he's robust, he's gentle. He has a good heart."

"I know. But we never thought of his mother. Sophie wanted him to marry me, even more than he did, I think. Maybe she even gave him the idea. When I told him I didn't want to, that night in the cemetery, he went home upset. His mother would have asked him the reason. When she found out, she assumed it was because he had no money. That's all the Marcuses think about. She figured that if Viktor already had his uncle's money, my father would say yes."

"But it still was her brother!"

"She's crazy, Meyer. And she hated him."

"How can you say such a thing?"

"She babbled to people. She told Frau Metzenbaum she wanted her son to get married as soon as he became twenty-five, so he wouldn't become a sissy, like his uncle Solomon. Bea Metzenbaum told Mama."

"Herr Gruen a sissy? Just because he never married?"

"Frau Marcus thought the whole Judengasse was gossiping about him. Laughing at her, behind her back. It's one of the things that was making her crazy."

"I never heard anyone say a word against Solomon Gruen. Or question his manliness. Just because he was kind… "

"The truth doesn't matter — it's what Sophie believed. She killed him so Viktor would inherit his money, but also to stop the gossip she imagined. Also for Viktor — so people wouldn't gossip about him, say he was a sissy like his uncle. Maybe she also wanted grandchildren."

"You're making me nervous, Guttle. And cold." Meyer stood and went up to his bedroom. He came down wearing slippers and a dark blue robe. "She lives toward the south end. He couldn't have walked far with the poison in him, Berkov said."

"Maybe she met him at the schul. Or near where he died. A friendly gesture, a glass of hot tea in the morning, with honey. And ratbane."

"Why are you telling me this now? Hersch goes on trial tomorrow."

"That's why I'm telling you. You have to stop the trial."

"I'd be a laughingstock."

"It doesn't matter. It's the right thing to do."

"But there's no evidence against her! Guttle, come up to the kitchen while I light a fire."

She was too upset to sit as she watched him add kindling and two logs and stoke the ashes smoldering in the woodstove. He put a kettle of water on the stove. "Guttle, Hersch Liebmann is the murderer. He stole from me. He stole from the schul. We know that as fact, we have the evidence. That's not a dream."

"That's theft. It's not murder."

"It gave him reason to murder — at least in his eyes. As I explained to you."

"What about my dream?"

"You don't like Frau Marcus, because she harasses you — so in your dream you killed her. It's that simple." He put his arm around her shoulder.

"Maybe that's why we sane ones sometimes do terrible things in dreams. So we don't do them in life."

"You also do terrible things in dreams?"

"Once I ate a pig. A whole pig."

"I don't believe you!"

"Well, most of it. Worse than that, it was some farm girl's pet."

"You'd never eat even a bratwurst."

"In a dream I would. What does that tell us? I have no idea. Except that dreams are even crazier than Sophie Marcus."

"I still think she did it." But her midnight certainty was melting away. She pressed her face into his chest. "You're making me feel like a child."

"Don't feel that way. It's just nerves. Tomorrow it will be over."

"I'm a fool."

"All of us are fools in the dark of night." He kissed the top of her head, inhaled her scent.

"I'd better go home," she said. "People will think I slept here."

"Imagine what Frau Marcus would do with that."

As he closed the door behind her, he heard the water in the kettle boiling. He went up to the kitchen and made his tea, and sat with it at the table. Waiting for it to cool, he looked up at the ceiling. He cracked his knuckles, and said: "Sophie Marcus? It's not possible — is it?"

24

O n the first day of the trial, snow light as pastry sugar sifted into the lane. With white frosting it coated the tops of the walls and the slopes of the ditch and the sills of the tenements. The cobbles became wet but not white as winter boots stirred the snow to slush. Among these were the boots of the twenty-three men of the jury, of the nine council members, of the scores of spectators who wanted to see this astonishing event, their boots turning slush to water as they walked or shuffled or hurried to the lecture hall of the yeshiva, which, except for the synagogue, was the largest room in the lane.

The oak table of the council had been positioned at one end of the hall. A witness chair stood to one side of it, the defendant's chair at the other. Forming two rows in front of the council table were the jurors' seats, and beyond them, two rows of chairs for witnesses. The remainder of the seats, perhaps two hundred, were available to spectators. The chairs had been crafted by the lane's carpenters thirteen years earlier, just before the smallpox came, for an appearance by the Ba'al Shem Tov; since then they'd been stacked high against the walls and arranged in the room only for special occasions.

Most of the jurors selected lived in the south end of the lane, where Hersch Liebmann was not so well known. The fire captain had spent two weeks choosing them after Meyer Amschel officially brought the charges. The number of jurors for a criminal trial was specified in the Talmud; at least thirteen of the twenty-three would have to vote "guilty" for the accused to be convicted.

Meyer felt apprehensive as he took his seat at the council table, to the right of the presiding Chairman, Wolf Schnapper. As he looked out at the witness section he knew that Guttle was even more nervous than he. Life had been a strain for her lately. The day before, he had overheard her talking to her mythical friend Melka of the South Gate, whom she only invoked in the most difficult of times.

"Sometimes I wish you hadn't done this," she had said to him on several occasions. Each time his reply had been much the same. "How can we let murder go unpunished?" Each time, she knew he was right — if he was right.

At the appointed hour, all the seats were filled; standing spectators crowded the rear, their boots staking their places with dark puddles; not even the eldest residents could remember a murder trial. Hiram Liebmann sat in the spectator area, Izzy Kracauer beside him to translate the testimony with his hands. Yetta Liebmann had chosen to remain beside her husband's bed at the hospital.

The Chairman asked Meyer Amschel if he was ready to proceed with the prosecution. Meyer, wearing his best coat and waistcoat, his unpowdered gray wig and a white yarmulke, said he was. Rabbi Eleazar was seated on the other side of the Chairman in his tall black hat. To the consternation of virtually everyone, the Chief Rabbi would be the advocate for the defense. By Talmudic tradition, someone on the council needed to fill that role — a man could not be tried without a defense — and Rabbi Eleazar had volunteered at once, as if he relished — almost as if he demanded — the assignment. No one, certainly not Meyer, knew why. Solomon Gruen had been his friend.

The Rabbi assured Chairman Schnapper that he, too, was ready. Banging his gavel several times, the Chairman called for silence from the gossiping spectators. He asked that Adonai bless the proceedings with justice and truth. Expanding his large chest, his gold watch chain looping across it, his eyes seeking out his daughter in the witness section with a dim foreboding he could not explain, he declared that the trial of Hersch Liebmann, on two charges of grand theft and one charge of murder without a witness, was now underway.

Hersch had been waiting calmly in an anteroom. When the fire captain opened the door and motioned for him to come out, he strode into the hall with his head held high while the spectators murmured. He would not give them the satisfaction of cowering. All his life he had been poor. For two months he had been a leper, shunned as he passed people, their eyes averted from him, their tongues silent. Very well, let them have their show. He could only wait and see what transpired. Deaf to their smug conceits, he would remain as mute as his brother.

He sat indifferent as Rothschild told the jury he would explore the thefts first, and then the murder; as he established by questioning Isidor Kracauer that a hundred gulden had disappeared from the synagogue while

Hersch was working there, and asserted that another hundred had disappeared from his own wooden chest while Hersch was working for him; how the fire captain had found two pouches of money containing a hundred gulden each in Leo Liebmann's mattress; how one of these bore the markings of his own shop.

"He did not even destroy the pouches," Hersch heard Rothschild tell the jury.

His defense advocate, the Chief Rabbi, established under cross examination that the office in the synagogue where the money was kept was never locked, nor the chest in which it was kept. The same for Meyer Rothschild's money. Every person in the lane had easy access to the money, Rabbi Eleazar pointed out. But with the gulden already found in Hersch's house, and exhibited to the jury, his defense seemed desultory.

Meyer Rothschild stood again. Hersch's skin seemed to tighten on him, he became more alert in his chair. Everyone in the hall became more alert. Theft was bad enough, but proof of murder, this all of them — including Hersch Liebmann — wanted to hear.

Meyer drank from a glass of water. He looked about until he had their attention, until not a sound could be heard. His experience speaking after the hanging at the Fair had given him confidence in his unexpected ability as an orator.

"Now we come to murder," he began. "Some of you may wonder why that word alone is not the formal charge, instead of 'Murder Without a Witness.' I will tell you why. There is a very important distinction. 'Thou Shalt Not Murder,' the Torah says — and it makes very clear that the punishment for murder is death. But… and this is the important part. The Talmud makes an exception. It says that if a person is convicted of a murder to which there were no witnesses, then the punishment is not death. It is incarceration for life. That is the charge here. I want to make it very clear: the defendant, Hersch Liebmann, is not on trial for his life. Even if he is convicted, he will not be put to death. Such a heavy responsibility will not be on your shoulders. That will rest with Elohim, where it belongs."

Meyer heard scraping among a few of the juror's chairs. He hoped he had eased their minds.

"Let us begin with the murder. On the morning of 29 March of this Christian year 1769, our beloved Schul-Klopper, Solomon Gruen, was found lying in the lane not far from the north gate. I shall direct several questions to Doctor Lev Berkov, who has been the chief Doctor here for more than four years, and is a member of the Judengasse Council.

"Doctor Berkov, on the morning we are discussing, you were summoned to attend to the person of Solomon Gruen, is that correct?"

Berkov spoke from his seat at the council table. "Yes."

"What did you discover?"

"Herr Gruen was dead."

"Subsequent to that, what else did you discover?"

"When I examined his corpse in the hospital, I found a suspicious white powder on the back of his tongue, and in his throat. On the Monday following, I took scrapings of this powder to a reliable chemist in town, to find out what it was. He assayed several tests, and told me the powder was arsenic."

Arsenic — the word swept in whispers through the spectators, as the snow, falling in thicker flakes, was sweeping against the stained-glass windows.

"What did you conclude from this?"

"That Solomon Gruen had died from arsenic poisoning — either by suicide or by murder."

"What did you do with this finding?"

"I told the Chief Rabbi, Rabbi Eleazar."

"What did he say to you?"

"He assured me in strong terms that he had known Herr Gruen very well, that Herr Gruen had not been upset or brooding, that it was not in his character to kill himself."

"What did you conclude from that?"

"That Herr Gruen most likely been given arsenic to drink by someone else. That he had been murdered."

"Why was that fact not made public?"

"Neither the Rabbi nor I could imagine who might want to kill the Schul-Klopper. Or why. The Rabbi decided there was no point in upsetting the lane, until or unless further evidence emerged."

"Did you do anything else in this matter?"

"I spoke with the neighbors at the north end of the lane, asking if anyone had seen anything unusual that morning. I did not tell them the death was suspicious. Without lying, I implied that I wanted to know what might have caused him to have a heart attack. Such as if he'd had an argument with someone. None of them had seen or heard anything unusual."

"Did you ever tell anyone else that Solomon Gruen had been murdered?"

"Not for several months. But increasingly it weighed on me that a murderer was going unpunished. One night, after having drunk several glasses of wine, I told two friends whom I trusted to keep the secret — just to unburden myself. That would be Yussel Kahn, and yourself, Meyer Rothschild."

"Thank you Doctor Berkov. I have no more questions."

As Meyer sat, the Chief Rabbi cleared his throat in preparation for cross-examination; this system had been mandated by the Talmud a thousand years before defense advocates were required most anywhere else. Hersch Liebmann leaned forward in his chair.

"Tell me, Doctor. If a person wanted to purchase arsenic, where might he do so?"

"At a chemist's shop in town."

"At any chemist's shop?"

"Pretty much."

"If this person did not want to purchase it, is it not true that arsenic is the principle ingredient of ratbane?"

"That is correct."

"What you found in Herr Gruen's throat might have been ratbane, which would test positively for arsenic. Is that right?"

"That's correct."

"Isn't it true that ratbane is found in virtually every house in the Judengasse?"

"I've never looked," the Doctor said.

A few in the audience laughed, but the laughter died quickly.

"Would you say that is general knowledge?"

"I've heard that. I will concede it is reasonable."

"So, to sum up: anyone with a few kreuzer could walk into any chemist shop and have no trouble purchasing arsenic. Anyone seeking ratbane could find it in almost every home in the lane. Not just in the home of the defendant — if, in fact, it can be found there. Is that a fair statement?"

"That's fair."

"Thank you, Doctor."

Meyer sipped again from his glass of water, and stood. "Very well," he said to the jury, "what have we established? We have established that Solomon Gruen was murdered; that the weapon was arsenic or ratbane, easily accessible to most anyone — including, I would point out, the defendant; and that, as far as we know, no one witnessed this murder. But the murder did occur — there can be no doubt of that. So the question is — what person or persons perpetrated it, and why."

Meyer walked around the table to get closer to the jurors in their two rows of chairs. The hall was quiet as a roomful of cobbles.

"I freely admit, there being no witnesses, that the charge against Hersch Liebmann rests on circumstances. I ask you to pay close attention to these circumstances. They are critical to this case.

"First of all, we have shown that a pouch containing a hundred gulden, belonging to the synagogue, was stolen from there while Solomon Gruen was the shammus — and while Hersch Liebmann was his assistant. Those two men had the easiest access to the money. Herr Gruen is dead — and the money was found in the home of Herr Liebmann.

"Let us suppose for a moment that the theft was discovered by the shammus — that he suspected that Hersch was the thief, and told him to return the money within, let's say a week — it could have been less — or the shammus would inform the Chief Rabbi. What would be the effect on Herr Liebmann if the shammus were to do this? Hersch Liebmann would be branded a thief. He would lose his caretaker job at the synagogue. He might be brought to trial.

"Would that have been reason enough for him to kill Herr Gruen?"

Meyer paced back and forth in front of the jury, looking from one face to another. Then he said quietly, "No. I don't think so. And you should not, either. It might have been reason enough for murder, but let us give the defendant the benefit of the doubt. Let us say not.

"So what, then? I'll tell you what. In the week before Solomon Gruen was murdered, I myself decided I needed an assistant in my coin and antiques business. Someone to run errands to the post, that sort of task. Immediately I thought of Hersch Liebmann. Why? Because he was a neighbor, because I knew his parents, because he might enjoy the job more than sweeping the schul. And I would pay a little more, which I knew his elderly parents could use.

"What happened then? I stopped Hersch in the lane on the twenty-eighth of March. I asked if he would be interested in coming to work for me. Hersch said he would. He seemed happy to be asked, as well he might. Then I told him that because I did not know him very well, I would be asking his employer, the Schul-Klopper, what kind of worker he was. If the report was good, he could have the job. I told him I would speak with him again as soon as I could talk with Herr Gruen."

A few murmurs were heard in the room as people anticipated what was coming. Then silence fell again like the snow, which had grown heavier still and was building on the sills of the windows, blocking from the bottom a line of exterior light.

"You can guess the rest. The very next morning, Solomon Gruen was found dead, not ten metres from the door to Hersch Liebmann's house. Before I got a chance to speak with him."

Murmuring among the spectators grew louder. The Chairman rapped his gavel for silence.

"I will ask the question I asked before. What would have been the effect on Hersch Liebmann if Solomon Gruen had not died that morning?

"When I spoke with the Schul-Klopper, he would have felt constrained to tell me the truth — that he suspected Hersch of stealing one hundred gulden from the schul. In which case I certainly would not have hired Hersch — as, without the opportunity to speak with Herr Gruen, I eventually did. Hersch would have lost his job at the schul. He would have lost the chance for a better job with more pay in my employ. A job, he might have been thinking already, where money was handled every day, a job from which he might be able to steal again. Which he later did, as you have seen. He would have been shamed before his family. Having told me of his suspicions, Herr Gruen no doubt would have told the Chief Rabbi — with all the consequences I have mentioned. Hersch Liebmann would have been disgraced — imagine, stealing from the schul! He might have been put on trial for thievery. Certainly he would never be hired for any job again. How would he live?

"Hersch Liebmann is not stupid. Hersch Liebmann knew all this.

"Are those reasons enough for him to murder Herr Gruen? This time I suggest that they are. He had to silence the Schul-Klopper. The easiest weapon at hand was ratbane. He would not even have to leave his house and risk being seen — he need only offer the Schul-Klopper a poisoned drink when he came knocking."

Meyer walked back to the table, drank more water, looked through some blank papers. Wanting the jurors to absorb his words, he stalled, glanced at the snow rising on the window sills.

"When Rabbi Eleazar presents his defense, he will tell you that what I have said is all speculation and supposition — that no one saw Hersch commit murder. I agree. What you must remember is that Solomon Gruen indeed was murdered — that is absolute fact. If not by Hersch Liebmann, who had such strong motives and such easy opportunity, then by whom?

"In a trial such as this, we must combine the physical evidence with logic. Remember, the Talmud agrees that a person can be tried for murder with no witnesses. That is the circumstance in which most murderers strike. If we insisted on witnesses, most murderers would go free. A terrible killing was committed in the lane on March 29th — and all logic points to Hersch Liebmann as the murderer."

He looked from one face to another among the jurors. Slowly he turned his back to them and walked to his seat. "Herr Chairman, that is the case for the prosecution."

The hall was silent with anticipation. Chairman Schnapper quietly asked the Chief Rabbi, "Do you want a rest before we proceed?"

"No, no, let's get on with it."

As Rabbi Eleazar stood, with his ship captain's demeanor, a disturbance erupted among the spectators — a scuffling of chairs, a loud, almost inhuman bellowing sound. Hiram Liebmann had climbed onto his chair and was waving his arms, signaling wildly, trying to shout with useless vocal chords. The Chairman banged his gavel several times. "What's going on back there?"

Hiram stopped his painful sounds, but continued to shout with his hands. All eyes in the hall were turned him.

"What does that man want?" Chairman Schnapper called out. "This is a trial we are conducting."

Izzy stood from his seat beside Hiram. He, too, began to signal rapidly, before he realized he must speak. "It's Hiram Liebmann. He wants to testify. He claims that he killed the Schul-Klopper."

A conflagration of voices erupted among the spectators at this unexpected turn. The Chairman repeatedly banged his gavel for order. The defendant looked across the room at his brother, consternation and sadness in his eyes.

"Nonsense," Meyer Amschel exclaimed. "He's just trying to save his brother!"

"Will you let him testify?" the Chief Rabbi asked.

"It's nonsense! He had no motive."

"He'll be under oath. Will you listen to him? What we want here is the truth."

"He'll just confuse the jury. He'll muddy the case."

"Isn't that for the jury to decide?"

"He's not on the witness list," the Chairman said. "It's up to you."

Meyer tossed papers in the air with angry resignation. "Let him testify. The jury already heard what he said."

Again and again the Chairman had to bang his gavel to restore order. "Let the witness come forward," he said. Izzy pointed to the witness chair. Hiram nodded and followed his friend to the front. Hiram sat, and Izzy stood beside him to interpret. The Chairman spoke the oath. Izzy nodded his head. Hiram did so as well.

"Very well," the Chief Rabbi said. "Hiram Liebmann, did you see who killed Solomon Gruen?"

Izzy enacted the question by pointing to Hiram, touching his eyes, mimicking someone handing a glass to another. Hiram shook his head, no.

"Then what is it that you have to contribute to this case?"

Izzy motioned to Hiram to say what he wanted. Hiram pointed to himself, then handed an imaginary glass. Izzy Interpreted: "I killed him, not my brother."

The jurors and spectators were leaning forward in their chairs to hear Izzy speak the deaf mute's confession.

"You're under oath!" Meyer shouted across the table, forgetting for the moment that Hiram could not hear, no matter how loud the shout.

"The witness knows he is under oath," the Rabbi said. "Now, Hiram, tell us. How did you kill the Schul-Klopper?"

Hiram enacted the scene like a mime. Izzy spoke the words. "He knocked on the door. I gave him a glass of milk, with ratbane in it. He drank it, then went outside. I put water to boil, and I poured a cup of tea. I took it to the window from which I watch the lane. He was lying on the cobbles. No one found him for six minutes, till the girl did."

The silence was intense. The whole room seemed to be growing darker, the oil lamps flickering, as if shaking their heads in dismay.

"Why did you kill him?" the Rabbi asked.

Izzy told the question. Hiram pointed to his chest, then knocked in the air as if with a hammer. "So I could become Schul-Klopper," Izzy interpreted.

"And are you now Schul-Klopper?"

"Assistant Schul-Klopper," Izzy said.

The Rabbi pondered a moment. "I have no more questions."

"Herr Rothschild?"

"I have just one. Why did you think you would become Schul-Klopper if Herr Gruen was dead?"

Izzy motioned the question, pointing at Hiram's chest and then at his temple, knocking with an imaginary hammer, shrugging his shoulders. Hiram beat his fist hard on his chest, several times. From their close friendship, Izzy interpreted the passion, the pleading eyes. "Because I deserved it. It's all I could do."

Meyer wanted to give him a withering glare — or perhaps a pitying one, he did not know which. Instead he looked down at the table, and sat. Was it possible?

"Are we finished, then?" Chairman Schnapper asked.

"Not at all," the Chief Rabbi said. "I still have a witness for the accused."

Izzy led Hiram back to the spectator section. Every manner of expression was directed at him — incredulity, anger, pity, curiosity, admiration.

Rabbi Eleazar's voice boomed out. "The advocate for the defense calls Guttle Schnapper."

Wearing a dark gray dress she thought appropriate for the trial, Guttle walked to the witness chair. As she was sworn, as Meyer looked across the table at her, she seemed to him — perhaps to everyone in the room — both vulnerable and mysterious. What could she contribute? She sat, smoothing her dress. Only she and the Chief Rabbi, who had questioned her weeks earlier, knew what she was going to say.

"Fräulein Schnapper," the Rabbi said, "please tell the jurors your movements on the morning of 29 March last, from the time you left your house."

"We had no milk for my little brother. I took a pitcher and crossed the lane and borrowed milk from Frau Metzenbaum."

"Was the sky still dark?"

"It was just beginning to brighten."

"Very well, go ahead."

"On my way back, I stumbled over something, and spilled some of the milk. I looked down and saw a man in a black coat lying there. When I looked closer, I saw a carved hammer in his hand. I realized it was the Schul-Klopper. I ran to get my mother, and almost bumped into Isidor Kracauer, who was coming out of the house next door."

"Let's pause there for a moment. Before you saw Izzy, did you see any other people nearby?"

"Yes."

"Who were they?"

"Three Gentile boys, about my age."

Meyer started in his seat. A murmur rippled among the spectators. Where, Meyer wondered, had three Gentile boys come from. He'd never heard of them.

"I must interrupt," Doctor Berkov said from his seat at the council table. "I spoke with this witness the day of the murder. She told me she had seen no one. Surely her memory was better that day than it is today."

Meyer nodded, astounded at his intended. What was Guttle doing? The Rabbi said, "Fräulein Schnapper, please respond to the good Doctor."

Guttle looked at Berkov, blushing slightly. "What Doctor Berkov asked me that day was had I seen anyone in the lane. I said no, which was the truth. I didn't even think of the Gentile boys. They were outside the gate."

The Rabbi looked at Berkov, who slumped back in his seat. She'd been understandably upset that day, the Doctor recalled. Still, she'd been right — those boys surely were irrelevant.

"What were the boys doing outside the gate?" the Rabbi asked.

"They were pointing at the Schul-Klopper, and laughing. I ran at them, and told them to show respect. They danced about, and ran away."

"Did you see anyone else outside the gate."

"Not then, but later. A constable who was new that morning, I had never seen him before. Later I learned his name was Fritz."

"When you saw these boys, was the gate open or closed?"

"It was closed."

"Was it locked?"

"I don't know. I didn't look that closely. I assumed it was locked. When it's closed, it's usually locked."

"But you don't know for certain. So isn't it possible, Fräulein Schnapper, that these three boys — about fifteen or sixteen years old, you say, about your age — that these three boys, or the new guard Fritz — came into the lane, and forced Herr Gruen to drink liquid that had arsenic in it, and then retreated outside the gate and watched him die. Is that possible?"

Guttle was reluctant to answer. Her eyes flicked across the table towards Meyer.

"Is that possible?" the Rabbi prodded.

"I suppose it's possible."

"If that were the case, Hersch Liebmann would not be guilty of murder, would he?"

"I suppose not."

"You suppose not? Can you be more certain than that?"

"If those boys or the Constable killed him, then obviously Hersch Liebmann did not. But there is no… "

"Thank you, I have no more questions."

Meyer leaped up at once, had to grab his yarmulke, which had begun to slide off. "Fräulein Schnapper" — those spectators who knew of their betrothal smiled — "did you at any time see those three boys in the lane, inside the gate?"

"No."

She felt terrible, she was eager to help him.

"Did you at any time that morning see a guard inside the gate?"

"No."

"Did you see Solomon Gruen outside the gate with them?"

"No."

"Did you at any time see any of those persons offer a drink to Herr Gruen?"

"No."

"Did you see any of them force a drink down his throat?"

"No."

"Solomon Gruen was the Schul-Klopper for more than thirty years. Do you know of any reason why any of those people — the new constable or those young boys — would decide to kill him that morning."

"No."

"Do you know of anything that any of them would have gained by killing him — such as preserving their own reputations in the lane, or gaining money, or avoiding being charged with theft?"

"No."

Meyer glared at the Chief Rabbi. "No more questions."

"Any rebuttal?" the Chairman asked Rabbi Eleazar.

"Just one question. Fräulein Schnapper, at any time that morning did you see Hersch Liebmann offer a drink to Solomon Gruen, or force one down his throat?"

"No."

The Rabbi nodded. "That concludes the defense, Chairman Schnapper."

The room sighed with the expelled breath of hundreds. The Chairman stood behind the table. "Men of the jury," he said. "The accuser has concluded his case, and the defender's advocate has concluded his. You have heard the testimony, and seen the evidence. You are now to discuss the case among yourselves, and decide the guilt or innocence of the defendant on each of the three charges against him. Should you find him guilty of any of the charges, you shall determine an appropriate punishment from those required by the Talmud.

"Of you twenty-three jurors, twelve votes of not guilty are needed to find the defendant innocent. Thirteen votes of guilty are required to find him guilty.

"Rabbi Simcha will remain with you as you deliberate, to answer any questions of Talmudic law that need explaining. The good ladies of the bakery — among them my wife Emmie, I might add — have prepared bread and meat for you to eat, and tea. You shall remain in this room to deliberate.

"I now must order all persons not on the jury to leave this hall. When the jury reaches its verdict, Rabbi Simcha will send word out into the lane, to allow you to come back and hear the verdict. The jurors will now convene among themselves."

He rapped his gavel once, sharply, on the table. The people began filing out, some discussing their views, others overwhelmed by what they had heard, trying to make sense of it, grateful they were not jurors.

As she donned her coat and walked slowly out into the falling snow, Guttle thought: what about Sophie Marcus, why did no one mention her?

25

The snow falling in thick flakes had covered the lane to a depth of several inches. Cobbles were visible only in patches, where little boys had been running about, pulling off one another's yarmulkes and rubbing snow into their hair, or trying to shove it inside their shirts, while little girls wearing wool caps stood in the shelter of doorways, giggling. The slopes of the ditch were white, and the crossing boards; flakes falling onto the sluggish waste clung to life briefly, then drowned. The people leaving the trial churned up the fresh snow with their boots even as new flakes settled on their coats. The lane was brighter to the eye than during those few sunny minutes of the clearest days.

In a first floor room at the rear of the hospital, Doctor Kirsch pulled a white sheet up over the vacant eyes of Leo Liebmann, while his Yetta cried noiselessly in a chair beside the bed, and Hersch and Hiram watched.

"He didn't want to wait for the verdict," Yetta said through her tears.

Hiram squeezed his mother's shoulder as Doctor Kirsch left the room, leaving the family to grieve in private.

"It was Rothschild who killed him," Hersch said bitterly.

"Don't say that." Frau Liebmann wiped her eyes with a handkerchief, looking at the form beneath the sheet that for more than thirty years had been her husband, her best friend, her joy, silly old fool that she loved. "Meyer Rothschild did not steal the synagogue's money. Or his own. Or hide it in Leo's bed."

"Are you saying that I killed Papa? Another accusation of murder?"

"No, my son. Nobody killed your father. Yahweh took him when Leo wanted to go."

"The money was to get away from this place. To start a life somewhere. Later on, after Papa and you ... were gone. I wouldn't have left till then."

Without looking at him she reached out and squeezed his hand.

"I didn't kill the Schul-Klopper. No matter what the jurors decide. I wouldn't kill anyone. But from now on people will look at me funny, even if the jury agrees I'm innocent. Some people will never be sure." He signaled his words for Hiram as he spoke. And he asked his brother, with his motions, "Why did you say you killed him? Were you trying to help me?"

Hiram stared straight ahead, and did not respond.

"Is it still snowing out?" Yetta asked. "When will we bury him?"

"In the morning. Under the snow."

"The grave?" Yetta said, a question in her voice.

"Hiram and I will dig it," Hersch said. "As soon as the verdict is done."

"How did the Rabbi learn about the Gentile boys?"

They were standing in the doorway of the Owl, brushing snow from their coats.

"He came and questioned me, because I had found the body. I never thought they were important, till he asked if I saw anyone outside the gate. Maybe running away."

"Why didn't you tell me? He made a fool of me in there."

"He said I couldn't tell anyone until the trial. Especially you, because you were the accuser. That was the law, he said."

"I don't know such a law."

"Don't be angry with me. I was only telling the truth. If you knew about the boys, would that have made you think Hersch was innocent?"

"No. He's still the only one with a reason to murder. Hiram was just trying to help his brother. The Rabbi was using those boys to confuse the issue."

"Why would he do that?"

"I have no idea," Meyer said. "Perhaps he'll tell us one day."

The snow was six inches deep late that afternoon when word spread that a verdict had been reached. Volunteers had shoveled the snow from in front of the synagogue and in front of the lecture hall, but the cobbles already were being freshly covered. The men had cleared the wide window sills of snow so it would not block the light from coming inside; the snow was re-establishing itself there as well.

The seats were filled as in the morning, the jurors in place, the defendant, summoned from the hospital by Rabbi Simcha, sitting without expression in his chair. The large room smelled of wet wool and apprehension. Many of the spectators seemed tired, having argued with one another for hours about whether Hersch Liebmann had killed the Schul-Klopper, debating how they would have voted had they been on the jury.

"Have the jurors selected a person to tell their verdict?" Chairman Schnapper asked.

One of the jurors stood, a man from the south end. "I have the verdict, Herr Chairman."

"Please convey it to us. The spectators shall remain silent till we have heard the verdicts on all three charges, as well as the sentences, if any. You may proceed."

The man opened a folded sheet of paper. Meyer could not remember such tension in his stomach as there was now — not even when he was dealing with the crown Prince. Hersch Liebmann appeared relaxed, as if, regardless of the verdicts, he had achieved some inner calm, but a close observer could see his left eye twitching. Guttle, seated in the witness section, did not know what to think, what to expect.

"On the first accusation of theft, in the matter of one hundred gulden stolen from the synagogue, we find the defendant guilty."

He paused while the briefest of murmurs swept among the spectators. Few seemed surprised, given the evidence.

"On the second accusation of theft, in the matter of one hundred gulden stolen from the business establishment of Meyer Amschel Rothschild, we find the defendant guilty."

The room remained silent. That verdict had been a certainty after the first.

Meyer held his breath, intent on the outcome of the murder charge. Guttle found her whole body trembling; she did not know which verdict she would prefer. The defendant leaned forward in his chair.

"On the charge of murder without a witness, in the death of Solomon Gruen, we find the defendant, Hersch Liebmann, not guilty."

Hardly a sound was heard. The room seemed to deflate even as Meyer did in his chair, Hersch by contrast squaring his shoulders, sitting tall, trying not to smile. Most of the spectators were too worn to talk, uncertain, as Guttle was, which outcome they had been hoping for. If Hersch Liebmann was not a murderer, that was good. But they had heard at the trial, for the first time, Doctor Berkov's evidence that Solomon Gruen had been murdered. That terrible fact had not changed.

"Have you decided on punishments for the two guilty verdicts?" Chairman Schnapper asked.

"We have, Herr Chairman. On the first charge of theft, we sentence the defendant to exile from the Judengasse for a period of seven years."

A collective inhaling of breath seemed almost to cause the room to implode. There had not been a criminal trial for so long that people had forgotten about exile.

"On the second charge of theft, we sentence the defendant to exile from the Judengasse also for seven years. Together, the defendant is sentenced to exile from the Judengasse for fourteen years. Such period of exile shall begin at sundown tomorrow.

"With the Chairman's permission," he continued, over a babble of chatter among the spectators, "the jurors have asked me to explain the sentence of exile, as follows." The room quieted at once, as he read from his paper. "Civilized behavior is based on trust. Because as Jews we can trust no one else, it is imperative that we be able to trust one another. Stealing from the synagogue, and stealing from one's employer, both are violations of sacred trusts. In such cases, as noted in the Talmud, the offender must be removed from society, in order to permit its congenial functioning. As for the accusation of murder, the majority of the jurors found that the charge had not been proven."

People in the rear were scrambling to their feet, like boys let out from heder. Doctor Berkov approached the Chairman and whispered in his ear. Meyer said to the Chairman, "Please ask him to tell the vote." The Chairman rapped his gavel, and did so.

"On the two charges of theft," the juror said, "the findings of guilt were unanimous. On the charge of murder without a witness, the votes were eight guilty and fifteen not guilty."

"Rabbi Simcha, are those the votes you saw in the jury room?"

"Those are correct, Herr Chairman."

Gaveling sharply three times to silence the departing spectators, Chairman Schnapper announced: "I have just been informed by Doctor Berkov that a few hours ago, having been ill for several months, Leo Liebmann passed away. Leo, as most of you know, was the father of the defendant. He will be buried after morning services tomorrow. In deference to the widow, the Chair will use its prerogative to delay the sentence, so that the defendant may comfort his mother at this difficult time. The sentence of the jury, of exile from the Judengasse for fourteen years, shall begin not tomorrow, but after the seven days of sitting shiva." He banged his gavel loud as a musket shot. "The court in these matters is now and forever adjourned."

Turning to his future son-in-law, as the people filed into the snow, Wolf Schnapper asked, "Are you satisfied with the sentence?"

"With the sentence, yes," Meyer said. "With the principal verdict, no. Solomon Gruen is dead — and someone murdered him. If not Hersch, who? If not Hersch, why?"

The snow had stopped falling, the clouds had blown away. The cemetery glowed from the ground up under a nearly full moon, which threw sharp shadows in front of each stone marker. The brothers worked alone and silent, clearing away the half-foot covering of snow in the family's ancient plot, purchased a century before by a forgotten ancestor. When the snow was piled like white ashes on the graves of others, they dug in the earth, which was not yet frozen, a grave for their father.

Pausing to rest when the hole was three feet deep, Hiram signaled to his brother, breaking the eerie silence without breaking it, asking him what he was going to do. Hersch both spoke and mimed his answer. "They'll give me five gulden. I'll ride some coach as far as it will take me. Then I'll walk. When I'm as far from this place as I can get, I'll look for work."

Hiram, reading Hersch's hands and to a lesser degree his lips, made a question with his fingers. *What kind of work?*

"I won't sweep floors. Or carry parcels. Maybe I'll become a highwayman. I'm good at stealing."

Hiram mimicked stealing, by picking the handkerchief from his brother's pocket. He grabbed that hand tightly with the other. *You're also good at getting caught.*

Hiram saw that his brother was glaring at him. The glare was the same as he had seen two months before when he had prowled around his father's bed to see what Hersch was stashing there, had found the hole in the mattress cover and pulled out the two pouches of coins from the straw. Had not heard, of course, his father coming in, standing behind him. His aged father had reached down, touched the pouches with stiff fingers, slumped to the floor a moment later, stricken. Hiram remembered shoving the pouches back into the straw, running to get Hersch, who ran for the Doctor. His brother never had blamed him for what happened. Until now.

Hersch only glared. He signaled nothing. Hiram broke the visual quiet by knocking in the air, then vigorously shaking his head. *I won't be Schul-Klopper anymore.*

"Why?"

They're sending you away, he mimed, pointing to Hersch and then over the wall. *I don't want to work for them.*

"You have to take care of Mama now. She'll need the money you make."

Hiram jumped into the hole, grabbed his spade, tore at the earth with a vicious chop, then another, and another.

"It's a different world for you now," Hersch said, "with Papa dead, and me going away." Whether out of carelessness or anger, he spoke only with his voice, not with his hands. Hiram heard nothing. Hersch knew his words did not need saying.

Few people came to see Hersch Liebmann take leave of the Judengasse for fourteen years. People did not want to shame him. Goodbyes, in the absence of love, would be inadequate.

As he stood near the north gate, Hersch had in his pocket five gulden from the synagogue's welfare fund. Beside him on the muddy, snow-crusted ground was a faded satchel stuffed with clothing. His mother was there, tears in her eyes, and his brother, and Wolf Schnapper, as chief officer of the sentencing court, and the fire captain, Joshua Lamb, in case of trouble. Meyer Amschel had agonized over whether to be present. Guttle had urged him to stay away, arguing that no good purpose would be served. Meyer had decided otherwise. He would not be going to gawk at a man being driven from his ancient home. Rather, he would present himself, and stand mute, and wait — to see if Hersch, who surely hated him, needed to divest himself of words, of anger. It was his obligation as a man, Meyer believed, to face this.

There was no oratory. Hersch hugged his mother, held her in his arms for a long time, her face pressed into his shoulder. Her legs for an instant collapsed under her, but Hersch held her up, and she regained her strength. Hiram embraced him ferociously; the brothers seemed locked in combat, like twin cobras. Flakes of snow began to fall, and they nourished an idea. Hiram ran to their house a few metres away, and up the stairs, and came down with his frayed black Schul-Klopper's coat, and held it out to Hersch. At first Hersch refused. Then, looking up at the gray winter sky, the falling flakes stinging his eyes, delighting in or ignoring a certain irony — that this had been Solomon Gruen's coat — he shrugged his sweatered arms into the sleeves, and let his mother straighten the collar.

Wolf Schnapper, eager to be off to Sachsen-Meiningen, stepped forward and shook Hersch's hand. The fire captain did the same. Five metres away, Meyer, who till then had been ignored by the Liebmanns, watched without moving, not wanting to offend, wanting merely to be available. To offer himself.

Hersch saw Meyer as if for the first time. He walked toward him, until they were face to face. Peeking at the scene from around the corner of the

Pfann, Guttle chewed on a knuckle, not noticing that she'd already chewed it raw.

"Are you here for forgiveness?" Hersch asked. HIs face seemed lit by flames.

Meyer was taken aback. "Not to receive it, nor to give it."

"You made people think I'm a murderer. I hope we will meet again."

Hersch loudly brought up from his throat a great gob of phlegm. Meyer did not flinch. He would receive whatever Hersch felt was his due. He permitted himself only to close his eyes.

Arrogance, Meyer thought, arrogance was my sin. Thinking I knew more than anyone. In this matter, someone knows more. To the Gentiles I must fawn in order to do business; they expect it. Perhaps the recoil of this fakery has been arrogance in the lane. I must remember to be my brother's keeper, not his judge.

The speed of thought is infinite. All this between the phlegm filling Hersch's mouth and his thick expectoration. Meyer flinched slightly, but felt no sodden blow, no sickly dripping on his face. Opening his eyes, he saw Hersch walking away in the Schul-Klopper's frayed black coat. The yellow-green glob of disgust was on the ground near Meyer's boot.

Watching without moving, he saw Hersch kiss his mother on the cheek, slap Hiram on the back, lift his bulging satchel in a strong hand and walk alone through the gate. Wolf Schnapper turned and left with the fire chief. Yetta Liebmann waited, to see her son turn and wave. When it was clear that he would not, she grasped Hiram's arm and leaned on it as she walked towards Meyer.

"Don't feel bad, Meyer Amschel," she told him in a shaky voice. "It isn't your fault. He did it to himself. When he was little, after Hiram came, he used to take things to get attention. This money, he took to escape from the Judengasse."

"It appears that he got his wish," Meyer said.

Nodding, turning, still leaning on Hiram, she walked across the lane to her house. Meyer could only imagine how vast and silent would be the emptiness inside.

As he watched Hersch's departing figure growing smaller, fading to white, Guttle came up behind him, circled his waist with her arms. Greedily he clasped her hands.

"You mustn't blame yourself," she said.

"Mustn't I?"

He did not turn to her, but continued to stare through the open gate as the distant black speck that was Hersch Liebmann melted to nothingness.

For a few days after the trial, some people in the lane looked at others with suspicion. If Hersch Liebmann had not killed the Schul-Klopper, who had? But soon this question almost disappeared, like smoke dissipating into the air. A new thought came to permeate the lane. Lev Berkov was a fine young man, a good Doctor, but he put too much faith in the new science. Suppose the chemist in Frankfurt had made a mistake, the powder in Solomon's throat had not been poison. Perhaps milk spilled by the girl had dried there. Or perhaps sometimes from a heart attack white powder from inside the lungs can erupt. No one in the lane would commit murder. No one hated Solomon Gruen. The answer was clear. Yahweh had simply decided that the Schul-Klopper had walked the lane enough. That it was time for his eternal rest. No one could call Adonai a murderer.

The Chief Rabbi did not discourage this line of thought. Not so Doctor Berkov, who was convinced a murder had taken place. But he saw no point in harping on the matter. Without a suspect, it would serve no purpose. Unless another suspicious death occurred in the lane.

26

At times, Guttle felt, the days hurried by as if they were late for evening service. At other times the hours dragged wearily, like the flour merchant's horse. Brisk mornings could be so robust with gossip that they seemed to have four dimensions. Dull afternoons could be narrow as the lane itself, and seem to have only two. One morning whose character was not yet determined, Guttle was sitting at the office desk, making entries in the ledger, when Meyer bounded down the stairs holding a small package wrapped in brown paper, a red ribbon around it. Eagerly, he handed it to her.

"What's this?"

"A gift."

"For what?"

"Today we've been betrothed for six months."

"Oh, Meyer." She stood and hugged him. "How nice. But I have nothing for you."

"Hardly a major oversight. A big kiss will be plenty. Open the wrapping."

"For a big kiss, this had better be good."

She untied the ribbon and tore apart the paper. In her hand she held a writing book, but one unlike Izzy's, one unlike any she had ever seen. The cover was made of wood. Carved into the wood were two stemmed roses, entwined.

"This is beautiful! Where did you find such a thing?"

"Do you like it?"

"I love it." She kissed, him lightly at first, then long and firmly.

"You're wanting another book already?"

She opened the cover and examined the pages of fine paper, patterned in faint swirls of white on white, like the underside of clouds. "It's much too beautiful to write in. Who made it?"

"At the September Fair, Yussel saw his bookbinder selling these books, but with plain paper covers. He got the idea to put carved wooden covers on them, but he never did. Then last week he told me he was going to try. I wanted his first one to be for you."

She traced her fingertips gently over roses. "I'll bet he could sell lots of these."

"He hopes to. With different designs, of course. He wants to carve figures from the Torah, Shakespearean heroes, loaves of bread. Those would be for recipe books. He's not making coffins anymore; he told the younger carpenters that's their responsibility now. Furniture he'll still make, but twice each week, on his way to Mainz, he'll pick up a few more empty books."

She pressed the cover to her cheek. "From coffins to flowers. It's good."

"He's a new man since he took up with Brendel Isaacs."

"What man wouldn't be?" Guttle said.

She looked down at the book, hesitant. Then she asked, shyly, "Do you still like her?"

"Is that a trick question?"

"No. I hope you do, because I like her a lot."

"Well, in that case, I do, too. There's something about her that's very agreeable."

"She's adorable, with those blonde ringlets and sparkling green eyes. She looks so innocent, but suggests a temptress. Which she's not. She's a good mother, a warm person. She's honest and real in a way that most of us aren't. Maybe because she didn't grow up between stone walls."

"You may be right. She's like a creature of nature, with a saucy quality that's unusual."

"Do I have a saucy quality?"

"I'd say you were more… impertinent."

"Is that like saucy?"

"About half way. But more refined."

"Is that good?"

"It's you. Which makes it wonderful." He took her hand, touched it with his lips.

"Should I try to be more saucy?"

"Don't you dare. Not until we're married, anyway. And then, only with me." His arms encircled her waist. "Anoint me with the sweet wine of your petulant lips, my impertinent love."

"You've been talking Shakespeare with Yussel again. The sonnets, no doubt. I'm afraid I'm still only me, Guttle Schnapper from across the lane."

"My own dark lady."

They kissed. She earned another book, and another, and another, before a client knocked on the door,

24 *March, 1770*

Forgive me, pretty book, for you are so beautiful and my lettering is not, and my thoughts surely are not. It has taken me five days to summon the courage to sully these lovely pages. But that's what you are for, so I shall will myself to begin.

Last night I lay awake wanting to curse Yahweh. To scream at Him for keeping us locked inside the walls. But cursing Him, I think, is not a good thing to do. So I talked with Melka of the South Gate. I asked her why Yahweh has done this to us. She said Yahweh did not do it, the Gentiles did. I asked her, isn't Adonai more powerful than the Gentiles? Melka did not answer.

Perhaps if Yahweh reads this journal He will answer me directly. But I doubt He has the time. Though I don't know what He does with His time, now that all has been created.

Melka said that as I get older I will stop being so angry, and will accept the way things are, just as my parents have. I'm not sure if that is a good thing.

26 *March*

Hannah Schlicter is going to make my wedding dress. This morning I went up to her shop to be measured. I had to wait a few minutes while she finished showing new fabrics to a Countess — a real one. She comes to Hannah every few months to order a new dress for her next fancy dinner or ball. I confess that I have been wondering since what it would be like to waltz my life away in a grand mansion with marble pillars and polished floors, with classic paintings on the walls and velvet on the chairs, with just the right kinds of dogs lounging on the floor for the painters to place in the corners of family portraits, with a maid serving tea to the ladies while the gentlemen ride to the hunt.

At sixteen I am an adult, but I still have childish thoughts.

28 *March*

Hardly a week goes by when I do not see Izzy strolling along, piping an invisible flute while a line of marching children, mostly girls, Amelia among them, follow behind, laughing and giggling. Today I was walking by the Chief Rabbi's study when I saw him standing in the doorway with Yussel Kahn, watching. The marching children waved at us. Only Yussel and I waved back. Surprised, I asked the Rabbi if he thought something more was happening here than just a silly children's game. Because in the legend, the Pied Piper led the children right out of Hamelin. The Rabbi said, 'I've been having similar thoughts — but it's even more problematic than that.'

I had never heard that word, problematic. I asked him what it meant.

'In the legend,' he said, 'the children never come back.'

I don't know if the Rabbi is afraid the children might leave the Judengasse one day — or that they might leave the Jewish faith.

29 *March*

It was a year ago today that I tripped on the Schul-Klopper. It is something I never will forget, and here, just in time, I have a book in which to write my feelings. Sometimes Meyer seems twice as clever as anyone needs to be.

My quill shakes in the ink, rattling the pretty bottle — Meyer gave me that, also — as I remember the Schul-Klopper lying dead on the cobbles, hammer in hand. Me not knowing then that there was poison in his mouth, his gut.

So much has flowed from his death! Izzy becoming Schul-Klopper. Hiram becoming his assistant. My foul encounter with the Kapitän. (Sometimes, when I am feeling squeamish, the memory of that still makes my stomach hurt.) Meyer hiring Hersch, and the ensuing theft of the money — which may have caused Leo Liebmann's death, and certainly caused the exile of his son. And most of all, Meyer. I first caught his eye, his admiration, he has told me, as a young woman no longer a child, when I rushed into the synagogue, among the astounded men, to hug and kiss Izzy, the new Schul-Klopper. Would we have become a couple if that had not occurred? Who is to say?

Other things may have been set in motion whose connections remain invisible. A year later we still don't know if the murderer was Hersch, or Hiram, or those three boys, or the young guard (why them? why then?) or Sophie Marcus. Or someone else, perhaps the murderer in the moon. Nor do we know why the Chief Rabbi was eager to defend Hersch. Perhaps we shall never know. I count that day, 29 March last, as the day I became an adult. Perhaps because, ever since, almost everything seems problematic.

The rag dealer Ephraim Hess, clearly agitated, rushed into the coin shop just before closing time and asked if he could speak with Meyer in private. Meyer nodded at Guttle, and said he could speak to both of them.

"I need to ask a favor of you," Ephraim said, breathing heavily, looking over his shoulder for a moment, as if he were being chased by dogs. "I hate to impose on you, you have helped me in the past, but that's why I come to you. If I ask too much, just send me away."

"First you'll have to tell me what this is about."

"This morning the Chief Rabbi came to my shop. He told me he had information that the Frankfurt Polizei are planning to raid the lane in the next day or two."

"He came to you, because … ?"

"I'm in my twenty-third year. Not old enough to marry. But we have the baby. If they check the records, they could haul me off to jail. Who knows for how long? I don't want Eva to be left alone with the child. They could even take the baby."

"Couldn't you hide him for a day? Leave him with another couple?"

"We thought of that. They haven't raided since Solomon was born. But what if they come again in a week? A month? We'd always be in fear. That's not a way to live."

"What is it you want me to do?"

"Eva and I have decided to leave. We've been saving money to do this for a long time, to get away from these walls, the cause of all our sorrow. We want to go to the British colony in America, where we've heard that Jews have freedom. We didn't plan to go until Solomon was older, until we had saved more money. But we're leaving tomorrow."

"And you need money?"

"No, no. We have enough to get to England. I'll find work there for a few years. Then we'll sail to America."

"What kind of work?"

"Whatever is there. We're leaving in the morning, before the Polizei come. The problem is, I have no time to sell the apartment, and the shop." He pulled a deed from his pocket. "I would like to sign this deed over to you. If you could sell the property in due course, you could forward the money to me when we have a proper address. Keeping a percentage for your trouble, of course."

Meyer closed his eyes, squeezing his lips with his fingers. Guttle did not speak, tried to be invisible.

"If I am presuming too much, please say so, and I will ask someone else."

"Be still," Meyer said. "I'm thinking." He glanced at the iron strongbox in the corner, with its huge padlock, the replacement for the old wooden box from which Hersch had stolen the purse. "How much do you want for the property?"

"I'm not greedy, Herr Rothschild, I'll take whatever you can get for it."

"I've told you before to call me Meyer. How about three thousand gulden?"

"That's a lot. I would gladly settle for two thousand."

"You don't know the demand for space in the Judengasse. A four-room house across the lane, with no air to breathe, just sold for six thousand." Meyer went to his desk, opened the drawer, pulled out a letter of credit. "Would you like to go directly to America?"

"Of course. But we can't."

"I have a proposition for you. I will buy the property right now. For three thousand gulden. A fair price. That will get you to America, with plenty left over to start a life. I could give you cash, but you wouldn't want to carry that much cash on your travels. Too many robbers out there. I'll make out a letter of credit in your name. No one else can use it. When you get to London, go to the bank I'm writing down. They'll have money for the voyage waiting for you. For the rest, they can give you a note on a bank in America, so you don't carry cash on the boat."

The rag dealer seemed amazed. "You can do all that?"

"A bank in Frankfurt can. They have an arrangement with a bank in London."

Ephraim did not know what to say. Meyer told him to just sign over the deed and take the letter of credit. Which Ephraim did, saying, "You're a good man, Herr Rothschild."

"As are you, Herr Hess."

Guttle finally spoke. "The baby is a year old. Is such a long voyage safe for him?"

"Eva's a good mother. She will keep him warm."

The rag dealer remained standing there, awkwardly, again looked anxiously over his shoulder toward the door, like a dog wanting out. Guttle hugged him, which made his face redden. "Kiss your wife for me," she said. "And darling Solomon."

Meyer shook the rag dealer's hand and led him to the door. "Have a safe journey. May Yahweh watch over you."

"Adonai will reward you for this," Ephraim said. Meyer waved him away, and he took off running down the alley.

Guttle put her arms around Meyer's neck. "That's a very small apartment for three thousand gulden."

Meyer replied, "The Atlantic is a very big ocean."

1 4 April

The police raided the lane today, just as the Chief Rabbi had warned. Four wagons clattered to a halt outside the north gate, two Constables in each. They did not carry the usual muskets, but had pistols tucked into their waist bands. From house to house they walked, making sure nothing that is prohibited, such as a printing shop, had opened, looking for high windows that should be boarded up. For several hours they were visible in the lane, like a foreign army. One officer spent the entire time in Rabbi Simcha's study, going over the community books. Luckily, when at last they left, no one had been arrested — and the Hesses were long gone. As the police wagons clattered off, the colorful banners over the shops seemed to flutter all at once, from everybody sighing. How the Rabbi knew they were coming, we have no idea.

1 6 April

I don't see how Meyer and I ever will tear down the walls. Today I had a thought I never had before. Why can't we go somewhere else, where there are no walls — as Ephraim and Eva have?

I remember when I was a child, not long after the time I got locked outside the lane, Papa with a special pass from his Prince took me on a carriage ride to see the city. We passed a lake with boats on it — people rowing in boats, boats with white sails that leaned in the wind and gleamed in the sun. I wondered what it would feel like to sail on water. Now I wonder again. What would it be like to sail to London? Or to America? To stand on the deck of a two-masted ship like those in the harbor, to wave goodbye to our friends as the seamen cast off the thick braided ropes from the quay, smoothly to sail down the gentle Main, and the Rhine, till the wind in the sails took us far out to sea, the waves pitching beneath us, the great ship dipping and yawing, foamy spray splashing across the deck, as the seamen talk about when they visit the lane, us holding on tight, knowing our destination is worth the discomfort, like Noah in the ark, like Jonah in the whale.

I wonder what Meyer would think. I am afraid to ask. I am afraid he would think me foolish.

1 7 April

Melka spoke to me in the night. She said that if Meyer and I love one another, there is nothing we should be afraid to discuss. That is easier for her to whisper, locked away in an attic, than for me to attempt.

While Meyer was drinking his morning coffee, Guttle, arriving for work, perched on the desk, started to speak, stopped herself.

"Is something wrong?" Meyer asked. "You seem upset."

"I want to ask you something. But you might get angry."

"I'm in a good mood this morning. Try me."

"What would you think about us leaving the Judengasse?"

"Today? Where would you want to go? Further than the market?"

"I don't mean that. I mean forever. After we're married. Sail away, like the Hesses did."

Meyer set down his cup, raised his eyebrows as he stood. This was a question, it appeared, that needed pacing room, though there wasn't much of it. Four steps and he reached the wall. An office with more room to pace — how much smarter would he be then?

"Our families are here."

"Papa has lots of money. We all could go."

"Start new businesses in a strange place? In a new language? With no contacts?"

"I know that would be hard. But I hate these walls so much!"

Meyer sat, reached for Guttle's hand, guided her onto his lap. "If we sailed away, we might find more freedom for ourselves. But what would that do for our fellow Jews?"

"What are we doing for them now?"

"Ten percent of my profits goes to the welfare fund, to help the poor families. When I make more money, there will be more for charity. When the time does come to tear down the walls, we won't be able to do it from London. Or America."

They sat in silence. When he pressed his face into the back of her neck, she asked, "Why do you love me? I'm so selfish."

"You're not selfish. You're just frustrated."

"Aren't you frustrated?"

"Of course. But I invest those feelings in the business. That's what gives me strength to bargain with the Gentiles, day after day."

"I really don't want us to sail away. I was just wondering."

"Do you ever think about why we're alive?"

"When I try to, it hurts my head."

"Remember that story book I gave you?"

"Don Quixote?"

"It was very long. Once you started reading it, why did you keep on?"

"To see what happened next."

"I think that's why we're alive. Yahweh likes stories. He wants to see what we do next."

"Like us painting our painting. But what happens after that?"

"After that, it hurts my head, too."

Her hand squeezed his knee. "Right now I know why I'm alive. To sit on your lap."

"There you go. And in six months —" his palm sliding up to her breast "— every night we'll escape on the ships of each other."

"Don't start!" She pulled his hand away. "Don't get me itchy again."

2 *2 April*

Dvorah is pregnant! She thought she might be when she started getting sick every morning, and now it is beginning to show. Doctor Kirsch says there is no doubt. Dvorah is so funny, she seems uncertain whether to hide the truth with loose dresses or proclaim it to the world with fitted waists. Sometimes I write nasty things about her — perhaps I am jealous of her beauty — but I love her very much. I can't imagine having grown up without her across the lane to giggle with, to confide in. We are closer than sisters. One time when we were little we made a pact that when we got married and cut off our hair, we would each wear wigs made from the other's locks. The idea was to see if we each became the other one. Children can be stranger than adults. Already the three midwives are competing for who will deliver Doctor Berkov's child. Dvorah loves the attention.

2 *3 April*

We girls in the lane grew up with only one question in our lives — whom will we marry? After that, there are only two other questions — how many children will we deliver, and how many of them will live. There should be something more. I don't know what it is.

Rumor swept through the lane that the boarded-up house at the south gate would soon be opened. "It's true," Guttle told Izzy as they stood in front of their adjacent doors.

"I don't believe there's any grotesque Melka locked away in the attic — but who would have the nerve to look?"

"Doctor Kirsch."

She began to tell him how it had come about. The young historian wanted to hear all the details. He opened his ever-present book to make notes.

"When Rebecca came to the lane last fall, she shared Doctor Berkov's apartment. But when he married Dvorah, Rebecca had to leave. She moved her things into the hospital, thinking it would be just for a few days. She's been sleeping there ever since."

"That must be unpleasant, it's like she's never away from her work," Izzy said, still looking down at his book, still writing. He had discovered that if you interjected such comments during an interview, it gained time to scrawl your notes.

"Especially now, with this outbreak of grippe," Guttle said. "The hospital is filled with people coughing. Anyway, a few weeks ago we were walking together, to stretch our leg muscles, and talk. I love to hear her talk of the outside world."

"I know. She speaks of the future — I research the past. We'd make a good team."

"Izzy, she's ten years older than you."

"I'm not talking about that kind of team. So what happened?"

"When we reached the south gate, Rebecca looked at the boarded up house, as if she'd never noticed it before, though she must have. She asked me why nobody lived there. I told her that somebody did. I told her about Melka."

"She must have smirked at that."

"She didn't express any judgment. She just listened. But the next day she went to see the banker Siegfried Salman, who owns the house. Last week she bought it from him. At a very low price, I imagine. She was so happy at the prospect of owning her own house, she didn't make them rip off the boards and show her the inside."

"Why not? She could have ended the Melka story right then."

"She knows the house must be filthy, and maybe falling apart. She also knows there might not be another house available for years. When she has time, she'll hire workers to clean it. To make repairs. Once she's not so busy with the grippe."

"I want to be there when she goes inside," Izzy said. "To watch the death of Melka."

"Just don't run away scared when you see her," Guttle said. "People might laugh."

2 *May*

The day his brother was exiled, Hiram quit as assistant Schul-Klopper. By giving Hersch his black coat he seemed to lose the confidence to face the world. He only does what he used to do, sits by his window looking down at the lane, timing things, noting them in his book; watching the fire captain, who took his place, knock on doors. Yetta appears to have survived the death of her husband better than Hiram has survived the loss of his brother.

Meyer still feels guilty about what happened. I remind him that Hersch was sent away because of thievery, of which he was surely guilty, not because of the murder charge. Meyer knows this, of course. Still, a small part of his heart may never mend. I will do my best to kiss the pain away.

4 May

Today we saw Madame Antoine, the young Archduchess of the Holy Roman Empire, pass through Frankfurt in an unimaginable procession of fifty-seven carriages filled with hundreds of nobles and servants. She is only fourteen, but she is on her way from Vienna to Versailles to marry the French Dauphin. One day most likely she will be queen of France.

Her mother, Maria Teresa, ordered the procession to pass in front of the cathedral here, where all of the Emperors are crowned. Peasants were urged to leave their fields and greet the Archduchess along country roads, and bid her farewell. Everyone in the Judengasse, by order of the Empress, was permitted to watch as well, to swell the crowds. Most of the men remained behind to do their work, Meyer among them. Dvorah and I left early, ahead of most of the women, and took up a good position, only a block from the church. Jews are not allowed to go closer to the cathedral than that.

We waited two hours for the procession to arrive, but the sight of that long line of glittering carriages was worth it. Trumpets and kettle drums played royal marches. The coach of the Archduchess was crimson and gold. Her complexion was pale and beautiful as she looked out through the window, luckily on our side. We could not see much of what she was wearing, but I could see her powdered hair piled high and studded with jewels, her pretty features, her high forehead, her blue-gray eyes; the carriage was that close, and had come almost to a stop.

I read in one of Meyer's newspapers that her trousseau, made in France, cost more than a hundred thousand gulden. I can't imagine having that much clothing. Dvorah said she could, if she didn't have to live in the Judengasse.

And the magnificent horses! One hundred and thirty seven of them, a guard said, to pull the coaches at one time — twenty thousand horses to complete the journey. The wealth of the Empress, who is paying for this, is hard to imagine. Yet according to the newspaper, it does not compare with the wealth of the King of France.

Still — Dvorah thinks I am crazy for this — I thought I saw sadness in the eyes of Madame Antoine. And why not? Fourteen years old, and she is being given in marriage for reasons of politics — to create an alliance between Austria and France. She may never see her family again. She has never met the man she will marry, who is only sixteen years old himself, and rather fat, they say. In the instant

*her carriage rolled slowly by, her eyes met mine. Our glances locked. I swear she
was wishing she could change places with me.*

"But she'll be Queen of France!" Dvorah said.

*We could not see what ceremony took place inside the cathedral. It was very
brief. Then with the creaking of hundreds of wheels the long line of carriages rolled
away, leaving behind only steaming horse droppings and the image of a sad,
innocent face that I shall never forget.*

*In a few days the procession will reach the border, and Madame Antoine will
be handed over to the French. At that moment her title and her name will change.
She will be called not the Archduchess, but the Dauphine. Her name will become
Marie Antoinette.*

*She is so young to be going so far, two years younger than I. Her situation is
like a fairy tale, or an opera — going off so grandly to marry a distant Prince. But
in that brief moment when our eyes locked together, I thought I saw deep sorrow.
As if she lived within walls that were higher than mine.*

*If that is true, then the walls of the Judengasse are not what the rag dealer
said. They are the creators of intense suffering — but they are not the origin of
sorrow.*

27

Spring rain was falling steadily, bouncing off the cobbles in florets, running into the sewage ditch that would carry it to the sluice and the river. In the narrow space between the front and rear rows of houses the drainage was not as good; the water building up outside the Hinterpfann was threatening to wash under the door and soak the office floor. Alone in the dank shop, Guttle fetched rags and stuffed them against the crack under the door to keep the water out, and climbed down to the small basement and carried up wood for the stove.

Returning to her chair, she soon became bored. Meyer had taken the morning coach to Speyer to show his coins to potential buyers. Not a single person had braved the rain to change money in the shop or to examine medals or antiques, and none was likely to. She enjoyed her job much more on days when Meyer was around, though she could hardly argue with what he said, that he made no profit, and no contacts, while sitting on his rear. She pictured him walking from a coin shop to a nobleman's house in the rain, if it was raining in Speyer, then to another coin shop, carrying his heavy case. She found herself drifting off to sleep — then bolted her head upright. An idea had occurred to her, a remedy.

The more she thought about it, the more she liked it. She could see no drawbacks. When Meyer returned late in the day and went upstairs to change into dry clothes, she was impatient to speak with him. She made tea for them both, and began to tell him of her idea while he drank, sipping the tea through a clump of honey crystals he held between his teeth. "It's an idea to save you time and money."

"So far I like it," Meyer mumbled around the honey.

"When you take your coins to a collector, suppose you show him a hundred coins, and tell him about them. Let's say he buys ten."

With his tongue, Meyer moved the clump into his cheek. "That would be a very good visit."

"Still, ninety percent of your time would have been wasted, showing him the coins he didn't buy."

"I can't expect them to buy every coin. Besides, one he doesn't buy today he might buy the next time."

"Let me continue. If he bought nothing, which happens sometimes, your whole visit was wasted. But suppose you did this. Suppose you prepared on parchment a list of your coins, with whatever descriptions you need. You have a few of these lists printed in a shop, and you send the them by post to the buyers, for them to examine. That way, when you call on them, they will already know which coins they are interested in. If they want to look at ten coins, you save ninety percent of your time. You return home that much earlier."

"Ah, I suspected there was a sweet Guttle motive here somewhere."

"Or you can see more clients in a day."

He sipped more tea through the diminishing crystals. Guttle was tense, waiting for a response. Endeavoring not to show it, letting him consider the idea, she heated more water, and poured him a second glass of tea.

"Suppose," he said, thinking aloud, "I make many copies of this list. I send it to nobles and other collectors far away. Farther even than I can travel in a day. They could let me know by post which coins they want to see. I send those coins to them. If they want to keep them, they send me the money — or we could bargain through the post about the price; they all love to bargain. If they are not interested in the coins once they examine them, they send them back. That would increase my profits twice. I save the time and the coach fare."

Guttle felt exhilarated. He not only liked her idea, he was expanding on it. He was getting so used to her ideas, it appeared, that he no longer felt it necessary to praise her. That was a mixed blessing; she was starting to feel hurt.

"But what if they keep the coins and don't pay for them?"

"They wouldn't." He was getting excited now. "These people have the money to pay. They wouldn't risk their reputations. On the contrary, they would see me trusting them, so they would return my trust. Which would build mutual confidence for bigger transactions in the future." He reached for her hand across the table. "Guttle, this is a wonderful idea. How did you come up with it?"

Her hurt vanished at once, an inner joy returned. "The rain brought it from the heavens. Or maybe it's from being with you."

Meyer nodded distractedly, still building on the idea. "After a buyer has made several purchases by post, I would pay him a visit. So we could get to know one another. So I could work my personal charm." He grinned.

His smile was self-deprecating, but his words, she knew, were true. Even Gentiles liked him, despite the Judengasse in his voice.

"Unfortunately," he said, "tomorrow you will begin to regret having this superb idea."

Guttle scrunched her face, as a child might. "Why would I regret it?"

He stood and bent behind her, and, lifting her French-style braid, kissed the warm nape of her neck. "Whom do you think, in handsome German script, will be making the lists for me?"

7 May

When I see Hiram at his third-floor window in the last house, I am often reminded of Melka — as if Hiram were born broken to offset her legend at the other end of the lane, a balanced configuration of the misbegotten. Perhaps he, too, will be a legend one day: Hiram of the North Gate. I can't imagine in what way, him being deaf and mute, but he remains close friends with Izzy — who will be the maker of our future myths. Izzy told me what Hiram said with his hands the day Hersch left the lane: 'You are my brother now.'

Guttle grabbed Izzy and they hurried down the lane. At the south end they found Doctor Kirsch waiting in front of her new house. Yussel Kahn and another carpenter arrived soon after.

The Doctor had warned all of them to bring large handkerchiefs. She made them tie the handkerchiefs over their mouths and noses, so they would not inhale too much acrid dust. Several metres up the lane the fire captain was stationed to keep the curious from getting too close till the Doctor knew what was inside. At once the ever-present Sophie Marcus gave him trouble, demanding that he let her pass. She began to shout, "Is that Schnapper whore better than me —just because she sleeps with Rothschild?" Her son the Cantor came out from their house and led her away. Guttle's face reddened with anger as she heard the insult, the lie.

The two carpenters began to pry loose the boards that covered the front door. The wood screeched and howled on rusted nails, but eventually came loose. The banker had given Rebecca a key for the front door. It was rusted, but not bent. Guttle and Izzy watched from close behind her as with a bit of jiggling she convinced the lock to turn. Still, the door was stuck shut. Yussel had to lean hard on it with his shoulder before it popped open. Rebecca pushed it wide, then jumped back, bumping into Guttle as, with the light flowing in like a scouring enemy, a cluster of brown rats scurried into the lane and scrambled downhill for the safety of the docks. There were not too many, because for a long time there had been no food or garbage in the house.

"They probably only sleep here in the daytime," Izzy said, "and go foraging on the docks at night."

"The Pied Piper would know," Guttle said.

"This means there are holes in the floor that will have to be filled with poison and boarded up," Yussel said. "Brown rats stay near the ground. If there are also black rats, they'll be in the attic."

Guttle shuddered. That's where Melka was.

Behind the running rats, a musty smell of dust and decomposed things rushed out through the open door like a long buried odor trying to flee from itself. Beyond the odor was darkness.

The north side of the house was protected by a thick fire wall., built by some previous rich owner to save his home should the adjacent buildings catch fire. Yussel and the other carpenter, called Doov, went around to the south side, which faced the curving ghetto wall and the river beyond. Rusted nails in the boards on the windows screamed like chickens in the slaughterhouse before loosening their grip. When the boards were pried off, the first sunlight in centuries sprayed pale rectangles on the dust that covered the ground floor like a rug. Rebecca entered slowly, followed by the others. The front room was large, had not been divided up; the home had been abandoned long before the Judengasse became crowded; Rebecca was delighted with its size. As their eyes became accustomed to the dim light they saw huge yellow spider webs hanging in every corner of ceiling and floor like the furnishings of tombs, webs made of thick strands woven around other strands. In the spun center of some, spiders hung motionless, dead or alive.

"They must live on vermin that ride in with the rats," Rebecca said.

Yussel moved closer for a better look. "Don't go near those things without gloves," he told the Doctor.

"I won't go near those things without a fire hose," she replied, tightening the blue kerchief that covered her dark hair, "and half a dozen strong men to aim it."

The carpenters had brought a ladder with them. "You might as well uncover the second and third floors," Rebecca said. "They're probably in the same condition."

Guttle felt herself getting anxious. Izzy was scrawling notes in his book.

"What about the attic?" Yussel asked. "As long as we have the ladder."

The Doctor led them out into the fresher air of the lane. Some in a small crowd of women and children who were gathered behind the fire captain cried out, asking what they had found. Rebecca told the carpenters, "Let's not do the attic today. I'm not comfortable preserving a myth — but I want to think about it." Turning to Guttle, she added, "If the attic is as nasty as what we just saw, your Melka is quite a girl."

2 4 June

This morning from my window I saw Izzy carrying into the Liebmann house long, thin sticks of wood, a roll of canvas, and what looked like jars of paint. Something is going on.

With Leo dead and Hersch in exile, a painful quiet emanated from the first house by the north gate. It had been weeks since Guttle had seen Yetta. Hiram's face had disappeared from his window. Concerned, Guttle decided to pay a visit, to make sure they were all right, to make sure Yetta would be coming to the wedding.

She crossed the lane and mounted the stairs. The familiar smell of boiled cabbage had been overcome by a more powerful one, the sharp aroma of paint and turpentine. Glancing at the door to Hiram's room, which was shut, Guttle asked after Yetta's health. Yetta said she was fine. But at once she seemed to change her mind. She pointed to the chairs in the kitchen, and they sat.

"I'm old, why should I lie to you?" Yetta said. "Old people don't have to lie. I miss my Leo." Guttle thought Frau Liebmann's eyes were reddening, but that may have been the flickering of the lamp. "There's no one else to talk to, I forget how my voice sounds. You should never know what it's like, Guttle, to lose your husband. Even though Leo's gone, I talk to him still. Sometimes we even fight."

Who could not smile at that? "And Hiram? I get the feeling he is painting something."

"To figure that out, you don't need such a young nose. It's wonderful, better than looking out the window all day. Isidor brings him paint and canvas and charcoal that Yussel Kahn buys near his bookbinder. From a window in Hiram's bedroom that faces to the north they tore off the boards, and replaced them with shutters he can open and close. The guard by the gate is too near to see up. The window looks only over the slaughterhouse. Nobody has complained so far, knock wood."

"What does he paint?"

"You shouldn't ask. Everything. You know how he used to clock things out the window, make little drawings in his book? It appears it wasn't such a waste. Now he looks at his book, and makes bigger drawings, from what he remembers. If he likes it, he tries a color painting. His eyes and his memory are good — as if to make up for the other."

"Can I see them? Can anyone?'"

Guttle was hoping she would say no. What if they were awful?

Yetta did say no. "He says nobody can see them until he is ready. Until he is good enough. He likes the drawings with charcoal, but paint is new to him. Every time he adds a color, he says, the other colors change. He has a lot to teach himself. I told him we could sell Hersch's bed so he would have more room to work. He said no. He wants to keep it till Hersch comes back."

"It sounds like he's doing fine," Guttle said.

Frau Liebmann closed her eyes, rubbed them with thinning hands. "Now, fine. What happens when I'm gone? There will be only Isidor he can talk with." She placed her hands on the table. "In two years he'll be old enough to marry. What girl will have him?" She found a handkerchief in her apron pocket and twisted it between her fingers. "Yahweh shouldn't hear this, but for Hiram, in one way it's been good that Hersch was sent away. He wouldn't have taken up painting with his brother around. But soon it won't be enough. Hersch was supposed to look after him when I'm gone."

Cold guilt blew through Guttle like a winter wind. Through all the years, she realized, it never once had occurred to her to learn Hiram's gestures, so she could converse with him. She had treated him as someone not worth talking to — just as most of the lane had.

Her next thought was to ask Yetta to teach her. But she held back. She needed to think about what future responsibility this might impose on her.

In that moment, she despised herself.

"The reason I came," she said, "I want to make sure you're coming to my wedding."

"Of course I'm coming. I've watched you grow up from a tiny thing. I used to mind you in your cradle when your Mama was at the bakery."

Guttle assured her that Hiram was invited, too. Yetta placed her hands, still clutching the handkerchief, in her lap. "For Hiram I can't speak," she said.

*N*ight. *A simple bedroom. Cassandra, a future bride, is admiring her wedding dress. She sits on the floor, leans her cheek against the hem of white lace. Mournfully, she sings an aria:*

> *Dear Melka above us, if you really love us*
> *I pray you will help me to reckon with Sophie;*

I spoke with the Cantor, he holds no more rancor,
It's just his sick Mama who plays out this drama;
Since I was a Nicht girl he's courting the Licht girl,
A sweet shining light who now brightens his night;
And here is a new find — he's says that he's inclined
(To prove his forgetting) to sing at my wedding!
And Jacob, his father, for reasons, I gather,
Of business intended, my pa has befriended;
Yet still there is Sophie, the devil's own trophy,
Intent on corrupting, befouling, disrupting,
Dismaying, waylaying, obscenely erupting.
Though lacking precision, I suffer from visions
Of bridal joy neutered, of nuptials disputed,
Of actions most foul when I leave the Owl.
Are these superstition or true premonition?
Where will she hide on the day I'm a bride?
What will she try to make sure that I cry?
Who will she be the day Meyer weds me?
Dear Melka above us, if you really love us,
While we plight love timeless you'll watch over me.

6 July

In Meyer's head there is a map of the entire world of finance to which I am not yet privy. I envision it as one of those engraved maps of the ancient Greek empire that Yussel bought from his bookbinder. In Meyer's head the map is not what the mercantile world looked like in the past, but how it will look in the future. On those unknown seas he is sailing when he seems most distracted.

9 July

Hannah fitted the pieces of my dress to me today. White silk with lots of lace, the fabric a gift from Meyer's brothers, ordered special from England. I'm getting excited about the wedding. If still a bit apprehensive.

Dvorah had grown huge. Each day she drifted slowly through the lane prow forward, Guttle thought, like Noah's ark. Both friends were busy at work, had not chatted for almost a week, till Guttle invited Dvorah to lunch. The day was warm, she fixed a cold meal of bread with cheese and a glass of borscht. They ate in the the courtyard of the synagogue.

"I'm so big," Dvorah acknowledged, easing herself onto a bench, grimacing. "Lev thinks it might be twins."

"Or two of every species."

Dvorah laughed, placing her hand on her belly to steady it as it shook. "Don't start," she said, "or I might have a donkey right here."

They took bites of their bread and cheese, washed it down with the borsht. "I hear you've settled on the names," Guttle said.

"David if it's a boy. Ruth if it's a girl."

"And Poland if it's a country?"

Dvorah was laughing again, although trying not to, her belly shaking more than before. She pressed her face into Guttle's shoulder, was crying now, or still laughing, Guttle couldn't tell. Perhaps an undecided mixture of both, like rain on a sunny day.

"I'm so happy," Dvorah blurted into her shoulder, through sobs. "But I hate being so huge."

Guttle held her tight and tried to calm her. "When I'm pregnant, I'm sure I'll be the same."

"Maybe." Dvorah sniffled. "But you won't have you to contend with."

You're wrong there, Guttle thought. I'll always have me to contend with.

1 3 July

Brendel Isaacs and her two little ones are moving here from Mainz — into the small apartment and shop Meyer bought from the rag dealer.

I'm not sure if the idea originated with Meyer or with Yussel. Strictly a business deal, Meyer says, keeping his face expressionless. According to the papers, Brendel is buying the property, with money she is borrowing from Yussel — who in turn is borrowing the money from Meyer. Brendel will run the rag shop, and make monthly payments to Yussel, who will pass them along to Meyer. Unless Brendel has no money, in which case Yussel will pay Meyer. Unless Yussel has no money, in which case no one will pay Meyer. The purchase price is two thousand six hundred gulden — four hundred less than Meyer paid.

Strictly a business deal.

That's what I mean about Brendel. She inspires men without really trying.

2 0 July

After we are married we shall have room in which to turn around. Meyer and his brothers have bought the three-eighths of his house owned by the Bauers, who will move in with relatives down the lane. The storage room adjoining the shop will become a bedroom for Meyer and me. This will give us privacy from Kalman, Moish and his family, who will have extra space two floors above. Meyer has ordered a new straw mattress, and feather pillows, from the Kracauer brothers. I hope the pillows won't smell of the slaughterhouse. I still share a bed with Avra. My chest prickles with apprehension when I think of Meyer beside me, but my face grows hot.

The day of the unveiling of the centuries-old Melka had arrived. Myth or corpse or something beyond human experience? Hundreds of women and a few men crowded toward the south gate. The fire chief and his volunteers formed a line across the lane to keep them away, to prevent a stampede. Anything could happen, depending on what was found. Climbing to the attic window up a long ladder that Izzy held steady, Yussel Kahn wearing his oldest clothes pried off the resisting boards. Inside the house, he removed more boards that sealed the attic doorway. Though he was no believer in Melka, he hesitated, took several deep breaths. Hamlet crept into his mind. *There are more things in Heaven and Earth, Horatio, than are dreamt of in your philosophies.* Shakespeare was a genius, yet he had peopled the world with ghosts. Who was he, Yussel, a mere cabinet maker, to demur? What seemed to him like hours were only seconds until he pushed open the door. Rebecca, Guttle and Izzy waited at the bottom of the narrow stairs, as if to leave room for a spirit, visible or not, to come flying or floating from the attic. When they saw nothing, heard nothing, they climbed to the attic and ducked under its sloping roof, and instinctively pressed backed against a wall, unafraid, they would claim later. Yussel was standing silently, staring at the center of the room. They followed his gaze. Bright sunlight slanted in through the uncovered window — the first sunlight in this room in nearly three hundred years. This was the only room in the lane into which the sun could stream at such an angle, the window being higher than the ghetto walls, and facing to the south. The floor was covered with dust, which their shoes stirred into the air. Golden motes danced in a shaft of sunlight. The sun illuminated a rectangular, dust-covered box. It was the size and shape of a coffin — a coffin that in the stream of light seemed to glow with a flame of its own.

"She's real — or was real!" Guttle blurted.

"Why would she be buried up here?" Izzy asked.

Guttle was trembling, glad they had not found a skeleton picked clean on the floor. She reached for Izzy's hand. He was shaking, too. Yussel and Rebecca looked at one another, hesitated, moved toward the box. Wearing an old hospital gown over her clothing, Rebecca ran a finger across the top; it left a streak in the dust. With the gown, heedless of getting it filthy, she wiped off more of the dust. Yussel knelt to examine what was clearly now a coffin.

"It's made of lead. The kind of coffin in which they preserve Kings."

Rebecca touched the lead, dull gray on the shadow side, gleaming in the sun. Guttle and Izzy stayed back. The fearful children of their beings held sway.

"They must have reinforced the floor to support this," Yussel said. "But how did they get it up here?"

"Will power?" the Doctor ventured.

"Shall we open it?'"

Izzy and Guttle, clinging, pressed their backs harder against the wall.

"Let me get a cloth," Rebecca said. She went down the squealing and creaking attic stairs, and the rat-soiled steps, to the ground floor. Guttle shivered when she returned holding two large rags. The Doctor and Yussel finished wiping the dust from the lid of the coffin, and the lighter layer that clung to the sides, trying not to swirl too much dust into the air. They are polishing eternity, Guttle thought. She and Izzy forced themselves to move closer, hearts thumping as if the Polizei were coming.

"The stench might be awful," Rebecca said. "Do you think you can cope?"

Yussel nodded. Guttle and Izzy remained silent. Yussel examined the coffin lid for fasteners. There were none. The heavy lid merely rested on top. Kneeling, he and Rebecca pushed at the lid; it moved only slightly. "We'll need your help," Yussel said over his shoulder. Izzy and Guttle knelt shakily beside them. All of them pushed. Slowly the lid moved. Thick musk invaded their nostrils, but nothing worse. Guttle prepared herself to see the dry brittle bones of Melka.

They strained and pushed harder. When the lid was half way across, Rebecca crept on her knees to the other side, to guide it to the floor. When it was safely off, they stood from aching knees and looked down. Whatever was inside the coffin was hidden beneath folds of canvas. Atop the canvas was a small scroll. Rebecca lifted it out. "Parchment," she said. "Almost like new."

She turned the rolled parchment in her hands. Guttle wondered: had Melka left a note? Finally Rebecca slipped off two gold-colored ribbons and unrolled the scroll. She perused it silently. Then she read it aloud, while Izzy scribbled the words into his notebook.

*T*o *future residents of the Judengasse—*

Jews newly arrived from Spain report that the Jewish faith has been forbidden in that country. All synagogues are being destroyed, all menorahs, Torahs and other artifacts being defaced and destroyed. Jews who do not convert to the Christian faith are tortured and put to death. Some are risking their lives by making false conversions and continuing to uphold their faith in shuttered basements.

In our synagogue here we have three Torahs, known to us affectionately, to distinguish among them, as Adonai, Eloheinu and Melekh. In this protective coffin lies Melekh, hidden here against the event that this persecution spreads to Frankfurt, that our synagogue, too, be razed. A scroll noting this location is secreted in the Chief Rabbi's house.

If you, our descendants, read this in time of strife, we pray for you. If you chance upon this for some other reason, leave Melekh undisturbed, against a future need.

For the two hundred and six living residents of the Judengasse,

Rabbi Yitzhak ben Levi,

21 December, 1492

They were silent, stunned. Rebecca knelt beside the coffin, gently lifted back the folds of canvas. Beneath them was the most beautiful Torah they had ever seen. Hebrew letters were embroidered in gold thread on maroon velvet. The elaborate crown covering the handles was gold as well, studded with gems, and indeed made Melekh look like a melekh — a king — from the words with which all their Jewish bruchas began: *Barukh attah Adonai Eloheinu Melekh ha-Olam…* Blessed Art Thou O Lord, Our God, King of the Universe.

Awed silence in the presence of living history, thick as the dust had been.

"So this is Melka," Rebecca said at last.

"Why not Melekh?" Izzy asked.

Still gazing into the coffin, Rebecca ventured, "Melekh is a hard word for little ones to pronounce, with the guttural sound at the end. Melka is easier. A transposition of syllables through the centuries. It could be as simple as that."

"Or perhaps on purpose — to make it female," Guttle said.

What to do next? Carefully, Rebecca smoothed the canvas flaps back over the Torah. After Izzy finished copying the words, she rolled the parchment scroll delicately, as if it were living flesh. She tied it with the ribbons and placed it in the coffin. From somewhere deep inside themselves they found the strength to lift the lid and place it as it had been. Except for the absent dust, Melka — Melekh, now — looked undisturbed.

"We have to agree to say nothing to anyone." Rebecca said. "To honor the scroll."

"In case he's ever needed," Izzy affirmed.

"People will want to know what we found," Yussel said. "Should we say the attic was empty?"

"That would destroy Melka," Guttle noted.

The Doctor rubbed her eyes with the back of her wrists, looking strained. "As I've said before, I have mixed feelings about preserving a legend. But perhaps that's the best course. I don't want to keep it alive with a lie. But it might be serving a purpose whose depth we cannot know. We'll say a partial truth — that a note on parchment from our ancestors warned us not to reveal what we found. We'll board up the door and window, and say we left the attic undisturbed. At least that part is true. Soon it will just be the top of my new house.

"People won't be happy," Guttle said.

The Doctor replied, "They live with worse."

One by one they moved to the window, knowing it would be their only opportunity to look out. They could see the Fahrtor gate, the river with its sailing ships, the entire serpentine length of the bridge, the land on the other side stretching away to the far horizon, rich with fields and farms. Before leaving the attic, with a hint of tears, each brushed the coffin with fingertips, and touched their fingers to their lips.

Guttle was correct. The waiting women were not happy. Some pleaded, cajoled, for information. "What was Melka like? What did she say?" The loudest was Sophie Marcus. "Look at them with their noses in the air! They're too good to talk to us!" Guttle and the others walked by stoically, but not without an ache in their chests.

2⁴ July

Mama and Avra asked me about Melka. I told them I had taken an oath not to speak of her. Surprisingly, they respected that, as if I had grown in stature in their eyes. Dvorah was very different. We have always told each other everything. She could not believe I would not confide. Refusing her was difficult. Now she is being sullen with me.

I still believe in Melka. I'm not sure why. Perhaps, because she has always lived in my brain, she will continue to live there, regardless of what we found in the attic.

The men lay tefillin every morning, dovaning to Yahweh, although they have never seen Him. Perhaps Melka is much the same.

Brendel Isaacs opened her rag shop with the inventory left behind by the Hesses, and their own personal clothing; she had no money to buy more stock. The day was hot and stifling, perspiration on every forehead. For the opening she wore a swishing dark green skirt that reached to her ankles, beige boots, a white blouse whose rectangular neckline ended barely above her breasts; the puffy short sleeves she'd slid off her shoulders. Her blonde ringlets fell from beneath a white mob cap. Hardly a man in the lane did not wander by to take a look at her goods.

"What do you think?" one man asked, trying on a heavy brown coat in the heat.

"It's perfect, it brings out the deep brown in your eyes," Brendel told him. "Your wife will fall in love with you — if she hasn't already."

"It's warm," the man said. He'd apparently just gotten warmer.

"When winter comes you'll thank me, guaranteed."

A young man tried on a blue wool sweater that had belonged to skinny Ephraim Hess. "It's a little snug," he said, wriggling his arms uncomfortably. Brendel came nearer, tugged at the hem of the sweater, smoothed it across the front with her slim hands. "Look how it shows off your sturdy chest. It will make the girls swoon."

Having come to congratulate her, Guttle and Meyer watched from nearby, with Yussel. "She's a born merchant," Guttle whispered.

"A racial inheritance," Meyer agreed. "Blonde hair notwithstanding."

"Yet nary a lie can pass those lovely lips without becoming truth." Yussel winked at Brendel as she glanced in his direction.

"Shakespeare?" Meyer asked.

"Yussel Kahn. She's turning me into a poet."

Brendel sold six wool sweaters that stifling day, and five wool coats. By late afternoon even the women were coming to see this merchant enchantress, while in many a household painful exchanges were taking place, among them:

—You have six children, and a wife! Don't you forget it!

As Guttle and Meyer walked back to the Hinterpfann, Meyer said drily, "There's no doubt she adds sparkle to the lane." Guttle took his arm. "If she pulled out a flute and started walking, half the men would line up behind her. I think we've imported The Piper of Desire."

"She wouldn't even need a flute," Meyer said.

The coin list was working. Every week, new orders arrived in the post for coins to be sent on approval. How many actually would sell was uncertain, but Meyer was optimistic, as always.

Opening the letters one day, Guttle found among the coin orders a short note, in an envelope bearing British stamps, which made her jump from her chair and read aloud to Meyer. It was from Ephraim Hess.

Dear Herr Rothschild and Future Missus. We are safely arrived in London. Such a splendid city! The letter of credit is fine at the bank. A Jewish community here has taken us in and helps with translations. We gave thought of staying here to learn English — but no. We sail on next boat to America! May Adonai bless you, and Tally Ho! E. Hess.

The note elicited smiles from both. Guttle walked to the synagogue to post it in the community room. As she did, people gathered to read it. They cheered and clapped and raised glasses of tea to the courage of the Hesses. Guttle told Meyer when she returned, "It feels as if the whole lane will be sailing with them."

4 August

I have been thinking about Melka — or Melekh. I suppose the lesson of the legend is simple, something children grope for in stories and myths, and adults are bound to learn: here in the Judengasse, it is our faith that keeps us sane.

But I wonder if that is true for Rebecca, for Brendel, for Dvorah. For Mama, even. I feel certain it was girls and women who created Melka — not an idol to worship, but a mirror of our minds: hidden away, not to be used except in time of trouble. The Torah would have women wielding pails and mops till the Messiah comes, while the men commune with Yahweh. Melka, perhaps, was our defiance. If so, in the dark attics of our souls she will live on.

10 August

My dress fits perfectly! Hannah is such a good seamstress! She and bulging Dvorah, who's left her hospital job to protect the babies, helped me try it on. I was standing in front of the tall mirror in Hannah's shop when in without knocking swept that Countess from the city, followed by her son. I had the feeling Paul came along in hopes of seeing Dvorah, because when she stepped in from the other room, with her belly the size of a Bavarian Alp, his mouth dropped open and he experienced a coughing fit. He excused himself and hurried down the stairs. Poor fellow, I think he was smitten with her beauty that first time he gave her his card, despite her being Jewish. He's a good-looking young man, I need shed no tears for him. I imagine he'd be quite a catch among Gentile girls. Perhaps his interest in Dvorah, though much too late, and against all the rules, shows strength of character.

Dvorah was amused by his arrival and quick exit. She grabbed me in the lane to talk. 'Isn't Paul von Brunwald cute?' she said. I patted her huge belly, and hurried on my way.

28

Guttle had submerged her body in the mikveh, the ritual bath, twelve times a year for three years — every month, right after her bleeding stopped, to purify herself, as the Talmud instructs. But the deep cavern where the mikveh was situated never before had glowed gold and silver. The fifty stone steps leading down to it were gray rock, the walls that supported the staircase were gray rock, the descent usually felt like immersion into a cave. Bathers had to walk carefully so as not to slip on the wet stones. The night before her wedding, Guttle was accompanied by Dvorah, as Guttle had accompanied her the night before she wed. Dvorah descended very slowly, holding on to the walls with each step. She had to be extra careful, with her belly protruding so far in front of her feet. She would be standing up for Guttle the next day — if she could stand at all.

Both doctors, Lev and Rebecca, had placed their ears to her belly. Both said they heard two separate heartbeats. They were sure Dvorah was carrying twins. The babies weren't due for several weeks, according to the doctors, but to Dvorah it often felt as if they already were fighting to come out.

The two young women washed themselves in a warm bath, then stepped into the mikveh itself, a square room with a square pool in the center. On Fridays it was reserved for men, to purify themselves before the Sabbath. Saturday evenings, like this one, were reserved for women. Several sat or stood on the stone border around the pool, helping one another dress, combing each other's wet hair. Guttle saw no one she knew well, but some seemed to know her, and told her Mazel tov, we'll see you at the synagogue tomorrow. Their greetings made her feel more than ever a part of the community. Few things were private in the lane, but three never were: a birth, a death, a wedding.

Dvorah set her clothing aside, and the towels she'd wrapped around herself. They had hardly covered her belly. Setting aside her own clothing and towels, Guttle knelt naked beside her and placed an ear to Dvorah's belly, stretched smooth as a giant grape. At first she heard only one tiny heart whispering within. Then she thought she heard three.

"Triplets for sure," she murmured.

Dvorah swatted a hand at her, large breasts jumping. "Bite your tongue," she said.

This is me in a year or less, Guttle thought. An innocent life growing inside me, as if I were a well-ploughed field. Does Yahweh want still more children in the lane? To skin their little knuckles on the walls? To skin their souls?

Together they moved to the edge of the pool. Steps beneath the water led to the deeper center, where a person could totally immerse. Unlike the cleansing bath, the mikveh was cold, as cold as the underground spring that fed it. Holding hands, they stepped in, shuddering at the water's rude touch. There was nothing to do but let it assault their every part. They lowered their heads beneath the surface, soaking their hair, before standing up and wading out, shivering but purified, in a ritual that went back thousands of years.

Guttle had not closed her eyes tightly enough before dunking her head, and water had seeped in. With a towel she rubbed it away. Perhaps that was why the room began to glow gold and silver — the amber of the kerosene lamps, the metal sheen of the water, commingling on the walls, turning the mikveh into one vast jewel, inside of which they were standing, naked, as if in an artist's vision. But after they had dried one another and dressed and climbed carefully up the stone stairs, the narrow sliver of sky, still light in August, also glowed. The Owl glowed. Guttle's bedroom glowed. The universe itself seemed to be donning unnatural glory, making outrageous preparation.

"Tomorrow I am getting married," Guttle told her cotton night dress as she pulled it on over her head. "That's all that is happening."

The day of the wedding was clear and dry, just as Wolf had promised nearly a year before. The Schnapper household crackled as the little ones ran about like chickens, seeking the help now of Avra, now of their mother, wriggling into the new clothing Emmie had made for the occasion, which invariably needed straightening. They knew enough not to bother Guttle, who had bathed and was trying to relax till her mother was ready to help her dress. To a lesser extent this crackling was extant in almost every house in the lane. Many people had been invited to the wedding, but this being a Sunday, with the gates of the Judengasse locked, almost everyone would be there; a cake or a plate of cookies to help feed the horde of celebrants would do as an invitation. And celebrants there would be. As a council member, Meyer was moderately known throughout the lane, and Guttle perhaps more so as The Girl Who Stopped the Horse.

Too nervous to eat breakfast, Guttle tried not to fidget as her mother pinned her hair in braids high atop her head, the highest they had ever been, affixing among them white lace flowers that matched her dress. Her mother was got up in blue silk, Avra in maroon. Her father and Meyer would be wearing matching gray coats and vests they had ordered from the tailor Max Levine, and white silk cravats.

The children having been warned to be on their best behavior, the family descended the stairs and walked proudly toward the courtyard of the synagogue. Neighbors in the lane, all walking in the same direction, called out Mazel tov and other good wishes. Several men had brought along their violins and were playing outside the temple, entertaining the gathering throng. Hannah Schlicter and Frau Metzenbaum from the bakery were bustling about, accepting cakes and trays of cookies, arranging them aesthetically on the white cloths that covered the large tables in the community room, which already were laden with the ruggelah and other desserts that Emmie and her friends had been baking for days. Guttle and her mother went in to wait. When the bride reached for a piece of ruggelah, her mother snatched it from her hand, afraid she might drop crumbs — or worse, apple filling — on her dress. Guttle relinquished it readily, had not even realized she was holding it. Just now she was more likely to wretch than to eat. Soon Avra hurried in to tell them everything was ready. The timing was perfect. Guttle stepped outside, into the brief bright sunlight of high noon. Her father was waiting. He escorted her slowly into the courtyard. The sun on her white dress was dazzling. "Adonai has blessed this marriage already," someone was heard to say.

To the soft sound of three violins, Wolf led her to the center of the courtyard, where the Chief Rabbi was waiting. The groom, looking somber, stood facing him. Yussel Kahn, standing up for Meyer, appeared tall and proud. Dvorah clearly was tired, bending an arm behind her to support her back, but was gamely standing up in a green maternity gown; a chair had been placed beside her if she needed to sit. Guttle smiled at Viktor Marcus, waiting behind the Rabbi to sing, as promised, and saw his father in the crowd. She did not see Sophie Marcus. Upset with herself, she realized that crazy Sophie was whom she'd been looking for.

As the invited guests pressed closer and hundreds of others peered in from the lane, Rabbi Simcha draped a single prayer shawl over the heads of the bride and groom. Around the waist of each he buckled large silver wedding belts. The men who had been playing violins in the lane ceased and came to look, with the exception of one who had been paid to provide the backdrop of a single slow melody.

Beneath her gown, Guttle's knees were trembling.

The Chief Rabbi, draped in his own large talis, lifted his book. In his strong voice he read the prayers and blessings of the marriage ceremony. A baby cried briefly in the arms of its mother, causing some guests to smile, as if that were a nice omen of things to come. Gazing above the Rabbi's head, Guttle saw on the low roof of the meeting room the figure of Hiram Liebmann, leading forward on his knees, sketching the wedding scene from above.

When he had finished the blessings, the Rabbi lowered his book and made a brief speech to the couple and the guests. "There are two points I want to emphasize to Meyer and Guttle on this sacred day," he began. "The first is a quotation from the Jerusalem Talmud, where we read: 'It is impossible for man to live without woman, and it is impossible for woman to live without man, and it is impossible for both to live without the Divine Presence.'

"Some couples have trouble with the third part — that it is impossible for a couple to live without the Divine Presence. The notion that Yahweh is present in their marriage makes some couples apprehensive, unable to be natural, fearful of enjoying life to the fullest. But that is not a valid concern. Because Yahweh is nothing if not natural.

"As proof, I shall quote from the Song of Songs, which says, 'Love is stronger than death, passion is as unyielding as the grave; its flames are flames of fire. A flame of God.'

"What does this tell the newly married couple? It tells them that despite the Divine Presence — or more accurately, because of the Divine Presence — they should enjoy their passion. Because passion does not fly in the face of Adonai. It is a gift from Him."

The Rabbi's words stripped Guttle naked. If until now only some in the crowd had been envisioning what Meyer would be doing to her that night, now, she was certain, everyone was. Her dress fell to her ankles — her chemise, her under things. She was as naked before these neighbors, friends, strangers — men! — as she had been in the bath with Dvorah the night before.

Unable to flee, or to cover herself, she blushed — not, she realized with horror, because they could see her, but because a part of her didn't mind.

"How else," the Rabbi was asking, "shall we all come to know the next generation of Schnappers and Rothschilds?"

The guests chuckled, or murmured their agreement. "The Chief Rabbi has gotten bawdier with age," someone whispered.

"On that joyful note," the Rabbi concluded, "the groom may place the ring on the finger of the bride."

Yussel gave the ring to Meyer. Guttle extended her hand, her long, slim fingers. The ring was large, featuring not a gem but a carving in the shape of a cottage. Owned by the synagogue, it was used in the marriage ceremony by every bride and groom. The small gold band Meyer had purchased would be exchanged for it later.

The ring slid easily onto her finger. Meyer said the words he had been memorizing for three nervous nights. "You are hereby sanctified unto me with this ring according to the laws of Moses and Israel."

Rabbi Simcha handed a scroll to the Chief Rabbi. It was the ketuba, the marriage contract, which Meyer had signed just before the ceremony in the presence of two witnesses, Lev and Yussel. In the age-old contract, he promised to provide Guttle with food, clothing and necessities, "and live with you as a husband according to universal custom."

The Rabbi offered the scroll to Guttle. Fully clothed again, she accepted it with a smile.

Yussel handed Meyer an empty wine glass. Imbedded in the wall of the courtyard was a small embossed stone that served as a target. Meyer hurled the glass at the stone. It smashed to fragments against the wall. If he missed the target slightly, no one commented. Most grooms missed. As the glass clattered in pieces to the cobbles, the Rabbi said, "Meyer and Guttle, you are now man and wife, till death do you part."

The guests began to cheer and shout Mazel tov as Meyer turned and kissed his Guttle. They held the kiss longer than the Rabbi appreciated, passion being a gift from Yahweh or not. He put his hand to his mouth and coughed, and the couple broke off their embrace.

The Cantor, Viktor Marcus, stepped beside him. With no accompaniment from the violin, he sang the wedding song, as Guttle held Meyer's hand. His tenor notes filled the courtyard and the entire lane, climbed the ghetto walls, must surely have reached the ears of heaven, Guttle thought. She favored him again with a smile.

Herr and Frau Schnapper hugged the newlyweds. Dvorah did the same, then lowered herself into the nearby chair. Yussel Kahn and Lev Berkov and

Doctor Kirsch and Brendel Isaacs and Yetta Liebmann and Izzy and his parents and Jacob Marcus, the moneylender, and Alexandre Licht, the shoemaker, and Emile Heckscher, a banker who was the richest man in the lane, and scores of others, rich and poor, old and not so old, lined up to shake hands with the smiling groom, to kiss on the cheek the happy bride.

Half a dozen men took up their violins and began to play. After starting with slow tunes they zipped into a hora. Guttle and Meyer joined hands with her parents and their friends and formed a circle and began to prance to their left. Other guests formed a larger circle around them, and danced to the right. The violins increased the tempo, the dancers pranced faster in a dizzying whirl of laughter, till shortness of breath caused some to break off and the two circles to unravel.

More dances followed, country dances well known in the lane, minuets known only by a few. Guests peeled off into the community room to drink wine or tea and eat of the cookies and cakes. Others remained outside, still dancing, as Guttle and Meyer watched and clapped in rhythm. The tireless violinists huddled together, then broke into a tune so fast it seemed impossible to dance to. People stood about, joking. No one took up the challenge, until Brendel Isaacs, in a bright yellow dress, moved to the center of the courtyard, paused to remove her shoes, began dancing then, rapidly, gracefully, alone, holding her skirts above her ankles, her blonde ringlets bouncing in counterpoint, her ankles crossing and recrossing in a blur of rhythmic grace, her stockinged calves flashing, her eyes closing, her mouth opening in a smile, her white teeth shining, her dance seeming to transport her to some other, better place. People had begun to clap with encouragement, men mostly, when to the surprise of everyone Doctor Rebecca Kirsch in a stunning pale blue dress stepped out and joined Brendel, first wearing her shoes, then kicking them off, whirling in her stockinged feet, a grin on her face, her hands high above her head, the two women facing one another not a metre apart, at once together in giddy liberation and mirrored in joyous competition, the skirts of their dresses swirling, Rebecca's pinned black hair disheveling, some onlookers at first shocked, then joining in the rhythmic clapping, first the young men, then some but not all of the older men, then some of the women as well, Rebecca surprisingly Brendel's match in speed and grace and endurance, Brendel impossibly increasing her speed to stay ahead, the two of them whirling, heads high, backs straight, chests taut, as if they had practiced this together, which they had not, whirling, whirling, till the music stopped suddenly as the musicians wore out, and the dancers collapsed, laughing and breathing hard, into one another's arms, and stumbled to a wall and collapsed against that, laughing still.

The fevered dance would be the talk of the lane for many weeks. Those who had missed it, to drink a glass of tea and devour a cookie, would forever have regrets. The exhausted musicians set down their violins. Guttle hugged the two dancers. She was grateful they had shifted attention from herself, at least for a while. No one had better friends.

"You should have joined us," Brendel said, still trying to catch her breath.

"And fall down dead on my wedding day?"

Guttle and Meyer led the rest of the guests into the community room for wine and cake. Toasts to the health and happiness of the bride and groom were offered. The couple mingled through the throng, laughing and joking and accepting good wishes. If a more well-liked pair had been married in recent years, few could remember. Their children, people predicted, drinking more wine — their children, praise Gott, would be something to see.

When the refreshed violinists took up their instruments again, Meyer whispered to Guttle that it was time they were alone. They hugged her parents and the children, and Meyer took a plate and filled it with cookies and ruggelah, and carried it with him as they waved and left the temple. Seeing the plate, a half-drunk Otto Kracauer called out, "This is no time to be thinking of your stomach, Meyer Amschel." The people around him laughed, and Guttle, eyes smiling with merriment, blushed. Holding hands, they walked up the lane for the first time as man and wife. Mercifully, no one, not even giggling children, followed; the adults made sure of that. The cookies were for the guards at the gate, Meyer told her, it never hurts to get on their good side.

The sun was gone but in Guttle's eyes the lane was gleaming with a unique light, as the mikveh had been the night before. She hoped that through her married eyes it would always be thus.

They had almost reached the Hinterpfann when Sophie Marcus stepped out of the alley and began to waddle toward them. She was holding something large, covered with a cloth. Guttle and Meyer paused. "A special gift for the bride," Frau Marcus said.

Meyer smiled, but Guttle's heart was pounding. Frau Marcus pulled the cloth from her gift. It was a white porcelain chamber pot, dotted with small pink flowers

"How thoughtful," Meyer said, bemused; it was an odd wedding gift, but practical.

Guttle grabbed the plate of cookies from Meyer's hands. Sophie Marcus lowered the chamber pot to her side. Just as her arms began to swing forward, to hurl its contents at the bride, Guttle threw the cookie plate in her face.

Instinctively, Sophie dropped the pot and raised her hands to protect her eyes. The porcelain shattered on the cobbles, the waste splashing in every direction. The plate smashed on the cobbles as well, cookies mingling with turds. Guttle jumped back, looked at her gown; it had remained spotless, had somehow escaped the assault. Sophie's own shoes and the bottom of her gray house dress were splattered. Seeing this, she fell to her knees, heedless of the stinking mess, and began to scream, to howl like an abandoned animal.

"Are you all right?" Guttle asked, turning to Meyer.

He was standing where he had been, astonished. "You expected this?"

"I expected something. I didn't know what."

"Why didn't you tell me?"

"I couldn't worry you. It might have been all in my head."

They were speaking loud over Sophie's howls. "You're my wife! From now on you'll tell me!"

"From now on!" Guttle agreed.

People were running up the lane in response to the howls. The fat Cantor was in the lead; he had recognized his mother's voice. Gazing at the smelly scene, taking in what had happened, he grabbed his mother and pulled her roughly to her feet. Jacob Marcus, not far behind, scanned the mess and shook his head. "I apologize for my wife," he said. "I hope you will forgive our family. I assure you, such a thing will not happen again."

"You assure us?" Meyer said. "How can you assure us?"

"You have my word."

Meyer nodded as the moneylender put his arm around his sobbing wife. With their son supporting her on the other side they half led and half dragged her, stumbling, down the lane.

Guttle felt tears begin to flow down her cheeks. Shuddering at what might have been, she pressed her face into Meyer's shoulder, and held it there. When she had calmed a little, she said, "I'm glad you were being generous."

"Generous?"

"The cookies for the guards."

The other spectators stayed back, allowing the newlyweds space in which to recover, opening a path through which the grieving Marcus family passed.

The Hinterpfann was empty. Kalman, and Moish's family, would be spending the night down the lane, crowded in with friends — a wedding gift sweeter than cake. Opening the door, Meyer made sure to lock it behind them. The couple smiled at one another shyly, and hugged, and kissed, and, tired from the dancing and the wine, exhausted by the assault, they lay together still clothed on the new bed with its feather pillows, and fell asleep in one another's arms.

After perhaps an hour, Guttle awoke. She crept quietly off the bed and heated water, bathed, slipped naked into an ivory silk night gown, a gift from Dvorah, and crawled back into bed. When Meyer awoke soon after, he had little trouble finding her in the silk.

Late the next afternoon, Guttle sat in the chair of the wigmaker and midwife Celia Levitan, a cloth draped over her neck and shoulders, wondering why she was crying. Hair hurts when you pull it, not when you cut it, so why these tears? She had not thought she would mind, as long as Meyer didn't. If Dvorah had hacked her auburn curls, they would have spurted real blood. Strike off Brendel's blonde ringlets and they likely would leak sunshine. But her hair was ordinary dark brown, the same as most of the hair in the lane, and it dropped to the floor of Celia's shop without a gurgle, without a murmur of dissent.

"You'll get used to it," Celia assured her.

"The rules were made by men," Guttle said. "I'd think they'd want us to keep our hair."

... and felt Meyer's gentle palms on her surging breasts.

"They need to feel trusting of their wives. For flirting, there are unmarried girls."

Guttle did not think Meyer would feel jealous if she kept her hair. She never had asked him. If you were a faithful Jew, this was just something a bride did without questioning, like lighting the Sabbath candles.

... like opening your thighs to his caress...

Her mother, who had come with her, dabbed the tears from her cheeks with a handkerchief.

"Just remember," Celia reminded them, "it was Samson whose strength was in his hair, not Delilah." To Guttle this sounded like trade talk, something Celia said to all the crying girls.

The wigmaker stopped snipping when she appeared to be half way through. Guttle was nowhere near bald as her mother was under her sheitl, as she assumed all married women were. Celia lifted the nearest wig from a shelf and fitted it on Guttle's head.

"What are you doing?" Emmie asked.

… moaning, moaning with pleasure…

"Trying it for size. Don't worry, I won't make her a blonde." She lifted off the yellow wig.

"But she still has hair."

Guttle's head remained covered by a dark crown, like many a newborn infant's. The wigmaker had lopped off all the locks that previously had fallen onto Guttle's neck and down her back; never again would she wear braids hanging in ribbons, or piled high, as she had at the wedding; there were no more long strands to get soaked in the rain. But a neatly trimmed cap of her own hair remained.

"This is how the girls are doing it now," Celia said.

"But the Talmud … " Emmie began.

"The Talmud says, 'A woman's hair is a private part of her.' That means you shouldn't show your hair in public, the Rabbis say. For a married woman to show her hair in public is like going about naked. But trimming is all that's necessary. The sheitl will cover this much."

Serenity settled upon Guttle. She had been willing to be bald — but this was better.

Meyer Amschel… her husband. What a strange word that was.

Her mother's eyebrows were raised, and seemed to stay that way, but she didn't argue with the wigmaker. Celia tried sheitl after sheitl on Guttle, in different shades of brown. All were styled the same, close-fitting on top, a simple roll at the neck; comfort was the important thing. They settled on a wig whose color was the same as her own hair — which made Guttle wonder again about this rule. She asked whose hair it was.

"We're not supposed to say," Celia replied.

When they had paid for the cutting and the sheitl, Celia swept the floor carefully, saving Guttle's long locks in a sack. Some day in the future, another bride would be wearing them.

3 0 August

Sorry, book, I was too tired last night to write. Or this morning. But one moment I must record. We were sitting on our bed. Meyer unbuttoned notch by notch my blue dress. Gently he folded it back off my shoulders. I imagined the curtains parting on a fine new play. A fine new opera. For only the second time, my breasts were revealed to him.

He sat gazing at them, as if they were treasures. Then he said, 'The circles of your nipples are like exquisite pink coins.' I flashed with anger. Coins? Even on our second night? I wanted to smack his face. But when I looked at him, something was different. His eyes were still on my breasts, but they were not the eyes that I knew, they were wider, softer, the large brown eyes of a child. As I realized this I felt a catch in my chest, as if some knowledge of his soul had passed directly into mine. It by-passed my understanding, I could not say what it was. Only my soul knew.

He shut his eyes for a moment. When he opened them, he was himself again. His lips fell upon my breast, his tongue played with it, his mouth engorged it. My anger melted away in a pleasure of such intensity as I had never felt before. It warms me still. I think in memory it always will. There is only one difficulty, I learned, with enjoying such fierce passion in the Judengasse. It is necessary to mute one's cries, to stuff one's fist into one's mouth, lest the entire lane hear.

Sophie Marcus, we have been told, has been locked away in the Marcus attic, the window boarded up against her own animal cries. They know of nothing else to do with her. Despite all that transpired, this saddens me. I cannot but think there was a time when she and her husband Jacob were young and in love, like Meyer and I.

Perhaps, in three hundred years, she will become a legend, like Melka.

Meyer is waiting for me. I must hurry. But first I want to see how my new name looks in writing.

Guttle Rothschild
Frau Meyer Amschel Rothschild
I like it.

Book Four: Wind in the Walls

Liberty of thought is the life of the soul.

Voltaire

A thinking man is a depraved animal.

— Rousseau

29

Guttle Rothschild was sitting on her bed, nursing her third child, Salomon, nine months old. Schönche, nearly four, was playing quietly on the floor with her favorite rag doll. Amschel, just turned two, was galloping about with a wooden horse that Yussel Kahn had carved for him. Delivering three children had broadened Guttle's slender hips, suckling one then another for four years had filled out her breasts. Judging by the glances she received from young men in the lane, this had not destroyed her appeal. Meyer certainly had not complained.

As the baby nursed, Guttle gazed with pleasure at a new addition to the bedroom — an oil painting of her wedding, which Meyer had purchased only a month before from Hiram Liebmann, as a gift for their fifth anniversary, and which now hung above their bed. Commissioned by Meyer, Hiram had rendered the scene just as she recalled it, even to the heaviness of Dvorah's body as she stood up for Guttle with difficulty a week before she was delivered of twins. Guttle wondered again at the artist's signature, nothing but Lieb, which Hiram had adopted as his painting name when he decided his work was good enough to sell. Who would have thought, she imagined Leo saying, that Hiram could paint as good as that young Wolf Mozart.

A knock on the front door evoked a mild epithet from her lips. A customer in search of coins would be good, but the timing was a bother. Gently she removed her breast from the baby, buttoned her blouse, and set the child in the middle of the bed, hoping he wouldn't cry.

The intruder turned out to be not a customer but Dvorah, holding a small white package. Guttle led her through the office into the bedroom and resumed nursing the infant. Her friend sat beside her, gazing at Hiram's painting.

"I discover new details every time I look at it," Dvorah said. "Who would have thought the deaf mute could make a painting like that?"

"People learn things. People grow."

Unwrapping her package, Dvorah held the book so Guttle could see the cover. "Do you know this story?"

"The Sorrows of Young Werther." Guttle shook her head. "Where did you get it?"

From the pocket of her dress Dvorah pulled a note she had shoved there. She smoothed the wrinkled paper and placed it in Guttle's hand. The note was brief, Guttle read it aloud. "I am Werther, you are Lotte. You must let me see you."

Guttle looked at the back of the note paper. It was blank. "That's all?"

"That's all. It was in the book."

She looked again at the note. "What does it mean? Who is it from?"

"It's from Paul."

Frowning, Guttle shifted the baby to her other breast. "I thought you told him a long time ago to stop writing."

"I did. Three years ago he told me was marrying a distant cousin, and would stop. Last spring he wrote again, and said he had gotten a divorce. I thought I told you that. He said he could not be married happily to anyone but me."

"And you answered that?"

"So as not to be rude. He is the son of the Countess, after all. Who is my mother's best customer."

"Doesn't he know you're married? That you have two children? That you're Jewish?"

"Of course he knows. He's been writing anyway. Of the wonderful things we could do together outside the ghetto."

"He's mad."

"He admits to that. Madly in love, he wrote in the last letter. That one I didn't answer."

"What about your mother? The letters used to upset her. With good reason."

"I warned him about that. I wrote him that Mama might become angry enough to tell the Countess. Or my husband."

"Yet he sent the book."

"Not to Mama's house. To Brendel, at the Café."

"What are you going to do?"

"Read it, I suppose. There's no harm in that. Did you see who wrote it? J. W. Goethe. That's Paul's friend Wolfgang. They came to the lane together that first time. You remember."

"I'm afraid I don't."

"It was right after that horse kicked you in the head."

"There you are. I remember Paul, but not his friend."

"They say the book has made him famous."

"Good for him." She lay Salomon down on the bed. "Dvorah, you seem a little too excited. It makes me nervous."

"Please don't worry about me," Dvorah said. She kissed Guttle's cheek, and squeezed her hand.

When Dvorah left, Guttle went upstairs and read a fairy tale to the other children until they fell asleep for their afternoon naps. Returning to the office, she sat at the desk and resumed work on Meyer's new catalogue. In five years it had grown from a single page to sixteen, a grand listing of Greek, Roman, Dutch, Russian and other coins, plus medals and statues. Some of the statues were encrusted with rubies or diamonds. To his best customers, Meyer now sent the catalogues bound in leather and embossed with their own names. No matter how costly the merchandise, he still sent it out on approval. None had yet been stolen.

As keeper of the ledgers, Guttle knew that Meyer was not getting rich, that he had nowhere near the money her father had, and nothing like the bankers at the south end. Most of the profits he poured back into the business, buying more coins, more antiques. But she was careful to keep household expenses down, and they were comfortable.

Carefully she transcribed in German on the catalogue form the descriptions of the unusual coins, which Meyer had scrawled on scraps of paper in Judendeutch. His spelling was bad, his grammar was worse — and when he went to call on nobles to make deals, his heavy Judengasse accent could hardly go unnoticed. Yet no one was better than Meyer about closing a deal — and he almost always did.

After half an hour of work, she stood up, feeling suddenly tired. Sometimes this was caused by the flickering flames in the lamps, but not today. She knew this feeling well. She had vomited the past three mornings while Meyer was in schul. More to the point, the Lady from Paris had not made an appearance in two months. Guttle had not yet told Meyer Amschel, but she was certain that once again she was with child.

Dread thoughts flashed through her mind, as they had for days now, as they had after Salomon was conceived. How Dvorah, still reveling in the twins, had lost two babies, with much bleeding. How Sara Greinz from the bakery had married one of the young heder teachers when she was eighteen years old, and had died in childbirth ten months later, along with her newborn son. With three healthy, if painful, deliveries in succession, Guttle could not help wondering when the fearful odds would turn on her.

Early that morning Meyer had hired a roan mare from Ziggy Zigmund's stable beyond the slaughterhouse and the herring shop and ridden it at an easy pace toward Hanau, ten kilometres southeast of Frankfurt. He was feeling buoyant, as he always did when a cache of new treasure loomed; he'd received word that a dealer in Hanau had been in receipt of a collection of rare coins from Sweden and Russia, and he hoped to get first look.

The coins at the Hanau dealer exceeded his expectations. He purchased most of the collection, which was the legacy of a Swedish Prince, along with a gold Russian sword, its handle studded with rubies. At once he thought of Wilhelm. If he could get to see the crown Prince today, he could offer him the sword at a good price, and still turn a fine profit for half a day's work; he would not have to list it in the new catalogue that Guttle had begun preparing, would not have to risk sending it out on approval.

The palace of the Crown Prince stood at the end of a long dirt lane lined on both sides with soaring poplar trees, two kilometres outside the town. It was a sweeping three-story building of cut stones, surrounded by hedges and gardens. The courtyards and pools were embraced by statuary of mythic females draped in veils, or not draped at all. Meyer left his horse at the stables, his new coin purchases in the saddle bags, except for the Russian sword in its scabbard, which he carried with him. He gained entry through the front gate by virtue of his status as court agent, as he had several times before. In the courtyards, he saw palace aides dressed in black and household servants in white moving among courtiers in bright plumage whose style echoed that of the Crown Prince, as if that might gain them favor in his eyes. The one exception was Carl Friedrich Buderus, the man Meyer had come to see. In his sparse office on the first level, Buderus, a clean-shaven young fellow, with wavy hair the color of fresh carrots, was dressed as always in chocolate brown. It lent him a serious air, Meyer thought, which no doubt he wanted to cultivate as an ambitious aide in the department of the treasury. He and Buderus had struck up an easy friendship on his previous visits, the young man undisturbed by the fact that Meyer was a Jew.

This day he would be of little assistance, however. When Meyer showed him the glittering Russian sword and explained the reason for his visit, Buderus admired it but handed it back. The Crown Prince was closeted in his apartments, Buderus said, and had left word that he was not to be disturbed. As he held Meyer's gaze, the thought passed between them that Wilhelm was entertaining a mistress — perhaps more than one. But no word was spoken on the subject. Instead, Buderus came around from behind his desk. "Are you riding back to Frankfurt?" he asked. "I have business there, and we could ride together if that is agreeable." Meyer replied that he would be honored by the company.

So it was that a short time later the two men on horseback were ambling down a road bisecting fields of pungent hay when their path was blocked by an officer of the Crown Prince's army. He was dressed in a deep blue coat, hat and breeches, a sword at his side, a musket in his hand. Buderus did not speak, merely wheeled his mount so the soldier could see Wilhelm's coat of arms embossed in red on the yellow saddle cloth. The officer stepped aside and let them pass.

"What was that encounter?" Meyer inquired.

Up ahead they could see a high-sided wagon, and a small cluster of blue-clad soldiers. "I suspect they're recruiting," Buderus said.

"Recruiting?"

"A regiment to lease to King George of England, Wilhelm's cousin. To help put down the uprising in America."

"I'd heard that his father the Landgrave often hired out troops at Hesse-Kassel. I didn't know that Wilhelm also did it."

"King George was having difficulty finding cannon fodder, to speak bluntly. Russia and Sweden turned him down. When the Crown Prince heard this, he quickly made an offer. At an advantageous price to himself. George had little recourse but to accept. The contract is being prepared as we speak."

They stopped beside the knot of soldiers in the road. Two young soldiers were walking to a small farm house. Two dogs began to bark, and ran at them from behind the red-painted house. The soldiers lowered their muskets, their bayonets fixed, and pointed them at the approaching dogs. The animals slowed their run, set their tails to wagging. From the house a peasant farmer emerged, wiping his hands on a cloth, as if he had been interrupted at lunch.

Meyer could not hear what was being said. The farmer began shaking his head. The soldiers began pushing him toward the house.

"It appears that he does not want to go," Meyer noted.

"They usually don't. But he has no choice. The Crown Prince owns him, body and soul."

A woman wearing an apron over her yellow dress came out of the house, two small children running to keep up. She spoke to her husband, looked at the soldiers, and began to wail. Her husband grabbed her and put a hand over her mouth, and hugged her, and knelt and hugged the children. He spoke to her, to them, quietly Then he turned and went into the house. In a short time he emerged carrying a sack. He stood beside his family and stared at the waiting wagon.

"Underwear and one change of clothes," Buderus said. "The regiment will provide a uniform."

The man hugged his wife and children again. Then, head held high, he walked between the soldiers to the road, and climbed into the empty wagon, which was surrounded by four more soldiers. The prisoner, Meyer thought — then he corrected himself — the recruit — appeared to be about Meyer's age.

"How long will he be gone from them?"

"As long as the fighting lasts. Assuming that he survives."

The wagon rolled off, pulled by two Clydesdales, surrounded by the four guards. The two recruiting officers walked beside it. A Kapitäin rode on horseback in the rear. In front of the farmhouse, the woman was pressing a large red handkerchief to her face. Even from a distance, Meyer could see her shoulders heaving. The two children, a boy and a girl, were waving their Papa goodbye.

"If I may ask," Meyer said, "how much does King George pay for these men?"

"Seventy-six gulden per year for each recruit. Another seventy-six for each man killed. Three wounded equals one killed. A simple formula."

"The money goes to the public treasury? With perhaps a stipend for the widows?"

"The money goes to Wilhelm."

Meyer absorbed this information silently. It was hardly his place to protest. But a question popped from his mouth regardless. "Why do the peasants not rebel?"

Buderus gave him a sidelong glance as they rode. "Why do the Jews not rebel?"

"Unlike the peasants, we are greatly outnumbered. There is a matter of the walls. And to date, although we are confined, we are not sent off to be killed. I suppose we should be grateful."

At a crossroads up ahead, the soldiers and the wagon maneuvered to the right, into a narrow dirt lane. Another farm house was not far away. Three more were visible further along.

"Have you seen enough of this?" Buderus asked.

"Perhaps one more, if you'll indulge me."

"It's hardly a state secret."

They reigned their horses twenty metres behind the guarded wagon as the two recruiters approached the first house. A woman with gray hair came to the door, then watched as they approached her husband, or son, who was at work in a field. The soldiers spoke to him. He appeared to argue, gesticulating with his arms. When one of the soldiers lowered his musket, his bayonet, the man had no choice to but to go with them. After procuring a sack from the house, he hugged the woman briefly, then walked with the soldiers to the wagon. The woman watched, silent, both hands covering her mouth.

"He must be fifty years old," Meyer whispered.

"The limits are sixteen to sixty. As long as they're able-bodied."

Suddenly one of the soldiers shouted, "There's another one!" They all looked toward the house. Beyond it a younger man on horseback was galloping away across the fields.

"Shall we give chase?" a soldier yelled.

"Let him go," the Kapitän said. "We'll come back for him another time."

The woman with graying hair was sitting in the dirt, appearing stunned, as she watched them move away. With the two recruits in the wagon, the soldiers strode on toward the next house, perhaps two hundred metres farther along. Buderus turned his horse towards the main road, and Meyer did the same.

"How many will they take?" he asked.

"The contract calls for twenty-five hundred. With the fees, and a number of dead and wounded, the Crown Prince likely will earn two million gulden. That's a lot of money. It's not as if the Crown Prince has no feelings. He would not do this for ten kreuzer."

Meyer, unsure if Buderus was being ironic, managed not to smile.

"Wilhelm's father, the Landgrave, will send twenty-five thousand men," Buderus said. "That's a lot more money."

They turned the horses onto the road to Frankfurt. The weak sun moved in and out among the clouds. Cows in a field on the left stood dumbly munching.

"That fellow who rode off," Meyer asked, "what will happen to him?"

"They won't shoot him for desertion. That would be costly. They'll make him run a gauntlet. Then they'll send him off to fight anyway."

"What if they don't find him?"

"Oh, they'll find him. If they don't, anyone who helped him escape will have to pay the fee. Or supply an able body to take his place."

When the boy escaped from the recruiters he leaped from the horse, which ran off, and burrowed into a stack of hay far out in a field. Bits of seed tickled his nose; he tried not to sneeze. His dog, a black mutt named Schnell, whimpered beside the hay but did not bark. He heard the army wagon creaking down the road and waited until much time had passed, until the sun was fading. He was hungry. At a neighboring farm, far from the house and barn, he found a field of carrots, and ate. He sent the dog home, fiercely, and in the falling dark set off across the fields in the direction of the city. It would take him much of the night to walk there, he knew, but in Frankfurt he could lose himself.

In recent years the lane had become overcrowded. Jews coming to Frankfurt for work were sent to the Judengasse, but by order of the lane council they could not be admitted. There were no apartments or houses available, they had been divided and redivided as much as was possible. So the newcomers began to sleep against the wall outside the north gate, and soon became a small community of beggars. At first Meyer would hand out coins as he passed, but they would only clamor for more. The Constables ordered him to stop, so the beggars would eventually move on.

The aroma of potato and onion stew greeted Meyer when he arrived home. He placed the sword and scabbard and his pouches of coins on the desk and hurried upstairs. Embracing Guttle, he sat on one of the kitchen chairs so that Schönche and Amschel, bursting in from their room shouting "Papa, Papa," could crawl over him while he kissed their hair, their cheeks. After the scenes he had witnessed, of fathers being ripped from their homes, he kissed them a few extra times. The baby Salomon was asleep in a small crib in the corner; those tender kisses he would save for later.

"You're upset," Guttle said, after he had shooed the children back to their room. "The coins weren't good?"

He took off his three-cornered hat and his gray wig, ran his hands through his hair. He put on the yarmulke she handed him. "The coins are a treasure. It's humanity that isn't good."

"That sounds serious." She pulled her skirt around her, sat across from him at the kitchen table as he recounted what he had witnessed. For a moment she closed her eyes, envisioning the scenes, and bit her lower lip. "Is it possible the peasants are treated worse than the Jews?"

"Sometimes," Meyer said.

"That's difficult to believe."

She took his hand and played with his fingers. They sat in silence, in sympathy with those being sent to a foreign war. Their God, she thought, is as harsh as ours.

Hesitant in the face of such imagery, she nonetheless forced herself to speak of other things. "I've got a potato stew simmering that might help cheer you up. But I don't think it will cheer you enough." She stood and came to his side. "So I'm going to tell you a secret."

Secrets made Meyer wary; he did not look up at her. "Well, I'm waiting."

"I'm think I'm carrying a child."

He looked up then, stared at this lovely, fertile being he had married. His worried face shattered into a grin. He stood, and he hugged her tightly. "Guttle, that's wonderful!"

She kissed his cheek, his ear. "I thought you would be pleased."

He placed his hand flat on her belly, to feel the child.

"It's much too early for that."

His hand rose to her breast. She eased it away. "It's much too early for that, also."

He kissed her forehead. "Perhaps that is Yahweh's ultimate plan," he said. "For the good people on earth eventually to outnumber the evil."

"Or maybe that's just an excuse for you to have your way with me."

Meyer swatted her rear. "I didn't realize we needed an excuse."

A stranger of striking appearance walked slowly across the arched bridge over the river Main on his way to the Judengasse. As he reached the Fahrtor Arch, he paused to look at the obscene drawing of the Judensau engraved high in the wall. He had been prepared for such a sight, he had seen such things in other places, though none as prominently displayed. He shook his head in sadness. As he stepped under the arch, he asked a tall, thin guard the amount of the toll required to enter the city. Setting down his bag, he handed over the eight kreuzer.

"Jew, what are you selling?" the guard asked. "I might want to buy something."

"You'll never want to buy from me," the stranger replied.

"And why is that? Tell me what you deal in."

"I deal in reason."

The puzzled guard cocked his head and squinted, but asked no more questions. The stranger began to walk up the lane, noting with incredulity the narrowness of the houses, less than three metres across; he had not seen their like anywhere. As he passed the fourth house a moneylender seated at an outdoor table rose and intercepted him. "Welcome, stranger," the man said. He was wearing a long black coat, a black hat, had an untrimmed black beard. "Jacob Marcus here." Marcus extended a hand, which the visitor shook lightly. "You'll be wanting to change your money to the local currency. Gulden and kreuzer, good in the Judengasse and all of Frankfurt. I offer the best rates in the lane."

Assuming that for the brokers to stay in business all rates in this narrow street would be the same — which they were — the stranger emptied his purse of notes and coins from Wiesbaden, where he had spent the past two days, and received gulden and kreuzer in return.

"Tell me — Herr Marcus, is it? — I've been riding a coach all day. Is there a place where a stranger can get a glass of tea?"

"Up ahead, not far past the hospital. Brendel's Café. Best eyeful of tea you could imagine."

The stranger assumed the man meant glassful, and was eager to be on his way. As he turned to go he heard a familiar intaking of breath, followed by astonished whispers and nervous giggles, as the children caught sight of his hump. Such sounds had trailed him all his life, would trail him, he knew, to the grave.

Brendel's Café was heralded by a blue and white banner. A good omen for his visit; he had a daughter named Brendel. When he reached it he found a quaint establishment, painted also white and blue, the first discernible attempt at a modern style he had seen within the gate. Three small tables, two chairs at each, stood on the cobbles; five more were arranged in a cozy front room, beside a counter covered with cookies and petite cakes on glass-covered trays. None of the chairs was occupied, the Café appeared deserted as he took a seat inside, as far as he could get from the sewage trench. Here the aromas of brewing coffee and warm chocolate overpowered the putrid smell outside. Barely had he set his traveling bag on the wooden floor when from a lighted doorway appeared one of the most appealing women he had ever seen — a woman not corseted and coifed and painted like the salon ladies of Berlin, but resembling a lovely, freshly scrubbed milkmaid, in a white cotton mob cap from which blonde ringlets peeked, a white apron over her blue peasant dress. An eyeful indeed, as the money changer had said.

When she brought out the glass of hot tea he ordered, she served with it on a small plate an enticing piece of ruggelah. "A free sample for a weary traveler," she said.

"Does my weariness show?"

"I'm afraid it does."

He bit into the pastry and chewed the tender crust, the sweet apple filling. "Delicious! You don't find ruggelah this moist in Berlin. I'll be wanting a few more. On my reckoning, of course."

From the counter she brought a small tray with several pieces on it. "You're a long way from home," she said.

"I've never seen the Rhine Valley. I thought it was time." He sipped his tea and ate another cake. "Not to be rude," he said, indicating the vacant room with his hand, "but your business seems slow. I gather the Café is new."

"People just ate their lunch. Some will come later, when they take a rest from work. It is new, though — eight weeks today. People here aren't used to coffee houses. We're forbidden to enter the ones in Frankfurt."

Sipping his tea, the visitor nodded.

"The lane is small enough so people walk home for tea," Brendel said. "For most, it's right upstairs from their shop. But that's not the same as relaxing in a Café, gossiping with your friends. Maybe having a good argument."

"Please, sit," the stranger said, indicating the vacant chair at his table.

Brendel sat, smoothing her dress beneath her. "I was a rag dealer before, but with my boys in heder now, I have time to bake." She reached for one of the ruggelah on the tray, and bit into it. "How rude," she said, brushing crumbs from her lips with her fingers. "Sharing your table, and I haven't introduced myself. I am Brendel Isaacs."

"The first part I could have guessed. Moses Mendelssohn." He offered his hand.

"Oh, my!" Her fingers flew to her mouth like birds to a nest.

"Is something wrong?"

"I'm sorry. I didn't recognize you."

"How could you? I've never been here before."

"I mean... you're a great man. I've been babbling on... I didn't realize... "

"You've been delightful, Frau Isaacs. Thanks to your babbling — and your ruggelah — I don't feel the least bit weary anymore."

"I haven't read your books — I'm sure I wouldn't understand a word — but my husband — he's not my husband, really — my friend Yussel Kahn — is a great admirer of yours. Will you be preaching here?"

"I don't preach, as such. But I do discuss my ideas in public, if I am invited."

"I'm sure the Chief Rabbi will invite you."

"Not necessarily. Most Rabbis don't like my views. They think of me as the enemy."

"The enemy of what?"

"Judaism."

"Oh." Brendel appeared shaken. She wiped her hands on her apron. "Are you?"

"Not in the least."

"I remember now. You don't believe in emotion."

"That's rather oversimplifying a complex idea." He placed his stubby hand on top of hers on the table, in a manner he tried to make fatherly. "I like you, Brendel Isaacs." He smiled at her for the first time. "That's an emotion. And I dare say I'm enjoying it. Also, I adore my wife. That's an emotion I would not want to live without. Fromet was a poor girl whom I married for love, not money — unlike most men."

"Do you have regrets?"

"Four grown children, no regrets. My ideas about replacing emotion with reason — that's in the context of philosophy, of religion. That's what upsets the Rabbis — for no good reason, in my view. But you don't need a speech right now." He withdrew his hand.

"How long will you be staying in the lane?"

"A week, perhaps two. If I'm tolerated."

"Do you have a place to stay? I would invite you, but I have one room, and two boys."

"I have a letter of introduction to a Doctor Kirsch. From her father, who is a teacher in Berlin. I'm hoping she will find a place for me."

"Don't you worry, Rebecca's a dear. I expect she'll put you up herself; she's one of the few people with room. They even hold intellectual discussions in her living room some nights. You might be asked to participate."

"A salon in the Judengasse? I thank you for warning me." He opened his purse and placed ten kreuzer on the table for the ruggelah "Now I should be going."

"That's too much money."

"Whatever is extra is for the company," Mendelssohn said.

30

Isidor Kracauer, wearing a butcher's apron that once had been white, emerged from the plucking room with a chicken dangling from each hand, hung one on a vacant hook and slapped the other on the counter. From the yard outside came the sounds of dozens more of the birds raising a ruckus — either fearing they would be next, or grateful they had lived to squawk another day; Izzy was never sure which. He held up the chicken so Frau Metzenbaum, across the counter, could look at it. "There you are, the freshest of the freshly killed."

Frau Metzenbaum looked at the chicken as Izzy, holding it by the legs, let it revolve in the air. When she voiced no objection, he tore a sheet from a roll of brown paper, quickly wrapped the chicken, placed it on a scale. He noted the poundage and told her the price.

"Your father used to weigh before he wrapped."

"I'm not my father. The paper weighs the same for every chicken. Next to nothing. You want me to unwrap it, the scale won't show any difference, I guarantee."

"Never mind, I'm in a hurry." She opened her purse. "I was just saying what your father used to do. So tell me, Isidor, how do you like being a butcher instead of a scholar?"

"It's much the same. Bloody battles, bloody beef."

It had been six months since his father's heart seizure, since Izzy — the only one of the three brothers who was "loafing around not doing anything, like a shmegeggi" — had been recruited to run the slaughterhouse. His father still handled the money at home and kept the ledgers, but under Doctor's orders he had slit the throat of his last chicken. Izzy had resigned as Schul-Klopper; the fire captain had that title now.

Like a shmegeggi, Izzy thought, he had been wasting his time reading Maimonides, the Kabbalah, tales of the Ba'al Shem Tov. Storing them in his

mind. Trying to make the disparate approaches to Judaism fit together. Now
he was done with all that. He did not mind dipping his fingers into the blood
of chickens and cows. He did not miss being the Schul-klopper, or the
shammus. What he missed was getting excited by what he read. Being
intrigued with life. He was twenty years old. He felt his mind had been
quicker at fifteen, and his heart more passionate.

The door to the dim slaughterhouse opened, tinkling the small brass
bell above it. Emerging from the rectangle of light was Doctor Kirsch,
followed by a stranger. Rebecca motioned Izzy out from behind the counter.
"Isidor, I'd like you to meet someone. This is Moses Mendelssohn."

"You're jesting." His instinct was to glance quickly at the man's back, to
see if there was a hump — but that would have been obscenely rude. Instead
he stood dumbfounded, not realizing that the visitor had extended his hand.

"I hear you're the local historian, when you're not killing chickens."

"Moses Mendelssohn?" Izzy swallowed hard, his Adam's apple
bobbing, before he could complete a sentence. He felt his face flushing. "I've
read all your books. I don't understand them, but I've read them."

"That's all a person can ask."

"Doctor Kirsch, do you know that this man is the German Socrates?"

"Hardly," Mendelssohn said.

"That's what the newspapers say. Sometimes they say the German
Plato."

"The newspapers like to exaggerate."

"He's changing Judaism!" This, too, directed at Rebecca, as if he were
not worthy of speaking directly to the philosopher.

"Not yet." She glanced at Mendelssohn. "I assume you would agree."

"Absolutely. I have theories, nothing more. Most people don't agree
with them."

"Including the Chief Rabbi," Rebecca told Izzy. "We stopped by his
study, to ask if Herr Mendelssohn could speak next week. The Rabbi said he
preferred that the people heard two sides. He suggested a debate."

"Here in the Judengasse? You're jesting!"

Behind them, unseen, the door opened slowly, without the bell tinkling.
Guttle had perfected the technique, to irritate Izzy, to surprise him
sometimes. To keep their old, teasing relationship alive. He seemed to need
it. She stood like a shade, unnoticed.

"We appear to be taxing your vocabulary," Rebecca said to Izzy. "The
presence of the great can do that." She touched his arm. "Why don't you get
me a chicken, so I can feed this man."

"For tonight? I don't have a salted one."

"There's no law against eating late," Mendelssohn said.

Guttle, overhearing, stepped forward and greeted Rebecca. "If you don't have supper ready, come join Meyer and me. We have plenty."

Rebecca made the introduction. "My good friend, Guttle Rothschild. This is Moses Mendelssohn."

As Guttle's mouth opened in wonder, Izzy, wrapping a chicken, called out from behind the counter, "Don't say 'You're jesting!' Herr Mendelssohn is tired of hearing that."

She recovered quickly. "I wasn't going to say that." She turned towards the visitor. "I was going to ask if he liked potato stew."

"I grew up on potato stew. It's my favorite."

"You're jesting!"

The stranger, his dark eyes merry, smiled agreeably.

"It has onions and carrots. And mushrooms."

"Just the way my Fromet makes it. With perhaps a pinch of garlic."

Relaxing, Guttle looked at Rebecca. "After evening services?"

"We'll bring a bread. And a bottle of wine."

"And some ruggelah," Mendelssohn said.

Noting the chicken on the Doctor's account, Izzy came around and handed it to her.

"The butcher is also invited," Guttle said, "if he promises to leave his bloody apron behind, and wear his scholar's cap."

Izzy flushed beneath his blond hair, which looked as always like a wild field of wheat. "I'm not a scholar any more."

"Being a kosher slaughterer is a fine and necessary profession," Mendelssohn said. "But it has been my experience that intelligence is a lifelong disease. Once you start thinking, it can be very hard to stop."

When Lev had not come home from the hospital by the time darkness fell, Dvorah fed the twins and put them to bed, assuring them, as she always did, that their Papa would kiss them goodnight when he got home; if she did not tell them so each time he was late, they would not go to sleep. Often she grew irritated waiting for him, but not tonight; she had only a few more pages to read in the book Paul had sent; she might be able to finish it and hide it among her things before Lev arrived. Lighting the oil lamp beside the chair in the bedroom, she fetched the book, and two carrots to eat that she had scraped clean, sat and began to read. The book enthralled her; how much this was because of the sad story, and how much because Paul had sent it as a gift along with that intimate note, she could not say. *I am Werther, you are Lotte.* The more she read, the more she realized what an expression of Paul's love that was. When she reached the end, her eyes were wet with tears. Poor Werther! How she understood his pain!

Pulling herself back to the real world, she hid the book in a drawer among her underthings, and she washed her face, lest Lev walk in and wonder why she'd been crying. She checked on the twins, making sure they both were asleep, then stripped off her clothing. Before donning her nightgown, she paused, naked, in front of her mirror, gazing at the body that had captured Lev and was now captivating Paul. She was twenty-five years old. Despite three pregnancies, she had been able to retain her voluptuous shape, partly with a diet of tea or coffee in the morning, carrots or an apple at night, and a small lunch between. She did not need more food than that; passion was her appetite.

Lifting her curls above her head, placing one alluring leg in front of the other, she saw in the mirror through her large dark eyes the eternal Jewess, but with red hair instead of black. Smiling seductively, she admitted that she admired her body as much as any male. Brendel Isaacs had a disarming way with men, but even Brendel's lovely body — she had seen it at the mikveh — could not quite compare with hers.

The click of the front door opening warned her that Lev was home; she had not heard him mount the stairs. For an instant she wavered between quickly pulling on her gown, or letting him find her like this, unabashedly admiring herself. Feeling brash, she stayed as she was, to see how he would react.

While Dvorah was reading The Sorrows of Young Werther, Lev had been examining a patient. Her large, bulbous tumor had reminded him of the Black Death, and he had been recalling its deadly history as he walked home: how in the thirteen hundreds it had wiped out in two years one-third of the population of Europe; how people had suffered horribly before they died, with painful buboes under their arms and in their groins; how the streets of the cities, Frankfurt included, had been littered with so many corpses the burial men could not keep up with them; how anyone who came near the victims became infected; how, seeking an explanation for this scourge, the populace of Europe had turned to its usual scapegoat: the Jews. They decided that the Jews had caused this suffering and death by poisoning the wells; never mind that Jews had been ravaged by the disease as much as anyone. Seeking revenge, mobs had begun attacking Jews, beating them, killing them.

The attacks became an excuse for herding the Jews behind walls and gates — for the Jews' own "protection." The Jews then were made to pay for this protection: in the Judengasse, twenty thousand gulden per year. Four centuries later, the medical schools still had no idea of what had caused the Black Death — or why it had disappeared.

All this was swirling through Berkov's mind as he climbed the stairs quietly, so as not to wake the twins, and opened the apartment door. Not seeing his wife in the kitchen, he looked in the bedroom, and found Dvorah standing naked in front of her mirror. The sight made his breath clutch. "At last, a healthy body," he said, wearily. Setting down his bag of instruments, he kissed her cheek, took her in his arms. He leaned down and pressed his face to her breast, and kissed her nipple.

"Is that all you see?" Dvorah asked into his hair. "A healthy body?"

"You know better," he murmured, and kissed the other nipple, again, again. "It's the body of my dreams."

"I hope it's the only one." Immediately she regretted the words. Paul von Brunwald was too much on her mind.

Discouraged by her tone, Lev withdrew his lips. She found her nightgown, pulled it over her head. He watched as it caught on her hair for a moment before she could pull it down.

"As a matter of fact, it's not. That's why I'm so tired these past few days."

Dvorah was astonished — not only that this could happen — that Lev could desire another woman — but that he would admit to it. For an instant, her mind reeled with dizziness.

"I've been dreaming of Mrs. Metzenbaum," he said, taking off his shirt to wash.

She still liked to see the dark hair on his chest, almost as thick and curly as the hair on his head. How she once had loved to rest her head on that chest! When — why — had she stopped enjoying that?

Her disbelief had become confusion. "Bea Metzenbaum? Isn't she rather large?"

"Too large. That's why I couldn't feel the growth in her stomach until the other day. It's as big as an apple. It's causing her terrible pain. And there's nothing I can do about it. I can call in a surgeon to amputate a shattered leg, a gangrenous arm. But you can't cut off a stomach."

"This is what you've been dreaming about?"

"Almost every night. In the dream she's already dead. I'm at the burial. Her husband picks up rocks and begins to throw them at me. At first he misses. Then they begin to hit."

"You've been kicking in your sleep. You never used to do that."

"Probably when the rocks hit. He begins to throw bigger ones. He tells me I killed his wife. Then he pulls a gravestone out of the ground — I think it's one of the Beckers — and he is going to crush me with it. That's when I wake up."

"Why would he say you killed his wife?"

"Because I know she's going to die — and I can't cure her."

Brushing her hair, Dvorah moved closer to him. "You've had patients before who you couldn't cure. Who died. Why is this time different?"

"I don't know." He pressed his face into her curls, something he loved to do, to smell the soap. "I don't know."

With unusual sudden insight, Dvorah knew. She shuddered, her nipples grew hard as seeds under her gown, as if she were cold. Unlike Guttle, she was not an inward thinker; she rarely considered what dreams might mean; they were much too confusing. But this once, she knew. The meaning scorched the room like lightning. It made her want to hide. His dream was not about Bea. It was about her — about them. Lev knew nothing, but some part of him, perhaps his trusting soul, knew everything. His soul suspected that her love for him was dying. And that he was guilty, because he could not cure her wanderlust.

She left him there to wash, went to the kitchen. So much for her own need. A stomach tumor had defeated all she had to offer. It was not the first time something like this had happened. She knew it would not be the last. She feared the competition of no woman except the dying. With them she could not compete.

When they went to bed, Lev fell asleep within minutes. Dvorah turned on her side, her eyelashes wet.

Flickering street lamps, newly installed in the center of the city, made the boy nervous. He slunk like a dog along the outskirts, till he could smell the river. In an open field he heard a pack of wild curs yelping as they tore something apart. Frightened, he circled a low building — and saw a Constable not twenty metres away, guarding a large iron gate. He ducked behind the building — and discerned in the darkness a narrow door. When he touched it lightly, paint splinters shed. He saw no windows, no lights, but heard chickens begin to squawk. It was a comforting sound. He yanked at the handle. The door was locked, but it creaked. He pulled again with all his strength. The door broke open. Quickly he slipped inside. The aroma of fresh sawdust enveloped him.

Guttle had fed the children early and put them to bed, so there would be room enough at the table. Also, so they would not find it necessary to comment on the visitor's hump.

Mendelssohn was filled with questions about the lane — the people, the restrictions, the houses, the heders, the businesses. Keeping their elbows close to their ribs — the table was more comfortable for four — the others answered his queries between spoonfuls of stew and bites of the bread Doctor Kirsch had brought, and sips of red wine. When the philosopher had run out of questions, Meyer Amschel, refilling the glasses, recounted the recruiting scene he had witnessed that afternoon.

"An abomination," Mendelssohn said. "Imagine what it must be like, the Prince owning your body. But there is a consistency to the recruiting — a consistency and an irony, both."

"How do you mean?" Rebecca asked.

"The colonists in America are fighting for their independence. The Boston Tea Party, Bunker Hill, I'm sure you've read of them in the newspapers. They're rebelling against the perceived tyranny of King George. Wilhelm is sending his peasants to fight the rebels. This is consistent with his position as Crown Prince. On the other hand, it is the opposite side of what the enslaved peasants might choose, were they given a choice."

"It make me wonder how the Crown Prince deals with his conscience," Guttle said, "knowing he is making money by sending men off to die. It's like selling souls to the devil."

"I don't imagine it troubles him," Mendelssohn said. "Such has been the behavior of Princes since men invented them — or, more accurately, since they invented themselves."

"These 'winds of freedom,' from America," Meyer asked, "—we've been hearing about them for years. Do you expect they will ever reach Europe?"

"Absolutely. I visited Paris last spring. Freedom and equality already are the talk of the salons. Soon the talk will reach the streets. It will be just idle chatter at first, but one day some spark will ignite it into action. Exactly when, no one can say."

"Aren't the people happy with the new King and Queen?" Guttle still felt the affection born five years earlier for the Archduchess Antoine, when during the royal procession their eyes had met with mutual empathy. She still felt an odd identification with the French Queen — something she dared not mention to anyone, not even Meyer, and could hardly explain to herself. The distant Antoine had joined Jennie Aron and the mythic Melka in Guttle's personal pantheon — someone in whom she could confide in absentia, without rebuke. Speaking to a Torah named Melekh had not sufficed.

"The young King was crowned last spring, while I was there," Mendelssohn said. "The Queen is a great favorite with the people, for her beauty and her compassion. She gives much charity, to help poor women and children. When she goes to the theatre, which she loves, even the cognoscenti stand and cheer for fifteen minutes. She is less popular at the court, however. Rival factions still call her 'the Austrian,' and are suspicious of her. As for the King, he is the object of unkind ridicule, because in five years of marriage he has not produced an heir — not a child of either sex. It is widely bruited about — only the French would discuss such a thing in public — that this absence of passion is his fault, not the Queen's." He glanced at Guttle and Rebecca. "I shall spare you ladies the details."

"Getting back to freedom, and equality," Izzy ventured, blushing, "when will those winds reach here?"

"The Holy Roman Empire? I love our homeland. I'm proud to be a German. But it's not in our character, I'm afraid, to rebel against authority. In the salons of Berlin, freedom is all the talk. But intellectuals rarely take up arms. That includes myself, of course. In any case, there aren't enough of us."

"What about the Jews?" Izzy asked. "Do you think we will be affected?"

"A fine question — which I will not answer now. That will be a major concern of my speech — my debate — next week with your Chief Rabbi. I hope you'll all be there. But I've prattled on enough for tonight. I fear I have taken advantage of your hospitality."

"Not at all," Guttle said.

"I will indulge myself, however, in another of your delightful Brendel's ruggelah." He reached to a tray and took one. "She is a genius with sweets, that woman. Were I to live here, I would get very fat."

A short time later, after Izzy had gone home and the women were gazing at baby Salomon in his crib, and saying their goodbyes, Meyer took Mendelssohn aside in the darkness of the lane. "Forgive me," he said, his usual propriety drowned by the alcohol, "but I am intrigued by the details you spared the ladies. About the potency, or lack of it, of the King of France."

Mendelssohn laughed, and clapped Meyer on the shoulder. "It's a decidedly un-Jewish problem. They say his foreskin is too tight, and is painful when he enters."

Swaying slightly, Meyer raised his eyebrows. "An odd appendage on which to hang the destiny of a nation." He hiccoughed. "But a problem easily solved, I would think."

"Truly, my friend? Would you care to be circumcised as an adult?"

Meyer winced, and stumbled slightly on the cobbles. "Herr Mendelssohn," he said, righting himself, "I see you are a true philosopher."

The next morning, Meyer lay in bed long after Guttle had risen to feed the children. His head ached, he felt as if his brain had been circumcised; he was glad he had no appointments scheduled.

"You drank a lot of wine last night," Guttle said, sitting on the bed when she saw that he was awake.

"So my head is telling me."

"Were you nervous entertaining Herr Mendelssohn?"

"I don't think so. Maybe a little. I was still shaken by the recruiting. The faces of those men, the wife, the children."

"I guess we're blessed to live in the Judengasse."

"That's more than a joke. At least the City of Frankfurt doesn't have an army."

Slowly he rose from the bed, holding his head; in the kitchen he drank a lot of water. Dressed, desiring the outdoor air, he walked to the post building near the town square, and found three envelopes — two orders for coins, and a letter from America addressed to Guttle. Immediately he became concerned. The only people they knew in the British colonies were the Hesses; Ephraim was always the one who wrote; this was addressed in a feminine hand. As he walked home he murmured a prayer that nothing bad had befallen his friend.

"Open it already," he urged Guttle as she studied the envelope front and back. It had been mailed a month before in the City of New York, where the Hesses lived in an apartment with their three young children. Guttle slit the thin envelope with a knife, pulled out a sheet of paper, and sat in a kitchen chair. Meyer sat across from her as she read aloud the delicate script.

"To dear Guttle and Herr Rothschild:

"Mostly before, my husband Ephraim Hess has sent letters to you. He has kept you interested about how we come to America by boat and find an apartment in which to live in City of New York on street called Canal. How he set up rag business here because that is what we know. How we birth two children in America, a girl and a boy, since Solomon, who in school has now started. I know Ephraim wrote you these things because he always speak letters to me before putting on stamps. Please excuse writing mistakes, five years here we learn good English, and always speak English with the children, but I forget some Judendeutch. In the lane I never learned to read. Here I learn good English, but if I write in English you not know how to read.

"First I to tell you not to worry, Ephraim is feeling fine. He ask me to write this letter because he in hurry to be off. Yesterday he enlisted (right word?) he joined the Continental Army to fight for America against the British and King George III. He go to Battery to sign papers, and he come back already wearing uniform, with a new friend wearing same uniform, to get personal items and kiss me and the children goodbye. His uniform is black three-corner hat, coat of blue, beige vest and breeches, black boot. He also carried musket with long barrel. I never think I would see Ephraim carry such. Solomon was much excited with musket. He want to be soldier and go with his Papa. Ephraim is gone to join General G. Washington or General B. Arnold, he was not sure yet when he left. He made me promise to write to you fine generous friends about this."

Guttle turned over the letter, wiping one eye with her hand as she did, and continued reading. "I am not looking to be happy without my Effie. The children will cry when they learn he be gone for maybe a long time. But I did not make to stop him go. Ephraim and me, we always believe if you want freedom you must fight for it, in the Judengasse or here. Now is time for him. He is eager to go and fight. May Adonai return him to me in fine health.

"We have friends here but not so many Jews as there. Perhaps it be suitable if I write you more when I feel lonely, as I know I shall? Last thing, Ephraim instructed me to remind you that America is land of opportunity. And will be more so after the war is won. So think about coming here, he says, it a better place to make your fortune than in the Judengasse.

"Please give thoughts to Herr Yussel Kahn and all others. Now I say goodbye, I must give nurse to little Meyer. Your true friend far away, Eva Hess."

Guttle set the letter on the table. Meyer picked it up, glanced at it, set it down. "Knowing Ephraim, it's not a surprise," he said.

She went into the children's room. Meyer could hear her speaking softly as he read the letter for himself. When he finished, he was shaking his head. "Little Meyer," he murmured. His eyes were blurred. "Don't let your Papa get killed, little Meyer."

31

The population of the Judengasse was growing. More newborn infants were surviving than were old people dying. This further intensified the crowding, and inspired an architectural innovation. The owners of first one, then another, then a dozen of the narrow tenements constructed outside staircases, rising from a window on the third floor to a window in the attic. This enabled the dwellers to tear out the indoor stairs, which cleared space for another bed or two. The outdoor staircases hanging over the lane were enclosed with wood, and further encroached on the light in the lane, casting shadows where none had been, darkening the twilight gloss.

No one was more conscious of these new shadows, this altered light, than Hiram Liebmann, as he sat over his first chocolate of the day at Brendel's Café. Still an early riser, Hiram was Brendel's first customer most every morning, sitting at an outdoor table when the weather was dry, immune to the early chill, sipping from the cup of warm chocolate, sketching on his pad a scene whose mood caught his attention: old men shuffling to the synagogue in black slippers, women emptying chamber pots into the trench, girls sweeping the cobbles, or the way a new staircase had altered a view that he had sketched before. The deaf mute was considered a vital part of the lane now that his drawings and paintings had begun to sell, not only to the inhabitants but to outsiders, to Gentiles. It was hard for people to imagine a time that he had not been there. They waved to him as they passed, and understood if he was too intent on his work to wave back. Guttle was one of many who shared the same thought: who would have predicted it — the deaf mute exhibiting such artistic talent, and a married man as well?

He had not yet touched his charcoal this morning when a man he had never seen approached the Café and sat at a table across from him. The man bore a hump on his back, which Hiram noted and quickly dismissed; he had realized, by age twenty-eight, that everyone had infirmities, visible or not.

What appealed to him as sketching material was the stranger's deep features, the unusual beard that hung from under his chin, his intense eyes as he bantered with Brendel, who appeared to know him, and who brought him a glass of tea and a slice of sweet.

"You enjoy my ruggelah so much," Brendel told the man, "that I thought you might sample my strudel."

The stranger smiled, and looked at the table. He'd never heard a Jewish woman — or a Gentile woman of the salons, for that matter — say anything so disconcertingly innocent. But perhaps he was imagining it; perhaps he was just missing Fromet.

Hiram, of course, could not hear Brendel's words, or know the stranger's thoughts, but her easy manner with the fellow dispelled what hesitancy he might have felt. He caught the man's attention with his eyes, held up a stick of charcoal, pointed to the stranger, to himself, and scrawled the charcoal above his sketch book.

"You want to draw me?" Moses Mendelssohn asked.

Hiram repeated his motions.

"Go right ahead," Mendelssohn said, then, realizing the artist could neither speak nor hear, shrugged, and nodded yes.

Hiram nodded his appreciation, and began to sketch on his pad. When his subject posed in a stiff position, looking directly at the artist, Hiram shook his head, mimed drinking and eating. Mendelssohn grasped the meaning, and paid no further attention to the artist.

Hiram worked quickly. By the time his subject had finished a second glass of tea and the strudel, the sketch was finished. Brendel came around behind, placed her hands on Hiram's shoulders, and looked at it. She was astonished not only at the accuracy of the rendering of Moses Mendelssohn drinking tea, but at the depth of feeling in the sketch. She took it from the table and showed it to the subject, who raised his eyebrows at the talent displayed, and nodded vigorously to Hiram. Brendel set it down in front of Hiram, pointed to herself, went to the kitchen and returned with her purse. She wanted to buy the sketch. She outlined a square with her hands — she would frame it — went to the wall and hung an imaginary drawing there.

"A memento of my most distinguished customer," she said to Mendelssohn.

She opened her purse and held it towards Hiram. He held up one finger. Brendel took a coin from her purse and placed it on the table — one kreuzer. Hiram grinned broadly — it was a good joke. She took the kreuzer back and replaced it with a gulden. Hiram did not take it, he appeared to be thinking.

Brendel added to the table another gulden, and another, until five gulden were stacked neatly. Hiram pushed the pile back in her direction.

"How much do you want? she asked. "I can't pay more than that." And turned her purse over, to show that it was empty.

Hiram pointed his index finger at her, then at himself, and made a sketching motion.

"You want to draw me? she asked, repeating his motions. "In trade for the sketch?"

Hiram hesitated, thinking how to convey his message. He turned his pad to a clean page, quickly drew the outline of a woman, placed dotted circles where the breasts would be.

"Hiram Liebmann!" She pointed to herself, motioned as if opening her blouse, saying. "You want to sketch me without my clothes?"

The artist nodded vigorously, and pushed the portrait of Mendelssohn towards her. Brendel's face flushed. She touched her fourth finger, where a wedding band would be — if she were married — and pointed across the lane toward the cabinet maker's shop. Hiram understood. *What would Yussel say?* He pointed toward the lane, toward himself, shook his own hand. *Yussel is my friend. He wouldn't mind.*

"Of course, it's my decision," Brendel said, for the benefit of Mendelssohn, who was observing the scene with delight.

Hiram was motioning toward Yussel's shop again, and to himself, and shaking his head. Brendel understood. *Yussel won't let me draw him. So he will let me draw you.*

This was one of the lesser but curious mysteries in the lives of both Hiram and Brendel. Of all the people in the lane whom the artist had wanted to draw during the past few years, only Yussel Kahn had refused. This seemed doubly odd, because Yussel still procured the paints, papers and canvas that Hiram needed, and the wooden stretcher bars. Yussel gave no reason for not wanting his portrait sketched. Even Brendel did not know why. She touched her ring finger again, pointed it at Hiram. "What would your wife say?"

Hiram nodded vigorously

"She would say yes?"

Hiram nodded again.

"You've asked her already?"

He shook his head no. He pointed to himself. He mimed sketching. He pointed over his shoulder to where he lived near the north gate. He shook his head no.

Having conversed with him every morning during the two months the Café had been open, Brendel could by now interpret Hiram's meaning almost as well as Isidor could. *I am the artist. My wife doesn't decide what I draw. I decide what I draw.*

Brendel pushed the portrait of the philosopher from her side of the table. He pushed it back at her. She picked it up and looked at it. "I really would love this on the wall. It would give the Café prestige." Looking at Hiram, she pointed to her temple. *I will think about it.*

The artist smiled and closed the sketch book, as if to end the conversation. Brendel held her new drawing. Standing, Hiram touched her face lightly, then raised his arms in a wide, circling motion. *Your beauty should be seen by the world.*

"My face the world can see," Brendel said, then motioned, *I didn't say yes.* Hiram merely smiled, as if to say, *You will.*

As he stood and paid his bill, Mendelssohn asked, "Is there a place to see his work?"

"First house by the north gate. His wife takes care of the selling."

The philosopher and the artist walked side by side up the lane. There was no attempt at conversation.

3 0 September

I was astonished by what I heard Meyer say this morning. He'd slept too late for morning services, so he put on his tefillin and did his dovaning at home. This rarely happened, and when it did I did not pay much attention; it was men's business, and I have the little ones to look after. But today when I entered the bedroom looking for his socks to darn, I heard him say, "Blessed are You, Lord our God, King of the universe, who has not created me as woman." I was struck dumb. When I did try to speak, he put a finger to his lips to silence me, and continued with his prayers, waiving me out of the room. I smoldered in the office, waiting for him to finish. When he did come out, uncoiling the tefillin from his hairy arm — at that moment the leather coils resembled a snake — he looked at me and said, "What?" Here is our conversation that followed:

"How could you say such a thing? Thanking God you weren't born a woman! What is wrong with being a woman?"

"Nothing, of course. It's not me who said it, it's in the prayer book. Every boy says it every morning from the day he is Bar Mitzvah'd. Till the day he dies. I didn't make it up."

"Who did?"

"I don't know. The ancient Rabbis, I assume."

"I don't want you to say that anymore."

"Guttle, it's part of the prayer. I have to say it."

"Do you believe it?"

"Do I enjoy being a man? Sure I do. I wouldn't make a very good woman."

"And what does that mean?"

"You of all people should be happy that I'm a man." He grinned and tried
to approach me, his favorite way to bury an argument, with a joke and a kiss, but
I backed away

"That's not the point!" I shouted.

Meyer did not know how to respond. He waved his arms in the air and
returned to the bedroom to put his tefillin away. When he did not come right out
I went upstairs to the children. I hugged Schönche especially. What kind of
religion do we have that would make men say such a thing? Surely Adonai would
not say that.

Would He?

Leaning against the first two houses at the north gate, angled so they could
be seen by visitors outside the gate as well as by people inside, were
twenty of Hiram's drawings, in wooden frames. One hand on his chin,
Mendelssohn moved from one to the other, gazing at each for several
minutes, as if memorizing them. All appeared to be scenes from the
Judengasse, vividly done in black and white, with an intriguing use of
shadows from the lamps. Behind women working in the bakery you could
feel the heat rising; the chief Rabbi at his desk was solid and massive as the
wood in front of him; a carpenter nailing together a coffin wore the stoic face
of death; a Constable leaning half asleep against a gate was menacing
nonetheless; a still life of a vacant bed was made oddly disturbing by the play
of darkness in the folds of the quilt; a row of grave stones in the cemetery
uncannily called to mind the houses in the lane. One drawing, suggesting the
myths of the Greeks, depicted a galloping horse and a running girl colliding,
while three unwary children played in the rear, muted, as if in a fog.
Mendelssohn turned to tell the artist how much he liked his work. He'd
vanished. The young wife approached him, a thin girl of perhaps nineteen,
with a sharp nose and chin, wearing a drab brown cotton dress.

"This is strong work," Mendelssohn said. "I don't even know the artist's
name. Lieb?"

"That's his signature. His name is Hiram Liebmann. I am his wife.
Avra."

"We Jews are not known as painters. I didn't know such work was being
done in here."

"It could hardly be done outside," Avra Liebmann, the former Avra Schnapper, said.

*T*he one with the sharp nose and the sharper tongue. That had been her reputation, she knew. She could not help her nose. Because of that she would not hold her tongue. Her parents had despaired that she would ever marry. (They thought she could not hear them, but she could.) Why should they not despair? With Guttle ahead of her, who'd made a solid catch in Meyer Rothschild. With Amelia behind her, the prettiest of them all — most likely she'd have a dozen suitors soon. While Avra swept the cobbles, emptied the slops, worked in the bakery, walked to the market, Avra do this, Avra do that. Avra a beast of burden after Guttle moved out.

Two houses away was Hiram Liebmann. The deaf mute in her childhood years, but an intriguing prospect after he became an artist. New confidence in his manner, yet still an awkwardness. A damaged vessel filled with artistry, to her unschooled but discerning eye. Seeming as innocent as she, though he was nine years older. The more she watched him, the more intrigued she became. He was no Meyer Rothschild, he had no money, he was not handsome. So much the better. She was no Guttle. She began to think of him as she lay in bed at night. His deafness, his muteness, became stimulating new challenges. But would their children be deaf and mute? They need not have children. Her narrow hips might make delivery difficult, Doctor Kirsch had warned. That was fine. His drawings would be their children. A charcoal for her, an oil for him. Guttle, the way things looked, would have plenty of real children for her to share.

She began to converse with him. She learned his language of hands. They became friends. Some days she would prepare a lunch for him. He allowed her into his studio to watch him paint.

One summer afternoon she resolved to teach him a new language. She followed him up the stairs and into his room after his mother had gone to market. He looked at her, waiting. As if he knew something different was about to occur. As if he had been waiting for this day.

It's hot, she indicated. Slowly she began to unbutton his shirt. He shuddered slightly, but did not resist. For each button of his she opened, she undid one of her own. He was ready before they were naked together. Her hand between his legs was a revelation to both of them.

If Yetta came home while they were thus engaged — which she did — and heard sounds emanating from Hiram's room that she had never heard from there before — which she did — and if she quietly entered her own room and closed the door, and sat on her bed, smiling, leaving the vegetables

from the market unattended in their sack in the kitchen — which she did —
the young lovers were unaware of it.

Yetta smiled happily through it all. Lying under a grayed sheet in her own
bed, gazing at the ceiling, she spoke to her dead husband. "Leo, did you
see that?"

"Did I see that? Who wants to see something like that? I heard, it was
plenty."

"It's a good thing, yes?"

"It's a wonderful thing. I could take some credit for it, too. I could tell
you I whispered a few things in that Avra's ear."

"You didn't! You did?"

"Of course I didn't. But I could tell you I did. How would you know
different?"

"Leo! If he weds her, she could feed him when I'm gone. You think
she'd marry him?"

"Of course she will."

"Why 'of course'?"

"I'll whisper it in her ear."

"Go back to sleep, Leo."

"Have good dreams, Eva."

Yetta sat upright from the pillows. "Eva? Who is Eva? What are you
doing up there?"

"Fooled you, Yetta. Have good dreams."

"Fooled me? I'll kill you, Leo Liebmann."

Eva, the rag-picker's wife with the nice breasts? Still he's thinking of
her? "You better go look in America!" she said. She lowered her head to the
pillow. "Men! The old are worse than the young. And the dead are worst of
all."

Avra and Hiram were married a month later. Avra's parents, Wolf and
Emmie Schnapper, did not object, were in fact enthusiastic. Avra was
eighteen already, no suitors were waiting in line. The dowry could be small.
"It's a match made by an observant Yahweh," Wolf confided to daughter
Guttle. "Avra can't stop complaining, and Hiram can't hear." Guttle told her
father that was a terrible thing to say — but she could not help smiling.

Gradually, something unforeseen occurred. Cooking Hiram's meals,
encouraging his work, sharing his bed, Avra Liebmann could not find a single
thing about which to complain. Life was beautiful. As was she, sharp nose
and all.

"I would love to purchase a drawing," Mendelssohn said. "Perhaps several. But I'll be traveling for weeks. They would be awkward to carry."

"We could send them by post. Hiram's work deserves to be seen in Berlin."

"How do you know I'm from Berlin?"

"My sister told me about your dinner."

"Doctor Kirsch?"

"Guttle Rothschild."

"Of course. A lovely and charming young woman."

"Those are rotten qualities in a sister."

"Why is that?"

"People compare."

"I see. Yet, if I may say so, you don't seem unhappy. Whereas at moments, in your sister's eyes, I detected a troubled place."

"Guttle told me you were smart. Few people notice that look. I'm happy, because I have a mission. I devote myself to Hiram's work. It will be appreciated, I think, for a long time. Guttle has three children, but no such mission. She wants to tear down the ghetto walls. What kind of goal is that? It's a fantasy."

"For the moment. Not for eternity."

"For eternity, we'll all be dead. But not Hiram's paintings."

"You're a forceful advocate."

"Let's see how successful. A special price if you take three."

Mendelssohn smiled ruefully. "In that case, I'll have to study them again."

Izzy came bursting out of the slaughterhouse, letting the door slam behind him, and ran across the cobbled square and in through the north gate, whirling to a stop when he saw Avra standing with Moses Mendelssohn. "Shalom," he said, breathing rapidly, "Avra, where's Guttle?"

"At home with the children, I imagine."

"Go get her. Quickly. Tell her I need her, right away. You watch the children for her."

"What's happened?"

"I can't talk now. Go!" Izzy ran back to the slaughterhouse.

"Please don't leave," Avra said to her distinguished customer, and scurried off, holding her skirt, in the direction of the Hinterpfann. Moses Mendelssohn, abandoned, stood bemused in the lane, like a disinterested prophet.

When Avra found her, Guttle hurried out the gate to the butcher shop. "What is it?" she asked as she pushed in through the door, the bell tinkling loud above her.

"Here, in the back," Izzy whispered.

"What's going on?"

"I don't know what to do. I need your advice."

"About what?"

"I found a man in the cold room. A boy. A Gentile."

"What's he doing in there?"

"Shivering."

"Why?"

"It's freezing in there."

"But why is he in there?"

"I locked him in."

"Why did you do that?"

"So he wouldn't get away."

"From what?"

"He's a deserter. From the Prince's recruiters. Like Meyer talked about."

"What do you expect me to do?"

"You're smart. Tell me what to do."

"First of all, don't freeze him to death."

"If I bring him out, people might see him."

"I'll go talk to him." She stepped towards the cold room. "Don't lock the door on me."

She pulled open the heavy wooden door and went inside. The room was small, barely two metres square. Two halves of a cow hung on large hooks. As her eyes accustomed to the dim light she saw a boy, about sixteen, cowering in a corner. He wore a shirt, with blood stains on it, but no jacket. Guttle opened the door a bit and called to Izzy. "Give me your apron!" She took it and handed it to the boy. "Pull it around your shoulders. You're shaking." The boy did as he was told. "We'll get out of this cold soon. First I need to know what's going on. What's your name?"

The boy's teeth chattered, but he said nothing. His face appeared red under the flickering lamps and in the reflection of the red meat. His eyes and hair were dark, his chin strong.

"The sooner we talk, the sooner you'll get warm."

"Georgi."

"Your whole name."

"Georgi Kremm."

"Tell me what happened. You're hiding from recruiters in Hesse-Hanau, is that right?"

The boy nodded.

"Why did you come here?"

"I don't want to fight in a war. I don't want to get killed. The war is not my business."

"I mean why here, to the Judengasse?"

"I heard Jews don't get recruited. I figured they wouldn't look for me here."

"No one in Frankfurt gets recruited. Do you like Jews?"

"I never met one."

"You met the butcher. You've met me. Will you trust us?"

"I don't want to go back."

"Can you stand the cold for five more minutes?"

"As long as it takes."

Suddenly the door opened a slit and Izzy whispered, "Quiet, the police!"

Hardly breathing, Guttle became aware of something dripping onto the floor. She could not tell if it was blood from the carcasses or water from the blocks of ice on a counter along one wall. Nor could she tell which was making her shake more, the cold on her skin or the nerves quivering inside her. The room was illuminated only by a small glass-covered square in the roof; the smoke from oil lamps would spoil the meat. As her eyes adjusted further she discerned two naked geese hanging by their feet in one corner, and terror in the eyes of the boy. Huddled in the room a bare two metres across with the Gentile and two halves of a cow and two dead geese and blood or water dripping, she felt trapped in a bible story, but could not think which: Jonah in the whale? Daniel in the lion's den? She had no answer for that, or for a larger question: why did she feel she must try to rescue the boy? And realized she did not so much feel she must help him as know she was going to. Unless the Polizei seized them all.

32

A Constable from the north gate shut the front door beneath the tinkling bell. His eyes roamed in both directions through the shop. Izzy hurried behind the counter.

"Good morning, officer. Is there anything I can get for you today?"

The Constable's belly pressed against the shirt of his uniform. Izzy could tell that he enjoyed his food. He hoped the visit was about a chicken.

"What have you got in your cold room?" the policeman asked.

"Excuse me?" Izzy almost choked on the words. Now he was in real trouble — for hiding a Gentile, no less. His father never would have done such a thing. How stupid could he be! How could the Constable know?

"All I see hanging here is chickens," the officer said.

"It's Friday," Izzy replied, uncertain if the officer was toying with him. "On Friday we sell lots of chickens."

"I know, I know. That's why I'm asking about the cold room. Do you have a nice fat goose in there? Or a duck? I would take even a turkey, if it's not too big. I'll go pick one out."

The Constable took several steps toward the end of the counter. The cold room was in that direction.

"Only chickens in there," Izzy blurted. "And beef. Next week I can get whatever you want."

"Next week?" The policeman stopped. "All right, next week. Get me a nice fat goose. My wife likes your Jewish birds better than the ones at the market. But to tell you the truth, she doesn't like buying from Jews."

"I'll tell you what," Izzy said. "Come back later, on your way home. I'll have a nice fresh chicken ready for you. Free of charge. That should make your wife happy."

"You're not married, butcher, I can tell. Nothing makes my wife happy. But free of charge — that will make me happy. And next week a goose, don't forget."

"Next week a goose," Izzy repeated.

"I'll come in before I lock the gates," the Constable said. The bell rang loudly as he left.

"Next week a goose," Izzy said in the policeman's wake. "Free of charge also, no doubt."

He wiped perspiration from his face with his apron. Would his father get angry? The cost of doing business, Izzy would tell him. No doubt Otto had done the same many times.

He knocked on the door and entered the cold room. Guttle was hiding near the hanging beef, with the boy. "He's gone. You can come out now."

Guttle stepped from the small room. She glanced about, saw that there were no

customers. Most of the women of the lane already would be home cleaning and salting their Friday night chickens. "Send your helper home for lunch, put up the Closed sign," she said. "Go to Avra at my house. Tell her to take a dress from my commode, and to wrap her head in a scarf. Tell her to put my dress and her sheitl in a shopping bag, as if she's coming to buy a chicken. You stay with my children while Avra comes here. Do you understand?"

"What's the dress and wig for?"

"I want to get Georgi into the lane. Past the Constable."

"Georgi?"

"That's the boy's name. You didn't even ask him? Never mind. Go do what I said."

She hid behind the counter. When the worker left she unlocked the cold room and told the boy to come out. He had a difficult time standing.

"Walk, get your legs working," she told him. "We'll get you out of here soon."

The boy obeyed, walking back and forth.

"There's blood on your shirt. Did you kill someone?"

"It's from the cow in there," he said.

Izzy did his job. Ten minutes later Guttle and Avra were pulling Guttle's dress over the boy's shoulders, settling Avra's wig on his head. He was no taller than Guttle, her dress covered the upper part his shoes. They thought of walking him in barefoot, but decided that would be more conspicuous. His strong chin was more of a problem, but there was nothing they could do about that.

"Pray to whatever God you have," Guttle told him. "We'll need all the help we can get."

Leaving the slaughterhouse through the back door, they circled it. With Guttle on one side, Avra on the other and Georgi in the middle, the three crossed the cobbles to the north gate. Guttle and Avra laughed wildly over a funny story to distract attention from the girl in the middle. The bored Constable paid them no mind.

They strode that way to the Hinterpfann, down the alley and into the office. Guttle locked the door behind her. They took off the wig, helped the boy wriggle out of his dress.

"Perhaps I should have gone to fight," he said.

"You're free to leave at any time."

Guttle's words stopped his mouth.

Izzy came down from the children's room. Avra pulled off the kerchief. She hesitated before donning her sheitl — it had just been on the head of a Gentile — but she put it on anyway. "Not a word to anyone," Guttle warned them. "Not till we decide what to do."

"He'd better be worth this," Avra said, looking at the boy. "Mendelssohn is gone from the paintings, without buying. We could have used the money."

"Mendelssohn will be here for a week," Guttle said.

When they left, she locked the office door again. "Upstairs with you," she told the boy. "There's a fire in the stove. Let's get you warm."

As he huddled in front of it, she put a kettle of water on to boil. "I'll bet a glass of hot tea would feel good."

"Do you have coffee?"

"He's fussy already." But she told him that she did.

They were sitting across from one another at the kitchen table, warming their hands in the steam of the beverages, assessing one another silently, each with his own thoughts. Guttle wondering what in God's eye she was doing.

"Tell me how you escaped," she said.

"At a neighbor's I was visiting. We heard my mother screaming. She is not the type to scream. I looked outside. The army recruiters were there. My older brother Arne they were taking away. I hid myself in a haystack. My mother kept screaming long after, a warning for me not to come back. My neighbor took me to town buried in his hay wagon." The boy's words were splashing out as if a winding stream had come unblocked. "I stayed on the narrow streets. When I got to the Judengasse, there was a Constable near the gate. I went in the butcher's, the back door, to hide there."

"Did you tell your neighbor where you were going?"

"No."

"Tell me something. Why do you think we should hide you here?"

"To save my life. I never hurt anyone."

Guttle pondered what to do next. For a moment she wished Meyer was at home, to make decisions, to take charge. Then she was glad he wasn't; she'd already taken charge. But her decision —which on some level she must have understood — went far deeper than that. For the first time in her life she was able to commit an act that connected to the outside world, to the civilization beyond the walls. It was beyond defiance, it was an affirmation, to that hostile society, of her own existence.

They heard a pounding on the office door.

"Sheist! They found me already."

"Nobody's found you. Be quiet as we go down. You can take your coffee."

Cut flush into the floor beside Meyer's desk was a square trap door that led to the basement storage space. Guttle knelt and lifted it open. "Be careful stepping down. We haven't got wood for the winter yet, so there's room. But be quiet. I'll send away who it is as quickly as I can."

The pounding was repeated, booming through the office like a kettle drum. The boy gave her his coffee mug and climbed backwards down the basement ladder. She handed down the coffee and closed the trap door. Looking about to make sure everything appeared normal, she unlocked the front door.

"Dvorah! Goodness, why all the pounding?"

Dvorah pushed past Guttle into the room. "You were expecting someone else?"

"I wasn't expecting anyone. I was napping with the children."

"Come," Dvorah said, entering the bedroom, sitting on the bed. She was waving about the gift copy of The Sorrows of Young Werther. "I read most of this last night, and finished it this morning. It made me cry. I have to tell you."

"Dvorah, this isn't the best time."

"With children there's never a good time. Guttle, sit. I'm busting my corset to talk. He kills himself!"

"Who kills himself?

Guttle decided to listen and get it done with, though the boy was right below.

"It's a love story. Werther and Lotte fall in love. But Lotte is betrothed to another, whom she will not renounce. Deeper and deeper their love grows. Lotte goes ahead with her marriage. Werther continues to love her. One time when her husband is away, he kisses her. The only time they have kissed. But she gets angry, and sends him away. And he kills himself for love. Isn't that sad? I cried all night. How can I not go see him?"

She felt as if through the thin soles of her shoes she could hear the boy breathing. "Go see who?"

"Paul, of course."

"Dvorah, you cannot go see Paul."

"I can't let him kill himself! I have to go. Tell him how hopeless it is. Tell him I care for him, but there is nothing we can do."

"You care for him? How can you care for him?"

"You don't know him as I do. I'll just tell him to have his carriage by the market. I can meet him there and go for a ride. Like that other... "

Dvorah had said too much, perhaps on purpose, needing to confide.

"Like what other? Dvorah, look at me! There's another?"

"Like that other time. Paul took me for a ride once. Well, twice. It was very innocent."

"I'm sure it was. The Jewish mother and the Gentile Count."

"He won't be the Count till his father dies."

"Excuse me. So what does Lev think about these innocent rides?"

"He's always so busy. There was no reason to tell him. They were just a way to see the city. Breathe fresh air. Get away from the lane for an hour or two."

From under the floor boards came a sound like a muffled sneeze.

"What was that?"

"Nothing. We have a rat in the woodpile."

"You ought to get rid of it."

"I know. You should, too."

"Guttle, that's not fair. Paul is very nice."

"So is Lev.

"It's true, he is. He's just not... exciting... any more."

"You'd better go now. Be careful what you're doing."

"I can't let him kill himself," Dvorah said.

When she had gone, Guttle took the boy upstairs and introduced him to Schönche and Amschel as her cousin, who was visiting. The boy watched her prepare chicken and vegetables for the Friday evening meal. She realized he must be hungry, and gave him bread and honey. With the children crawling all over Meyer when he returned from business in the city, Guttle told him, "This is my cousin, Georgi Pinsky, visiting from Wiesbaden. My aunt Katie's son."

Meyer looked the boy over and shook his hand. "Georgi Pinsky? Of course. Guttle speaks of you often. About your mother Katie as well. I see you have your mother's chin."

The boy looked at Meyer as if he were a lunatic. There was also fear in his eyes that Guttle had not seen before Meyer arrived.

"There's blood on your shirt," Meyer said.

"From a c-cow," the boy explained. "In the b-butcher's."

"Downstairs, please," Meyer said to Guttle.

In the office she told him what had happened, and everything she knew about the boy. Meyer kept silent, as if calculating the situation from all directions. As if it were a business deal. Then he exploded in anger. He tried to keep his voice down so the neighbors wouldn't hear, but he was barely able to as he paced about, raising his arms over his head, dropping them, signaling disbelief in what she had done.

"Are you crazy? Bringing a runaway goy into the lane? Into my house? Are you trying to bring the police down on our heads? Or worse yet, the Crown Prince, whom I've been cultivating for five years? Are you trying to destroy my business? And what about the neighbors, the Rabbis? Do you think they want a goy in the lane? I can't believe you did this."

She was shaken by his outburst; her lower lip trembled.

"Do you know that if you're caught, there's a large fine for hiding him? Seventy-six gulden! Or else you must supply an able-bodied replacement — which will not be me, I assure you. I suggest you get rid of him now, before they lock the gates." He took his handkerchief from his pocket, wiped flecks of foam from his lips.

"I won't."

"You won't? What's gotten into you? I am your husband, you will do as I say!"

"Not this time."

"Not this time? How dare you? Why not this time?"

"Because the boy's life could be at stake. Listen to me, Meyer. You have a happy life, I know. You get to travel through the city, through the countryside, every day. You get to show off your children in schul. The business is doing well. I'm happy for all of that. You know that I am. But do you ever think of my life?" She stood, as if uncertain how far to proceed, then sat again. "While you're riding around on horses buying coins, I'm stuck here in the lane. I can never go further than the market. In the house, I cook, I clean, I take care of the children." With her hand she wiped a single tear from her cheek. "I have no complaint about that, those are the duties of a wife. I'm happy, even proud, to be your wife. But I am not just a wife. I'm a person, with needs of my own." She paused, and her voice softened then, from anger to earnestness. "Do you remember how we used to talk when we were betrothed? How together we would try to tear down the walls? I don't see us doing that any time soon. But here I have a chance to save a life. We have a chance. And I can't let that opportunity pass. We are so religious here, following all the customs — but what was it Mendelssohn said? True religion is to be a moral person. Now is my chance to prove to myself that I am. If being moral comes with risks, I'm ready to face them."

Angry and confused, Meyer could only reply, "But he's a goy!"

"All the more reason to save him. Any Jew would save a fellow Jew."

With intense effort he let his breathing slow, he calmed his voice. "So this is what comes from allowing a philosopher into the lane."

He reached for a chair and sat. He shook his head, rested his elbow on the desk, amid a small pile of coins. With his other hand he rubbed his forehead, trying to deny a headache. "I didn't know you were so unhappy," he said.

"I'm not so unhappy. I love you. I love being your wife. I love our children. But sometimes I need to do things separate from you. I read my history books, when I can squeeze in the time, when the children are asleep. But to save a boy from going to war — this in itself could be a little bit of history. It's something I must do, to be true to Guttle Schnapper. More important, to be true to Guttle Rothschild."

Meyer sat silently, his eyes closed. To Guttle it seemed as if hours passed. Perhaps it was only minutes. Meyer stood, took off the gray coat he still was wearing, draped it over his chair, as if he had just arrived home on a normal day. His voice was reserved when he spoke. "Where will he stay, till the danger passes? He can't sleep crowded in with the wood."

"I thought Rebecca might take him in."

"She's got Mendelssohn there. We can't put the great man at risk."

"Perhaps your brother Kalman can stay a few nights with a friend. Or at Rebecca's. The boy could have his bed."

"Have you asked Kalman?"

"I wouldn't do that without speaking to you."

Rubbing the back of his neck, Meyer said, "I don't suppose they'll come looking for him here. Wilhelm has plenty of other peasants." He took a deep breath, exhaled forcefully, as if trying to exhale the boy. "Give him one of my yarmulkes, just in case. And tell him to start growing a beard — if he can."

"He's got dark hair and eyes. If he wants to stay in the lane, maybe he could

really pass as my cousin."

"Or as your long-lost sister. Did he make a handsome lass?"

She took his hand and kissed his knuckles, smiled inwardly in triumph, accepting his weak joke as his surrender. She offered peace with irony. "I'm glad you agree with me."

Meyer responded in kind; both understood intuitively that wry humor, as much as passion, was a substance of their love. "When do we not agree?" he said.

On the Sabbath they made him stay in the house. On Sunday, with the gates locked and a police raid unlikely, they tested him at their end of the lane, among the neighbors they knew well. "Guttle's cousin, Georgi Pinsky, visiting from Wiesbaden. Katie's boy."

Of course, the neighbors said. Katie, who married into the Wiesbaden Pinskys. Nice to meet you, Georgi Pinsky (wink). From the very first there was the wink, directed at Meyer or Guttle or at the boy himself. Who did not remember Emmie Schnapper's sister Katie — the one she never had mentioned, the one no one had ever seen? But there was a definite family resemblance. Avra's nose merely had dropped to his chin. They knew, of course. Whether Izzy had told someone, or Avra, or if the butcher's helper had overheard, Guttle could not say. Her guess was Izzy. How could he not boast to his brothers, or his Papa, of what he had found? And once his father Otto knew, the whole lane knew.

On Monday the young man walked freely in the lane, wearing Kalman's clothes, a yarmulke on his head, a hint of stubble on his cheeks. In the north-end houses many people might refer to him as the Gentile, or the Runaway. But in the street he was Georgi Pinsky (wink.) Katie's boy. As if it were all a good joke. They had no fear for themselves; they had done nothing. And the Crown Prince seemed far away.

Not all were so accepting, however. Otto Kracauer was not. Nor were Jacob Marcus, the moneylender, nor Alexandre Licht, the shoemaker, nor most of the south end. Guttle's own mother was appalled at what she had done, though her father said nothing.

A torrent of angry gossip washed along the cobbles like summer rain stirring the dirt.

— Can you imagine such a thing? Who would bring a goy into the lane?

—Meshuganah Guttle Rothschild, of course.

33

The debate, held in the lecture hall of the yeshiva, attracted the largest crowd, outside of the synagogue, since the murder trial of Hersch Liebmann nearly six years earlier. Guttle, Meyer and their friends arrived early, and took up half of the third row. Guttle sat between Meyer and Yussel Kahn. Beside Yussel were Brendel and Doctor Kirsch. Beside Meyer were Dvorah, Doctor Berkov and Isidor. At the hospital, the aides on duty knew where to find the two doctors if there was an emergency. Throughout the lane, younger sisters were acting as baby sitters. Amelia, now thirteen years old, was watching Guttle's children, along with the Gentile boy.

At the prescribed time of eight o'clock, every seat was filled, and people were standing without complaint at the sides and across the rear. Two lecterns had been placed at the front of the hall, two metres apart. Rabbi Simcha introduced the debaters. The Chief Rabbi was dressed in his constant black, the visitor in Berlin beige. Herr Mendelssohn would speak first on the subject for the evening, the future of the Jews, Rabbi Simcha said.

"Thank you, Rabbi," Moses Mendelssohn began. "I am grateful for this opportunity to convey my views to the people of the Judengasse, many of whom I have met personally during the past few days. The throng in this hall is a fine testimony to the civic awareness in this lane.

"What, then, is the future of the Jews? How much of the answer depends on forces outside of our control, and how much depends on ourselves?

"The good news is that the forces out of our control are now running in our favor, like a river rushing downhill. The time in which we live is perhaps the first time we Jews can say that in seven hundred years — since the slayings of the first crusade inaugurated all these centuries of religious prejudice, of atrocities rooted in so-called faith.

"The time in which we live already is being called, by journalists and scholars, the Age of Enlightenment. There is a heavy irony in speaking such words here in the Judengasse, with its high walls, with its gates that are locked against us even as I speak. There is irony in saying those words anywhere in the City of Frankfurt, where the treatment of we Jews — of you forced to live in this ghetto — is the most restrictive and obscene in all of Europe, from the marital and legal restrictions to that despicable Judensau I saw as I entered the city. But the fact remains that enlightenment has been born in the world like a young lion — and it is moving in this direction.

"Now, what do I mean by enlightenment? It is, quite simply, the application of human reason to all things. The first important thing that reason shows us is that the treatment of men by their fellowmen down through the centuries has not been reasonable. There is no way to defend with reason why some men should be born Princes and others should be born slaves. There is no way to demonstrate with reason that one religion contains the whole truth about God, and is superior to all others.

"Modern science has shown us that the blood of nobles is no different than the blood of peasants. Yet all around us, the Princes, under their own laws, which benefit only themselves, own the very bodies and souls of their fellow men. Reason tells us that at heart, the essential message of all religions is that man should live a moral life, and treat his fellow men well. Yet we see nothing but war and hatred among Catholic, Lutheran, Muslim, Jew.

"These ideas are not new. They trace back at least as far as the British philosopher John Locke a century ago, who suggested that the true determinant of government should be the will of the majority — not the whim of a Prince or a King. Like an underground river, these enlightened ideas have been gaining strength ever since, aided by the writings of such men as the French philosopher Voltaire, and others. These writings have influenced the British colonists in America who are rebelling against their King. These ideas are the talk of Paris. They cannot but swamp the Holy Roman Empire before long. When they do, the gates of this lane will be unlocked forever.

"But what will happen then? Are you people of this crowded lane prepared for the new opportunities that will come?

"I am sorry to say that, from my observation, you are not. In your heders and in your fine yeshiva, the only things taught are the Pentateuch and the Talmud. The only language spoken besides Hebrew is the hybrid Judendeutch. But the Gentiles, at least in the learned classes, are teaching their children science and medicine, history, philosophy, languages such as Latin, Greek and French. I hope you will not take this wrong, but the fact is that many of you men of the Judengasse cannot speak or read pure German — the language of our country.

"I was going to save this talk for Berlin, but I think not. I propose here tonight that the time has come for nothing less than a Haskalah, a Jewish enlightenment.

"It is essential that our Jewish schools broaden their curricula, so that our children will be able to take advantage of a new equality when it arrives. Girls should be educated as well as boys — in separate schools if that is desired, but educated nonetheless. In an enlightened future there will be freedom to choose any profession, to live anywhere one desires. But this opportunity will be worthless if you are not prepared to use it, to throw off the shackles of the ghetto. Unless you are ready to act, the gates will remain locked, the walls will stand, life here will remain unchanged. The Gentiles will continue to view us as some curious, subhuman race.

"All of that is at stake in the coming years."

Guttle sat enthralled, her mouth slightly open, her lower lip loose. In all the years of her yearning for the destruction of the walls, she never once had focused on what would follow. Mendelssohn was right, she thought. Without any walls the ghetto might still be a ghetto if the people let it remain so, if they were not prepared to live in the changing world.

She glanced at Meyer. He was listening intently, but she could not read his thoughts.

"I have more to say," Mendelssohn concluded, "but I shall pause here, to drink some water, and to permit your learned Chief Rabbi to respond."

Rabbi Eleazar sipped from his water glass, cleared his throat. Engrossed by Mendelssohn's words, eager for their Rabbi's rejoinder, most in the hall had ceased to notice a flickering of the lamps.

The Chief Rabbi's voice was deep and confident as he began.

"I must beg to differ with our distinguished visitor, on almost everything he said."

Pockets of laugher erupted in the audience. Even Mendelssohn smiled.

"The future of the Jewish nation is not an open question. It is all written down in this book — in the Pentateuch." He held up the book for them to see. "So long as we adhere to Yahweh's laws as set down in the five books of Moses, and to the teachings of this other book, the Talmud"— he held that up as well — "we Jews shall survive as a nation. I would point out that many nations of history are no longer with us — the Hittites, the Philistines, the Canaanites, and so forth. All have perished, along with their beliefs. The pagan gods of the Greeks and the Romans have perished. Yet we Jews have survived, despite all the attempts to destroy us, despite the destruction of our sacred temple, and the diaspora that followed.

"Why have we survived? Precisely because we did not try to be like the others, as Herr Mendelssohn would have us do. Precisely because we have preserved our separate identity. Precisely because we have followed Yahweh's laws to the letter. Because when we do, He watches over us, no matter our earthly travail. The books of Moses do not instruct us to become scientists or philosophers, to learn Latin or Geek. They instruct us to retain our faith, and obey the laws that Yahweh has given to us. By doing so, we have survived for six thousand years. By doing so we shall continue to survive, until the Messiah comes.

"Let us take a look at the world Herr Mendelssohn is offering as a desirable future for the Jews. He wants us to move out of the ghetto, to live among the Gentiles as equals. He wants us to speak pure German, so our Hebrew accents will not distinguish us as Jews — as if we should be ashamed of the way we speak! What would be the logical next step? The logical next step is that our Jewish men would see nothing wrong with marrying Gentile girls. Our Jewish girls would happily — so they might think — marry Gentile men.

"Our visitor presents all this as a future to be desired — but what then would happen to the Jewish race? We would be absorbed into the larger population. We would throw onto the trash heap the sacred laws of the Sabbath, of circumcision, of kosher, and all the rest. In short, we would no longer be Jews. We would have violated our sacred covenant with Adonai — and who will watch over us then?"

Guttle felt Meyer's hand on her knee, his breath on her cheek, as he leaned towards her. "It's true," he whispered.

"Many Gentile thinkers," the Rabbi continued, "who agree with Herr Mendelssohn, have suggested publicly that because of his stated beliefs, he ought to convert to Christianity. Because, knowingly or not, that is the cause he serves."

A tense intaking of breath swept parts of the audience.

"I would like to ask him to tell us why he has not done so."

Mendelssohn grasped the lectern on both sides. As he leaned forward, from Guttle's view his hump seemed to alternate dark and light as a lamp on the wall behind him flickered.

"Some of you in the audience gasped at the Rabbi's question," he said. "I assure you, it does not offend me. I relish the chance to explain my position.

"I am a Jew. I was born a Jew. My wife is a Jew. I shall be a Jew until I die. I believe in Yahweh, and in the books of Moses, and in the teachings of the Talmud. I do not believe that Jesus was the son of God, as a Christian must believe. I shall explain why. And I shall do so on the basis of reason, not of faith.

"Tomorrow morning, go to the south gate of your lane and look out. Look at the sun in the sky, and the clouds. Look at the river Main flowing by, and the fertile fields across the river, and the shapes of the distant mountains. Look at your wives, your children. Think of the miracle of birth. Think of the incredibly complex functioning of the human body, which we humans cannot begin to understand. Think of the birds and the fish, think of all the animals that you know to exist, even if you cannot see them through the walls. What do all these things tell us? Because they exist, they tell us they have been created. And what does our reason tell us about that? It tells us that because all these birds and elephants and humans have been created, there must have been an entity — an intelligence — a super intelligence — that created them. I say a super intelligence because surely no man, no amount of men, could have done so. We have not the intelligence nor the power. That super intelligence — that undeniable creator — is what we call God.

"I said that I believe in the books of Moses. Many so-called miracles are described in those books. If I believe only in reason, you might reasonably ask, how can I believe in such miracles — the ten plagues in Egypt, the parting of the Red Sea, the acquiring by Moses of the Commandments? I shall tell you how. Because almost every miracle described in the Pentateuch was witnessed by the entire Jewish nation — by tens of thousands of people who could tell the tale. Reason tells me that an event witnessed by so many people must have taken place. Who would believe in an eclipse of the sun, had it not been witnessed by millions?

"Where I take issue with my Gentile friends, in Berlin and elsewhere — and I have many of them, and I am glad that I do — is that I do not believe that Jesus was the son of God. My God-given reason does not let me believe that. Each of the so-called miracles attributed to Jesus, as described in the New Testament, was witnessed by only a handful of people — mostly by his few original followers. Even those followers did not declare him the son of God — not when he was alive. It was more than three centuries later before the Catholic church declared that Jesus was of divine origin — and even then there was much dispute. I tell my Christian friends that we Jews will gladly accept Jesus as a major Jewish teacher, an important prophet — but my reason finds no evidence that Jesus was the Messiah, that he was the son of God.

"That, my friends, is ample reason why I retain the faith of my fathers, and only their faith. I observe the Jewish holy days. I go to schul. I do not write on the Sabbath. I keep a kosher home. I am as much a Jew as anyone in this room. But these things have not prevented me from participating in the increasingly modern world. By living a moral life I have tried to show the Gentiles what we Jews truly are. We do not have to segregate ourselves in order to do that. Indeed, if we demonstrate to them up close that we are clean and moral beings, their prejudices against us, which are based on ignorance, might vanish."

As the Rabbi began his rejoinder, Guttle saw that his neck had become thick with knotted tendons, as if an ancient, rough landscape were reasserting itself there.

"Our visitor — and I underline that word, visitor — just suggested that we have segregated ourselves. I would like him to tell me what Jew built these walls, or locked these gates. Or wants to be confined in such a way. Let him name one. Is there anyone in this room who enjoys being a prisoner of the Gentiles? Stand and show your face."

Nobody stirred. Mendelssohn's face flushed. Drops of perspiration glistened on the foreheads of both men, glowing in the lamplight, Guttle thought, like semiprecious gems. Like their words — or was one speaking pearls, the other, paste? She wasn't sure.

"Jews did not physically build the walls or lock the gates, of course," Mendelssohn said. "The Rabbi knows I did not mean to suggest that they did. We Jews are not responsible for the actions of those who oppress us — or are we, in fact, a little bit responsible?"

He paused to make sure he had their attention. Not a sound could be heard.

"We look at Catholics, Lutherans, Muslims. They are Gentiles. That is simple fact. That means simply that they are not Jews. So far, so good. But how do many of us refer to them among ourselves? We call them goyim. That has a demeaning sound. The word Gentile distinguishes us from them. But when we use the word goyim, we are placing them beneath us, we are holding them in contempt — just as, too often, they use the word Jew as if it carries within itself a negative adjective. Dirty Jew. Filthy Jew. Scurvy Jew. Damn Jew. By moving among them in modern life, as I suggested earlier, we will show them that we are not dirty, not filthy, that — though we may like our herring — we do not have scurvy, or any other disease. We would become their equals in science and philosophy and mathematics and literature — in all modes of learned human endeavor. But just as they must stop condemning us for being Jews, we most stop calling them goyim, and pretending we are superior."

The Chief Rabbi smiled, and stroked his broad beard, as if he had a winning point to make. "You said you believe in the books of Moses. In those books we are given a special covenant from God. Do you believe that? Does it not make us superior?"

Many in the audience were nodding slightly as the visitor prepared to respond.

"I said before that I believe in the Pentateuch, and I do. I like to picture all of religion as a broad house. We Jews, and the Christians, and the Muslims, all believe in the same God. We all believe we are descended from Abraham. So we all live together in the first floor of this vast house of religion. The way we best serve this God, as I said before, is to live a moral life, and to help others. All religions teach this. But living a moral life does not depend on believing that a glass of wine is the blood of Jesus — or that women must cover their faces — or on not eating meat with milk. These separate practices should not turn us away from the laws of morality in which we all claim to believe. Reason tells us that.

"Now, on top of this house, I see a second story, much smaller than the first. In this house, Yahweh has prescribed special laws for the Jews. Because they were given to us by Him, we have accepted them. They are a sacred trust, and a sacred burden. Non-Jews do not have to accept them in order to lead moral lives. Just as accepting this special relationship with Yahweh does not make us superior moral beings. Only our actions do that — not our prayers."

He paused for a long drink of water.

"I think that concludes the principal ideas I want to convey. Unless the Chief Rabbi has further questions of me."

The Rabbi had none. "The people here know my views, I shall not belabor them," Eleazar said. "I shall just repeat what I said before. Our faith is what has sustained us for six thousand years. We must not do anything that undermines that faith. Our faith is who we are. Our faith is who we shall become."

Applause was not permitted in the synagogue, and so, by force of habit, there was no applause in the lecture hall. Its absence left tension hanging in the air — coughing, chairs scraping, silence. When Rabbi Simcha asked if anyone in the audience had a question, Yussel Kahn stood. "I've heard it said that this period of enlightenment is already ending. That a reaction already is setting in against pure reason. Can Herr Mendelssohn comment on that?"

"I would be glad to," Mendelssohn said. "Unfortunately, there is some truth to what you've heard. More so here in Germany than in England or France. A new sentimentality appears to be rising. The other day, in your wonderful Café — the best ruggelah in all of Europe, I dare say — a young woman asked me if I had read the book that is the talk of the land. It is called *The Sorrows of Young Werther*. I have indeed read it. It is perhaps the prime example of this new sentimentality. There is not a hint of intelligent thought or reason anywhere in the book. It is pure emotion. A young man, Werther, falls in love with a woman who is already betrothed to another. Soon after she marries her betrothed, Werther kills himself. End of story. In between is what I can only term garbage — a worshipping of nature and emotion over progress and reason."

Guttle leaned forward, looked past Meyer at Dvorah, trying to discern her reaction. Dvorah's face in the dim light was tense. Seeming to sense that Guttle was looking at her, she turned her head. Guttle saw in her friend's eyes a fierce anger, combined somehow with frustration, with helplessness, as if she wanted to shout a response, but could not. As if, even if she had the chutzpah to respond, she did not have the words.

Mendelssohn was continuing. "This book celebrates what the Frenchman Rousseau has been saying, as against the views of a far superior thinker, Voltaire. Rousseau would have us seek the ideal man in a state of nature. This is naive. The truth is that man, when he is not acting as a thinking being, goes out and kills and tortures other men — and women and children — for no defensible reason. For some sick emotional release, for a misguided faith — as we have seen throughout history. Similarly, Werther, instead of understanding with his reason that his pain will pass, acts on his emotion alone, and shoots himself."

"Werther, of course, is a fictional character. The author, Herr Goethe, who appears to know well what it is to have loved and lost, did not kill himself. He wrote a book. The act of writing a book is filled with hope. Yet he makes his nature-loving character commit suicide — an unnatural act. The worst part is that there have been reports from all over Germany of young men killing themselves after reading this book. As if that makes them romantic heroes. The fact is, I half suspect that the author meant us to see Werther as pitiful, not heroic. To use a wonderful Yiddish word, Goethe's young man is a schlemiel — as are all his real-life worshipers."

Guttle heard someone nearby gasp. She leaned forward. It had been Dvorah, whose hand was pressed to her mouth as she shook her head. Catching sight of Guttle, she continued shaking 'no.' To Guttle, her friend seemed powerless to stop, as if she did not realize she was doing it.

"Nonetheless," Mendelssohn went on, "the book's popularity does suggest a resurgence of unreasoning sentiment — which can be a deadly and violent state of mind. It is a state of mind that is particularly perilous to us Jews.

"I have responded at some length about this because it suggests an important point regarding the future of Jewry. We must earn new respect, and new freedom — we must make what progress we can — while the ideas of the enlightenment are still ascendant. If unreasoned emotion regains sway, then once more we shall be called dirty Jews, once more the gates, having opened, will swing shut. The God in which we believe has given us free will with which to choose our actions. He has shown many times that, no matter how sincere our faith, he will not take those actions for us."

"He will!" someone shouted from the midst of the audience. Heads turned, but no one echoed the cry.

"He won't," Guttle said to herself.

"Are there any more questions?" Rabbi Simcha asked. When there were none, he thanked the learned men for their provocative exchange. "The debate tonight is ended," he told the audience, "but the ideas expressed by our speakers most likely will vie for our souls for years to come."

Standing with the others, the lingering arguments flashing and dying and flashing again in conversations all around her, Guttle suspected that Rabbi Simcha was right. But never mind years to come. The lane might well be fiercely divided tomorrow.

34

S he hit him, I tell you.

—She hit who?

—The philosopher.

— Everyone in the lane is a philosopher.

— Don't play games. The one who gets paid for it. Moses Mendelssohn.

— Who hit him?

— The Doctor's wife. Dvorah Schlicter.

— Dvorah Berkov?

— That's the one.

— What do you mean, she hit him. Where did she hit him?

— Alongside the temple.

— By his ear? Where, inside the schul?

— I told you, alongside the schul. In the dark. She bloodied his nose.

— She hit him so hard?

— With a book.

— Why did the Doctor's wife hit the philosopher?

—Is that a riddle?

— It's a riddle unless you know the answer.

— She didn't like what he said.

— A lot of people didn't like what he said. I didn't like so much what he said. Girls in the schools? What for? But I didn't hit him.

— She didn't like what he said about the book.

— The Talmud?

— Not the Talmud. That Gentile book.

— The Worth of Young Sorrow?

— That's the one.

— Why would she care that he didn't like the book?

— She liked it.

— For that you hit a philosopher?

— They're blaming it on the schnapps.

— What schnapps?

— Not the schnapps she wasn't drinking.

— The Doctor's wife drinks a little?

— Lately, they say.

— Who says?

— People who see. From a flask, yet.

— So she hit him with a book. Did he hit back?

— Of course not. He's a philosopher.

— He turned the other cheek?

— His nose she bloodied, I told you. He has only one nose.

— So what did he do? She's a big girl.

— With those she wasn't hitting him, I don't think. He put out his hands to block her. She kept hitting with the book, and yelling.

— It's a good thing she didn't use the flask. She could have broken it.

— It was made of silver.

His nose she could have broken. You saw?

— I didn't see. I heard from someone who saw. Most people went home after his speech.

— Like me.

— But a few stayed in the lane, schmoozing. Yussel Kahn and Brendel from the Café were there, Meyer Rothschild and his wife.

— Guttle?

— Guttle heard, and ran to see — she's a friend of the Schlicter girl. She grabbed her around the waist, and pulled her away from Mendelssohn. The Doctor's wife still was yelling, struggling, and they fell down together, the sane one on top of the crazy one, grabbing her wrists, and the book went flying, splash, into the ditch. The very same Worthies of Sorrow. So now she was yelling even louder. She crawled on her knees and grabbed for her book in the ditch. A handful of you know what, she got.

—A handful of shmutz? Oy, vey.

—She lay there crying while the book floated away with the turds.

— Ashes to ashes. What about the Doctor? Didn't he do something?

— He was in the hospital. Someone went to get him, he quick came running.

— I would think.

— He kneeled by his wife and talked to her. He stood her up and walked her to their house. She was leaning on him.

— That's all?

— The woman Doctor fixed Mendelssohn's nose.

— It won't be the end of it.

— How do you know?

— You don't hit a philosopher and that's the end of it. Otherwise they all would get hit.

Thus did gossip pre-empt, that first day, discussion of the debate.

Guttle's beige cotton dress, one of her favorites — what else do you wear to such a distinguished debate? — was soiled with mud, her left sleeve was torn half off. Her bare shoulder gleamed in the lamplight from the windows as they walked home. Neither she nor Meyer spoke. Her insides felt muddy as her dress, her heart had been torn from its moorings and cast adrift like a small boat in a storm.

Amelia and the Gentile boy were talking in the kitchen when they arrived. The boy said goodnight and went upstairs to his room.

"What happened!" Amelia asked, startled to see mud on her sister's cheek.

"She's fine," Meyer said. "Please go home now. Thank you for watching the children."

Amelia peered at Guttle, who said nothing, who was too upset to speak. "She doesn't look fine."

"Go," Guttle said, softly. She kissed her sister's forehead, keeping her dirty hands at her sides. "We'll talk tomorrow."

When Amelia had gone, Guttle sat at the table, staring at nothing. Meyer made tea and placed a glass in front of her, and sat beside her with his own glass. From outside they heard a light rain beginning to bounce off the chimney. Meyer stroked Guttle's hand. The knuckles were scraped raw. Drying blood streaked the drying mud. "You should wash that," he said. Guttle did not respond. Her mind was in a different place, seeking Melka, or Jennie Aron, or Madame Antoine — any secret female friend. "I'm going to lose her," she murmured.

"Lose who? Do you know what that was about?"

She did not realize she had spoken aloud. Meyer's question brought her back to the crying of her knuckles, and the rain. She shook her head.

"You're her best friend, surely you know something. A person doesn't just break down like that, for no reason."

Her eyes still were far away, her voice a monotone. "It's woman business."

"Mein Gott! Is she sick?"

Guttle closed her eyes, breathed deeply. "Not how you mean."

"If it's a woman's thing, I won't pry." He stood, leaving his glass of tea untouched. "I go to Mannheim tomorrow. I need to go to bed. Shall I help you clean yourself?"

She touched his arm, her torn sleeve hanging like a broken limb. "I can do it. You go. I may sit up awhile, if that's all right."

Never in the five years of their marriage had she not come to bed with him. They would lie together, hand in hand, discussing the events of the day, till gently he turned toward her with a slowly rising passion, or away from her to sleep.

"Of course." He kissed her hair. "Don't stay up too long. The baby will be crying early."

She sipped her tea, now cold. The scrape on her knuckles was stinging worse. She rose and took off her muddied dress and dropped it on the floor, removed her scuffed shoes and soiled stockings. In her chemise, she poured water from a pitcher over the back of her hands, blotted them with a towel, sat again at the table, sucking her knuckles for solace. Absorbing the skin and blood of Dvorah's pain.

By the time she went to bed faint light was crawling in over the window sill. She slept through Meyer's departure for schul and then for work — a rarity. Only the baby's hungry cries awakened her. As she cradled him to her breast, sympathy for Dvorah's plight gave way to anger. The world was a meaner place this morning than it had been the day before, and it was Dvorah's fault. Guttle had no hunger for breakfast. Meyer had fed the children — another rarity. Dressing quickly, she asked Georgi to stay with Schönche and Amschel, and she carried the baby into the alley. When she saw Dvorah's daughter Ruthie pass on the way to her sewing lesson, Guttle walked down the lane to where Dvorah and Lev and the twins resided, past the communal baths, above a shoemaker's shop. The twin boy David would be in heder. She lingered amid the smell of tanned leather, nodded to the cobbler, Alexandre Licht, as he hammered at his bench, wearing his familiar red beret, unused nails protruding from his mouth, then climbed a flight of stairs and knocked on the door.

"Go away." Dvorah's voice sounded as if it were coming from Mainz, or beyond.

"It's Guttle. Let me in."

"Go away."

"I'm not leaving. You need to talk before you explode."

She stood there till she heard the padding of feet across the wooden floor. The door was unlocked from inside, and opened. Dvorah still was wearing her lavender dress from the night before, covered with dried mud and now a grid of wrinkles from being slept in as well. It looked like one of those plowed fields across the river that were visible through the south gate. Her hair resembled an auburn mop. Guttle closed the door and followed Dvorah into her bedroom, and watched as she climbed into bed and pulled the floral quilt to her chin. Guttle shifted baby Salomon from one arm to the other.

"I already exploded, don't you think?"

"That was outward. If you explode inward it could be worse."

"How could it be worse? I don't dare show my face in the lane."

"So you'll spend the rest of your life in bed?"

Dvorah made no response.

"Those rides you've been taking with Paul. I've been wanting to ask you. The last time, you came home with white powder on your shoulders. On your collar. What was that?"

"White powder? Are you sure?"

"I'm sure."

"Oh. I know. It must have been powder from his wig."

"So, you lied to me!" Guttle said. "Those rides. They were not just rides."

Her head on the pillow, Dvorah closed her eyes. She did not say Guttle was right. She did not say Guttle was wrong.

"How could you do that?"

"You don't know what it's like."

"Tell me, then."

Dvorah opened her eyes, raised herself on the bed, sat with her legs crossed in front of her. "When I'm making supper, Paul is in my head. When we're having conversation at the table with the twins, I have to fight to concentrate. My head is thinking of where Paul is. The same when Lev talks to me — which is rare enough. I want it to be Paul, making me laugh. Making me feel wanted. Even now, talking to you, I'm wondering what he's doing. Who he's with." Flushed, as if overheated, she pushed away the quilt. Her toenails were painted red. Guttle had never seen that before. "All morning I've been picturing that beautiful book floating away with the turds. It's probably in the river by now, being eaten by fish."

"Fish don't eat books. Bookworms, maybe."

"That's not funny."

"I know. What did you tell Lev?"

"Nothing. Just that I've been under a strain. He gave me a powder to sleep."

"That's all? No questions?"

"He's got a serious case in the hospital. Someone may die. I don't even know who. He always has a serious case to think about."

"He's a Doctor. He helps people."

"That doesn't help me. He married a selfish person."

"So what will you do?"

"I don't know. One day I'll have to tell Lev. Ask him to grant me a divorce. Take the twins and move into the town, and marry Paul."

"A divorce? How can you even think such a thing? I've never heard of a divorce in the lane."

"I don't know what else to do."

"Are you sure Paul wants that? You're not just his Jewish doxy?"

"You think that little of me? He's already proposed marriage."

"To marry him, you would have to convert. Become a Christian."

"It won't change what's in my heart."

"I've never heard you say that before — that Adonai is in your heart."

"Guttle, Guttle. Three children, a fourth on the way, and you're still an innocent." She put her hands on Guttle's shoulders. "I didn't say Adonai was in my heart. Haven't you been listening? It's Paul who's in my heart."

"Suppose what you're feeling is the lure of forbidden fruit. You won't be able to come back when you've had enough."

"I've thought of that. Am I supposed to be stronger than Eve was?"

Guttle began to arrange Dvorah's curls. "Well, it's not the Garden of Eden you'd be leaving." She pressed her thumb hard against Dvorah's lips. "Aside from, you should pardon the expression, Jesus, what does Paul offer that Lev doesn't?"

"You need me to tell you? Theater. Picnics in the park. Fancy dress balls. Silk every day of the week, if I want. Fresh air for me and my children to breathe — they own a chateau in the Black Forest. Sailing on lakes in the mountains. A trip every year to Paris, where the fashions are. But I can put it in a simpler way. No walls. No gates. That's what Paul has to offer."

"He's your Melka."

"But he's not, don't you see? He's real."

Guttle breathed deeply, looked around the room, then, reluctantly, back at her friend. She wished Paul von Brunwald never had entered the lane. He had come, like almost all the Gentiles who passed through the gates, just out of curiosity. To look at the Jews in the zoo. Now this. "You make it sound so nice. Mountains. Lakes. Paris. Who wouldn't want those things? It makes me a little jealous, I hate to admit. But look at the price. Look what you'd be giving up."

"Look out the window, Guttle. That's what I'd be giving up."

"That, and your children."

"What are you talking about? The children are coming with me."

"Paul wants that?"

"Of course. We're a family."

"What about Lev? He'll never let you take them."

"Of course he will. He can hardly raise them by himself."

Something glistening and bright beneath the edge of the bed had been distracting Guttle. She reached to the floor, drew up a small silver flask. Liquid sloshed inside it. She peered at an engraving on one face — two standing lions holding aloft a quarter moon. If pressed, she would guess it was the escutcheon of the House of Brunwald. "And this? "

Dvorah took the flask, shoved it under her pillow. "It keeps me from shaking. Sometimes it keeps me from screaming."

"Not last night."

"Don't remind me."

"Why did you have the book with you?"

"It's always in my purse. It's like having a bit of Paul with me." She ran her fingers along the pattern of a white flower on the quilt. "That's why I lost control. When he attacked the book, it was as if were attacking Paul. When he called it garbage, I felt he was trying to destroy our love. It was a dumb thing to do, I know. But I couldn't stop myself."

Guttle closed her eyes. Such consuming, distracting passion must be terrible, like a deadly disease. But was it also wonderful?

"What did people say?" Dvorah asked.

"I was too busy wrestling to listen. Most people already were gone."

"Then there won't be a lot of gossip?"

"I wouldn't count on that. It's the ones who didn't see that whisper."

Lying down again, Dvorah pulled the quilt over her face.

"When will you do all this?"

From beneath the quilt she mumbled a muffled, "I don't know." She exposed her face, tucked the quilt beneath her chin. "Not during the High Holy Days. That would make people hate me. After that, Paul is going to Rome for a month with his mother; she has a sister there. I have to wait until they come back."

Guttle stretched her legs as if they were cramped. The weight on her heart was pulling on her tongue; she did not know what more to say.

"Don't be angry with me, Guttle. I'm not as strong as you are. You could live in the lane for a hundred years, if you had to. I can't. I need to get out."

Strong? Is it really strength that lets me endure, Guttle wondered, or is it the same complacency I see all around?

"The children will be missing me," she said. "Georgi is watching them. I have to go." Lifting the baby into her arms, she kissed Dvorah's cheek, very lightly, and tried to ignore the tears she thought she could see forming in Dvorah's eyes.

Down in the lane, she was angry with herself. She had gone to Dvorah planning to yell at her, to tell her to stop destroying her family, to shake righteousness into her. That wasn't what she had done. Why not?

"It's not my life," she told the baby in her arms.

But she knew that Dvorah's absence, if indeed she left, would leave a gap in her life as long and as foul as the ditch. She felt now as she had felt six years earlier, in the instant when she saw the black stallion bearing hard upon her. There was no way to escape the impact — not then, not now. She could only try to minimize the hurt. It was to absorb pain that women had been made. Only Lev could stop Dvorah, by not granting her a divorce. But what Jewish man would not, if his wife flung in his face her naked body entwined in sunny meadows or bleak hotels with the naked body of another man — a Christian, no less? Not that the shape of his uncut manhood would matter. Guttle shuddered; she had heard that Gentile men demanded all manner of obscene behavior; she wasn't sure if this was true, or a libel, like the blood libel against the Jews.

Back then she'd been told she had saved three children by stopping the galloping horse. Now she saw no way of stopping anything.

Youngsters were playing in the lane. She had passed a dozen or more, but now she took notice of them. The twins — Dvorah had said she would take the twins. That won't happen. Lev would never agree. And without them, Dvorah would stay. Would put her precious nobleman behind her, would get her senses back. Lev might still divorce her, but she would stay in the lane to be with David and Ruth. She was only twenty-four. The men would be lining up.

But what kind of men? Those who thought she was a whore?

She nuzzled Salomon's cheek. "I hope you didn't listen at Dvorah's," she told his large and trusting brown eyes. "I would never do that to you." The baby gurgled happily, as if he understood.

When she reached the Café, Brendel was standing outside; it was midmorning, there were no customers. Brendel raised her eyebrows, a question clear as the spoken word, asking if Guttle had found out anything. Guttle merely shrugged. Then she paused, asked a question herself. "Do you know if Herr Mendelssohn is all right? Did he come to the Café this morning?"

"Ate four ruggelah. Said he was glad he doesn't eat with his nose. 'Then you'll live?' I asked him. He said he would — so long as there are no more critics lurking."

Brendel chucked the baby under the chin. "Reminds me of mine when they were babes. How is Dvorah? You want some tea or something?"

Guttle sighed, long and deep. "A glass of tea would be nice."

"With milk?"

"With milk. But Brendel — please, no questions."

"Sit, dearie," Brendel said. "It's on the way. One hot tea, sans questions."

"Sans? What is sans?"

"It means without, in French. Herr Mendelssohn told me."

Guttle sat, cradling the baby in her arm. "Sans," she echoed, as Brendel went for the tea. The lane *sans* Dvorah. It had a softer sweeter sound then the Hebrew, bli, or the German, ohne. But was that a sentence that should be soft? It sounded better the other ways. The lane *bli* Dvorah. The lane *ohne* Dvorah. Whatever the language, she could not picture it. She saw only emptiness. Blowing her breath across the top of the glass that Brendel had set before her, she sipped at her tea and formulated her first philosophic principle, Guttle's First Law of Probabilities: If it is impossible to conceive of, it will not happen. She hoped her philosophy was better than her French.

Early that afternoon, holding his small satchel of clothing in one hand and a bag of ruggeleh in the other, a plaster on his injured nose, Moses Mendelssohn left the lane. He was escorted to the north gate by some of his new friends, most of them women — Guttle, Brendel, Rebecca, Avra, and a few of the younger men— Izzy, Hiram, Rabbi Simcha. The women waved handkerchiefs as he passed through the gate. The Constables sneered at his hump. Some of the beggars who were sprawled outside the gate offered to eat it. When the philosopher was perhaps thirty metres away, he turned and nodded, and the women again waved their handkerchiefs, which resembled small windblown flags.

The Judengasse, after three centuries, would never be the same.

35

Guttle dreamed that night about the Schul-Klopper. This had not happened for a long time. In her dream she tripped over Solomon Gruen's outstretched leg, just as she had in real life when she was younger. But when she peered at him in the dream, he began to raise his head, to sit up on the cobbles. Angry, Guttle swung her pitcher of milk at him, slammed him in the head, hard, again, again, till he fell back to the cobbles. Until he was truly dead

She awoke chilled from perspiration. She did not know if dreams still meant anything, as they did in the books of Moses. Usually she gave herself a headache if she tried to figure them out. But this one she thought was obvious. The Schul-Klopper represented all the traditions of the lane — which in fact he had. But she had been much impressed with Moses Mendelssohn's remarks, especially about girls going to school. Would that, as Rabbi Eleazar had suggested, be a death blow to the Jewish people?.

Later, preoccupied with this question, she went out and walked the lane. Knots of old men with beards could be overheard ridiculing what Herr Mendelssohn had said. But no women were discussing it. She knew why. If women opposed what he'd said, they might offend their female friends who welcomed it. If they sided with what he had said, they would earn the fierce anger of their husbands, fathers, brothers. So they remained silent, as she had with Meyer during their breakfast — a silence that left tension thick as fog clogging the lane.

1 9 October

Locked in an attic for five years now, Sophie Marcus has become, for the children, a mirror image of Melka. They flee from her in exaggerated terror when every few days either her husband or her son Viktor or Viktor's wife, the former

Leah Licht, one hand firmly gripping Sophie's arm, walks her in the lane for fresh air and exercise. Sometimes she is well behaved, and the walk passes without incident. Other days, with no immediate provocation, she begins to hurl epithets and curses at anyone she might encounter. At such times the hand of her escort tightens firmly around her arm and she is led back to the Marcus home, to the attic with its boarded window. While we in our innocence turned to Melka for solace, the children today use Sophie as a threat, warning in their games that "Sophie is right behind you, Sophie's gonna steal you away."

Should I happen to be in the lane when Sophie is walking, I quickly duck into the nearest shop, so as not to set her off like fireworks. On those rare occasions when I wander far toward the south gate and pass the Marcus house, I cannot help but glance up at the boarded window behind which she sits — or prowls like a caged beast, or whatever it is she does. For hours afterward, as happened today, I am riven by guilt over my role in her imprisonment all those years ago. Though what I could have done differently, other than marry her son, I do not know.

Georgi Kremm began an apprenticeship to the cabinet maker, starting off by sweeping floors and oiling furniture, then taking instruction in the fine art of carving. As weeks passed, the boy began to show an aptitude for the craft. Wood shavings curled and disappeared like the days, October became November. One mild evening in early December, Yussel came to the Hinterpfann with his apprentice to ask Guttle and Meyer for advice. He had heard from the Chief Rabbi, he said, that the Polizei would be inspecting the lane in a few days. He didn't know if Georgi should be hidden, after so long a time, or should continue working as if nothing were amiss. They all quickly agreed that if he hid and were found, a lot of questions would be asked; that it would be better for him to work in plain sight, wearing his yarmulke. Most likely the boy would not be noticed.

"The Rabbi warned you of this raid?" Meyer asked. "We haven't heard of it."

Yussel's face colored unaccountably. They had never known him to blush about anything other than Brendel. "He must have told me first because of the boy."

"That must be it," Meyer said. He did not mention the cabinet maker's evident discomfort, though he continued to wonder about it.

The next morning, after Meyer had gone to the city, Guttle left baby Salomon with Amelia and walked to the bakery to buy bread. She saw a commotion going on in front of the cabinet maker's shop. Several dozen men and a few women were gathered there, remonstrating about something with Yussel. As she got closer she could make out their words, spoken in loud and nasty tones. "The goy has to leave… What do we need him for?… We don't owe the Gentiles anything."

"The boy is my apprentice, he's not harming anyone," Yussel told them, standing in front of the shop.

Guttle reached the edge of the gathering. It was growing larger as people heard the shouts and came to watch. She didn't understand why this was happening now, Georgi had been here two months without a problem.

"There's never been a goy living in the lane," a man shouted. He wore a long black coat and a yarmulke, and had an untrimmed black beard, and seemed to be the leader of the group. Guttle recognized him as Jacob Marcus.

"He'll bring bad luck," a woman called out.

"As opposed to the good luck we have living here?" Yussel asked calmly.

"Never mind luck," a man said. It was Alexandre Licht, the shoemaker, wearing his red beret. "The police are coming tomorrow, the Rabbi says. What if they find the boy? We could all be in trouble."

"The council should throw him out," someone yelled.

"There's the Chairman, let's ask him," another said as Lev Berkov strolled over from the hospital to observe the trouble. Doctor Berkov was the council's rotating Chairman this year.

"What about that, Doctor?"

"The council has discussed this informally," Lev told them. "There was no mood to order him out, as long as he behaves himself."

Guttle had not seen much of Lev in recent weeks. His face was drawn, weary, as if he knew there was trouble in his marriage, but could not be certain why.

"What are we arguing for?" Jacob Marcus said. "When the police come tomorrow, we'll just denounce him. The police will take him away, good riddance."

Guttle's face reddened. She felt as if a window in her brain had blown open, and in a searing instant twenty-two years of training to be a proper woman had taken flight, like doves at the sound of a musket shot. In front of the cabinet maker's a spruce coffin rested on the cobbles. She registered that Yussel had stopped making these, that he must be teaching the boy, and with both of them working, there would be no room to keep it inside. Sacrilege or not, she lifted her long skirt and climbed onto the coffin, one hand supporting her growing belly.

"Gentlemen, listen to me!"

"Look at her, she stands on a coffin," a woman said loudly. "For shame! To insult the dead like that."

"I don't mean to insult the dead," Guttle said, as they quieted to listen. "I don't know who this coffin is for. I apologize to the family if it is already marked. But I must be heard. Right now this coffin is empty. If we send Georgi away, we might be sending him to his grave. He's only sixteen years old."

"Who cares? He's a goy."

"Yes, Georgi is a Gentile. But he was not around when three quarters of Frankfurt's Jews were slaughtered before the ghetto was built. He was not alive when these walls were erected. He did not take part in the Fettmilch riots more than a hundred years ago."

"His ancestors did."

"His ancestors most likely did not! They are country people. He is from a peasant family. They're treated as badly as we are. Maybe worse."

"How could it be worse?" a man yelled.

"Because he is being recruited to fight in a war. At least they don't take our sons away."

A slight murmur ran through the crowd.

"There's another reason." Guttle had never spoken before a crowd like this, but passion had muted her nerves. "The American colonists are fighting for their freedom. There are Jews among them, who are equal citizens in America. Most of you remember Ephraim Hess. He is now in America, fighting there. Crown Prince Wilhelm is forcing his peasants to go and fight against freedom. Is that the side we want to support?"

"It's not a question of America's freedom," the shoemaker said. "It's for our own safety. If the police find him here, we all will suffer. Harboring a runaway is against the law."

Guttle began shaking her head before he finished. "There is no reason for the Frankfurt Constables to seek him out," she said. "They don't work for the Crown Prince of Hesse-Hanau. But if they do realize he's not a Jew, the whole lane will not suffer. Yussel Kahn here will stand forth, I'm sure. He is the one employing the boy."

Yussel nodded, though he seemed to half wish she had not brought that up.

"And I will step forward," Guttle said, "because he is living in my house. No one else can be accused of harboring him."

Over the heads of the crowd she noticed several women in their aprons standing in front of the bakery, watching. One of them was her mother. Beside her was Yetta Liebmann.

"They still could accuse the whole lane," Marcus said. "They can do whatever they want. Listen, I'm tired of arguing. When the police come, we'll denounce him. The police will take him. End of problem." He turned as if to walk away.

Guttle could not accept what she had heard. "Wait! My ears can't believe what you said. You would denounce this boy to the police? Since when do Jews denounce people to the police because of their faith? They've been doing that to us for a thousand years. More. Now you would have us begin? Shame on you! Shame on any of you who would dare to do such a thing."

Her chest was heaving, as if she had just run the length of the lane. She stopped speaking. Her head was wet with perspiration under her sheitl. Her armpits, her thighs, were moist. She looked at their faces, silent now — ashamed, she hoped — and climbed down from the coffin with shaky knees. She felt a fluttering in her womb. The baby alone was applauding.

Murmuring among themselves, the people began to disperse. Guttle hoped she had won them over. Then Jacob Marcus fired his voice at her like a stone. "The goy has got to go!"

Guttle walked home alone. She needed to wash. She wondered what Meyer would think of his wife, the public speaker, when he heard what she had done.

Between the time he entered through the gate and the time he reached the Hinterpfann, Meyer heard. From Yetta Liebmann: "You sent my son Hersch from the lane, five years I haven't seen him, just a few letters, and you take in a goy? Your wife makes such a speech, on a dead body? It's a sin!" From Otto Kracauer he heard. "You'd better control your wife. People are asking who wears the tzitzis in that family." Before even removing his coat, his three-cornered hat, Meyer asked Guttle, who was preparing dinner in the kitchen, "You actually did that? You stood on a coffin — a coffin! — and harangued people? How could you have done such a thing?"

Guttle continued to stir with a long wooden spoon a stew that was simmering. "The coffin was empty," she said calmly. "An empty coffin is just a box. Was I to remain silent? It was the right thing to do."

"It was not proper! You are a woman, and you were haranguing men. Men twice your age, three times. Scholars. Grandfathers. What happened to your manners?"

"They want to denounce Georgi to the police. Do you think that's right? How would you feel if the Constables took him away, sent him off to war."

"No matter what they want, your behavior was not proper."

He sat heavily on a chair, removed his hat, his wig, ran his hands through his hair. He stepped to the wash basin, rinsed his hands, dried them on a towel. In a weary voice, he murmured, "It was, perhaps, the moral thing to do."

Guttle turned to look at him, spoon in hand. "Therefore?"

"I suppose it raises a question. Which is more important when there is a conflict between them — propriety, or morality?"

"Is that such a hard question?"

"Not for you. Maybe not for me. But lack of propriety makes people more upset."

"Lack of morality makes Yahweh more upset."

"Of course. But propriety has rules. Morality is subjective."

"Therefore propriety is the superior good? That doesn't follow."

"I know," Meyer said. "But propriety is visible in the lane. Morality exists only in the mind. It's a rare case where the invisible has substance, and the visible does not."

Guttle turned back to stir her stew. Meyer came up behind her. "Did you really tell them that if the boy were caught, you would take responsibility?"

"Whether I told them or not, I would have to do it. He's in the lane because of me."

"What if they arrested you? Took you away to prison? What would happen to the children? Not to say me?"

"This is a conversation we could have had two months ago. While Georgi was hiding in the slaughterhouse. Now there isn't a point. It's too late."

Meyer closed his eyes wearily, and stroked his short brown beard between his thumb and forefinger. "Unfortunately, with that I agree."

Putting down her spoon, Guttle took his hand in both of hers. "They won't arrest him. Or me. Adonai won't let that happen."

"Let's hope not." He put his arms around her, each absorbing the body warmth of the other. After seven years, this contact still shortened their breath. "What I wish," Meyer said, "since you made your speech, is that I were there to see their faces."

Easing her rounded belly back slightly, touching his cheek, his beard, Guttle conceded, "If you were there, I might not have dared."

The police arrived the next morning, as Rabbi Eleazar had warned. Four Constables entered through the north gate and ambled down the lane, two on each side. Some houses they entered and inspected, others they passed by. Leaving baby Salomon with Moish's wife, Guttle hurried to the bakery. She wanted to see what would happen with Georgi.

The women in the lane were wearing their drabbest clothing, and no jewelry, which, like silk, was forbidden except for the Sabbath. The shoemaker, standing outside his shop, wore on his head not his red beret but a yarmulke; Frankfurt had forbidden Jews to wear berets. Violators of any rules could be fined. More serious infractions — such as a secret printing press — could send the owner to prison for life.

Watching from the bakery, Guttle saw the police emerge from the first house. She hoped Avra had remembered to lock the shutters on Hiram's window, the one that offered north light for his work. They appeared to skip the second house, but entered the Owl. She was confident they would find nothing amiss there. Georgi, working with Yussel across the lane, was her only concern. When they reached the Café, which was new since their last inspection, the officers stopped, and huddled together. Were they perceiving some violation? But starting businesses within the gates was permitted. Perhaps they were only debating whether to rest and drink coffee now, or on their way back. She saw Brendel take one step into the lane and smile at the Constables. Their decision made without another word, they followed her into the Café. Guttle grinned. Clever Brendel, doing her best to lift the Polizei into a pleasant mood.

Guttle visited with her mother in the bakery. Emmie had not said a word about her speech, and did not do so now; she acted as if it had not occurred. Ten minutes passed before the Constables had finished their coffee — free of charge, most likely — and continued with their inspections. Every shopkeeper wished they would hurry; people tended to stay at home, and not shop, while the police were in the lane. But the Constables were in no rush. They paused to look in the window of every pawnbroker, seeking a good bargain; there were more pawnbrokers in the lane than in the rest of Frankfurt combined; they were the principal attraction in the Judengasse for Gentiles in need of cash. They by-passed the hospital, not wanting to expose themselves to disease. That's where we could have put the boy, Guttle thought, much too late. Further along, they entered the shoemaker's shop. When they emerged, one of the policeman was holding by the edge, as if it were a dead skunk, the cobbler's red beret. "I wasn't wearing it," he protested.

"That's why there's no fine —but we must save you from temptation," the officer said, and he tossed the cap into the flowing ditch. Alexandre Licht had spoken against the Gentile boy, but still Guttle felt sad for him as he stepped to the ditch and watched his proud possession, a part of his identity, curl with liquid and sink into the passing morass.

The officers across the lane had been taking longer with their inspections, perhaps being more thorough — but now they were approaching the cabinet maker's. Guttle saw Jacob Marcus leave his table and begin to meander up the lane. Her pulse quickened. Was he merely curious, or would he denounce the boy?

Wanting to see what transpired inside, she crossed the lane and entered the shop. "I'm just a customer," she said to Yussel, at the same time waving to Georgi. She began to examine a carved table. To her glancing eye, Georgi, in his yarmulke and tzitzis, looked as Jewish as anyone; after two months out of the sunlight, his skin already had faded to the Judengasse pallor above an incipient beard.

The boy picked up a broom and began to sweep up the curls of wood shavings on the floor, just as the two Constables entered. Nodding to Yussel, they seemed to inhale with pleasure the wood smells of the shop, an oasis from the sewage stench, as their eyes roamed about, taking in the tools, the pieces in progress, the cans of polish. Then one of them focused on the boy.

"You never had an apprentice before," the officer, a thin, pinch-faced fellow, said.

Guttle was stricken with fear. She wanted to close her eyes, but forced herself to watch.

"You've got a good memory," Yussel said.

"How long has he been working for you?"

Turning away, she became engrossed in a half-finished mahogany desk.

"About two months."

"What is your name?" the officer said to the boy, and he sniffed the air, as if at the body odor of a Jew.

The boy stopped sweeping. If he was afraid, he did not show it. "Georgi Pinsky."

"Did you make that coffin?"

Georgi nodded.

"He's got a lot to learn," the Constable said to Yussel. "This looks like a trough for pigs."

Georgi's face flushed. The second officer, a shorter, rounder fellow, appeared to find the remark very funny. He laughed loudly. He asked, "Are you hiding any pigs in the Judengasse?" He laughed again, at his own joke.

"Upstairs," the first officer said, pointing. "Let's see if there are thirsty pigs up there."

As they climbed the stairs, Guttle tried to relax. Turning to leave, she saw Jacob Marcus across the lane, talking with the shoemaker. She decided to stay where she was. If they were going to denounce the boy, they would have to do it in front of her.

She could hear the footsteps of the police moving higher, to the top floor. Immediately, strong words filtered down, loud but indistinct. There was some kind of problem. She looked at Yussel, questioningly. He put a finger to his lips. A moment later they heard the sound of hammering. Guttle was afraid for the boy again.

The footstep descended the three flights of stairs. The thin policeman was holding several gulden notes. He paused to fold them into a pouch on his belt, then turned and yelled up the stairwell. "Ten gulden today. Next time, you go to prison."

He looked at Yussel and Guttle. "Air for the children!" he muttered, shaking his head, and without another glance at Georgi he led the other Constable out of the shop.

Guttle stepped closer to Yussel and whispered, loud enough for Georgi to hear, "What do you think happened up there?"

"They had a window unboarded. Overlooking the park and the city."

"But they must have known the police were coming."

Yussel did not reply, turning instead to a partial bookshelf. He bent to insert a dowel.

"You knew about the window," Guttle said. "You must have told them to leave the boards off. So the officers would focus on that, and not on Georgi. I'll bet you're going to reimburse them for the fine."

Yussel continued working, inserting a second dowel, tapping it in softly with a wooden mallet, saying nothing.

"The boss must like your work," Guttle said to Georgi. The boy grinned.

"I guess I'm not needed here," Guttle said. She stepped outside. The officers were passing the synagogue, moving into the south end. Licht the cobbler and Marcus the moneylender were still across the way, watching them. Guttle grew agitated. The boy would not be safe until the Constables were gone

She was too impatient to wait. She needed to confront the issue. Crossing the ditch on a shaky board, she approached the men. "There was no problem about the boy," she told him.

"This time," the moneylender said.

"Do you still plan to turn him in?"

Jacob Marcus looked away, stared down the lane. His eyes would not meet hers. "I've heard that good Jews don't do that."

Guttle remained expressionless, though her eyes smiled.

"Besides," the shoemaker Licht said, "the bastards ruined my hat."

36

In mid-December, a short letter arrived from America, from Eva Hess, the rag-picker's wife. Guttle read it to Doctor Kirsch in her office at the hospital.

"November, 1775

"*Dearest Friends. You may have heard in the newspapers that the terrible smallpox to America has come. Here is called God's Country, but the pox has come regardless of God. Many people die, including some in the army. This short letter is to let you know not to worry about us, that Ephraim and me are fine. We both had the pox a little bit as children in the lane, and newspapers here say if you had it once you cannot again. We worry for our children, of course, but the pox has thus far not been bad in New York. We pray it does not come to Europe or the Judengasse. Ephraim is with the troops of General Washington, he has not been injured. We think of you often with much feeling. Eva Hess.*"

Rebecca frowned behind her desk. "I'd heard that the pox was there."

"Is it true what she says? That if you had it once you can't get it again?"

"It seems to be true. We don't know why. It would be nice if we could give everyone a very small case. Then no one would die if it comes back."

"Could you do that?"

"If we tried, we might start an epidemic."

"What I came to ask you is, should I post the letter in the community room? I do with all their letters, but I don't want to frighten people."

"Certainly, post it. If the pox comes — and it very well may not — denying it won't do any good. Knowledge is always better than ignorance."

"You truly believe that?"

"Of course."

"Then let's start a heder for girls," Guttle blurted

"Us? Here? Would the Chief Rabbi approve?"

"Most likely not."

"Would Meyer approve?"

"I'm not sure."

The Doctor stood and lifted a notebook from her desk. "I have patients to see. That's an interesting idea, Guttle, but it raises a dozen questions. Let's discuss it when I have more time."

"You'll think about it?"

"Absolutely."

Walking to the synagogue to tack up the letter, Guttle had to pause to battle a moment of dizziness. The cupola seemed to swirl above her. What had she done? The idea of a heder for girls had leaped into her brain on the instant. Why had she spoken it? She with a baby due in April.

Still, she had begun teaching Schönche to read. Why not teach other girls as well? She paused again when she felt a flutter, a gentle kick, in her womb. Little Leah — she was convinced that, after two boys, it would be a girl this time — little Leah was ready to enroll.

17 December

For weeks now, something has been wrong with Mama. At times she does not remember things. Or starts conversations in the middle. Today as we walked together to the market to buy onions and potatoes, she startled me with what she said. "I had a friend named Sophie," she began. "We were like sisters. She wanted to marry a handsome young man with good prospects, Wolf Schnapper. But his father did not care for her; she came from a poor family. He wanted to betroth Wolf to me instead. When my father agreed, Sophie's heart was broken. She pushed me from her life. She never spoke to me again, not one word. Later she was married to someone else, I forget his name. I wonder what happened to Sophie. I wonder where she is. Do you know, Guttle?"

"I don't know, Mama," I lied.

How could I have explained? I was too astonished to think.

"To have a friend who acts as if you are dead, that is a terrible thing," Mama said.

Late in the afternoon I stood by the north gate, waiting for Papa to return from court. When he did, I pulled him aside and told him what Mama had said. I asked it if was true — that long ago, he, or his father, had rejected the hand of Sophie Marcus. I had never heard that before, I didn't know if Mama in some deluded way was making it up.

Papa admitted it was true. "When Sophie wanted so desperately for her son to marry you, I wondered if there was a connection," Papa said. "Some need to undo the past. But the mind is too complex to figure out. What did it matter, after all? It was Meyer you wanted."

As I watched him hurry up the stairs to Mama, my inner world turned upside down. For the first time, I understood why poor Sophie Marcus views us Schnappers as the devil's handmaidens.

December turned cold as Hanukah approached. Menorahs appeared in a window of every apartment, a single candle burning, plus the shamash candle on top, honoring the miracle of the one-day flask of purified oil in the temple in Jerusalem that had burned for eight days.

"I'm not happy," Dvorah told her husband.

"I know," Lev said. "But it's been more than a year since the baby died. We have to get on with our lives. In bed and everywhere."

Two candles, side by side, like flaming lovers, glowed in the windows. Candles honoring the Maccabees, who rescued the temple from the Syrians. "I hate being locked in the lane," Dvorah said.

"Who doesn't? But it's a fact of life." He lifted his yarmulke, ran his hand through his hair. "There's not much we can do about it." He rolled the muscles of his back, still tight from a surgery he had performed that day.

Three candles cast a brighter light. Illuminating the hatred of the Syrians, who had made Judaism a crime, punishable by death. "I'm serious," Dvorah said. "I have to get away from here, or I'll go mad."

"Perhaps you need a journey. We'll get permission for you to leave. Go for a week to Belgium, or France. Two weeks, even. Take Guttle, or Brendel. The grandmothers can watch the children."

Four candles burning. Revealing that the enemy had sacrificed swine in the sacred temple. The twins, David and Ruth, six years old, placed the menorah on the floor and jumped over the burning candles, an ancient Hanukah game, and laughed. Hanukah half gone, and Dvorah still twisted like the flames. "I want a divorce," she said.

"What! I never heard such nonsense! I know I've been busy at the hospital, but I love you, Dvorah. You've got David and Ruthie to raise. Why should you want a divorce? Why would I give you one?"

Five candles and one on top cast a light as bright as a lamp. In the lane, a light snow began to fall, the flakes glowing orange outside the window panes. "I'm in love with someone else."

"I don't believe you! With whom?"

"His name doesn't matter."

"Is that so? Well, you had better fall out of love. And quickly, if you know what's good for you."

The flames bent in their direction, as if the better to hear. So, too, did ears behind the apartment walls.

"I won't fall out of love. To you, Lev, everything is simple. Life is not so simple. Listen to what I'm saying." She hesitated, then plunged on; it was the only thing he would understand. "I've been sleeping with him."

Lev's face reddened. "You what!" He grabbed a sharp knife from the table. He was shouting now. "Tell me who it is! I'll kill him!"

She stared at him, not moving.

He looked at the knife in his hand, as if uncertain how it had gotten there. He looked at her. "It's you I should kill! Or scar that pretty face of yours! Keep you out of trouble."

Dvorah didn't flinch. She knew her husband better than that. She was not afraid. "I want you to give me a divorce. I want to leave the lane and marry him."

"Leave the lane? Then he's not Jewish?" Saliva was spluttering Lev's beard. "Mixed marriage is forbidden! You would have to convert!"

"I'm planning to," she said, calmly.

"You really have gone meshuganah!" Again he looked at the knife in his hand, as if it were a stranger. He tossed it onto the table. "Attacking Mendelssohn with some stupid book, now this! You've been shtupping some goy behind my back? Sure, I'll give you a divorce. Why don't you leave right now? I should throw you down the stairs, without another word."

"But you won't."

Six candles in a row. The Doctor's hand shook as he lighted them in front of the twins, and said the Hanukah prayer. The children spun a dreidl. Spinning, spinning, slanting crazily on the slatted wooden floor, it clattered to a stop with the letter nun showing — no one wins.

"Is something wrong, Papa?" Ruthie asked. "I heard you and Mama shouting."

"We'll talk about it tomorrow."

When the twins were asleep, he asked her, "So, when are you leaving, Jezebel?"

"At the end of the week. So David won't miss heder."

"David? What does David have to do with this?"

"I'm taking the twins with me, of course. They need their mother."

"Like they need a viper, they need their mother! Over my dead body you'll take the children, and turn them into goys. David loves to learn. He might be a Rabbi some day. You worry about him missing heder, but you plan to take him to a church? Your mind is gone, Dvorah!"

"You know you can't raise them alone. Think about it."

A candle for every day of the week. Room left for only one more. The lane was bright with them, so pretty. Lev had sent the children to their grandmother Hannah's for the night.

"I have a compromise," Dvorah said. "We can be friendly about this. I'll only take Ruth. You can bring up David however you want."

"You're a regular King Solomon! If you go, David and Ruthie will lose their mother. Now you want them to lose each other as well? The other half of themselves? You've turned into a whore, Dvorah, and a selfish one at that. Go open your legs for your goy, see if I care. Don't forget to pocket his money, I'm sure he's rich."

Now Dvorah began to shout. "Don't point fingers, I always was your whore! You didn't want me for anything else! You didn't think I was good for anything else! It's time I had some love in my life!"

"Love? Don't fool yourself, Dvorah. This is not about love. This is your passage out of the lane. Behind those breasts you have no heart. You're weak. You can't deal with life. That's fine. But the twins stay with me, or no divorce. And don't expect to come visit them. I doubt you'll be very welcome in the lane. You know what they'll call you? The Jewish shiksa whore!"

The flickering candles sputtered and died, sending to heaven eight twists of smoke, the smell of wax. No matter, tomorrow evening there would be nine, a full cheerful lineup, in every home in the lane. But first, in the daylight, there was talk.

—You heard?

—The walls are thin, who didn't hear? Who doesn't know someone who heard?

— So what do you think?

—What's to think? The Jewish shiksa whore!"

Perhaps it was not exactly that way, the days of Hanukah, a detail different here or there, but that is how, each year after that, Lev Berkov would remember it, as he lit the candles, while David and Ruthie watched, and the flames burned holes in his heart.

The candles, eight days worth, all forty-four of them, were gone. The menorahs soon would be put away for another year. Dvorah Berkov, nee Schlicter, soon to be Dvorah von Brunwald, stood inside the gate, hugging her children goodbye. Her mother was there, too, and her sisters. Tears were on every cheek except Dvorah's. A satchel was at her side, she would send for the rest of her things later on. She would write.

She needed to leave, not to prolong this, Paul was waiting with his carriage by the town square. But she couldn't step through the open gate.

Not yet. Her eyes looked toward the Hinterpfann, or rather towards the alley that led to the Hinterpfann. No one appeared.

With a sudden, hopeful thought, she looked towards the Owl. Towards the third floor window of Guttle's old room. Between the curtains she saw her friend, watching.

Guttle did not stir. Guttle did not come running down the stairs to embrace her, to shed a tear together. Guttle did not wave goodbye.

Dvorah decided not to wave, either. She hugged her children one last time, and carried her satchel through the gate.

When Dvorah was out of sight, past the slaughterhouse, past the Zig-Zig Stables, past the herring shop, into the Gentile world, Guttle sat on the bed she used to share with Avra. She had come here to watch through the window as Dvorah left; she had not been able to stop herself from seeking this pain.

She wondered at the changes wrought by time and love. Now she sleeps in Meyer's bed, Avra sleeps with Hiram, this same straw mattress belongs to Amelia, whom Izzy hopes to wed in five years, when he reaches marrying age — though her father might have other ideas. But she could not separate her mind long from Dvorah. Everything her friend had done was terrible, was sinful, was against the will of Yahweh: indulging in an adulterous affair, divorcing her husband, abandoning her children, abandoning her God. Of the latter two she was not sure which was worse. Her reason told her that the worse was to abandon almighty Yahweh, creator of the universe, giver of the laws, instructor of the patriarchs. Her heart told her that one's children should come before everything.

Yet look what Dvorah had obtained in return, Guttle thought, standing, peering at the gate through which her friend had left. She had achieved what Guttle had dreamed of since she was a child, what still she craved in the core of her being. By piling sin upon sin upon sin upon sin, Dvorah had escaped from the lane.

37

The winter had been harsher than usual, with low temperatures and frequent snows that turned the outlying roads into ice-filled ruts, treacherous for the thin legs and fragile ankles of the horses. Meyer had remained close to home, doing most of his business by post, and even that had been slowed by the storms, the post messengers no more eager than anyone to be trapped in a blizzard. So when the first Friday in March dawned unexpectedly mild, offering a foretaste of spring, Meyer was restless. After morning services, he kissed Guttle's cheek and belly — she was in her seventh month — rented a mare from Ziggy Zigmund and set off for the palace at Hesse-Hanau. He had no pending business with the Crown Prince, but he did not like many months to pass between visits to Carl Buderus in the treasury office. That young man, Meyer had sensed for some time, could be his gateway to future wealth.

The door to Buderus's office was open when Meyer knocked on it. Looking up from his desk, at which he'd been writing, Buderus welcomed him without standing, and motioned him to a chair. "Meyer Rothschild, what a coincidence. I was just writing to you. Now you've saved me the trouble."

"I was in the vicinity…"

"That's good luck, then." Buderus, whose serious demeanor was in constant warfare with his flaming hair, sipped from a cup of steaming coffee. Meyer had skipped breakfast in his restlessness and after his ride would have welcomed a cup of refreshment, but the treasury man did not offer. Doing business with a Jew, even being friendly, was no problem for Buderus, but hospitality, Meyer knew, was too much to expect.

"I'll explain what has occurred," Buderus said, setting down his cup and wiping his lips with a napkin. "You may recall that some time ago — in September, I believe it was — you and I encountered regiment recruiters on the road to Frankfurt."

"I remember well."

"We have received notification that the first payment for the recruits has left England. It should arrive within the month — a nice, round one hundred thousand gulden. With King George struggling to outfit his troops, the notes are not payable until August. The Crown Prince wishes to discount them, and invest the money at once, to maximize his profits."

"Of course."

"How does this involve a coin dealer from the Judengasse, you may well wonder."

Meyer remained silent, concealing the elation that was budding in his chest like the scent of spring.

"Yesterday, Wilhelm gave me the names of three bankers with whom he planned to divide the business — one here in Hanau, two in Frankfurt. He has summoned them to meet here at eleven in the morning of Tuesday next, to offer the terms. They will be the standard. The six-month notes will be discounted at ten percent. Profits on the ninety percent that is invested shall go to the banker at an additional ten percent. I know you are not a banker as such, but I assume that you understand."

"It is quite clear," Meyer said.

"I thought it would be. As Wilhelm spoke, I recalled our encounter with the recruiters. I suggested to His Serenity that he divide the business four ways, assigning one fourth to you, if you are interested."

"I am gratified," Meyer said. "Also flattered."

"Well you might be. When I made the suggestion, Wilhelm replied, 'The Jew Rothschild? He deals in coins. What does he know of banking?' I allowed that you were hoping to expand your business in that direction. I assume I was correct."

"You were quite correct, sir."

"Never mind the sir. I told the crown Prince that I had confidence in your financial skills, and that this would be a good test of them. He was not enthusiastic, I tell you honestly. 'Very well, Buderus, test your wings,' were his exact words. Then he added, 'If this is a disaster, I shall remember who suggested the Jew.' I tell you this, Rothschild, only to make clear that if you agree to participate, my future could be at risk as well as yours."

"May I ask why you are doing this?"

"I have asked myself that question all morning." He glanced towards the open door, got up and closed it before resuming his seat. "In strict confidence, I will tell you that there are several treasury officers more senior than I — but none with much understanding of the burgeoning world of trade. I have been seeking a way to call attention to my abilities. These British notes are an opportunity for me. The other bankers no doubt were selected by my superiors. You will be my iron in the fire. If you agree."

"That's a great deal of confidence you place in me."

"I've watched how you operate your coin business. Your instincts are impeccable. My instinct is to harness your instinct. For the benefit of us both. And of the Crown Prince, of course — for the benefit of Wilhelm most of all." He sipped at his coffee, the steam no longer visible. "There, that was much better than writing it all down. You see — it must have been instinct that brought you here today."

"Or the warming of the weather."

"Don't belittle yourself. Do you have any questions?"

Meyer twisted a loose button on his coat; he would have to show it to Guttle. "Only one. Several times you hinted that I might not agree to this wonderful opportunity. Why is that?"

"How shall I phrase it?" Buderus scratched idly on the unfinished letter with his quill. "I understand that you Jews are not averse to making money, only to enjoying it."

Meyer studied the young man, who was at least five years his junior. "Perhaps I am the exception."

Nodding twice, Buderus stood and came out from behind his desk. "We shall expect you here at eleven on Tuesday next. Should you decide not to participate, don't bother with a courier. If you don't appear, I will know your decision."

"If I may, you have doubted me again. Perhaps you think I fear such a test."

Buderus escorted him to the door. "Perhaps that's it," he said.

On his way home, Meyer stopped at the small farm of the widow Kremm, Georgi's mother. Yussel had begun paying the boy for his work, and Georgi was sending most of his pay home. The widow had graying hair and a haggard appearance, like a rag doll discarded in the rain.

"He is well?" she asked, as she took the envelope of money.

"He is very well, Frau Kremm."

"He hasn't turned into a Jew yet? Hasn't grown horns, or a tail?"

Anger flashed through him. He fought to control it. This ignorant woman was not worthy of his rage. He did not speak.

"Better my boy should go for a soldier. He's not a coward, you know. You shouldn't think that. His father was killed in the Seven Years' War, and Georgi is just as brave. It's the beatings by his uncle he's hiding from."

"Beatings?"

"Listen to my mouth. I have to go sweep the floor."

"Shall I give Georgi your greetings?"

"If he wants my greetings he can come home, where he belongs."

She disappeared inside the small house, whose outer walls were badly in need of paint; Georgi's uncle clearly had little concern about that. Leaving the unkempt yard and a brown field beside it waiting for seed, Meyer felt new sadness for the boy. Family tyrants could be as evil as princely ones. Georgi might be in no hurry to leave.

The branches of the lindens and the poplars alongside the road were not yet budding, but Meyer, trying to recapture his earlier mood, envisioned their future greenery. Carriage traffic was heavy on the highway to Frankfurt. His progress slowed. He grew impatient to tell Guttle of his good fortune. He had no doubt that he could invest as well — most likely better — than the other bankers. His joy at this unexpected stake was a limitless balm until, where two roads intersected, he was stalled completely by the traffic of coaches and wagons and defecating horses, and he recalled the odd words of Buderus at the palace. *Jews are not averse to making money — only to enjoying it.* What did he mean by that? Only a fool would not enjoy it. Never mind spending, it was the making itself, the accumulation, that gladdened the blood.

As Meyer rode home to the lane, Guttle walked slowly from the bakery carrying a challah for the erev Shabbas meal. Her back ached from supporting the seven-month child in her womb. Her breasts were sore. Her swollen ankles throbbed. She was tired. Not yet twenty-three years old, she felt this day like an elderly woman, grumpy and out of sorts. Worse, she feared that something was wrong with the child inside her.

Rebecca had assured her that the baby was alive. The midwife had told her that all women felt this way. But her pregnancy felt somehow different from the ones before. It was Dvorah she wanted to talk to. Dvorah would understand. They would hug, her fears would dissipate, soon she would be making jokes, making Dvorah giggle.

Yet her mood did not improve when Hannah Schlicter intercepted her in front of the Pfann.

"Guttle, did you see the carriage of the Countess outside the gate this morning?"

Guttle hadn't. "Was she ordering more dresses?"

"She tried on the dress I made her for Dvorah's wedding. It will be in three weeks, you know."

Guttle said nothing.

"The dress fit perfectly, but it was a disaster. I lost my best customer. The Countess said she won't be coming back. She said I'll be family now, Paul's mother-in-law, so she can't be treating me like some poor dressmaker. I told her that would only make me a poorer dressmaker. She didn't think it was funny. Why should she, it wasn't meant to be funny."

"I'm sorry," Guttle said, shifting her challah from her right arm to her left.

"Listen, darling, I had a letter from Dvorah today. Would you like to read it?"

"Another time."

"That's what you said the last time. But you never did. She wants to come see you, take you for a ride in her coach, talk to you."

"I can't do that."

"She's your best friend."

"She was."

"So she became a Christian. She doesn't really believe in it. Besides, what's that to you? You have a Gentile boy living in your house."

"He didn't abandon God. He didn't abandon his children."

"He abandoned his mother, I understand."

"He didn't. He sends his pay to her."

"Never mind, this is about Dvorah. You love her. She loves you. She didn't abandon the twins, they go to see her once a month, that's all Lev would allow. He won't let her come to the lane. She's nervous about the wedding, you need to see her, listen to her talk. Like in the old days."

"She's out of my life now. It was her choice."

"You'll at least write to her, then? That much you owe her."

"I can't."

"You think I was not hurt by what she did? Her mother? Moving away. Becoming a Christian. Leaving the twins like that. I cried my heart out for days. But then it was over. We get on with life. We accept. Who are you to condemn her so?"

Cold sweat broke out on Guttle's face. She began to feel faint. Hannah did not appear to notice.

"I'm ashamed of you, Guttle Schnapper. That you would ignore a friend in need."

"My name is Rothschild."

"You're a cruel woman, young lady. By any name."

Guttle put her hand against the wall for support. Faintness melted her muscles. The bread dropped to the cobbles. Hannah looked at her pale face and at the round bread rolling on the stones toward the ditch, and turned abruptly and walked back to her house. Barely able to move, her belly fluttering, Guttle watched the challah come to a stop just short of the ditch. Her body was drenched in sweat. She did not know if she could fetch the bread, if she could bend over without toppling. She dared not let go of the wall.

Who was she to condemn Dvorah so? Was Hannah right? Was she being stupid in cutting off the friend she loved so much? The friend for whom she longed?

No! There were laws of morality. There were lines you could not cross. Without moral restraints, without a conscience, humans would not be worthy. Not of one another, and not of Yahweh. Dvorah had crossed those lines beyond all measuring, simply for her own pleasure — hurting her children, her husband, her mother, her sisters. Aside from killing another human, how much worse could a person act?

And so —No!

Her body was trembling within a skin of sweat as she leaned against the wall and thought these thoughts. She wiped her brow with her sleeve.

She wanted to hug Dvorah.

A young girl ran to the challah and carried it to Guttle. She was Reba Schlicter, Hannah's youngest, one of Guttle's favorites. Guttle thanked her. "Do you miss your sister?"

"A lot."

"Me, too," Guttle said.

When Meyer entered the lane moments later, he found his wife leaning against the wall, holding the bread. "You look like you've seen a ghost, Guttle. What's wrong?"

"I'm feeling faint, that's all. Help me to the house. I need to lie down."

Meyer took the bread, she leaned on his shoulder as they walked down the alley. In the house he removed her shoes and she lay on the bed, shivering. He covered her with a blanket. Her eyes were closed as he stood watching her, tinged with fear.

The children he would send across to Guttle's mother for Sabbath dinner. The wonderful news from Buderus he would have to store in his chest till she felt better.

Brendel would come on a Saturday morning, she had told Avra, when the Café was closed, when the men and many of the women were in schul, when few would notice her visit. Would that be all right? That would be fine; the artist worked every day; he did not respect the Sabbath. Bereft of ears, tongue, father, brother, he felt that he owed God nothing.

She could come this Sabbath, Brendel had told Avra, would that be convenient? That would be fine. He was eager to start on figure studies, as the great masters had done.

North light streamed through the open shutters. Paper was piled neatly beside his easel, alongside sharpened charcoal sticks. He did not hear her light, flying footsteps on the stairs — he would not have heard had they been slow and heavy — but he saw Avra open the door. He saw a smile both shy and adventurous beneath her blonde ringlets and blue cap. She said something to his wife. Avra nodded, they chatted in a world to which he was not privy, a world beyond the open studio door through which he was watching. In her animated face, her sparkling green eyes, she exuded what sunlight there was in the lane, even on the darkest days. It was her face, more than her chocolate, that inspired him each morning to wrestle with another day.

He would not sketch her face. That was their agreement. Her torso must be headless, she had a reputation to protect, and two young boys. Her portrait would be fine another time. Without her body.

Where would she undress? Avra led her into Yetta's room; his mother was at schul.

He had known that the cabinet maker would not object. Could not. It was Yussel who had brought him as a wedding gift a book of etchings of the masters. Most of them had sketched the female form. He allowed himself a private smile. None had sketched Brendel Isaacs.

Barefoot, she stepped into his room, his studio, wearing one of Avra's robes. His wife watched from the doorway, to see if she was needed. He motioned Brendel to a place two metres in front of him, where they had positioned Hersch's old bed in the gray light pouring from the window. He nodded to her, very slightly, as if he were an old hand at this. Her face flushed a pale pink, but only for a moment, as she opened the robe and let it drop to the floor. The light caressed her body with sheen and shadow. His room, not the schul, had become God's temple.

He raised a hand for her not to move as he studied her, as he began to sketch. He noted the angle at which her shoulders sloped. How her breasts offered themselves, two matching undercurves, one slightly smaller than the other, something he had not expected. Around her nipples were not magenta discs, like Avra's, but pale pink flowers of soft flesh, the petals uneven, a pinkness made by a cherry dropped in milk; the pink nipples themselves shyly trying to hide their emerging heads. He sketched the slope of her flesh as it curved into her waist and out again to her hips. Beneath her navel her nether hair was a pale brown fuzz, a perfect triangle, unlike his wife's dark diamond. Her left thigh caught the light from the window, then rounded into deep shadow. He drew, smudged the charcoal for shading with his fingers, with the side of his hand, stepped back from the easel, looked at the sketch and at her, idly noticed Avra still watching from the doorway, returned to the easel to add a line here, to soften a line there. Unclipped the paper from the easel, set it on the floor, clipped another sheet in place. He motioned her to the bed. She sat, resting for a moment, then reclined on her side, facing him, moving her lithe arms slowly, sensuously, as if posing unclothed had come as a birthright with her form. He raised a hand when he saw what he wanted, not just her shape but the negative space beyond and between, and she paused and held the pose. Quickly he began to sketch. His manhood, he was glad to note, was behaving itself. Avra, not only his wife but his manager, had been wise in making love to him at dawn.

He placed the sketch on the floor, fastened another sheet of paper on the easel. Her back, her buttocks, her legs extended, her legs bent at the knee, one by one the sketch pile grew, each drawing without a head. A terrible image occurred to him — the severed head of the blacksmith from Mainz lying on the beach. And then a connection he had never made before — that the head had belonged to Brendel's husband, the father of her boys.

He set the charcoal down and waved at her to relax. She slipped into the robe, they entered the kitchen, he gave her a glass of water. They found his wife in his mother's room, where much of his work — framed by Yussel Kahn — was stacked in the space where his father 's bed had been. Avra was removing his sketches of the lane from their frames.

"Why are you doing that?" He saw Brendel's lips move as she spoke to Avra and motioned the question to him.

"To put the new sketches in. The ones that Hiram likes. We'll display them in the lane on Monday."

"In the lane?"

"Where else?"

"People will be shocked. Are you sure that's a good idea?"

"We could use some excitement," Avra said.

"But the Rabbis… the children. What will you tell them?"

"Art needs no defense. Besides, your body is the work of Yahweh. How can they be ashamed of that?"

"But they will be."

"So, let them do the defending."

"I didn't realize… " Brendel said.

"No face, as you and Hiram agreed."

"It will become a guessing game!"

Avra grinned. "I wouldn't be surprised."

"How awful!" She was rubbing her forehead with her hand.

"Listen to me," Avra said. "The lane is awful. The locked gates are awful. The laws against the Jews are awful. Your beauty is not awful. The beauty inside our clothing is revealed only in bedrooms, at night, in the dark. But it's a part of the life of the lane, and that is Hiram's subject. How can he not show that? The children you're concerned about — they don't come from starter dough."

"I don't see you posing nude."

"My body no one would look at twice."

Following the conversation by reading their lips and their hand motions, Hiram stepped closer to Avra, kissed her temple, pointed to himself, smiling. He would look at her twice.

"You can't sell them!" Brendel was near to tears now. "I never agreed to that! Imagine men hanging these in their bedrooms. Their wives would hate me!"

"I doubt any married man would dare."

"Who, then? Bachelors? That would be worse!"

Avra pondered, looked at Hiram. "Very well, we'll just display his talent. They won't be for sale."

"It's more than his talent you're displaying!"

Hiram spoke to Avra quickly with his hands. Avra frowned, but translated. "He doesn't want to upset you. He says he won't show them without your permission."

Brendel wiped perspiration from her forehead, tried to slow her breathing, the rise and fall of her chest beneath her robe.

"It's not as if you're ashamed of your body," Avra said.

Brendel's eyes flashed at her. "Why should I be ashamed of it!"

"Exactly. Why should anyone?"

Cocking her head to the side, squinting at Avra, Brendel said, "I think I know Guttle well. You I don't know at all."

"Few people do."

Slowly Brendel began to look at the drawings, one by one. Most she placed carefully in one pile. A few she set aside — those that showed the confluence of her thighs, her triangle of private hair. "You can show all but these," she said.

Hiram, understanding, nodded his head.

"A guessing game." Brendel turned to Avra. "Will you help me bake this week? I suspect I'll be selling lots of ruggelah. And mun cake. And strudel. Lots of everything."

Hiram raised two fingers at her, pointed to the studio. Two more drawings? Brendel shook her head, no, and went to Yetta's bedroom to dress.

Guttle remained in bed most of the Sabbath. After morning services, while the children played in the lane, Meyer strolled to the south gate and gazed out at the river, his mind dancing with numbers. He could not put pencil to paper on Shabbas, but nothing could prevent his mind from spinning its mathematical polka to the sweet music provided by Buderus, the carrot-haired Gentile angel. To discount notes of twenty-five thousand gulden at ten percent, he would need to put up twenty two thousand five hundred. He had been able to put away twenty thousand from his profits of the past five years, with the help of Guttle's efficient housework — keeping their clothing in good repair, preparing simple meals. He'd been saving the money for just such an opportunity. The difference he could borrow from one of his brothers.

On the river, while gray and white gulls whirled against the winter sky, he saw seamen from a three-masted ship that lay at anchor unloading huge bundles of cloth — cotton and silk that had been turned into bolts of fabric in the mills of England. Kalman and Moish made a nice living importing such cloth; if they could order in greater bulk, they would obtain a lower wholesale price, their own profits would increase, and he could turn a substantial profit for the Crown Prince. The Gentile bankers, he felt certain, would invest in bank notes or safe foreign currencies, items that carried little risk. Investing in the expanding import business could earn far larger profits — assuming a ship carrying your merchandise did not go down at sea, or get highjacked by pirates to a distant port. Though ordered in bulk, the fabric would be sold to merchants and tailors and dressmakers only in small lots, so the market would not be flooded and the price driven down.

The wisp of a cloud floated through him. What if he lost money for the Prince, instead of making a profit? The answer to that was simple. He would make sure that he did not. He would read the markets as he read the Torah. Just as religiously.

And Buderus not withstanding, he would not feel guilt about getting rich. Why should he?

Watching the schooner unload at the busy quay stoked his effervescence. His good fortune, he felt certain, would help cure Guttle's malaise, whatever it was that ailed her, as soon as she felt well enough to listen.

Sunday morning, Guttle arose from her bed to feed the children breakfast. When they had gone out to play, and the baby Salomon was gurgling contentedly in his crib, Meyer sat across from her at the kitchen table, both of them sipping tea through crystals of honey; she was still in her robe, he had donned dark blue knee-breeches and a matching vest. Unable to hold back any longer, he told her of the offer from Buderus, from the Crown Prince. Guttle broke off a braid from the leftover challah on the table. When she spoke, it was not with the excitement he had expected.

"You're not going to do this, of course."

Meyer looked at her warily. This must be one of her teases; she was so good at that. But her lips held no hint of a smile.

"Not going to do this? What do you mean?"

"I mean you're going to thank the Crown Prince for his gracious offer, but tell him thank you, no. Aren't you?"

"I don't understand what you're saying. This is the opportunity I've been seeking for years. Why would I say no?."

Guttle lay her piece of challah on the table. "Meyer, this money is in payment for the peasants sent to fight in America. Like Georgi's brother. You said so yourself. Surely you don't want to get involved in that."

"I won't be getting involved in anything." His left hand rubbed his head in frustration, leaving his hair in disarray, giving him a rare unkempt look. "I'll just be investing some money."

"Meyer, it's not just some money. Surely you see that. This money pays for the bodies of the peasants. It pays for their blood."

"That's not relevant, Guttle. The men already are in England. Maybe already on their way to America. If I turned down the offer, it wouldn't change anything. The ships still would sail. Some of the men still would die. The only difference would be that Gentile bankers would be investing the money, would be making profits, would be earning the gratitude of the Crown Prince. Whether I do this or not doesn't affect the peasants at all."

Guttle folded the collar of her gray robe up under her chin. "The money comes with blood on it. There's no way to avoid acknowledging that."

"Nonsense." Meyer stood and paced about. He was trying hard not to lose control, not to become overbearing. "This is the opportunity I've been waiting for. If I invest this money wisely, I'm sure to get more of Wilhelm's business. Our lives could take a turn for the better."

"Our lives are fine now. We don't need blood on our hands."

"Stop with the blood already." Now he was truly angry, his face was reddening. A different kind of man, he thought, would slap her. "When Wilhelm's father dies, Wilhelm will become the Landgrave of Hesse-Kassel. The treasury there is a hundred times bigger than at Hanau. Friedrich has been hiring out his peasants to fight in every war in Europe for forty years.

The money is in his treasury — along with his rents, his profits from his fields, from his investments. If one day I am offered to invest that money, how would I separate one source from another? It's all intermingled."

"That's in the future. If it happens, you're smart enough to figure out something."

"Guttle, in business everything is intermingled. Besides, if I turn down this offer from Wilhelm, there won't be any future for me. Not with him. Not now, not later."

"It won't be the end of the world."

"It would be the end my dream! Of our dreams! If the law ever changes, if the gates are unlocked, only those with money will be able to move out. This is our chance to stop adding to our money, and start multiplying it. That's what's at stake here."

"You won't just be sending men off to die, which is bad enough," Guttle said. "You'll be sending them off to kill other men."

"I won't be sending them anywhere! They're already sent!" He gripped the back of his chair. "I have to say this, Guttle. Today, maybe for the first time since we've known each other, you have disappointed me."

"I have disappointed you?" She lost control, began to shout at him. "How can you say such a thing? What about being a good person! What about morality!"

His voice rose to the anger of hers. "This is not about morality! This is business!"

Shaking her head, Guttle stood, hugged herself as if she were chilled. When she spoke her voice sounded tired, worn out. "My ankles are hurting. I'm going back to bed." At the top of the stairs, before she descended, she said quietly, "I hope you won't disappoint me."

"What? What was that you said?" But she was gone, moving carefully down the stairs, gripping the rope balustrade tightly, as if below her were an abyss.

He slammed his fist against the table. The challah and the two tea glasses jumped. He sprang down the stairs two at a time and out into the lane without a coat. A chill wind blowing from the south rippled the loose white sleeves of his shirt. Angrily he strode down the lane, ignoring people who offered greetings. Not stopping till he reached the locked south gate, locked because it was Sunday. He gripped its iron bars like a prisoner in a cell. He looked at the gray river trembling beneath the wind. The ship from yesterday was gone. Turning, he entered the cemetery, walked about among the stones of all the thousands who had been born in the lane, and had died in the lane.

He read names. He read dates. He read encomiums. Hours passed before his anger abated, before he dared return to the Hinterpfann.

38

—Oh mein Gott! Do you see?

—For shame! For shame!

—Look at that one. And that one.

—And this one here, do you see?

—If you'd get your nose out of the way, I could see.

—How could he draw such things?

—How could she display such things?

—Women will see.

—And children!

—He left off her face. Whom do you think it is?

—I tell you one thing, my wife it's not.

—Look at her... her you-knows. It's someone young.

—But not too young.

—He almost shows... oh, mein goodness!

—And he's deaf, he won't hear the children cry.

—Why would you think the children will cry when they look?

—They'll cry when their mamas spank them.

—Here comes the Chief Rabbi, and Simcha. Someone must have sent for them.

Rabbi Eleazar took a quick gander at the drawings, and approached Avra, who was standing in the doorway. "You must put those away. At once."

"Why?"

"They are a disgrace. They are obscene."

"They depict the creation of God. Was Adonai a disgrace? Was Adonai obscene?"

The throng around the drawings was growing larger as word spread. People stood on their toes to see over the heads of those in front of them.

"You go too far, young lady. Adam and Eve, though created naked, put on clothes."

"You know better than I do, Rabbi — they put on clothes because they ate of the forbidden fruit. Because they disobeyed the will of God — and became ashamed of their bodies. It was not Yahweh's intent that they be ashamed of His work."

"That was in Paradise. Does the Judengasse look like Paradise to you?"

"All the more reason we need to look at beauty. Why must anyone get upset at these images? Women see them every month, for real, in the mikveh. Men see them every night, in their wives. And touch them."

"Not children."

"What house is so large that a boy has not glimpsed his mother washing, or a girl her father?"

"Such drawings undermine the Jewish spirit. The life of the mind."

"Only if we allow them to."

"Enough talking. As the Chief Rabbi, I order you to take them down."

"You have no such authority. Where is it written that you do?"

"It is by common consent."

"My husband is an artist. Artists work beyond common consent."

His face darkening beneath his high black hat like a beet from the fields, the Chief Rabbi turned to Rabbi Simcha for help. Simcha, one palm on a pockmarked cheek, said nothing. The Chief Rabbi turned and strode off angrily towards his study. Simcha took a few moments to look at the drawings. Before following his superior, he rolled his eyes at Doctor Kirsch, whom he noticed in the crowd wearing an amused expression. Rebecca, ever curious, left the throng and intercepted Simcha before he had gone ten metres. "What do you think, Rabbi?" she asked him.

"What do I think? I think Moses Mendelssohn has struck again."

"Mendelssohn?"

"The Mendelssohn Rebellion, I call it. Time was when the women in the lane were content to scrub the floors and cook the chickens and have the babies, and bring the children up to be like their mothers and fathers — the boys as students of the Torah, the girls as, well, as their wives. Then Mendelssohn came here — what, about six months ago? Look what's happened since. We have a Gentile living in the lane — invited in by the daughter of the Court Jew; she even mounts a coffin and harangues the old men who don't want him here, who consider his presence an abomination. The Doctor's wife runs off from her husband and children to marry a

Christian — the son of a Count, no less. A Café owned by a woman — a woman more or less living in sin — which most people had been shunning, suddenly begins to prosper after Mendelssohn gives it his blessing. Now some other woman — I hope I never know who, how could I look her in the eye again? — some woman has disrobed to her skin for the artist, and another daughter of the Court Jew flaunts the drawings in public; she disobeys the Chief Rabbi, even argues with him. Nothing like this has happened in the lane in three hundred years."

"Is that so bad?"

"I didn't say if it was good or bad. Only that it was new."

The Doctor ran her fingers through her lustrous black hair. "I never though to link those things. Perhaps because I've been close with some of these women, and seen their ambivalence, their pain. Tell me, Rabbi, what you think of this Mendelssohn's Rebellion, if that's what it is."

"What do I think?" He glanced down the lane, where the sturdy black figure of the Chief Rabbi was diminishing in size as he neared the synagogue. "Clearly it's scandalous. It's like a wind blowing the yarmulkes right off our heads, as the Chief Rabbi might say."

"I know what the Chief Rabbi would say. I just heard him. What about Emil Simcha?"

He glanced toward the synagogue, then back at Rebecca. Lowering his voice, he said, "Just between us, Doctor, it's making life interesting. There are worse things than scandalous." He touched the top of his head, making sure his yarmulke was still on. With a small, rueful smile that softened his scarred face, he added, "Not that it wasn't interesting before. The compression from the walls makes sure of that."

Together they began to walk down the lane, the Doctor towards the hospital, the Rabbi towards his study. "At least I became a Doctor long before Mendelssohn spoke," Rebecca said. "I'd hate to be a crowd follower."

"That was in Berlin, am I right?"

"Correct."

"Your father encouraged you?"

"Pretty much."

"Isn't your father an acquaintance of Mendelssohn?"

Taken by surprise, Rebecca inclined her head, smiling gamely in defeat, her dark eyes merry. As they reached the hospital, she said, "You've really thought this through."

Simcha shrugged modestly. "That's what we Rabbis do. That's what we're for."

Up the lane, in front of Hiram's drawings, some art lovers had left, others had come to look, and the old men, with nothing better to do, continued to speculate.

—The question remains, who is it?

—It's not skinny Avra.

—It could be her sister, Guttle Rothschild.

—Except Guttle is pregnant out to here.

—You know what I think? A lot of wives will get pregnant tonight.

—From looking at pictures you don't get pregnant.

—You'd be surprised.

—I know who! There's only one woman who would drop her drawers in front of the deaf mute.

—Who is that?

—The shiksa whore. The Doctor's former wife.

—She left the lane months ago.

—Maybe he drew her months ago.

—Then why not show them before?

—He waited till she wasn't Jewish.

—What, something changes then?

—You know what? Looking at these is making my mouth go dry.

—I know what you mean. You want to go to the Café?

—My thought precisely. We'll have Brendel fix us a nice glass of tea.

Guttle lay awake in the dark. She and Meyer had not said a word to one another since their fight. In the morning it would be two days. Nothing like this had ever happened before. She was frightened for her marriage. He was due at Hesse-Hanau at eleven in the morning — if he was going. He would have to leave early. He lay beside her, his broad back turned. She did not know if he was awake or asleep. She did not want to find out. Her body was stiff, tense. Not, she assumed, like the naked torso in the drawings in the lane. She had heard about them from Avra, who had come to see how she was feeling. Avra who had faced down the Chief Rabbi — the Chief Rabbi! — with chutzpah. Or had it been true courage? Guttle was not sure about the prerogatives of art. All she knew was that just now her own body was not a thing of beauty. She felt heavier than when she had borne the other children;

her arms and legs were thicker, her every movement was sluggish. She felt more like a cow in a barn than a wife in bed. Why did she have to become pregnant every time Meyer sneezed? It was not his fault, a man had to sneeze, Yahweh had made him that way. She loved her three children, like Meyer she wanted more, and yet… She felt a pain wrack through her womb and her back, as if it would cut her spine in half.

When she had fallen asleep she had dreamed of the trench running red with her menstrual blood. She'd been awakened by pain and sat upright, near to tears, from the pain or the nightmare, she was not certain which. Something was wrong with the baby inside her; she could tell. Something was different this time. That was why she could not get warm, why her entire body ached, why she was so tired. She had tried talking to Melka, but Melka was Melekh, a King, a Torah, a man, and didn't want to hear of such things. She tried talking to Jennie Aron, but Jennie was a virgin, knew nothing of giving birth — burned to death, a far worse pain And the Archduchess, Marie Antoinette, ridiculed for being childless after six years of marriage. Guttle wondered which was worse, the pain of ridicule or the pain of labor, of giving birth, the punishment visited by Yahweh on Eve. "I am not Eve!" she cried aloud. Beside her Meyer stirred, but when she became silent again he did not turn to her.

My soul is divided, she thought. I am twenty-three years old and I am still a child, talking to girls who are imaginary, or distant, or dead — yet I am becoming a mother to my sisters, and to their friends; they come to me for advice, as if I had the wisdom of someone twice my years. Is that because I am Meyer's wife? Because I am my father's daughter? "Let's see what Guttle thinks," they say. But why? Is this wisdom, that I believe in Torah and Talmud and all the traditions of my people, yet I stand upon a coffin and scold the elders? Is this wisdom, that I cut myself off from the friend I love the most, and then pine for her smile, her touch, the very color of her hair? Is this wisdom, that the man I married is a tireless worker who wants to make us rich, and I meddle in the business he knows so well?

But how can I not speak the truth — at least the truth as it seems to me? If I don't, then I cease to exist. The 'me' in me disappears. I become just a tiny part of a pointless untruthful beast called the Judengasse. Or called humanity. Surely that can't be what Yahweh wanted when He created us in His image. If I do not speak the truth, and my children don't, and their children don't, then what is the purpose of bearing children at all? Then humans are only an endless procession of lies. That can't be what Yahweh intended.

Another spasm in her womb. Something bad was happening — not just the child kicking, she could feel that, but something else. Another spasm. If she did not know she had two months yet, she would think she had started labor. But she felt as if the child inside her had a mind of its own. A sharp contraction ripped through her like an animal with claws. Is the child doing this, or is my mind doing this to my body, out of anger at Meyer Amschel? To punish him — for what? It cannot be. Just ask anyone, they will tell you, I would not do such a thing. I am the perfect one. Not as selfish as Dvorah, not as flirtatious as Brendel, not as brilliant as Rebecca, not as sharp-tongued as Avra, not as skinny as some or as heavy as others, clever but not clownish, born to be, if not everyone's mother, then everyone's big sister — not just Avra's and Amelia's and Mira's and Benjy's but also Izzy's, and Dvorah's — who is older than me — and Georgi — my own doing, but why did I do it? — and now even big sister to Mama, who is disappearing into a vapor of fear as her children get older. "Let's see what Guttle thinks." I am tired of living up to my name. Guttle. The Good.

Yet that is not entirely true. Bringing Georgi into the lane, haranguing the elders from a coffin, even, when I was younger, intruding on the men in the synagogue. Plenty of men in the lane, and women, too, must whisper of Guttle the Bad. Even to Meyer I must be a curse when I speak of the blood on Wilhelm's wealth.

Already I hear the Chief Rabbi rebutting my thoughts: You have read the Torah, Guttle. Yahweh did not create you in His image. He created man in His image. He created woman from Adam's rib, to serve. To multiply. Not to criticize. Not to harangue. Not to intrude.

Yes, I have read the Torah, but why do I have a mind, if not to think? If I do not think, I do not exist, except as a slave — and that I cannot accept. Yet women all around me accept. My mother. Dvorah's mother. The rebbetzin. Almost every woman in the lane accepts. Only my sisters and my friends do not. Is there something wrong with us?

I used to joke, to tease, in order to ease the pressure of the walls. That has become more difficult to do. The stakes increase in sorrow. How does one joke about Georgi? Or Dvorah? Or money stained with blood? To tease and joke and sing arias through the sorrow of life, with honor and honesty — that would be a worthy goal. But is it possible?

For twenty-three years I have lived. I have borne three children. How old, dear Yahweh, how fecund must I be before I understand?

Enough, my twisting brain. I'm tired. So tired…

"Mein Gott!" Half asleep, Guttle woke and winced at yet another strong contraction. And then another. "It's too early!" she yelled at the ceiling, arching her back.

This time Meyer turned, groped for her hand. "What is it?"

"Run and get the midwife." She gasped at another wave of pain. "The baby's coming!"

"Not for two months."

"It's coming now!" she screamed. "Just go!"

Jumping out of bed, stumbling in a moment of dizziness, Meyer quickly donned a robe and slippers, unlocked the door and hurried into the lane, ran in the darkness, his slippers flapping, past the hospital and the baths to Celia Levine's wig shop, began to pound on the door. He pounded until Celia sleepily came to the front, a robe over her shift, wearing slippers. She lighted a lantern, saw through the window who it was, opened the door.

"You've got to come! Guttle is having her baby!"

"Guttle? It's too soon!"

"I know it's too soon. Please, come now!"

She handed the lantern to Meyer. "You'd better get the Doctor," she said, grabbed a sheitl from the nearest shelf — it was black — pulled it over her light brown hair and hurried off along the cobbles, not bothering to lug her birthing chair. "Please,Yahweh, don't let me lose her. Don't let me lose my wife," Meyer said in supplication. He hurried to the south end, the lantern with its single candle dangling at his side. At Rebecca's, too, he pounded on the door until it opened. He could hardly speak. "Guttle… baby… coming now." Rebecca grabbed her medical bag from the table beside the door and was gone before he could say more, running the length of the lane, barefoot on the cobbles, holding her sleep shift above her knees, barelegged, black hair flying behind her. She and the midwife reached the Hinterpfann together, dashed to Guttle, who was crying out in her bed. Moish's wife, having heard her cries from the third floor, was with her. "I'll look after the children," she told Guttle, and went upstairs.

"Cramps, stomach, belly, back — it's labor, I know," Guttle said.

The Doctor lit the lamp on the wall, raised the hem of Guttle's gray shift to her knees, leaned in. "It's too soon, she's not dilated nearly enough." The midwife peered close, agreed. "How can we stop the uterus from pushing it out?" Guttle could not tell which had spoken. "We can't… it could tear her… I know… Guttle, try to relax, honey. It won't be as big as full term, it might not hurt as much." Guttle moaned as another spasm came and went. She groped for a hand, found Rebecca's, squeezed it hard.

Meyer sat at his desk in the office outside the bedroom, hearing Guttle's cries. There was nothing he could do but murmur prayers. Celia came out, asked him to heat water, dip rags or towels in it. He went up to the kitchen, to the woodstove, added a small log to the embers, did as he was told. He could hear the children talking in their room, went in to comfort them while his sister-in-law prepared their porridge. Through the second-floor window, between the house and the ghetto wall less than a metre away, he could see the gray of the new day slumping in.

He would have to leave soon for Hesse-Hanau. How could he leave with Guttle in such throes? How could he not? His life's dream depended on his being there, the culmination of seven years of trying. "Thank you, Yahweh, thank you for your timing," he muttered bitterly. A new experience for Meyer — being sarcastic with the Lord.

He had left fresh clothing in the office, so as not to disturb Guttle if she were sleeping. He went downstairs. Her cries were muted, but still he heard them as he dressed.

He could not leave her this way.

He dared not humiliate Buderus, and offend the Crown Prince.

You Jews are not averse to making money — only to enjoying it.

Already he was perspiring in his fresh clothes. He could not sit but paced about, went upstairs to the kitchen to drink some water, then down to the office again.

A small cry from the bedroom. Not Guttle's, another. A baby! He hurried in. The midwife was holding an infant, covered with blood, the smallest human creature he had ever seen. "A girl," Celia said, as she wiped the child's body with a warm wet rag.

"Leah's here!" Guttle said, seeing Meyer from the bed.

Meyer winced. You were not supposed to use the name till it was given to her in the synagogue, eight days later.

The Doctor was working between Guttle's legs, using towels to inhibit bleeding. Meyer grabbed for the wall when he saw a towel turn red. "Will she be all right?"

"It's torn tissue, not a hemorrhage," Rebecca said, turning her head to Meyer, her hands still between Guttle's thighs. "I think we can get it stopped."

"You think!" His frustration burst out at the Doctor, which he knew was not fair; he would not be shouting at Doctor Berkov. "That's all? You just think?"

"I'll get it stopped," Rebecca said, calmly, her eyes on her work. "It's slowing already."

"Thank Gott! And the baby?" Meyer looked at his fourth child, still in Celia's arms.

"Her lungs will be small," the Doctor said. "I wouldn't count too much on the baby."

Meyer closed his eyes at her words. He murmured a desperate prayer. Opening them, he bent over the bed. Guttle's hair and face were wet, her eyes closed; clearly she was exhausted. He pressed his lips to her forehead. "I love you," he said.

Her eyes seemed drained of all feeling when she opened them. "I know you do." She paused for breath between each utterance. "I'm sorry about Leah... I couldn't keep her long enough... I don't know why."

"It's not your fault."

She closed her eyes, weary. "It's no one else's. I hate to blame Yahweh for everything."

Meyer touched his lips to hers. "You just rest," he said. "There will be plenty of others."

Guttle closed her eyes against his words. A flash of anger was extinguished by grief. She was too weary to deal with that now.

39

Buderus was pacing in his office when Meyer burst in, sweating, his wig askew under his tricorne, as the hats were now called, courtesy of the French, his heart shaken loose by his frantic ride and adrift now like a raft in a sea of guilt, guilt not over the blood of peasants — this day he had not given that a thought — but over the blood of the wife and child he had left, if only for the morning. It might be, he was aware, the only morning his newborn infant would know.

"I'd just about given up on you," Buderus said. "I thought your conscience had tied your hands."

"Conscience? What does conscience have to do with anything?" You sound like my wife, he wanted to say, but he didn't

"It doesn't to me if it doesn't to you."

"Am I late?"

"It's two minutes to eleven. The others are waiting. I think you should straighten your wig, and dry your face. He is wary enough already."

When Meyer had done so, Buderus led the way up a marble staircase, with carved mahogany balustrades, to a spacious anteroom. Crown Prince Wilhelm, standing behind a gilt writing table, talking quietly with an aide, was got up in his usual outlandish colors; he would have been born a jester, Meyer thought, if he had not been born a Prince. But the room was rich and tasteful, its golds and beiges accented with soft red velvet drapes that echoed the seats and backs of the chairs. The walls were painted red, with gold trim on a series of plaster arches. Gold chandeliers supporting red candles hung from the white ceiling. A red rug covered the floor. Meyer had never been in such a room. He'd never even imagined one. The room gave the Judengasse the aspect of a stable.

The three Gentile bankers, chatting in a corner, all were dressed in black and white — black coats and knee-breeches, white vests, shirts and hose, polished black shoes without buckles. Except for his white shirt, Meyer was all in brown, the same as Buderus. He preferred to leave black to the Rabbis.

Seeing that Wilhelm was occupied, Buderus introduced Meyer to the bankers. "Herr Schoenbrunn, Herr Krapp, Herr Krupp, this is Meyer Rothschild." Herr Krapp was a tall, thin man with a sallow face. Herr Krupp was a short, round man with a pudgy, pink face. Herr Schoenbrunn was neither tall nor short; his pointed face evinced a bluish cast. The bankers glanced at Meyer as they might at a passing cockroach, and turned back to their own circle.

"Do all Jews sweat like that?" Herr Krapp asked his colleagues, in a reedy voice from his lofty height.

"Only in the presence of money," Herr Krupp replied, in frog like tones, from not far above Herr Krapp's waist.

"Like dogs on a hot day, lapping up grease," Herr Schoenbrunn offered definitively.

Though not facing Meyer, they were speaking loud enough for him and Buderus to hear. That was the point. Meyer stood silently, but the coils of his brain were sizzling. He decided to resurrect an idea that had come to him during the ride — an idea he had discarded as perhaps too provocative.

When Wilhelm's aide left the room, the Crown Prince motioned to Buderus, who led Meyer and the others to the front of the writing desk. "Your Excellency, you are acquainted with Herrs Krupp, Krapp and Schoenbrunn. Perhaps you remember Herr Rothschild."

"Of course, the Jew Meyer. He has a way with coins. But Buderus, how many times have I told you that I am not yet Your Excellency. My father is His Excellency. I am only Your Serenity."

"I'm sorry, Your Ex... Your Serenity."

"You seem nervous, Carl Friedrich. As well you might be." The Crown Prince looked directly at Meyer while speaking to Buderus." Do you want to withdraw your recommendation? There is still time."

"Not at all, Your Serenity. I have full confidence in Herr Rothschild."

Meyer noticed something he had not seen before in the Crown Prince — a twitch that closed his right eye in a kind of grimace every few seconds. He wondered what the Prince had to be nervous about, beyond that which makes every man nervous, his own mortality. Perhaps, Meyer thought, conscripting his peasants into a foreign war does not agree with him.

"Very well, let's proceed. I'm sure Buderus has informed you all of the conditions of the discounting. If there are no questions, you may sign in my presence the contracts here on the desk, each for the discounting of one fourth of one hundred thousand gulden, at ten percent."

Krapp, Krupp and Schoenbrunn remained silent. Meyer glanced at Buderus, then spoke, oblivious of his Judengasse accent, which evoked smirks from the three financiers. "I would like to thank Your Gracious Serenity for including me in this august company. As a token of my esteem for Your Serenity, but also to demonstrate sound financial practice, I am prepared to discount the notes assigned to me at eight percent, instead of ten. If it please Your Serenity."

The three men in black looked aghast. The Crown Prince raised his eyebrows, glanced at Buderus, who merely shrugged. "Is there a catch to this, Buderus? Some kind of Jewish trick?"

"This is the first I hear of it, Your Serenity. I wish Herr Rothschild had informed me earlier of this proposal, but he did not." He turned to Meyer. "I assume that you would not attempt to swindle His Serenity in some way."

"Of course not. It's a simple matter of fairness. I believe I can earn a fair profit at eight percent."

Wilhelm pursed his lips, nodded, twitched, brushed a fleck of white dust from his orange coat. "Interesting," he said. "The fact is, I have been thinking along the same lines myself, for future contracts." He turned to the others. "What about you gentlemen? Are you prepared to match the offer of the Jew, and discount at eight percent?"

The bankers coughed in unison, raised fists to their mouths as their faces reddened. "Your Serenity, I doubt that is possible in the current climate," Krapp said.

"I would have to check with my bank," Schoenbrunn offered, "however..."

"This is an alarming proposal, undoubtedly a Jew plot," Krupp barked. He pulled a large handkerchief from his pocket and wiped his perspiring forehead. "I must urge His Serenity to cast the Jew from among us, and divide the notes three ways, at the standard ten percent. The fiscal stability of Frankfurt could be at stake."

Wilhelm summoned Buderus to his side. The aide's red hair was a close match to the Crown Prince's coat. They turned their backs and conferred briefly. Facing the group again, Wilhelm said: "I appreciate your concern for the fiscal stability of Frankfurt, Herr Krupp. As you may know, however, I am the Crown Prince of Hesse-Hanau, which does not include Frankfurt. While I wish my neighbors well, their financial stability is hardly my concern — certainly not as opposed to the health of my own treasury. I would point out that some of our citizens may be sacrificing their lives in defense of our treasury, as it were. It behooves me, therefore, not to let them down."

The Crown Prince reached for a gold goblet of water that stood on his desk, and drank, looking over its rim at the bankers, his eye twitching faster. Neither Meyer nor the others knew where this was leading.

Setting the goblet down, wiping his lips with a white lace handkerchief, Wilhelm continued. "A more reckless ruler than I might dismiss the three of you at once and offer all of the notes to Herr Rothschild at eight percent. Prudence, however, dictates that I continue to spread the investments about. I therefore have determined to amend the contracts only slightly in deference to this unexpected offer. You gentlemen in black will discount at ten percent, as previously agreed, but only on fifty percent of the notes, which shall be divided equally among you. The other fifty percent will go to Herr Rothschild, at eight percent. I assume that is agreeable."

"But. . ."

"But . . . "

Buderus leaned close and whispered to Meyer, "Can you cover fifty percent?"

"Absolutely," Meyer whispered back — without a notion, just then, as to where he would obtain the money.

"Very well, then," the Crown Prince said. "There being no objection, Carl Friedrich will amend the figures before you sign the contracts. It has been a pleasure doing business with you."

Wilhelm glided, as only silken nobility can, through a doorway to his inner sanctum. "Please wait down in my office, gentlemen," Buderus told the bankers. "It will only be a moment. Herr Rothschild, remain here, if you will."

The eyes of Krapp, Krupp and Schoenbrunn flashed murderous hatred at Meyer as they filed out.

"You were afraid they would tear me apart?" Meyer asked.

"Something like that. You've made a good start with His Serenity — but I wish you had warned me ahead of time."

"I did not think of this ahead of time."

"Herr Rothschild — Meyer, if I may call you that — I doubt that you do anything without thinking of it ahead of time. But I want to be certain again that you can pay for the notes. Fifty thousand gulden is a lot. You don't have a bank behind you, like the others."

"I can borrow what I need in the Judengasse. At four percent. Five the most. That still leaves me three percent profit."

"That's not much, for the risk you'll be taking when you invest Wilhelm's funds."

"Ten percent of twenty-five thousand gulden," Meyer said, "is a profit of twenty-five hundred. Obviously. Whereas eight percent of twenty-five thousand, plus three percent of an additional twenty-five thousand, amounts to a combined profit of twenty-seven hundred and fifty gulden. That's an additional two hundred and fifty gulden."

"You figured that in your head, while Wilhelm was speaking?"

"With all respect, did you see me using my toes?"

"I would have liked to," Buderus said, grinning at the image.

"I have a motto, Herr Buderus."

"You may call me Carl."

"My motto is, Slow but Steady."

"Not very original. Those bankers would agree with it."

"Of course they would. But I don't mean slow in the head."

Smiling, Buderus asked, "What would you have done, in their place?"

"Me? I would have met my eight percent. I would have come down to seven percent. Even six. To drive out the upstart Jew, as they would put it. But because they did not do that, in future discounting, God willing, they will have Meyer Amschel Rothschild to contend with."

"God willing? Does your Jewish God take an interest in money matters?"

"To tell the truth, I have no idea. I should have said Carl Friedrich Buderus willing. Also, his Excellency willing."

"His Serenity."

"To me, today he is an Excellency."

Buderus moved behind the writing table, sat, dipped a quill into an inkwell, and amended Meyer's contract from twenty-five to fifty percent of the notes. Meyer scrawled his signature at the bottom of the two copies.

"Should your transactions please the Crown Prince," Buderus said, "it's possible that in future dealings we would be able to offer you a line of credit, so you would not have to borrow." He slid one copy of the contract into a drawer, handed the other to Meyer. "I would ask you where you're planning to invest Wilhelm's money — but I don't think I want to know."

"Then I'll give a little hint. 'Slow but steady' is my motto only sometimes."

"I suspected as much," Buderus said.

Leaving the palace, reclaiming his mount, the contract tucked carefully into his waistcoat, Meyer was exultant. Fifty percent of the notes! He could never have planned it that way. His instincts had served him well. Would he have dropped to eight percent if they had not been so smug, had not insulted him? He could not be sure. It was possible — one glimpse had assured him they would be no threat, would not bargain down; they were too pompous for that. Now he was in the chase. Now he was 'Meyer' to Carl Buderus, and he was 'Herr Rothschild' — no longer 'the Jew Meyer' — to the Crown Prince. He'd been amused by the titles owed the nobility, by the difference between Serenity and Excellency. Never mind noble blood, he thought: with enough money you could become an Excellency. If he invested Wilhelm's notes well, if he had good luck — and luck was three-fourths information, he reminded himself — he soon might truly stop adding his money, as he had said to Guttle, and begin multiplying it.

His mind was filled with prancing numbers and galloping investments till he was half way home, when he recalled the grim early morning, Guttle's blood, Leah's too-tiny face, and a rush of guilt so overwhelmed him, like a blow to his head, that he almost fell off his horse. Only by slowing the mare to a walk and clinging to the saddle horn could he balance himself on her back the rest of the way.

The infant was curled on Guttle's breast as Guttle lay on the bed, her head on the pillow, the quilt of muted colors in disarray. The newborn wrinkled her nose, tried to suck at a distended nipple. Guttle could hear her taking in air.

"She's not getting much."

"She won't need much milk the first day. So long as she keeps breathing."

"There's nothing we can do to make sure?"

"Nothing," Rebecca said. "It's up to Yahweh and Leah."

"Then she'll be fine," Guttle said.

Rebecca had sent the midwife home, asked her to stop at the hospital and tell Doctor Berkov where she was. Her own body was wet with sweat, her shift clinging to her breasts.

"Do you want children?" Guttle asked.

Rebecca straightened the quilt, sat on the bed, looking at the infant. "I don't know. I'm thirty years old. It's a little late to start. Especially without a husband."

"But would you want them?"

"I'm not sure."

"What about love? You care about your patients, but that's not love. Not what I feel for this baby. My heart already is so full, I would gladly die if that would let her live."

"That's no way to talk. You have other responsibilities … if Leah doesn't survive."

"Don't you ever get tired of responsibilities?"

"Every day. But ... "

"But what?"

"What else is there? Pleasure? I love to dance. But how long can you dance? And who does it help?"

"Don't you want a man?"

"A man would be nice. But I haven't met a man yet who could accept my being a Doctor. Really accept it, with all his heart."

"When you first came here, I thought maybe you and Yussel Kahn ... "

Rebecca ran her fingers along the pieces of the quilt. "Yussel could have accepted it, perhaps. As he got used to the idea. But Yussel has Brendel — whom I adore."

"I'll never forget you two dancing at my wedding. The spirit, the joy."

"Neither will I."

"It's too bad we Jews don't have saints."

"Why do you say that?"

"I would nominate you."

"What a thing to say! Saint Rebecca, sweaty and stark naked under her shift. Maybe Hiram Liebmann could draw me. For the ages."

"You heard about that? I wonder who it was who posed."

"When you see the drawings, you'll know."

"I will? I heard there aren't faces."

"In the mikveh, who looks at faces?"

"The mikveh. I never thought of that. I wonder if the model thought of that."

Guttle groaned, shifted the infant to her other breast. "It still hurts. Between my legs."

"That will take time to heal. Where the tissue tore."

"This little one really wanted to come out, I don't know why. In the lane, life is not so pleasant she needed to hurry." Guttle kissed the infant's moist head. "Why don't you go upstairs and wash, Rebecca? Take one of my clean shifts."

The Doctor looked at the baby. Her face, with its strong cheek bones, hardened. She turned her eyes from Guttle. They lighted on the painting of the wedding.

"Go up and wash. Leah and I will be fine."

Still the Doctor did not speak.

"What is it?"

Rebecca knelt beside the bed, gently took the infant from Guttle's breast. She held it to her cheek, she pressed her hand to its chest. She stood and held the infant's face near a small mirror on the wall. Trembling, Guttle sat up in the bed, grabbed her soaked hair with her fingers, pulled at it instead of screaming.

"I think she's gone," the Doctor said.

"Give her to me! She can't be gone. She just needs her mother's milk."

Holding the infant in both hands, Rebecca handed her to Guttle, who pressed her to her breast. "Nooo," she murmured, a long, low moan of pain. "Drink, Leah, drink!" The infant did not suckle. Guttle pressed the infant's face hard into her breast. "Drink, Leah! Listen to your mother!"

Closing her eyes, Guttle lay back on the pillow, one hand cupped around the child. Gently the Doctor lifted the dead baby away. Guttle turned onto her side, her face toward the wall.

"Her little lungs couldn't hold the air. It was to be expected."

Guttle did not reply.

"I have to take her away. I'll send Avra to be with you."

Still barefoot, the Doctor left the room, holding the small body wrapped in a towel

They all came. Jennie Aron came, in a simple brown shift, her hair cut short, her bare arms pale from prison. Melka came, a woman again, in a velvet robe of maroon and gold, a simple gold crown on her head. Madame Antoine came, in a gown of pastel blue, her bodice cut low, combs of diamonds piled in her hair. Guttle's tears quenched the flames that licked at Jennie's knees. Melka breathed life into a baby girl, Guttle handed her carefully to the Queen. Marie Antoinette smiled, touched its chin, her fingers burdened with gold and diamond rings. Madame Leah, she cooed, and lifted the child, lovingly, high in the air.

Meyer entered the room. Still she faced the wall, but through the colors of her dream she sensed his presence.

He moved close to the bed, he gazed at her back as it rose and fell evenly. His heavy eyes scoured the shadowed folds of the quilt she had made while pregnant, from odd bits of cotton and wool; she'd made a smaller one for the child. He looked beside the bed for a cradle, looked in the corners of the room for a pulled-out drawer.

"She's gone," Guttle murmured, without turning.

He sat on the bed, the straw in the mattress sighing. He touched her hip through the quilt. She did not stir. He noticed the child's quilt blending in near the edge of the bed. Pulling it closer, he pressed his fingers to its useless folds. He did not speak. He squeezed her hip, then stood and left the room, quietly closing the door.

Upstairs, in the kitchen, he hugged Avra and the children to him, together, his encompassing arms his only speech; they, too, knew to remain quiet; Avra had explained. This loss, his reason whispered, was common; more than half the babies ever born died quickly, not only in the lane but everywhere; the doctors had warned them all.

Reason offered little comfort. Meyer felt that Yahweh could do better.

Eyes closed, lids weighted with guilt, his mind groped in the dark at a pinpoint of light as from a distant star — the light of the most recent happiness he'd known. It had been so long ago. With intense effort, he recalled when it was. It had been in Hesse-Hanau, at noon.

They never spoke of the baby's death. For weeks it was a wall between them; then a curtain; then a fragile mist, in which like tentative lovers they started holding hands. Peering into their souls, they saw a cradle, empty, pleading. Seeking surcease, they went to see Rabbi Simcha. "It's been my experience," he said, "that the soul, to flourish, needs both love and sorrow — much as a tree needs sun and water."

"Love," Guttle said. "Why sorrow?"

"Look about the lane," Simcha said. "It appears to be a building block."

Nor did they speak again of Wilhelm's money — not till Guttle referred to it eleven months later, after a letter arrived from Ephraim Hess in America. The letter was longer than the others they'd received. Meyer read it silently at the kitchen table, after the children had gone to bed.

3 January 1777

*D*ear Meyer Rothschild and Frau R..

I feel sorry I have not written you in much time, but I have been busy fighting the war. My Eva has written to you, I know. Now I have time to write because I am in a hospital with a wound. Do not be frightened, it is not a serious wound. I shall return to my company before too long. Meanwhile, I thought you would be interested to hear the story of how this wound came about. It has to do with the Judengasse.

I have been fighting in a regiment under the command of General George Washington. It seems that the other George, King George of England, has hired many thousands of soldiers from Germany to come fight his war for pay. We call them Hessians — and guess why. Because most of them come from Hesse-Kassel and Hesse-Hanau, not very far from Frankfurt. I do not know if you know of this. It seems very strange to me.

Until not long ago my regiment had not encountered them. Then General Washington learned, from his spies or scouts, that a large army of these Hessians was making winter camp at a place called Trenton, across a river called the Delaware, where we were hidden. General Washington decided on a surprise attack. On Christmas night, my regiment and others, led by a Kernel named John Glover, ferried across the river. The night was dark, without a moon. The river was clogged with ice. Many times our boats hit floating chunks of ice in the black current. I nearly tumbled into the water once, but I did not.

When we reached the other shore we marched to Trenton and attacked the Hessian camp from three directions. They were caught by surprise, and many surrendered, but most fought. Moving along the grass among bushes and trees I think I may have wounded a few with my shots. Toward morning as the battle raged some distance away I crept around a large stand of bushes and came face to face with one of the enemy as he was crawling around from the other side. We both jumped up. Suddenly we were facing each other from four feet apart. Whoever shot first or lunged first with his bayonet could have killed the other. Instead we crouched there with our knees bent, looking into each other's face. Who goes? he said in German. He was one of the Hessians, of course. I answered him in Judendeutch, which was close enough to German for him to understand. I am from Frankfurt, I said.

I did not mean for him to think I was also a Hessian fighter, of course — our uniforms are so different. We both wear blue coats but theirs are trimmed with red, and we have beige pants and they have white pants (you could guess I was once a rag dealer, no?) And their hats are taller, red with gold fronts, like cathedral doors. I asked where he was from. He was suspicious at first. All I was trying to do was be friendly, so we would not kill each other, with the sounds of the battle dying down, and him not British at all. We were still staring, our weapons aimed at each other. He said he was from Hesse-Hanau. I lived only a few kilometres from there, I told him, in the Judengasse. The fellow nodded. Our arms were getting tired, so we lowered our muskets so the stocks were resting on the ground.

I said to him — in Judendeutch, he did not speak English — there is no point killing each other, why don't you go back to your regiment and I will go back to mine. He thought a moment and said that was a good plan. I even wanted to shake hands with him but he seemed to think it was some kind of trick. So I shrugged and turned to walk away, and heard a twig snap under him and I leaped to the side just as he lunged at my back with his bayonet, at the same time saying, in an ugly voice — Dirty Jew!

If I had not lunged to the side I most likely would have been dead. His bayonet could have pierced my lungs or heart from the back. As it was, his bayonet drove into the back of my shoulder. I pulled away and whirled and thrust my bayonet into his belly. I pulled it out and drove it hard into his his chest. Blood spurted everywhere, including on my uniform. I must have burst his heart. He fell to the ground on his back. In his eyes was an expression of surprise, as if he was asking me why I had killed him. As if he was asking me how could a Jew do that? Then his eyes rolled back in his head and he died.

I write in such detail mainly to point out what happened at the end. I sailed all the way to America six years ago, only to be almost killed by a German from Hesse-Hanau — not because I was an enemy soldier, but because I am a Jew!

The bayonet wound is in my left shoulder, so I am able to write this letter with my right hand. The shoulder is healing well, the Doctors say. In a few weeks I should be fighting again. I will address this envelope only to you, Meyer Rothschild, because I don't know if women, like your Guttle, will be too upset reading about how I killed this man. I leave that up to you. (I never asked his name. I wish I had. Though I don't know why.) In the battle, I found out later, we Americans had only ten casualties and the Hessians had a hundred. We also took a thousand prisoners. Of course, in other battles we have had to retreat. These I have not written about.

I hope this letter finds everyone well in the Judengasse.

I remain your former neighbor and fellow Jew,

—Cpl. Ephraim Hess

Finishing the letter, Meyer was incensed at the irony — as Ephraim no doubt meant him to be. He was grateful that the rag dealer was alive. Without hesitation, he handed the letter across the table to where Guttle was knitting. She glanced at him questioningly, then put down her needles and read it.

When she was done, she set the letter on the table, and resumed her work. The ivory needles clacked faintly as her deft fingers dipped and pulled. Using pale blue yarn, she was knitting a sweater for an infant.

"Another Hessian killed," she murmured, as she spread the stitches on the needle. "Seventy-six more gulden to invest."

Meyer reacted as if a bomb had exploded in the kitchen. The bomb took his breath, he could not speak. He stood and turned from her and glared at the whitewashed wall hung with black pans, as if they would tell him what to say. He was furious, yet he dared not upset her. Not when she was with child.

His chest was burning, he was trying to calm himself. He waited, his back to her, wanting her to apologize. All he heard was the sound of her needles clicking. "I'm sorry" was something Guttle rarely said.

He wanted his anger to pass. He willed it to pass. It hung about like an unwanted dog. It nipped at his heart.

He had chosen her to marry, he knew, because she had a mind. Because she thinks. He cannot control what she thinks. Now he suddenly understood: neither can she. What she thinks is who she is. Even when she is wrong.

He turned and approached the table where she knitted, and touched her shoulder. She looked up from her needles, a question in her eyes. He saw her read the answer in his gaze, the answer to her unspoken question: love triumphant over pain. She set down her knitting and stood, and accepted his arms around her, and let her head rest against his chest. For a long time they stood that way, bloodied survivors beneath the tree of life.

Book Five: The Killing

The resurrection of the dead is one of the cardinal principles established by Moses our Teacher. A person who does not believe in the principle has no real religion, certainly not Judaism. However, resurrection is only for the righteous.

—Maimonides

40

9 April 1785

*M*y *dear Herr Mendelssohn,*

Meyer Amschel and I have learned about your illness in the Berlin newspaper. Please accept our fervent wishes for a full recovery. We had been planning to congratulate you on the publication of your new book, Morning Hours, but we had not known until today that you chose that title because your health permitted you to write only in the morning. We hope you will be well enough to visit the Judengasse next year on the tenth anniversary of your first visit, as we have discussed. I guarantee that no one will assault you next time, though perhaps you should leave your Goethe books at home.

You asked in your recent note for me to tell you the status of our friend Isidor Kracauer, the scholar turned butcher, saying you may want to send him something. Izzy is still the kosher slaughterer, though I know he is increasingly restless. He wants to marry my younger sister Amelia, but though she loves Izzy she is not eager to marry a butcher. Stubbornness runs in our Schnapper veins — as you know from the hard bargain my sister Avra drives whenever you purchase another of Hiram's drawings. Several of your friends have come here recently to buy his paintings and drawings, as well as Gentiles from Frankfurt, and even a collector from Le Marais, in Paris. This has been a blessing. By keeping Hiram and Avra busy, it has helped them to accept the death last year of his mother, Yetta. She was a wonderful woman.

Recently it occurred to me that perhaps Amelia is jealous of Avra — that would be a first! — and wants to be someone's muse, just as Avra has become Hiram's muse. I can see where it would be difficult even for a beauty like Amelia to be the muse of a slaughterer. Most of the girls in the lane are content to repeat the lives of our mothers, to marry and have children and gain weight and keep house, in the traditional way, and let their husbands make all the decisions, with few yearnings beyond food on the table for their children. For the rebellious ones, such as myself and Brendel Isaacs and Doctor Kirsch and a few others, who want something more, the old men tend to blame you. It's not your fault, of course — I suspect that thirty-one years ago I wanted to tear down the walls of my mother's womb. But such blame that they put on you is, in my view, not a criticism but a compliment.

I had hoped to start a school for girls here with Doctor Kirsch. But Rebecca has been too busy at the hospital and I have been too busy being pregnant and raising the children, and no one else would get take charge, so that has not come to pass. Meyer has his eye on a larger house for us that might become vacant. I told him I don't want to hear about it until it happens. There is no point getting excited over nothing.

What else might interest you? The Gentile boy Georgi Kremm is still here, working as a carpenter in Yussel Kahn's shop. He rents a room from Doctor Kirsch, and meets every afternoon with Rabbi Simcha; he is studying to convert and become a Jew. Georgi says that no people outside the lane ever treated him as well (which makes me wonder — half the lane has yet to accept him.) According to gossip, he has his eye on the daughter of one of the money lenders at the south end. I have not asked Georgi about this girl, Misha Marcus, because converting only in order to marry is not encouraged, and I don't want to know the answer. Rabbi Simcha will be the one to judge how serious Georgi is. Meyer Amschel says that anyone willing to be circumcised at age twenty-five certainly is serious — but might also be insane.

We have six children, as you know, but I don't think I ever mentioned the three that died at birth. Why Adonai needs dead babies is a question that I imagine you, with all your wisdom, cannot answer any more than we. Rabbi Eleazar and Rabbi Jonah say it is to test our faith. That is too easy an explanation for everything bad. When I asked you in my last letter to please define the difference between suffering and sorrow, you replied that you would rather first hear what I thought. I am embarrassed to discuss philosophical questions with such as you, but here is what I think. Suffering is a condition of the body or the mind. It can be temporary or permanent. Usually we know its cause — a painful disease, for instance, or the death of a beloved. Or the death of one's newborn. Sorrow, however, may well reside in the soul itself. It seems to endure, although its presence can be submerged some of the time beneath love and laughter. I don't know if any of this is correct, but if it is, that still leaves a question for you about which I have always wondered: what is the source of this sorrow that dwells within us, us attached to no visible cause?

Now look, the oil in the lamp is burning low, sputtering wildly. I look forward to learning what your surprise for Izzy might be. (Since he became thirty years of age he prefers to be called Isidor, but nobody besides Amelia pays attention.)

  From this day forth, your health shall be in our daily prayers.
    Your dedicated friend,
    Guttle, wife of Meyer Rothschild

Sprinkling sand on the sheets of paper to blot them, Guttle looked fondly at Meyer across the table. She'd been planning to show him what she had written, but with the overhead lamp dying, the Talmud still open, and his head leaning awkwardly against the back of the chair, her husband had fallen asleep. She would wake him soon, or his neck would be stiff in the morning.

Four weeks later they were moving to a larger home, a few houses south of the synagogue, at the midpoint of the lane. Guttle was not sure why her exhilaration was tempered by guilt as she watched Meyer and Moish, Yussel and Georgi carry beds and tables and chairs from the old house to the new, watched Schönche and Amschel push wheelbarrows filled with linens and clothing, as she stood in the entryway of their new home and directed things — the children's beds up to the two attic rooms, girls to the left, boys to the right, the linens here in our bedroom off the entryway, the heavy strongbox to the counting house, Meyer's new office off the vestibule. There was no reason for guilt, the house was not that much larger. If the Hinterpfann was less than three metres across, the House at the Green Shield was only four and a half. Room for perhaps an extra bed in each room, but that was all. It faced the street, and had three tall windows on each floor, including in a parlor, which they had never had before. And a water pump inside the stone vestibule that was the marvel; they would be able to pump water without going outside. It was one of only a handful of indoor pumps in the lane.

"How did you manage to buy it?" Guttle had asked Meyer when with a smile like a bashful heder boy with a secret he'd first shown it to her. It was only half of a large, gabled house, the other half was called The Arch because of its rounded entryway, but still…

"The Kornfeld brothers are tired of the lane. They're moving their families to Amsterdam. They have cousins there who have a business."

"How much did you pay?"

"Eleven thousand."

"Eleven thousand gulden? Meyer, that's a fortune! I saw in the *Zeitung* that Goethe's father bought a twenty room mansion, in the nicest part of Frankfurt, for half of that."

"This is the Judengasse. He couldn't have gotten that price here."

"Can you picture the Goethes living here?" Her eyes sparkled, less from that odd image, no doubt, than from the giddy prospect of enjoying a new home that was not tucked away as if ashamed of itself, in the rear, in the dark.

House at the Green Shield. A nice name, a bit more space, and different smells than the humid musk of the Hinterpfann. The stone vestibule smelled like the masonry, where the monuments for the cemetery were engraved. The upstairs, she believed, smelled like the sea, though she had never smelled the sea; it was an illusion of the gray light pouring in, she knew; they had moved from darkness into welcome glare. With Meyer's approval she had ordered furniture upholstered in green for the parlor. But their bedroom was no larger than before, and the kitchen seemed even smaller, the stove holding only one pot, so why this guilt? Meyer had worked hard for the money.

This sturdy, one-hundred-and-seventy-year old house, so close to the synagogue, seemed to Guttle more than just a place to live; it seemed like a proclamation: the Rothschilds are Somebody. Meyer might feel that way, but Guttle didn't feel special — not with her body adding perhaps a pound each year — fifteen since their wedding day — to her once slim figure, not with the marks of stretched skin that criss-crossed her hips like spider webs, souvenirs from each of the children, the living and the dead. Meyer's eagerness in bed had not diminished, nor had hers; for this enduring mutual attraction she was grateful. But some mornings she felt as old as this house, and needed two glasses of strong tea to reawaken her spirit. Doctor Kirsch had told her this was normal: a baby almost every year would wear down anyone. Guttle had taken this as a challenge. She vowed to be an exception.

Amelia took Guttle's hands in hers. "I want you of all people to understand. Isidor has an exceptional mind. You know that. I just want him to use it, not just cut meat all day. I won't be able to make him happy until he's happy with himself. Is that so selfish?"

"You're a wise one, little sister. It reminds me of something you astonished me with when you were a child. You said Jews always go around in circles, because if they didn't, they would bump into a wall."

"I said that?"

"When you were seven years old. I just wonder how long you and Izzy can go around and around like a hora without getting dizzy. Without starting to hate each other."

"We would never do that."

"People do," Guttle said.

They'd been standing near the doorway. They stepped out of the way as ten-year-old Salomon struggled with a wheelbarrow filled with logs from the old cellar. As he tried to steer it into the vestibule, he lost control, the barrow toppled sideways and most of the logs spilled out. Salomon punched himself in the forehead with his fist, and began to retrieve the logs. Young Nathan, seven years old, who had been following along, stood watching.

"Help your brother," Guttle told him.

"If he had piled the logs like I said, they wouldn't have spilled."

Salomon pushed Nathan in the chest. The younger boy kicked his brother hard in the knee. Salomon fell to the floor, holding his knee, crying. Nathan began to pick up the logs and pile them in the wheelbarrow with precision.

Guttle and Amelia moved farther into the lane and turned their backs on the boys. "Nathan has a ruthless streak," Amelia said.

"Meyer can hardly wait to teach him finance. 'Isn't that rushing things,' I told Meyer. He said I shouldn't worry, each boy in turn, first Amschel when he turns twelve next month, then Salomon, only then Nathan. 'Already the boy loves arithmetic,' Meyer said. 'And he loves to be in charge. With that touch of meanness he has, Nathan is a born banker.'"

"It could be worse," Amelia said. "He could be a born butcher."

"Did I detect a subtle insult to my husband?"

"Guttle, I adore Meyer, you know that. Besides, he's not mostly a banker, he's mostly a dealer in antiquities. And an importer."

"Mostly."

"But do you know what he really is?" Amelia, brushing a lock of dark hair off of her eye, looked about to make sure no one was nearby. "Meyer is a small boy collecting coins. He always will be."

"He wouldn't like to hear that."

"I'm not telling him, I'm telling you."

"He's got six children, he would say. He makes a lot of money."

"No matter."

15 May, 1785

*M*y *dear Guttle:*

I am in receipt of your letter of 9 April. Thank you for your kind solicitations regarding my health. It is unlikely I will get the opportunity to visit the Judengasse next year, because the doctors, though they try to disguise their belief, do not think I shall last till Hanukah. I am being sickened by some sort of nerve disease which they can neither name nor cure. Their only prescription is rest, with which I am happy to oblige them, having no choice but to take to my bed each day around the noon hour. My mood is sanguine, however, because I view death not as an ending, as some people do, but as an opportunity to enter the afterlife that Moses promised. If Maimonides was right, that in time we become like the moon and the stars in our proximity to God, then why fear death at all?

Your comments about Isidor Kracauer confirm me in my intention. I shall explain. Over the years I have gathered a vast library of spiritual and philosophical works, as you might imagine. My dearest possession is my ancient copy of The Guide of the Perplexed, by Maimonides, whom I believe was the most insightful Jewish thinker of all; his writings certainly shaped my views. It is said that this copy was handled by the Rambam himself, though of this I have no proof. My son Joseph has given up his Hebrew studies — I am letting him go his own way, being no friend of coercion — so it would be foolish to leave this book to him when I am gone. Since your Isidor seems as Perplexed as anyone, and strongly in need of a guide, I plan to send him this treasured book as a gift; perhaps it will encourage him to return to his scholarship, and join the long line of Jewish thinkers.

Because I do not feel comfortable posting this irreplaceable book to a slaughterhouse, with all the possibilities of damage, I shall send the package to you, knowing you will get it to him.

I think you have hit the nail on the head, as your carpenter friend Yussel might say, in defining the difference between sorrow and suffering. As for the origin of that lingering inner state of sadness that we call sorrow, I think it is vital that each thinking man and woman seek the answer for themselves. It may be, indeed, that the correct answer is different for each of us.

Alas, my hand tires. I shall try to summarize briefly how I personally try to deal with both suffering and sorrow at this penultimate stage of my life. I choose from the systems of the philosophers that which will make me happier and at the same time can make me better. I rejoice in every religious custom which does not lead to intolerance and misanthropy; rejoice in every ceremony that has something true and good for its basis; endeavor as far as possible to eliminate the false, and abolish nothing until I am able to replace its good effect by something better.

Now I am back to bed, at noon. The Guide of the Perplexed I shall have Fromet send in a separate parcel. Please extend my warmest regards to your loving Meyer, to winsome Brendel, to generous Doctor Kirsch, to anyone else in your bustling lane who remembers me kindly.

        As always, your humble servant,
        Moses Mendelssohn

As Yussel Kahn turned the corner of Linden Street into the Heldenplatz, in Frankfurt, he stopped suddenly. He had been here hundreds of times before, but now he felt cold sweat break out on his forehead and a thumping begin in his chest, as he saw at an angle across the square a police wagon blocking the street in front of Johannes Gluck, Bookseller. Three more officers sat on horses that were standing impatiently, pawing the muddy cobbles, in front of and behind the wagon. Yussel shrank back against the window of a pawn shop and watched, his view partially blocked by the trunks of several lindens in the square. In two directions the foot traffic seemed almost normal. Bankers in dark coats and knee-breeches and silk hose and powdered wigs crossed the manure-strewn streets, lost in their important conversations; shoppers carried bolts of fabrics, or smaller packages, as they emerged from the stores. An ice wagon stood in front of an ale house while the driver, using large tongs, hauled an opaque block of ice inside. But a few people, he saw, had gathered near the police wagon, curious to see what had brought the Constables there. Yussel's first impulse was to join the little group and hope he would not be recognized. But that might be suicidal. His next impulse was to leave at once, to hurry back to the lane. But that would be cowardice, and would leave him dangling in ignorance. Rejecting both ideas, he stayed where he was, leaned against the window of the pawn shop like a bystander without any cares, and waited to see what would happen.

So it has come to this, he thought. After sixteen years, they have found out. He wondered how.

He thought painfully of Brendel, of her two boys, to whom he had become like a father. If he were arrested, imprisoned, how could he live apart from her, when she dwelled with loving and sensuous force in his soul? When the Chief Rabbi had approached him far in the past, he had been happy to accept the task, honored and excited. He was alone then, often in despair, his life a salacious daydream of pretty women half his age. This would be a chance to do something meaningful, he had decided, and his decision had felt right; even if he were some day to lose his life, as the Schul-Klopper had, it would be no great loss. But things were different now, with Brendel, with the boys. Now he did not choose to rot in prison, or to hang by his neck until dead.

The procedure had been so simple. The bookseller, who secretly sold Nahum Baum's poetry along with his Shakespeare and his Milton and his histories and his maps, was still willing. Widely read, he had long been outraged by the treatment of the Jews; as a matter of honor he was willing to continue taking a risk to help. Gluck had been in business for years, not far from the headquarters of the Frankfurt Constabulary, and had good relations with a sympathetic officer of the police or the judiciary — to this day Yussel did not know which; he never had needed to know. Twice each week Yussel had come to the Heldenplatz on business. Sometimes he would enter the book-seller's to buy glue for his carpentry, sometimes to purchase a book. Other times they just would chat, about public affairs, about an interesting new book that was being published. If he saw through the window that Gluck was busy with a customer, Yussel would just pass by — but only after glancing at the books in the window. In the center of the window was a low table on which there were always three books displayed — a Goethe, a Schiller, translations of Voltaire or Rousseau, the Holy Bible, whatever. What Yussel looked for was books about art. If any of the three books featured on the table was about a painter — Leonardo, Michelangelo, Rembrandt, it did not matter who — Yussel hurried back to the Judengasse, to the Chief Rabbi's study, and gave him the warning: the police would be raiding the Judengasse in the next few days. Both Yussel and Gluck believed that the risk of anyone noticing this obscure code was minimal.

So many years had passed without discovery that Yussel no longer thought about danger — until he came upon the police wagon and its two dray horses standing in front of the bookseller's shop. Had the police somehow discovered the officer among them who was sympathetic to the Jews? Had someone recognized the code? He had no notion of how they might have found out, but apparently they had.

His mind sizzled like oil in a hot iron pan as more people crowded around the police wagon to see what was happening. They were looking toward the shop. Officers must be inside. Did they know that he, Yussel, was the go-between? He did not think Gluck would tell them, Gluck was a gentleman who had become through the years a friend. But the Polizei, he knew, had ways to get information from even the most resisting soul.

An old, suppressed image came to mind: the music and gaiety of the Frankfurt Fair, of one particular Fair, of the gallows, of the blacksmith from Mainz. It always had been difficult to accept the connection, that this had been Brendel's husband, the father of her sons. Was that now to be the fate of the bookseller? Or of himself? He did not deny to himself that suddenly he was afraid. His fear was not so much for himself —the dead felt neither pain nor desire — but what would his arrest, and what might follow, do to Brendel? How could she withstand a second horror? Dear, sweet Brendel. And the boys — what would she tell her sons this time?

He saw a stirring in the crowd near the wagon, heard a murmuring. He inched his way further into the square, seeking a better view. Johannes Gluck, his gray hair thinning, wearing his usual gray apron, was being led out of his shop between two Constables, his hands bound behind him. Yussel watched with agony for his friend, head turned half away from the scene to hide his face, as the bookseller, under prodding by a Constable, climbed into the wagon. Yussel in the time it takes to turn a page in a book imagined what would happen in the next few seconds. Johannes Gluck standing in the wagon on the way to jail would realize what lay ahead: he would be tortured to reveal the names of his contacts — the high official who knew of the planned raids ahead of time, the man from the Judengasse to whom he informed. Johannes would want to endure neither the torture nor the inevitable betrayal; realizing this, he would find the right moment to leap from the wagon, run down the street; the pursuing officers would fire their muskets; blood would erupt like flowers all over his back; he would fall to the cobbles, to a satisfying death, a man with honor to the end. All this the bookseller would do in a moment, Yussel convinced himself.

His heart and breath were hurtling as if he himself were running down the street. But the bookseller was not. The horses slowly began to walk. The wheels of the wagon slowly began to turn, like the earth. Flanked by two officers holding muskets, the bookseller stared straight ahead.

Circling the Heldenplatz — the Place of Heroes, except that there were no statues of heroes, only three squat bases that stood truncated on the grassy center — as if the city had scoured the history of the Holy Roman Empire and found as yet no hero worthy of bronze — the police wagon came directly at Yussel. He turned to the wall, bent over, adjusted his hose, till the wagon with its human cargo had passed. As he bent the blood had rushed to his head, and now Yussel felt trapped in a fog. Were they, even now, looking for him in the lane? Should he hire a horse, flee to Berlin, or even further, to Vienna, and start another life? Should he risk going back, quickly sign over the shop to Georgi, explain the danger to Brendel and the boys, see if they wanted to come with him? Brendel surely would.

One decision came easily. He would not flee from here, without a proper farewell. If the police already were waiting for him... he would have to take that chance.

He started walking home. Shaken with every step, images created by his nerves drifted through his brain in many colors, like a patch of spent oil on the surface of the sewage ditch — slick purples, yellows, blues, greens, floating toward oblivion with the muck.

While Yussel walked home, uncertain of the future, Izzy sat beside Amelia in the Rothschild parlor, to discuss with Guttle and Meyer his own plans for the future. He was not wearing his butcher's apron. His blonde hair no longer stood up like a wheat field, but lay flat on his head, and had begun to darken. This had happened several years before, literally overnight. One night he had stolen his first kiss from Amelia, and the next morning he had awakened with altered hair, a change that no one could explain. In his years at the butcher shop his chest and arms had thickened, which Amelia liked, and his hands were acquiring a permanent bloody tint, which she didn't.

Receiving the Guide of the Perplexed from Moses Mendelssohn — the philosopher's own copy, possibly even handled by the Rambam himself — had had a profound effect, Izzy told them. He had decided he had been put on earth by Yahveh to do Jewish scholarship; that's how he must spend the rest of his life.

"So I have made plans," he said firmly, trying to sound like the man of thirty he now was, though he still appeared much younger, and often acted so. Holding the hand of Amelia, who was blushing, and looking at Guttle, he went on, "Because you were responsible for my receiving the book, Guttle, I want you to be the first to know." He felt pressure on his palm from Amelia. "Well, not exactly the first. Amelia knows." She squeezed his hand again. "And Meyer knows." He saw Guttle give Meyer a questioning look, as she wondered what her husband had held back from her. Amelia dug her fingernails into Izzy's palm. "And my two brothers also know. And my mother, of course. And Rabbi Simcha. But besides them, I want you to be the first."

"I'm honored," Guttle said.

Smiling slightly, she thought: so they have overcome their fears at last. Loving each other for so long — since they were children and Amelia used to follow Izzy's Pied Piper of a Schul-Klopper through the lane — each as they grew older silently becoming terrified of joining together as man and wife — each making profound excuses behind which to hide. How many times have I wanted to tell them they were merely afraid, that they should look within themselves, that they should confess their concerns to each other? How many times have I held back, my mouth tightly shut, deciding they must face and accept and subdue their trepidations on their own, without my interference — when they were ready to, and not before. Perhaps, now, they are ready.

"Here are my plans," Izzy was saying. "You know that when my father died he left the slaughterhouse in three equal shares, to me, Eli and Aaron, even though I am running it. And he left their feather business in three shares as well. I have agreed to trade my share of the slaughterhouse, which makes good money, to my brothers, in return for their two shares of the feather business, which is going bankrupt, now that nearly everyone in the lane has feather beds."

"It wasn't Meyer who gave you this business advice, of that I'm sure," Guttle said.

"As a matter of fact, Meyer worked it out for us. He has agreed to buy the feather business from me."

Again Guttle looked at Meyer, furrowing her brow. A dying feather business? Had he lost his senses? Her husband's features betrayed only slight amusement at her puzzled look.

"Meyer plans to close the feather shop and use the space for his office," Izzy continued. "He needs more room, now that he'll be taking Amschel into the business. Also, he will have more storage space for imports."

Guttle had not taken her eyes off Meyer. "Again I'm honored that I'm the first to know."

She had been aware of Meyer's hopes, of course — but not of this sudden reality.

"With the money from Meyer," Izzy said, "and with whatever dowry your father sees fit to provide, Amelia and I will be married. She will remain here in the lane while I go away for a year to a rabbinical school — one that Rabbi Simcha will suggest. To be taken seriously as a scholar, I need to be a Rabbi."

Guttle looked at each of their faces. "It's amazing what can go on in the lane right under one's nose. In a single day."

"Everyone always asks your advice," Izzy said. "We decided it was time we made decisions on our own."

Adjusting her skirt more comfortably on the love seat, Amelia said, "This was after we couldn't find you anywhere."

"I was at the cemetery with Mama," she said. "Little Benjy would have been eighteen today." She reached into her skirt pocket for her handkerchief, but did not withdraw it, merely grasped it. "Mama wouldn't leave. For a time she didn't know where she was. We could hear the river running. She thought we were on a boat. She thought that if we left the cemetery we would drown." Hidden in her pocket, her fist was squeezing the handkerchief with force, squeezing away the tears she refused to let form in her eyes. "But back to your news. You're telling me all this now, because?"

"We're asking your approval," Amelia said.

"You don't need my approval for any of it. For marriage, you need Papa's approval."

"Oh, I forgot to mention," Izzy said. "Your father also knows."

Guttle felt her tears welling up, despair for her mother — today had been the worst episode by far — overwhelmed by joy for her sister. She sat on the love seat beside Amelia, forcing Izzy to move to the edge, and hugged her close. "I'm so happy for you," she said. And to Izzy, "You don't deserve her — making her wait this long."

"I didn't make her wait. She made... "

Meyer stood and shook Izzy's hand. "The Schnapper girls have a strange sense of humor. You'll get used to it.'"

"Get used to it? I've been suffering barbs from Guttle since we were kids. I never get used to it." He turned to his betrothed. "But no more waiting. Let's go to Simcha and choose a school for Rabbis."

"And a wedding date." To Guttle she said, "Papa is leaving the date up to us."

"He's growing soft, it appears." Because of Mama, she knew; the little rules didn't matter any more.

"It's thanks to you, Guttle. He said to us last night, 'Guttle made a good match with Meyer. Soon he'll be richer than I am. That's why Avra could have her starving artist. That's why you can have your starving scholar. When you need money, you'll be able to turn to Rothschild, instead of your poor old Papa.'"

Guttle grinned and said, "He was joking."

"I'm not so sure," Meyer said drily.

When her sister and Izzy had gone, Guttle led Meyer to the loveseat, and they sat together, Meyer's arm around her shoulder. "Did you see how happy they are?" she said.

"She'll make a beautiful rebbetzin."

"Thank you for helping them. It's a mitzvah."

"You think so? A feather-business in my cap?"

"For that, you owe me a kiss."

"Maybe two," Meyer said.

"It all happened so fast. My head is buzzing like a fly."

"Are you angry that you weren't consulted?"

"A little. But the news is so good — I would have to be a sourpuss to show it."

"Once Izzy made up his mind, they were like wild horses to figure things out."

From the floor above, the sound of violins stumbled down the stairs, burrowed through the ceiling, music, noise, a battle between the two. The three eldest children, Schönche, Amschel and Salomon, all were learning to play the violin, and, hearing the guests leave, had begun to practice, all at once, in a manner sure to claim attention. The sweet melody of Schönche's Mozart sonata — his newest, recently published — struggled to hold its line against the ragged scales of the boys. Skinny Nathan came racing down the stairs, the index finger of each hand pressed into his ear, and threw himself to his knees in front of his parents. "Mama, Papa, make them stop," he pleaded, popping his blue eyes wide in aesthetic pain.

"Sometimes," Meyer said, "I wish we had room for a piano."

Guttle winced at a particularly sour note in the fiddle cacophony that was pouring down upon them like an indoor storm. "Have you heard Rebecca play? She plays beautifully. She learned as a child in Berlin." Guttle glanced around the living room. "If not a piano, perhaps we could fit a harp. I would love to learn."

His fingers having made his point, Nathan stretched out at their feet on the dark green rug, which contrasted starkly with his head of curly auburn hair.

"Your friend Marie Antoinette plays the harp," Meyer said

Abruptly, Guttle raised her cheek from his chest. "How do you know about her?"

"That she plays a harp?"

"That she's my friend."

"Sometimes, when you think I'm asleep, you speak to her."

"You listen? That's very rude."

How could that be? In sleep, she knew, he descended so deep into the night world that the entire Judengasse could burn and he would not awaken. While she would be roused from slumber by the slightest cough of one of her children two stories above.

"The bed is very small, Guttela."

"Have you heard anything you shouldn't have?"

"Not that I'm aware."

Guttle rubbed a hand across her eyes, feeling foolish. "You must think I'm still a child."

"Not at all. Friends are good." He kissed her lightly on the forehead. "Especially royalty."

Guttle punched his knee, reached down, pulled Nathan up onto her lap.

"They're still playing," the boy whined.

"What about you? What instrument would you like to play?"

"If I absolutely had to?"

She pressed a spiraling curl into place among the others. "If you absolutely had to."

"Artillery!" Bouncing on her lap, he yanked at an imaginary cord. "Cha-boom!"

Meyer could not help laughing. He rumpled the boy's hair.

"Don't encourage him," Guttle said.

Then it happened, as it happened so often — his hair — the color, the exact auburn shade as Dvorah's — whom she had not seen since she walked out of the ghetto nine years ago — Dvorah, who had cast her aside — or whom she had cast aside, no longer was she sure which — whom she would never see again — whom she was doing everything possible to forget, which was the only sane thing to do — the running together on the ramparts of childhood, the secret giddy laughter, the mutual nakedness of the mikveh, the birth of children, whom they had assumed would be raised like cousins — the total trust, the love — all this memory encapsulated in a vibrant shade of auburn. How was a woman to cut off the past, when the past lived on in the hair of her own child?

Guttle pressed her lips to the offending locks.

Meyer knew well the look that now sculpted his wife's face — the stillness of white marble, a visage of a long-gone Greek, of a bereaved sister looking out to sea. "It's returned?" he murmured, with sympathy.

Her chin remained pressed to the boy's hair. She closed her eyes, tightly.

"Who knocks?"

"Good evening, rebbetzin. I need to see the Rabbi."

"He's sick in bed, Yussel. I thought everybody knows that."

"I wouldn't disturb him, but it's important."

"Everybody's problem is always important. Go see Simcha, he's important, too."

"Rabbi Simcha doesn't know about this. Only your husband knows. There may be danger to the lane."

"Danger? Danger he would want to know about. I'll go make him ready. But this had better be serious danger."

He found Rabbi Eleazar in a dark bedroom with blankets hung over the windows, the only illumination a candle on a bedside table. The Rabbi's head was propped up on three pillows. His face was haggard, his eyes seemed watery in the flickering light.

"Rabbi, I hope you're feeling better," Yussel said.

"Better?" The Chief Rabbi's stentorian voice was weak, cracked, like a bass fiddle left too close to a fire. "Better I won't be feeling till I get to the afterlife. I know that, Berkov knows that. Now you know that. So tell me what's happened. What danger?"

Yussel described the scene of the policemen taking away the bookseller.

"After, what, sixteen years, they found out?" he said. "How?"

"I don't know, Rabbi. The question is, what to do?"

"Do they know about you?"

"I don't know."

"Will the bookseller tell? He will if they torture him." His voice was increasingly hoarse. "You want me to say whether you should stay or run away? I don't know the answer. At least it's a choice. Poor Solomon Gruen, peace be upon him, never had a choice."

"You still believe he was killed because of that?"

The Rabbi twisted his torso beneath the covers, reached with difficulty to his bedside table, lifted a glass of water. His hand trembled as he raised it to his lips, and drank. He had trouble reaching the table again. Yussel took the glass from his shaking hand and set it down on the wet circle where it had been.

"I have always believed that," the Rabbi said, his voice smoothed by the water. "Only one thing kept me from being certain. Why was the bookseller not seized at the same time? They would have tortured Solomon to learn his source. Still, I recruited you, and put you at risk."

"I had no family then. I was honored to be chosen."

"Now this. You never know what Frankfurt will do." He made a dismissive motion with his hand, as if in disgust. Yussel had never noticed how gnarled it was. "For some reason they preferred not to bring charges last time. Not to have a trial. Just to poison him. I have a suspicion why, but it doesn't matter."

"Perhaps it does matter. Will you tell me?"

"No. I don't know what to advise you, Yussel, it was always a risk. What you did all these years was wonderful. Who knows how much trouble you saved the people in the lane? How many beatings, or worse, were avoided? I won't even describe what the Constables used to do in the old days, if they found a violation. Now, without the bookseller… I suppose nothing can be done. Anyway, that will soon be up to my successor, Jonah or Simcha".

"Everyone expects the new Chief Rabbi will be Rabbi Simcha," Yussel said. "He's been your assistant for so long."

"Not everyone expects. You young people expect. Simcha is very modern. The old people like Jonah better. He's been head of the yeshiva for many years. That's what I'm waiting for. To hear who is chosen."

"To hear? Rabbi, it's you who chooses."

The Rabbi's dry lips formed a slight smile. He winced, and Yussel could imagine the cutting discomfort. "You think my mind is going, eh Yussel? It is not me who chooses. I am only the messenger. It is Yahweh who chooses."

Yussel did not know what to say. He felt better than when he had entered this dark room; his mind had been distracted from the bookseller. From his own fate.

"That's all I'm waiting for," the Rabbi said wearily. "For Yahweh to tell me. Then I will give the word, and move on."

"Rabbi, I need to discuss my situation with someone. I need advice. I can't keep it secret anymore."

"Tell whomever you trust. May Adonai look after you, Yussel Kahn. Now I must rest, and listen for His word."

Yussel stood, and turned to leave.

"But one more thing, Yussel. Maybe it's not what you think. Maybe they arrested the bookseller for something else, something less important. Maybe he killed his wife."

"I don't think he killed his wife."

"Well, we can always hope," the Rabbi said.

41

The four walls were solid stone, without windows. The ceiling was thick spruce. The floor was hard earth, upon which a thin mattress had been thrown. The only illumination was a single candle. The only furnishing beyond the mattress and the candleholder was a chamber pot. Stretched on the mattress, naked, his head near a corner, Yussel could touch two of the intersecting walls. They were cold and damp.

I am Odysseus, who spied for the Greeks against the Trojans. Now I am trapped in this island cave, a prisoner of the beautiful Calypso. I can hear the sea sloshing, teasing my desire to escape. Seven years I am doomed to be imprisoned here. Some would call it Paradise. We make love, a goddess and a man. Yet it is a prison still. I long for home, for my fair Penelope. I feel her breath, as if she were here with me.

Asleep in his arms, Brendel stirred. He pulled the rough sheet higher over her naked form, against the chill of the cellar. Her blonde ringlets whispered against his arm as she slept, like daffodils. He could feel each apple breath on his skin against the fetid smell of the earthen floor.

Water sloshed in the well beneath the pump in the vestibule. At least, he thought, I am not in the Frankfurt prison across the river, with its stone rats and vermin and sadistic guards. Before they take me there, shall I flee?

I am Socrates, convicted of treason, condemned to die in three days. Crito visits me in prison, urges me to escape. It would not take much money to buy off certain people, he says, and he has plenty. No. I shall not try to escape my prison. There is no time when injustice is justified. It is wrong to answer injustice with injustice. And surely, to bribe my captors so that they let me escape, is an injustice. I shall die as I have lived, unafraid. If hemlock is my fate, so be it. I shall drink it without pause. I shall not run.

"What will you do?" Brendel had asked, her eyes rimmed red from her tears. "Where will you go? How will I find you? When could you come back? Should I go with you?"

"I won't leave you," he had said, "except at the point of a sword."

"Perhaps you could hide, till they forget." She implored him. "We need advice from clearer minds."

Her legs could hardly support her as she clung to him, as they walked slowly along the cobbles in the falling dusk.

"We could hide you," Guttle had said.

"I will not hide."

"Just for tonight," Brendel pleaded. "Till we see if they come. So we can think."

"Perhaps they will accept payment to leave you be," Meyer said. "It would profit them more than putting you in prison."

"And if they rejected your bribe? You would join me in an adjacent cell. Bribing an officer of the law is also considered treason. I won't let you take that risk."

"You could hide in our cellar, at least tonight," Guttle said. "I'll throw a rug over the trap door. There's already a mattress, the boys sometimes play down there."

"I have to be with him tonight! What if it's our last night together?" The tears cascaded down Brendel's cheeks. She did not wipe them away.

"I'll give you a key," Guttle said, wrapping her arms around her trembling friend.

I am Boethius, in my Italian prison cell, under sentence of death. The charges of treason are false. But soft, here is the fair Philosophy, come to comfort me. "You are complaining of your condition, your treatment by Fortune. But it is your attitude that makes things seem wretched. Endure all with a calm mind and you will find yourself blessed." "How can I feel blessed, imprisoned as I am?" Philosophy says, "Men seek riches, gems, beautiful clothes, which are good only in themselves and do not extend their goodness to their possessor. All other creatures of God are satisfied by their own intrinsic good; only humans, who should be above other creatures, lower themselves to seek value in worthless things. You all seek happiness, which indeed is the highest good. Happiness is to desire nothing further." I reply, "I do not desire further — only not to be separated from the woman I love." Consolation of Philosophy, I call the book that I am writing in prison. But do I still find consolation after they twist a cord around my forehead tighter and tighter, until my eyes pop? And then, without trial or evidence, summon an executioner, who clubs me in body and head until I am dead?

"What if they stick you in that prison across the river?" Brendel had asked. "Will they let me see you? What if they hang you!"

"It won't be like that." He had tried to assure her, unable to assure himself. "I'll have an advocate. I' ll have a trial. They'll see what a piddling thing it was, to get early notice of inspections. Who was hurt by it?"

To himself, he said: they will paint it as a corruption of the system. Therein will they find their treason.

Brendel sniffled, wiped her cheek with the back of her hand, smearing the tears. "The old Schul-Klopper. Before I came to the lane. Did he have an advocate? A trial?"

Yussel looked at the dark green rug. None of them dared to answer.

Reaching out in the cellar, he felt again the cold of the stone behind his head. His hand recoiled, as if he had touched his own mortality.

Odysseus, Socrates, Boethius. Living these thousand years in poetry, in dialogues, in their own philosophies. Who will mourn the death of a carpenter?

"Why did the Chief Rabbi need a spy?" Guttle asked.

She and Meyer were standing on the terrace behind the vestibule — another rare attraction of the Green Shield. There had not been enough room for a second house to be built in the rear — just enough for a small structure that housed a privy, and a small room, in which the girls played house. The high ghetto wall separated the terrace from the city, but the view of the sky was wider here than in the lane, and Guttle liked to come out at night to look at the stars — which, according to Mendelssohn, knew God. Sometimes, when she was alone, she talked to them.

Meyer, gazing at a three-quarter moon high in the night sky, replied, "My father used to tell me how, in the old days, the police would storm through the lane unannounced, carrying clubs, and beat up anyone who was violating the law. Some of the beatings were quite severe. Eleazar is old enough to remember them. I imagine he determined that so long as he was Chief Rabbi, we would not be surprised again."

"Was it worth it to risk Yussel's life?"

"Perhaps not. But who knows what terrible sight might be burned into Eleazar's brain?"

"What do you think will happen?"

"I think Yussel should leave, before the police come. But he's stubborn, and proud. I don't think he will."

"He and Brendel could go together. With her boys. To Berlin, maybe. There's no ghetto there."

"Isn't that where Dvorah is living?"

"She's isn't Dvorah any more."

"I know how you feel, Guttela. I... "

"That's not what I meant. I mean she's changed her name."

"Changed her name? How do you know?"

"From her mother. We still don't speak, but every time I pass near, she makes sure she's telling someone, in a loud voice, about what a grand life Dvorah has in Berlin. Her big house, with a marble staircase and a grand ballroom, where they have parties that last until morning, and fancy dress balls thick with nobility. 'My daughter, the Countess,' Hannah says, so proudly. She thinks people here are impressed."

"No doubt some of them are."

"She's calls herself Countess Madeleine von Brunwald."

"Madeleine?"

"There's not one thing remaining of the girl I used to love."

Meyer put his arm around her shoulder. "I think there is one thing."

"And what is that?"

"Your love."

She pulled away from him. "Have you been reading my diary?"

"You ask me such a thing? In all the years since I gave you that first empty book, I have never once looked. What do you have now, a dozen books? That's your private domain. You think I don't respect that?"

"I have sixteen books."

"I don't have to read your books, you know. After all these years, I can read your face."

"Not always."

"Always about Dvorah. But what is that sly look you're giving me?"

"Some things you never guess until I tell you."

As he studied her face, his jaw fell open. "Guttela! You're pregnant!"

Looking up at the stars, she spoke to a particularly bright one. "I have to admit, he's getting to know me better."

His arms encircled her waist while she still gazed heavenward. Perhaps it was not a star, it did not twinkle like one. Perhaps it was a planet. Venus.

"What's wrong?" she asked.

"For a moment, I wanted to dance. Now that we have our own dance floor, under the sky. Isn't that terrible? For a moment I forgot about Yussel, and the police. The mind tries to flee from such things."

Chastely, he kissed her cheek.

"I, too, just had an awful thought," Guttle said. "While I was looking at that star. Or maybe it's a wonderful thought. I'm not sure."

"How can you not be sure?"

"If I was Brendel… if I was afraid the police might take Yussel away… the thought struck me that, down in the cellar, they might have started a baby."

Meyer took her hand. Together in silence, slowly, they walked the length of the terrace to the ghetto wall, their sharp moon shadows beside them, rippling on the terrace stones. Guttle touched the wall, peered along its base. "Is there someplace we can buy good earth?"

"How do you mean, earth?"

"Fertile soil."

"I imagine Zig Zigmund could get some, where he buys his hay. What for?"

"I want to fill pots with earth, and plant flowers out here."

"Will they receive enough sunlight to live?"

"I'm not sure. It's like getting pregnant. We plant a seed, and take our chances."

"Shhhh. Don't talk like that."

"It's all right, Meyer, it's just the truth. We both know that by now."

He put a finger to her lips, and held her close.

After a few moments, Guttle said, "Wait a minute! That must be what he meant."

"What who meant?"

"What you said before, about how the Chief Rabbi may have seen people beaten. I can never forget what he told me when I found the Schul-Klopper's body. He said, 'Perhaps he died that another might live.' I always assumed he meant some specific person. But it must have been because of his spying — that he died because of that, and maybe someone in the lane — anyone — was not killed because of that."

"It makes sense."

"Yes, it does."

"What's the matter? You look sad."

"Not sad. Wistful, perhaps. It was more mysterious the other way. More romantic. When I took it as a prediction. About a certain unknown individual."

"Unfortunately, life is not romantic."

"You think not?" She took his hand, her eyes returning to the stars. "Perhaps it depends on how we view it."

"Do you think I've grown too pragmatic?" He drew her hand to his lips, kissed it, then kissed her temple. "Lucky for me, you are romantic enough for both of us."

Leading him toward the house, her gaze still exploring the night sky, Guttle said, "It's time we went to bed. Don't you agree?"

With his eyes open, Rabbi Avram Eleazar could not see Adonai; only with his eyes closed could he see Adonai. At such times, he could see that Adonai was invisible.

Angels, on the other hand, were not invisible, just difficult to see with his eyes closed — which was the only time they appeared. Once he passed away, he assumed, this would change; that's how he would know he was dead.

His eyes were closed now, his head resting on his pillows, while in the kitchen Gilda heated chicken soup; he had been able to eat nothing else for days.

When he heard the voice, he was elated and frightened at once.

"Sorry to bother you, Rabbi, but it is time for you to choose."

The voice sounded familiar. He could barely discern a shape in the misty blue field behind his eyes. "Who speaks to me like that? Who gives me orders?"

"It is the cherub Leo."

"The cherub Leo? I've never heard of a cherub Leo."

"Tell him your whole name. There are a thousand Leos." This voice was feminine, and sounded further away.

"It is the cherub Leo Liebmann."

"Leo Liebmann? From the Judengasse? Good for you, Leo! And whose was that other voice I heard?"

"You heard? She's not supposed to talk to humans. That was the angel Yetta."

"Angel? You mean your Yetta is not yet a cherub?"

"What can I tell you?" the cherub Leo said.

The voice in the background spoke up. "Tell him the truth. You'd better."

"The truth is, an angel is higher than a cherub."

"How can they be higher?"

"Cherubs can talk to humans. Angels can talk to God."

"Leo, if angels can talk to Yahweh, have Yetta ask Him about the Judengasse. How much longer before the gates go away?"

"She asked him the first day she was here. He has it under consideration."

"Under consideration? It's been three hundred and fifteen years already."

"It seems He has many things to consider. Which reminds me of why I'm talking to you. It's time for you to pick your new Chief Rabbi. If you understand what I mean."

"I'm afraid I understand. So tell me, does death hurt?"

"No need to be afraid. Just name Rabbi Simcha as your choice, and you can join us, without pain."

"Simcha? Why Rabbi Simcha? He's much too modern. My choice is Rabbi Jonah."

"You don't understand how it works, Rabbi. I thought you would. Yahweh's choice is Rabbi Simcha."

"That's the wrong choice. How do you know that's Yahweh's choice? You just said you can't speak to Him."

"Yahweh told the angel Yetta. She instructed me to tell you."

"It's a mistake. Let me speak to Him."

"Speak to Yahweh? I just told you, only angels speak to Him. You tell me. I tell the angel Yetta. Yetta tells Yahweh."

"Only if it's important," he heard her voice in the background say.

"The new Chief Rabbi? Of course it's important. Listen, Leo, tell Yetta to tell Yahweh that I'm choosing Rabbi Jonah. Tell Him I'm closer to the situation."

"Closer than Adonai?"

"Just tell Him."

"He might not appreciate it."

"I'm still the Chief Rabbi, am I not? Jonah will do just fine."

"Jonah will do what fine?" The voice was Gilda's as she carried into the room a bowl of hot soup.

"You heard me, rebbetzin?"

"You were talking in your sleep."

"I wasn't sleeping."

"Have it your way. Look, I brought you some nice soup, to make you well."

The Rabbi thought: It's decided now. I won't be getting well. But there's no need to alarm Gilda. Instead, he told her, "The soup is delicious."

"You haven't tasted it yet," Gilda said.

"You can't ask him, of course," Guttle had said. "But you can tell him that if he happened to be interested, you would be interested. But if not, then to ignore what you said. He'll be flattered, without having to give a direct answer."

Rebecca hugged Guttle, kissed her cheek. "I wished I'd had the nerve to speak with you last week. I bought a bottle of this new wine from France — champagne, they call it. I was going to ask him then. But I became frightened. What if he has no such thoughts about me? I would feel like a fool. So I sat all through dinner and I didn't dare."

"Nothing's lost," Guttle said. "You'll tell him tonight. If he becomes Chief Rabbi, he ought to have a wife."

"Wife. The word alone sends chills through my body. I'm thirty-nine years old. What were you, sixteen when you married? I think it's easier then."

Guttle smiled at Rebecca's flushed cheek. The Doctor seemed to be a young girl again. "You'll be fine."

"If he's interested."

"You can only let him know your feelings. I would think he would know them already, but with men you can never tell. Sometimes they wear blinders, like a horse. Once you open his eyes, it's up to him. I never asked why you preferred to be alone all these years. And I never asked him. About some things you don't pry."

"My work."

"I know. And his work. But Lev got married."

"Look what happened."

Guttle had turned away to look at the river. Rebecca's eyes followed. With much shouting, sailors were hauling up the anchor on a large two-masted sailing ship that would be setting off towards the Rhine, its cargo to Frankfurt delivered.

The tea water was boiling. The bubbling brought Rebecca back to the moment. Simcha was in the dining room. She removed the kettle from the stove — and heard a knocking at the front door.

"Who could that be?" she said to Simcha as she passed, wiping her hands on a dish rag. She opened the door to find Brendel standing there, looking agitated, her hair disheveled.

"Rebecca, is Georgi in his room?"

"I think so."

"I need to run up and see him for a moment. It won't take long."

"Is something wrong?"

"No. Yes. I can't talk now. Can I go on up?"

"Of course."

The Doctor stepped aside as Brendel hurried by. Her feet flew lightly up two flights. Rebecca heard her knock on Georgi's door, exchange a few sentences with him. When Brendel came down, looking about for Rebecca, she found her in the dining room.

"Oh! I didn't know you had company. Good evening, Rabbi. I'm sorry to interrupt."

"It's not a problem," Rebecca said. "We're about to have tea. And some of your mun cake. Would you like to join us?"

"I wish I could. But I have to go now."

She turned and was out through the door before they could ask her anything else.

"What was that about?" Simcha wondered.

"I don't know. I've never seen Brendel so flustered. Something is wrong."

"She went up to see Georgi, so it must be about the shop."

"Perhaps. But why didn't Yussel come?"

Neither had an answer. Rebecca returned to the kitchen and poured two glasses of tea. She set them on the table. Simcha sliced off a piece of cake, yellow cake marbled with poppy seed mun, and put it on a plate for her, took a slice for himself.

"So," Rebecca said. Her stomach was thumping as if it had a heart of its own. Now was the time, she thought, if ever she was going to speak.

"Emil…"

"Rebecca…"

They had spoken at the same time. Both of them smiled.

"You first," Simcha said.

Rebecca could hardly speak. "No, you first. You're my guest."

"Very well. I have an important question I want to ask you." Simcha sipped at his tea.

Her blood was pounding in her ears, her wrists, her groin. For a moment she closed her eyes. Perhaps Yahweh was being kind, and she would not have to confess her feelings first. She glanced at the framed drawing on the wall behind Simcha's head, Hiram's charcoal sketch of she and Brendel whirling about at Guttle's wedding. Her heart was whirling even faster now. Where, she asked herself, has the calm and competent Doctor gone? My body is acting sixteen.

"I have been thinking about marriage," Simcha said.

Yes! Her heart wanted to sing out the news like a songbird heralding the dawn; she still remembered such sounds. Yes! She kept her trembling hands beneath the table.

"I know that will sound strange to you. I'm fifty-one years old, I never thought to wed."

"Not at all," she managed to say, her voice sounding to herself like a dry rasp, plaster being ripped off a wound.

"But some think I may soon become the Chief Rabbi."

"Of course you will."

"Not necessarily. Rabbi Jonah is of the old school, the same as Rabbi Eleazar. I think he will be the choice."

"Jonah is almost as old as Eleazar."

"He still has a few years left, I would imagine. The point is, I've thought about it, and decided that the Chief Rabbi, whomever he is, ought to have a wife. He would seem more solid, more trustworthy, with a wife behind him. Then I thought more, and decided that whether I am named Chief Rabbi or not, Emil Simcha ought to have a wife. It's time."

She didn't trust herself to speak.

"I was wondering how you feel about that."

"About you taking a wife? If you want to, I think it would be wonderful!"

"Good." He bit into the soft cake, chewed, swallowed. "I don't need your permission, of course, but we've become quite close, and I wanted to see how you felt."

Permission?

"Several times now I have had lunch with the widow Baumgarten. Thelma, her name is. The food was fine. Her house is very clean. She is a bit on the portly side, compared to you, for instance— "

Compared to me...

" —but I think she would do nicely as a Rabbi's wife. Should I become Chief Rabbi, I would need someone to keep that large house clean. And to cook dinner for guests. The Chief Rabbi must entertain, after all. So I am planning to ask Thelma tomorrow if she will marry me. I wanted you to be the first to know."

Rebecca gripped the table, trying to stop the room from spinning. To gain time, to think straight, she tried to drink some tea, but her hand was trembling on the glass.

"I'm glad you have no problem with that," Simcha said.

"Why would I have a problem?" She was sure her voice was quivering, but he seemed not to notice.

"Of course, we'll still be friends, you and I." He took another bite of cake. "You want to hear something funny?" His mouth was half full of mun. "When I first got the idea to marry... " He swallowed the chewed cake "... I thought of you."

The intake of her breath was sharp, as if someone had grabbed a private part of her. She coughed, to cover the sound.

"Then I had to laugh at myself. Imagine, Doctor Kirsch cleaning house for me, while her patients wait at the hospital. Imagine her scrubbing floors on her knees, instead of cleaning people's wounds. How selfish could I be?"

Rebecca said nothing.

"You're being quiet. I was not wrong, was I? You would not want to dust my house and scrub my floors, would you?"

She forced a smile. "I would not."

"Or wash my shirts and things? Of course you wouldn't."

"I have my work at the hospital. I think that's more important."

"Exactly. That's what I told myself. That's when I decided on Thelma. She and I don't converse as you and I do, but she's a good woman. She has children already, they're grown, so we won't have to deal with that part. Me with my scar and the pits on my face, it's just as well."

Rebecca pictured the bottle of champagne, leaning alongside the block of ice in the ice box. Her fingers felt at least as cold. She was holding her emotions rigid, as if they were not fluid, but brittle bones; as she did before scraping a gangrenous leg, while her assistants fought to hold the patient still. She had last done that ... was it only yesterday?

"I'm sure she'll make a good wife," Rebecca said.

"I'm happy to hear you say that." He placed his napkin on the table. "Thank you for a wonderful dinner, as always." He stood. "But now I must be going. It's getting late, we wouldn't want people to talk."

"We wouldn't want that," she said, escorting him to the door.

"Good night, Doctor," he said, as he stepped into the lane.

"Good night, Rabbi."

The freshet of night air that swept in from the river felt good, but she did not want to go into the lane. Closing the door behind him, she returned to the dining room, took up the tea glasses and the cake plates and carried them to the kitchen. She would wash them in the morning. She pictured again the champagne; she could pop it open, a bit of alcohol would be relaxing. But the whole bottle would make her sick, and once she started, she might not stop. Turning down the lamps until the flames died, she climbed the stairs to her bedroom, took off her shoes, her stockings, her dress, her corset. In her pale blue shift she lay on top of her quilt, breathing evenly, looking at the ceiling.

Scrubbing floors. Washing shirts. At least she hadn't made a fool of herself.

On the floor above her, Georgi Pinsky also lay on top of his quilt, staring at the ceiling, thinking again and again of what Brendel had said to him. "When you open the shop in the morning, Yussel won't be there. If the police come looking for him, tell them you don't know where he is. Nothing else. You don't know where he is."

That was all. She wouldn't answer questions. She said she couldn't, not yet.

"I don't know where he is."

What would the police want with Yussel?

"Rabbi, it's me, the cherub Leo. I have a message."

"From Yahweh?"

"The angel Yetta informed Yahweh that you were planning to choose Rabbi Jonah. Yahweh had an idea — He's good at that sometimes. He instructed Yetta to tell me to tell you that since He created man with free will, you are free to choose whomever you desire. You may select Rabbi Jonah over Rabbi Simcha, if that's what you want."

"I knew He would be reasonable. We've always been on good terms, Yahweh and I."

"Wait, I'm not finished. Yahweh said I should ask you whether, since He created man in His image, that means that He, Yahweh, also has free will."

"Of course it does. Who could have more free will than Adonai?"

"Good. Because He said that if you choose Rabbi Jonah as the new Chief Rabbi, He, Yahweh, will strike Jonah dead. On the instant."

"On the instant?"

"That's what He said."

"You mean, with lightning, like in the Bible?"

"Lightning He finds too dramatic nowadays. An affliction of the heart, most likely."

"He would do that?"

"Joking He wasn't."

"That's some free will I have."

"The choice remains yours, Yahweh said."

"Tell Yetta to thank Him for me."

The Rabbi's irony was lost on the cherub.

"Once you announce your successor, you'll be able tell Him yourself."

"Tell Him myself? I thought only angels…"

"Are you listening to me? You will be able to tell him yourself, angel Avram."

"Angel Avram?"

"Dummkopf!" It was the female voice in the distance.

"Oy, vey. I wasn't supposed to tell you yet."

"That's all right, I won't tell a soul. I'll die quicker, before He changes his mind. But I wouldn't tell anyone."

"What wouldn't you tell anyone?" Gilda asked, carrying in a small bowl of porridge, to see if he could keep it down.

"Sit, Gilda, sit. Have I got news!"

"About the new Chief Rabbi?"

"That, too."

The candle had burned out during the night, and Brendel awoke in a darkness more complete than she had ever known. Not a morsel of light penetrated the stone cellar, not even along the edges of the trap door, which Guttle had covered with a rug. At first she had no remembrance of where she was. Normally happy and eager upon awakening, she sat up slowly, filled with an undefined grief from the past. She tried to wriggle from under it, as she wriggled her long legs from under the sheet that covered her. Reaching out, touching a cold stone wall, she was shocked into the present, the danger to Yussel. Only then did she hear him snoring. The absence of light had banished time, but her body had grown used to waking when it was the hour to go the Café and light the wood stove to bake her daily breads. Yussel's snores, too, were an indicator of morning; he only snored towards dawn, on those mornings when inner anguish had kept him awake through the night. Patting about in the dark, seeking her undergarments, her hand touched the candleholder. Her fingers found the tin of matches. Wick enough remained on the candle to hold a flame as she dressed, climbed the steps to the trap door, managed to push it open despite the weight of the rug that covered it. Yussel still was snoring as she left the cellar and lowered the door beneath her.

Her body had been true to the time, much like a sleeping animal's. Dawn had awoken, the lane was lurching to life as she clutched her shawl around her and hurried to the Café. A few steps ahead of her she saw Rebecca, dressed in black, as she walked to the hospital. Brendel strode quickly, tugged at the Doctor's sleeve. When Rebecca turned, she seemed at first not to recognize her friend, as if her mind was far away, as if she was in a trance.

"Are you all right?" Brendel asked. "You look as if you're grieving."

"I'm fine," Rebecca said, clearing her throat of morning phlegm. "But you — you've been crying."

Brendel shook her head, not wanting to speak of Yussel. She kissed Rebecca's cheek and hurried on towards the Café, wondering what was wrong with the Doctor. She knew Rebecca would never confess to a problem, would say that nothing was wrong even if she were dying; her feelings were as hidden as Brendel's were obvious.

She was a little bit late in opening, she realized when she found Hiram Liebmann waiting outside the Café, arms folded, sketch pad leaning against the wall. She unlocked the door, motioned to him to enter, and quickly lit the stove in the kitchen. After putting up water for his chocolate, she went to wash herself. She felt bereaved, as if Yussel already had been taken by the police. When she checked her face in the mirror, near the bed she rarely used, she looked it, with charcoal smudges beneath her eyes, red circles rimming her whites. Like most women in the lane, she did not wear powder. She splashed cold water on her face, hoping that would help.

She was glad her boys had rented a room from Moish Rothschild in the Hinterpfann; she would not want them to see her like this. Daniel, who was nineteen, was working at the Zig-Zig stable as a blacksmith, following his father's path, though she did not like to think of it that way; the smell of molten iron, the sizzle as it was cooled, must have crept into his veins when he was little. Joshua, seventeen, was in his final year at the yeshiva. Drying her face with a towel, she vowed to cry no more, to look her best when the boys came for supper.

When she stepped back into the Café she found that Hiram had helped her by opening the shutters wide and moving the outdoor tables into place. She carried his chocolate to him as he sat in his favorite spot, with a view down the lane. Trying to calm herself, to rest for a moment, she sat across the small table from him. Hiram frowned at her, pointing to her eyes, his brow furrowing, asking in his silent manner what was wrong. She squeezed his hand upon the table, thanking him for his concern. She shook her head, not wanting to speak of it, not with her voice, not with her hands. After a glance up the lane — the Polizei could come at any time — she returned to the kitchen to mold her breads. Her hands were shaky as she kneaded the dough. She hoped Yussel would sleep in the cellar all day. Perhaps, if the police came while he was there, she could tell them he had fled, that he had gone to Hesse-Kassel, or Hanover, somewhere beyond their jurisdiction; perhaps even to France. If they believed her, perhaps they would not come again.

Perhaps.

R abbi Emil Simcha had just left the synagogue after conducting morning services when he saw the Chief Rabbi's wife looking out the second story window of their adjacent house. Gilda Eleazar called to him, told him to get Rabbi Jonah and come upstairs, her husband wanted to speak to them together. Raising a dark eyebrow, Simcha wondered what that could mean. Surely Eleazar was not yet dying. And even if he had made his choice, why call in the two of them?

They found the Chief Rabbi propped up on his pillows, smiling, appearing more cheerful than he had for weeks. Rabbi Jonah, a large man with a full white beard and a full head of white hair, went to the side of the Chief Rabbi's bed. Simcha, much younger than the other two, stood respectfully at the foot of the bed.

"So much wisdom in one bedroom," the rebbetzin said, entering to see if they wanted tea. "Maybe not seen since Sarah and Abraham conceived."

Simcha smiled at this rare public display of the wit with which Gilda Hoerner had won the heart of Avram Eleazar more than fifty years earlier; the rebbetzin had been content to bury her light in her husband's massive shadow ever since. Rabbi Jonah did not smile at her joke; perhaps, Simcha thought, after thirty years as head of the yeshiva, he no longer registered the voices of women. Or perhaps he found her remark blasphemous.

"No tea, Gilda," the Chief Rabbi said. "I have here a circumcision to perform."

Simcha and Jonah glanced at one another, wondering if their mutual friend had lost his senses. Gilda left the room, a smile spreading across her wooden teeth.

"Don't be frightened, I have no knife," the Chief Rabbi said. "Besides, you both were circumcised long ago." He reached to his bedside table, lifted a glass of water, drank from it, set it down. "I only meant that you are both dear to me, as its foreskin is to an infant — but in the matter of choosing my successor, I have no choice but to cut one of you off."

Simcha and Jonah could hardly relax; what they had suspected this meeting might be about was correct. The chair beside the Rabbi's bed beckoned; neither dared to sit.

"Instead of telling my successor in private, I have summoned you both so you could hear my reasoning. I decided that would be the best thing to do to ensure your future cooperation in the service of the Judengasse."

Simcha thought: Joint Chief Rabbis? That would hardly work. What if they disagreed on some important issue?

"Rabbi Jonah, you have been a wonderful director of the yeshiva. For three decades you and your staff have turned out fine scholars. Ever since we attended rabbinical school together in Hanover, you have been my closest friend. If I choose you, I told myself, you will make a fine successor in upholding the sacred traditions."

Jonah nodded with pursed lips, acknowledging Eleazar's words.

"And you, Rabbi Simcha," the Chief Rabbi said, gazing toward the foot of the bed. "Despite the difference in our ages, we have worked closely together for almost twenty years. By this time, you know all that I know about presiding over the lane. The young people in particular love you, perhaps more than they respect me — don't think I'm not aware of that — and the young, of course, are the future. So there was ample reason to choose you as well."

Impassive, Simcha said nothing.

"I am not King Solomon. I came up with no brilliant answer. I had to choose between you. My choice was Rabbi Jonah."

Jonah coughed to conceal his delight at the achievement of his lifelong ambition. Simcha, knowing Eleazar's precision in speech, wondered at his choice of words.

"I say my choice 'was,'" the Chief Rabbi continued, "because I have been overruled."

Jonah could not contain his question, it popped from his mouth like a live animal. "Who can overrule the Chief Rabbi?"

"Adonai, of course."

He went on to recount what had happened, the threat to Jonah's heart if he were chosen. "Unlike Abraham with Isaac," the Chief Rabbi said, "I did not think it was a chance I should take."

Rabbi Jonah was holding one hand to his chest. "Of course not," he said, his voice sounding hoarse.

"So now you know why I summoned both of you. Both of you were chosen, as it were. But it is Simcha who shall serve. You, Jonah, shall remain director of the yeshiva, with the knowledge that Adonai is indeed watching. Jonah, tell the Schul-Klopper to announce the decision at evening services today. I shall not last the week. Very likely I shall not last the night."

"That can't be true," Simcha blurted. "You're looking much better. You're sounding much better."

"That may be," the Rabbi said, nestling his head more comfortably into his pillows. "But the angels are waiting." He closed his eyes, no longer needing to be strong, his responsibilities drifting away like the smoke from all the chimneys in the lane.

42

In mid-afternoon, Guttle began to wonder about Yussel Kahn. She had seen Brendel leave in the morning, but she had not heard Yussel go. It was possible, with the younger children running up and down the stairs and in and out the door, shouting and playing, that he had left without her hearing him. But she decided to go down to the cellar and check. Pulling away the rug, lifting the trap door, she called down to him. There was no response. The open trap illuminated the ladder. Careful not to trip on her skirt, she climbed down, and turned, saying his name. As her eyes adjusted to the dark, she discerned his form on the dirt floor. Reaching to touch him, to make sure he was well, to see if he was hungry, she recoiled suddenly with shame, and turned away. Yussel was naked. And so silent, he might be dead.

She shooed the thought away like a rat, but heard herself whimpering as she climbed the ladder to the vestibule. She left the trap open and hurried out the door. Wanting to run, not wanting to attract attention in case the police were in the lane, she forced herself to appear calm, but walked with rapid strides. At the hospital she hurried in and looked for Doctor Berkov in his office; it was empty. In the next office she found Rebecca at her desk.

"Where's Lev? I need him to come quickly.,"

"He's with a patient. What's wrong?"

"It's Yussel Kahn. He's on the ground. He's not moving."

Rebecca quickly came around from her desk.

"We need Lev. He's naked," Guttle said.

"Stop being silly!"

Guttle led the way from the hospital to the Green Shield, and pointed to the trap door.

"Did he fall in?"

"No. Go look. But don't look "

Rebecca already was climbing down the latter. "Give me some light," she called.

Guttle grabbed the vestibule lamp and the tin of matches beside it, lit the wick and placed the lamp in Rebecca's upstretched hand. As she did, she heard a deep moan from below. "He's alive!" she blurted, and started to climb down the ladder, then stopped. "Is he covered?"

"He's covered," Rebecca said.

The Doctor was kneeling beside Yussel, holding the lamp near his face, peering into his eyes. "Yussel, can you hear me?"

Yussel moaned.

"What happened?" the Doctor asked.

Slowly, Yussel raised himself to his elbows, peered around the cellar at the stone walls flickering yellow, as if trying to remember where he was. He placed his hand on his forehead. "I had a dream. A mob was chasing me, to hang me. The leader was Voltaire. He tried to grab me, saying 'the Jew must die'. I wrenched myself from his grasp — and I woke up just before my head slammed into the wall."

Rebecca peered at his forehead, where the skin had swelled and already was darkening. "He's got a nasty bruise," she said, as Guttle knelt beside her.

Yussel raised himself higher. "Voltaire — the hypocritical fraud."

The Doctor checked each of his limbs, and found no damage.

Yussel sat up gingerly. "My head hurts." He grimaced as he touched his scalp.

"Can you dress yourself?"

"I want to see Brendel."

"Put your clothes on. I want to look at that bruise in the light."

Watching his eyes narrow, then widen again, Guttle could see the dawning within him.

"I'm not going to hide anymore. Have the police come to take me away?"

"Nobody's taking you away," Rebecca said.

Guttle touched the Doctor's shoulder. To Yussel, she said, "They haven't come yet."

Rebecca turned to Guttle, her face in the dim light a dark question mark.

"I'll explain later," Guttle said.

In the cabinet maker's shop, Georgi Kremm was making a bookcase, inserting dowels, copying the precise style of his employer. Yussel had told him once how all the great painters had apprentices. Sometimes their paintings were labeled "From the School of Rembrandt." Or whoever. This bookcase, Georgi vowed, would be from the School of Kahn. Few would be able to distinguish it from the master's work.

Today, however, he was Yussel Kahn. Or would be, if the police came. Only two officers could recognize him, the two that had come to the lane that time, the tall one with the thin face and the shorter one with the round face. Those two he would not be able fool. But any others... He had thought about it much of the night. He did not know why the police wanted Yussel, but it could not be for anything terrible; Yussel was too good a man, too good a citizen. Yet apparently it was serious enough to cause Yussel to hide. Georgi had stuffed a roll of gulden into his pocket, money he'd earned in the shop. If there was a fine for what Yussel had done, he was prepared to pay it. A cheap enough price for all that he had learned. If the punishment were something more serious, perhaps a few months in jail... well, he might be dead if the Judengasse had not taken him in; he owed them something. Becoming Yussel, he would become a Jew even before the Rabbi sanctioned it. He would prove himself worthy. Worthiness, he had learned in his lessons with Rabbi Simcha, was what being a Jew was about. Worthiness not to your neighbors, not even to God. Worthiness to yourself.

In the morning he had been nervous, but as the hours passed with no police, he had relaxed. He liked himself better for his decision. Even if the police did not come, he had proved to himself his courage.

"Is Yussel Kahn here?"

Bent behind the bookcase, sandpapering the bottom shelf, he choked on sawdust as he heard the words. They had come at last. At least the voice of the officer sounded mild, not brutish. Georgi stood to face the unknown.

The officer was not wearing a uniform. He was dressed in a brown coat, beige breeches, white stockings. He was older than Georgi had expected, white hair showing around his ears beneath his tricorne. Perhaps he sat at a desk at the headquarters on the Fahrgasse.

"Is Yussel Kahn here?" the man repeated.

Georgi stepped from behind the bookcase, squared his shoulders. He had rehearsed this scene for hours in his bed. For a former peasant boy, the noblest moment of his life. "I am Yussel Kahn." His voice did not waver.

"You are Yussel Kahn?" The stranger sounded disbelieving.

"At your service, officer."

"Indeed. What is this masquerade?"

"If you'll look at the banner outside, sir, you will see my name and profession. Yussel Kahn, Fine Wood Work."

"Young man, I don't know who you are. You could pretend to be Saint Peter, for all that I care. But I have known Yussel for more than twenty years. I have sold him dozens of books, and loaned him hundreds. I've furnished the very glue you're using for those dowels. And you are not Yussel Kahn. Can we agree on that?"

Georgi looked at his feet, his face flushing. When he looked up again, he said, "I'm sorry, sir. I thought you were the police."

"Do I look like the police? What would the police want with Yussel ?"

"I don't know."

"I see. I'm sure Yussel did not put you up to this impersonation. In any event, can you tell me where to find him?"

"I would guess he's at Brendel's Café, up the lane."

"Ah, Fraülein Brendel. I've been hearing about her for years. And, young man…"

"Yes?"

"Do a good job with that bookshelf. I suspect it's for my shop."

Georgi was speechless as the bookseller walked out. He felt like a fish with a hook in his mouth, in the pond near their farm. Did this mean the police might still come for Yussel? He hoped not. He could feel his embarrassment melting his resolve. His act of courage had been a declaration of stupidity; he could see that now, and felt ashamed. Despite his Talmudic studies he had not yet overcome the unlearned peasant within.

"Some day!" he vowed, speaking aloud in the empty shop, and he resumed work with vigor on the bookseller's new shelves. As he worked, he felt his mother watching him, heard her laughing raucously through broken teeth.

Doctor Kirsch had plastered a cut on Yussel's forehead. Perched as it was on a large purple bruise, it was earning him sympathetic questions as he sat in the Café, drinking tea. Guttle had stayed with him. Meyer joined them upon returning from the city.

The cobbler Alexandre Licht, buying a piece of strudel to take to his shop, noticed the plaster and the bruise, and asked Yussel, "Did Brendel hit you with her frying pan?"

"Voltaire hit me," Yussel said, "with his duplicity."

The shoemaker peered, shrugged, not comprehending, and left, his belief affirmed that those people who read too much think too much.

The lane was busy with shoppers, with women returning from the market or the bakery, with children running about, the crowd now redoubling as the heder boys and the yeshiva boys were released from school and their younger siblings ran in and out among longer legs to meet them, the boys sometimes stopping suddenly to retrieve a fallen yarmulke, causing collisions of flesh and bone, sometimes causing tears. Brendel brought a fresh pot of tea to the table and refilled the glasses of Yussel, Meyer and Guttle. Yussel blinked, then rubbed his eyes, as from the passing mass of people a figure emerged that he recognized, but could not place. The bookseller spotted Yussel at once, and approached the table. Yussel jumped up, almost knocking over the table and all three glasses, which wobbled but held steady.

"Gluck! What are you doing here?"

"A nice greeting. Am I not welcome, then?"

"No one has ever been more welcome in my life. Unless you brought the police."

"What is all this with the police?"

Remembering his manners, Yussel introduced the bookseller to Meyer, Guttle and Brendel, all of whom were too surprised to speak.

"Fräulein Isaacs," Gluck said, "what a pleasure. You are even lovelier than in Yussel's descriptions."

"Am I?" She chucked Yussel's shoulder.

"Sit," Yussel said. "What are you doing here? I thought you were in prison."

"Why would I be in prison?"

"Because of... "Yussel stopped and looked around. "Because of the art books. I saw you arrested yesterday."

"Ah." The bookseller finally sat. Yussel, still standing, also sat. "Yes, I was arrested. It had nothing to do with that."

"Nothing... ?"

Brendel almost swooned. "Thank God," she said. Standing behind Yussel, her knees weakening, she squeezed his shoulders. "We were terrified — for nothing."

Guttle and Meyer looked at one another. Meyer squeezed her hand.

"What, then?" Yussel said. "Why else would they take you away?"

"Nathan the Wise."

"Nathan the... It's banned! You were selling it!"

"I had them in the cellar. Someone saw me bring one up, and informed."

"That's wonderful!" Meyer said, laughing.

"Wonderful?" The bookseller looked puzzled, then hurt.

"What did they do to you?" Yussel asked.

"Do to me? Nothing. A fine of ten gulden. And a warning — next time a hundred gulden. That I cannot afford."

"Gluck, I'm glad you came here. More than glad. But, if I may, why did you come?"

"To talk about the art books. The authorities will be watching me now. I can't take the risk anymore. I'm sorry."

"Don't be sorry! You've brought us wonderful news. We thought… I thought… never mind what I thought. Cowards die many times before their deaths."

"Are you saying you're a coward?" Meyer asked.

"Not me. Shakespeare."

"Shakespeare did not live in the Judengasse."

"We're not cowards," Guttle said, "yet we die every day when the gates are locked."

"Enough about death!" Brendel said. "Yussel is safe. We're all safe. That's what matters."

Yussel kissed the midsection of her sky-blue dress, just above her apron. "A bottle of wine," he said, looking up into her smile. "That new champagne. To celebrate!"

She bent and kissed the top of his head, between his bruise and his yarmulke, disappeared into the kitchen, returned with a bottle of Moët — which the French had recently begun exporting — and four wine glasses. Yussel with his strong hands popped the cork, and poured.

"What shall we toast?" Guttle asked.

"How about Mendelssohn?" the bookseller suggested, pointing to the framed drawing on the wall. "The real Nathan the Wise."

"No," Yussel said. He stood. "I will make the toast." He held up his glass. "The simplest and the oldest toast in the world. And the most profound. L' Chaim!"

"L' Chaim!" the others echoed in unison, and sipped the champagne. Brendel's smiling lips sipped from Yussel's glass.

Yussel sat. "L' Chaim," he repeated softly, in a voice both weary and relieved. Never before had the commonplace toast meant so much to him. L' Chaim. To life.

"About your helper," the bookseller said. He motioned to Yussel's bruise. "Did you and he knock heads together? He seems to think he is you."

"He thinks he is me?"

"That's not acceptable," Brendel said. "Not without proof." She winked at the bookseller, and went to attend to the customers now streaming in.

Yussel's eyes followed her with adoration. "L' Chaim!" he said again, and he raised his glass and drank, the bubbles of the odd new wine tickling the roof of his mouth. Licking his lips for the last drop, setting down the glass, he murmured it quietly, again. To life.

D octor Kirsch was sitting behind her desk, in the black dress that without her quite realizing it was her mourning for the future, the acknowledgment of a loneliness that she had not permitted herself to feel in fifteen years. The hospital was almost empty. She never wanted people to be ill, but today more work would have helped her keep her mind from feeding on itself. This rarely had been a problem for her, but had become one in recent weeks as she began to recognize and accept her feelings for Emil Simcha. She thought she had buried feelings like that when she was nineteen years old. Then last night her longings had been exposed for the foolishness they were.

Footsteps on the wooden floor broke her indulgent reverie; more than broke it, shattered it like a China plate. She looked up to see the last person she expected in her doorway. Caught halfway between pleasure and anger, her face remained without a clear expression.

"If you're not busy," Rabbi Simcha said, "I'd like you to come and walk with me. I have something to talk about."

Rebecca raised her eyebrows without realizing it and left her desk and moved past him in the doorway and out through the entrance into the lane. Simcha started toward the south end, and she walked beside him.

"Rebecca, why did you come to the Judengasse?"

"That's an odd question after fifteen years. To be a Doctor, of course."

"Of course. And I came to teach at the yeshiva. In the twenty years I've been here, only three people besides myself have come to live here voluntarily. Brendel Isaacs, who came to be with Yussel. Georgi Kremm, who was escaping a war. And you."

"Your point being?"

They were threading their way among shoppers in the lane and children playing noisily.

"My point being, I used to think no one would come here unless they were hiding from something. There were a dozen yeshivas I could have chosen, but I came to the most oppressed ghetto in the German lands. You could have chosen a dozen hospitals, but you came here — a place where we get locked in at night. I've been asking myself why we both did this. I haven't entirely abandoned my earlier theory, but I've come up with a new one, at least for the two of us. Perhaps Yahweh meant for us to be together."

She stopped and turned to face him. Her face flushed, then paled. Her features became stony with anger, but her voice was controlled. "How can you say such a thing? After what you told me last night. I saw you going into Frau Baumgarten's house today. What happened, did she turn you down? "

"A fair question. No. She did not turn me down." They had reached the south gate. The noise from the docks was rushing into the lane like an angry wind. "I wish we could go walking on the river rampart. But if you'll bear with me, the cemetery will have to do. For quiet."

"You have me very confused. I'm not accustomed to being confused."

He took her elbow and guided her through the cemetery gate, to one of the paths among the stones. As the ghetto wall rose between them and the docks, the rushing noise diminished, but not the fury snapping in her brain.

"I spent a restless night," Simcha said, "thinking of the things I said to you at dinner. Again and again they twisted through my sleep. Absurd images of you scrubbing floors. Washing my shirts. Till the truth dawned on me. What I was seeking was not a wife, but a housekeeper."

Rebecca glanced at his face, still controlling her anger. "Why are you telling me this?"

"By the time I went to Thelma Baumgarten's place for lunch — as you apparently saw me entering — I had made a decision. Frau Baumgarten was happy to accept my offer."

"I see."

"I asked her to be my housekeeper. To come a few times a week, to clean and to cook. For suitable wages, of course. And she agreed. How could I have thought she could be my wife? We would not have been a good match."

They were in the center of the cemetery, near the Beckers. They stopped walking. Rebecca ran her hand along the top of a grave marker. She willed her throbbing nerves to be as hard as the stone her fingers were caressing.

"Which brings me to my central point."

She waited.

A movement caught her eye, a gray cat slinking among the stones. She picked up a pebble and threw it. The cat scampered off. They didn't need cats from the dock digging among the graves. And throwing rocks at a Rabbi would be frowned upon.

"With the housework done by Frau Baumgarten," Simcha said, "your work at the hospital would not be diminished. We could continue to enjoy our talks, as we do every Tuesday — but we could talk every night. If... "

She looked at the ground, at the few early weeds sprouting among the graves. She turned to him, her face chiseled stone. Her voice was harsh when she spoke. "If what?"

"If you would agree to be my wife."

Rebecca turned away, looked at the acres of graves between them and the wall. Gulls from the river swirled overhead, dipped and disappeared. She felt anger, not joy. After the wound of the previous night, her defenses were in place, like a porcupine's.

"You don't have to decide now," Simcha said. "And I want to make clear, this would be for companionship only. To fend off loneliness. I wouldn't expect us to... I wouldn't expect you too... not with my pocked face, my scar. I'm fifty-one years old, I've learned to live without that. Our bedrooms would be separate."

Rebecca turned to him, her anger unexpectedly dissipating beneath his words, like a spring shower beneath the sun. He had never revealed himself this way before. "No," she said.

"I see. You have no need to think. Just... no."

"Do you want to know why?"

He reached up and held his yarmulke in place against a breeze that swirled among the stones. She could see a heaviness weighting his eyes. "If you care to tell me."

"When I marry," Rebecca said, "if I marry, it will not be a marriage in name only. I would expect to feel the warmth of my husband's body alongside mine in the night. I would expect him to desire me, in the way a woman wants to be desired. Without that, I see no point in marriage."

"I see."

"I love you as a friend. But unless you desire me as a woman, we should remain friends."

The sky darkened suddenly, a dense gray cloud hiding the sun. The tombstones lost their shadows. Weeds began to whisper, a swirling wind scratching them against the soapstone markers. Here and there, puffs of dirt took flight. Rebecca turned from him, as if rubbing a speck of soil from her eye.

The Rabbi moved his hands toward her shoulders, took them down, did not know what to do with them. "Unless I desire you? Surely you're making a joke. You think inside this Rabbi's black that I wear is not a man?" Carefully he risked one hand on her shoulder. He realized he was grateful that she had turned away; it was easier to speak to her back. "Don't you realize how desirable you are? You don't know how hard I have been battling not to respond to it. Not to risk losing your friendship. You are so beautiful — your lean face, your flashing eyes, your hair, your manner. Everything about you. But long ago the pox had its way with me. I can hardly expect you to want to kiss a face such as mine."

For the first time during this long, tormenting day, the Doctor allowed herself a smile. Turning to face him, raising herself slightly on her toes, she kissed his lips, lightly. Then she settled back.

The Rabbi could feel his eyes clouding over with unexpected joy; he closed them so she would not read the depth of his feelings. "Was that to prove a point," he asked, his eyes still closed, "or was that an answer to my question?"

She raised herself on her toes, pressed her lips to his, held them there, until his arms tightened around her, and his lips pressed back, and they were locked in embrace. She broke it only in order to breathe, and pressed her cheek to his.

"That was a yes," she said. "But only on my terms."

He felt a wetness on his cheek. He did not know if it were his tears, or hers. Perhaps it was both, commingled. "I like your terms better," he whispered hoarsely

When they had kissed again, their fingers gripping each other's backs, and had separated, breathing rapidly, and had taken each other's hands, Simcha said, "There's one more thing I have to tell you. If we do this, you will be the Chief Rabbi's wife. People will look at you as… I don't know as what. Not only as a Doctor, but also as the rebbetzin."

"I had already guessed that."

He touched her cheek, looked into her deep, dark eyes. "How long shall we keep our betrothal a secret?"

"Ten minutes. More I couldn't stand." Tears were drifting down her face. She ignored them. "People will look at the stoic Doctor Kirsch, who never shows her feelings, and they will know anyway. Especially when they see that my feet no longer touch the cobbles."

The new Chief Rabbi grinned.

"Let's go," she said, pulling on his hand. "I want to tell Guttle. And Brendel. I want to tell all my friends. Let's go to the Café. Is that all right?"

"I want to tell the world," Simcha said.

When they were twenty steps into the lane, with the sun shining again, the applause began, and the shouting. Word already had circulated about Simcha's promotion. "Mazel tov! Mazel tov! Long life to the new Chief Rabbi!" Women leaned out of second and third floor windows to cheer. From the doorways of shops the owners and their customers spilled out and began to applaud and call out greetings. As Simcha walked up the lane, Rebecca at his side, the hurrahs moved along with him like a rumble of thunder — which drew more people into the lane, and more applause.

"It wasn't to be announced until evening services," Simcha shouted into the Doctor's ear.

"You know there are no secrets in the lane!"

On and on the applause continued as they passed the synagogue and the hospital. People began to follow behind them, clapping their hands in rhythm. As they neared the Café and Brendel's customers saw who it was, they, too, stood and began to cheer and to shout Mazel tov to the new Chief Rabbi, Guttle and Meyer and Yussel among them. The lane in front of the Café became crowded, as did the Café itself. The Rabbi and the Doctor both appeared flushed. Simcha raised his hands and asked for quiet. Gradually the shouts faded away.

"I'm not sure what all this Mazel tov is for," he told them. "The new Chief Rabbi will not be announced by the Schul-Klopper until evening services — about half an hour from now."

"We know it's you!" someone called out. "The Rabbi is out of the bag!"

Amid laughter, Simcha raised his arms again for silence. "But I do want to make a different kind of announcement."

Talking ceased. People wanted to hear the first thing their new Chief Rabbi — whether he admitted it or not — would say. His hand at his side, Rabbi Simcha gripped Rebecca's hand, out of sight of most of the crowd.

"I suspect that this will come as a surprise to most of you. The truth is, it comes as a surprise to me. Just a few minutes ago, Doctor Kirsch — Rebecca, here — agreed to become my wife."

For a moment there was silence while this unexpected news circled inside the Café like a bird. Then shouts and cheers exploded, deafening as artillery.

"Long life to the Doctor rebbetzin!" someone shouted.

"Long life to the rebbetzin Doctor!"

Laughter and cheers and the buzz of shouted whispers spilled out into the lane. Already the identity of the new Chief Rabbi was ancient history; this new news sizzled up and down the lane like the aroma of frying chicken fat, a tasty and unexpected treat. Guttle pushed forward to hug Rebecca, cheek against cheek. Meyer and Yussel shook hands vigorously with Rabbi Simcha. Others pressed around the betrothed couple to do the same. Behind the counter, Brendel turned to her younger son, Joshua, and whispered in his ear. He worked his way through the crowd and out into the lane and ran a few houses south and up a flight of stairs. A few minutes later the noisy throng quieted as talk and laughter was sliced like butter by the sharp sound of a violin. The crowd parted to make way for Pinchas Cohen, the oldest fiddler in the lane, who was well into his eighties. He stepped from the cobbles into the Café without pausing in his tune.

"A dance! A dance by the betrothed!" someone shouted.

People pulled the Café's small tables to the sides, creating a space in the center. Rebecca Kirsch took Emil Simcha's hand and led him to it, and while hundreds of eyes watched, people in the back urging those in front to kneel so they could see, the couple began a slow and stately dance, while some of the onlookers whistled and cheered. Soon others began to dance, not in the Café — there was no room there — but in the lane, across the sewage trench.

When the betrothal dance ended, people cheered the fiddler, whose grin showed his mottled pink gums; he'd been so excited to come lead the celebration that he'd forgotten to put in his teeth. Brendel sidled up to him and whispered in his ear. Pinchas Cohen grinned even wider. He lifted his violin to his chin, took a deep breath into his skinny chest, then another, pulled several slow notes across the strings with his bow. Slowly, infinitesimally, he began to bow faster, then faster still. Brendel motioned away people who were clogging the impromptu dance floor. She approached Rebecca and held out her hand. Rebecca hesitated, shook her head 'no' while allowing Brendel to pull her into the open space. Brendel kicked off one shoe, then the other. The crowd — those who remembered — began to shout encouragement.

Rebecca wagged a finger at them, then removed her shoes as well. Brendel did a few trial steps on the wooden floor in her stockinged feet, as if to loosen her muscles. Rebecca, shaking her head ruefully, did the same. Brendel raised her skirt above her ankles and began to dance, slowly at first, then quickly catching up to the music. Rebecca, frowning, shaking her head, nonetheless followed her lead. Soon the two women were stepping and whirling about one another, mirror images, Brendel in her pale blue dress and white apron, Rebecca all in black, Brendel's blonde ringlets bouncing on her shoulders, Rebecca's black hair flying off her neck. The onlookers clapped in time to the music that kept getting faster and faster. Guttle, watching, hugged Meyer, pressed her face into his chest, wetting his shirt with her tears. Faster and faster the old fiddler played in a frenzied display, people marveling at his dexterity. Gradually the clapping fell away like pebbles, people could not clap that fast, but the two women danced faster and faster, until suddenly the music exploded into a stunning silence. Abruptly the dance was over, and as they had done fifteen years earlier at Guttle's wedding Brendel and Rebecca fell into one another's arms, holding each other up as they tried to catch their breath, laughing, kissing one another on the cheek, wobbling as they struggled to remain on their feet.

"More music," someone yelled, but in the silence the fiddler shook his head and pointed to his watch pocket. Just then they heard the fire chief, now the elderly Schul-Klopper, calling out as he walked by in the lane that it was time for evening services, calling out because amid the frenzied rhythm of the fiddle no one had hear him knocking. The throng began to dissipate, the women and children to their homes to prepare the evening meal, the men toward the synagogue.

Following the men, Pinchas Cohen paused in front of the house of the Chief Rabbi, and thought of Avram lying ill in bed, and began to play for his friend a gentle concert of mournful melodies.

Of all the men, only Yussel Kahn held back. He watched Brendel hang the "Closed" sign and lock the door of the Café, and close the dark blue curtains. Together they moved the tables back into place. Then Yussel took her hand. "Tired?"

"Very."

"It's been a memorable day. To begin so badly, and to end so well."

"It's only the end that counts."

"I was afraid I might be in prison by now. That I might never see you again."

"I know."

He sat on the nearest chair, guided her onto his lap. He nuzzled the sweet, grassy smell of her faintly perfumed sweat. "I think it's time," he said. "Simcha shamed me into the spirit. Gluck scared me half to death. I told you once that I would know if the time came. I think it's time."

Brendel touched his face with her slim fingers. "Are you sure? Just because of Simcha and Rebecca, we don't… "

"Not because of them. For us. If you want to think about it… "

"I've had fifteen years to think about it." She tugged on the point of his short reddish beard, lately lightened by a hint of gray. "What about your vow not to marry again?"

"Yahweh will understand."

She hesitated. "And Lainie?"

"Lainie, too, will understand."

Straightening the collar of her dress, he added, "You do have one thing to consider. It might destroy your reputation."

Brendel grinned. "The Judengasse will survive." She lightly kissed his nose. "But wait a moment. You don't expect me to stop being me, just because of a wedding band."

"Not for a minute."

"Good. Because that would be bad for business."

His hands encircled her waist, a moment's kiss away. She whispered, "What about evening services?" His hands were untying her apron. "That, too, Yahweh will understand."

Fifteen minutes earlier, hearing applause and shouting from below, Gilda Eleazar had made sure her sheitl was on straight and had looked out the third floor window. Rabbi Simcha, the new Chief Rabbi, was being hailed by his admirers as he walked up the lane. For a moment she began to shake with anger; her husband was not yet dead, and already they were cheering his successor. She told herself to be fair, knowing it was Avram who had made the changeover immediate, but still, they could have some consideration as they walked by the house where he was asleep. She thought of shushing them, but knew she would not be heard, and was afraid it could be taken wrong, taken as if she resented Rabbi Simcha. She did not. Only Yahweh she resented, for taking her husband before her.

She left the window and looked in on him; he was sleeping peacefully; between his gray beard and his gray mustache was the suggestion of a smile. As she sat heavily in a chair in the parlor, she said aloud, to the walls, "Me, I'm not smiling. Where will I live, Avram, the house is for Simcha now? To whom will I kvetch when my ankles hurt.?"

"Now music!" she had muttered as the sound of a violin blew in through the window. She tried to minimize her anger. "Let them play, let them cheer, they have little enough to cheer about."

Her trembling hands were wrinkled, covered with ugly brown spots. "Adonai," she said, gazing at the ceiling, "if we get married forever, why not take us together? Wouldn't that be an improvement? Why should I sit helpless and see my Avram go? They'll expect me to watch him buried into the earth. Watch them shovel dirt on top of him. More than fifty years we've lived together. How can I watch that?"

The fiddle notes continued to intrude. Wearily, she pulled herself up from her chair and went to the window to lower the glass, to close the shutters, to block out the sound. But at the window, she stopped. The music had changed. It had become a slow, mournful melody. Below in the lane she saw Pinchas Cohen gently working his bow, playing his oldest friend into heaven.

A light rain began to fall. Pinchas Cohen ignored it, continued to play.

Gilda felt a chill. She was in no hurry to shuffle to the bedroom. She knew.

43

Helmut Mann leaned against the base of a great black oak on the bank of the river Fulda, holding a fishing pole, its line drifting lazily in the current. Dragonflies buzzed along the silver surface, dipped and spun away. Beyond the muddy banks on both sides, spikey wild grasses, mostly cord grass and blue stem, sun bleached pale green in September, climbed the face of the hills. High above, to the fisherman's left, its shadow hanging over the river just as the oak's black branches did — just as Helmut's fake Christian name hung over his Jewish self — was Riesenburg, the tall stone Castle of Thieves.

It had been nearly fifteen years since Hersch Liebmann, tired of being known to other highwaymen as the Judengasse Jew, had taken a different name. No longer did anyone even call him Helmut the Jew, as a few had done at first; the last cutthroat who had done so still carried a scar on his neck. Hersch did not mind his religion being known — a fair number of the highwaymen were Jews, including practicing ones who would not commit robbery on Saturdays. But when he left the cover of the hills and entered a town to have a woman, Helmut Mann suited him better on the hostel register.

The fish weren't biting. Hersch, feeling lazy, didn't care. He'd eaten a large breakfast of eggs stolen from a nearby chicken coop, and for dinner he could always approach the cooking fire of one band of thieves or another. His shoulders, arms and chest had grown thick enough, the blade in his boot was sharp enough, his willingness to use it notorious enough, that he was welcome to share a meal wherever he chose. He had learned quickly that for a Jew to survive in the wild he needed to be twice as mean as a Christian. In the early years several men had tested his Jewish mettle. No one had done so twice. Reputation was everything among thieves, just as it was in the ghetto; that was why he had not returned home when his fourteen years of exile had ended a year ago. In the lane he still would be looked down upon as a thief; here he was honored for it. In the ghetto he still would be suspected of murder, no matter that a jury had cleared him; here the rumor enhanced his safety.

He would have liked to visit his mother, but Yetta would be eighty-eight years old; most likely she was long dead. He had heard tales of a popular deaf mute artist called Lieb; he could not picture his brother as a painter, but he had not been eager to go and see. There would be questions of what he, Hersch, had been doing all these years. He was forty years old; he was not about to defend his life to bearded old men.

Pulling his fishing line from the river, he wrapped it around the pole. The fish would bite better at dawn, he knew, but he did not care to rise at dawn; in the real world there were no morning services. Although, out of habit, he still kept his head covered at all times — not with a yarmulke, but with a red cloth cap that was serviceable against sun and rain. He'd bought the cap from a shopkeeper in Göttingen, who told him they were popular among the working men of France.

In a linden across the river, a pale green woodpecker, with a cap as red as his, was tapping noisily. Hersch adjusted his own cap to fit more snugly, and as he climbed a worn path through the brush toward the castle, he reflected with contentment on his life as Helmut Mann: he rode on horseback far and wide under the German sky, stealing a new mount whenever his horse stepped into a rut or a gopher hole and went lame; he slept under the stars, or in a cliffside cave, or in an abandoned castle of his choosing; when he was short of coins he stopped a coach, or a solitary rider, and often did not have to rob again for weeks; he had not dug a grave in fifteen years — not since the snowy day he'd dug his father's.

"That you?" A thin, womanly voice rose from within the bushes.

Leni. A whore who'd taken a liking to him a month back, and had stolen a mare from in front of a bridle shop and followed him into the hills. Not a real beauty, not enough meat on her bones, hair mousy brown instead of the blondes he preferred, but for now she suited him. Saved his weekly trip into some snide town. In return he made sure she was fed.

"Any news?" he said into the brush.

Leni emerged from the bushes, finished with her business, adjusting her faded dress, once-dark gray, dotted with yellow buttercups. "Fellow come in from Kassel a while ago. Says the Landgrave ain't dead yet."

"It's just a matter of time."

"What's it to you if the Landgrave dies?"

"I told you already." Leni wasn't as smart as the girls in the lane, though she had other attributes. "When the old man dies, the nobles and the traders will be rushing in like grasshoppers for his funeral. And for the crowning of his fat son Wilhelm. Licking royal ass. Then they'll have to ride home again. Easy pickings, coming and going."

"What if you get caught? What will happen to me?"

You'll go back to whoring, he thought, which you will do any day now, regardless. But he didn't say it. "Never been caught yet. Why start now?"

He turned her around and gently pushed her up the narrow dirt path, following an arm's length behind. Leafless branches grabbed their clothing like needy beggars, and had to be dislodged from shirt and skirt.

"Fellow rode up a while ago, looking for you," she said. "Had a big black horse, a fancy sword on his saddle."

"Who was it? Turn around and look at me when you talk."

But he already knew who it was.

She turned to him, squinting into the late afternoon sun. "Said his name was Klaus. Said he's your partner. I thought I'm your partner."

"It's different."

More reliable than sunrise, Hersch thought. Klaus Fettmilch never is late when the pickings are easy. Word must have flown like a crow from here to Hanau, from Göttingen to Wiesenbad, from the highest hills to the river valleys. Prince Friedrich, the Landgrave of Hesse-Kassel, had a stroke. His Excellency is expected to die.

Leni giggled, dirty fingers covering her mouth.

"What's so funny?"

"It's different, you said. I sure do hope it's different."

"Your mind is filth." He took her by the shoulders, turned her around, shoved her again towards the castle. Gently. She stumbled nonetheless before righting herself by grabbing hold of a bush from which the buds of purple berries grew.

"What's so special with you and this Klaus?" she asked, looking over her shoulder.

"We've got history."

The air suddenly chilled as they entered the shadow of the castle tower. They scrambled down a wall of rust-colored earth into a dry moat. Chunks of castle stone littered the bottom; the moat had not been filled with water in three hundred years.

Leni brushed soil from her dress. "What kinda history?"

"Let's go find him."

But they did not find him.

Riesenburg meant Giant Castle to the literal, who saw its tower soaring impossibly high into the sky since the twelfth century, and Castle of Giants to the superstitious serfs in the valley, who were convinced that mere humans could not have raised a stone fortress so high. Lord Adolph Rumpf, who built the castle and owned the serfs, assuring them that not only could they gather within the castle walls in the event of a barbarian attack, but that the unseen giants would help to defend the castle. For three centuries the enclosed stone structure was home to Lord Rumpf and his descendants, to servants, administrators of the fields and taxes, horses, soldiers, chickens, pigs and other livestock, for each of the four outer walls was nearly a thousand metres long. Neither the barbarians nor anyone else ever attacked, and in the year 1462, even as the Jews of Frankfurt were being walled into the Judengasse, the Rumpf descendants ceded their property to the Landgrave and his new state of Hesse and moved to a warmer and sunnier chateau they built on the Rhine.

The castle stood untouched for two hundred years. Then the former serfs — now called peasants — having not seen a giant in the vicinity for generations, began to vandalize the walls and turrets and doors for wood and stone with which to build sturdier huts of their own. The drawbridge over the dry moat was torn away, as were the great doors and much of the surrounding walls. Only in recent years had the remains of the castle been put to use again, as a gathering place for highwaymen. Here the thieves in the region slept easily between robberies. No police forces existed in the open lands, and should Constables from Hesse-Kassel, twenty kilometres to the north, or Hesse-Hanau, a hundred and fifty kilometres, to the south, or even the Landgrave's personal troops, try to march against them, the highwaymen could easily hold out in the two hundred fortified rooms still standing, until the officers of the law became tired, or hungry, and went home.

Decaying castles scattered all along the river Fulda had fallen into similar disrepair and disrepute, and Hersch Liebmann, alias Helmut Mann, from time to time had taken his ease in many of their cold and mournful, windowless stone-floored rooms. At the moment, Riesenburg suited Hersch's purposes best. It was the nearest castle to Hesse-Kassel, and only two kilometres from the north-south road leading in and out of that city.

The castle remains were so vast, with their rooms and half rooms, their walls and half walls, their shadows and half shadows, that Hersch Liebmann and Klaus Fettmilch did not find one another that night. Made generous by a full purse, Hersch tossed a coin to a couple of thieves roasting a rabbit over a fire in the dry moat, and he and Leni were invited to partake. Afterward, the two of them bedded down on saddle blankets in the castle keep, in a large room that once had been the chambers of a lord.

Rebecca and Simcha were lying together in a new feather bed they had purchased. She was looking at the ceiling, its wooden planks, a dark knot in one board shaped like the head of a horse. Her chest filled with remembered uncertainty, and she shuddered. The night was mild, only a thin sheet covered them. The lamps were off, a ghostly light from the moon, creeping in through the window, gave the many folds of the sheet a blue-white dimension.

"Are you tired, Simcha? Can I talk?"

His eyes were closed, but he seemed alert. "You can talk any time."

She found his hand, took it in hers. For comfort, or to better monitor his reaction — she was not sure.

"That day in the cemetery, when you asked me to marry you, you said something we both let pass. You said anyone who comes to live in the Judengasse voluntarily must be running away from something."

"Or hiding. Yes."

"You were speaking of yourself?"

"I was including myself."

"It's true of me as well."

"I know. I don't know what, or who, but I've always believed there was something."

Opening his eyes, he turned on his side to look at her, the new Rebecca, her black hair cropped short to fit under the caps and hats she had decided to wear in public instead of a sheitl — white caps while she was at work, large straw hats to complement her dresses on the Sabbath. They both felt the requirement in the Talmud for women to hide their hair was pointless, but they had agreed that as the wife of the Chief Rabbi she must follow the ancient tradition; if she wanted to break with the past, she should save her rebellions for more important matters.

"For you to stay here this long," he said, "to deny all men your beauty for fifteen years — it could not have been just your work."

"I've never told anyone what happened. I want to tell you, but I'm also hesitant. I want to keep your respect."

The room darkened from blue-white to gray as a cloud covered the moon. From the forbidden park beyond the wall they heard a dog's lonely howl.

"Somebody famous — whom I can't recall, that's how famous he was — wrote that 'the past is prologue.' Anything that brought you to me cannot be so bad."

She squeezed his hand for a moment. The room lightened to ghostly, the horse-head knot blinked at her memory.

"I was sixteen. I met a boy." She felt Simcha skip a breath, but she went on. "His name was Lucas. We met at a synagogue dance, while he was visiting a cousin on our street. He had the deepest brown eyes, the longest lashes, the smoothest skin, the… " She covered her eyes with her hand as his fingers tensed "I'm sorry, Emil." She twisted her body violently, pressed her face into his neck. "I'm sorry."

"Don't be. Go on with your story."

"You know that I belong to you now."

"Yes."

She touched his beard. This close, the graying hairs were a blur.

"We began to spend time together. We fell in love. When we were eighteen, he wanted us to marry. I had won admittance to Göttingen, which was difficult for girls. And for Jews. I told him I wanted to go to medical school, that we could marry afterward. He was very smart, interested in ideas. I suggested he come with me, study philosophy. We could be together until we received our degrees, then return to Berlin and marry. My father knew some of the faculty, and he managed to get Luke a late admission.

"He lived across the city. The day we were to leave for Göttingen, with our trunks of clothing, we were to meet at the coach station. It would be a long ride, with two nights spent at inns. My father took me to the coach house in his carriage. The morning skies were gray, I remember, and as we neared the station a light rain began to fall. We were early. Father and his driver put my heavy trunk in the waiting coach. I watched from a bench on a covered porch as four gray horses, each a different shade, were watered, and hitched to the coach. Every twenty miles we would stop at a post station to get fresh horses, the driver said. On the second day we would get a new coachman as well. I had never been far from Berlin, I was interested in what he was saying. Then I looked at my watch. It was almost time for the coach to leave. My heart started racing. Lucas had not yet arrived."

She looked at Simcha. He was listening intently, though saying nothing.

"Two other passengers had appeared, two merchants, or bankers, in black coats and white stockings, with white lace jabots at their necks. They, too, would be traveling to Göttingen. I left the bench and stood at the edge of the platform and peered down the road. The rain was heavier now. There was no sign of Lucas. I grabbed my father's arm, asked where Lucas was. He had no idea, of course.

"I saw one of the merchants look at his watch. I hurried inside to the driver, told him that my betrothed — I exaggerated, we were not officially betrothed — I told him my betrothed was coming as well, had bought a ticket, and would be along any moment. Checking his own watch, the driver said he could delay the departure five minutes, no more. That was a rule of the company, he said. In Berlin they are very punctual.

"I ran outside. I was becoming frantic. I ran a down the road in the rain, as if that would make Lucas appear. I was not thinking clearly, as you might imagine. I was wearing a large straw hat, bright yellow, tied under my chin with a green ribbon, and the rain rolled off it, wetting mostly my shoulders, and the hem of my dress. It was a white dress, the hem turning dark in the rain, just as my life was, I remember thinking. I climbed back onto the platform and asked my father, Where is he? Where is he? How was my father to know?

"The five minutes passed. The driver must have taken pity on me, because he stalled, adjusting the reins and bridles, checking the large wooden wheels, for another five minutes. I told my father I would not leave without Lucas. Father pointed out that I was due at the university in two days, that no other coach would leave today. One of the merchants overheard, and approached us. He was not a merchant at all, but a professor at Göttingen, going back for the new term. Rather than risk losing my place in the medical school, he told me, I must go, and tell them that my friend had been delayed, and would be arriving late. I didn't want to leave without him, but it made sense. Papa promised to wait at the coach station for another hour. When Lucas arrived, Papa would tell him to hire a fast horse and catch up with the coach down the road — certainly at the first post exchange. His trunk could be sent on later. I had no choice but to climb into the coach with the professor. We left without Lucas."

Rebecca's mouth was dry, she was not used to talking so much.

"And he didn't come?" Simcha asked. "He didn't overtake you on the road?"

Silent, remembering, Rebecca under the sheet moved her fingers among the hairs on her husband's abdomen. Finally she said, "I never saw him again."

Simcha closed his eyes, leaving the words hanging in the blue, attempting something he had learned from Rabbi Eleazar: trying to put himself into her body, her mind, at that time, trying feel what she must have felt. He stroked her hand.

"Those two nights at the coach house inns, I paced the floor, crying, afraid to sleep. I had no idea what had happened to him. Instead I slept as we rode, my head on the shoulder of the professor. At Göttingen, I moved as in a gypsy's trance. Every day I expected him to appear. Or at least to receive a letter, explaining. Every day was a disappointment. How I got through my studies I don't know. Some days I was furious with him. How could he abandon me like that? What had I done to him? Then I would be furious at myself for feeling that way — of course he would not abandon me. We loved one another. Something terrible must have happened to him that morning. Perhaps he had been waylaid by highwaymen, who stole his trunk and broke his skull. Or shot him, and left him in a forest. Then I would get into a rage at myself. Because it was my fault."

Simcha heard her despair. It was as if the young man's disappearance had happened yesterday. "Becca, Becca, how could it be your fault?"

"Because Lucas did not want to go."

"To the university?"

"He wanted to be a merchant, like his father. Import valuable antiques. From China. From India. From Persia. Make money for us, so we could be comfortable when we married. I told him that money was not important to me, that at the university we could be together."

"That didn't make you responsible for whatever happened."

"It did. If he was waylaid on the way to the coach — he would not have been there if I had not convinced him. If he fled on a ship, to China, to India — then I had been overbearing, had driven him away. For three months I wrestled with those thoughts, every night."

"Three months?"

"Then I received a letter."

Simcha took a deep breath, let it out silently, and waited.

"It was a complete rejection of me. Of everything about me. He never wanted to be a philosopher, he wrote. He never wanted to study at the university. He wanted to go to sea as a merchant. He didn't want a Doctor for a wife. He wanted a real woman, not a walking brain. A woman who would open her legs — he actually wrote that — and bear his children and raise them while he was off traveling."

She stopped, wiping tears from her cheeks, tears hot with memory.

"He was a fool," Simcha said softly.

"He wasn't a fool. He was honest. He had come to hate me for what I had done to him."

"What you had done to him? You hadn't done anything!"

"He didn't know the words. But I had taken away his manhood."

"That's nonsense. Look what you do to me." He kissed her cheek. "So you came here to forget."

"I managed to get through school. I felt awful every morning for years, but I wouldn't let him take my career from me. Afterward, I couldn't live in Berlin. Everywhere there would be memories. When I saw Lev Berkov's posting about a position here, I decided this would be the perfect place. I could hide myself inside the walls. Here I would not expect to see him around every corner — since there are no corners. I was a good Doctor — and an awful person. Here I could put up my own wall."

"You feared being betrayed again."

"Yes."

"And excised your emotions."

"When possible."

"When you first arrived here, Yussel Kahn liked you, as I recall."

"We used to talk. I was not ready for more. When Brendel came along, and rejuvenated him, it was clear I'd made the right decision."

"But all these years … "

"Sometimes in bed at night I wanted to die, I needed so badly to be touched. To be held. Calm Doctor Kirsch, always in control. But you know the men in the lane. Most of them feel the way Lucas did. The way almost all men do. I refused to go through that again. My work had to be enough."

"And now?"

She took his hand, placed his palm on her breast. "When your heart still beats, fifteen years is a long time to be dead."

Her roaming eyes found the horse-head knot, barely visible; the moon's reflected light had vanished. "Though part of me hates Lucas, every year, as Yom Kippur approaches, I think I should light a Yahrzeit candle in his memory. I once heard a rumor that he was on a ship that went down at sea. But I never have. Because he might still be alive."

"Perhaps this year you should light one. Not for him, but for you. To signify that he is dead in your heart."

Unable to contain a smile in the dark, Rebecca wondered if all men were that transparent, or only her Simcha. "I think I will do that," she said.

Birds were heralding the dawn with an avian orchestra. A skylark and a nightingale piped a fugue, a gold-fronted leaf bird fluted in harmony, a woodpecker tapped on an oak-trunk drum, pink and blue fruit doves, a colorful chorus, cooed. Lying on the grass, his hands behind his head, Hersch was reminded of his brother; like Hiram, the birds could make every sound but words. Yet he envied the freedom of their flight. Perhaps that's what Hiram was doing when he painted the pictures that Hersch had heard about. Perhaps the pictures were Hiram's wings.

"Damn birds!" Klaus Fettmilch, who had been sleeping on the grass a few metres away, sat up, muttering. "They kept me awake all night."

"You snored from dark to dawn."

As Klaus meandered down the path to the river, Leni came up behind Hersch and kissed the top of his head. "Why do you stay around that Klaus. I don't like him."

"I hate the cocky whore-son. But I've got a use for him. When the old Landgrave dies — a few days after — we can go away without him."

"What kind of a use for him?"

"I need him to tell somebody something. It's important. Don't worry your pretty head, find some twigs for a fire. We'll make some coffee."

The birds were chirping at the risen sun when they finished. "My horse is going lame," Hersch said. "I'm gonna go down the road a ways, see if I can find a nice horse in a pasture, that nobody's watching."

"I'll go with you," Klaus said. "See if I can find a young girl milking, that nobody's watching."

"Watch your mouth. There's a lady present."

Klaus looked directly at Leni, then around and behind him. "I don't see any lady," he said, and he grinned at them both. Hersch found a small stone on the ground, fired it at Klaus. It struck him in the knee. "That hurt!"

"Next time I'll make you eat it."

Klaus stood, rubbing his knee. "Some day, Jew, I'll hurt you bad. When you're not expecting it." He started to walk away, to find his black stallion.

Hersch turned to Leni, but spoke loudly. "That's the only time he'll try anything. When I'm not looking. Hey, Fettmilch, I know you won't poison me! You don't have three little boys to hold me down!"

Behind thick bushes ten metres away, Klaus bent and found a stone. In one motion he stood and fired it at Hersch. His aim was errant, the stone struck Leni in the face. From her knees she pitched forward, both hands covering her eyes, her long hair falling over her face like a curtain, almost into the dying fire. Hersch with his arms around her waist dragged her away from the smoking twigs, told her to lie back on the grass. Blood was trickling from high on her cheek, just below one eye. He looked at her small face, her pug nose, saw pain in her pale blue eyes. She had not made a sound since being struck. "Are you all right? You're not much for complaining."

"I don't like that man," Leni said.

The children were asleep. Guttle was strumming her harp, Meyer was reading the Talmud in his favorite chair, half listening to the tender chords. As the light burned low, he stood and adjusted the wick, and sat again. Hesitant, her heart beating rapidly, Guttle said, "We have to discuss something."

"I'm listening." He did not raise his eyes from his book.

"Many years ago, I got the idea to start a school for girls. I never acted on it."

"Which was very wise of you." He turned a page.

Guttle let her fingers rest on the strings. "Now I want to do it."

"Not a good idea." He put a marker in his book and set it aside. "What is different now than back then, when you first mentioned it?"

"Two things. Now we have the older children, who can watch the little ones. I'm thinking perhaps three mornings each week."

"And the other thing?"

"Rabbi Eleazar is gone. I was afraid back then that he would forbid it."

"You think Rabbi Simcha would approve? He still has to uphold the Torah, The Talmud."

"I don't know that he would approve. But it is not his nature to forbid."

"I'm not so sure. Have you asked him?"

"I wanted to speak with you first. Then I'll go to Rebecca for help. Surely he wouldn't forbid his wife. I want her to teach science. I plan to teach the girls to read and write German. And perhaps French history. Yussel would teach literature, and other history. Perhaps Brendel could teach them to dance."

"You have it all planned. Have you considered that asking Rebecca would put her on the spot? She's the Chief Rabbi's rebbetzin."

"People have to act on what they believe. If she agrees, she could talk to Simcha."

"Of course. And that would put Simcha on the spot. You want to come between man and wife? Sometimes what seems like a good idea can lead to disaster."

Guttle stood from her round stool beside the harp. "It doesn't have to be that way! Why do you see it like that?"

"I see things as they are. You've told me that often enough." He lifted his yarmulke, ran his hand through his hair. "Listen to me, Guttle. You have not thought this through. This is a dangerous thing you are proposing. It will divide the lane into opposing factions — divide it as perhaps it has never been divided before."

"There are always factions over something. Look what happened when I brought in Georgi. Some were upset, but they learned to live with him. They even like him now, if they admit the truth."

"Georgi was different. The idea of him upset people, but they could ignore him if they wanted. A school to teach girls — teach them subjects that even the boys are not taught? Think about it. It goes against five thousand years of tradition. That is sufficient reason right there. But consider what would happen. Some girls will want to attend the school, and their parents won't let them. This will cause unhappiness for both. Those girls who are not allowed to attend might become envious of those who do. Worse than that — it could upset the entire social order in the lane. What young man will want to marry a girl who is more worldly wise than he is? These girls you teach — the more you educate them, the less marriageable they become."

Guttle was stunned by his diatribe — by the obvious truth of it. "Not necessarily," she said, weakly. "Look at Rebecca."

"Fine, look at Rebecca. She's, what, forty years old? It took her that long to find a husband. Perhaps too long to have children."

"She doesn't want children."

"There you go. I admire Rebecca Kirsch — Frau Simcha now..."

"Doctor Simcha."

"Right. Doctor Simcha. I admire her as much as anyone. But turn girls into scholars, and where will mothers come from? And babies — the future Jews? And who was strong enough to marry her, in the end? The new Chief Rabbi! For your plan, we don't have enough Chief Rabbis."

"You married me!"

"Exceptions there always are."

"Who is the exception, you or I?"

"No doubt both of us."

He seemed to run out of words suddenly, like a carriage horse pulling up short at the post house. Guttle sat, feeling almost as if she had been physically beaten. "What if everything you say is true," she said, her voice hoarse, "and what I want to do is the right thing to do?"

"Who says it is right?"

"Mendelssohn, for one."

"He is just one man."

"Sometimes acting morally has consequences. But it is still acting morally."

"That's true. But in this case, most of the lane will not agree with you."

Meyer picked up the Talmud from the small table beside him, looked at its worn leather cover, set it down again. He pulled his watch from his pocket. "It's late. I have to go to bed. Promise me you won't do this."

"I can't promise so much."

"So much? Am I asking so much — that you listen to your husband? What can you promise then, if not that much?"

"I can promise to consider what you said. To consider the consequences."

"Fair enough." He stood from his chair. "You're the smartest woman I know. If you consider the consequences, you'll come to the right decision." He leaned over, kissed her forehead. "Now, if you'll come to bed, we can put this disagreement behind us."

"You go. I have considering to do."

"Can't it wait until morning?"

"It wouldn't let me sleep. Of that I'm sure."

Meyer moved toward the top of the stairs. "You'll turn down the lamp?"

"I'll turn down the lamp."

As Meyer descended, Guttle exhaled deeply, rested her head on the back of her chair, tried to breathe slowly, deliberately. To the empty room she said, "Now the battle begins."

Rebecca and Guttle were sitting in the Café after closing time. Brendel had shut the doors, was washing dishes in the kitchen, while her two friends drank tea and talked.

"What Meyer says is true, Guttle. Everything he predicted is likely to happen. Are you sure you want that?"

"Are you saying you won't help me?"

"That's not what I said."

"You know it's the right thing for us to do."

"You're putting me in a difficult position. I'm not alone anymore. This will reflect on my husband. He could even forbid it. How would that look, if I am involved?"

"There's no place large enough to to do it except your old house, with Melekh sleeping in the attic."

"What about the community room?"

"They would never allow that. It's part of the synagogue."

Rebecca sipped her tea, bit into a macaroon. Guttle was tense as she awaited a response. The shouts of children playing in the lane were distracting. There seemed to be a fight taking place.

"I have an idea," Rebecca said, sounding uncertain. "But first you need to think this through again. Bitterness could run in the lane like the sewage."

"Then you'll help? We can use your house?"

"You have to request the community room."

"Why? That will require a public meeting. Public approval."

"So? You might as well see what you'll be up against."

"I don't see…"

Rebecca put her hand on Guttle's. "This question is not about you, or me. It's about the Chief Rabbi. Trust me."

Drying her hands on a towel, Brendel entered the Café from the kitchen. "So, what have you two conspirators decided? Are we going to assault the bastions?"

Guttle sighed, closing her eyes wearily, trying to rub pain from her forehead. "I don't know," she murmured. "Someone must."

44

1 3 October

Consider the consequences. Think this through. How could I not?

Three women came to visit last night. Whether I was awake or asleep I cannot say.

We met in the bakery, long after it had closed for the night. Joan of Arc was there — not my imaginary Jennie — and Madame Antoine, is now Queen Marie Antoinette — but not Melka, or Melekh; to my surprise, Mama was there instead. The fires in the stoves had been banked, with embers left glowing for the bakery women to stoke up easily in the dawn. Perhaps that is why Mama came; she no longer works there, but it is one of the few places where she still feels comfortable. The embers cast an orange glow over all of us as Mama pulled her gray robe tight around her, the hem of her white nightgown showing beneath, and sat on the stone bench where so many years ago I used to search for beetles. Madame Antoine made a throne for herself of one of the tables on which by day the flour and eggs and yeast are rolled into braided challah, which, oddly, her pale brown hair seemed got up to resemble, though no challah braids, I think, were ever studded with emeralds. For Joan of Arc no makeshift seat sufficed to contain her. Dressed in men's clothing, covered shoulder to boot in heavy armor that glinted a fiery orange, she preferred to pace near the entry, as far from the stoves as possible — because of the heat, she said, though the glow of the embers may have been reason enough. I did not recognize her at first, and thought she might be an impostor. The Joan of Arc depicted by all the painters is tall and thin, blue-eyed, fair and pretty; in person or spirit she was none of these; she was short, stocky, brown-eyed and dark, as befit the French peasant girl she was.

"But I had lovely breasts," she said when I questioned these discrepancies. For a moment I feared she would strip off her clothing to prove this. She did no such thing, modest maid that she was, and it was not long before a certain

magnetism emanating from her person dispersed my doubts. "Your artists fit glory into their own notions of beauty," she said, with benign acceptance. "Lean and weak I could not have done what I did. It was essential that I was a woman, of course, which is why I speak of breasts; a man with my accomplishments would long since have been forgotten. If the artists need make me tall and fair, let them; I would have burned equally well."

I was startled by her easy manner about the flames; perhaps it was because, though dead, she lives on.

"But my appearance is not why you summoned me here," she continued. "You are torn about how to proceed in some conflicted matter. Spare me the Jewish details, which I surely would not understand. And those involving learning; I never learned to read — though this proves nothing, except that God chooses whom He will to do His work. My simple message is this: oppose the authorities and there will be consequences, there is never doubt of that. But if your inner voices tell you to fight, then you must fight. How else to remain in a state of grace, not only with your God but with yourself?"

As I absorbed from her own lips the words she'd lived by, my blood stirred like the blood of a warrior. But Madame Antoine, smoothing the shadows of her stunning skirt, did not agree. "There is such a fine thing as compromise," she said, examining the painted nails of her fingers. "I offer myself as a prime example. The people of France are suffering. Drought has caused a terrible shortage of bread. When I ride along the roads in my chariot I do what I can; I stop and give money to the women, to feed their children; I love children; to see them hungry tugs at my heart. But what of the jewels I wear? The diamonds on one necklace could feed an entire province for a year. No one knows that better than I. But they brought me from Vienna to Versailles to be a Queen; they expect me to act like one, to look like one. A poor symbol of France I would be without rubies, sapphires, emeralds, pearls, without ivory combs and lapis buttons, without trains of the finest silk, without the rarest feathers in my hair. I give the courtiers the Queen they demand — while quietly I give the poor at least some of the livres they need. In every conflict there is a place for compromise." She glanced at Joan, who was listening while she paced, her armor crackling at times. "If nothing else," the Queen said, "it is a way to avoid the fire."

I saw Joan wince. She started to speak, then changed her mind and turned away, her sword clanking against her metal thigh. As for myself, I felt confused.

"Compromise? I cannot start half a school for girls. They will not burn me if I proceed. But people have been shunned for less. Why should I invite such trouble?"

"Exactly, bubbelah." It was Mama answering; I had not realized I had spoken that last thought aloud. "Why go looking for trouble? It will find you often *enough without you looking for it." How Mama allowed herself to speak in such company I didn't know. Perhaps the loosening of her hold on life had loosened her fears, her deference, as well.*

"Because it's the right thing to do."

"Are you so sure of that?" Mama asked. "Why not listen to the wisdom of the Queen, and compromise? Teach a few girls in your home, as you do already with your own daughters. Don't call it a school, and people will look the other way. That's the first thing we learn in the lane — to look the other way. One day some man will start a school for girls, and then perhaps few will object."

I could feel Joan seething. With anger she thrust her sword hard into a flour sack. The brown flour running out suggested, in the orange darkness, blood from a belly. "Then it will be charity," she said, and spat. "A woman must do it, to show other women the way. There's more than milk in a woman's breasts, there's courage. You need to find it."

"And burn in the fire?" the Queen asked.

"There are compensations. They have shown me the future. I shall be called Saint Joan. The church that condemned me shall canonize me."

"We Jews don't have saints," I mused, and smiled at the notion of Saint Guttle. Hardly.

"Surely you have the wise, the valiant, the heroic," Joan said.

"Mostly we honor tzadiks."

"What are they?"

"Very righteous men."

"And the name for very righteous women?"

I had to think a bit. "We don't have such a word."

"Maybe no word," Mama put in, "but there are many honored women in the Torah. Sarai, Rachel… "

"Did they oppose the will of men?" Joan asked.

"They bore righteous sons!"

Joan of Arc, Marie Antoinette, said nothing,

Mama turned to me with a pleading look. "Guttle, darling, you, too, have borne sons. No doubt you will bear more. You have suckled them at your breasts. Will you be instructed about a woman's proper function, a breast's proper use, by a virgin? By a Queen who surely employs wet nurses? You have a righteous man; he will raise your sons righteously. Why must you want more?"

After the disarray of Mama's mind in recent months, I felt an unaccountable fear at her lucidity. Declining rapidly, she has been regressing into Biblical yesterdays; this morning she called the River Main the Red Sea. The scientific name for this condition is dementia, Rebecca says. But Mama does have her lucid hours. For these midnight arguments, to what distant fount of wisdom had she traveled?

For one final moment before they disappeared, the Queen spoke. "I must tell you this. I never said it. About eating cake. Never. That's a canard invented by those who want my head. If your enemies will speak ill of you no matter what you do, why not do as you like?"

I had no response. I lay awake most of the night, long after they all had vanished, writhing in search of an answer.

14 October

It was Melekh after all who led me to decide. I recalled the day we found him there in his lead coffin in the attic of the River View — me and Izzy, Yussel and Rebecca. It struck me like a revelation — two men and two women! Given the most sacred secret of the lane! Surely this would not have been so if women were to remain inferior in knowledge, and in Yahweh's eyes. He had prepared this lesson for me so long ago — right there in Rebecca's house! — but only now did I interpret the meaning. Unless some deeper part of me understood it, has been responding to it, has been leading me to this, all along.

What was Brendel's phrase? We will assault the bastions.

Yes!

Having finished work in his counting house, reckoning their net worth, Meyer summoned Guttle to tell her the final tally privately. He spoke without preamble, calmly, but in a voice tinged with excitement. "We have one hundred and fifty thousand gulden."

"Meyer, that's wonderful! We must be the richest people in the lane!"

"Oh, far from that. The south end banker, Emil Hecksher, has more than four hundred thousand, I would guess."

"That much?"

"Still, it's a good accumulation. We've surpassed your father, I think. I would estimate we're among the ten wealthiest families in the Judengasse. But the amount is our secret. You can't tell anyone."

"Not even Papa?"

"Not even him. Something three people know is no more a secret."

She placed her hands on the back of his neck to rub away the knots she could feel. "Whatever you say, Herr Genius."

He wriggled his shoulders gratefully. "It doesn't take genius. Just concentration."

"But what about that?" She was peering over his shoulder at a ledger that lay open on the slanting table. "The ledger says sixty thousand."

"That's for the tax assessors. About the rest they don't have to know."

"You've done that before?"

"There wasn't so much cash before." He looked at her. "Does that bother you?"

"The way they treat us, they don't deserve a kreuzer."

"My feeling exactly."

A rapping on the door, by small knuckles, interrupted them. Guttle opened it and found Nathan there, in trousers she had made for him after the fashion of the sailors on the docks, and scuffed shoes, and a hand-me-down shirt from Salomon, and an oversized yarmulke — the eager boy unable to be still, standing first on one foot, then hopping to the other. "There's a messenger here for Papa. From the Crown Prince!"

He said the last words with awe and admiration. Puzzled, Meyer raised an eyebrow as he eased his way past Guttle into the vestibule. At the arched doorway he accepted a small brown envelope from the courier, checked that the wax seal was unbroken, and from his pocket withdrew a coin and gave it to the man for his trouble. Peering at the seal as Guttle joined him in the bright vestibule, Meyer said, "It's not from Wilhelm, it's from the treasury office. That means Buderus." He broke the seal, and with mounting anticipation — for he suddenly had an inkling of what it might contain — he pulled out a single piece of note paper. He scanned it quickly, then read it to her.

"Wilhelm's father, the Landgrave Friedrich, is dead. The funeral is Wednesday. Wilhelm will be crowned on Thursday. You might want to be there. Buderus."

Both remained silent as they absorbed the news. Meyer was not completely surprised, he had heard rumors of an illness.

"That means in Hesse-Kassel," Guttle said. "That's a long way."

"One hundred and fifty kilometres. A two-day trip each way. I should leave tomorrow to be in time for the funeral. After the coronation, I would have to stay over, so as not to ride on Shabbas. That's all right, I can make good contacts there. I would be back in a week."

"You've never stayed away overnight before. Not even once. The children will be upset."

"I'll talk to them. Guttle, do you realize what this means? As Crown Prince, Wilhelm has a fortune. As Landgrave, he'll inherit twenty times as much. Beyond counting, almost. When I get his investments — and I will — I'll have something real to work with. Then maybe you'll see a genius."

"But you haven't had his investments for ten years. Not since you discounted the British bills for his soldiers. He's acted as if you lost his money, instead of doubling it."

"I know. I don't know why. Neither does Buderus. But Buderus is still there. Look what he wrote, 'You might want to be there.' It's easy enough to finish the sentence. '... if you know what's good for you.' To Buderus, I still have opportunity."

"I don't want you to go. It's too dangerous. Besides, you're clinging to an old hope. Wilhelm clearly isn't interested."

"Then I have to make him interested. All my life Yahweh has told me to work hard and take risks and get rich. I can't tell you why, there's no place to spend in the lane. Still ... "

She had never forgotten Amelia's view of Meyer years ago: that the money he accumulates represents his lost mother's love. She dared not say that to him. Instead she asked, "Yahweh speaks with you?" He had never said such a thing before.

"Not with a voice, like your Jennie Aron."

"You've heard me speak to her as well?"

"Only in the night. She heard heavenly voices, and look what happened to her. Some God that was. I don't hear Adonai's voice, it's just a feeling I have. Ever since my parents died. To collect coins, to make money. It seems important — for what purpose, I'm not sure."

"But it's been ten years!"

"Buderus says it will be worth my while. Maybe Yahweh speaks to Buderus."

"He's Jewish?"

"No. But Adonai may be open-minded."

"I've never met this Buderus. Does he even exist?"

"He just sent a messenger with this note, no? I have to go. I can't disobey my feelings."

"What about my feelings? Seven days? It frightens me. There are highwaymen. I don't want to be left a widow."

"And my feelings about you starting a school? That frightens me. You have to follow your heart, you told me. You'd better make your heart strong for the meeting tonight, I doubt it will be pleasant. But I have to follow my feelings as well. I have to go to Kassel." Meyer took her arms in his hands. "I'll be safe. Adonai will look after me."

"Everyone thinks that." She turned away from him. "Go then, if you must. I will miss you."

"And I, you." He wrapped his arms around her waist from behind, lightly kissed the back of her neck, imbibed his favorite scent.

"You'd better hurry."

"I have till tomorrow."

"To Ziggy's. To hire a horse and carriage, before he has none left."

"I was thinking the regular coach."

"They might be full. You won't be the only one going."

Meyer kissed her cheek, and said, "Where would I be without you?" Still in his shirt sleeves, he hurried out the door.

Hersch Liebmann was riding the twenty kilometres from Riesenburg Castle into Kassel for two reasons. He wanted to hear if there was any news, and he wanted to build the stamina of his new filly, a dappled gray no more than three years old, with a sleek but promising build. In his fifteen years in the wilds he had become a good judge of horseflesh; even Ziggy Zigmund would have found no fault with this one. Because he had to call her something, Hersch had named her Yetta, after his mother. He let the filly walk easily, galloped her, walked her more, interrupting that with an occasional sprint. He liked a horse that could change speeds quickly; back on the castle grounds he would work on her change of directions. As horse and rider reached the outskirts of Kassel, Hersch pulled lightly on the reins. The sound was unmistakable now. Church bells. He thought he'd been hearing them for the last kilometre; now he was certain. They were not tolling the hour, something had happened. He could guess what it was. He touched Yetta's flanks and the horse moved forward. Around a bend a farmer on an empty wagon that smelled like hay was approaching.

"What are the bells for?" Hersch called out as they came together.

"The Landgrave is gone."

"Are you sure?"

"I hope so, for his sake. They're gonna bury him Wednesday."

Hersch grinned at the tired joke, touched his cap and moved on, leading Yetta deeper into the city. He wanted to make sure. He was peering at the Landgrave's palace about four streets away when he had to pull up sharply to avoid running down a town crier. The fellow was walking in the road holding a sign on a pole. "Landgrave Friedrich Is Dead — Funeral Wednesday Noon," the sign said, black letters on a white background. As the man walked he cried out the news for the masses who could not read. When Hersch had passed the man and looked back, he could read the other side. In red letters against gold, it proclaimed, "Long Live Landgrave Wilhelm — Coronation Thursday Noon."

Farther along the street he saw criers walking in every direction, dressed like the first in the Landgrave's colors, red and gold, carrying similar signs as they moved through the town. The streets were becoming crowded, people streaming toward the palace. Hersch turned the filly and threaded back against the incoming tide. He knew all he needed.

He found Klaus Fettmilch sitting by a dead fire, polishing his already gleaming sword. The former Kapitäin stood and waved the sword about, causing Yetta to back off skittishly.

"Where's Leni?"

"Probably in the castle keep. She doesn't seem to like my company."

"Who can blame her?" Hersch swung off the filly's back, tied the reins to a tree. "But never mind that. Friedrich is dead. Soon the roads will be crawling with easy marks."

"Is the deal still good? I get three-fourths of the take?"

"If you do what I said."

"I know, I know. Tell this Jew Rothberg what happened. But how come you're so sure he'll show?"

"Rothschild. I told you. He was kissing Wilhelm's ass way back then. He's not going to miss the coronation."

"And I have to tell him what I did, why?"

"Do you ever pay attention? He's the one who accused me of murder, got me thrown out of the Judengasse. I want him to hear the truth, from your own mouth."

"And after I tell him, you expect me to let him live? Let him spread the story about? I'd sooner slice open his bowels."

"After you tell him, I don't care what you do."

Fettmilch raised his sword above his head. Holding it with both hands, he plunged it viciously into the ground, as if his worst enemy were lying there.

"A clean kill," Hersch said, "so long as the fellow was asleep." He patted the flank of the filly, who was grazing calmly, and he said to Klaus, "I'm going to find Leni."

As Hersch walked off towards the ruined castle, Klaus called out, "I'll give you some advice. Don't believe a word the whore says!"

45

—Did you hear? Levi and Cohen are not speaking.

—If they're not speaking, how could I hear? What are they not speaking about?

—That school for girls, of course.

—How can you tell?

— That's what everyone's not talking about.

—Everyone's not talking?

—Steinbaum's not talking to Greenbaum. Rosenbaum's not talking to Cedarbaum. Frau Schwartz is not talking to Herr Schwartz. Julia Licht isn't talking to her father.

—Come to think of it, the lane sounds pretty quiet.

—Except for the ones who are arguing. Kahn is arguing with Schultz. Mincus is arguing with Steinbaum.

—… who isn't talking to Rosenbaum.

—No, to Rosenbaum he's talking. To Berger he isn't talking.

—Berger's also not talking? What's the big deal, they want a school? So what?

—That's what you think, so what? Are you meshuganah? Feh, maybe I'm not talking to you!

—Is that so! How will I know you're not talking to me?

—I'll tell you.

—Listen, find someone else not to talk to. I'm busy.

The yeshiva auditorium had not been this crowded since the debate between Moses Mendelssohn and Rabbi Eleazar nearly ten years earlier. The extra chairs normally stacked high against the walls had been set out behind the permanent ones. Hundreds of men and a few dozen women filled the seats; most of the women of the lane had stayed at home with their children, and would abide by whatever rules the men decided upon, as was the custom.

The Chief Rabbi, who at the end of the evening would rule on the question, sat alone at a small table; Rabbi Joshua would preside over the meeting. Guttle, as the chief proponent of the school for girls, sat in the front row, to the right, in a dark blue dress. To her surprise, her father had taken a seat beside her. Meyer Amschel, busy preparing for his journey to Hesse-Kassel, had arrived late, and stood with scores of others at the rear.

The leader of the opposition, the moneylender Jacob Marcus, wearing a black suit and a brown yarmulke, sat in the front row to the left. The shoemaker Alexandre Licht, still in his leather apron, sat beside him. The two had become unlikely family when their children married.

Banging a gavel several times to silence the chatter that filled the hall, Rabbi Joshua stated the resolution that had been the talk of the lane for days: "That a secular school for girls should be permitted to function in the community room." He explained the rules: that speakers on each side would alternate; that the opposed faction would speak first, since they had demanded the meeting; that each argument should be presented only once, because the Chief Rabbi would decide the case on the merits, not on the number of supporters pro and con; repetition would be ruled out of order, lest the meeting last till dawn.

With that, he called on the first speaker for the opposition. Jacob Marcus ascended to the lectern. Guttle, breathing deeply to calm herself, wondered why she and the Marcus family seemed fated always to be enemies. She felt her father squeeze her hand.

"Put them in their place, Jacob!" a man's voice shouted from the rear.

Marcus nodded, raised a hand for silence. He stroked his gray beard several times, in a manner that reminded some of the late Chief Rabbi Eleazar. Perhaps that was his intent.

"I shall be brief," he began. "The law, the Halakah, is on our side. There can be no overruling it. According to the Halakah, Adonai enjoined, and I quote, 'fathers to teach their sons.' It mentions nothing of their daughters, or their wives. Just 'fathers to teach their sons.' Scholars of the Torah, the Talmud, the Mishna, have noted for five millennia that the sacred writings are concise, that they do not waste a word — that omissions are as significant as inclusions. The omission of the words 'and daughters' is a clear statement that they were specifically excluded; it is no different than if the Halakah said, in so many words, 'they shall not teach their daughters.' For this reason, I ask the Chief Rabbi to declare this meeting over, and rule according to the law."

The crowd murmured with approval as Marcus looked at Rabbi Simcha. The Chief Rabbi waved his hand in a circle in the air, indicating that the meeting should continue. When Rabbi Jonah tried to approach the lectern, Marcus remained where he was. "I don't know what a wave of the hand means," he said. "Could the Chief Rabbi speak?"

"We are here to listen to arguments, not to silence them," Simcha said from his table, impatience in his voice. "If this speaker has finished, let us proceed to the rebuttal."

Guttle clenched her hands into fists. She could not respond to every argument herself, each speaker was allowed but one turn. She needed her allies to speak. Rebecca had told her she would not participate, because her husband was the judge. Guttle turned, seeking Yussel Kahn in the audience. Instead, she felt her father rise beside her, watched as he walked to the podium. He had not told her he would do this.

"The honorable Jacob Marcus has quoted the Halakah correctly," Wolf Schnapper began. Guttle realized he had dressed in his best black suit, the one he wore to special occasions at court. "But Marcus errs when he says it cannot be changed. It has been changed, has evolved, in the past. I shall limit myself to one example.

"Our honored forebears, whose lives are recited in the Torah, practiced polygamy. They were permitted to have many wives — as was also the case in non-Jewish tribes. Perhaps the best-known example is Jacob, son of Isaac, grandson of Avram. Jacob took four wives — four sisters, in fact — Leah, Rachel, Zilpah and Bilhah. No one argues that Jacob sinned. Certainly the Torah does not. Taking many wives was common practice among the Jews of the time. Yet I wonder why it was accepted."

He paused, poured water from a pitcher into a glass, and drank. Smiling sheepishly, Guttle found herself filling with pride as her father defended her school. She had not felt so wonderfully close to him since the night of her betrothal, when he'd entrusted her to Meyer.

"Here is why I raise this question. We all know that in the beginning, Adonai created Adam and Eve. But wait a moment. That is one man and one wife. The Torah does not say God created Adam and Eve and Emmie. Or Adam and Eve and Guttle."

"Thank God for His wisdom," someone yelled.

Schnapper flushed. "Or Adam and Eve and Sophie," he said, looking at Marcus, who turned away. "Just Adam and Eve. One man, one woman. The learned Herr Marcus has pointed out that omissions in the sacred writings are as important as things stated. Very well. Where are Adam's other wives, if Yahweh intended men to have more than one? They have been omitted, because they did not exist. It is clear from this that He intended man to be monogamous.

"A second citation. The Torah says in Genesis, 'Therefore shall a man leave his father and mother and cleave to his wife, and they shall be one flesh.' The wording is singular. One wife. One flesh. Is that not a clear instruction for monogamy?

"But for thousands of years, the compilers of the Halakah, the Jewish law, did not make this interpretation. Why not? Because it would have gone against the common practice. It was not until eight hundred years ago that Rabbi Gershom ben Judah, just down the road in Mainz, issued his famous ruling that banned polygamy among Jews. Why did he do that? What had changed?"

No sound could be heard as Schnapper paused again for a sip of water.

"What had changed was that the civilizations around us gave up polygamy. Most Jews gave it up as well. But some continued to practice it — and the learned Rabbi from Mainz saw that this was being held against us by our neighbors. They viewed us as having a lower morality. So he changed the law. He ruled that taking more than one wife was a sin. My point here is that the law can evolve. As to whether girls should be educated — I leave that to future speakers."

Light applause sprinkled through the room like rain. Most of the audience did not stir; they anticipated juicier arguments to come. Guttle squeezed her father's hand as he sat, and pressed her forehead into his shoulder, in silent thanks. He had been so well-meaning — even if his example could be turned against her.

Rabbi Jonah called for the next speaker for the opposition. People looked toward Alexandre Licht, but he did not rise from his seat. Instead it was Hannah Schlicter who approached the lectern. Pleased to see a woman on their side, many of the men applauded even before she began.

"My neighbor, Wolf Schnapper, did not speak of the education of girls," she said. "But that is why we are here. So I shall speak of it. I have had two tragedies in my life. I lost my husband to highwaymen. And I lost my first-born daughter to education. Yes, to education! Many of you know the story, it has been whispered about often enough. It is time for me to speak up publicly — to save some of you from suffering the same tragedy.

"My daughter, Dvorah, was a good girl. She had no fancy notions. When her best friend, Guttle Schnapper, taught herself to read German, Dvorah wanted to do the same; you know how jealous girls can be of one another. It was a struggle, but she managed, with Guttle's help. I thought little of it at the time. Dvorah married our fine Doctor, Lev Berkov. They had wonderful twins. Then what happened? A Christian gentleman came into the lane one day and took a liking to my Dvorah. What man wouldn't, with her lovely face and figure? He sent her a book — a German book, some kind of love story — and with this book the goy made love to her, from afar, and turned her head."

Hannah passed her hands in front of her eyes, as if brushing away a cobweb from the past, a spider's lair of indecency.

"It hurts me to speak of the rest — how my Dvorah, under a Christian spell, ran off with that man, leaving her husband and children behind. Dvorah's life, and my life, and Lev Berkov's life have been ruined, because Guttle Schnapper, now Guttle Rothschild — the same person who wants to start this school for girls — because she taught my daughter to read German! And what has Guttle Rothschild done since? She refuses to answer Dvorah's letters — her best friend! — as if Dvorah, not she herself, is the sinner. If this school is approved, your daughters, like mine, will be the prey of Christian gentleman. The goys do not want good girls steeped in Jewish prayers, they want 'educated' girls they can flaunt before the world. If we let this school open, our daughters will be educated out of the lane, out of their families, out of our lives."

Sympathy followed Hannah Schlicter to her seat, and murmurs of assent. Guttle felt as if she had been kicked in the stomach. She could barely breathe. Such nonsense, she thought — wasn't it? It was not the book that had seduced Dvorah, but the opportunity for wealth, the chance to flee the lane. Did Hannah not know her own daughter? Had she convinced herself that what she spoke was the truth? Guttle needed to answer, to defend herself, but she could not; she was not about to waste her allotted turn besmirching Dvorah, any more than her mother had already done. But to leave that fairy tale unanswered?

She felt the warmth in the room overcoming her, the smell of sweat, of stale breath, of wool, of camphor from clothing newly rescued from cedar chests against October's chill.

Rabbi Jonah asked for the third time if there was a rebuttal speaker. He was about to call for the opposition to speak again when the crowd, especially the women, oohed with pleasure as Doctor Lev Berkov strode to the lectern, still lean and handsome despite the worry lines in his face, the streaks of gray in his hair and goatee. Quivering with curiosity, the women leaned forward, gossip creating more rapture than Godliness, even here.

"Despite my profession, I am not a public person," the Doctor began. "It pains me to acknowledge in any way the statements you just heard from my former mother-in-law. It pains me even more to spell out the truth, which until now has been my personal preserve. But slander against the teaching of reading, in any language, is something no intelligent man can let stand. Revealing my own personal shortcomings is nothing before that."

Guttle recalled Dvorah's drooling over Paul von Brunwald. Watching Lev now, she admired his courage in speaking out.

"So," the Doctor said. "I must make it clear that what came between my former wife and myself was not a book. No made-up story can destroy a marriage — except, perhaps, whispered lies. The guilty person in my divorce was not the German writer Goethe. Nor was it Dvorah. It certainly was not Guttle Rothschild. It was myself. I was guilty of ignoring my wife, in favor of my work at the hospital. Blaming it on reading, blaming it on Guttle Rothschild in order to oppose a school — that is either malice or ignorance. I should have made clearer to Dvorah, before we married, my dedication to the hospital, to the health of each one of you, and your parents, and your children."

"Hoorah for the good Doctor," a woman yelled.

"Please," Berkov said, "I did not come up here for your approval, merely to tell the facts. As long as I am here, however, I would like to point out where educating a woman can lead."

"You tell them, Doctor," Alexandre Licht shouted, sensing an unexpected ally.

Berkov peered into the audience, and pointed. "Will you please stand up?"

Rebecca had not wanted to be part of the argument; she saw no choice now but to stand.

"You all know this woman, Doctor Rebecca Simcha," Berkov said. "Some of you in this room would be dead by now had not Rebecca, a long time ago, learned to read."

Murmurs and nods. Berkov left the lectern, returned to his seat beside Rebecca.

The room grew warmer still from so many bodies. One of the lamps began to flicker, as if doused by perspiration, the illusion of flames dancing on the wall. Guttle's nerves grew taut as harp strings as her turn to speak drew nearer. Rabbi Jonah had told her he would be the final speaker for the opposition; she would follow him. She smoothed her belly to calm the tense child inside.

A woman whom Guttle did not know said what Meyer had predicted days before. "What man will marry a woman who knows more about the world than he does? How will I marry off my four daughters? I'll have a house full of old maids. Is that how to improve our lives? Better their wombs should be full of babies than their brains full of facts." The loudest cheers of the evening surged through the hall, men and women alike joining in. Rabbi Jonah had to rap his gavel to restore silence.

Again Guttle fretted when, at first, no one responded. Then Brendel Isaacs strode forward, shapely in a plain gray dress, a subdued style for her. "The school will not be mandatory," she said from the podium. "No girl will have to come. That woman's daughters will not have to attend if she does not want them to." The Café owner took a step away from the lectern, tucked a stray blonde ringlet under her wide-brimmed purple hat, then added, "No old maid will be forced to take dancing lessons from me."

Men in the audience laughed; others raised eyebrows. Despite her fifteen years in the lane, Brendel's wit still was overshadowed by her sensuality. She winked at Guttle as she left the podium.

Alexandre Licht spoke next. Guttle braced for a personal attack; the shoemaker had disliked her ever since their confrontation over Georgi Kremm. But Licht, gray hair showing beneath his familiar beret, took a different approach.

"Today, my youngest daughter told me she hates me," he said.

She could feel the attention of the audience quicken.

"You all know me, I make good shoes and boots. This I do without knowing what a bunch of dead Greeks wore on their feet. I was able to provide a fine dowry for my older girl, Leah, when she married our fine Cantor, Viktor Marcus. Every day in the schul I thank Adonai for their happy marriage, for their two healthy children, and a third on the way. My wife Sonia, peace be upon her, must be qvelling up in heaven. I have had a good life. Until today. Today my youngest said she hates my kishkas, my guts." The shoemaker paused, rubbed his eyes with his scarred hands, as if brushing away tears, plunged his hands into the pockets of his apron. "What did I do to deserve this? She begged me for the third time to let her attend this new school her friends are talking about. And for the third time, I did what I had to do, what Adonai tells me to do. I told her no. If there is such a school, her two best friends will be attending, she says. I told her I didn't care, that Yahweh's word is more important. So thanks to talk of this so-called school, my daughter hates me." He paused, glanced around the room. "I can see by some of your nodding faces that I am not alone."

Licht seemed about to say more, but turned and left the platform. Guttle swallowed with difficulty. Who could respond to that? Who could tell a father it is all right that his daughter doesn't like him anymore?

She was right; no one stood to respond. She slumped, feeling miserable, abject. Then like a lovely bird a girl's voice flew over the audience from among those standing in the rear. "No daughter will hate a father who truly loves her!"

Amazed, knowing the voice, Guttle swiveled to look. Schönche was standing beside Meyer. Had he told her what to say? Of course not! Till now a shy girl, Schönche at thirteen was blossoming quickly. Guttle felt her own courage renewing itself.

Turning back, she saw that the cobbler had not yet taken his seat, but was staring at the rear with hard, squinting eyes.

No one else signaled to speak. Rabbi Jonah, his long white beard touching the lectern, began, raising one hand toward the ceiling and the heavens beyond, his forefinger extended.

"You have heard powerful arguments against this school," he began. "I shall give you the most important one." His voice seemed to be shaking with anger; his raised finger began to tremble; he resembled drawings of prophets from the Bible. His voice rose to a roar. "Ideas such as this school could mean the end of the Jewish people!"

Guttle was nonplussed by the thunderous claim; it was absurd. She wondered if his trembling was a trick he had learned. But from many in the hall came mumblings of agreement.

"Our religion, which is primary to our nature, is distinct from that of all other nations," Jonah intoned. "We Jews, as trained by Moses and the prophets, set for the world a moral and social example. Our system is unique. It has been tested by time. The ancient Greeks are gone, and the Romans, and the Assyrians, and and a host of other civilizations. But we Jews are still here. In a ghetto, yes, but still here.

"Our religion is one of humility. 'Thou shalt walk humbly with thy God.' That's all that is required of us in this life. Walk humbly with Yahweh. We do this in our daily prayers, in our devotion to study of the Torah, the Talmud, the Mishna. We need not study philosophy, or science, or other current fashions. We need only lead moral lives, and walk with our God.

"This is not a question of girls versus boys, of women versus men. In our yeshiva, of which I am the proud head — in every yeshiva in the world — we teach and study only our religion. That is what has enabled us to survive.

ROBERT MAYER

Now a movement is beginning, of which this proposed school is a part, to change that; to study what the goyim study, so we will be able to mingle with them. The truth is, at this time in our history we are lucky to be surrounded by high walls and iron gates. They don't permit us to mingle, we can hardly give up our Jewishness. But once the walls come down — and some day, however long in the future, they must — if we mingle, we intermarry. And then the Jewish race, the Jewish nation, disappears. Secular study will supersede Jewish studies. And in the eyes of Adonai, our Jewish hearts will be dead.

"You may think I exaggerate. I know that the fine women who propose to run this school for girls — this secular school, which is the larger point — I know they do not intend such consequences. But throw a single pebble, and the entire pond ripples. Let us cling to Adonai, who supported us under the severest trials, who conducted us safely through numberless perils, who smoothed our passage through the most tempestuous paths, and let us be impressed with the radiant message, that the beauties of nature shall fade, that science will bring catastrophe, that the whole visible world will sink into endless night — but that Israel shall survive, and be 'saved an everlasting salvation.' That we have been promised. That we must accept as sufficient. We must reject this school as we would reject tossing a match into a river of oil. All we need in our lives, men and women both, is the eternal flame of Yahweh's grace."

The Rabbi stopped, drank water, was done. The lecture hall filled with applause, men and women stood at their seats. "Thank God for Rabbi Jonah!" someone yelled. Guttle's chin sunk. She shook her head, battled the need for tears. How could she follow that?

Her father nudged her shoulder. "It's your turn," he whispered.

"I can't. He's right."

"Do you really believe that?"

"They do. Listen to them."

"They had their moment. Now it's your moment."

"What I had planned to say — it will sound petty after that."

"Then say something else. Open up your heart. The words will come."

"Guttle Rothschild?" Rabbi Jonah was calling her name for the second time. "Do you want to speak, or not?"

"Yes." Her voice was hoarse, the word came out as a croak. She cleared her throat so hard it hurt. "Yes!" Her knees felt soft as fresh challah as she climbed the two steps to the podium.

Challah! A new idea lit her face. She would choke them on challah!

She poured herself water with a shaky hand while the crowd quieted. Her thoughts were born as if independent of herself. She would pick them out one by one, like beetles.

"Give her a coffin to stand on, that's what she likes!" a woman's voice cried out

"The coffin of the Jewish people," a man yelled.

Their words stung like lashes across her face. Looking out at the audience, she saw a pack of snarling dogs, like those in the rubble beyond the walls, teeth ready to devour a mother hare. She wanted to step down, go home. Who was she to oppose their will? Who was any woman?

The thought stiffened her. But she must not harangue them. She must be reasonable.

"I agree with Rabbi Jonah to a large extent," she began quietly, "just as most of you do. I agree that the essence of our being as Jews is our Jewishness. Our devotion to Adonai as the only God. Our moral qualities as expressed in our deeds, and in our prayers, and in our following of Jewish law as set forth in the Torah and the Halakah. Why then, do I stand before you now to advocate a secular school for girls?

"When I was young I worked in the bakery. I picked the beetles out of the flour, before my mother and the other women baked our bread and challah. It was a necessary job. But it did not occupy my mind very much. I hope you will concede that Yahweh did give us women minds." She paused to let nervous laughter pass among a few in the crowd. "What did I think about as I picked out the beetles so we would all eat pure challah on Friday nights? Not of the pain in my knees from kneeling on the stone floor, or the strain in my eyes from wanting to spot every insect. I am fortunate to have a wonderful father, who goes out into the world most days as the Court Jew in Sachsen-Meiningen. I would point out, in passing, that his business with the outside world has not corrupted his faith. Nor has it corrupted the faith of my husband, Meyer Rothschild. My Papa used to bring home German newspapers. He taught me to read German from them. This opened to me the world of books, in addition to our fine religious teachings. It enabled me, while cleaning the flour for your challah, to think of worlds beyond our walls — to escape into them, just as you men escape in schul into the ancient world of the Israelites.

"Now I am married, I have six children. You can see that another is on the way. I cook for them, I clean house, I do whatever is required. I light the Sabbath candles, I go to the mikvah every month. Am I less of a Jew, then, because I also know the names of the Roman emperors? Am I less of a Jew because I have studied the French kings? As long as I follow Halakah, am I less of a Jew because I have read a book called Don Quixote?

"As a grown woman I no longer pick out beetles. Some other girl does that. But, like picking the beetles, cleaning house and cooking for my family does not fill all of my mind. The rest of my brain needs to be used for something, or Adonai would not have given it to me. I don't think this makes me less of a Jew. But I shall tell you what does.

"I am less of a Jew than you men because I am not allowed to study Talmud. According to the Torah, men have an obligation to study Torah and Talmud day and night, and have to account for every second 'wasted' on matters not involving Torah. We women are exempt from this obligation, because our other duties take so much time. At least, that is the reason usually given. More likely, our forefathers thought we were not smart enough. So we are taught only enough Jewish law to run our homes.

"What else makes me less of a Jew? Not that I know the story of a Catholic girl called Joan of Arc — but that I cannot sit in the schul, I have to stand in the back. Not that I can read a German newspaper — but that I am not allowed to read from the Torah, as you men do every week. Perhaps if I were allowed to study and argue Talmud in the schul, my mind would be fully occupied, and I would not long for other knowledge.

"So I have a simple proposal to make. I will gladly withdraw our plans to establish a secular school for girls, if you will allow me and my daughters and all the women in the lane to be complete Jews — to sit in the schul with you, to pray with you, to attend heder and yeshiva, to do all the religious things you do. Then perhaps our minds will be filled with Adonai, as our hearts already are, and we would need nothing else."

"Noooo." The audience seem to moo like a herd of cows. Guttle looked down at the lectern and waited before continuing; she had anticipated some such response.

"Just say this will be so, that we can study Halakah as you do, and we will start no school. But until you say that, we must proceed. We women and girls, your mothers and your wives and your daughters, are looked upon as lesser beings. We are viewed as the beetles in God's flour. Especially here in the Judengasse, where we all suffer confinement together, that is no longer enough. We are not intruding insects. Like you men, we are the flour itself. We must be allowed to rise. Our school will be a bit of yeast, nothing more."

The horses in her breast were running wild. In the small of her back her chemise was soaked. Her head was perspiring under her sheitl, her gray hat. Her legs were shaky. She stepped from the lectern and managed to walk to her seat. There was no applause.

Rabbi Jonah declared a brief recess. People stood in small knots and talked, debated, joked. Brendel and Yussel congratulated Guttle on her speech. Meyer approached, Schönche beside him. He nodded at Guttle, and said, "That was superb strategy. You and Rebecca would do well in business." His highest compliment.

"What do you mean, Papa?" Schönche asked.

"They offered up an expensive antique. Simcha can please the crowd by refusing it — then buy what your Mama wanted to sell him all along."

"How do you know?" the girl asked, as Rabbi Simcha approached the lectern and motioned for all to be seated.

"Listen," Meyer whispered.

The Chief Rabbi waited for silence. When he spoke, his voice was calm. "We have heard an interesting discussion," he said. "I shall not respond to each argument, but will simply present my decision, and the reasons for it. At first we had one question before us; now, after the last speaker, we have two. I will address the second question first — the question of admitting girls to heder and yeshiva, women to read from the Torah. I have been Chief Rabbi for a short time. Whatever merit might be in these suggestions — I am not indicating if they have merit — it is not my place to overrule the traditions of our people for five thousand years. That will not happen."

The audience was silent. Guttle had expected nothing less from Simcha, from any Rabbi.

"This also relates to the question of the evening — shall a school for girls be established in the community room. That room is part of the synagogue. It belongs to the community, as its name suggests. While educating girls and women might not violate the letter of the Torah, it once again would overturn long practice, and would clearly go against the will of the majority. That, too, I am not going to do. My ruling is that such use is inappropriate, and is denied."

Applause rolled though the room like thunder, with lightning shouts of praise for the Rabbi. People stood, began to put on their coats, while others still applauded, shouted, shook hands. The majority was thrilled, as if the Messiah had come.

Simcha banged the gavel on the lectern, banged it again, restored a curious quiet. "Please," he said. "I have not finished." The remaining talkers settled down.

"If the school in question were planning to teach the Talmud to females," the Chief Rabbi said, "I would have to consider whether an absolute prohibition were appropriate. But it is my understanding that what is proposed is secular studies. The synagogue and its facilities are no place for that, so, again, that request is denied. Beyond that, secular questions are not in the purview of the rabbinate." He paused. "Now I have finished. Shalom to you all."

More applause, also whispers, cheers. In the front row on the left, Alexandre Licht turned to Jacob Marcus. "A fair man, the new Chief Rabbi, a wonderful man. An important victory."

"Victory? We lost," Marcus said.

"What do you mean, we lost? We won."

"Didn't you hear his last words? He gave them permission to run their school anywhere else but the synagogue."

"There isn't room for a school anyplace else."

Marcus looked across the aisle, where the female Doctor was talking quietly with Guttle Rothschild. "If they didn't already have a place," he said, "they wouldn't have put us through all this meshugas."

46

Meyer had not seen so many powdered wigs in his entire life as paraded at Landgrave Wilhelm's coronation ball, in the gold-painted great hall of the palace at Hesse-Kassel. Older men wore the traditional campaign-stye wig, full white hair falling down both sides of their head from a part in the center. Most popular was the Ramillies wig, the hair pulled back tightly into a braid that hung down the back, with just a single curl above each ear. A bowl-shaped toupee, with curls running around the back of the neck from ear to ear, was visible on some. Most striking, particularly on the younger men, was the new hedgehog style, in which the hair stood straight out on all sides, and leaned back, as if it were being blown by a breeze. How it got its name was clear, and only the most confident had adopted it so quickly. One of these was Carl Buderus. Meyer felt it a shame that the young man, for the decorum of the ball, had covered his own flaming locks. Perhaps, as treasurer to the Landgrave, he did not want to appear so young anymore. As for the women, Meyer thought many of their upswept wigs were ridiculous. It was as if they had tried to outdo one another in a contest for a prize. The wigs rose to enormous heights; many were entwined with looping ropes of pearls, or amethysts, or diamonds. These were the conservative ones. Younger women had all manner of plumes and feathers growing out of their wigs, a decoration, he was told, popularized by the reigning Queen of France. Most outrageous of all was a woman whose tall white wig was crowned by a model of a clipper ship under full sail. Who she was and why she had a ship on her head he determined to find out.

Nor had he ever seen such décolletage. The ball gowns of the women, no matter what shade of lavender or green or blue or white, whether of silk or velvet or taffeta, all were cut in a square deep below the neck, displaying surprising amounts of powdered bosom. The older women wore necklaces of diamonds, rubies, emeralds, often several tiers dangling, not only to flaunt their wealth but to distract from the mottled or wattled skin of their necks. The young, pretty ones had left their throats bare, so as not to detract from their appealing natural beauty while they had it. Of the gowns, many were brocaded and widely hooped, in the French style, their wearers seeming to glide upon layers of petticoats when they walked, as if wearing their own private oceans. A few gowns were narrower, in the less giddy style of Vienna. Meyer was not sure if this less flamboyant style attracted mostly older women, or if it made all women look older, and therefore wiser. He was trying to impress in his memory every detail of fashion, because Guttle would be eager to hear them, as would their daughters, and her sisters. He imagined what Guttle would look like got up in such finery. He sensed that she would feel embarrassed.

Everything about Hesse-Kassel was new and wondrous to him. On the second day of his journey he had entered the broad valley of the river Fulda; as he neared the city, steep hills rose on either side of the river. Half way up one of the hills stood the palace of the Landgrave, a great stone edifice with many turrets, much larger even than Wilhelm's palace in Hanau. The throngs at Friedrich's funeral had been exceeded only by those at Wilhelm's coronation. To both events Meyer had worn the gray linen coat, vest and breeches in which he had married Guttle fifteen years earlier. They still fit well enough, only the breeches had required letting out at the waist, though not much; Guttle with her ever present needle had seen to it. For the first time, he had powdered his wig, so he would blend in with the Christian dignitaries. What was forbidden to the Jews in Frankfurt was not forbidden here.

At both events the Landgrave's private militia had been much in evidence in their

blue and red coats, white breeches, high black boots, tall red hats with gold shields — the same uniforms, Meyer recalled from Ephraim Hess's letters from America, that the Hessian troops had worn while fighting there. In the day between the funeral and the coronation he had roamed the streets of Kassel. It was the prettiest city he had ever seen, with magnificent buildings and museums and wide boulevards lined with trees, which ended at green parks. Clearly, the riches that had flowed into Friedrich's coffers from the sale of soldiers to the English king had been put to use in Kassel, if not in the rest of the state of Hesse, where the peasants were as poor as anywhere. Hundreds, if not thousands of them had lined the road into the city, begging alms from the dignitaries arriving in their coaches. Against his instincts, Meyer had not thrown them any coins; he did not want to attract the eye of highwaymen who might be on the lookout for victims with money to spare.

He had brought along enough cash to pay for the hotel room Buderus had reserved for him — only visiting nobles were put up in the palace — plus kosher meals in the Jewish quarter and other eventualities. At the last minute he had added a small extra pouch of gulden to mollify any highwaymen who might accost him.

In the afternoon before the coronation ball, Meyer had found Buderus surveying the offices of the royal treasury. Pleased to see him, Buderus had given Meyer a tour of the palace, and of terraced gardens that rose behind it step-like into the hills. The final terrace was dominated by a tall cylinder of stone that overlooked the city. Crowning this monument was a statue of a man, almost naked, wielding a huge club.

"Of whom is that statue?" Meyer had asked. "Surely not the first Landgrave."

Buderus had laughed appreciatively. "I'm afraid not. That's Hercules."

"Ah. The Greek god."

"Well, not exactly. He was the son of a god and a mortal woman."

"Like your Jesus."

Hesitant, considering, Buderus did not respond directly. "He was the strongest man who ever lived."

"And he is up on that stone because?"

"As a symbol of power, I imagine."

Meyer turned and surveyed the magnificent palace below them. "With all this money, who needs symbols?"

Buderus led him back down through the terraced gardens. Leafy plants of every description, whose names Meyer did not know, perfumed the air, the unaccustomed sweet scents making his nostrils itch. "At a time like this," Meyer said, "it would be out of place to ask how much the Crown Prince will be inheriting. I say that just so you know I am interested in doing business with the new Landgrave."

"It would also be premature. It will take time to do a reckoning. Let me say that I never doubted your interest."

> "Of course. But if an expert were to make a
> premature guess, he would say…?"

Buderus glanced about to make sure they were alone. "He might say, at the low end, forty million gulden."

"That is a nice low end. And at the high end?"

"A hundred and twenty million."

Meyer paused, and inhaled deeply.

"This height can take your breath away," Buderus said.

"Yes. May I sit here on the terrace for a bit?"

"Of course. If you have trouble finding your way out, there are guards everywhere. Shall I see you and your wife at the ball tonight? I don't believe I've met her."

"My wife is not with me."

"Most women love these things. She's not ill, I hope."

"She does not have a pass to leave the Judengasse."

Buderus closed his eyes, frowned. "Of course. That was thoughtless of me."

"It is life that is thoughtless."

When Buderus had disappeared inside the palace, Meyer sat on a wooden bench and looked about. A hundred and twenty million gulden! Even forty million! If he could handle even a small fraction of Wilhelm's investments, he could become a rich man. But did he envision himself one day living in a mansion draped in gold, framed by gardens, manned by servants? He did not. Life in the Judengasse did not encourage such thoughts. What he did envision was the iron chest in his counting house overflowing with cash, so much so that he had to pile another strong box on top of the first, then another beside it, until there was hardly room to turn about. Enough money to double or triple his business, to give shares to the boys as they came of age, to give nice dowries to the girls when they married.

"Excuse me. Aren't you Meyer Rothschild?"

The question drew him back to the present, to the ballroom to which he had descended as to a golden magnet, where an orchestra dressed in gold and red was playing, where the wigs and the décolletage were dancing, where he was sipping from a flute of champagne, where in front of him a beautiful woman stood, wearing a powdered white wig bedecked with strings of pearls, her powdered bosom floating white under his eyes from within a purple dress of the finest silk. The quality of fabrics he could tell just by looking.

"Excuse me, have we met before?" She looked familiar, but…

"That's wonderful! You don't recognize me." The woman laughed musically. "I'm Dvorah. From the Judengasse."

"Dvorah Schlicter? Of course! I just didn't… "

"You expect red hair!"

"Yes, that's it." His heart was fluttering uncertainly, at once glad to see her, guilty to be speaking with her.

"It's Madeleine von Brunwald now, of course. And the hair is still red under the wig."

"I just didn't expect… you live in Berlin… of course, you are a Countess now. All the nobles must have been invited."

They had to speak loudly over the music. Couples were dancing sedately just a few feet from them. Dvorah looked about. "Is Guttle here?"

"Already you've forgotten the laws of Frankfurt? What has it been, nine years?"

"Don't be cross with me. Of course I have not forgotten. I guess I was just hoping, since you are here... " She shrugged.

The dance ended. People began moving about, selecting partners for the next.

"Will you dance with me?" Dvorah asked.

"Where is your husband. Paul, isn't it?"

"He's over there, talking with some friends. He was thrown from a horse last week during a hunt. His leg is badly bruised, he's leaning on a crutch. And I do so love to dance."

"I'm not much of a dancer."

He was thinking: speaking with her is one thing. To dance — that would break faith with Guttle. Seeming to read his face, Dvorah did not insist. He was grateful for that. Instead, he asked her about the wigs and fashions on display. It was a good choice of subject, Dvorah seemed to know everything about fashion from her life in Berlin. But she soon turned the subject.

"You and Guttle have a lot of children. I get letters from my mother."

"We have six. Another on the way. And you?"

"Paul and I have two, a boy and a girl."

An awkward silence fell between them. All safe subjects had been completed. Meyer tried to think of a way to excuse himself.

"Meyer... " She put her hand on his arm. "I stood up for Guttle at your wedding, though I could hardly stand. Why is she being so stubborn all these years? When you are not?"

"I can't speak for Guttle. Perhaps it's because I am not a mother."

"That's cruel. Here I thought you were being nice."

"You asked me, Dvorah. I should say, Countess."

Already he was feeling a slight nausea, the beginning of indigestion. When he returned home, would he tell Guttle of this encounter? She would get upset. But if he did not, she might hear of it from some one else. From Dvorah's mother. That would be worse.

"Let me ask you something." He had lowered his voice. Dvorah leaned close, as if expecting some intimacy from the lane. Her face was inches from his, her bosom brushed his lapel, her perfumed powder made him light-headed. "That woman over there. With the boat on her head. Do you know who she is?"

Disappointed, Dvorah glanced away. "That's Wilhelm's mistress, Rosalie Ritter. She's Swedish. Mother of seven of his children."

"I didn't know he had so many."

"That's only with her. The rumor is there are seventy, altogether."

"The Crown Prince? Does he have such a handsome face? Does he cut such a dashing figure?"

"You're funny, Meyer Rothschild. It's not his face or his figure that's on his millions of gulden."

Meyer's eyes sparkled, the skin beside them crinkled with delight. That was something Guttle might have said. He had often wondered, in the old days, at the depth of her friendship with Dvorah. Perhaps there was more to Dvorah than he had noticed back then, something obscured by her buoyant shapeliness. Something that perhaps had blossomed when removed from Guttle's shadow.

"Come, let me introduce you to Paul." Taking his hand, she led him across the ballroom. They passed beside the mistress with the clipper ship atop her wig. From up close Meyer could see, on the deck and climbing the masts, tiny Hessian soldiers. He could not help but smile at her taste; she was flaunting at his coronation the source of Wilhelm's inheritance.

They approached a gentleman who was leaning on a wooden crutch. Dvorah introduced Meyer to her husband, and to the man with whom he was conversing, a clean-shaven fellow in a blue coat and yellow breeches. Both were sipping champagne. "Meyer Rothschild, an old friend from Frankfurt, this is Wolfgang von Goethe."

"The writer," Meyer said, offering his hand. Goethe nodded politely, but did not see — or pretended he did not see — the proffered hand. Ignoring Goethe's slight, or trying to, Meyer said, "Dvorah here is your most violent reader."

"Yes, I know that story."

Dvorah lightly slapped her husband's arm. "Paul! I asked you never to tell about that."

"I didn't. And Herr Rothschild, my wife's name is Madeleine, if you please."

"Paul didn't tell me," Goethe assured her. "It was Mendelssohn himself, years ago. He found it quite amusing, in retrospect. They say he's dying now, poor fellow, from a disease of the nerves. He made quite a name for himself, for a Jew."

Meyer Amschel studied the flute of bubbling liquid in his hand, as if trying to decide if his cautious self should respond, or if he should let the champagne speak. He was tired of acting properly. The drink declined to wait for his decision. "You're a learned man, Herr Goethe. Do you have a problem with Jews?"

Goethe, too, had been drinking champagne, had consumed several flutes, and his response was unthinking, something he had said many times before, in different company, as if it were a little joke. "Let's just say I wouldn't want to marry one."

The three listeners tensed. Goethe realized his mistake. "Present company excepted, of course. The Countess has long since renounced the heresy into which she was born."

Seeing Dvorah's face redden, and emboldened by the poet's faux pas, Meyer said, "There is talk that some cities may end the prohibition on marriages between Christians and Jews."

Goethe waved the hand holding his drink. Paul lurched back to avoid flying drops, almost losing his balance on his crutch. "You're speaking of Vienna. Not Weimar. As for my native Frankfurt — never. That's one reason I fight this so-called Enlightenment. It goes too far. Marriage is an affair of emotion, not reason. The gut tells us that marriage with a Jew is unacceptable."

Paul was looking at Goethe with a mixture of astonishment and hurt, like a friendly dog suddenly smacked.

"Stop looking at me that way. Your wife became a Christian before you married her. No one has a problem with that."

"Are you married, sir?" Meyer asked.

"I don't have to be a donkey to bray like one."

Giggling, Dvorah covered her mouth. Meyer could think of no better response than to leave the statement hanging in the air.

It still was hanging when a cluster of finery that had been moving slowly nearer enveloped them. Wilhelm, the portly former Crown Prince of Hesse-Hanau, as of today the powerful Landgrave of Hesse-Kassel, was greeting his guests. With Buderus at his side, he shook hands with Count Paul von Brunwald, nodded to his wife, shook the hand of the poet. Glancing at Meyer Amschel, he paused uncertainly, as if he recognized him from somewhere but could not recall from where; nine years had passed since Meyer had invested his conscription funds and earned him sizable profits. Buderus leaned close to the Landgrave, whispered in his ear. Still looking at Meyer, Wilhelm narrowed his eyes, but with no further offer of recognition, moved on.

Meyer was astonished, then furious. Turning away from the others to conceal his anger, he thought: he didn't know who I was! When Buderus reminded him, he didn't care!

The orchestra resumed playing. Dvorah wandered away to find more champagne. Meyer, seething at both Wilhelm and Goethe, walked off in a different direction, out onto the marble terrace. Bonfires illuminated the rising gardens in the night. A quarter moon mocked him with its slashing grin. Fighting a quiet rage that was burning in his chest with the champagne, he rose from one deserted terrace to the next.

Without planning to climb so high he soon found himself on the topmost tier, gazing at the statue of Hercules against a dome of dark sky and white stars. More astonishing, he soon found himself doing what Guttle might have been expected to do, but not he, not Meyer Rothschild. He found himself speaking to the huge stone figure that held aloft an ominous club.

"So, Hercules. Do you have a last name? Never mind. They say you are half a man, half a god. Does one half worship the other? Which half needs that club?" Meyer looked about, to make sure the terrace still was deserted except for himself. He gazed again at the towering figure. "You want to know something? I'll tell you a secret. We have something in common, you and I. I, too, am half a man. But what is my other half? Where I shall find him? Where is my powerful club?"

Hercules with unblinking eyes stared out over the Landgrave's palace, over the river Fulda, over all of Kassel. He took no more notice of Meyer Amschel than Wilhelm had.

Friday was the first day of school. Excitement warred with trepidation in Guttle's breast as she walked down the lane with Schönche, past men in doorways or open windows wearing their prayer shawls, tefillin wrapped around their arms and foreheads, dovaning, the lilting chants continuing from house to house as they had each morning for centuries, the birdless songbird sound of the Judengasse. The shutters of shops were being thrown open by rag dealers, pawn brokers, tailors, money lenders, hairdressers, carpenters — and in a moment she would open the door to a new world for the girls of the lane. As the German instructor, she would preside over the first class each morning, because learning to read German was the key that would unlock for the girls the literature that Yussel would teach them, the books about science that Rebecca would obtain for them, all the subjects they might want to study later. Teaching them to read German was essential; only religious texts were printed in Hebrew; nothing was printed in Judendeutch.

"How many girls will there be besides me?" Schönche asked as the smell of the river reached their nostrils, as they drew closer to the River View, where a knot of people, men and women both, waited. She hoped they were parents waiting to greet them, to introduce their children, to thank the teachers for volunteering their time.

"Twelve registered yesterday," Guttle said. "More might come."

"There she is!" a man shouted, and as Guttle, approaching, smiled, the group lined up three deep across the lane in front of the school. Then the shouts began. Guttle at first recognized no faces, saw just lips and teeth and tongues mouthing accusatory words.

"No school for girls!"

"Ruin your own daughters, not ours!"

Someone even invoked the painful scourge of the lane: "Women need learning like men need hemorrhoids." The bitterness in their voices, the stupidity — she had not expected that, not after Rabbi Simcha's ruling.

Schönche, frightened, turned her head into her mother's shoulder. Guttle took her hand, stunned by the confrontation. She looked from face to face, seeing among the men Jacob Marcus and Alexandre Licht, her old adversaries. She could read the bitterness in the moneylender's face, bitterness related not only to the school; his daughter Misha had been mooning over Georgi Kremm . Alongside Marcus a wide woman turned and Guttle was astonished to see it was Sophie Marcus herself, let out of her attic lockaway. The other women shouting were mostly from the south end; Guttle hardly knew them.

With the corner of her eye she saw Hiram Liebmann leaning against a wall, pad and charcoal in hand, sketching the angry faces, the open mouths. Such was his success that no one took notice of him anymore, no one took umbrage at whatever he wanted to draw.

Watching from across the lane in his cylindrical black hat, not smiling, was Rabbi Jonah. Two metres from him a group of men stood wearing white prayer shawls trimmed in black, and holding prayer books. At their feet was a spruce coffin, borrowed or snatched from the shop of one of the carpenters. To the coffin someone had affixed a paper sign that said, in black letters: "Jewish Nation." As Guttle approached, the men began to chant, *Yisgadahl ve yisgadash, shemay rabo*...

Kaddish — the mourners' prayer for the dead.

"Mama, Mama, why are they yelling at you?"

She turned and saw Nathan a few feet away, tears running down his face. Her resolve began to falter, she did not want her children involved.

"What are you doing here?" she said to her seven-year-old. "You should be in heder!"

"I wanted to see your school. Why are they angry with you?" he said, crying.

He confronted the rank of women blocking the school. "You leave my Mama alone!" He raised his fists in front of his skinny chest, as if he would box with them. Schönche took Nathan's hand. "I'll take him back," she said, and began to pull him away.

Guttle felt grateful to her daughter, but the boy threw off her grasp. "I hate them! I hate them!"

"Go back to heder," Guttle ordered. "Now!"

He stared at her. She could read the hurt her in little boy's eyes before he turned and ran.

Heart palpitating wildly, Guttle faced the others. Logistics flashed through her brain the way numbers must flash through Meyer's: what would happen if she moved toward the door? Would they make her push her way through their massed flesh? Arguments were a staple of life in the Judengasse — but physical force? Never!

She could see some of the girls who had registered for school clustering near the south gate, watching uncertainly. If she did not open today, Guttle thought, her foes would be emboldened, and the school might be lost forever. She needed to be resolute — but did that include pushing, shoving? She was the wife of Meyer Rothschild, the mother of six children. She was not about to roll in the mud.

She knew not to argue with them, not here, not now. But Avra, who had come up beside her, could not contain her tongue. "There's a whole world out there we know nothing about! Our minds must be wider than the lane!"

"Not wider than the Torah!" a yeshiva boy yelled back.

His words ignited the anger with which Guttle had been prepared to harangue them at the meeting the other night. "Do you want to live in the lane forever? Do you prefer it here? If not, why lock the minds of our daughters behind mental walls, mental gates? Do you feel safer in here? Are you afraid to experience the outer world, is that it? After three centuries we have been conditioned like barnyard animals to accept this smelly lane as our home. Must we not fight against that acceptance? Must we not yearn to be free?"

The fierceness of her attack stunned them into silence. For a moment she thought she'd won them to her side. Then a man's voice yelled, "Go home and dump your litter!"

Whirling about, she faced the crowd that blocked the door. The central obstacle was Sophie Marcus, who looked to have gained a hundred pounds since she threw excrement at Guttle on her wedding day. Guttle looked at her eyes, tiny in her fleshy face. Their glassy glow suggested neither anger nor sorrow, only the absence of clarity. Sophie was not shouting imprecations, but she was blocking the door like a snuffling hog. Bracing for a collision, hands protecting her belly, Guttle directed her gait at the barely visible space between Sophie's bulk and that of Hannah Schlicter beside her. One step, two, three. Sophie didn't budge, but at the last instant Frau Schlicter — perhaps out of some muscular memory of the days when Guttle had been like a daughter to her — moved aside, and Guttle edged past Sophie Marcus with only a bumping of hips. The others backed away and let her pass. Taking a key from a pocket of her coat, she unlocked the door, and waved to the girls huddling near the gate, calling them forward. Timidly they threaded through the crowd.

"Don't go in!" some in the crowd chanted.

"It's the devil's house!" a voice — it sounded like the shoemaker's — yelled.

The girls hesitated. Standing beside the door, Guttle saw Schönche take the hand of one of them and gently lead her through the crowd. The others followed, silent, their eyes cast down to the cobbles.

When they were safely inside, some remained quiet, others chattered nervously. Guttle locked the door behind them as a chorus of nasty cries poured down from outside. Something thudded against the door. It could have been mud; it could have been something foul.

Guttle motioned the girls to wooden chairs that had been arranged in a semicircle. Taking off their coats, leaving on their hats, they sought seats beside girls they knew. Guttle's body was tense, her mind burning with the insults that had been hurled at her. Closing her eyes, she willed her body to calm. She had to be strong for them, not show her own fear. When they stopped fidgeting she stood before them, showed them a broad smile. How nice they looked, their hair freshly washed and combed, wearing their best blouses and skirts.

"Someone out there just told you this is the devil's house," Guttle began. "Looking at all your brave faces, I would say it's a house of angels."

"My little sister was brave," one girl said, "but Mama wouldn't let her come."

"Perhaps she will when things calm down."

Shafts of gray light slanted into the room from the double-high south windows. The devil's house! Guttle's mind leaped to Melekh sleeping in his lead coffin three floors above, a secret that none of the girls knew, that none of the people outside knew — a sacred presence, which, for her, consecrated this house, this school. Shouts that continued outside were muffled now by the door, the walls. Her chest filled with the sweetness of victory, the sweetness of challah dipped in honey and blessed by Elohim. The best moments of her life blew through her mind like the golden autumn leaves that sometimes tumbled windblown through the gates and settled on the cobbles like offerings. Her first sight of the Frankfurt Fair. Her betrothal. The first book she read. Her wedding night. Her first birthing — it had been Schönche, now a grown girl, almost a woman, sitting in front of her with the others, waiting eagerly. Such was the miracle of life.

She began again, more formally, with a talk she had rehearsed the night before. "Welcome, ladies, to the Moses Mendelssohn Academy for Girls — the first Jewish school for girls in the four centuries of the Judengasse. Most likely, one of the first in the Holy Roman Empire."

Unbidden, the pupils, these eight daughters of the lane, sat taller in their seats, and began to clap.

"Here you will learn much about the world outside the lane," Guttle said. "It will not make you lesser Jews — just better educated ones. Don't you think that Yahweh, who is omniscient — who knows everything — will appreciate the company of girls who know *something?*"

They laughed at that, the tension breaking cleanly, like an egg on the side of a pan. They looked at one another, drawing strength, as Schönche led a second round of applause.

When they stopped clapping they could hear a knocking at the door, sounding loud as thunder, though it was soft. Instantly the tension was back. All breathing in the room seemed to stop. Guttle approached the door. "What do you want?" she said with irritation. "This is a school in progress."

"It's me," a muffled female voice said. "Rebecca."

Relieved, Guttle opened the door slightly, then further, to let the Doctor in. Behind her the lane was empty now, as if she had imagined it all; she could see the gates of the cemetery across the way.

"I heard there was trouble," Rebecca whispered, as Guttle locked the door behind her. "Are you all right?"

Nodding, Guttle turned and introduced the class to their new science teacher.

Rebecca had just begun saying a few words about the importance of science in the modern world when there was another knock on the door. Annoyed, Guttle went to the door, unlocked it. Brendel and Yussel Kahn stepped in, looked about.

"Everything looks calm," Yussel said. "There's no problem?"

"Not anymore."

"We heard you were in danger."

"Heard from who?"

"Little Nathan." Brendel took Guttle's arm. "He was crying. He said they were going to hurt his Mama."

She introduced the rest of the faculty. Each said a few words about their classes. The girls listened raptly. "When d-do we s-start to d-dance," the youngest, nine years old, asked Brendel. The dance teacher looked at Guttle, then said, "Next week, I imagine." The girl rocked in her seat with delight.

"I think there's been too much excitement today to begin a real lesson," Guttle said. "You were very brave to come, with those angry people outside. Just remember — they may disagree with the school, but they would never hurt you." A murmur of uncertain assent; who could predict what grown-ups would do? "Tomorrow is Shabbas, so no school. Be sure and be good, so your parents don't think we've corrupted you. We'll see you here Sunday morning, with your thinking caps on."

"Is that like a yarmulke?" one girl asked.

Amid laughter, Guttle said, "Very much so. Like a mental yarmulke."

Near the ruins of the castle, a pair of ravens glided to a perch high in a black oak. Watching their silhouettes against the afternoon sky, Hersch Liebmann, sitting on a patch of browning grass, was struck not by their blackness — he was familiar with that — but by their two-ness. The world in pairs. Noah's Ark.

"Where's your bitch?" Klaus asked, as if reading his mind. "I haven't seen her around for days."

Tempted to say he had sent her away, Hersch in his bitterness was honest. "She rode off."

"Got tired of you so soon?"

"She was in a rage that I didn't kill you, after what you did to her. I would have, if I didn't need you to enlighten" — he found an odd pleasure in the word — "to enlighten Meyer Rothschild on Sunday."

"What did I do? She's a whore. Oh, I get it." Klaus reached into his waistcoat pocket, pulled out a kreuzer, tossed it at Hersch. It fell in the grass beside him. "You see her again, give her that. Tell her we're fair and square."

Hersch strode a few steps to the river to hide the anger that was reddening his face. Kneeling, he scooped water into his palms and poured it over his head, and ran his hands through his hair. He could see small fish darting beneath the surface, leaving silver trails. The truth was, he missed her. That had never happened before, there was always an easy girl in the next town.

But with her — a shiksa whore - could he ever return to the lane?

It had been two months since he had gone back — almost. He had ridden to Frankfurt, left his horse at a stable, walked through the streets to the Judengasse. More beggars than he remembered had been camped outside the north gate, but the odor of chicken shit from the yard of the slaughterhouse was the same. He might have been one of these grubby beggars, he told himself, had he not become a highwayman.

His exile had ended months before, but he'd been hesitant to enter. His parents were dead. The cloud of the Schul-Klopper's murder so long ago would still hang over him like an evil sign. Yet as he stood outside the open gate, looking in, he was surprised by the magnetic pull he felt. He recalled the years of playing near the ditch with Hiram when they were little. But those had not been so wonderful, he reminded himself, astonished to find himself longing for the past in this prison he despised, when for years now he had been sentenced only to freedom, to roaming the outer world, to sleeping amid the fresh smells of grass and trees and flowers, to sporting with almost any girl he wanted. Gentile girls, who expected nothing more.

He could walk the length of the lane for the sake of old times, he'd thought, see what had changed, what shops had closed, what new ones had opened; perhaps no one would recognize him after fifteen years. But as he hesitated he had seen through the gate a woman emerge from the first house — his old house — and begin to set paintings and drawings along the front wall. A moment later Hiram had emerged, carrying another batch. Hersch had been surprised by the confident way Hiram carried himself; he looked older, of course, and was wearing a short beard now, but appeared strong, secure, despite his infirmities. And this must be his woman. Hersch had heard long ago that the artist Lieb was married, but he had not known to whom; he recognized her narrow face now, she had been a neighbor. Her name was Amelia — no that, had been the pretty little one. This was Avra. Hardly a beauty like the others, too skinny for his taste, but a Schnapper nonetheless. He watched as Hiram disappeared inside and Avra set up a chair beside the paintings. His pockets were bulging with gulden notes, he could go in and buy the biggest of the lot, pass himself off as a wealthy collector — but what would he do with it?

For a long time he stood with the beggars, admiring the business of the lane — the rag dealers hawking old clothes, the money-changers offering deals, the women carrying bread from the bakery. Little ever changed in the Judengasse. Growing somber, he turned away and went to reclaim his horse, and he left the city rapidly. He would not return until the suspicion of him as a murderer, planted so long ago by the hateful Meyer Rothschild, was gone. Which might be never.

Then last week the Landgrave had died, and like a forgiving angel his idea had come to him in the night, while Lena slept at his side.

Walking up the slope from the river, Hersch picked up the coin Klaus had thrown, and tossed it to him. "You wouldn't want to leave your fortune lying about."

Catching the coin, Klaus grinned through yellow teeth and hurled it as high as he could, watched it come down in the branches of the black oak, sending the ravens flapping, dropping into the river. "That was from your share," he said.

"I told you that you could keep all of it."

"First I keep three quarters, now all of it. I always heard Jews were good at business.

Guess you can't believe what people say." Klaus stretched his arms over his head, lay back on the scratchy grass. "What if your rich Jew goes home tomorrow, and we miss him?"

"I told you, he won't ride on a Saturday. Sunday we'll be waiting. A one-horse carriage, black, with red moldings. I followed him in the town and got a look."

"I never heard of waylaying a man to tell him a story." Klaus pinched a bug that was crawling across his shirt, and threw it off. "I thought of something funny, though."

"What's that?"

"It's a story he'll be dying to hear!"

Puffs of white clouds passing low overhead hid behind the heights of the hills. A crow cawed high in a linden tree.

"That's funny," Hersch said. But in his voice nor his visage was there a hint of mirth.

Guttle lit the Shabbas candles and fed the children. The first Shabbas since their wedding that they had been apart. Later, sitting alone at the kitchen table in front of a bowl of cold borscht, she was too upset to eat, the morning's confrontation at the school still weighing on her, causing pain in her belly. No matter. She closed her eyes and said the brucha for food. She added an improvised prayer for Meyer Amschel's safe return. Late into the night she sat by candlelight, then in smoky darkness. His return was still three days away.

47

A heavy mist hung over the Fulda valley like a blanket of wet cotton. The hillside palace was invisible from the streets of Hesse-Kassel, as if it existed only in the Landgrave's mind. Leaving the city at dawn in his rented one-horse carriage, black with red trim, Meyer let the roan mare walk slowly; it was impossible to see up the road more than fifty metres; collision with incoming traffic was a definite danger. Meyer was glad it was Sunday morning; few Gentiles would be on the road.

He had gone about ten kilometres when a breeze came up, shredding the fog into what the rag dealers called odds and ends. On the hillside across the river, rounded bits of fog shone brightly against the green grass, until he realized that the mist was gone and that it was a flock of sheep at which he was gazing. At that moment the rising sun climbed over the hill and set the moist grass to sparkling like bits of ice — or diamonds — and illuminated swirling swatches of lavender wildflowers. A swift shadow crossed the flank of the roan and Meyer saw an eagle diving from the sky, towards the river bank; no doubt it would rise in a moment with some small animal in its talons. Meyer hoped for some reason that it would come up empty; this time it did, soaring skyward carrying no visible prey, gliding further along the river in search of a catchable meal.

With the morning clear now, Meyer flicked the reins and the mare increased its pace to a slow trot as the road veered away from the river. He marveled at the infinite beauty of the universe that Yahweh had created — then was overcome with sadness. Guttle, he realized, would never in her life see such scenes as he had just witnessed, unless confinement to the Judengasse was lifted; nor would Schönche, Amschel, any of the children, so long as the gates were locked and the stone walls stood. For hundreds of kilometres in every direction there must be beauty like this, and to the cloistered Jews it did not exist. His sadness turned to anger, first an indiscriminate and, he knew, useless anger at the unfairness of it all, then an anger focused on Wilhelm, who had slighted him so at the ball. In Meyer's mind money and freedom were entwined like a woman's braid, though he could not unravel a connection so long as the Judengasse stood. Anxious now to get home to those he loved, he flicked his whip lightly on the rump of the mare, who responded with a faster trot. The increased speed whipped freshets of cool and calming air across his face.

Far to the left he could see the remains of an old stone castle — a remnant from Ivanhoe's day, he thought. The castle disappeared as the road wound through a copse of trees and tall brush. He heard voices and galloping hooves behind him, and out of the brush on either side came a horse and rider, stirring up the dusty surface of the dirt road, one on a large black stallion, the other on a brown filly, the faces of the riders covered by masks as they raced past his carriage until they were about fifty metres ahead. They wheeled their mounts and blocked the road and he had to pull on the reins, hard.

His face broke out in sweat as his carriage creaked to a halt. He waited for them to speak, to demand his cash. They said nothing. The one on the black stallion, a silver sword hanging from his saddle, came close, leaned over and yanked at the reins of the carriage, which flew from Meyer's hands like twisting snakes. Holding the reins, the robber moved beside the roan and began to lead the horse to the left. Meyer could see a narrow dirt path that led through the trees.

"What's this?" Meyer asked loudly. "You want my money? I have some. Not a lot."

The fellow on the stallion did not answer, did not bother to turn his head, continued to lead Meyer's carriage away from the main road. The other drew up beside the carriage on the other side. Meyer was becoming frightened now. Did they mean to steal his horse, leave him alone out here in the wilderness? But horses were cheap, he'd heard that nobles paid more for a pineapple from the New World than for a horse. What did they want with him?

The narrow path wound deeper into the shadows of trees and brush, slightly downhill. Then it burst into bright sunlight and crossed a scraggy field. Meyer could smell the river Fulda, and saw up ahead the half-fallen castle that he had spied not long ago, from afar. They led his carriage half way around the castle remains, to a place shadowed by irregular walls, broken in places but still standing. Two large crows cawed as they flew off from a roosting place in the castle tower high overhead, then glided in circles in the blue, as if curious to see what would transpire below

Be calm, it would be a simple business transaction, Meyer told his throbbing heart; they just don't want to stay by the road in case another coach, or a Constable, comes along. But they had been well hidden from the road in the trees through which they had passed; there had been no need to come this far.

The fellow on the stallion dismounted and tied his horse and Meyer's to a weathered post that seemed to have been hammered into the ground long ago for that purpose. The morning had grown warm and the man was sweating as he pulled off his mask and tossed it on the ground. His face seemed vaguely familiar, from the distant past, Meyer thought, but he had no idea who it was. The other man dismounted, wrapped his horse's reins around a fallen rock.

"Get down," the first man told him. "And bring that money you mentioned."

Meyer did as he was told, his knees shaky as they absorbed his weight. He took his purse from the pocket of his coat and tossed it to the robber; coins clanked as he caught it in the air. The robber seemed to weigh it in his hand. "Not much for a rich man."

"I'm not so rich," Meyer said.

"Forget about the money." The voice was the other highwayman's as he came around the carriage, and it resonated in Meyer's ears in an eerie way. The man pulled off his mask.

"Is it possible? You resemble Hersch Liebmann. From the Judengasse."

Allowing himself an ironic grin, Hersch bent in a mocking half bow. Meyer saw the handle of a pistol protruding from the waistband of his trousers. He looked at the other fellow, who was counting the coins and notes in the pouch. In the context of the Judengasse Meyer remembered him now, though his face was rounder than Meyer recalled, and his stomach larger. "You were the guard Klaus."

Grinning, Klaus finished counting, returned the money to the pouch, tied the pouch to the saddle of his horse. Untying the reins, he swung up into the saddle. "Hardly worth the effort," he muttered.

Quickly Hersch confronted the mounted highwayman, his long barreled pistol aimed at arm's length at Klaus's chest. "Aren't you forgetting something?" he said.

"You're not serious," Klaus replied. "You'd shoot me over that old turd?"

"Climb down, or you'll find out fast," Hersch said.

Meyer had no notion of what was being played out in front of him. He was relieved when Klaus, after staring hard at Hersch to read his intent, shrugged and swung off the horse. Meyer had never seen a person shot, had no desire to. Violence against a fellow human — anything more than a light swat on a child's tush — was one of life's prime evils.

Yet he was aware of a twinge of exhilaration at the sight of a Jew holding a pistol and pointing it in anger.

"Let's get it done, then," Klaus said. He unsheathed his sword from his saddle and carried it with him through a low opening in the castle wall. Hersch motioned Meyer to follow. Unnerved by Klaus's sword, Meyer stared at Hersch, who remained expressionless and waved him through the opening, his pistol still in his hand. With no choice but to obey, Meyer found himself in a stone room from which the roof was missing. A raven asleep in a crevice high in the wall screeched and flapped its shadow across the earthen floor as it lunged in heavy flight through the absent roof. A lizard, invisible against the pale dirt floor until it moved, skittered around Meyer's dusty shoes and disappeared.

"If it's more money you want, I can get it at home," Meyer said.

"I told you before, this is not about money," Hersch said. "Fettmilch here has a story I want you to hear."

"For that he needs a sword?" And then: "Fettmilch, as in the riots?" Meyer looked from one to the other. Klaus Fettmilch grinned.

"The captain thought Fettmilch on my tag would have been an unnecessary provocation, as he put it. I couldn't give a turd."

"The story is about the Schul-Klopper who was poisoned," Hersch said. "Fifteen years ago. Do you remember?"

"Of course I remember."

"Of course you do. You accused me of killing him. Fettmilch remembers, too." He motioned to Klaus with his pistol. "Tell him what happened."

Klaus lifted his sword, plunged it into the earth. He leaned on it as if it were a walking stick. "The old Jew was a spy."

"I know that."

Hersch interjected, "You know that?"

"I found out only recently. Why didn't they arrest him? Bring him to trial?"

"It was a mess of slops," Klaus said. "When raid after raid found no violations, produced no nice fines, headquarters suspected the Jews were being tipped off. The informer was a Leutnant at the gate, name of Gruber. He was seized the day before the killing."

"Fritz, the young one, took his place!" Meyer said.

"He's got a good memory," Klaus said to Hersch, then turned back to Meyer. "Gruber was taken into the forest and shot. He never confessed, but they had made the Jew Klopper talk."

Meyer did not know why he was being told this now. He felt droplets of sweat running down his back beneath his shirt. "I still don't see… "

"The Kommandant of the Polizei wanted to keep things quiet. He was embarrassed to have an informer on the force. He didn't want the Frankfurt Council to know. Or the Empress. So he ordered that they both be killed, the Leutnant and the Jew. I did what I was told to do." He turned to Hersch. "Is that enough for you?"

"Tell him the rest."

"How they got caught? They were buggering each other, the faggots. Once or twice a week they were going at it. In a field behind the Judengasse. That's when the Jew got his information about the coming inspections. After someone saw them at it, and they were seized — and maybe toyed with a little — the Jew confessed."

Meyer's face was flushed. He had heard talk of such things. He'd assumed it only happened among the nobility; among the Gentiles. Among the ancient Greeks. But Solomon Gruen? Was it possible he truly enjoyed such behavior — or had he sacrificed his body in the service of his fellow Jews?

"That's not the part I meant. Tell him about the killing."

His mouth taut, his lips a thin, bloodless line, Klaus pulled his sword from the dirt, slowly wiped it clean. He jammed it again into the earth. A raven fluttered out of the sky to the edge of the roof, discerned the human presence, took flight.

"The Kommandant wanted the Jew dead. But with no trial, no testimony of a depraved Leutnant. He wanted it to appear a natural death. Or a murder among the Jews."

"Go on," Hersch said, when Klaus paused. "You're awfully shy today, considering all you've done since."

"Shut your mouth. I'm almost done. Then the Jew here is done."

Sweating heavily, Meyer tried not to accept Klaus Fettmilch's meaning. Surely this could not be happening to him. Where was he to run, where was he to hide, how was he to fight?

"The Kommandant ordered me to arrange the killing. But not to be seen doing it. I bought rat poison, found three boys who were willing. Gave them a key to the gate."

"For money?" Meyer asked, nervously, not knowing what difference it made, not knowing if he was speaking of Solomon Gruen's murder or his own.

"For fun," Klaus said, looking directly at Meyer, who saw madness in his eyes, as if he, too, were uncertain which murder they were talking about, the one fifteen years ago or one he would soon commit.

"Two of them held him, forced his mouth open. The third poured poisoned milk down his throat. He squirmed for a few minutes, then died. If anyone had seen from their windows, it was just some hooligans. Who never would be found."

"The boys Guttle saw outside the gate," Meyer murmured.

"Which, thank God, she told the Rabbi about," Hersch said.

At first Meyer felt the story made no sense. He had met the informant at Brendel's Café just the other day. The bookseller Gluck. Then he understood. When he was arrested, Solomon Gruen implicated Leutnant Gruber in order to protect the bookseller and the real source.

Had he been forced by the Leutnant into disgusting sex? Or had the Schul-Klopper been using Gruber all along, as an emergency cover story if needed? Surrendering his body to protect the lane? To keep the bookseller in place?

Meyer turned to Hersch. "I owe you a strong apology. I owe you more than that."

Klaus pulled his sword from the earth. He wiped the blade on his trousers. Facing Meyer, he spoke to Hersch. "Is that what this was about? An apology? You Jews are madder than I thought. You create the great plague, wiping out half the people of Europe, but I have to go through this nonsense for an apology?"

"What are you talking about?" Hersch said.

"The Black Death, of course. When you Jews poisoned the wells".

"We caused the plague? You're meshuganah," Hersch said.

"Who told you such things?" Meyer asked.

"Who told me? No one told me, everyone knows. I heard it at school. Among the Constables. It's not a secret. My great grandfather, at least, was one who wouldn't stand for it. He led a raid into the Judengasse to kill the Jews."

"Who fought back well," Meyer said. "The Fettmilch riots — that was your grandfather? The Frankfurt council did not agree with him. He was arrested, tried, and hanged."

"The council were fools. But today, thanks to Helmut, or Hersch here, I can take my revenge, in my family's name. I can hardly let you live, to spread what I just told you. The Polizei Kommandant — he's still the same — would not be pleased. As for me, I was only following orders. But when the dripping head of that Jewish thief was stolen from the Fahrtor gate, and smuggled into the Judengasse, all the guards, including me, were fired. The Kommandant was afraid there might be another collaborator. We were told to leave Frankfurt and not return."

Klaus was babbling on, as if the impending sight of Jewish blood had loosened his tongue. "I assume the Polizei know what I've been doing. They could find me, if the wrong word got about. So you see, Jew, you have to die. Even your friend Hersch here has agreed to that."

Grinning, Fettmilch ran a finger along the blade of his sword. Meyer backed away. In two steps his shoulder blades were pressed against the castle wall of stone. He looked at Hersch, who had not stirred. He thought to start saying the She'ma, but refused to accept his imminent death. Images of Guttle and the children flashed through his mind in an unspoken visual prayer. For him to die here, now — this could not be Yahweh's plan.

One of the horses whinnied, another answered.

"Enough talk," Klaus said. "Now you will die, Jew — in the name of Fettmilch!"

He raised his sword parallel to the ground. Meyer twisted and cringed, trying to cover himself with his arms. Klaus was about to lunge forward, to plunge the sword into Meyer's bowels, when with a sudden swift motion Hersch holding his heavy pistol by its long barrel swung the iron grip with a crunching thud into the side of Klaus's head. The sword fell to the earth as Klaus collapsed, fell on his side, twisted onto his back, lay still. Meyer dropped to his knees on the gray earth, turned his head, pressed his face to the stone wall, as if uncertain if he were alive or dead.

Hersch stuck his pistol in the waistband of his trousers, lifted Klaus's sword, leaned it against a wall. Meyer, on his haunches, was breathing evenly, trying to recover control.

"Danke schoën," he said, hoarsely.

"I didn't do it for you. I need you alive."

"You need me?"

"What do you think this was, a game? You know the truth now. From the killer's mouth. You will return to the Judengasse and tell what happened. Tell them that Hersch Liebmann is not a murderer, and never was. You will make sure that everyone knows."

"Of course. I could do no less."

"Good. You owe your life to that."

Meyer nodded, used protruding stones from the wall to pull himself to his feet. His knees still were shaky.

"I've hated you for years, for accusing me," Hersch said. "But you didn't deserve to die for it. Not by the sword of scum like this." He kicked the boot of the fallen Klaus, who moaned, turned his head slightly, then lay inert.

"He's alive," Meyer said. "I thought you had killed him."

"I didn't want to kill him."

Meyer nodded, wiped pale stone dust from his beard.

"That, you shall do."

Not comprehending, or trying not to, Meyer looked at Hersch. "You expect me to kill him? Surely not. I couldn't do such a thing."

"Why not? He's lying at your feet. It's time you dirtied your hands, like the rest of us."

"Adonai forbids it. The Sixth Commandment. Thou shalt not murder."

"The punishment for murder is death. Is that not what the Talmud says? If we must never kill, who is to put a murderer to death?"

"The Torah does not prohibit killing. Only murder — unjustified killing."

"Surely killing is permitted to defend oneself."

"It is."

"He just tried to kill you."

"But now he lies defenseless. Weaponless."

Hersch stepped to the wall, lifted Klaus's sword. "Plunge it into his chest, or his bowels — as he tried to do to you." He handed the sword to Meyer, who did not grasp it but let it fall to the earth, as if he were being handed a venomous snake.

"You think we should let him live?" Hersch asked. "So that when he finds me, he can plunge his sword into my back for what I just did? So that he can come to the Judengasse and slaughter you. Or your wife? Or your children? After first raping them? Do you think he won't do that, after what he told you? After I cracked his skull?"

Meyer closed his eyes, not knowing what to think, what to feel. Hersch pulled his pistol from his trousers. "Do I have to force you to do it? Do I have to threaten to kill you if you don't? Is that what's necessary? Here, take the pistol." He pressed it into Meyer's hands. He spread his own arms wide, so he was defenseless. "There. Now you have a choice. You can kill me, if you prefer. A fellow Jew. Who has not murdered anyone. Or you can kill Klaus Fettmilch. Who murdered the Schul-Klopper, as he just told you. Who rapes women and young girls whenever he feels the urge. He raped my woman five days ago. I would have killed him on the spot, but I wanted him alive, to speak his confession to you. I knew he would die today. I saved your life so you could take his."

"Why not kill himself yourself?" Meyer said, managing somehow to keep his voice strong.

"Because there is sweet revenge in making you do it. You accused me falsely of murder. Now you can see what it feels like to truly kill."

"So that you can accuse me? Is that your plan?"

"I'll never speak of what happens here. I don't need anyone else to know. It's enough that I will know, and you will know. Perhaps it won't be much of a burden for you to carry. The bastard deserves to die."

Meyer looked at the pistol in his hand, its long barrel, felt the heavy weight of it in his palms, on his fingers. He never thought that in his life he would even touch such a thing. Is this, he wondered, what the scales of justice weigh?

"Use the pistol, if you're squeamish about the sword. Point it at his chest and squeeze the trigger. Look, he's opening his eyes. It won't be safe to let him live."

"Thou shalt not murder," Meyer said, shaking his head from side to side.

He raised the pistol with both hands, pointed it at Klaus's chest. His hands were not steady. He turned to look at Hersch. Their brown eyes met. Neither turned away. Perhaps this is just a test, Meyer thought, perhaps there is no powder in the pistol, or no ball. A test, like Abraham and Isaac. I will squeeze the trigger and hear only a dull click. Then Hersch will load the weapon and do the killing. From the Schul-Klopper's death it was Hersch, among the living, who had suffered most; it is Hersch who needs revenge.

The thoughts flew through his mind in an instant, were displaced by others like a swarm of gnats, which restored an itchy rage in him — the slight by Wilhelm at the coronation ball, the hateful Herr Goethe. Then another vision, from long ago — the scene Guttle had described to him one night long after they were married, of what had happened the night of the Schul-Klopper's death, when she had run by mistake to the south gate. How Kapitän Klaus had tried to lure her outside to rape her. What if he had had succeeded? How would Guttle have been affected? Would she have carried Klaus's child? Would she have come to hate all men? Would she have turned Meyer's troth aside? Would she still be joyful on their sheets? If the guard had succeeded in raping her, their six children might not even exist!

A question sprung from his lips without anticipation. "Does he rape girls who are fifteen years old?"

"He likes virgins. That's his favorite age. Though he's not always picky."

Hersch's final word was obliterated by an explosion of noise and dust as Meyer, while still looking at Hersch, squeezed the trigger of the pistol, with or without intent, and the small stone room recoiled into its own deafening echoes. The backward force of the weapon jolted Meyer's wrist and elbow, wrenched the long pistol from his hand. As it dropped to the earth Meyer turned his head and looked at Klaus, lying in the dirt, and saw through a haze of gunpowder the former guard's chest and face bubbling with blood, the ground around him splattered red, as if the pistol ball had torn through his ribs and exploded his heart. His eyes were rotated back in his head, only the whites showing. Before Meyer could be sick he turned away and ducked through the opening in the stone wall and out into the shade, and walked to the post to which the horses were tied and held it with both hands for support. A songbird, he somehow noticed, was warbling in a nearby tree.

Hersch came out and approached the horses, holding his pistol and Klaus's sword. He returned the sword to its sheath, which hung from the saddle on the black stallion, and laid the pistol on a rock; he would clean it and load it before leaving. "You see. It wasn't so difficult."

Wiping his moist upper lip and mustache with his handkerchief, Meyer turned his head and spoke. "Your word is good? You will never mention this?"

"You accused me of a murder, when I was innocent. I will never say a word, though you are guilty. What remains is for you to ponder who is the better man."

Meyer lowered his arms and unhooked the reins of the roan from the post. The white droppings of a large bird splattered the ground beside him. He looked up but saw nothing except blue sky. *I killed a man but nature didn't notice.* Feeling dazed, he climbed onto the carriage seat. His ears felt plugged from the resounding shot.

"Will you be returning to the Judengasse?" he said, without looking at Hersch.

"Who can tell? First there's a woman I need to find."

Meyer Amschel flicked the reins, the roan stirred, the large wooden wheels of the carriage began to turn and creak.

"You forgot your money," Hersch called.

Meyer heard but did not respond. He flicked the reins again and the horse left the shade of the castle wall and turned onto the narrow path down which they had come. The

heat of the sun bore down. Meyer wriggled out of his coat. As he did he saw that his white stockings were splattered with spots of red; he would have to stop and change his clothes and bury the stockings before he reached the post exchange half way to Frankfurt, where he would spend the night. The horse moved through the welcome cool of the copse of trees, then, guided by Meyer's pull, turned south onto the main road. Wiping his sweaty forehead with his shirt sleeve, Meyer tried to block from his mind the ragged red image of Klaus Fettmilch's exploded heart. He couldn't, and leaned over the side of the carriage and vomited, pulling the horse to a stop. He climbed down and knelt in the grass beside the road and vomited more, until his sides and his back hurt from the effort. When he was done he sat beneath a tree beside the carriage to gather his strength. Before leaving Kassel he had filled an earthen jar with drinking water, and he used the water now to rinse the residue of vomit from his mouth. The odor left, but the memory of blood remained. The smell of gunpowder still filled his nostrils. The belief that from all Hersch had told him, Klaus Fettmilch deserved to die, did not stop his hands from trembling. He tried to tell himself he had not meant to pull the trigger, that he was looking at Hersch at the time, that his hand had simply contracted in anger with the pistol pointed at Klaus.

Though he never would be put on trial, would a jury believe such a story? Of course not! He spat the taste of blood into the road.

Would he have squeezed the trigger had Guttle never told him of her encounter with Klaus that night at the south gate? He didn't know. But Klaus had only been frightening her. Had he intended to rape her, he would have seduced her out the gate without mentioning barter. He recalled how innocent Guttle had looked earlier that evening, running into the schul and hugging Izzy. And how defiant. The night he had fallen for her. He felt now as if Guttle had been at his side in the castle. But Guttle would not have fired the pistol.

The sound of rippling water reached Meyer's ears. Either the river had curved back toward the road, or the road had sought out the river. He walked the roan through sloping grass to the fast-flowing Fulda and let her drink. He washed his hands in the river. He washed them again. Pulling off his blood-pocked stockings he wound them tight in a ball and dug a hole with his hands in the mud at the river's edge and buried them. From his trunk in the carriage he pulled out another pair, the silk ones he had worn to the coronation four days earlier. To put them on he sat on a rock near a clear, shallow pool where the river had overflowed. Glimpsing the still reflection of a tree limb in the pool, he knelt beside it, leaned over — and was startled by what he saw. In the shallow pool he saw the reflection of white-bearded Moses peering back at him. Fascinated, he stared at the ancient prophet, until he found in the water his own dark eyes, his own full lips, his own shorter beard, but white now instead of brown; it was not Moses he was looking at, but himself in old age.

Why was Yahweh showing him this now? He ran his fingers through the water, disrupting the image. When the ripples settled, the white-bearded face still was there. Suddenly he was overcome with terrible grief for what he had done; the awful weight of the killing struck him with a crushing force; had he not already been on his knees he would have fallen to them. Tears trickled down his cheeks, dissolved into his beard.

Why had he not thrown down the pistol, as he had thrown down the sword? Would Hersch really have killed him? He felt certain the answer was no; he would have killed Fettmilch. But he had not thought of that, in the moment. In the moment, he, Meyer Amschel Rothschild, whatever the tangled reasons, must have wanted to kill.

He sat on his haunches, dipped his hand in the pool, wiped his eyes, his cheeks — and felt grit on his fingers. He looked at his hand, stroked his beard; his hand came away with a residue of powder. Understanding, he leaned over the pool, cupped his hands, splashed water onto his face, rubbed away the gunpowder that had been assaulting his nostrils, that had whitened his whiskers. When he peered again into the water the image he saw was of himself, his beard its usual brown: the ambitious court agent, forty-one years old, husband, father, dealer in antiquities.

Standing shakily, he let his eye follow the sparkling river as it curled around a bend. Tormented, he tried to ponder the future. First, he would do what was fair and just for Hersch. As soon as he reached the lane, he would tell the true story of the death of the Shul-Klopper. He would tell it everywhere, from the north gate to the south, from the synagogue to the Café, like a prophet of old. If he withheld salacious details, out of respect for the dead, they were not so important.

Of the murder in the castle ruins he would not speak. Not to Guttle. Not to the children. Not to anyone. Only Yahweh would know.

"I did what I was told," Fettmilch had said.

It was not an adequate defense. Not for the Gentile, not for himself. Who was he, neither judge nor jury, to wield the sword of justice — a terrible, bloody justice, stained and irrevocable?

Thou shalt not murder. Now he was in his heart, and would always be, one thing above all else: a man who had disobeyed God.

48

On Sunday, the second day of classes at the Moses Mendelssohn Academy for Girls, Guttle's antagonists sputtered remarks as she passed, but there were only half as many as on the first day; none of the leaders had returned. Guttle was pleased — but an ominous feeling settled in her gut. Why had they surrendered so easily? It was not like them.

Two new, younger girls in braids, about eight years old, had braved the controversy — or their parents had — and had shown up, appearing only mildly frightened, along with the previous eight. After giving her first German lesson, watching the pupils squirm, their faces distorted in pain and puzzlement as she explained the complications of *der, die* and *das,* Guttle let them stand and stretch. Rebecca would be teaching the science class next, but she was treating a critically ill patient and had warned Guttle that she might be late. Five minutes passed, then ten. Guttle decided she had better tell them something about science, from what little she knew, until Rebecca appeared.

"When we talk about learning science," she began, as the girls settled into the chairs, "it is different than learning a language, such as German. With a language, we begin with correct answers. Der Dummkopf is correct. Die Dummkopf is not. No one argues about it. Except, perhaps, der Dummkopf."

The girls laughed. School could be fun, if the grown-ups stopped fighting about it, stopped making everybody nervous.

"But in science, we begin with questions, and we look for the answers. We don't know what they are ahead of time. Sometimes people disagree on the answer."

She saw puzzlement in some faces. One girl raised her hand. "So how do we know who is right?

"A very good question, Katya. We don't know who or what to believe, until there is proof. Science is about finding proof."

They waited, attentive. Guttle could understand their confusion. In the lane everything they were taught was already known, it was either right or wrong and had been for thousands of years. Only at the highest levels of Talmudic argument was there room to disagree. That was why so many viewed her as a nuisance. For the second time — the first had been with Georgi — she had brought serious debate to the kitchen table, and out onto the cobbles.

"Let me give you an example of what I'm talking about," she said. "For thousands of years, most people have believed that the sun up in the sky revolves around the earth. Correct? We can see it every day, rising over the eastern wall, passing straight overhead at noon, then, at evening, setting over the western wall."

Ruthie Berkov raised her hand and spoke. "That's not what Galileo said."

"Very good, Ruthie. Who was Galileo?"

"An Italian philosopher."

"Yes. Philosopher, or scientist, as they are starting to be called now. How do you know about him?"

"I heard my Papa and Yussel Kahn discussing him once."

"Does anyone else know about Galileo?"

"He lived a long time ago," Schönche said. "But I don't know what he did."

"Ruthie, do you?"

"Not exactly."

"I'll tell you what he did. It was only a hundred and fifty years ago — well, I guess that is a long time. Galileo proved that the sun does not move around the earth. He proved that, instead, it is the sun that stands still, and the earth that moves around it."

Several of the girls giggled. Others murmured in disagreement.

"I know," Guttle said, "you think that if that were true, we would all be falling down. Doctor Simcha will tell you more about that during the week. For today, can you accept my word that it is true? Can you do that? Just for a few minutes?"

The pupils hesitated, then agreed, reluctantly.

They all turned towards the door as it began to open. For an instant Guttle was frightened; she had neglected to lock it. Then Rebecca entered the room, closing the door quietly behind her. She apologized to the girls for being so busy, and stood off to the side, asking Guttle to continue. In the Doctor's constricted face Guttle read that she had just lost a patient.

She turned back to the class. "As scientists — we are all scientists now, right? — we know, because Galileo proved it scientifically, that it is the earth that moves around the sun, and not vice versa. But a problem quickly arose. 'Wait a minute,' the Pope said — he's the head of the Catholic church — 'that can't be true.'"

"'Why can't it be true?' we ask.

"Because we're not falling down?" Katya said.

"That was not the Pope's concern. The Pope said. 'This cannot be true, because the Bible says otherwise. King Solomon wrote, "The sun also riseth, and the sun goeth down." Clearly, the sun is moving. Are you saying that King Solomon, in the Bible, lied?'"

The pupils sat silent, transfixed. Hiding a smile, Guttle looked away from them, toward the window, through which about ten metres away she could see the ghetto wall. She noticed that Rebecca had her eyes closed, as if in pain.

"So," Guttle said. "Which should we believe? As scientists, do we concede that Galileo made a mistake, and agree with the Pope that the Bible is always right? Or do we stick to our scientific beliefs, and decide that the great Solomon was wrong?"

No one responded. Their faces looked even more puzzled than during der die das.

"I'll tell you what the Catholic church did when it was faced with this problem," Guttle said. "It banned Galileo's writings on the subject. It made him renounce his discovery that the earth moves. Because the Pope found it in conflict with the teachings of the church. If Galileo hadn't done what they wanted, they would have put him to death." She paused for a moment, to let the girls ponder the import of that. "But years later, when Galileo was an old man, dying a natural death, do you know what his last words were? At least, what legend has it? I was not there, of course."

Too rapt even to acknowledge her little joke, the students waited.

"According to legend, Galileo's dying words were: 'And yet, it moves.'"

Silence. She looked from one face to another. Several girls who had been holding their breaths now breathed audibly. She saw Ruthie and Schönche, the two eldest, exchanging glances.

From outside, the sound of a horse neighing, an unusual voice in the lane, shattered the quiet. Guttle went to a window and looked out, giving the girls time to think, to absorb the story. A carriage driver who had brought an elderly banker to his home was having trouble getting his gray roan to maneuver out the south gate alongside the ditch; the horse seemed to fear losing his footing near the trench, and wouldn't move. Horses, like

Christians, rarely were at ease in the Judengasse. Finally the driver got down from the carriage and led the roan out by walking in front of him with the reins.

Her mind distracted, Guttle was taken back to the time she had been kicked by the stallion as it careened into the ditch. Rushing down the alley, the children playing — had she really noticed the children there, so long ago, those blurred colored shapes in the corner of her eye? She still could not be sure.

Uncertain if minutes had passed or only a few seconds, she turned to the class. Her daughter was raising her hand.

"Yes, Schönche?"

"I think I would believe Galileo rather than the Catholic church. But what if the Chief Rabbi said King Solomon was right? Who should we believe then?"

"That's right," Ruthie Berkov added. "The chief Rabbi wouldn't lie. That would be a sin."

Guttle bit her lip. What had she done? How could she not have seen this coming? She looked to Rebecca for help. The Doctor merely shook her head. The older girls smiled; they knew the Chief Rabbi was Rebecca's husband.

Guttle felt trapped — even a bit afraid, though she could not put a name to the fear. "I'm going to stop for today," she said. "You have a lot to think about. The truth is, I, too, have a lot to think about. That's what science does. It makes you think." She felt cold sweat break out on her brow. "Tomorrow, perhaps Doctor Simcha will tell you how Galileo proved what he did. About what is called the scientific method. We'll also learn some more German words."

She moved to the door and pulled it open. The girls donned their coats and filed out into the lane, inured, like everyone, to the stench. Rebecca approached Guttle with a shake of her head. "You had to start with that? By contradicting Solomon? By dark it will be everywhere."

"I was only marking time for you. The lesson didn't go as I'd planned."

"With smart students it never will."

"My own daughter! I wanted to slap her face. I also wanted to kiss her." Guttle slipped into her coat. "Still, we might as well get all the fighting behind us now. Establish our freedom to teach the truth, right at the beginning."

"You're more of a troublemaker than I thought."

"Is that bad?"

Rebecca kissed Guttle's cheek. "I didn't say it was bad."

Guttle put her arms around the Doctor; in Meyer's absence she longed for human touch. "Did you see their faces?" she asked. "The glow in their eyes? They just got their first little glimpse over the walls."

Walking home, putting Schönche's question from her mind, Guttle felt exhilarated. A confusion that had undermined her understanding of herself for as far back as she could remember seemed to have been resolved through her defiance in starting the school. She had often wondered which was the essence of her, the true Guttle: her fantasies and dreams, her conversations with Melka and Jennie Aron and Madame Antoine, her whimsical inner opera — or the things she did each day in the lane: making a home for Meyer, raising the children, cooking, cleaning. But the school itself had begun as one of her fantasies — which after ten years she and Rebecca had made real. She saw now that the opposing parts of her were of equal significance — were not even opposing. She would not be Guttle Schnapper Rothschild without escaping into her fantasies when desired — and emptying life's chamber pots when necessary. She would not be whole without the interplay of the physical universe and her imagined one — just as the world would not be the world without the earth, but it also would not be the world without the heavens. Perhaps this is the burden and the challenge of human life: the task of choosing, every instant, between infinite dualities. Perhaps she would not end up insane after all

That evening, with the children in bed, she sat again in Meyer's chair, wearing a white sleeping gown and her pale blue robe, and turned to a passage in Numbers that she had been trying to read the night before. Something in it was calling to her, something related to the sadness she had seen in so many of the faces of the girls at the school. They were eager and excited, but when their faces were at rest they acquired a faraway burden beyond reckoning. She saw in them the same sadness that had lived within her when she was their age, a sadness beyond words or understanding, a perpetual sorrow that dwelled even now in a pocket of her heart.

She read again where Moses and Aaron sought water for their people in the desert:

> *And Yahweh spoke to Moses, saying:*
> *Take the staff*
> *and assemble the community, you and Aaron your brother;*
> *you are to speak to the boulder before their eyes*
> *so that it gives forth water,*
> *thus you are to bring out for them water from the boulder,*

that you may give drink to the assembly and their cattle.
So Moses took the staff from before the presence of Yahweh,
as he had commanded him.
And Moses and Aaron assembled the assembly facing the
boulder.
He said to them:
Now hear, you rebels,
from this boulder must we bring out water?
And Moses raised his hand
and struck the boulder with his staff, twice,
so that abundant water came out;
and the community and their cattle drank.
Now Yahweh said to Moses and to Aaron:
Because you did not have trust in me
To treat me as holy before the eyes of the children of Israel,
therefore:
You shall not bring this assembly into the land that I am
giving them.

Guttle paused. She read the passage again. She pondered Yahveh's
stern words, wondered at them, and grew disturbed. She knew that Moses
had not been allowed to enter the Promised Land, the Land of Israel, with his
followers; he had died in sight of it. She had always heard he was being
punished for some terrible sin. But no, this was the place in the Torah where
Yahweh had decided to keep him out! Exactly here!

She read the passage yet another time, with mounting trepidation. God
had told Moses to speak to the boulder so that it would give water; instead,
Moses had hit it with his staff. In this small manner he had disobeyed God.
But was that so terrible an offense, in the context of his life? Moses, who upon
Yahweh's instruction had led the children of Israel out of bondage in Egypt?
Who had stopped them from worshipping idols? Who had been entrusted
with the Ten Commandments by Yahweh Himself? Moses, who would
guide his people across the desert for forty years? The supreme leader of the
Jews! Yet in the eyes of God — in one angry instant — Moses was found not
worthy of the Promised Land, the land that flowed with milk and honey.
Because just this once — in this one small action — he had disobeyed.

Guttle found her lower lip trembling, pressed her fingers to it, felt an
avalanche of insight about to crash down upon her. If Moses was not good
enough in the eyes of Yahweh, how could any of us hope to be? What are we,
compared to the great Prophet? To surpass Moses we would have to be

perfect. But God Himself had made us flawed! We can never hope to please Him entirely.

This unexpected understanding watered her eyes, as if they were a garden in need. The walls enclosing the lane, the locked gates, were unjust, obscene, hateful, the cause of infinite sadness stoically borne. Some day they must be torn down; she and Meyer must pledge themselves anew to that goal, must work to lead their people, one bright day, out of the Judengasse. But the walls, she now understood, were not the true cause of unutterable regret. In this one unfair passage in the Torah lay the reason for Melka and Jennie Aron and her other fantasies. This one passage was why Pincus Cohen played his mournful fiddle tunes, why Hiram Liebmann drew his dark pictures, why Viktor Marcus sang sad arias alone in the cemetery, perhaps even why the Gentile Goethe wrote his unforgiving books. Because, like herself, deep in their souls they knew they were not good enough. They knew that no Promised Land awaited them.

In this one dire passage in Numbers, it appeared, lay the origin of sorrow.

Only her husband, she thought, seemed to be an exception. Of all the people she knew, only Meyer Amschel had never evinced a reason to doubt himself.

"Mama!"

It was Nathan again, frightening himself with a dream. She set down the book and hurried, barefoot, up the stairs to him, her toughest child by day, the most in need at night. She kissed his forehead and sat beside him while he drifted off again into his nocturnal caves. She wished she knew how to light a lamp in them.

Returning to the chair, exhausted from the emotions and confrontations of the past few days, Guttle herself fell asleep, the sacred book open in her lap.

She was awakened by the most dread word in the Judengasse. At first she thought it was part of a nightmare, the kind that made her clutch Meyer's arm for comfort, in the hope that he would turn to her in his sleep and embrace and distract and protect her. But Meyer was not there, and when she heard the terrible word a second time she knew she was awake.

"Fire!" someone was shouting down below. "There's a fire in the lane!"

Could this be true? A whimper of panic sliced through her grogginess like a sharp knife through brisket. She rose from her chair too quickly, grabbed her belly as she felt the baby move. A moment later she was climbing the stairs, looking in on the children. Both of the bedrooms were dark, no sign of flames. "Baruch atau Adonai," she murmured. Blessed art Thou, O Lord. In the kitchen she made sure the woodstove was properly damped, then hurried down to the bedroom where she put on her slippers with growing apprehension; fire had destroyed large sections of the Judengasse three times in the century. Pulling her robe tighter around her, she stepped out into the lane. At first all looked normal. Then she saw the glow of lamps starting to illuminate many apartment windows, realized that people were scurrying over the cobbles. They were running from the north, as if fleeing a fire's heat, but in that direction she saw no flames. Following the crowd as it flowed with unspoken fear around the scimitar curve of the lane, she saw the illusion of flames shadow-dancing on the last house before the cemetery — but not the terrible brightness of unconfined fire. She began to walk quickly; were it not for the baby in her she would have run.

A hand gripped her shoulder. It was Rebecca. "Do you think?" the Doctor shouted over the noise in the lane. Guttle didn't answer. When they curled around the bend they could see it for themselves, and smell its appetite. The last house on the east side — the River View — the two-day-old Moses Mendelssohn Academy for Girls — was clothed in orange and yellow flames. A breeze off the river was carrying to them the smell of smoke, and something more sinister.

"This can't be!" Guttle cried out, weakly, wanting to vomit, and she began to run in spite of her swollen belly, the Doctor running behind her, passing silhouettes of men, women and some children hurrying along the cobbles. As they got closer they saw the flames reflected like an undulating line in the sewage ditch, heard the voice of Joshua Lamb, the fire captain, shouting, "More water! Every man get a pail and carry water!" Men already were scurrying behind the last house near the cemetery, where there was a pump and buckets, and hauling filled buckets across the lane. When Guttle and Rebecca were within ten metres of the school they saw that the filled buckets were not being emptied onto the flames, but were were being splashed on the wood facade of the adjoining house. It was clear that the River View, with flames already licking at the third floor, could not be saved; the men were trying to prevent the fire from grabbing hold of the adjoining house, and moving up the lane like a ravenous beast.

"Someone really hates us," Rebecca muttered, shaking her head from side to side.

"No one would do that!" Guttle stared into the blinding white centers of the flames as she pressed behind a crowd of onlookers. She looked toward the heavens for an answer, her eyes beginning to tear from smoke and grief.

She recalled something Meyer had told her the Talmud claimed — that the Torah had been written with black fire on white fire.

"Do you smell it?" Rebecca said into her ear. "Burning oil."

The two women pushed through the crowd to the front. They could hear the fire devouring the inside now, had to shield their eyes against the ash-blown heat.

"The fire wall is holding," a familiar man, his face dark with soot, shouted to the fire

captain, clanking down an empty pail. They realized it was Yussel.

"So far," Lamb replied.

Yelling above the crackling roar, which could devour words as well as wood and paint, Guttle, her eyes shut by thick smoke, asked the captain, "Was it purposely lit?"

"It appears that way." He had to shout back, though he stood not a metre away.

"How could anyone do such a thing?"

"A splash of oil. A match."

"Did anyone see who?"

"I doubt it, in the dark. With only the cemetery across the way."

"You'll try to find out?"

"Of course."

Turning to to Rebecca, she said, "A short-lived school," and wiped streams of tears from her cheeks. The two women embraced, held each other, their faces flickering yellow and orange, heat pouring over them, bits of floating ash settling on their shoulders. The throng behind them stood mute as it watched with respect the flames devour the house like a great orange rat devouring cheese; they were tense, waiting to see if the metal fire wall would hold until the end. If it melted, or collapsed, and the next building caught, they would rush back to their homes, awaken all the children, begin hauling their dearest possessions into the lane while praying the flames didn't leap across the ditch to the other side; if it did, the entire Judengasse could burn to the ground; they would have no place to live.

Guttle felt that somehow the scene was Biblical. Was this a punishment, a plague? "Was Yahweh opposed to the school?" she wondered aloud. Her tears had stopped. There was no point.

"It wasn't Yahweh who splashed the oil," Rebecca said.

From within the burning house they heard a heavy beam crashing down. With sudden remembrance, Guttle screamed. "Georgi! Where's Georgi?"

Trembling, she scanned the crowd. The fire had turned their faces into pumpkins. She pushed among them, calling "Georgi! Georgi Kremm! Are you out here?"

A murmur swirled like an eddy of smoke through those who remembered that the Christian boy lived on the third floor. Guttle rushed to the front, grabbed the arm of Joshua Lamb. "Georgi Kremm lives up there! Have you seen him come out?"

"Not since I arrived," the captain shouted over the fire's roar.

"Mein Gott!, he might still be in there! Can someone go in?" But her soot-filled eyes told her the answer before the captain spoke, and as if in response another large beam exploded onto the floor inside the house, a fireworks of sparks visible through the gaps in the flames.

"No one can go in," the captain yelled. "The upper floors will soon collapse, and the roof."

"He might be trapped up there!"

"Then he'd best be praying," the captain said.

Sweating men in nightshirts or dark robes still were hauling water across the lane, splashing the adjoining house; its facade glinted wet in the firelight. Some of the men, suddenly too weary to hurl their buckets, set them down and stood to rest their arms. Others were scurrying into the second adjoining house, climbing to its roof, emptying buckets onto the roof of the first. Occasionally a lone woman or child shrieked in fear.

"We should get things out of the house!" one wife could be heard urging during a momentary lull in the roar.

"And put them where?" Her husband tried to calm her. "Everyone will lose everything — or no one will. It's up to Yahweh now."

People were coughing, moving further up the smoke-filled lane, away from the fire. Frantic, having trouble breathing, Guttle searched for Rebecca with her arms outstretched, like a blind person, found her, grabbed the sleeve of her blouse. She realized that Rebecca was dressed, must have been at the hospital. "Georgi may be up there," she said, trying not to clench her teeth around the words, not to clench her mind around the prospect of Georgi's fate. The Doctor, her face a grim and forlorn mask, said nothing.

The boy, no longer a boy, would in three days no longer be a Christian. Georgi Kremm was twenty-six years old; in three days he would complete his year of Jewish studies with Rabbi Simcha and would be circumcised; his name would become Georgi ben Avram. As he lay in bed that night on the third floor of the River View, he was deeply content. In the lane he had become far more comfortable with life than he ever had been on the farm with his mother and the "uncles" who came and went like flies in August and were just as welcome. He was glad that now when he was troubled he could talk directly to God, instead of seeking out a priest, which he had never done. He was not eager to be circumcised, the thought of it made him wince, he did not understand why the God of the Jews demanded this, but if Abraham had withstood the pain at the age of ninety-nine and become father to a nation, then he, Georgi, would drink a lot of schnapps, put a piece of spruce molding between his teeth, and survive. When his skin had healed he would be able to ask for the hand of Misha Marcus. To endure both the pain of study and the pain of the knife to become a Jew — surely her father would accept him then.

He had drifted off to sleep on a vision of Misha's lovely hands. Now, hours later, waking, he felt too warm — from his lustful dream, he thought — and threw off his blanket. But he grew even warmer, and then he heard crackling sounds and getting out of bed saw the image of flames on the ghetto wall across from his third-floor window, and knew that something was burning. From the window he could not see what it was — he could see nothing but the wall flickering orange in the night. He turned toward the closed door; smoke had begun to seep under it; he began to cough, at the same time realizing that the school itself was on fire.

He threw open the window to see if he should jump. The drop was high, he might break his legs. He leaned out to breathe fresh air, and looking down saw a mass of flames rising toward him, as if the ground below were a pool of burning oil. He dared not jump into that.

The smoke from under the door was thickening, clouding the room. Grabbing the blanket from his bed he wrapped it over his nightshirt and pulled open the door. A beaded curtain of flame hung in his path. Through it he glimpsed the staircase smoldering but not yet gone. Holding the blanket around him with one hand he threw his other arm across his eyes and hurled himself into the fire. He smelled a foul smell that was his own hair being singed. The floor boards of the landing were beginning to burn, flames licking at his feet through the gaps. He reached the top of the stairs and started down. The heat was intense. The banister was crumbling charcoal, he could not hold on. At the first landing he batted at flames as if they were swarms of hornets and continued down, and stepped into vacant air where the steps were gone and fell to the smoldering floor among burning chairs. The fire danced all around him; three of the four walls were blazing. He lay still for a moment, rubbed a throbbing ankle, twisted his torso in each direction, seeking a way out. A roar like crackling thunder rumbled above and a huge object crashed to the ground, seemed to break apart as it landed, one side falling off, a white form spilling onto the floor as the fallen object settled on its side, reflecting flames. Struggling to his feet, bending low, Georgi edged closer and saw what looked like a metal coffin among the smoking boards, and beside it a Torah scroll, its crown of gold flashing white in the flames like a cry for help. He tried to grasp this miracle, a Torah falling from Heaven — I need to rescue it, he thought, it is the sacred word of Yahweh, it saved me from… so much. But his body was jolted with pain as his blanket caught fire. Throwing it off, he rushed headlong through the flames, head tucked into his chest, neck seared now by a falling ember, and saw a gap where the front door had been. He rushed through it and burst out into the lane, where he stumbled, fell to the cobbles, gasping, realizing he had been holding his breath inside against the thickening smoke till his chest felt ready to explode out through his nose, his mouth, his throat, even his eyes. On his hands and knees, he inhaled the air like a dog lapping water.

"**M**ein Gott! It's him!" Seeing this apparition expel itself from the burning school like a cannon ball Guttle ran to him, too close to the fire, wanted to hug him, was afraid she'd touch a place where he was burned and cause him agony. He smelled only of smoke, not of man. Seeing a bucket of water left by one of the men she dipped her hands in it, scooped up what her palms would hold, offered him drink. He shook his head, pushed himself up, gulping smokier air. She saw that his hair had been singed, that part of his nightshirt had burned away. He bent and gripped his right ankle, pressed it tenderly. Guttle felt faint when she saw a piece of bone sticking through the blistered skin.

"You're hurt, but thank God you're alive," she said. "We thought you were… I should have run in but. . ."

Georgi leaned on her, wincing when weight came down on his right foot. "Water," he rasped, pointing to the bucket.

Guttle knelt and cupped her hands in it again and let him lap it from between her palms.

"Your robe," he said. The hoarse sound of his voice was painful. "Take off your robe."

"Why? I have only a nightshirt on."

What was she thinking? He must be cold! She opened her robe and slipped out of it, handed it to him, crossed her arms over her breasts. Georgi rolled the robe into a ball and pushed it deep into the bucket of water, and held it there, then pulled it out, dripping, and stretched it over his shoulders. Of course, she thought, he was burning, not cold.

"Hand me the bucket," he said.

Others were trying to crowd around. The fire captain was shoving them back. "Give him room," he was saying. "Let him breathe. He almost died in there."

Rebecca pushed through to see if she could help. After a quick look she said, "We need to get him to the hospital. On a board. He can't walk on that leg."

"The bucket," Georgi said again.

Guttle shrugged and picked up the bucket. Half the water was gone.

"Pour it over my head."

Guttle looked at Rebecca. The Doctor nodded. She overturned the bucket above his head, watched it soak his blackened hair, his face, drip onto her soaking robe. He took a step toward the burning house, a grimace visible in his flickering face, then another step.

"Wait!" Guttle shouted into the fire's rushing wind. "This way!" She reached out a hand to him; she feared stepping closer, burning planks from the front wall were falling beside him. He ignored her proffered hand.

"He's disoriented," Rebecca said. "The heat, the smoke."

"No," Georgi yelled. "I have to go back in."

"What?" Guttle and Rebecca cried the word at once.

"There's a Torah in there. I have to rescue it."

He was waving smoke from in front of his face.

Melekh!

The fire captain had come near to pull them back. "Get him away from there."

With a crash a burning plank fell in front of the captain, just missing him as he leaned back. It blazed between Guttle and Georgi, flames from the board obscuring Georgi's legs.

"We've got lots of Torahs!" Guttle screamed. "You can't go back in."

"It's the sacred word of Yahweh!"

"Melka!" a woman in the crowd wailed. "Melka is burning! What will we do now?"

"Georgi!" Rebecca shouted, but he was not listening any more. Turning away from them, pulling Guttle's wet robe over his head, he pushed into the the mass of flames where for centuries the door to the River View had been, and disappeared.

"Stop him!" Guttle cried, her face in the face of the fire captain, her eyes wild with fear, but she knew it was too late, that nothing could be done.

The captain took her hand. "Frau Rothschild, Yahweh saved the lad a moment ago. Maybe He will save him again. There's none of us humans can."

Blistered segment of skin sizzles on his scalp. He staggers under the soaked blanket, heavy as the past. Finds the black hole of a fiery door, pushes through, ankle cutting like a butcher's knife, eyes stinging in the smoke, peers this way, that, all ways burning, smoke thick as morning fog, smelly as musket spit — coughs, coughs again, mouth dry as autumn hay — sees the gleaming crown between the flames — that way! — ember ashes hot beneath his feet, booming sounds above like artillery. Peering up into ash falling like snow he sees flames wrestling beams, his ankle twists, scalds on a blackened pan. He falls to a knee, hot handle poking his groin, drops to his other knee, sweat coating his body like grease, his uncle's hand pushing him down, stinking like rotted cheese or chicken shit, doesn't the bastard ever wash? Twisting from the hot metal — palm stings as he pushes down on hot ash — turn away will you I'll shove a musket up your ass, squeeze the trigger I will. Heat or suck making him dizzy. He turns — where is the Torah, the coffin? Lashes out with a punch to his uncle's groin, uncle screaming as he falls or is that him screaming from a burning board bouncing off his back? Eyes tearing from smoke and flame and shame — run, hide, say you ran from the recruiters, no one need know the truth. Flames like angel wings point, he sees the gleam of the coffin, stumbles toward it, trips over the fallen lid, the soaked blanket catches on a post as on a restraining hand, twists away, pulls itself half off, he is exposed. There is the Torah. Flames surround it. He cannot breathe he must get out the pain is too much he must get both of them out. Hurls himself through a storm of fire to a clearing of white ash, falls to his knees, ankle like a smith's hot iron in his leg. Lifts the Torah still wearing its crown of gold, scroll heavy as lead itself, have to get it out — works blistering hands beneath the scroll, it budges off the ground, he strains to pull it higher, cradles it to his chest, tries to stand, to drag his shattered leg through the ember glow, ignoring the pain, stooped by the weight, but moving. When like a tree falling unseen a roof beam falling knocks him prone, his body covering the Torah like a lover. Has to get up but the beam won't lift. No feeling in his hands. His back is broken. Cries for help but only croaks — no matter, no one can rush in now. Cradles the Torah beneath him, the warm parchment, the soft sweet cheek of God, as the roof collapses, crashes down, a burning wooden tent covers him, pain ascendant like a shofar's wail till in the highest octave of scream it calls down upon itself a cooling light. His blistered forehead falls into the melting Torah crown. One leg twitches, stops. His face is white as a Jew.

Late that afternoon, as Meyer returned from his journey, the horse reacted first, rearing up, refusing to enter the stable, before Meyer smelled the residual smoke. Zig Zigmund grabbed the reins, somehow calmed the horse and led him in, told Meyer about the fire. His mind still stuck in the castle killing, Meyer could barely comprehend. "Burned to the ground?" After all of Guttle's work… "I don't believe it." But in the wind rushing up from the river like a teller of tales he smelled the truth of it. "In the night? Then it was empty, no one was hurt."

"Just the Christian fellow."

"Georgi lives there! Not badly?"

"He's gone. Rushed into the burning house like a Dummkopf, and the roof collapsed."

"Georgi was no dummy!"

"Maybe Adonai doesn't want converts."

The story did not make sense. Meyer told Zig he would settle his bill later, and he hurried into the lane, carrying the case of clothing he had taken to Hesse-Kassel. He saw Guttle's father standing in front of the Owl, looking toward a faint spiral of smoke still rising at the south end.

"Guttle — how is Guttle?" Meyer asked.

"Papa! Papa's home!" Nathan shrieked as he ran out of the Owl doorway and leaped into Meyer's arms. Meyer pulled the boy's head to his chest, knelt and covered his face with kisses.

"There was a fire, Papa! Georgi went to heaven, because he tried to save the Torah."

"Yes, I heard," Meyer said. To Wolf Schnapper he added, "Where is Guttle?"

"Sleeping," Nathan answered. "She told us not to bother her."

Meyer stood and rubbed the boy's red hair and looked at Schnapper. "I can't believe it. And what's this about a Torah?" The court Jew told him what details were known, and about the funeral for Georgi Kremm that would begin in an hour.

"They poured oil and lit a match?" Meyer was incredulous.

Schnapper shrugged, as if to say, What is there to say?

Meyer told Nathan to stay with his grandpa, that he wanted to speak with Guttle alone, Walking down the lane, he left his case in front of the Green Shield, continued toward the south end. He realized what was strange about the lane. No one was visible. It was as if the fire had sucked out all the air and driven the people inside.

As he neared the south gate the smell of smoke and the sickening sight assaulted his nose, his eyes, like acid. There was no more River View, no

Mendelssohn Academy, just this wide sore pocked with ash and rubble, spits of smoke rising here and there, the ash blackened by water so the fire would not flare. A woodstove still stood, its bent pipe leaning into the air like unfinished business. Twisted metal poked from the ash, the remains of lamps, of pots from the kitchen. The lead coffin lay on its side, the lid in the rubble not far away. The metal fire wall was charred in places, had buckled in other places, but gleamed in the afternoon light. "Thank you, Adonai, at least for that," Meyer murmured, but bit his lip in memory of the boy whom Guttle had saved.

He found her in their bed, curled like a fetus around the fetus in her belly, elbows guarding the sides of her head, a blanket drawn to her waist. Her eyes were closed, the skin around them puffed. Her sheitl was askew, her short dark hair peeking out like a frightened animal. He set down his case, exchanged his hat for a yarmulke, and sat on the bed beside her. He could tell she was not asleep. Gently he took her hand. "I'm sorry," he said.

"I killed him."

She did not stir, did not open her eyes to look at him.

"You didn't kill him. Whomever set the fire killed him."

He leaned over, kissed her shoulder, the only part of her he could reach. Her shift smelled of wood and smoke.

"I brought him into the lane so he would not die in a war. Instead his death was worse."

"You couldn't foresee that."

"If I hadn't started the school, he would be alive. He would have become a Jew. He would have married, started a family."

"Guttle, it's terrible what happened. But you shouldn't torment yourself. Who could predict a Jew could do such a terrible thing?"

Sweat bathed his forehead as he said those words. Who could predict a Jew could shoot a pistol?

"I provoked them with my new ideas."

"Perhaps they needed provoking."

She opened her eyes. "This from you?"

"There are sins and there are sins."

"Georgi was my little brother, replacing Benjy. Perhaps that's why I took him in." She was sniffling; she pressed a balled handkerchief to her nose.

"I know." Feeling helpless, Meyer stroked the light down on her arm, as he had done a thousand times in happier days, sensual nights.

She set the handkerchief aside, took his hand, attempted a brave smile.

"They say he ran into the flames to save a Torah. Surely that was not your fault."

"I should have held him back. I wanted to."

"You knew of this Torah?"

She nodded like a guilty child. "Melka. Hidden in the attic. For us women, a symbol of the madness of adapting to the lane. Now we have fire and ash. Complete insanity."

"You never told me about the Torah. I didn't know we kept secrets from each other."

"We were forbidden to speak of it — those who knew."

Meyer exhaled, closed his eyes, ran his hand across his forehead. He thought: I, too, now have a secret. "The funeral will be soon," he said. "Will you be able to go?"

"I must."

He moved aside as she pushed away the blanket, held her belly with one hand, put her legs with difficulty over the edge of the bed. He took her in his arms, held her.

"I haven't asked about your journey."

"There is plenty of time for that."

"At least you got home safely."

"Yes."

He looked away, at the window, at a slit between the curtains, saw Fettmilch's drawn sword, his bloody heart exploding, smelled again the gunpowder in his beard. The pressure of the pistol shot returned to his ears, warning him it would never go away. Not entirely.

"Look," she said, touching above his ear. "You have some gray hairs."

"Was I gone that long?"

"It seemed so to me."

He pressed his lips to her cheek. "Have you heard what Simcha decided? About Georgi's burial? Your Papa told me."

She shook her head, shivered, pulled her gown tight around her breasts. "I haven't been out… since morning. I sent the children to Mama. To Amelia. Someplace."

"The Torah in the River View was partly burned. They found Georgi's body… what was left… curled over it. As if to shield the parchment from the flames."

"I know." Tears slid down her cheeks. She pressed her fists to her eyes. She felt as if she were acting like a little girl, not a woman who herself had lost three babies.

"I'm sorry to speak of this… his remains," Meyer said. "But you'll want to hear. When a Torah is damaged, it must be buried in a coffin, like a person. The Chief Rabbi has given an astonishing honor. Because Georgi gave up his life trying to save the scroll, his bones and the Torah will be buried together. In one box. I've never heard of such a thing."

Guttle sniffled. "He was so excited about becoming a Jew. He'll like... He would have liked..."

Meyer put his arm around her, hugged her close as they sat side by side.

"Hesse-Kassel," Guttle asked after a time, "it went well?"

"I'll tell you later." Some of it, he thought, helping her to her feet. "Now we must get ready for the services. But the school — where will you hold your classes?"

"The school? The school is dead," Guttle said. "That, too, will be buried in the box with Georgi."

49

Meyer mourned the death of Georgi, but he believed that Guttle was punishing herself for something that was not her fault. He saw a vagueness in her eyes that had never been there before; it obscured her inner light the way morning fog sometimes hid ships on the river. She dressed in the same shift day after day, put on a gray coat and walked the lane hour after hour, while Schönche did the cooking and directed the other girls in the cleaning. His attempts to talk to her were drowned in vacant stares. He could only hope that her despair would pass with time, that it would not affect the health of the child she was carrying.

His own guilt was undeniable. He had pulled the trigger with his own finger, a man's heart had exploded. The body had not been buried, had been left as carrion for birds or wolves. Thou Shalt Not Murder. Of his journey he had told Guttle of meeting Dvorah and Goethe. But the killing he did not mention. It occurred to him that if he confessed it, she might let go of her own assumed guilt. But he could not do so. Some day, perhaps — if the proper time came. He had always prided himself on his morality. It was a fixture of who he was as much as the coins he sold, the profits he made. Now, to anyone who knew of the murder, his moral acts could appear fraudulent, a facade to hide his guilt, or a penance to atone for it.

If Hersch keeps his word, Meyer thought, no one need ever know; my moral actions will be a fraud only to myself.

For seven days he sat shiva for Georgi at the Chief Rabbi's house, with Simcha and Yussel and Lev Berkov and enough other sympathetic men to make up a rotating minyan. In her own way, he understood, that was what Guttle was doing. She was sitting shiva by herself, perhaps with her companions of the mind. He would try to be patient.

When the shiva for Georgi was done, Meyer turned to the other task that burdened him: to reveal to the lane the truth of the Schul-Klopper's murder so long ago; to clear Hersch Liebmann's name. Out of courtesy he told it first to the Chief Rabbi, in his study. The Rabbi listened silently. When Meyer finished, Simcha said, "Rabbi Eleazar must have guessed right away. Maybe not whom, but why. That the Schul-Klopper was killed because of his spying. Eleazar carried guilt to his grave."

Like a minstrel without a lyre, Meyer roamed the lane and told the story again and again of his meeting in the ruined castle with Hersch Liebmann and Klaus Fettmilch. He made no mention of weapons, only of the words that were spoken. He told the tale in the community room and in the Café, in the courtyard of the schul and to knots of men gathered outside shops and houses. Always his concluding words were the same: "Should Hersch ever return to the lane, please remember: although he did commit theft in a youthful error, he has paid the penalty. He is not a murderer. Wrongful charges that I rashly made long ago, each evening with my bread and wine I now taste bitterly."

Which was true.

After each telling, the same questions and comments were hurled at him by the listeners. Why did the bastard confess now? I wish he'd told me — I would have killed the sleazy dog!

"Why did he tell me?" Meyer would reply. "Perhaps to clear his conscience. He didn't look well when I left."

Where is he now? they growled.

Meyer would pause, silently ask Yahweh to forgive him for speaking in metaphors. Then he would say: "He rode off into the woods on a pale horse. I don't think we shall see him again."

And they would erupt: if we see him, we'll hang him! Hanging is not good enough, we'll tear him limb from limb! We'll butcher him, if we see him again!

In the crescendo of their bravado Meyer would turn and walk away, and find another group to whom to tell his tale.

No one spoke to Guttle as she trod the cobbles from the south gate where the ashes of the school still smelled of death to the north gate through which she had first escorted the boy, dressed as a girl, into the lane. She recalled Amelia's childhood wisdom, why Jews walk in a circle, though hers was not a circle but a straight line endlessly doubling back upon itself. Her friends knew not to approach her; those she considered her enemies were respectful enough to turn away, now that the deed was done. She could not have said why she walked the lane hour after hour as if in a trance, or like a ghost, but with each passing day she came to represent, to some, the lane's collective guilt.

Meyer was wrong, she was not communing with her spirits. Melka was dead, buried with Georgi — she still could hear the earth dropping onto his coffin like desolate rain. Mortality's ultimate sound. Jennie Aron, alias Joan of Arc, had died anew in the flames of the River View, with Georgi; Guttle could not witness with her mind's eye the burning of one without acknowledging the burning of the other. She had not banished Madame Antoine, but the Queen of France offered no consolation, only a willing ear. The people she passed in the lane saw her lips moving but caught only a word, a phrase, as she drifted by in conversation with the Queen, day after day making the same comments, the same accusations.

"I likened them to animals, I likened the lane — which is their home — to a barn. I cast doubt on the wisdom of Solomon, and in doing so, murdered Georgi. In his innocence, Meyer, so worldly wise, could never kill. But with words I have slain Georgi as surely as if I had splashed the oil and lit the match. My words were the match."

Marie Antoinette answered, "Do you plan to have them cut out your tongue?"

Guttle shuddered, continued walking, trying to see what her mother had lately begun to see in her dementia: the River Main as the Red Sea, the walls as the hills of Galilee, the south gate a passage from Egypt to the desert. She tried to escape into the world of the ancients, to become one of them, but she could not. All she saw was the school devoured by fire, with Georgi trapped inside.

The Chief Rabbi was coping no better. One day Meyer accosted him outside his study after, for the second week in a row, Simcha had let the younger Rabbis lead the daily prayers. "If I may say so, Rabbi," Meyer told him, "you seem as morose as my wife. I suppose more than anyone in the lane you and Guttle, and perhaps Yussel Kahn, were closest to Georgi Kremm. Still…

"Georgi ben Avram."

"Yes. Still, you have presided at many funerals, even of Jewish infants without number. Infants without names. For this... accident... to undermine your spirit so..."

The Rabbi led Meyer into his study, closed the door behind them. It was virtually unchanged since Rabbi Eleazar had presided over the lane. He motioned to a chair; Meyer sat as the Rabbi settled behind the desk.

"You have, what, three sons, Meyer? Six children, a seventh coming. I loved Georgi like the son I will never have. But we sat shiva, I will say yizkor for eleven months, in time I will get over his death. That is the way of life, as you well know. What I may not get over is my failure in my first testing as Chief Rabbi — a failure that led to his death, that has divided the lane into warring camps."

"You exaggerate, Rabbi."

"Do I? Is not arson an act of war?"

"With all due respect, you sound like my Guttle. She also claims responsibility. As if guilt were a prize. You both can't both be guilty — especially when you are both innocent. Why do you say you failed? At what?"

"Had I allowed them to start their school in the community room, there would have been no fire. The synagogue is stone, it has survived fire for centuries. Georgi would still be alive."

"But you said that would have been wrong."

"It would have. But I knew, of course, their plans for the River View. I played a game. Had I banned the girls school altogether, then Georgi my student — would be alive."

"But you felt a ban was unwarranted — your true feeling, I would guess."

"Of course. I am not a king, a landgrave, a pope. Just the Chief Rabbi. I do not rule, however I may rant."

Meyer grinned, glad Simcha could still make a joke. "So you had no choice." Just as I had no choice, he thought. "You did what you believed was right."

"And look what happened. The fact is, I had another choice, which I did not think of then. That is where I failed. That is why I am considering resigning my position. The thought of which makes me morose, as you have observed."

"Resign? You cannot resign. The lane needs you to guide us."

"Rabbi Jonah would make a capable replacement, till one of the younger Rabbis gains stature. I might even leave the lane, move to Mainz, to Berlin, were it not for Rebecca. She is the one who is needed."

Meyer lifted off his yarmulke, ran a hand through his hair, felt sweat on his scalp. "Your reasoning escapes me, Rabbi. I still don't see where you failed."

"I should not have made any decision. This I realized long before the fire — as soon as I saw the demonstrations outside the school. The lane was divided, like a cleft cow at the slaughterer's. That was clear at our meeting. It was the duty of the Chief Rabbi to heal this division, to bring the two sides together — not to split them further apart. It was my job to restore the arm of Jew around Jew."

"How could you have done that?"

"I could have expressed my own view of secular education. The spectre raised at the school meeting was that we will lose our faith if we study the outside world. It seems to me that Adonai would not have created the outside world if we were not to know of it. He would not have driven Adam and Eve from the Garden of Eden if He did not want them to see the rest. Yahweh gave us Jews brains large enough to encompass both religious and secular studies. Since all creation is the work of God, studies of His creation — what we call secular studies — cannot be deemed irreligious."

"Do you think that would have swayed them?"

"Some of them. But it is not my place to address secular matters."

"So what could you have done?"

"That is the problem. I do not know. I am not King Solomon."

"According to my eldest daughter, even Solomon was wrong sometimes."

"Yes, it was the talk of the lane that Sunday afternoon. Someone with a match disagreed."

"Resigning as Chief Rabbi will solve nothing."

"My successor might solve everything."

"What does Rebecca say?"

"I don't treat her patients. She doesn't make my decisions."

"There must be a way to bring the people together. To end this bitterness."

"When you think of it, Meyer, let me know."

As he left the Rabbi's study, Guttle was passing in the lane. She did not greet him. Perhaps, Meyer told himself, she had not seen him. Though he believed she had.

She was not so different from Meyer, she thought. If her school had been a ten-year fantasy that lasted less than a week, his dream of extreme wealth was a similar fantasy. Anger had flushed his face when he told her how Crown Prince Wilhelm, now the Landgrave of Hesse-Kassel, had not even recognized him at the coronation ball. Meyer had come back with no new investments, not even the promise of profits in the future. The defeat had aged him, she felt; not just the beginning of gray in his hair, but a new sobriety in his manner. She could not tell how much he was mourning for Georgi, for her school, how much for his own shattered hopes.

The gray silence in which they were trapped frightened her. This was something new in their marriage. The ashes of the River View had extinguished her bright world. Wilhelm's indifference had extinguished his. But they had to pass beyond this darkness soon, if only for the children. They were old already — Meyer was forty-one, she thirty-one — but the young must be raised with hope, or they would wilt like an orchard without rain; their fruit, which was their intelligence, would molder.

The baby kicked, as if he could hear. Perhaps, she thought, he could.

——Where have you been? It's been weeks since I saw you.

—In bed with the grippe.

—Tell me something. If you weren't sick, would you have gone to the goy's funeral?

Certainly not! A goy buried with a Torah? It's a sin! What kind of Chief Rabbi do we have?

—He was only three days from being a Jew.

—A ger! A convert! A cross they should have buried him with. Maybe in three days he would have risen.

—It's true, they didn't bury Rabbi Eleazar with a Torah.

—Or Rashi, or Maimonides. Just this goy.

—Still, the fire was a terrible thing. Whom do you think?

—Whom do I think? What am I, an eye in the back of your head? The moneylender Marcus, maybe. He didn't want the school, he didn't want the goy to marry his Misha. Two kugel with one match.

—Such a rich man? He wouldn't do such a thing.

—His meshuganah Sophie, then. It had to be a crazy, to risk burning the gansa lane.

—I think the cobbler Licht. You heard at the meeting, his daughter hated him from the school. That could make you crazy.

—Or the seamstress Hannah Schlicter, whose daughter was shtupped by a book. She maybe was setting fire to Guttle Rothschild.

—Half the lane hated the school, it could have been anybody. It could have been more than one. A plot.

—Whomever, they made a mitzvah. Good riddance to the school. And the goy. Now they can build three new houses on that land, there's so many people wanting to buy. The rebbetzin will be rich.

—Then the buyers will sell off apartments, and they, too, will be rich.

—If they could afford to buy, they already were rich.

—So they'll be richer. It's the way of the world. But they might just build another school.

—So someone could burn it down again? They wouldn't take a chance.

—I suppose. What's that?

—What's what?

—Under your sleeve. When you waved your arm just now. It looked like a bandage wrap. You fell and hurt your wrist?

—Oh, that. A little burn, from lighting the woodstove. It's nothing.

—Your wife doesn't light the stove?

—Not that time.

—What did the Doctor say?

—Who are you, the Inquisition? I told you it's nothing. So what's been going on, while I was sick with the grippe?

—The Chief Rabbi, I hear, is planning a meeting.

—Of course there will be a meeting. There always will be a meeting, until the Messiah comes.

—And then?

—That's how we'll know He's the true Messiah. If He doesn't call a meeting.

—That's a good one. So tell me, was it a nasty burn?

—Forget that already. I have a question. In our holy Jewish cemetery, where did they bury the goy?

—Right in the middle, I heard. They made a little room among the Beckers.

Yussel Kahn was waiting for Guttle to appear. When she did, the cabinet maker stepped into the lane, holding a book. "Good morning," he said. "If you have a moment, there is something I would like to show you."

Guttle with her vacant stare paused, waited.

"I was reading an essay last night by a French writer, Montaigne. I would like to show you one sentence." He opened the book to a marked page

— marked with a sliver of wood from the last table Georgi had carved. Yussel read aloud: "He owed his life not to himself but to the world as an example."

The carpenter lowered the book. "He's talking about the death of Socrates. But when I read that, I couldn't help thinking of Georgi, rushing into the flames. That's how he, too, died. As an example to the world."

Yussel saw no expression on Guttle's face — this lively face that had once enchanted him, which appeared so worn now. She took the book from his hands, opened to the marked page, stared at it. When she handed him the book, her face still was empty. "Thank you, Yussel," she said, in a voice without emotion, a voice that seemed far away, and she nodded to him, almost like a curtsy, Yussel thought, and resumed walking up the lane. He did not know if she had understood. The fair Ophelia.

The shaking of the earth rippled the sleep in which she was drowning. She clawed her way to the surface. It was not the earth shaking, it was the bed; it was not Samson shaking the pillars of the deep, but Meyer Amschel beside her, head and shoulders racking, as if in pain. His back was to her. She placed a hand on him. His shivering skin stung her fingertips.

"Meyer! What is it?"

He did not reply. His torso trembled. She heard his tears as if they were shrieks.

"Meyer! Tell me!"

She had never seen him cry. She moved beside him, slipped her arm around his hip, pressed her belly to the curve of his back. He gripped her hand, held it to his chest.

"You have married a horrible man," he murmured.

His words were muffled by the pillow, by the dark, by their own absurdity.

"What are you saying?" Her mouth was at his shoulder. "You had a dream."

He squeezed her hand as if to break her bones. As if clinging to it for life. "I wish a thousand dreams. Instead of a single truth." He pressed her hand to his lips. On her knuckles she could feel his tears.

"You are a wonderful man. A wonderful husband. A wonderful father."

"I have done something terrible."

"What? When?"

"In Hesse-Kassel."

The bottom fell from her stomach. The child within her had no support. She could hardly utter the words. "With a woman?"

He twisted at once to face her, touched her hair. "No, Guttle, never! I would never betray you. You should never think such a thing."

"Then what?" Her relief gave way at once to deeper fright. What could be worse than that?

"It was not you whom I betrayed. It was Yahweh."

The tightness in her body began to ease, leaving mild aching in its place. Surely, this he was imagining. "How can that be, Meyer? You are a man of God."

Breathing deeply, he did not answer, but lay his head upon her chest. With her fingers she smoothed his hair, damp with sweat.

"You haven't told me," she whispered.

He offered no response, as if he had not heard, though his ear was near her lips. When at last he spoke she felt the words on her breast as much as she heard them through the dark.

"I cannot speak of it."

She would have pulled him nearer if that were possible. "Not to me?"

His silent sobs had leveled into breathing. His body no longer shook.

"Not to anyone." His words were heavy, like iron. "Perhaps, some time — if there comes a time."

Her own eyes began to water. She pressed her lips to his hair. What was this secret that blindly she now must help him carry?

He revealed no more. He was asleep.

How long she lay awake, his breath on her breast rippling in sluggish rhythm the lace of her gown, she could not say.

In the darkness she sought her confidantes — Melka, Jennie. But they were gone, destroyed for her by the fire. Would Yahveh reveal to her Meyer's betrayal?

He appeared — if it were He — behind the closed lids of her waking eyes, in the image of a golden Torah, floating beneath a pewter cloud. Hiram was painting the Torah on canvas. Beside him, Izzy pointed at something she could not see.

There was nothing of Meyer's betrayal.

Pondering what this image signified, she drifted to sleep on the rhythm of Meyer's heart.

When she awoke, in the damp and dark of morning, she knew she could not bear for one more day to view the remains of the fire. She put on an old house dress, tied a babushka around her head, lifted the bucket from beside the woodstove, and grabbed the scoop that she used to shovel ashes out of the stove. At once she set the scoop back where it had been, hanging from a nail on the wall beside the stove; it was much too small. Quietly, so as not to wake Meyer or the children, she left the house and walked the empty lane. First light was just visible in the sky above the walls when she reached the cemetery. She took one of the spades left inside the gates, carried it and the bucket across the lane to the ashen remains of the vanished River View. The lead coffin still was there, the charred woodstove, pieces of half-burned rafters, ashes ankle deep over the land. Setting the bucket down, she scooped ashes with the spade that normally was used for digging graves, and dumped them into the bucket. She scooped another shovelful, another. When the bucket was filled she carried it to the sewage trench and dumped the ashes in, just inside the south gate, where the trench sloped sharply down towards the river. She filled and emptied the bucket, again, again. Her body began to perspire. The work felt good. She felt cleaner for it somehow, even as her hands — and when she wiped her brow, her face — became smudged with gray.

The sky brightened slightly, but she could smell rain coming. As she worked near the center of where the school had been, she noticed someone watching her from the cobbles. Then another person, and another. She did not know who they were, did not care, merely continued her work. But when a few minutes later she paused to rest, leaning on the shovel, wiping her sweaty forehead with her forearms, she saw that Meyer had joined the onlookers. Beside him was Rabbi Simcha, and a moment later Rebecca — as Doctor or friend she could not tell. They seemed to be restraining her husband, urging him not to wade across the ashes to her. She brushed at droplets on her cheek, thought the rain had come. She was weeping for Meyer's unknown grief.

Taking up the spade, she filled the bucket, carried it to the trench and emptied it. When she turned back, her satisfaction waned. She had made only a narrow trough in the ashes; clearing the land would take her all day; perhaps many days. Ignoring feelings of defeat, she resumed her work, till she heard scraping in the gravel beneath the ashes at the opposite edge of the property, twenty metres away. She looked in that direction. A woman — no, a girl, also wearing a babushka — had materialized with a scoop and bucket of her own, was kneeling and scooping ashes. When her bucket was full she left footsteps in the ashes till she reached the path Guttle had made and followed it to the trench and emptied her bucket. As the girl passed on her way back, Guttle recognized her as Misha Marcus, who had hoped to marry Georgi. Up close, Misha's face, framed by her dark blue kerchief, was softer than Guttle had remembered; in her eyes was a sadness that matched her own.

As the two of them worked, without exchanging words, another girl appeared with a bucket and a scoop. Guttle recognized her as Reba Schlicter, Hannah's youngest, now fourteen. Reba waved to Guttle, then without a word began to scoop the ashes. As the morning warmed, more kerchiefed women joined in; some Guttle did not know, others she recognized. Leah Marcus, who had married the Cantor, appeared with her rebellious younger sister — the one who had told her father the shoemaker that she hated him. They allowed much space around Guttle as they worked. No word was uttered as they shoveled the ashes, filled the buckets, emptied them into the sluggish current of the ditch, returned to scoop more ash.

As the number of shovelers, all women, increased, working with the silence of the dead, Guttle saw that the number of onlookers also had grown. Rebecca, who owned this land, was gone, no doubt to the hospital, but Meyer and the Chief Rabbi still watched. It could not be such an entertaining spectacle, Guttle was thinking, when her bucket was darkened by a shadow. She stood upright to see who had come so near, and was startled to find herself facing the vast bulk of Sophie Marcus. Guttle tensed. Her grip on the shovel tightened. Was she going to have to hit this woman at last?

Sophie did not speak, just gazed at Guttle. She extended her flabby arm. When Guttle didn't understand, Sophie indicated the shovel. Guttle hesitated — should she arm her enemy? — and felt a cramp in her belly, the baby protesting the work she was doing. She peered into Sophie's eyes, could read nothing there —neither hostility nor friendship. She handed her the spade. Sophie took it, reached for Guttle's bucket, carried both several metres away, and began to scoop up ashes, like the others. Guttle watched her for a moment, looked around at all the women working, slowly made her way to the cobbles, to where Meyer stood.

"Look how you all appear," he said, pointing. "The ashes rising like mist, into the silence. It's a painting."

"Except for the stove in the middle," Guttle said, wiping her face on her sleeve. "I want to move that. But it's heavy."

"I'll help you."

Meyer stepped into the ashes, getting his black shoes and white stockings covered with soot. Guttle looked down, patted her belly.

"Of course, what was I thinking?" Meyer said. "I'll go find the boys."

Leaning forward, she kissed his cheek. "Thank you for loving me," she said. "Thank you for putting up with me."

His torment of the night, she knew, she must forget.

Meyer folded her hands into his, looked into the eyes that had ensnared him so long ago, and at the sultry, down-curving lips. He said, "My pleasure, Madame R."

She watched in silence as he set off in search of their sons.

Turning to resume her work, she noticed Jacob Marcus standing across the lane, inside the cemetery, watching from a distance the silent women working. With new resolve she crossed the sewage trench and approached the moneylender, who nodded in greeting but said nothing.

"Herr Marcus," Guttle asked, "would you do me the honor, this afternoon, of coming to my home for a glass of tea?"

Marcus studied her face, raised his glance to where his Sophie was scooping ashes with women from the length the lane. He spoke then from behind his beard, saying, "Yes, Frau Rothschild. I think I could do that."

The event would be significant. That was clear from the way Yussel and the other carpenters lay a board floor in the center of the property, and built a platform with a lectern that stood just off the cobbles, and for days hammered together long rows of tiered benches at the rear and along both sides of the River View land. On the appointed day, music summoned them all, music from the instruments of the newly formed Judengasse Gratuitous Orchestra, so identified by a painted sign propped near where the players stood, between the tiers of benches and the outdoor wooden floor. Arshel Cohen was there, and six other men, playing violins, a bass fiddle, a saxophone, a trumpet. Brendel Kahn in a new green dress puffed at the shoulders gracefully glided her hands in front of them, her arms encased in white gloves to her elbows suggesting the necks of swans.

The music swirling through the lane like a breeze lured them to the south end. It was a Sunday afternoon, the gates were locked, but they would have been there anyway. Tier after tier of the wooden benches filled quickly, almost all the men wearing black suits, the women in pastel Shabbas dresses of blue or green or lavender. Children climbed up and down the tiers until the seats were filled, then sat or sprawled on the ground or on the strange outdoor floor. The sky was a dark gray, and Rabbi Simcha was praying that rain would not fall, as he walked about, asking one person and then another to sit in a row of chairs, borrowed from the yeshiva, which had been lined up near the lectern: Guttle and Meyer, Jacob Marcus, Hiram Liebmann, and Isidor Kracauer, who had interrupted his rabbinical studies at Furth to return to the lane, amid hugs from Guttle and endless kisses from his young wife, Amelia.

When the tiers were filled, and latecomers had crowded in the lane behind the lectern, Rabbi Simcha mounted the platform and welcomed them. "First of all, I want to thank the members of the Judengasse Gratuitous Orchestra for their invigorating music. Several weeks ago I asked Brendel Kahn, whom we know is a wonderful dancer, to form a small orchestra, because I wanted this occasion, though solemn, not to be somber. When I mentioned my idea to Brendel she was eager. But she was concerned that some people would object, would say that an orchestra is the last thing we need in the lane — that it would be gratuitous. To meet such objections, in a spirit of compromise, she has named the group the Judengasse Gratuitous Orchestra. We shall hear more music from them today, and I hope for a long time to come."

Brendel waved her baton and the musicians stroked and blasted three raucous chords of thanks, drawing laughter and cheers from the crowd, creating, at least for the moment, just the mood of good feeling that the Chief Rabbi wanted.

"We are here today, as you know, because of what happened on this spot a month ago. We are here not to fight, I hope, but to come together. As I have said before, the existence, or not, of a secular school in the Judengasse is not among the official concerns of the Chief Rabbi. But the morale of the lane, the unity of we Jews, certainly is. With that explained, I will turn the discussion over to Frau Meyer Rothschild, the creator of the school for girls."

Guttle, wearing a loose blue dress over her convex belly, left her seat and moved behind the lectern. What whispering there was in the crowd she could not make out.

"We all were horrified by what happened here," she began, her hands clutching the lectern. "The terrible blaze that destroyed the Moses Mendelssohn Academy for Girls was not an accident. The fire captain has told us that. We do not know who lit the match. I no longer want to know. Adonai knows. The guilty person will have to answer to Him.

"But as I watched a few weeks ago women from all over the lane working together to clear the ashes, a deeper understanding of the fire came to me. At first it startled me. But I have come to believe it is true. Adonai, who is all powerful and all-knowing, in His wisdom created the blaze Himself."

There were gasps in the crowd, and cries of "Impossible." Guttle had expected this, she had chosen her words to hold their attention.

"Let me tell you why I believe this. The school for girls had become an unfortunate symbol in the lane. It was dividing neighbor from neighbor, child from parent. This was largely my fault, and I have grieved over it. But Adonai, if he grieved, also acted. He did not want Jew hating Jew, Jew fighting Jew. So in His wisdom He allowed the school to burn — not because he opposed the educating of girls, I believe, but to give us a chance to do it properly, in a way that unites us, not divides us.

"With some trepidation, I must admit, I took this idea to the honorable Jacob Marcus. After several intense discussions, he agreed. Together we took our thoughts to Rabbi Simcha. Our mutual decision was that together we must rebuild the school."

"No! No! No!" came shouts from the crowd. Most remained silent, listening.

"Here is why. Because if we do not, those opposed to the school would have won a victory over those who favored it — at the cost of a life, and a historic Torah — and bitterness would remain deep. But we have to rebuild it in a different manner, with more widespread approval. We discussed some of the objections to the school. One was that giving our girls a secular education that is denied to our boys could cause grave problems in the relations between the two, in future marriages — in the bedroom, if I may put it delicately. We agreed there is reason for concern. So the new secular school, we decided, should be available to both boys and girls."

"Shame! Shame!" someone yelled. Guttle held up her hand for silence.

"Do not misunderstand — the boys and girls will not share a classroom. They will not even be in the school at the same time. The plan is that three days a week the school would be for boys, and the other three days for girls."

"What about heder?" a voice called out.

"I am getting to that. While girls could enroll at any age after seven years, boys would first have to complete their heder studies. This will ensure that for the boys, religious education will take precedence. They will have to complete that before moving on to secular studies. And for both boys and girls, of course, the school would be voluntary."

"Secular study goes against Jewish law!" someone shouted.

Guttle turned to the Chief Rabbi. He approached the lectern and told them of his view — that because all of creation is the work of Yahweh, no realm of study could be sinful.

"You haven't answered the main point." Another voice from the crowd. "The Bible says not to teach girls."

Simcha nodded, waited for quiet. "Those of you who attended the school meeting some weeks ago heard a spirited debate about that. While the Talmud says that fathers must teach their sons, it does not explicitly forbid the teaching of girls. I lean toward the belief that girls, too, have minds. Perhaps because I married a brilliant one."

"We hope you've married her body, too," someone yelled, sending laughter circling the tiers.

Guttle straightened her hat, purple with a matching feather, and gripped the lectern. Her hands were sweating, and her scalp beneath her sheitl. Her back had begun to ache from standing so long with her protruding belly. Her mind flashed for an instant to her wedding day, to Dvorah more than eight months pregnant standing beside her. Dvorah whom Meyer had seen at Hesse-Kassel. Whom she would never see again. Dvorah, who ought to be here in the crowd.

"I have one important question for the Chief Rabbi to address," she told them, "a question that I know is on many of your minds: how can we be sure that a rebuilt school will not be burned again?"

An emotional leaning forward in the tiers. This they very much wanted to hear. Simcha was smiling, nodding, as Guttle stepped down from the podium and returned to her seat beside Meyer, who gripped her hand in support.

"I will be happy to respond," Simcha said. "To do so, I would like two men to join me up here." He motioned to the chairs below. Hiram Liebmann and Isidor Kracauer climbed agilely onto the podium, and stood one on each side of the Rabbi.

"This idea was brought to me by Frau Rothschild, who is too modest to explain it. So I shall do so. It begins with the Torah. As everything does. We all know that the Five Books of Moses, which make up the Torah, are the sacred word of Adonai; that each of the fifty-two sections we read, one each week, is sacred. We lost a magnificent Torah in the fire, a scroll bequeathed to us by our forebears in the Judengasse in the year 1492. I have decided to replace that scroll by one that will be a special treasure for us all.

"As you know, each Torah must be written by hand. I have asked Hiram Liebmann here, the finest artist the Judengasse has known, to put his delicate hand to the task of transcribing a new Torah. I am happy to say that he has agreed."

"It's a mitzvah!" some yelled.

"Yes, it will be a wonderful mitzvah," Simcha continued. "But I am not ashamed to say, and I know Hiram will not be embarrassed if I point out, that he is not the most studious man in the lane regarding the Torah, nor is his attendance at schul exemplary. But the Torah must be penned with the heart, not just the hand. What to do? I have written to the Chief Rabbi at Furth to see if he would permit our Isidor Kracauer, his rabbinical student, to return to the lane and sit beside Hiram, and work with him every day on the meaning of each word, of each character, as Hiram writes. The Rabbi of Furth responded that if Izzy were to spend a year explaining to Hiram every nuance of the words he is writing — a year is how long it normally takes for a scroll to be created — then at the end of that year Isidor would be even more qualified to be a Rabbi than if he finished his studies at Furth. With that glad news, I wrote to Isidor. He has returned to the lane, as you can see. These two fine young men — whom you will recall once shared the Schul-Klopper's job — together will create for us a magnificent scroll."

Hearing a murmur run through the crowd, Simcha said: "I know, you wonder what this has to do with the fire. I am coming to that. We plan to have the carpenters build a small Aron Kodesh under the roof of the new school. It will be a cabinet of wood, not a coffin of lead. It will burn easily, should there be a fire."

"I don't understand," a man cried out. "We can't read from it up there. We can't even see it up there."

"Let me finish," the Rabbi said. "When the scroll is completed, and the women of the lane have made a fine velvet case for it, and the jewelers of the lane have made a fitting gold crown, we each one of us will get to see and admire the scroll work, which I know will be magnificent. We each will get to kiss the Torah. Then we shall place it as I have described. But here is the difference between this Torah and the one we lost in the fire. The one that partially burned was a secret. But the future location of this new Torah I am making public now. Everyone will see where we are placing it. I am confident that no one in the lane — no Jew anywhere — would knowingly put a torch to a Torah, or to a building that contains a Torah. There can be no greater sin in the eyes of God."

Nods of approval bent the heads of many, like a breeze humbling the heads of tulips.

"What about during the first year?" a man yelled.

"I'm glad you brought that up. Because the Torah will take a year to inscribe, I have instructed the carpenters to wait a year before constructing the school. During that time, we shall use this vacant space to celebrate our unity, with parties and dances. It was for this reason I asked Brendel Isaacs — Brendel Kahn — to form the Judengasse Orchestra. Personally, I do not find it gratuitous. The orchestra will entertain us at these parties and dances, just as, if there are no more questions, they shall entertain us now, as we celebrate the birth of a new school, and a new unity, upon the ashes of the old."

"We have no unity!" someone cried out.

People turned to look. It was the shoemaker, Alexandre Licht.

"Bah!" he shouted, "Bah on your school for girls."

With many eyes watching he descended from the second tier and strode across the wooden floor, past the lectern, out into the lane. Another man, then another, climbed down and followed him out of the meeting, as did several women. Another man, another, leaving in protest.

Guttle held her breath as they left. The Rabbi could think of no way to stop them.

A moment of expectant silence, the pause between lightning and thunder.

Then the exodus stopped. Only a few dozen had departed. Hundreds remained.

The Chief Rabbi held up his hand for their attention. "To tell you the truth," he said, "I am glad that some of our friends have left. That they were not afraid to speak their minds with their feet. If ever all Jews agree on something, we will know the end of the world is upon us."

Many in the crowd laughed, and began to applaud. Seizing the moment, Simcha waved his arm, and Brendel, seeing this, turned to the musicians and punched the air, and in an instant the Judengasse Gratuitous Orchestra filled the tiers with the opening notes of an old and lively tune.

Hesitant at first, one couple and then another moved onto the wooden floor. Those who were not dancing watched, chatted, laughed, applauded. The orchestra followed with a country dance, then a demure waltz.

After a deliberate pause, when the dance floor cleared, Brendel held up five fingers to her musicians, and they began a slow tune that gradually began to increase in tempo. It was the same challenge dance that Brendel and Rebecca had danced twice, once at Guttle's wedding long ago, once in the Café on the evening of their betrothals.

The floor remained empty. Who could keep up with such music?

The first to try was Schönche Rothschild. Stepping down from the second tier of seats, pulling off her shoes, she edged onto a corner of the boards and began to dance, slowly at first, listening intently to the music, trying to increase her speed. Itchy in her own seat, Leah Marcus, the shoemaker's daughter, the Cantor's wife, ran down three tiers and out onto the floor and began to challenge Schönche. Two metres apart, they danced, their feet flashing, their forms moving closer together. Delighted by Schönche's courage, Guttle began to applaud. Many in the crowd joined in. The young women were not nearly as good as Brendel and Rebecca had been, but they would improve.

Seeing the two dancers slowing, their untrained legs growing weary, Brendel curtly silenced the orchestra. Schönche and Leah fell into one another's arms, sweating, breathless. "Let's practice that," Leah managed to whisper. Schönche, too breathless to speak, could only nod.

Brendel pointed her baton across the dance floor. "What about the rebbetzin?"

Grinning, Rebecca waved her hands, palms outward, in front of her chest. "I'm too old for that," she called out. "What about you?"

Brendel, too, grinned, and ran a hand across her slightly thickened middle, barely noticeable. "I'm too pregnant for that."

Rebecca's eyes widened. Those who heard checked with their neighbors to see if they had understood. They turned and whispered to those behind them. The news rose like perfume from the lowest tier to the highest. "Brendel and Yussel are pregnant!" People began to cheer. Some of the older women, who knew of Yussel's sad history with babies, found tears moistening their cheeks.

The Chief Rabbi was watching from the podium. Rebecca turned to look at him. He smiled, shrugged, nodded, as if to say: if you want. Rebecca waved her hand to silence the crowd. Her motion went unnoticed by all but the trumpet player, who blasted a high C long and loud, bringing chatter to a halt. Rebecca moved to the center of the dance floor. "Since this seems to be a day for celebrating," she said, blushing a bright red, "I am happy to announce that the Chief Rabbi and I also are pregnant."

Consternation, uncertainty. Could this be a joke? They were so old! He was fifty-one! She was, what, thirty-nine? Old, yes, but not exactly Sarai and Abraham. Cheers erupted, and whistles, and clapping, louder even than for Brendel and Yussel. Brendel ran across the floor to Rebecca and the two women hugged. Simcha stepped down from the podium; he and Yussel embraced.

"A dance to celebrate," someone yelled.

The Chief Rabbi huddled with Brendel, hummed a tune, moving his right hand in rhythm as if to demonstrate the music. Brendel called Arshel Cohen over. The lead fiddler said he knew it well. He returned to the orchestra, spoke to the other players. Brendel cleared the floor save for the Rabbi and her husband, turned to the orchestra, raised her baton and swung it down. Led by the fiddler, the orchestra began to play a Jewish folk tune from Vilna, the Rabbi's place of birth, the city where he had grown up. Slowly the Rabbi, all in black, began to dance, and motioned to Yussel to join him.

"I don't know what to do," Yussel said.

"Just copy me."

Simcha squatted, shot first one leg out in front of him, then the other. Yussel tried to do the same, and fell on his side. Righting himself, he tried again. This time he succeeded. As the music continued and the two prospective fathers danced, Guttle and Meyer, watching, linked arms. Yussel and Simcha were joined on the dance boards by the Cantor and the fire marshall, by a heder teacher and a pawnbroker, by men from all over the lane, squatting and kicking, throwing out their arms for balance, copying one another, falling, resuming — this peasant dance having existed dormant in the marrow of their bones — locking arms and walking like ducks, becoming red in the face, while their wives ringed the wooden floor or stood on the tiers to see better, and laughed, and clapped. The Gratuitous Orchestra improvised, and the tiers of onlookers rising toward the gray November sky applauded, and a hundred children in the lane, boys and girls together, tried to imitate the dancing men and careened to the cobbles, laughing, unhurt. Watching through the locked south gate, his musket at his side, even the Constable on duty smiled.

Overheated, perspiring, Rabbi Simcha sat, trying to catch his breath, wiping his face with his handkerchief. Amid the lilting music and the throbbing in his temples he thought he heard heavenly voices. "They're happy!" he heard the cherub Leo exclaim. Whereupon the angel Yetta replied, "They'll just have to live with it."

Epilogue: A Birthday — 1848

H er hand quivering slightly — how she hated that — Guttle touched her cheek. Mrs. R. Never before that day among the ashes had he called her that. Later he would call her Mrs. R. or Guttle or Gutteleh, depending on his mood, though she could never calculate precisely which mood induced which endearment. On his part it was a rare inconsistency. The closest she could come to discerning a pattern, he used Mrs. R. was when he was optimistic about his future fortunes; to refine it even more, when he was optimistic with little visible reason. As if to say, "That is what the entire civilized world will know you as some day, my Gutteleh. Mrs. R."

He was wrong about that. Nowadays the civilized world called her Madame Rothschild.

The dregs of her tea were cold. She stood and walked to the kitchen with her glass, and heard a knocking on the door downstairs. She did not put much stock in clocks — at her age, it mattered little what the time was, except when they were going to the opera and didn't want to miss the beginning. Though often the proprietors would hold the curtain if the first mezzanine box on the right was not yet occupied. This was an embarrassment to her, but they insisted. Which is why, if she did not care to attend a performance, she made sure that someone sat in her seat. Preferably a woman. In that way she could create many "Madame Rothschilds" to be whispered about. One is never too old for games.

Another series of knocks on the door. Surely it was too early for her daughters to bring the cake. She went to the top of the stairs. "Who pounds on my door?"

"It's Doctor Weitz."

The Doctor? She had not summoned him. This would be an odd birthday visitor.

"Come up, Doctor, the door is not locked."

She heard him enter the vestibule and climb the stairs. He was a young man, not forty yet, with ginger hair that reminded her of Yussel Kahn, peace be upon him.

"To what do I owe this visit?" she asked as the Doctor set his black leather bag on a table.

He removed his hat, revealing a white yarmulke underneath. His blue suit was the latest fashion among the young. "Your daughter Julie came to my office the other day. She..."

"Julie? What is wrong with her?"

"It's nothing, a minor ailment, don't trouble yourself. But when I asked about you, she said you had been complaining about aches and pains. With a patient of your years, I thought I should stop by."

"My years? Yes, I suppose I have years. I can tell mostly when I walk to the river. When you were young, Doctor, you and your sisters attended the River Academy, did you not?"

"I was there for one year, right after heder. Then it closed. I continued school in Frankfurt. What prompts your question?"

"No reason. I was just reliving memories." She moved to a chair, eased herself into it. "Those aches and pains — also when I stand too long." She adjusted the skirt of her green silk dress to a more graceful shape over her thick ankles.

"I was upset when the academy shut down," the Doctor said. "I liked it. I still remember the myths and legends that building held. But too many Jews had moved from the lane. There weren't enough students left."

"To what legends are you referring?"

"The myth of the three heroes, mostly. We heard that before the academy was built, a school for girls stood on that spot. Someone who opposed the educating of girls set it afire. A fellow named Georgi ran into the flames, trying to save a Torah. Supposedly, he was burned to death."

"You don't believe that happened?"

"The problem was, each time we heard the story there was a different hero. I still remember the names. Sometimes the fellow was Georgi Kremm. Other times it was Georgi ben Avram. Other times it was Georgi Pinsky. But none of them ever existed — the older boys checked in the birth books. It was a good story, though. We used to frighten the girls with tales of his ghost."

She thought of Georgi's grave in the cemetery. They had neglected to look there, among the Beckers.

"There was another good story," the Doctor said. "We used to hear that under the roof there was a special Torah. Some woman's idea of preventing another fire. Because no Jew would burn down a building knowing there was a Torah inside. It's what caused the academy to survive, they used to say."

"Aren't all Torahs special?"

"This one supposedly had been hand lettered by the great artist Lieb. But because he wasn't pious enough, he was tutored in every word, every letter, by the famous Rabbi I. Kracauer. In his younger days, of course. Before he became Chief Rabbi."

"This, too, you boys didn't believe?"

"Do you know what a Torah by Lieb would be worth today? Anyway, why do you ask about the academy?"

"I walked down there yesterday," Guttle said. "I need my exercise, as you have told me."

"You didn't go in, I hope," the Doctor said with a grin. "Do you mind if I sit?" He pulled a chair closer to her.

"Of course I went in. Why walk so far and not go in?"

"To the River Tavern? It's a den of roughnecks. Foreign sailors. The dregs of humanity. People get killed in there."

"But they serve good beer."

"You drink beer there?"

"If I'm feeling well. They have good stories. I've always enjoyed good stories."

"You buy a round of beers, and in exchange they tell you of their adventures?"

"Doctor Weitz! Shame on you! That would hardly be seemly — to buy beer for younger men." She grinned, hoped her new teeth were straight. "The sailors buy for me. 'Another chilled for Madame R.,' they shout."

"They know who you are?"

"Of course. I suppose I remind them of their mothers. Or — I'll say it first, Doctor — of their grandmothers." Feeling a breeze through the window, she pulled her sleeve cuffs down from her elbows to her wrists. "No doubt I'm the only woman in the River View who won't give them disease."

"The River Tavern. And you — do you tell them stories?"

She waved a shaky hand. "What would seamen want with an old lady's memories? I have wonderful memories, of course. Mostly of Meyer. Of how together we lived our dream, by seeing the walls come down. Not by our hands, of course, but with gelt. The French army helped, when they invaded Frankfurt. Their cannons destroyed a third of the Judengasse. The Council had no choice but to let those Jews without homes move into the city. The

French already had given equality to their Jews, by the way, after their revolution. After they beheaded...but never mind that. The Frankfurt Council was not in a hurry to open the lane, until Meyer raised for them 290,000 gulden. A lot of money. A tax that was a bribe. No matter. It also helped ease the laws for the Jews. More than anything, that crowned Meyer's life. But the seamen at the tavern don't care about such things, and the journalists already know."

"The journalists?"

"They shall be here later. Today is my birthday. For some reason they keep track. Ninety-six, if I don't lie."

"I didn't know. Mazel tov!"

"Thank you, Doctor."

"And they will ask you why you still live in the lane, I suppose. When your five sons own palaces and banks not only in Frankfurt but in London, Paris, Vienna, Naples. When the Rothschilds are richer than kings. The richest family in the world. When kings try to borrow money to make war, it's your sons who decide if there will be a war."

"It's true. One by one in his little countinghouse Meyer taught each of them the business of banking. When they came of age he sent them abroad, to blanket Europe with their influence."

"But once again you will not tell the journalists why you still live here, with all that wealth available? The very last resident of the Judengasse?"

"A soul must have secrets, or it is no longer a soul."

"Will you tell me? There are healthier places to live, you know. Cleaner air to breathe than here among these warehouses. Surely your sons have invited you."

"I'm old-fashioned, Doctor. I remain loyal to my husband."

"I know he's buried in the cemetery here, but..."

"For thirty-six years already. As I said, Meyer taught our sons to make money, and sent them out to the Promised Lands. But he never went himself, not even after he opened up the gates. He stayed here. But it's more than that. It's the Judengasse itself. Someone needs to remember. People from all over the world come here to visit Madame Rothschild, as they call me. Not long ago that nice writer from Denmark, Herr Anderson, came. Would they visit me someplace else? By remaining here, I keep the memory of the Judengasse alive. Someone needs to."

The Doctor could think of no reply. There was a moment of silence.

"So. About your aches and pains. What hurts when you stand too long? Your muscles? Your joints? Your back, perhaps?"

"You name it, I feel it. Also when I sit too long."

"I see."

"Also when I lie down too long." She smiled shyly at him. "That's three of a kind. Too bad I'm not playing poker."

"In that case, I won't be poking you," the Doctor said. "I could poke here, poke there, ask you where it hurts. But you say it hurts everywhere, so poking wouldn't tell me a thing. I doubt it's anything treatable — muscles, bones, joints, they all wear out with age."

The Doctor pulled a silver watch on a chain from his pocket. "I must move along, I have another patient to see a few streets away." He stood, gripped his leather bag, took his hat in his hand. Guttle followed him to the top of the stairs. He took one step down and turned to her. "You should have a very happy birthday, Madame. Eat a piece of cake for me. As for the aches and pains, I'm sorry I can't help you. I can't make you any younger."

Guttle shook her head, her wry smile peeking out again from her wrinkled face. "You misunderstand, Doctor," she said. "It's older I want to become."

The Doctor grinned, then said, "If it won't offend you, Madame, there is one question I've been wanting to ask."

"Well, speak up. At my age I don't offend."

"The story goes that your husband made his first fortune by investing funds for nearby Princes — profits they obtained by selling peasants to fight in foreign wars. That was the seed for the magnificent wealth of your family. The story goes that you were against Meyer's making money that way."

"It's true. It was the worst fight we ever had. So, what is it you want to know?"

"After all these years, does that still bother you?"

"Such a question," Guttle said. "I still live here, do I not?"

Author's Note

Many sources contributed to the factual foundation upon which this novel is built. Two in particular must be acknowledged: the biographies *Founder,* by Amos Elon, and *The House of Rothschild,* by Niall Ferguson. For anyone seeking further factual information, Elon is stronger on daily life in the Judengasse, Ferguson on the detailed financial history of the Rothschilds.

Though this book is a work of fiction, many of the characters, notably Guttle Schnapper and Meyer Rothschild, were real people. Others, and many of the scenes, are wholly imaginary. Lives and incidents in the Judengasse may have unrolled as portrayed, but, to quote Ira Gershwin on the Bible, it ain't necessarily so.

Since completing the manuscript, I frequently have heard a complaint from the cherub Leo, usually around four in the morning. "Why did you end where you did?" he asks. "There's a lot more to the story." Whereupon the angel Yetta invariably reassures me. "You told the important parts. The rest concerns only money."

If the mingling of history and fiction needs any defense, I rely on the words of the Nobel Laureate Elie Wiesel, who wrote — attributing the concept to the Baal Shem Tov — "The real and the imagined, one like the other, are part of history; one is its shell, the other its core."

—Robert Mayer
February 22, 2010

Made in the USA
Lexington, KY
07 November 2011